the fiction of experience

MODERN SHORT STORIES

M. X. LESSER
Rutgers University

JOHN N. MORRIS
Columbia University

MC GRAW-HILL BOOK COMPANY, INC.
New York San Francisco Toronto London 1962

07-037336-1

303132333435 MMN MMN 909876543210

Library of Congress Catalog ***Card*** *Number: 62–17644*

"The Downward Path to Wisdom," from *The Leaning Tower and Other Stories,* Katherine Anne Porter, copyright 1339 by the author. Permission of Harcourt, Brace & World, Inc.

"My Oedipus Complex," from *The Stories of Frank O'Connor,* Frank O'Connor, copyright 1950, 1952 by the author. Permission of Alfred A. Knopf, Inc. and Harold Matson Company.

"The Use of Force," from *The Farmers' Daughters,* William Carlos Williams, copyright © 1961 by New Directions. Reprinted by permission of New Directions, Publishers.

"The Tree," from *Adventures in the Skin Trade,* Dylan Thomas, copyright 1955 by New Directions. Permission of the publisher and David Higham Associates, Ltd.

"Songs My Father Sang Me," from *Ivy Gripped the Steps* and *The Demon Lover,* Elizabeth Bowen, copyright 1941, 1946 by the author. Permission of Alfred A. Knopf, Inc. and Jonathan Capt Ltd.

"The Rocking-Horse Winner," from *The Portable D. H. Lawrence,* D. H. Lawrence, copyright 1933 by The Estate of D. H. Lawrence. Permission of The Viking Press, Inc.

"Blackberry Winter," from *The Circus in the Attic and Other Stories,* Robert Penn Warren, copyright 1947 by the author. Permission of Harcourt, Brace & World, Inc.

"The Sorrows of Gin," from *The Housebreaker of Shady Hill* and Other *Stories,* John Cheever, copyright 1953 by the author. Permission of Harper & Brothers.

"The Celestial Omnibus," from *The Collected Tales of E. M. Forster,* E. M. Forster, copyright 1947 by Alfred A. Knopf, Inc. Permission of the author's representatives and of the publishers Sidgwick & Jackson, Ltd.

"The Artificial Nigger," from *A Good Man Is Hard to Find and Other Stories,* Flannery O'Connor, copyright 1955 by the author. Permission of Harcourt, Brace & World, Inc.

"The Innocent," from *Nineteen Stories* and *Twenty-one Stories,* Graham

Greene, copyright 1946 by the author. Permission of The Viking Press, Inc. and Messrs. William Heinemann, Ltd.

"Barn Burning," from *Collected Stories of William Faulkner*, William Faulkner, copyright 1939 by the author. Permission of Random House, Inc.

"Silent Snow, Secret Snow," from *The Collected Short Stories of Conrad Aiken*, Conrad Aiken, copyright 1932 and © 1960 by the author. Permission of The World Publishing Company.

"The Conversion of the Jews," from *Goodbye, Columbus*, Philip Roth, copyright 1957, 1959 by the author. Permission of Houghton Mifflin Company.

"Araby," from *Dubliners*, James Joyce (B. W. Heubsch, 1916). Reprinted by permission of The Viking Press, Inc.

"A Visit of Charity," from *A Curtain of Green and Other Stories*, Eudora Welty, copyright 1941 by the author. Permission of Harcourt, Brace & World, Inc.

"The Capital of the World," from *The Fifth Column and the First Forty-nine Stories*, Ernest Hemingway, copyright 1936 by the author. First published in *Esquire* under the title "The Horns of the Bull." Permission of Charles Scribner's Sons.

"Wunderkind," from *The Ballad of the Sad Café*, Carson McCullers, copyright 1951 by the author. Permission of Houghton Mifflin Company.

"Susanna at the Beach," from *Love and Like*, Herbert Gold, copyright 1954, 1960 by the author. Permission of The Dial Press, Inc.

"The Freshest Boy," from *Taps at Reveille*, F. Scott Fitzgerald, copyright 1928 by the Curtis Publishing Company and © 1956 by Frances Scott Fitzgerald Lanahan. Permission of Charles Scribner's Sons.

"The Garden Party," from *The Short Stories of Katherine Mansfield*, Katherine Mansfield, copyright 1922, 1937 by Alfred A. Knopf, Inc. Permission of the publisher and The Society of Authors as the literary representative of the estate of the late Miss Katherine Mansfield.

"Tomorrow and Tomorrow and So Forth," from *The Same Door*, John Updike, copyright 1955, 1959 by the author. Permission of Alfred A. Knopf, Inc.

"Paul's Case," from *Youth and the Bright Medusa*, Willa Cather, copyright 1905, 1932 by the author. Permission of Alfred A. Knopf, Inc.

"Your Body Is a Jewel Box," from *The White Horses of Vienna and Other Stories*, Kay Boyle, copyright 1936 by the author. Permission of Harcourt, Brace & World, Inc.

"Ah, the University," John Collier, copyright 1939 by the author. Permission of Harold Matson Company.

"Of This Time, Of That Place," reprinted from *Partisan Review* (Jan.–Feb., 1943), Lionel Trilling. Permission of the author.

"I'm a Fool," from *Horses and Men*, Sherwood Anderson, copyright 1924 by Eleanor Anderson. Permission of Harold Ober Associates, Inc.

"Flight," from *The Long Valley*, John Steinbeck, copyright 1938 by the author. Permission of The Viking Press, Inc.

"A Summer's Reading," from *The Magic Barrel*, Bernard Malamud, copyright 1956, 1958 by Bernard Malamud. First published in *The New Yorker*. Permission of Farrar, Straus and Cudahy, Inc.

"A Tree of Night," from *A Tree of Night and Other Stories*, Truman Capote, copyright 1945 by the author. Permission of Random House, Inc.

"Youth," Joseph Conrad. Reprinted by permission of J. M. Dent & Sons, Ltd.

"In Dreams Begin Responsibilities," from *The World Is a Wedding*, Delmore Schwartz, copyright 1948 by the author. Permission of New Directions.

PREFACE

In ancient shadows and twilights
Where childhood had stray'd,
The world's great sorrows were born
And its heroes were made.
In the lost boyhood of Judas
Christ was betray'd.

GEORGE WILLIAM RUSSELL (Æ), "GERMINAL"

FOR most of us that "lost boyhood"—however ancient, however shadowy—remains a nagging point of return. Though we know we cannot be what once we were, we are forced by the urgencies of the present to understand, to go back. For we realize growth is rooted in a sense of the past: to predicate a future without it is to grow old without aging. And, it must follow, literature that searches these memories, the substance of what we are and will be, involves and informs us. This volume reflects that assumption.

Such a sampling of modern American and British short stories about young people has its own variety—in range, in technique, in theme. Besides such familiar names as Conrad, Joyce, Hemingway, and Faulkner, new writers are represented here: Flannery O'Connor, Philip Roth, and John Updike, to name three who since the war have found the short story a peculiarly roomy form in which to exercise their talents. More important, perhaps, is the fact that in technique these stories, old as well as new, differ remarkably. Compare, for example, D. H. Lawrence's "The Rocking-Horse Winner," a sombre fantasy, with Sherwood Anderson's "I'm a Fool," in which the communication of the felt meaning depends upon the almost stenographic recording of meticulously observed social fact. Or, among more recent examples, note the differences of treatment in Dylan Thomas's "The Tree," a highly charged though thoroughly elusive "poem" of religious intensity, and John Cheever's "The Sorrows of Gin," an insistent catalogue of suburbia. Stories similar in theme suggest even more clearly the richness of difference the form is capable of. Modern writers are especially concerned with the memory's manipulation of reality: to contrast the cinematic sense of time in Delmore Schwartz's "In Dreams Begin Responsibilities" with the fluid sense of it in Robert Penn Warren's "Blackberry Winter" is to cast light on each story—and on many modern novels as well. Another recurrent theme is the quest for love, the subject of James Joyce's "Araby" and Graham Greene's "The Innocent." Although movement is scarcely perceptible in each, one ends in disillusion, the other in damnation.

The notes preceding each story follow Wordsworth's dictum for those who feel "the weight of too much liberty." In this narrow space we have sought to sketch the author's life and work and to offer an implication rather than explication of his story: long enough to be instructive, short enough to avoid irritation.

The stories are arranged approximately in the order of the age of the central character. They deal with the familiar circumstances and sensitive reflections of children and adolescents—the world of fantasy and imagination, love and fear, and growth. Our notion is that in them the reader will find characters akin to himself and situations that, by the imaginative extension of his experience, he can conceive possible.

We hope that in the scope of this book, as well as in the merit of individual stories, the reader will discover the immediacy of his past and the diversity of serious pleasures that modern fiction affords.

M. X. L.
J. N. M.

CONTENTS

MODERN SHORT STORIES

by Katherine Anne Porter

THE DOWNWARD PATH TO WISDOM

Katherine Anne Porter, born on May 15, 1894, at Indian Creek, Texas, is the great-great-great-granddaughter of Daniel Boone. She was educated in small convent schools in Texas and Louisiana. Although she has written continuously from her earliest years, she withheld her work from publication until she was thirty. Her first collection of stories, Flowering Judas, *appeared in 1930. Three others have followed. She has also published five novelettes and a collection of essays. Miss Porter has received two Guggenheim fellowships (1931 and 1938) and three honorary doctorates (University of North Carolina, 1949, University of Michigan, 1954, and Smith College, 1958). A former vice-president of the National Institute of Arts and Letters, Miss Porter has taught at Stanford, Chicago, Michigan, Washington and Lee, and Liège, Belgium, the last as a Fulbright lecturer. In 1962 she published her long-awaited novel,* Ship of Fools.

"The Downward Path to Wisdom," like a number of Miss Porter's other stories, recalls to us the mysterious terrors of childhood. Capricious and irresponsible elders—Uncle David, Old Janet, that two-headed monster "Mommanpoppa"—use the little boy against one another like a club. He learns shame and experiences unusually early the masculine predicament of lacking a penny to buy licorice for a girl who is tired of blowing up balloons. He is a human being, or is becoming one; but no one will believe it—and least of all himself. It is only in the litany of his last words that he both asserts and distorts his being.

IN the square bedroom with the big window Mama and Papa were lolling back on their pillows handing each other things from the wide black tray on the small table with crossed legs. They were smiling and they smiled even more when the little boy, with the feeling of sleep still in his skin and hair, came in and walked up to the bed. Leaning against it, his bare toes wriggling in the white fur rug, he went on eating peanuts which he took from his pajama pocket. He was four years old.

"Here's my baby," said Mama. "Lift him up, will you?"

He went limp as a rag for Papa to take him under the arms and swing him up over a broad, tough chest. He sank between his parents like a bear cub in a warm litter, and lay there comfortably. He took another peanut between his teeth, cracked the shell, picked out the nut whole and ate it.

"Running around without his slippers again," said Mama. "His feet are like icicles."

"He crunches like a horse," said Papa. "Eating peanuts before breakfast will ruin his stomach. Where did he get them?"

"You brought them yesterday," said Mama with exact memory, "in a grisly little cellophane sack. I have asked you dozens of times not to bring him things to eat. Put him out, will you? He's spilling shells all over me."

Almost at once the little boy found himself on the floor again. He moved around to Mama's side of the bed and leaned confidingly near her and began another peanut. As he chewed he gazed solemnly in her eyes.

"Bright-looking specimen, isn't he?" asked Papa, stretching his long legs and reaching for his bathrobe. "I suppose you'll say it's my fault he's dumb as an ox."

"He's my little baby, my only baby," said Mama richly, hugging him, "and he's a dear lamb." His neck and shoulders were quite boneless in her firm embrace. He stopped chewing long enough to receive a kiss on his crumby chin. "He's sweet as clover," said Mama. The baby went on chewing.

"Look at him staring like an owl," said Papa.

Mama said, "He's an angel and I'll never get used to having him."

"We'd be better off if we never *had* had him," said Papa. He was walking about the room and his back was turned when he said that. There was silence for a moment. The little boy stopped eating, and stared deeply at his Mama. She was looking at the back of Papa's head, and her eyes were almost black. "You're going to say that just once too often," she told him in a low voice. "I hate you when you say that."

Papa said, "You spoil him to death. You never correct him for anything. And you don't take care of him. You let him run around eating peanuts before breakfast."

"You gave him the peanuts, remember that," said Mama. She sat up and hugged her only baby once more. He nuzzled softly in the pit of her arm. "Run along, my darling," she told him in her gentlest voice, smiling at him straight in the eyes. "Run along," she said, her arms falling away from him. "Get your breakfast."

The little boy had to pass his father on the way to the door. He shrank into himself when he saw the big hand raised above him. "Yes, get out of here and stay out," said Papa, giving him a little shove toward the door. It was not a hard shove, but it hurt the little boy. He slunk out, and trotted down the hall trying not to look back. He was afraid something was coming after him, he could not imagine what. Something hurt him all over, he did not know why.

He did not want his breakfast; he would not have it. He sat and stirred it round in the yellow bowl, letting it stream off the spoon and spill on the table, on his front, on the chair. He liked seeing it spill. It was hateful stuff, but looked funny running in white rivulets down his pajamas.

"Now look what you're doing, dirty boy," said Marjory. "You dirty little old boy."

The little boy opened his mouth to speak for the first time. "You're dirty yourself," he told her.

"That's right," said Marjory, leaning over him and speaking so her voice would not carry. "That's right, just like your papa. Mean," she whispered, "mean."

The little boy took up his yellow bowl full of cream and oatmeal and sugar with both hands and brought it down with a crash on the table. It burst and some of the wreck lay in chunks and some of it ran all over everything. He felt better.

"You see?" said Marjory, dragging him out of the chair and scrubbing him with a napkin. She scrubbed him as roughly as she dared until he cried out. "That's just what I said. That's exactly it." Through his tears he saw her face terribly near, red and frowning under a stiff white band, looking like the face of somebody who came at night and stood over him and scolded him when he could not move or get away. "Just like your papa, *mean.*"

The little boy went out into the garden and sat on a green bench dangling his legs. He was clean. His hair was wet and his blue woolly pull-over made his nose itch. His face felt stiff from the soap. He saw Marjory going past a window with the black tray. The curtains were still closed at the window he knew opened into Mama's room. Papa's room. Mommanpoppasroom, the word was pleasant, it made a mumbling snapping noise between his lips; it ran in his mind while his eyes wandered about looking for something to do, something to play with.

Mommanpoppas' voices kept attracting his attention. Mama was being cross with Papa again. He could tell by the sound. That was what Marjory always said when their voices rose and fell and shot up to a point and crashed and rolled like the two tomcats who fought at night. Papa was being cross, too, much crosser than Mama this time. He grew cold and disturbed and sat very still, wanting to go to the bathroom, but it was just next to Mommanpoppasroom; he didn't dare think of it. As the voices grew louder he could hardly hear them any more, he wanted so badly to go to the bathroom. The kitchen door opened suddenly and Marjory ran out, making the motion with her hand that meant he was to come to her. He didn't move. She came to him, her face still red and frowning, but she was not angry; she was scared just as he was. She said, "Come on, honey, we've got to go to your gran'ma's again." She took his hand and pulled him. "Come on quick, your gran'ma is waiting for you." He slid off the bench. His mother's voice rose in a terrible scream, screaming something he could not understand, but she was furious; he had seen her clenching her fists and stamping in one spot, screaming with her eyes shut; he knew how she looked. She was screaming in a tantrum, just as he remembered having heard himself. He stood still, doubled over, and all his body seemed to dissolve, sickly, from the pit of his stomach.

"Oh, my God," said Marjory. "Oh, my God. Now look at you. Oh, my God. I can't stop to clean you up."

He did not know how he got to his grandma's house, but he was there at last, wet and soiled, being handled with disgust in the big bathtub. His grandma was there in long black skirts saying, "Maybe he's sick; maybe we should send for the doctor."

"I don't think so, m'am," said Marjory. "He hasn't et anything; he's just scared."

The little boy couldn't raise his eyes, he was so heavy with shame. "Take this note to his mother," said Grandma.

She sat in a wide chair and ran her hands over his head, combing his hair with her fingers; she lifted his chin and kissed him. "Poor little fellow," she said. "Never you mind. You always have a good time at your grandma's, don't you? You're going to have a nice little visit, just like the last time."

The little boy leaned against the stiff, dry-smelling clothes and felt horribly grieved about something. He began to whimper and said, "I'm hungry. I want something to eat." This reminded him. He began to bellow at the top of his voice; he threw himself upon the carpet and rubbed his nose in a dusty woolly bouquet of roses. "I want my peanuts," he howled. "Somebody took my peanuts."

His grandma knelt beside him and gathered him up so tightly he could hardly move. She called in a calm voice above his howls to Old Janet in the doorway, "Bring me some bread and butter with strawberry jam."

"I want peanuts," yelled the little boy desperately.

"No, you don't, darling," said his grandma. "You don't want horrid old peanuts to make you sick. You're going to have some of grandma's nice fresh bread with good strawberries on it. That's what you're going to have." He sat afterward very quietly and ate and ate. His grandma sat near him and Old Janet stood by, near a tray with a loaf and a glass bowl of jam upon the table at the window. Outside there was a trellis with tube-shaped red flowers clinging all over it, and brown bees singing.

"I hardly know what to do," said Grandma, "it's very . . ."

"Yes, m'am," said Old Janet, "it certainly is . . ."

Grandma said, "I can't possibly see the end of it. It's a terrible . . ."

"It certainly is bad," said Old Janet, "all this upset all the time and him such a baby."

Their voices ran on soothingly. The little boy ate and forgot to listen. He did not know these women, except by name. He could not understand what they were talking about; their hands and their clothes and their voices were dry and far away; they examined him with crinkled eyes without any expression that he could see. He sat there waiting for whatever they would do next with him. He hoped they would let him go out and play in the yard. The room was full of flowers and dark red curtains and big soft chairs, and the windows were open, but it was still dark in there somehow; dark, and a place he did not know, or trust.

"Now drink your milk," said Old Janet, holding out a silver cup.

"I don't want any milk," he said, turning his head away.

"Very well, Janet, he doesn't have to drink it," said Grandma quickly. "Now run out in the garden and play, darling. Janet, get his hoop."

A big strange man came home in the evenings who treated the little boy very confusingly. "Say 'please,' and 'thank you,' young man," he would roar, terrifyingly, when he gave any smallest object to the little boy. "Well, fellow, are you ready for a fight?" he would say, again, doubling up huge, hairy fists and making passes at him. "Come on now, you must learn to box." After the first few times this was fun.

"Don't teach him to be rough," said Grandma. "Time enough for all that."

"Now, Mother, we don't want him to be a sissy," said the big man. "He's got to toughen up early. Come on now, fellow, put up your mitts." The little boy liked this new word for hands. He learned to throw himself upon the strange big man, whose name was Uncle David, and hit him on the chest as hard as he could; the big man would laugh and hit him back with his huge, loose fists. Sometimes, but not often, Uncle David came home in the middle of the day. The little boy missed him on the other days, and would hang on the gate looking down the street for him. One evening he brought a large square package under his arm.

"Come over here, fellow, and see what I've got," he said, pulling off quantities of green paper and string from the box which was full of flat, folded colors. He put something in the little boy's hand. It was limp and silky and bright green with a tube on the end. "Thank you," said the little boy nicely, but not knowing what to do with it.

"Balloons," said Uncle David in triumph. "Now just put your mouth here and blow hard." The little boy blew hard and the green thing began to grow round and thin and silvery.

"Good for your chest," said Uncle David. "Blow some more." The little boy went on blowing and the balloon swelled steadily.

"Stop," said Uncle David, "that's enough." He twisted the tube to keep the air in. "That's the way," he said. "Now I'll blow one, and you blow one, and let's see who can blow up a big balloon the fastest."

They blew and blew, especially Uncle David. He puffed and panted and blew with all his might, but the little boy won. His balloon was perfectly round before Uncle David could even get started. The little boy was so proud he began to dance and shout, "I beat, I beat," and blew in his balloon again. It burst in his face and frightened him so he felt sick. "Ha ha, ho ho ho," whooped Uncle David. "That's the boy. I bet I can't do that. Now let's see." He blew until the beautiful bubble grew and wavered and burst into thin air, and there was only a small colored rag in his hand. This was a fine game. They went on with it until Grandma came in and said, "Time for supper now. No, you can't blow balloons at the table. Tomorrow maybe." And it was all over.

The next day, instead of being given balloons, he was hustled out of bed early, bathed in warm soapy water and given a big breakfast of soft-boiled eggs with toast and jam and milk. His grandma came in to kiss him good morning. "And I hope you'll be a good boy and obey your teacher," she told him.

"What's teacher?" asked the little boy.

"Teacher is at school," said Grandma. "She'll tell you all sorts of things and you must do as she says."

Mama and Papa had talked a great deal about School, and how they must send him there. They had told him it was a fine place with all kinds of toys and other children to play with. He felt he knew about School. "I didn't know it was time, Grandma," he said. "Is it today?"

"It's this very minute," said Grandma. "I told you a week ago."

Old Janet came in with her bonnet on. It was a prickly looking bundle held with a black rubber band under her back hair. "Come on," she said. "This is my busy day." She wore a dead cat slung around her neck, its sharp ears bent over under her baggy chin.

The little boy was excited and wanted to run ahead. "Hold to my hand like I told you," said Old Janet. "Don't go running off like that and get yourself killed."

"I'm going to get killed, I'm going to get killed," sang the little boy, making a tune of his own.

"Don't say that, you give me the creeps," said Old Janet. "Hold to my hand now." She bent over and looked at him, not at his face but at something on his clothes. His eyes followed hers.

"I declare," said Old Janet, "I did forget. I was going to sew it up.

I might have known. I *told* your grandma it would be that way from now on."

"What?" asked the little boy.

"Just look at yourself," said Old Janet crossly. He looked at himself. There was a little end of him showing through the slit in his short blue flannel trousers. The trousers came halfway to his knees above, and his socks came halfway to his knees below, and all winter long his knees were cold. He remembered now how cold his knees were in cold weather. And how sometimes he would have to put the part of him that came through the slit back again, because he was cold there too. He saw at once what was wrong, and tried to arrange himself, but his mittens got in the way. Janet said, "Stop that, you bad boy," and with a firm thumb she set him in order, at the same time reaching under his belt to pull down and fold his knit undershirt over his front.

"There now," she said, "try not to disgrace yourself today." He felt guilty and red all over, because he had something that showed when he was dressed that was not supposed to show then. The different women who bathed him always wrapped him quickly in towels and hurried him into his clothes, because they saw something about him he could not see for himself. They hurried him so he never had a chance to see whatever it was they saw, and though he looked at himself when his clothes were off, he could not find out what was wrong with him. Outside, in his clothes, he knew he looked like everybody else, but inside his clothes there was something bad the matter with him. It worried him and confused him and he wondered about it. The only people who never seemed to notice there was something wrong with him were Mommanpoppa. They never called him a bad boy, and all summer long they had taken all his clothes off and let him run in the sand beside a big ocean.

"Look at him, isn't he a love?" Mama would say and Papa would look, and say, "He's got a back like a prize fighter." Uncle David was a prize fighter when he doubled up his mitts and said, "Come on, fellow."

Old Janet held him firmly and took long steps under her big rustling skirts. He did not like Old Janet's smell. It made him a little quivery in the stomach; it was just like wet chicken feathers.

School was easy. Teacher was a square-shaped woman with square short hair and short skirts. She got in the way sometimes, but not often. The people around him were his size; he didn't have always to be stretching his neck up to faces bent over him, and he could sit on the chairs without having to climb. All the children had names, like Frances and Evelyn and Agatha and Edward and Martin, and his own name was Stephen. He was not Mama's "Baby," nor Papa's "Old Man"; he was not Uncle David's "Fellow" or Grandma's "Darling," or even Old Janet's "Bad Boy." He was Stephen. He was learning to read, and to sing a tune to some strange-looking letters or marks written in chalk on a blackboard. You talked one kind of lettering, and you sang another. All the children talked and sang in turn, and then all together. Stephen thought it a fine game. He felt awake and happy. They had soft clay and paper and wires and squares of colors in tin boxes to play with, colored blocks to build houses with. Afterward they all danced in a big ring, and then they danced in pairs, boys with girls. Stephen danced with Frances, and Frances kept saying, "Now you just follow me." She was a little taller than he was, and her hair stood up in short, shiny curls, the color of an ash tray on Papa's desk. She would say, "You can't dance." "I can dance too," said Stephen, jumping around holding her hands, "I can, too, dance." He was certain of it. "*You* can't dance," he told Frances, "you can't dance at all."

Then they had to change partners, and when they came round again, Frances said, "I don't *like* the way you dance." This was different. He felt uneasy about it. He didn't jump quite so high when the phonograph record started going dumdiddy dumdiddy again. "Go ahead, Stephen, you're doing fine," said Teacher, waving her hands together very fast. The dance ended, and they all played "relaxing" for five minutes. They relaxed by swinging their arms back and forth, then rolling their heads round and round. When Old Janet came for him he didn't want to go home. At lunch his grandma told him twice to keep his face out of his plate. "Is that what they teach you at school?" she asked. Uncle David was at home. "Here you are, fellow," he said and gave Stephen two balloons. "Thank you," said Stephen. He put the balloons in his pocket and forgot about them. "I told you that boy could learn something," said Uncle David to Grandma. "Hear him say 'thank you'?"

In the afternoon at school Teacher handed out big wads of clay and told the children to make something out of it. Anything they liked. Stephen decided to make a cat, like Mama's Meeow at home. He did not like Meeow, but he thought it would be easy to make a cat. He could not get the clay to work at all. It simply fell into one lump after another. So he stopped, wiped his hands on his pull-over, remembered his balloons and began blowing one.

"Look at Stephen's horse," said Frances. "Just look at it."

"It's not a horse, it's a cat," said Stephen. The other children gathered around. "It looks like a horse, a little," said Martin.

"It is a cat," said Stephen, stamping his foot, feeling his face turning hot. The other children all laughed and exclaimed over Stephen's cat that looked like a horse. Teacher came down among them. She sat usually at the top of the room before a big table covered with papers and playthings. She picked up Stephen's lump of clay and turned it round and examined it with her kind eyes. "Now, children," she said, "everybody has the right to make anything the way he pleases. If Stephen says this is a cat, it *is* a cat. Maybe you were thinking about a horse, Stephen?"

"It's a *cat,*" said Stephen. He was aching all over. He knew then he should have said at first, "Yes, it's a horse." Then they would have let him alone. They would never have known he was trying to make a cat. "It's Meeow," he said in a trembling voice, "but I forgot how she looks."

His balloon was perfectly flat. He started blowing it up again, trying not to cry. Then it was time to go home, and Old Janet came looking for him. While Teacher was talking to other grown-up people who came to take other children home, Frances said, "Give me your balloon; I haven't got a balloon." Stephen handed it to her. He was happy to give it. He reached in his pocket and took out the other. Happily, he gave her that one too. Frances took it, then handed it back. "Now you blow up one and I'll blow up the other, and let's have a race," she said. When their balloons were only half filled Old Janet took Stephen by the arm and said, "Come on here, this is my busy day."

Frances ran after them, calling, "Stephen, you give me back my balloon," and snatched it away. Stephen did not know whether he was surprised to find himself going away with Frances' balloon, or whether he was surprised to see her snatching it as if it really belonged to her. He was badly mixed up in his mind, and Old Janet was hauling him along. One thing he knew, he liked Frances, he was going to see her again tomorrow, and he was going to bring her more balloons.

That evening Stephen boxed awhile with his uncle David, and

Uncle David gave him a beautiful orange. "Eat that," he said, "it's good for your health."

"Uncle David, may I have some more balloons?" asked Stephen.

"Well, what do you say first?" asked Uncle David, reaching for the box on the top bookshelf.

"Please," said Stephen.

"That's the word," said Uncle David. He brought out two balloons, a red and a yellow one. Stephen noticed for the first time they had letters on them, very small letters that grew taller and wider as the balloon grew rounder. "Now that's all, fellow," said Uncle David. "Don't ask for any more because that's all." He put the box back on the bookshelf, but not before Stephen had seen that the box was almost full of balloons. He didn't say a word, but went on blowing, and Uncle David blew also. Stephen thought it was the nicest game he had ever known.

He had only one left, the next day, but he took it to school and gave it to Frances. "There are a lot," he said, feeling very proud and warm; "I'll bring you a lot of them."

Frances blew it up until it made a beautiful bubble, and said, "Look, I want to show you something." She took a sharp-pointed stick they used in working the clay; she poked the balloon, and it exploded. "Look at that," she said.

"That's nothing," said Stephen, "I'll bring you some more."

After school, before Uncle David came home, while Grandma was resting, when Old Janet had given him his milk and told him to run away and not bother her, Stephen dragged a chair to the bookshelf, stood upon it and reached into the box. He did not take three or four as he believed he intended; once his hands were upon them he seized what they could hold and jumped off the chair, hugging them to him. He stuffed them into his reefer pocket where they folded down and hardly made a lump.

He gave them all to Frances. There were so many, Frances gave most of them away to the other children. Stephen, flushed with his new joy, the lavish pleasure of giving presents, found almost at once still another happiness. Suddenly he was popular among the children; they invited him specially to join whatever games were up; they fell in at once with his own notions for play, and asked him what he would like to do next. They had festivals of blowing up the beautiful globes, fuller and rounder and thinner, changing as they went from deep color to lighter, paler tones, growing glassy thin, bubbly thin, then bursting with a thrilling loud noise like a toy pistol.

For the first time in his life Stephen had almost too much of something he wanted, and his head was so turned he forgot how this fullness came about, and no longer thought of it as a secret. The next day was Saturday, and Frances came to visit him with her nurse. The nurse and Old Janet sat in Old Janet's room drinking coffee and gossiping, and the children sat on the side porch blowing balloons. Stephen chose an apple-colored one and Frances a pale green one. Between them on the bench lay a tumbled heap of delights still to come.

"I once had a silver balloon," said Frances, "a beyootiful silver one, not round like these; it was a long one. But these are even nicer, I think," she added quickly, for she did want to be polite.

"When you get through with that one," said Stephen, gazing at her with the pure bliss of giving added to loving, "you can blow up a blue one and then a pink one and a yellow one and a purple one." He pushed the heap of limp objects toward her. Her clear-looking eyes, with fine little rays of brown in them like the spokes of a wheel, were full of approval for Stephen. "I wouldn't want to be greedy, though, and blow up all your balloons."

"There'll be plenty more left," said Stephen, and his heart rose under his thin ribs. He felt his ribs with his fingers and discovered with some surprise that they stopped somewhere in front, while Frances sat blowing balloons rather halfheartedly. The truth was, she was tired of balloons. After you blow six or seven your chest gets hollow and your lips feel puckery. She had been blowing balloons steadily for three days now. She had begun to hope they were giving out. "There's boxes and boxes more of them, Frances," said Stephen happily. "Millions more. I guess they'd last and last if we didn't blow too many every day."

Frances said somewhat timidly, "I tell you what. Let's rest awhile and fix some liquish water. Do you like liquish?"

"Yes, I do," said Stephen, "but I haven't got any."

"Couldn't we buy some?" asked Frances. "It's only a cent a stick, the nice rubbery, twisty kind. We can put it in a bottle with some water, and shake it and shake it, and it makes foam on top like soda pop and we can drink it. I'm kind of thirsty," she said in a small, weak voice. "Blowing balloons all the time makes you thirsty, I think."

Stephen, in silence, realized a dreadful truth and a numb feeling crept over him. He did not have a cent to buy licorice for Frances and she was tired of his balloons. This was the first real dismay of his whole life, and he aged at least a year in the next minute, huddled, with his deep, serious blue eyes focused down his nose in intense speculation. What could he do to please Frances that would not cost money? Only yesterday Uncle David had given him a nickel, and he had thrown it away on gumdrops. He regretted that nickel so bitterly his neck and forehead were damp. He was thirsty too.

"I tell you what," he said, brightening with a splendid idea, lamely trailing off on second thought, "I know something we can do, I'll—I . . ."

"I *am* thirsty," said Frances with gentle persistence. "I think I'm so thirsty maybe I'll have to go home." She did not leave the bench, though, but sat, turning her grieved mouth toward Stephen.

Stephen quivered with the terrors of the adventure before him, but he said boldly, "I'll make some lemonade. I'll get sugar and lemon and some ice and we'll have lemonade."

"Oh, I love lemonade," cried Frances. "I'd rather have lemonade than liquish."

"You stay right here," said Stephen, "and I'll get everything."

He ran around the house, and under Old Janet's window he heard the dry, chattering voices of the two old women whom he must outwit. He sneaked on tiptoe to the pantry, took a lemon lying there by itself, a handful of lump sugar and a china teapot, smooth, round, with flowers and leaves all over it. These he left on the kitchen table while he broke a piece of ice with a sharp metal pick he had been forbidden to touch. He put the ice in the pot, cut the lemon and squeezed it as well as he could—a lemon was tougher and more slippery than he had thought—and mixed sugar and water. He decided there was not enough sugar so he sneaked back and took another handful. He was back on the porch in an astonishingly short time, his face tight, his knees trembling, carrying iced lemonade to thirsty Frances with both his devoted hands.

A pace distant from her he stopped, literally stabbed through with a thought. Here he stood in broad daylight carrying a teapot with lemonade in it, and his grandma or Old Janet might walk through the door at any moment.

"Come on, Frances," he whispered loudly. "Let's go round to the back behind the rose bushes where it's shady." Frances leaped up and ran like a deer beside him, her face wise with knowledge of why they ran; Stephen ran stiffly, cherishing his teapot with clenched hands.

It was shady behind the rose bushes, and much safer. They sat side by side on the dampish ground, legs doubled under, drinking in turn from the slender spout. Stephen took his just share in large, cool, delicious swallows. When Frances drank she set her round pink mouth daintily to the spout and her throat beat steadily as a heart. Stephen was thinking he had really done something pretty nice for Frances. He did not know where his own happiness was; it was mixed with the sweet-sour taste in his mouth and a cool feeling in his bosom because Frances was there drinking his lemonade which he had got for her with great danger.

Frances said, "My, what big swallows you take," when his turn came next.

"No bigger than yours," he told her downrightly. "You take awfully big swallows."

"Well," said Frances, turning this criticism into an argument for her rightness about things, "that's the way to drink lemonade anyway." She peered into the teapot. There was quite a lot of lemonade left and she was beginning to feel she had enough. "Let's make up a game and see who can take the biggest swallows."

This was such a wonderful notion they grew reckless, tipping the spout into their opened mouths above their heads until lemonade welled up and ran over their chins in rills down their fronts. When they tired of this there was still lemonade left in the pot. They played first at giving the rosebush a drink and ended by baptizing it. "Name father son holygoat," shouted Stephen, pouring. At this sound Old Janet's face appeared over the low hedge, with the tan, disgusted-looking face of Frances' nurse hanging over her shoulder.

"Well, just as I thought," said Old Janet. "Just as I expected." The bag under her chin waggled.

"We were thirsty," he said; "we were awfully thirsty." Frances said nothing, but she gazed steadily at the toes of her shoes.

"Give me that teapot," said Old Janet, taking it with a rude snatch. "Just because you're thirsty is no reason," said Old Janet. "You can ask for things. You don't have to steal."

"We didn't steal," cried Frances suddenly. "We didn't. We didn't!"

"That's enough from you, missy," said her nurse. "Come straight out of there. You have nothing to do with this."

"Oh, I don't know," said Old Janet with a hard stare at Frances' nurse. "*He* never did such a thing before, by himself."

"Come on," said the nurse to Frances, "this is no place for you." She held Frances by the wrist and started walking away so fast Frances had to run to keep up. "Nobody can call *us* thieves and get away with it."

"You don't have to steal, even if others do," said Old Janet to Stephen, in a high carrying voice. "If you so much as pick up a lemon in somebody else's house you're a little thief." She lowered her voice then and said, "Now I'm going to tell your grandma and you'll see what you get."

"He went in the icebox and left it open," Janet told Grandma, "and he got into the lump sugar and spilt it all over the floor. Lumps everywhere underfoot. He dribbled water all over the clean kitchen floor, and he baptized the rose bush, blaspheming. And he took your Spode teapot."

"I didn't either," said Stephen loudly, trying to free his hand from Old Janet's big hard fist.

"Don't tell fibs," said Old Janet; "that's the last straw."

"Oh, dear," said Grandma. "He's not a baby any more." She shut the book she was reading and pulled the wet front of his pull-over toward her. "What's this sticky stuff on him?" she asked and straightened her glasses.

"Lemonade," said Old Janet. "He took the last lemon."

They were in the big dark room with the red curtains. Uncle David walked in from the room with the bookcases, holding a box in his uplifted hand. "Look here," he said to Stephen. "What's become of all my balloons?"

Stephen knew well that Uncle David was not really asking a question.

Stephen, sitting on a footstool at his grandma's knee, felt sleepy. He leaned heavily and wished he could put his head on her lap, but he might go to sleep, and it would be wrong to go to sleep while Uncle David was still talking. Uncle David walked about the room with his hands in his pockets, talking to Grandma. Now and then he would walk over to a lamp and, leaning, peer into the top of the shade, winking in the light, as if he expected to find something there.

"It's simply in the blood, I told her," said Uncle David. "I told her she would simply have to come and get him, and keep him. She asked me if I meant to call him a thief and I said if she could think of a more exact word I'd be glad to hear it."

"You shouldn't have said that," commented Grandma calmly.

"Why not? She might as well know the facts. . . . I suppose he can't help it," said Uncle David, stopping now in front of Stephen and dropping his chin into his collar, "I shouldn't expect too much of him, but you can't begin too early—"

"The trouble is," said Grandma, and while she spoke she took Stephen by the chin and held it up so that he had to meet her eye; she talked steadily in a mournful tone, but Stephen could not understand. She ended, "It's not just about the balloons, of course."

"It *is* about the balloons," said Uncle David angrily, "because balloons now mean something worse later. But what can you expect? His father—well, it's in the blood. He—"

"That's your sister's husband you're talking about," said Grandma, "and there is no use making things worse. Besides, you don't really *know*."

"I *do* know," said Uncle David. And he talked again very fast, walking up and down. Stephen tried to understand, but the sounds were strange and floating just over his head. They were talking about his father, and they did not like him. Uncle David came over and stood above Stephen and Grandma. He hunched over them with a frowning face, a long, crooked shadow from him falling across them to the wall. To Stephen he looked like his father, and he shrank against his grandma's skirts.

"The question is, what to do with him now?" asked Uncle David. "If we keep him here, he'd just be a—I won't be bothered with him. Why can't they take care of their own child? That house is crazy. Too far gone already, I'm afraid. No training. No example."

"You're right, they must take him and keep him," said Grandma. She ran her hands over Stephen's head; tenderly she pinched the nape of his neck between thumb and forefinger. "You're your Grandma's darling," she told him, "and you've had a nice long visit, and now you're going home. Mama is coming for you in a few minutes. Won't that be nice?"

"I want my mama," said Stephen, whimpering, for his grandma's face frightened him. There was something wrong with her smile.

Uncle David sat down. "Come over here, fellow," he said, wagging a forefinger at Stephen. Stephen went over slowly, and Uncle David drew him between his wide knees in their loose, rough clothes. "You ought to be ashamed of yourself," he said, "stealing Uncle David's balloons when he had already given you so many."

"It wasn't that," said Grandma quickly. "Don't say that. It will make an impression—"

"I hope it does," said Uncle David in a louder voice; "I hope he remembers it all his life. If he belonged to me I'd give him a good thrashing."

Stephen felt his mouth, his chin, his whole face jerking. He opened his mouth to take a breath, and tears and noise burst from him. "Stop that, fellow, stop that," said Uncle David, shaking him gently by the shoulders, but Stephen could not stop. He drew his breath again and it came back in a howl. Old Janet came to the door.

"Bring me some cold water," called Grandma. There was a flurry, a commotion, a breath of cool air from the hall, the door slammed, and Stephen heard his mother's voice. His howl died away, his breath sobbed and fluttered, he turned his dimmed eyes and saw her standing there. His heart turned over within him and he bleated like a lamb, "Maaaaama," running toward her. Uncle David stood back as Mama swooped in and fell on her knees beside Stephen. She gathered him to her and stood up with him in her arms.

"What are you doing to my baby?" she asked Uncle David in a thickened voice. "I should never have let him come here. I should have known better—"

"You always should know better," said Uncle David, "and you never do. And you never will. You haven't got it here," he told her, tapping his forehead.

"David," said Grandma, "that's your—"

"Yes, I know, she's my sister," said Uncle David. "I know it. But if she must run away and marry a—"

"Shut up," said Mama.

"And bring more like him into the world, let her keep them at home. I say let her keep—"

Mama set Stephen on the floor and, holding him by the hand, she said to Grandma all in a rush as if she were reading something, "Good-by, Mother. This is the last time, really the last. I can't bear it any longer. Say good-by to Stephen; you'll never see him again. You let this happen. It's your fault. You know David was a coward and a bully and a self-righteous little beast all his life and you never crossed him in anything. You let him bully me all my life and you let him slander my husband and call my baby a thief, and now this is the end. . . . He calls my baby a thief over a few horrible little balloons because he doesn't like my husband. . . ."

She was panting and staring about from one to the other. They were all standing. Now Grandma said, "Go home, daughter. Go away, David. I'm sick of your quarreling. I've never had a day's peace or comfort from either of you. I'm sick of you both. Now let me alone and stop this noise. Go away," said Grandma in a wavering voice. She took out her handkerchief and wiped first one eye and then the other and said, "All this hate, hate—what is it for? . . . So this is the way it turns out. Well, let me alone."

"You and your little advertising balloons," said Mama to Uncle David. "The big honest businessman advertises with balloons and if he loses one he'll be ruined. And your beastly little moral notions . . ."

Grandma went to the door to meet Old Janet, who handed her a glass of water. Grandma drank it all, standing there.

"Is your husband coming for you, or are you going home by yourself?" she asked Mama.

"I'm driving myself," said Mama in a far-away voice as if her mind had wandered. "You know he wouldn't set foot in this house."

"I should think not," said Uncle David.

"Come on, Stephen darling," said Mama. "It's far past his bedtime," she said, to no one in particular. "Imagine keeping a baby up to torture him about a few miserable little bits of colored rubber." She smiled at Uncle David with both rows of teeth as she passed him on the way to the door, keeping between him and Stephen. "Ah, where would we be without high moral standards," she said, and then to Grandma, "Good night, Mother," in quite her usual voice. "I'll see you in a day or so."

"Yes, indeed," said Grandma cheerfully, coming out into the hall with Stephen and Mama. "Let me hear from you. Ring me up tomorrow. I hope you'll be feeling better."

"I feel very well now," said Mama brightly, laughing. She bent down and kissed Stephen. "Sleepy, darling? Papa's waiting to see you. Don't go to sleep until you've kissed your papa good night."

Stephen woke with a sharp jerk. He raised his head and put out his chin a little. "I don't want to go home," he said; "I want to go to school. I don't want to see Papa, I don't like him."

Mama laid her palm over his mouth softly. "Darling, don't."

Uncle David put his head out with a kind of snort. "There you are," he said. "There you've got a statement from headquarters."

Mama opened the door and ran, almost carrying Stephen. She ran across the sidewalk, jerking open the car door and dragging Stephen in after her. She spun the car around and dashed forward so sharply Stephen was almost flung out of the seat. He sat braced then with all his might, hands digging into the cushions. The car speeded up and the trees and houses whizzed by all flattened out. Stephen began suddenly to sing to himself, a quiet, inside song so Mama would not hear. He sang his new secret; it was a comfortable, sleepy song: "I hate Papa, I hate Mama, I hate Grandma, I hate Uncle David, I hate Old Janet, I hate Marjory, I hate Papa, I hate Mama . . ."

His head bobbed, leaned, came to rest on Mama's knee, eyes closed. Mama drew him closer and slowed down, driving with one hand.

by Frank O'Connor

MY OEDIPUS COMPLEX

Frank O'Connor (pseudonym of Michael O'Donovan) was born in 1903 in County Cork and attended the Christian Brothers' school there. At twelve he had written enough poems, biographies, and essays on Irish history to "publish" a collected edition. Too poor to go to the university, he worked as a librarian in Cork and Dublin and later directed and collaborated on plays for the famous Abbey Theatre until 1939. He has taught at Harvard and Northwestern and has traveled extensively through Ireland, England, France, and the United States. He has published several volumes of criticism and more than fifteen collections of short stories.

"My Oedipus Complex," one of O'Connor's best known pieces, is told from a child's point of view; that is, the action is purposely limited by what the boy understands and sees. Thus his mother is "simple" and "exclusive" because she claims she cannot "afford" the price of a baby, even a "cheap" one, until the boy's father returns from the war. His father, "awkward and hairy," glares down at him "like a mountain out for murder." In other hands, the situation might have occasioned a mere exercise in sensitivity, but O'Connor avoids that, controlling it with a completely adult vocabulary. And his wit disinfects it.

FATHER was in the army all through the war—the first war, I mean—so, up to the age of five, I never saw much of him, and what I saw did not worry me. Sometimes I woke and there was a big figure in khaki peering down at me in the candlelight. Sometimes in the early morning I heard the slamming of the front door and the clatter of nailed boots down the cobbles of the lane. These were Father's entrances and exits. Like Santa Claus he came and went mysteriously.

In fact, I rather liked his visits, though it was an uncomfortable squeeze between Mother and him when I got into the big bed in the early morning. He smoked, which gave him a pleasant musty smell, and shaved, an operation of astounding interest. Each time he left a trail of souvenirs—model tanks and Gurkha knives with handles made of bullet cases, and German helmets and cap badges and button-sticks, and all sorts of military equipment—carefully stowed away in a long box on top of the wardrobe, in case they ever came in handy. There was a bit of the magpie about Father; he expected everything to come in handy. When his back was turned, Mother let me get a chair and rummage through his treasures. She didn't seem to think so highly of them as he did.

The war was the most peaceful period of my life. The window of my attic faced southeast. My mother had curtained it, but that had small effect. I always woke with the first light and, with all the responsibilities of the previous day melted, feeling myself rather like the sun, ready to illumine and rejoice. Life never seemed so simple and clear and full of possibilities as then. I put my feet out from under the clothes—I called them Mrs. Left and Mrs. Right—and invented dramatic situations for them in which they discussed the problems of the day. At least Mrs. Right did; she was very demonstrative, but I hadn't the same control of Mrs. Left, so she mostly contented herself with nodding agreement.

They discussed what Mother and I should do during the day, what Santa Claus should give a fellow for Christmas, and what steps should be taken to brighten the home. There was that little matter of the baby, for instance. Mother and I could never agree about that. Ours was the only house in the terrace without a new baby, and Mother said we couldn't afford one till Father came back from the war because they cost seventeen and six. That showed how simple she was. The Geneys up the road had a baby, and everyone knew they couldn't afford seventeen and six. It was probably a cheap baby, and Mother wanted something really good, but I felt she was too exclusive. The Geney's baby would have done us fine.

Having settled my plans for the day, I got up, put a chair under the attic window, and lifted the frame high enough to stick out my head. The window overlooked the front gardens of the terrace behind ours, and beyond these it looked over a deep valley to the tall, red-brick houses terraced up the opposite hillside, which were all still in shadow, while those at our side of the valley were all lit up, though with long strange shadows that made them seem unfamiliar; rigid and painted.

After that I went into Mother's room and climbed into the big bed. She woke and I began to tell her of my schemes. By this time, though I never seem to have noticed it, I was petrified in my nightshirt, and I thawed as I talked until, the last frost melted, I fell asleep beside her and woke again only when I heard her below in the kitchen, making the breakfast.

After breakfast we went into town; heard Mass at St. Augustine's and said a prayer for Father, and did the shopping. If the afternoon was fine we either went for a walk in the country or a visit to Mother's great friend in the convent, Mother St. Dominic. Mother had them all praying for Father, and every night, going to bed, I asked God to send him back safe from the war to us. Little, indeed, did I know what I was praying for!

One morning, I got into the big bed, and there, sure enough, was Father in his usual Santa Claus manner, but later, instead of uniform, he put on his best blue suit, and Mother was as pleased as anything. I saw nothing to be pleased about, because, out of uniform, Father was altogether less interesting, but she only beamed, and explained that our prayers had been answered, and off we went to Mass to thank God for having brought Father safely home.

The irony of it! That very day when he came in to dinner he took off his boots and put on his slippers, donned the dirty old cap he wore about the house to save him from colds, crossed his legs, and began to talk gravely to Mother, who looked anxious. Naturally, I disliked her looking anxious, because it destroyed her good looks, so I interrupted him.

"Just a moment, Larry!" she said gently.

This was only what she said when we had boring visitors, so I attached no importance to it and went on talking.

"Do be quiet, Larry!" she said impatiently. "Don't you hear me talking to Daddy?"

This was the first time I had heard those ominous words, "talking to Daddy," and I couldn't help feeling that if this was how God answered prayers, he couldn't listen to them very attentively.

"Why are you talking to Daddy?" I asked with as great a show of indifference as I could muster.

"Because Daddy and I have business to discuss. Now, don't interrupt again!"

In the afternoon, at Mother's request, Father took me for a walk. This time we went into town instead of out the country, and I thought at first, in my usual optimistic way, that it might be an improvement. It was nothing of the sort. Father and I had quite different notions of a walk in town. He had no proper interest in trams, ships, and horses, and the only thing that seemed to divert him was talking to fellows as old as himself. When I wanted to stop he simply went on, dragging me behind him by the hand; when he wanted to stop I had no alternative but to do the same. I noticed that it seemed to be a sign that he wanted to stop for a long time whenever he leaned against a wall. The second time I saw him do it I got wild. He seemed to be settling himself forever. I pulled him by the coat and trousers, but, unlike Mother who, if you were too persistent, got into a wax and said: "Larry, if you don't behave yourself, I'll give you a good slap," Father had an extraordinary capacity for amiable inattention. I sized him up and wondered would I cry, but he seemed to be too remote to be annoyed even by that. Really, it was like going for a walk with a mountain! He either ignored the wrenching and pummeling entirely, or else glanced down with a grin of amusement from his peak. I had never met anyone so absorbed in himself as he seemed.

At teatime, "talking to Daddy" began again, complicated this time by the fact that he had an evening paper, and every few minutes he put it down and told Mother something new out of it. I felt this was foul play. Man for man, I was prepared to compete with him any time for Mother's attention, but when he had it all made up for him by other people it left me no chance. Several times I tried to change the subject without success.

"You must be quiet while Daddy is reading, Larry," Mother said impatiently.

It was clear that she either genuinely liked talking to Father better than talking to me, or else that he had some terrible hold on her which made her afraid to admit the truth.

"Mummy," I said that night when she was tucking me up, "do you think if I prayed hard God would send Daddy back to the war?"

She seemed to think about that for a moment.

"No dear," she said with a smile. "I don't think he would."

"Why wouldn't he, Mummy?"

"Because there isn't a war any longer, dear."

"But, Mummy, couldn't God make another war, if He liked?"

"He wouldn't like to, dear. It's not God who makes wars, but bad people."

"Oh!" I said.

I was disappointed about that. I began to think that God wasn't quite what he was cracked up to be.

Next morning I woke at my usual hour, feeling like a bottle of champagne. I put out my feet and invented a long conversation in which Mrs. Right talked of the trouble she had with her own father till she put him in the Home. I didn't quite know what the Home was but it sounded the right place for Father. Then I got my chair and stuck my head out of the attic window. Dawn was just breaking, with a guilty air that made me feel I had caught it in the act. My head bursting with stories and schemes, I stumbled in next door, and in the half-darkness scrambled into the big bed. There was no room at Mother's side so I had to get between her and Father. For the time being I had forgotten about him, and for several minutes I sat bolt upright, racking my brains to know what I could do with him. He was taking up more than his fair share of the bed, and I couldn't get comfortable, so I gave him several kicks that made him grunt and stretch. He made room all right, though. Mother waked and felt for me. I settled back comfortably in the warmth of the bed with my thumb in my mouth.

"Mummy!" I hummed, loudly and contentedly.

"Sssh! dear," she whispered. "Don't wake Daddy!"

This was a new development, which threatened to be even more serious than "talking to Daddy." Life without my early-morning conferences was unthinkable.

"Why?" I asked severely.

"Because poor Daddy is tired."

This seemed to me a quite inadequate reason, and I was sickened by the sentimentality of her "poor Daddy." I never liked that sort of gush; it always struck me as insincere.

"Oh!" I said lightly. Then in my most winning tone: "Do you know where I want to go with you today, Mummy?"

"No, dear," she sighed.

"I want to go down the Glen and fish for thornybacks with my new net, and then I want to go out to the Fox and Hounds, and—"

"Don't-wake-Daddy!" she hissed angrily, clapping her hand across my mouth.

But it was too late. He was awake, or nearly so. He grunted and reached for the matches. Then he stared incredulously at his watch.

"Like a cup of tea, dear?" asked Mother in a meek, hushed voice I had never heard her use before. It sounded almost as though she were afraid.

"Tea?" he exclaimed indignantly. "Do you know what the time is?"

"And after that I want to go up the Rathcooney Road," I said loudly, afraid I'd forget something in all those interruptions.

"Go to sleep at once, Larry!" she said sharply.

I began to snivel. I couldn't concentrate, the way that pair went on, and smothering my early-morning schemes was like burying a family from the cradle.

Father said nothing, but lit his pipe and sucked it, looking out into the shadows without minding Mother or me. I knew he was mad. Every time I made a remark Mother hushed me irritably. I was mortified. I felt it wasn't fair; there was even something sinister in it. Every time I had pointed out to her the waste of making two beds when we could both sleep in one, she had told me it was healthier like that, and now here was this man, this stranger, sleeping with her without the least regard for her health!

He got up early and made tea, but though he brought Mother a cup he brought none for me.

"Mummy," I shouted, "I want a cup of tea, too."

"Yes, dear," she said patiently. "You can drink from Mummy's saucer."

That settled it. Either Father or I would have to leave the house. I didn't want to drink from Mother's saucer; I wanted to be treated as an equal in my own home, so, just to spite her, I drank it all and left none for her. She took that quietly, too.

But that night when she was putting me to bed she said gently:

"Larry, I want you to promise me something."

"What is it?" I asked.

"Not to come in and disturb poor Daddy in the morning. Promise?"

"Poor Daddy" again! I was becoming suspicious of everything involving that quite impossible man.

"Why?" I asked.

"Because poor Daddy is worried and tired and he doesn't sleep well."

"Why doesn't he, Mummy?"

"Well, you know, don't you, that while he was at the war Mummy got the pennies from the Post Office?"

"From Miss MacCarthy?"

"That's right. But now, you see, Miss MacCarthy hasn't any more pennies, so Daddy must go out and find us some. You know what would happen if he couldn't?"

"No," I said, "tell us."

"Well, I think we might have to go out and beg for them like the poor old woman on Fridays. We wouldn't like that, would we?"

"No," I agreed. "We wouldn't."

"So you'll promise not to come in and wake him?"

"Promise."

Mind you, I meant that. I knew pennies were a serious matter, and I was all against having to go out and beg like the old woman on Fridays. Mother laid out all my toys in a complete ring round the bed so that, whatever way I got out, I was bound to fall over one of them.

When I woke I remembered my promise all right. I got up and sat on the floor and played—for hours, it seemed to me. Then I got my chair and looked out the attic window for more hours. I wished it was time for Father to wake; I wished someone would make me a cup of tea. I didn't feel in the least like the sun; instead, I was bored and so very, very cold! I simply longed for the warmth and depth of the big featherbed.

At last I could stand it no longer. I went into the next room. As there was still no room at Mother's side I climbed over her and she woke with a start.

"Larry," she whispered, gripping my arm very tightly, "what did you promise?"

"But I did, Mummy," I wailed, caught in the very act. "I was quiet for ever so long."

"Oh, dear, and you're perished!" she said sadly, feeling me all over. "Now, if I let you stay will you promise not to talk?"

"But I want to talk, Mummy," I wailed.

"That has nothing to do with it," she said with a firmness that was new to me. "Daddy wants to sleep. Now, do you understand that?"

I understood it only too well. I wanted to talk, he wanted to sleep—whose house was it, anyway?

"Mummy," I said with equal firmness, "I think it would be healthier for Daddy to sleep in his own bed."

That seemed to stagger her, because she said nothing for a while.

"Now, once for all," she went on, "you're to be perfectly quiet or go back to your own bed. Which is it to be?"

The injustice of it got me down. I had convicted her out of her own mouth of inconsistency and unreasonableness, and she hadn't even attempted to reply. Full of spite, I gave Father a kick, which she didn't notice but which made him grunt and open his eyes in alarm.

"What time is it?" he asked in a panic-stricken voice, not looking at Mother but at the door, as if he saw someone there.

"It's early yet," she replied soothingly. "It's only the child. Go to sleep again. . . . Now, Larry," she added, getting out of bed, "you've wakened Daddy and you must go back."

This time, for all her quiet air, I knew she meant it, and knew that my principal rights and privileges were as good as lost unless I asserted them at once. As she lifted me, I gave a screech, enough to wake the dead, not to mind Father. He groaned.

"That damn child! Doesn't he ever sleep?"

"It's only a habit, dear," she said quietly, though I could see she was vexed.

"Well, it's time he got out of it," shouted Father, beginning to heave in the bed. He suddenly gathered all the bedclothes about him, turned to the wall, and then looked back over his shoulder with nothing showing only two small, spiteful, dark eyes. The man looked very wicked.

To open the bedroom door, Mother had to let me down, and I broke free and dashed for the farthest corner, screeching. Father sat bolt upright in bed.

"Shut up, you little puppy!" he said in a choking voice.

I was so astonished that I stopped screeching. Never, never had anyone spoken to me in that tone before. I looked at him incredulously and saw his face convulsed with rage. It was only then that I fully realized how God had coddled me, listening to my prayers for the safe return of this monster.

"Shut up, you!" I bawled, beside myself.

"What's that you said?" shouted Father, making a wild leap out of the bed.

"Mick, Mick!" cried Mother. "Don't you see the child isn't used to you?"

"I see he's better fed than taught," snarled Father, waving his arms wildly. "He wants his bottom smacked."

All his previous shouting was as nothing to these obscene words referring to my person. They really made my blood boil.

"Smack your own!" I screamed hysterically. "Smack your own! Shut up! Shut up!"

At this he lost his patience and let fly at me. He did it with the lack of conviction you'd expect of a man under Mother's horrified eyes, and it ended up as a mere tap, but the sheer indignity of being struck at all by a stranger, a total stranger who had cajoled his way back from the war into our big bed as a result of my innocent intercession, made me completely dotty. I shrieked and shrieked, and danced in my bare feet, and Father, looking awkward and hairy in nothing but a short grey army shirt, glared down at me like a mountain out for murder. I think it must have been then that I realized he was jealous too. And there stood Mother in her nightdress, looking as if her heart was broken between us. I hoped she felt as she looked. It seemed to me that she deserved it all.

From that morning out my life was a hell. Father and I were enemies, open and avowed. We conducted a series of skirmishes against one another, he trying to steal my time with Mother and I his. When she was sitting on my bed, telling me a story, he took to looking for some pair of old boots which he alleged he had left behind him at the beginning of the war. While he talked to Mother I played loudly with my toys to show my total lack of concern. He created a terrible scene one evening when he came in from work and found me at his box, playing with his regimental badges, Gurkha knives and button-sticks. Mother got up and took the box from me.

"You mustn't play with Daddy's toys unless he lets you, Larry," she said severely. "Daddy doesn't play with yours."

For some reason Father looked at her as if she had struck him and then turned away with a scowl.

"Those are not toys," he growled, taking down the box again to see had I lifted anything. "Some of those curios are very rare and valuable."

But as time went on I saw more and more how he managed to alienate Mother and me. What made it worse was that I couldn't grasp his method or see what attraction he had for Mother. In every possible way he was less winning than I. He had a common accent and made noises at his tea. I thought for a while that it might be the newspapers she was interested in, so I made up bits of news of my own to read to her. Then I thought it might be the smoking, which I personally thought attractive, and took his pipes and went round the house dribbling into them till he caught me. I even made noises at my tea, but Mother only told me I was disgusting. It all seemed to hinge round that unhealthy habit of sleeping together, so I made a point of dropping into their bedroom and nosing round, talking to myself, so that they wouldn't know I was watching them, but they were never up to anything that I could see. In the end it beat me. It seemed to depend on being grown-up and giving people rings, and I realized I'd have to wait.

But at the same time I wanted him to see that I was only waiting, not giving up the fight. One evening when he was being particularly obnoxious, chattering away well above my head, I let him have it.

"Mummy," I said, "do you know what I'm going to do when I grow up?"

"No, dear," she replied. "What?"

"I'm going to marry you," I said quietly.

Father gave a great guffaw out of him, but he didn't take me in. I knew it must only be pretence. And Mother, in spite of everything, was pleased. I felt she was probably relieved to know that one day Father's hold on her would be broken.

"Won't that be nice?" she said with a smile.

"It'll be very nice," I said confidently. "Because we're going to have lots and lots of babies."

"That's right, dear," she said placidly. "I think we'll have one soon, and then you'll have plenty of company."

I was no end pleased about that because it showed that in spite of the way she gave in to Father she still considered my wishes. Besides, it would put the Geneys in their place.

It didn't turn out like that, though. To begin with, she was very preoccupied—I supposed about where she would get the seventeen and six—and though Father took to staying out late in the evenings it did me no particular good. She stopped taking me for walks, became as touchy as blazes, and smacked me for nothing at all. Sometimes I wished I'd never mentioned the confounded baby—I seemed to have a genius for bringing calamity on myself.

And calamity it was! Sonny arrived in the most appalling hullabaloo—even that much he couldn't do without a fuss—and from the first moment I disliked him. He was a difficult child—so far as I was concerned he was always difficult—and demanded far too much attention. Mother was simply silly about him, and couldn't see when he was only showing off. As company he was worse than useless. He slept all day, and I had to go round the house on tiptoe to avoid waking him. It wasn't any longer a question of not waking Father. The slogan now was "Don't-wake-Sonny!" I couldn't understand why the child wouldn't sleep at the proper time, so whenever Mother's back was turned I woke him. Sometimes to keep him awake I pinched him as well. Mother caught me at it one day and gave me a most unmerciful flaking.

One evening, when Father was coming in from work, I was playing trains in the front garden. I let on not to notice him; instead, I pretended to be talking to myself, and said in a loud voice: "If another bloody baby comes into this house, I'm going out."

Father stopped dead and looked at me over his shoulder.

"What's that you said?" he asked sternly.

"I was only talking to myself," I replied, trying to conceal my panic. "It's private."

He turned and went in without a word. Mind you, I intended it as a solemn warning, but its effect was quite different. Father started being quite nice to me. I could understand that, of course. Mother was quite sickening about Sonny. Even at mealtimes she'd get up and gawk at him in the cradle with an idiotic smile, and tell Father to do the same. He was always polite about it, but he looked so puzzled you could see he didn't know what she was talking about. He complained of the way Sonny cried at night, but she only got cross and said that Sonny never cried except when there was something up with him—which was a flaming lie, because Sonny never had anything up with him, and only cried for attention. It was really painful to see how simple-minded she was. Father wasn't attractive, but he had a fine intelligence. He saw through Sonny, and now he knew that I saw through him as well.

One night I woke with a start. There was someone beside me in the bed. For one wild moment I felt sure it must be Mother, having come to her senses and left Father for good, but then I heard Sonny in convulsions in the next room, and Mother saying: "There! There! There!" and I knew it wasn't she. It was Father. He was lying beside me, wide awake, breathing hard and apparently as mad as hell.

After a while it came to me what he was mad about. It was his turn now. After turning me out of the big bed, he had been turned out himself. Mother had no consideration now for anyone but that poisonous pup, Sonny. I couldn't help feeling sorry for Father. I had been through it all myself, and even at that age I was magnanimous. I began to stroke him down and say: "There! There!" He wasn't exactly responsive.

"Aren't you asleep either?" he snarled.

"Ah, come on and put your arm around us, can't you?" I said, and he did, in a sort of way. Gingerly, I suppose, is how you'd describe it. He was very bony but better than nothing.

At Christmas he went out of his way to buy me a really nice model railway.

by William Carlos Williams

THE USE OF FORCE

William Carlos Williams was born on September 17, 1883, in Rutherford, New Jersey. He received his M.D. degree from the University of Pennsylvania in 1906 and studied pediatrics at the University of Leipzig. His poetry won early recognition and awards from the Dial *in 1926 and* Poetry *in 1931, and more recently from the National Institute of Arts and Letters (1948) and the Bollingen Prize Committee (1952). In 1952 Dr. Williams was appointed (but did not serve) as Consultant in Poetry to the Library of Congress. Besides his many volumes of verse, he has published seven novels, an autobiography, and a number of collections of his essays and stories. He died on March 4, 1963.*

"The Use of Force," like the other stories in Life Along the Passaic River, *exploits Dr. Williams' experience as a physician practicing among the distressed poor during the thirties. Unlike some fiction of that decade, it is more than a sociological tract. It concerns the stubborn force of the human will, lodged in however small and fevered a body, and that will's power to confront and defeat, morally at least, a physically more powerful opponent.*

THEY were new patients to me, all I had was the name, Olson. Please come down as soon as you can, my daughter is very sick.

When I arrived I was met by the mother, a big startled looking woman, very clean and apologetic who merely said, Is this the doctor? and let me in. In the back, she added. You must excuse us, doctor, we have her in the kitchen where it is warm. It is very damp here sometimes.

The child was fully dressed and sitting on her father's lap near the kitchen table. He tried to get up, but I motioned for him not to bother, took off my overcoat and started to look things over. I could see that they were all very nervous, eyeing me up and down distrustfully. As often, in such cases, they weren't telling me more than they had to, it was up to me to tell them; that's why they were spending three dollars on me.

The child was fairly eating me up with her cold, steady eyes, and no expression to her face whatever. She did not move and seemed, inwardly, quiet; an unusually attractive little thing, and as strong as a heifer in appearance. But her face was flushed, she was breathing rapidly, and I realized that she had a high fever. She had magnificent blonde hair, in profusion. One of those picture children often reproduced in advertising leaflets and the photogravure sections of the Sunday papers.

She's had a fever for three days, began the father and we don't know what it comes from. My wife has given her things, you know, like people do, but it don't do no good. And there's been a lot of sickness around. So we tho't you'd better look her over and tell us what is the matter.

As doctors often do I took a trial shot at it as a point of departure. Has she had a sore throat?

Both parents answered me together, No . . . No, she says her throat don't hurt her.

Does your throat hurt you? added the mother to the child. But the little girl's expression didn't change nor did she move her eyes from my face.

Have you looked?

I tried to, said the mother, but I couldn't see.

As it happens we had been having a number of cases of diphtheria in the school to which this child went during that month and we were all, quite apparently, thinking of that, though no one had as yet spoken of the thing.

Well, I said, suppose we take a look at the throat first. I smiled in my best professional manner and asking for the child's first name I said, come on, Mathilda, open your mouth and let's take a look at your throat.

Nothing doing.

Aw, come on, I coaxed, just open your mouth wide and let me take a look. Look, I said opening both hands wide, I haven't anything in my hands. Just open up and let me see.

Such a nice man, put in the mother. Look how kind he is to you. Come on, do what he tells you to. He won't hurt you.

At that I ground my teeth in disgust. If only they wouldn't use the word "hurt" I might be able to get somewhere. But I did not allow myself to be hurried or disturbed but speaking quietly and slowly I approached the child again.

As I moved my chair a little nearer suddenly with one cat-like movement both her hands clawed instinctively for my eyes and she almost reached them too. In fact she knocked my glasses flying and they fell, though unbroken, several feet away from me on the kitchen floor.

Both the mother and father almost turned themselves inside out in embarrassment and apology. You bad girl, said the mother, taking her and shaking her by one arm. Look what you've done. The nice man . . .

For heaven's sake, I broke in. Don't call me a nice man to her. I'm here to look at her throat on the chance that she might have diphtheria and possibly die of it. But that's nothing to her. Look here, I said to the child, we're going to look at your throat. You're old enough to understand what I'm saying. Will you open it now by yourself or shall we have to open it for you?

Not a move. Even her expression hadn't changed. Her breaths however were coming faster and faster. Then the battle began. I had to do it. I had to have a throat culture for her own protection. But first I told the parents that it was entirely up to them. I explained the danger but said that I would not insist on a throat examination so long as they would take the responsibility.

If you don't do what the doctor says you'll have to go to the hospital, the mother admonished her severely.

Oh yeah? I had to smile to myself. After all, I had already fallen in love with the savage brat, the parents were contemptible to me. In the ensuing struggle they grew more and more abject, crushed, exhausted while she surely rose to magnificent heights of insane fury of effort bred of her terror of me.

The father tried his best, and he was a big man but the fact that she was his daughter, his shame at her behavior and his dread of hurting her made him release her just at the critical moment several times when I had almost achieved success, till I wanted to kill him. But his dread also that she might have diphtheria made him tell me to go on, go on though he himself was almost fainting, while the mother moved back and forth behind us raising and lowering her hands in an agony of apprehension.

Put her in front of you on your lap, I ordered, and hold both her wrists.

But as soon as he did the child let out a scream. Don't, you're hurting me. Let go of my hands. Let them go I tell you. Then she shrieked terrifyingly, hysterically. Stop it! Stop it! You're killing me!

Do you think she can stand it, doctor! said the mother.

You get out, said the husband to his wife. Do you want her to die of diphtheria?

Come on now, hold her, I said.

Then I grasped the child's head with my left hand and tried to get the wooden tongue depressor between her teeth. She fought, with clenched teeth, desperately! But now I also had grown furious—at a child. I tried to hold myself down but I couldn't. I know how to expose a throat for inspection. And I did my best. When finally I got the wooden spatula behind the last teeth and just the point of it into the mouth cavity, she opened up for an instant but before I could see anything she came down again and gripping the wooden blade between her molars she reduced it to splinters before I could get it out again.

Aren't you ashamed, the mother yelled at her. Aren't you ashamed to act like that in front of the doctor?

Get me a smooth-handled spoon of some sort, I told the mother. We're going through with this. The child's mouth was already bleeding. Her tongue was cut and she was screaming in wild hysterical shrieks. Perhaps I should have desisted and come back in an hour or more. No doubt it would have been better. But I have seen at least two children lying dead in bed of neglect in such cases, and feeling that I must get a diagnosis now or never I went at it again. But the worst of it was that I too had got beyond reason. I could have torn the child apart in my own fury and enjoyed it. It was a pleasure to attack her. My face was burning with it.

The damned little brat must be protected against her own idiocy, one says to one's self at such time. Others must be protected against her. It is social necessity. And all these things are true. But a blind fury, a feeling of adult shame, bred of a longing for muscular release are the operatives. One goes on to the end.

In a final unreasoning assault I overpowered the child's neck and jaws. I forced the heavy silver spoon back of her teeth and down her throat till she gagged. And there it was—both tonsils covered with membrane. She had fought valiantly to keep me from knowing her secret. She had been hiding that sore throat for three days at least and lying to her parents in order to escape just such an outcome as this.

Now truly she *was* furious. She had been on the defensive before but now she attacked. Tried to get off her father's lap and fly at me while tears of defeat blinded her eyes.

by Dylan Thomas

THE TREE

Dylan Thomas was born on October 27, 1914, at Swansea, Wales, and educated at the Swansea Grammar School, where his father taught English. His first book, 18 Poems, *appeared when he was nineteen. At various times Thomas was a journalist, an odd-job man, a film script writer, and an anti-aircraft artillery observer—but always a poet. His fine voice got him work reading his poems and those of other poets over the B.B.C. Third Programme. He came to the United States in 1950, 1952, and 1953, to read poetry at colleges and universities across the country. On November 9, 1953, at St. Vincent's Hospital in New York, he died, at the age of thirty-nine. "The Tree" appears in* Adventures in the Skin Trade, *a collection of his experiments in the short story, published posthumously.*

Thomas once described his poetry as "the rhythmic, inevitably narrative, movement from an over-clothed blindness to a naked vision." To this end his poems deal with a psychic, almost, at times, an apocalyptic reality. In the story presented here these elements are fused, for he suggests that there is a deeply felt psychological aptness in the principal religious symbol, the tree. It is Adam's and Christ's and the Druids'. The boy and the idiot—"naturals" in an old sense of that word—apprehend that fact and respond to it, terribly but appropriately.

RISING from the house that faced Jarvis hills in the long distance, there was a tower for the day-birds to build in and for the owls to fly around at night. From the village the light of the tower window shone like a glowworm through the panes; but the room under the sparrows' nests was rarely lit; webs were spun over its unwashed ceilings; it stared over twenty miles of the up-and-down county, and the corners kept their secrets where there were claw marks in the dust.

The child knew the house from roof to cellar; he knew the irregular lawns and the gardener's shed where flowers burst out of their jars; but he could not find the key that opened the door of the tower.

The house changed to his moods, and a lawn was the sea or the shore or the sky or whatever he wished it. When a lawn was a sad mile of water, and he was sailing on a broken flower down the waves, the gardener would come out of his shed near the island of bushes. He, too, would take a stalk, and sail. Straddling a garden broom, he would fly wherever the child wished. He knew every story from the beginning of the world.

In the beginning, he would say, there was a tree.

What kind of tree?

The tree where that blackbird's whistling.

A hawk, a hawk, cried the child.

The gardener would look up at the tree, seeing a monstrous hawk perched on a bough or an eagle swinging in the wind.

The gardener loved the Bible. When the sun sank and the garden was full of people, he would sit with a candle in his shed, reading of the first love and the legend of apples and serpents. But the death of Christ on a tree he loved most. Trees made a fence around him, and he knew of the changing of the seasons by the hues on the bark and the rushing of sap through the covered roots. His world moved and changed as spring moved along the branches, changing their nakedness; his God grew up like a tree from the apple-shaped earth, giving bud to His children and letting His children be blown from their places by the breezes of winter; winter and death moved in one wind. He would sit in his shed and read of the crucifixion, looking over the jars on his window-shelf into the winter nights. He would think that love fails on such nights, and that many of its children are cut down.

The child transfigured the blowsy lawns with his playing. The gardener called him by his mother's name, and seated him on his knee, and talked to him of the wonders of Jerusalem and the birth in the manger.

In the beginning was the village of Bethlehem, he whispered to the child before the bell rang for tea out of the growing darkness.

Where is Bethlehem?

Far away, said the gardener, in the East.

To the east stood the Jarvis hills, hiding the sun, their trees drawing up the moon out of the grass.

The child lay in bed. He watched the rocking horse and wished that it would grow wings so that he could mount it and ride into the Arabian sky. But the winds of Wales blew at the curtains, and crickets made a noise in the untidy plot under the window. His toys were dead. He started to cry and then stopped, knowing no reason for tears. The night was windy and cold, he was warm under the sheets; the night was as big as a hill, he was a boy in bed.

Closing his eyes, he stared into a spinning cavern deeper than the darkness of the garden where the first tree on which the unreal birds had fastened stood alone and bright as fire. The tears ran back under his lids as he thought of the first tree that was planted so near him, like a friend in the garden. He crept out of bed and tiptoed to the door. The rocking horse bounded forward on its springs, startling the child into a noiseless scamper back to bed. The child looked at the horse and the horse was quiet; he tiptoed again along the carpet, and reached the door, and turned the knob around, and ran on to the landing. Feeling blindly in front of him, he made his way to the top of the stairs; he looked down the dark stairs into the hall, seeing a host of shadows curve in and out of the corners, hearing their sinuous voices, imagining the pits of their eyes and their lean arms. But they would be little and secret and bloodless, not cased in invisible armour but wound around with cloths as thin as a web; they would whisper as he walked, touch him on the shoulder, and say S in his ear. He went down the stairs; not a shadow moved in the hall, the corners were empty. He put out his hand and patted the darkness, thinking to feel some dry and velvet head creep under the fingers and edge, like a mist, into the nails. But there was nothing. He opened the front door, and the shadows swept into the garden.

Once on the path, his fears left him. The moon had lain down on the unweeded beds, and her frosts were spread on the grass. At last he came to the illuminated tree at the long gravel end, older even than the marvel of light, with the woodlice asleep under the bark, with the boughs standing out from the body like the frozen arms of a woman. The child touched the tree; it bent as to his touch. He saw a star, brighter than any in the sky, burn steadily above the first birds' tower, and shine on nowhere but on the leafless boughs and the trunk and the travelling roots.

The child had not doubted the tree. He said his prayers to it, with knees bent on the blackened twigs the night wind fetched to the ground. Then, trembling with love and cold, he ran back over the lawns towards the house.

There was an idiot to the east of the county who walked the land like a beggar. Now at a farmhouse and now at a widow's cottage he begged for his bread. A parson gave him a suit, and it lopped round his hungry ribs and shoulders and waved in the wind as he shambled over the fields. But his eyes were so wide and his neck so clear of the country dirt that no one refused him what he asked. And asking for water, he was given milk.

Where do you come from?

From the east, he said.

So they knew he was an idiot, and gave him a meal to clean the yards.

As he bent with a rake over the dung and the trodden grain, he heard a voice rise in his heart. He put his hand into the cattle's hay, caught a mouse, rubbed his hand over its muzzle, and let it go away.

All day the thought of the tree was with the child; all night it stood up in his dreams as the star stood above its plot. One morning towards the middle of December, when the wind from the farthest hills was rushing around the house, and the snow of the dark hours had not dissolved from lawns and roofs, he ran to the gardener's shed. The gardener was repairing a rake he had found broken. Without a word, the child sat on a seedbox at his feet, and watched him tie the teeth, and knew that the wire would not keep them together. He looked at the gardener's boots, wet with snow, at the patched knees of his trousers, at the undone buttons of his coat, and the folds of his belly under the patched flannel shirt. He looked at his hands as they busied themselves over the garden knots of wire; they were hard, brown hands, with the stains of the soil under the broken nails and the stains of tobacco on the tips of the fingers. Now the lines of the gardener's face were set in determination as time upon time he knotted the iron teeth only to feel them shake insecurely from the handle. The child was frightened of the strength and uncleanliness of the old man; but, looking at the long, thick beard, unstained and white as fleece, he soon became reassured. The beard was the beard of an apostle.

I prayed to the tree, said the child.

Always pray to a tree, said the gardener, thinking of Calvary and Eden.

I pray to the tree every night.

Pray to a tree.

The wire slid over the teeth.

I pray to that tree.

The wire snapped.

The child was pointing over the glasshouse flowers to the tree that, alone of all the trees in the garden, had no sign of snow.

An elder, said the gardener, but the child stood up from his box and shouted so loud that the unmended rake fell with a clatter on the floor.

The first tree. The first tree you told me of. In the beginning was the tree, you said. I heard you, the child shouted.

The elder is as good as another, said the gardener, lowering his voice to humour the child.

The first tree of all, said the child in a whisper.

Reassured again by the gardener's voice, he smiled through the window at the tree, and again the wire crept over the broken rake.

God grows in strange trees, said the old man. His trees come to rest in strange places.

As he unfolded the story of the twelve stages of the cross, the tree waved its boughs to the child. An apostle's voice rose out of the tarred lungs.

So they hoisted him up on a tree, and drove nails through his belly and his feet.

There was the blood of the noon sun on the trunk of the elder, staining the bark.

The idiot stood on the Jarvis hills, looking down into the immaculate valley from whose waters and grasses the mists of morning rose and were lost. He saw the dew dissolving, the cattle staring into the stream, and the dark clouds flying away at the rumour of the sun.

The sun turned at the edges of the thin and watery sky like a sweet in a glass of water. He was hungry for light as the first and almost invisible rain fell on his lips; he plucked at the grass, and, tasting it, felt it lie green on his tongue. So there was light in his mouth, and light was a sound at his ears, and the whole dominion of light in the valley that had such a curious name. He had known of the Jarvis hills; their shapes rose over the slopes of the county to be seen for miles around, but no one had told him of the valley lying under the hills. Bethlehem, said the idiot to the valley, turning over the sounds of the word and giving it all the glory of the Welsh morning. He brothered the world around him, sipped at the air as a child newly born sips and brothers the light. The life of the Jarvis valley, steaming up from the body of the grass and the trees and the long hand of the stream, lent him a new blood. Night had emptied the idiot's veins, and dawn in the valley filled them again.

Bethlehem, said the idiot to the valley.

The gardener had no present to give the child, so he took out a key from his pocket and said, This is the key to the tower. On Christmas Eve I will unlock the door for you.

Before it was dark, he and the child climbed the stairs to the tower, the key turned in the lock, and the door, like the lid of a secret box, opened and let them in. The room was empty. Where are the secrets? asked the child, staring up at the matted rafters and into the spiders' corners and along the leaden panes of the window.

It is enough that I have given you the key, said the gardener, who believed the key of the universe to be hidden in his pocket along with the feathers of birds and the seeds of flowers.

The child began to cry because there were no secrets. Over and over again he explored the empty room, kicking up the dust to look for a colourless trap-door, tapping the unpanelled walls for the hollow voice of a room beyond the tower. He brushed the webs from the window, and looked out through the dust into the snowing Christmas Eve. A world of hills stretched far away into the measured sky, and the tops of the hills he had never seen climbed up to meet the falling flakes. Woods and rocks, wide seas of barren land, and a new tide of mountain sky sweeping through the black beeches, lay before him. To the east were the outlines of nameless hill creatures and a den of trees.

Who are they? Who are they?

They are the Jarvis hills, said the gardener, which have been from the beginning.

He took the child by the hand and led him away from the window. The key turned in the lock.

That night the child slept well; there was power in snow and darkness; there was unalterable music in the silence of the stars; there was a silence in the hurrying wind. And Bethlehem had been nearer than he expected.

On Christmas morning the idiot walked into the garden. His hair was wet and his flaked and ragged shoes were thick with the dirt of the fields. Tired from the long journey from the Jarvis hills, and weak for the want of food, he sat down under the elder-tree where the gardener had rolled a log. Clasping his hands in front of him, he saw the desolation of the flower-beds and the weeds that grew in profusion on the edges of the paths. The tower stood up like a tree of stone and glass over the red eaves. He pulled his coat-collar round his neck as a fresh wind sprang up and struck the tree; he looked down at his hands and saw that they were praying. Then a fear of the garden came over him, the shrubs were his enemies, and the trees that made an avenue down to the gate lifted their arms in horror. The place was too high, peering down onto the tall hills; the place was too low, shivering up at the plumed shoulders of a new mountain. Here the wind was too wild, fuming about the silence, raising a Jewish voice out of the elder boughs; here the silence beat like a human heart. And as he sat under the cruel hills, he heard a voice that was in him cry out: Why did you bring me here?

He could not tell why he had come; they had told him to come and had guided him, but he did not know who they were. The voice of a people rose out of the garden beds, and rain swooped down from heaven.

Let me be, said the idiot, and made a little gesture against the sky. There is rain on my face, there is wind on my cheeks. He brothered the rain.

So the child found him under the shelter of the tree, bearing the torture of the weather with a divine patience, letting his long hair blow where it would, with his mouth set in a sad smile.

Who was the stranger? He had fires in his eyes, the flesh of his neck under the gathered coat was bare. Yet he smiled as he sat in his rags under a tree on Christmas Day.

Where do you come from? asked the child.

From the east, answered the idiot.

The gardener had not lied, and the secret of the tower was true; this dark and shabby tree, that glistened only in the night, was the first tree of all.

But he asked again:

Where do you come from?

From the Jarvis hills.

Stand up against the tree.

The idiot, still smiling, stood up with his back to the elder.

Put out your arms like this.

The idiot put out his arms.

The child ran as fast as he could to the gardener's shed, and, returning over the sodden lawns, saw that the idiot had not moved but stood, straight and smiling, with his back to the tree and his arms stretched out.

Let me tie your hands.

The idiot felt the wire that had not mended the rake close round his wrists. It cut into the flesh, and the blood from the cuts fell shining on to the tree.

Brother, he said. He saw that the child held silver nails in the palm of his hand.

by Elizabeth Bowen

SONGS MY FATHER SANG ME

Elizabeth Bowen was born on June 7, 1899, in Dublin, but spent most of her school years in the south of England. She wrote her first short stories when she was twenty; her first book appeared in 1923. She has published six collections of stories, eight novels, and three volumes of essays. Miss Bowen has been awarded honorary degrees by Oxford and Trinity College, Dublin.

During World War II Miss Bowen worked days for the Ministry of Information and nights as an air raid warden in London. She was also at work on a novel and the stories collected in Ivy Gripped the Steps *(1946), of which "Songs My Father Sang Me" is one. In her preface to that collection, Miss Bowen, speaking of the "climate" of the war years, says, "The search for indestructible landmarks in a destructible world led many down strange paths. The attachment to these when they had been found produced small worlds-within-worlds of hallucination—in most cases, saving hallucination." Certainly part of this statement applies to the girl in "Songs My Father Sang Me." To her, at least at times, her father is twenty-six (though she must be nearly that age herself); and wartime London is not nearly so real to her as one summer afternoon in 1925. It is less certain, however, that her hallucination is a "saving" one.*

"WHAT'S the matter," he asked, "have I said something?"

Not troubling to get him quite into focus, she turned her head and said, "No, why—did you say anything?"

"Or p'r'aps you don't like this place?"

"I don't mind it—why?" she said, looking round the night club, which was not quite as dark as a church, as though for the first time. At some tables you had to look twice, to see who was there; what lights there were were dissolved in a haze of smoke; the walls were rather vault-like, with no mirrors; on the floor dancers drifted like pairs of vertical fish. He, meanwhile, studied her from across their table with neither anxiety nor acute interest, but with a dreamlike caricature of both. Then he raised the bottle between them and said, "Mm-mm?" to which she replied by placing the flat of her hand mutely, mulishly, across the top of her glass. Not annoyed, he shrugged, filled up his own and continued, "Then anything isn't really the matter then?"

"This tune, this song, is the matter."

"Oh—shall we dance?"

"No." Behind her agelessly girlish face, sleekly framed by the cut of her fawn-blonde hair, there passed a wave of genuine trouble for which her features had no vocabulary. "It's what they're playing—this tune."

"It's pre-war," he said knowledgeably.

"It's last war."

"Well, last war's pre-war."

"It's the tune my father remembered he used to dance to; it's the tune I remember him always trying to sing."

"Why, is your father dead?"

"No, I don't suppose so; why?"

"Sorry," he said quickly, "I mean, if . . ."

"Sorry, why are you sorry?" she said, raising her eyebrows. "Didn't I ever tell you about my father? I always thought he made me rather a bore. Wasn't it you I was telling about my father?"

"No. I suppose it must have been someone else. One meets so many people."

"Oh, what," she said, "have I hurt your feelings? But you haven't got any feelings about me."

"Only because you haven't got any feelings about me."

"Haven't I?" she said, as though really wanting to know. "Still, it hasn't seemed all the time as though we were quite a flop."

"Look," he said, "don't be awkward. Tell me about your father."

"He was twenty-six."

"When?"

"How do you mean, 'when'? Twenty-six was my father's age. He was tall and lean and leggy, with a casual sort of way of swinging himself about. He was fair, and the shape of his face was a rather long narrow square. Sometimes his eyes faded in until you could hardly see them; sometimes he seemed to be wearing a blank mask. You really only quite got the plan of his face when it was turned halfway between a light and a shadow—*then* his eyebrows and eyehollows, the dints just over his nostrils, the cut of his upper lip and the cleft of his chin, and the broken in-and-out outline down from his temple past his cheekbone into his jaw all came out at you, like a message you had to read in a single flash."

She paused and lighted a cigarette. He said, "You sound as though you had never got used to him."

She went on, "My father was one of the young men who were not killed in the last war. He was a man in the last war until that stopped; then I don't quite know what he was, and I don't think he ever quite knew either. He got his commission and first went out to France about 1915, I think he said. When he got leaves he got back to London and had good times, by which I mean something larky but quite romantic, in the course of one of which, I don't know which one, he fell in love with my mother and they used to go dancing, and got engaged in that leave and got married the next. My mother was a flapper, if you knew about flappers? They were the pin-ups *de ses jours*, and at the same time inspired idealistic feeling. My mother was dark and fluffy and as slim as a wraith; a great *glacé* ribbon bow tied her hair back and stood out like a calyx behind her face, and her hair itself hung down in a plume so long that it tickled my father's hand while he held her while they were dancing and while she sometimes swam up at him with her violet eyes. Each time he had to go back to the front again she was miserable, and had to put her hair up, because her relations said it was high time. But sometimes when he got back again on leave she returned to being a flapper again, to please him. Between his leaves she had to go back to live with her mother and sisters in West Kensington; and her sisters had a whole pack of business friends who had somehow never had to go near the front, and all these combined in an effort to cheer her up, but, as she always wrote to my father, nothing did any good. I suppose everyone felt it was for the best when they knew there was going to be the patter of little feet. I wasn't actually *born* till the summer of 1918. If you remember, I told you my age last night.

"The first thing *I* remember, upon becoming conscious, was living in one of those bungalows on the flats near Staines. The river must have been somewhere, but I don't think I saw it. The only point about that region is that it has no point and that it goes on and on. I think there are floods there sometimes, there would be nothing to stop them; a forest fire would be what is needed really, but that would not be possible as there are no trees. It would have looked better, really, just left as primeval marsh, but someone had once said, 'Let there be bungalows.' If you ever motored anywhere near it you probably asked yourself who lives there, and why. Well, my father and mother and I did, and why?—because it was cheap, and there was no one to criticize how you were getting on. Our bungalow was tucked well away in the middle, got at by a sort of maze of in those days unmade roads. I'm glad to say I've forgotten which one it was. Most of our neighbours kept themselves to themselves for, probably, like ours, the best reasons, but most of them kept hens also; we didn't even do that. All round us, nature ran riot between corrugated iron, clothes-lines and creosoted lean-to sheds.

"I know that our bungalow had been taken furnished; the only things we seemed to have of our own were a number of satin cushions with satin fruits stitched on. In order to dislodge my biscuit crumbs from the satin apples my mother used to shake the cushions out of the window on to the lawn. Except for the prettiness of the dandelions, our lawn got to look and feel rather like a hearth-rug; I mean, it got covered with threads and cinders and shreds; once when I was crawling on it I got a pin in my hand, another time I got sharp glass beads in my knee. The next-door hens used to slip through and pick about; never, apparently, quite in vain. At the far end, some Dorothy Perkins roses tried to climb up a pergola that was always falling down. I remember my father reaching up in his shirt-sleeves, trying to nail it up. Another thing he had to do in our home was apply the whole of his strength to the doors, french window and windows, which warped until they would not open nor shut. I used to come up behind him and push too.

"The war by now, of course, had been over for some years; my father was out of the British Army and was what was called taking his time and looking around. For how long he had been doing so I can't exactly tell you. He not only read all the 'post vacant' advertisements every day but composed and succeeded in getting printed an advertisement of himself, which he read aloud to me: it said he was prepared to go anywhere and try anything. I said, 'But what's an ex-officer?', and he said, 'I am.' Our dining-room table, which was for some reason possibly me, sticky, was always spread with new newspapers he had just brought home, and he used to be leaning over them on his elbows, biting harder and harder on the stem of his pipe. I don't think I discovered for some years later that the principal reason for newspapers is news. My father never looked at them for that reason—just as he always lost interest in any book in which he had lost his place. Or perhaps he was not in the mood for world events. My mother had never cared much for them at the best of times. 'To think of all we expected after the war,' she used to say to my father, from day to day.

"My mother, by this time, had had her hair shingled—in fact, *I* never remember her any other way than with a dark shaved point tapered down the back of her neck. I don't know when she'd begun to be jealous of him and me. Every time he came back from an interview that he hadn't got to or from an interview that hadn't come to anything, he used to bring me back something, to cheer himself up, and the wheels off all the mechanical toys got mixed with the beads and the threads and the cinders into our lawn. What my mother was really most afraid of was that my father would bundle us all off into the great open spaces, in order to start fresh somewhere and grow something. I imagine he knew several chaps who had, or were going to. After one or two starts on the subject he shut up, but I could see she could see he was nursing it. It frustrated her from nagging at him all out about not succeeding in getting a job in England: she was anxious not to provide an opening for him to say, 'Well, there's always one thing we *could* do . . .' The hard glassy look her eyes got made them look like doll's eyes, which may partly have been what kept me from liking dolls. So they practically never talked about anything. I don't think she even knew he minded about her hair.

"You may be going to ask when my father sang. He often *began* to sing—when he hammered away at the pergola, when something he thought of suddenly struck him as good, when the heave he gave at the warped french window sent it flying open into the garden. He was constantly starting to sing, but he never got very far—you see, he had no place where he could sing unheard. The walls were thin and the lawn was tiny and the air round the bungalow was so silent and heavy that my mother was forced to listen to every note. The lordly way my father would burst out singing, like the lordly way he cocked his hat over one eye, had come to annoy her, in view of everything else. But the still more unfortunate thing was that my father only knew, or else only liked, two tunes, which were two tunes out of the bygone years which made him think of the war and being in love. Yes, they were dance tunes; yes, we have just heard one; yes, they also reminded my mother of war and love. So when he had got to the fourth or fifth bar of either, she would call out to know if he wanted to drive her mad. He would say and say, 'Sorry,' but if he was in the mood he'd be well away, the next minute, with the alternative tune, and she would be put to the trouble of stopping that.

"Mother did not know what to look like now she was not a flapper. Mostly she looked like nothing—I wonder whether she knew. Perhaps that was what she saw in the satin cushions: they looked like something—at least, to her. The day she and I so suddenly went to London to call on her sister's friend she did certainly manage, however, to look like something. My father, watching us down the garden path, ventured no comment on her or my appearance. However, which ought to have cheered me up, we created quite a furore in the train. We went sailing into the richly-appointed office of mother's sister's friend, who was one of those who, during the war, had felt mother should be cheered up. Can I, need I, describe him? The usual kind of business pudge, in a suit. He looked in a reluctant way at my mother, and reluctantly, slightly morbidly, at me. I don't know how I got the impression mother held all the cards. The conversation, of course, flowed over my head—I just cruised round and round the room, knocking objects over. But the outcome—as I gathered when we got home—was that mother's sister's friend said he'd give my father a job. He had said he could use an ex-officer, provided it was an ex-officer with charm. What my father would have to do was to interest housewives, not in himself but in vacuum cleaners. If it helped to interest some housewives in vacuum cleaners, he could interest them just a little bit in himself. Mother's sister's friend called this, using judgment of character.

"When my mother, that evening, put all this to my father, he did not say anything but simply stood and stared. *She* said, 'Then I suppose you want us to starve?'

"So my father stopped being a problem and became a travelling salesman. The best part was that the firm allowed him a car.

"I must say for my mother that she did not ask my father how he was getting on. At least she had much less trouble about the singing: sometimes he'd be away for two or three days together; when he was home he simply sprawled in his chair, now and then asking when there'd be something to eat, as unmusical as a gramophone with the spring broken. When I came filtering in he sometimes opened one eye and said, 'And what have *you* been doing?'—as though he'd just finished telling me what he'd been doing himself. He garaged the car some way down the next road, and in the mornings when he was starting off I used to walk with him to the garage. He used to get into the car, start up the engine, back out, then look round at me and say, 'Like to come out on the job?—yes, I bet you would,' then let the clutch in and whizz off. Something about this always made me feel sick.

"I don't of course clearly remember when this began, or how long it went on for; but I know when it stopped. The night before my seventh birthday was a June night, because my birthdays are in June. The people who lived all round us were sitting out, on the verandas or on their lawns, but my mother had sent me to bed early because she was having a party for me next day and did not want to get me over-excited. My birthday cake which had arrived from the shop was on the dining-room sideboard, with a teacloth over it to keep the flies off, and my father and mother were in the lounge with the french window shut, because she had several things to say to him that she did not want the people all round to hear. The heat travelled through the roof into all the rooms, so that I could not sleep: also, my bed was against the wall of my room, and the lounge was the other side of the wall. My mother went on like someone who has been saving up—just some touch, I suppose, had been needed to set her off. She said she would like to know why there was not more money—my father's job, I suppose now, was on a commission basis. Or, she said, was he keeping another woman?—a thing she had heard that most travelling salesmen did. She said she really felt quite ashamed of having foisted my father on to her sister's friend, and that she only wondered how long the firm would stand for it. She said her sisters pitied her, though she had tried to conceal from them that her life was hell. My father, who had as usual got home late and as usual had not yet had any supper, could not be heard saying anything. My mother then said she wished she knew why she had married him, and would like still more to know why he had married her.

"My father said, 'You were so lovely—you've no idea.'

"Next morning there was a heat-haze over everything. I bustled into the dining-room to see if there was anything on my plate. I forget what my mother had given me, but her richest sister had sent me a manicure-set in a purple box: all the objects had purple handles and lay in grooves on white velvet. While I was taking them out and putting them back again, my father suddenly looked up from his coffee and said *his* present for me was in the car, and that I'd have to come out and fetch it. My mother could hardly say no to this, though of course I saw her opening her mouth. So out we set, I gripping the manicure-set. I don't think my father seemed odder than usual, though he was on the point of doing an unexpected thing—when he had got the car started and backed out he suddenly held open the other door and said, 'Come on, nip in, look sharp; my present to you is a day trip.' So then I nipped in and we drove off, as though this were the most natural thing in the world.

"The car was a two-seater, with a let-down hood . . . No, of course I cannot remember what make it was. That morning, the hood was down. Locked up in the dickie behind my father kept the specimen vacuum cleaner he interested women in. He drove fast, and as we hit the bumps in the road I heard the parts of the cleaner clonking about. As we drove, the sun began to burn its way through the haze, making the roses in some of the grander gardens look almost impossibly large and bright. My bare knees began to grill on the leather cushion, and the crumples eased out of the front of my cotton frock.

"I had never been with my father when he was driving a car—it felt as though speed and power were streaming out of him, and as if he and I were devouring everything that we passed. I sat slumped round with my cheek against the hot cushion and sometimes stared at his profile, sometimes stared at his wrists, till he squinted round and said, 'Anything wrong with *me*?' Later on, he added, 'Why not look at the scenery?' By that time there *was* some scenery, if that means grass and trees; in fact, these had been going on for some time, in a green band streaming behind my father's face. When I said, 'Where are we going?' he said, 'Well, where *are* we going?' At that point I saw quite a large hill, in fact a whole party of them, lapping into each other as though they would never stop, and never having seen anything of the kind before I could not help saying, 'Oh, I say, look!'

"My father gave a nod, without stopping singing—I told you he had begun to sing? He had not only started but gone on: when he came to the end of his first tune he said, 'Pom-*pom*,' like a drum, then started through it again; after that he worked around to the second, which he sang two or three times, with me joining in. We both liked the second still better, and how right we were—and it's worn well, hasn't it? That's what this band's just played."

"Oh, what they've just played?" he said, and looked narrowly at the band; while, reaching round for the bottle on the table between them he lifted it to replenish her glass and his. This time she did not see or did not bother to stop him: she looked at her full glass vaguely, then vaguely drank. After a minute she went on:

"Ginger beer, sausage rolls, chocolate—that was what we bought when we stopped at the village shop. Also my father bought a blue comb off a card of combs, with which he attempted to do my hair, which had blown into tags and ratstails over my eyes and face. He looked at me while he combed in a puzzled way, as though something about me that hadn't struck him became a problem to him for the first time. I said, 'Aren't we going to sell any vacuum cleaners?' and he said, 'We'll try and interest the Berkshire Downs.' I thought that meant, meet a family; but all we did was turn out of the village and start up a rough track, to where there could not be any people at all. The car climbed with a slow but exciting roar; from the heat of the engine and the heat of the sun the chocolate in the paper bag in my hands was melting by the time we came to the top.

"From the top, where we lay on our stomachs in the shade of the car, we could see—oh well, can't you imagine, can't you? It was an outsize June day. The country below us looked all colours, and was washed over in the most reckless way with light; going on and on into the distance the clumps of trees and the roofs of villages and the church towers had quivering glimmers round them; but most of all there was space, sort of moulded space, and the blue of earth ran into the blue of sky.

"My father's face was turned away from me, propped up on his hand. I finally said to him, 'What's that?'

" 'What's what?' he said, startled.

" 'What we're looking at.'

" 'England,' he said, 'that's England. I thought I'd like to see her again.'

" 'But don't we live in England?'

"He took no notice. 'How I loved her,' he said.

" 'Oh, but don't you now?'

" 'I've lost her,' he said, 'or she's lost me; I don't quite know which; I don't understand what's happened.' He rolled round and looked at me and said, 'But *you* like it, don't you? I thought I'd like you to see, if just once, what I once saw.'

"I was well into the third of my sausage rolls: my mouth was full, I could only stare at my father. He said, 'And there's something else down there—see it?' I screwed my eyes up but still only saw the distance. 'Peace,' he said. 'Look hard at it; don't forget it.'

" 'What's peace?' I said.

" 'An idea you have when there's a war on, to make you fight well. An idea that gets lost when there isn't a war.'

"I licked pastry-crumbs off my chin and began on chocolate. By this time my father lay on his back, with his fingers thatched together over his eyes: he talked, but more to the sky than me. None of the things he was saying now went anywhere near my brain—a child's brain, how could they?—his actual words are gone as though I had never heard them, but his meaning lodged itself in some part of my inside, and is still there and has grown up with me. He talked about war and how he had once felt, and about leaves and love and dancing and going back to the war, then the birth of me—'Seven years ago to-day,' he said, 'seven years; I remember how they brought me the telegram.'

"Something else, on top of the sausage and heat and chocolate suddenly made me feel sick and begin to cry. 'Oh please, oh please don't,' I said, 'it's my birthday.'

" 'Don't what?' he said. I, naturally, didn't know. My father again looked at me, with the same expression he had worn when attempting to comb my hair. Something about me—my age?—was a proposition. Then he shut his eyes, like—I saw later, not at the time —somebody finally banishing an idea. 'No; it wouldn't work,' he said. 'It simply couldn't be done. You can wait for me if you want. I can't wait for you.'

"Then he began acting like somebody very sleepy: he yawned and yawned at me till I yawned at him. I didn't feel sick any more, but the heat of the afternoon came down like a grey-blue blanket over my head. 'What you and I want,' my father said, watching me, 'is a good sleep.'

"I wish I could tell you at *which* moment I fell asleep, and stopped blurrily looking at him between my eyelids, because *that* was the moment when I last saw my father.

"When I woke, there was no more shadow on my side of the car; the light had changed and everything looked bright yellow. I called to my father but he did not answer, for the adequate reason that he was not there. He was gone. For some reason I wasn't at all frightened; I thought he must have gone to look for something for us for tea. I remembered that I was not at my birthday party, and I must say I thought twice about that pink cake. I was more bored than anything, till I remembered my manicure-set, which owing to the funniness of the day I had not been able to open a second time. I took the objects out of their velvet bedding and began to prod at my nails, as I'd seen my mother do. Then I got up and walked, once more, all the way round the car. It was then that I noticed what I had missed before: a piece of white paper twisted into the radiator. I couldn't read handwriting very well, but did at last make out what my father had put. '*The car and the vacuum cleaner are the property of Messrs. X and X*' (the firm of my mother's sister's friend), '*the child is the property of Mrs. So-and-so, of Such-and-such*' (I needn't bother to give you my mother's name and the name of our bungalow), '*the manicure-set, the comb and anything still left in the paper bags are the property of the child. Signed——*' It was signed with my father's name.

"The two dots I saw starting zigzag up the side of the down turned out to be two sweating policemen. What happened when they came to where I was was interesting at the moment but is not interesting now. They checked up on the message on the front of the car, then told me my father had telephoned to the police station, and that I was to be a good girl and come with them. When they had checked up on the cleaner, we all drove down. I remember the constable's knobbly, sticky red hands looked queer on the wheel where my father's had lately been . . . At the police station, someone or other's wife made quite a fuss about me and gave me tea, then we piled into another car and drove on again. I was soon dead asleep; and I only woke when we stopped in the dark at the gate of the bungalow.

"Having tottered down the path, in the light from the front door, my mother clawed me out of the car, sobbing. I noticed her breath smelt unusual. We and the policeman then trooped into the lounge, where the policeman kept nodding and jotting things on a pad. To cheer up my mother he said that England was very small—'And he's not, so far as you know, in possession of a passport?' I sucked blobs of chocolate off the front of my frock while my mother described my father to the policeman. 'But no doubt,' the policeman said, 'he'll be thinking better of this. A man's home is a man's home, I always say.'

"When my mother and I were left alone in the lounge, we stared at each other in the electric light. While she asked if I knew how unnatural my father was, she kept pouring out a little more from the bottle: she said she had to have medicine to settle her nerves, but it seemed to act on her nerves just the opposite way. That I wouldn't say what my father had said and done set her off fairly raving against my father. To put it mildly, she lost all kind of control. She finished up with: 'And such a fool, too—a fool, a fool!'

" 'He is not a fool,' I said, 'he's my father.'

" 'He is not your father,' she screamed, 'and he is a fool.'

"That made me stare at her, and her stare at me.

" 'How do you mean,' I said, 'my father is not my father?'

"My mother's reaction to this was exactly like as if someone had suddenly pitched a pail of cold water over her. She pulled herself up and something jumped in her eyes. She said she had not said anything of the sort, and that if I ever said she had I was a wicked girl. I said I hadn't said she had, but she had said so. She put on a worried look and put a hand on my forehead and said she could feel I'd got a touch of the sun. A touch of the sun, she said, would make me imagine things—and no wonder, after the day I'd had.

"All next day I was kept in bed; not as a punishment but as a kind of treat. My mother was ever so nice to me; she kept coming in to put a hand on my forehead. The one thing she did not do was get the doctor. And afterwards, when I was let get up, nothing was good enough for me; until really anyone would have thought that my mother felt she was in my power. Shortly after, her rich sister came down, and my mother then had a fine time, crying, talking and crying; the sister then took us back with her to London, where my mother talked and cried even more. Of course I asked my aunt about what my mother had said, but my aunt said that if I imagined such wicked things they would have to think there was something wrong with my brain. So I did not re-open the subject, and am not doing so now. In the course of time my mother succeeded in divorcing my father for desertion; she was unable to marry her sister's friend because he was married and apparently always had been, but she did marry a friend of her sister's friend's, and was soon respectably settled in Bermuda, where as far as I know she still is."

"But your father?" he said.

"Well, what about my father?"

"You don't mean you never heard anything more of him?"

"I never said so—he sent me two picture postcards. The last"—she counted back—"arrived fourteen years ago. But there probably have been others that went astray. The way I've always lived, I'm not long at any address."

He essayed, rashly, "Been a bit of a waif?"

The look he got back for this was halfway between glass and ice. "A waif's the first thing I learned not to be. No, more likely my father decided, better leave it at that. People don't, on the whole, come back, and I've never blamed them. No, why should he be dead? Why should not he be—any place?"

"Here, for instance?"

"To-night, you mean?"

"Why not?" he said. "Why not—as you say?"

"Here?" She looked round the tables, as though she hardly knew where she was herself. She looked round the tables, over which smoke thickened, round which khaki melted into the khaki gloom. Then her eyes returned, to fix, with unsparing attention, an addled trio of men round the fifty-five mark. "Here?" she repeated, "my father?—I hope not."

"But I thought," he said, watching her watching the old buffers, "I thought we were looking for someone of twenty-six?"

"Give me a cigarette," she said, "and, also, don't be cruel."

"I wouldn't be," he said, as he lighted the cigarette, "if you had any feeling for me."

by D. H. Lawrence

THE ROCKING-HORSE WINNER

D. H. Lawrence was born on September 11, 1885, in Eastwood, a coal-mining village in Nottinghamshire. He managed to secure a fairly good education. His early poems were published in the English Review, *and in 1911 his first novel,* The White Peacock, *appeared. In 1914 Lawrence married Frieda von Richtofen, with whom he had earlier eloped when she was still the wife of a Nottingham professor. The notoriety of this affair did not help him in his struggle against the suppression of his allegedly obscene novel,* The Rainbow, *published in 1915. Such battles continued throughout his lifetime as he brought out such novels as* Women in Love *(1921) and* Aaron's Rod *(1922). Only recently has it become possible to buy* Lady Chatterley's Lover *in either the United States or Great Britain. On March 2, 1930, Lawrence died of tuberculosis near Nice.*

Lawrence's ideas, Diana Trilling has remarked, "are essentially poetic ideas . . . [that] suggest more than they state. . . ." "The Rocking-horse Winner," certainly, is poetic in some sense of the word. One need read no further than the opening sentence, which suggests the conventional beginning of a fairy tale, to know that what is to follow is not a piece of naturalistic fiction. It is fantasy. Its quality recalls the Elizabethan "Tom o' Bedlam's Song."

> *With a burning speare, and a horse of aire,*
> *To the wildernesse I wander.*
> *By a knight of ghosts and shadowes*
> *I summon'd am to tourney*
> *Ten leagues beyond the wide world's end.*
> *Me thinke it is noe journey.*

THERE was a woman who was beautiful, who started with all the advantages, yet she had no luck. She married for love, and the love turned to dust. She had bonny children, yet she felt they had been thrust upon her, and she could not love them. They looked at her coldly, as if they were finding fault with her. And hurriedly she felt she must cover up some fault in herself. Yet what it was that she must cover up she never knew. Nevertheless, when her children were present, she always felt the centre of her heart go hard. This troubled her, and in her manner she was all the more gentle and anxious for her children, as if she loved them very much. Only she herself knew that at the centre of her heart was a hard little place that could not feel love, no, not for anybody. Everybody else said of her: "She is such a good mother. She adores her children." Only she herself, and her children themselves, knew it was not so. They read it in each other's eyes.

There were a boy and two little girls. They lived in a pleasant house, with a garden, and they had discreet servants, and felt themselves superior to anyone in the neighbourhood.

Although they lived in style, they felt always an anxiety in the house. There was never enough money. The mother had a small income, and the father had a small income, but not nearly enough for the social position which they had to keep up. The father went in to town to some office. But though he had good prospects, these prospects never materialized. There was always the grinding sense of the shortage of money, though the style was always kept up.

At last the mother said: "I will see if *I* can't make something." But she did not know where to begin. She racked her brains, and tried this thing and the other, but could not find anything successful. The failure made deep lines come into her face. Her children were growing up, they would have to go to school. There must be more money, there must be more money. The father, who was always very handsome and expensive in his tastes, seemed as if he never *would* be able to do anything worth doing. And the mother, who had a great belief in herself, did not succeed any better, and her tastes were just as expensive.

And so the house came to be haunted by the unspoken phrase: *There must be more money! There must be more money!* The children could hear it all the time, though nobody said it aloud. They heard it at Christmas, when the expensive and splendid toys filled the nursery. Behind the shining modern rocking-horse, behind the smart doll's-house, a voice would start whispering: "There *must* be more money! There *must* be more money!" And the children would stop playing, to listen for a moment. They would look into each other's eyes, to see if they had all heard. And each one saw in the eyes of the other two that they too had heard. "There *must* be more money! There *must* be more money!"

It came whispering from the springs of the still-swaying rocking-horse, and even the horse, bending his wooden, champing head, heard it. The big doll, sitting so pink and smirking in her new pram, could hear it quite plainly, and seemed to be smirking all the more self-consciously because of it. The foolish puppy, too, that took the place of the teddy-bear, he was looking so extraordinarily foolish for no other reason but that he heard the secret whisper all over the house: "There *must* be more money!"

Yet nobody ever said it aloud. The whisper was everywhere, and therefore no one spoke it. Just as no one ever says: "We are breathing!" in spite of the fact that breath is coming and going all the time.

"Mother," said the boy Paul one day, "why don't we keep a car of our own? Why do we always use uncle's, or else a taxi?"

"Because we're the poor members of the family," said the mother.

"But why *are* we, mother?"

"Well—I suppose," she said slowly and bitterly, "it's because your father has no luck."

The boy was silent for some time.

"Is luck money, mother?" he asked rather timidly.

"No, Paul. Not quite. It's what causes you to have money."

"Oh!" said Paul vaguely. "I thought when Uncle Oscar said *filthy lucker,* it meant money."

"*Filthy lucre* does mean money," said the mother. "But it's lucre, not luck."

"Oh!" said the boy. "Then what *is* luck, mother?"

"It's what causes you to have money. If you're lucky you have money. That's why it's better to be born lucky than rich. If you're rich, you may lose your money. But if you're lucky, you will always get more money."

"Oh! Will you? And is father not lucky?"

"Very unlucky, I should say," she said bitterly.

The boy watched her with unsure eyes.

"Why?" he asked.

"I don't know. Nobody ever knows why one person is lucky and another unlucky."

"Don't they? Nobody at all? Does *nobody* know?"

"Perhaps God. But He never tells."

"He ought to, then. And aren't you lucky either, mother?"

"I can't be, if I married an unlucky husband."

"But by yourself, aren't you?"

"I used to think I was, before I married. Now I think I am very unlucky indeed."

"Why?"

"Well—never mind! Perhaps I'm not really," she said.

The child looked at her, to see if she meant it. But he saw, by the lines of her mouth, that she was only trying to hide something from him.

"Well, anyhow," he said stoutly, "I'm a lucky person."

"Why?" said his mother, with a sudden laugh.

He stared at her. He didn't even know why he had said it.

"God told me," he asserted, brazening it out.

"I hope He did, dear!" she said, again with a laugh, but rather bitter.

"He did, mother!"

"Excellent!" said the mother, using one of her husband's exclamations.

The boy saw she did not believe him; or, rather, that she paid no attention to his assertion. This angered him somewhat, and made him want to compel her attention.

He went off by himself, vaguely, in a childish way, seeking for the clue to "luck." Absorbed, taking no heed of other people, he went about with a sort of stealth, seeking inwardly for luck. He wanted luck, he wanted it, he wanted it. When the two girls were playing dolls in the nursery, he would sit on his big rocking-horse, charging madly into space, with a frenzy that made the little girls peer at him uneasily. Wildly the horse careered, the waving dark hair of the boy tossed, his eyes had a strange glare in them. The little girls dared not speak to him.

When he had ridden to the end of his mad little journey, he climbed down and stood in front of his rocking-horse, staring fixedly into its lowered face. Its red mouth was slightly open, its big eye was wide and glassy-bright.

"Now!" he would silently command the snorting steed. "Now, take me to where there is luck! Now take me!"

And he would slash the horse on the neck with the little whip he had asked Uncle Oscar for. He *knew* the horse could take him to where there was luck, if only he forced it. So he would mount again, and start on his furious ride, hoping at last to get there. He knew he could get there.

"You'll break your horse, Paul!" said the nurse.

"He's always riding like that! I wish he'd leave off!" said his elder sister Joan.

But he only glared down on them in silence. Nurse gave him up. She could make nothing of him. Anyhow he was growing beyond her.

One day his mother and his Uncle Oscar came in when he was on one of his furious rides. He did not speak to them.

"Hallo, you young jockey! Riding a winner?" said his uncle.

"Aren't you growing too big for a rocking-horse? You're not a very little boy any longer, you know," said his mother.

But Paul only gave a blue glare from his big, rather close-set eyes. He would speak to nobody when he was in full tilt. His mother watched him with an anxious expression on her face.

At last he suddenly stopped forcing his horse into the mechanical gallop, and slid down.

"Well, I got there!" he announced fiercely, his blue eyes still flaring, and his sturdy long legs straddling apart.

"Where did you get to?" asked his mother.

"Where I wanted to go," he flared back at her.

"That's right, son!" said Uncle Oscar. "Don't you stop till you get there. What's the horse's name?"

"He doesn't have a name," said the boy.

"Gets on without all right?" asked the uncle.

"Well, he has different names. He was called Sansovino last week."

"Sansovino, eh? Won the Ascot. How did you know his name?"

"He always talks about horse-races with Bassett," said Joan.

The uncle was delighted to find that his small nephew was posted with all the racing news. Bassett, the young gardener, who had been wounded in the left foot in the war and had got his present job through Oscar Cresswell, whose batman he had been, was a perfect blade of the "turf." He lived in the racing events, and the small boy lived with him.

Oscar Cresswell got it all from Bassett.

"Master Paul comes and asks me, so I can't do more than tell him, sir," said Bassett, his face terribly serious, as if he were speaking of religious matters.

"And does he ever put anything on a horse he fancies?"

"Well—I don't want to give him away—he's a young sport, a fine sport, sir. Would you mind asking him himself? He sort of takes a pleasure in it, and perhaps he'd feel I was giving him away, sir, if you don't mind."

Bassett was serious as a church.

The uncle went back to his nephew and took him off for a ride in the car.

"Say, Paul, old man, do you ever put anything on a horse?" the uncle asked.

The boy watched the handsome man closely.

"Why, do you think I oughtn't to?" he parried.

"Not a bit of it! I thought perhaps you might give me a tip for the Lincoln."

The car sped on into the country, going down to Uncle Oscar's place in Hampshire.

"Honour bright?" said the nephew.

"Honour bright, son!" said the uncle.

"Well, then, Daffodil."

"Daffodil! I doubt it, sonny. What about Mirza?"

"I only know the winner," said the boy. "That's Daffodil."

"Daffodil, eh?"

There was a pause. Daffodil was an obscure horse comparatively.

"Uncle!"

"Yes, son?"

"You won't let it go any further, will you? I promised Bassett."

"Bassett be damned, old man! What's he got to do with it?"

"We're partners. We've been partners from the first. Uncle, he lent me my first five shillings, which I lost. I promised him, honour bright, it was only between me and him; only you gave me that ten-shilling note I started winning with, so I thought you were lucky. You won't let it go any further, will you?"

The boy gazed at his uncle from those big, hot, blue eyes, set rather close together. The uncle stirred and laughed uneasily.

"Right you are, son! I'll keep your tip private. Daffodil, eh? How much are you putting on him?"

"All except twenty pounds," said the boy. "I keep that in reserve."

The uncle thought it a good joke.

"You keep twenty pounds in reserve, do you, you young romancer? What are you betting, then?"

"I'm betting three hundred," said the boy gravely. "But it's between you and me, Uncle Oscar! Honour bright?"

The uncle burst into a roar of laughter.

"It's between you and me all right, you young Nat Gould," he said, laughing. "But where's your three hundred?"

"Bassett keeps it for me. We're partners."

"You are, are you! And what is Bassett putting on Daffodil?"

"He won't go quite as high as I do, I expect. Perhaps he'll go a hundred and fifty."

"What, pennies?" laughed the uncle.

"Pounds," said the child, with a surprised look at his uncle. "Bassett keeps a bigger reserve than I do."

Between wonder and amusement Uncle Oscar was silent. He pursued the matter no further, but he determined to take his nephew with him to the Lincoln races.

"Now, son," he said, "I'm putting twenty on Mirza, and I'll put five for you on any horse you fancy. What's your pick?"

"Daffodil, uncle."

"No, not the fiver on Daffodil!"

"I should if it was my own fiver," said the child.

"Good! Good! Right you are! A fiver for me and a fiver for you on Daffodil."

The child had never been to a race-meeting before, and his eyes were blue fire. He pursed his mouth tight, and watched. A Frenchman just in front had put his money on Lancelot. Wild with excitement, he flayed his arms up and down, yelling "*Lancelot! Lancelot!*" in his French accent.

Daffodil came in first, Lancelot second, Mirza third. The child, flushed and with eyes blazing, was curiously serene. His uncle brought him four five-pound notes, four to one.

"What am I to do with these?" he cried, waving them before the boy's eyes.

"I suppose we'll talk to Bassett," said the boy. "I expect I have fifteen hundred now; and twenty in reserve; and this twenty."

His uncle studied him for some moments.

"Look here, son!" he said. "You're not serious about Bassett and that fifteen hundred, are you?"

"Yes, I am. But it's between you and me, uncle. Honour bright!"

"Honour bright all right, son! But I must talk to Bassett."

"If you'd like to be a partner, uncle, with Bassett and me, we could all be partners. Only, you'd have to promise, honour bright, uncle, not to let it go beyond us three. Bassett and I are lucky, and you must be lucky, because it was your ten shillings I started winning with. . . ."

Uncle Oscar took both Bassett and Paul into Richmond Park for an afternoon, and there they talked.

"It's like this, you see, sir," Bassett said. "Master Paul would get me talking about racing events, spinning yarns, you know, sir. And he was always keen on knowing if I'd made or if I'd lost. It's about a year since, now, that I put five shilling on Blush of Dawn for him—and we lost. Then the luck turned, with that ten shillings he had from you, that we put on Singhalese. And since that time, it's been pretty steady, all things considering. What do you say, Master Paul?"

"We're all right when we're sure," said Paul. "It's when we're not quite sure that we go down."

"Oh, but we're careful then," said Bassett.

"But when are you *sure?*" smiled Uncle Oscar.

"It's Master Paul, sir," said Bassett, in a secret, religious voice. "It's as if he had it from heaven. Like Daffodil, now, for the Lincoln. That was as sure as eggs."

"Did you put anything on Daffodil?" asked Oscar Cresswell.

"Yes, sir. I made my bit."

"And my nephew?"

Bassett was obstinately silent, looking at Paul.

"I made twelve hundred, didn't I, Bassett? I told uncle I was putting three hundred on Daffodil."

"That's right," said Bassett, nodding.

"But where's the money?" asked the uncle.

"I keep it safe locked up, sir. Master Paul he can have it any minute he likes to ask for it."

"What, fifteen hundred pounds?"

"And twenty! And *forty,* that is, with the twenty he made on the course."

"It's amazing!" said the uncle.

"If Master Paul offers you to be partners, sir, I would, if I were you; if you'll excuse me," said Bassett.

Oscar Cresswell thought about it.

"I'll see the money," he said.

They drove home again, and sure enough, Bassett came round to the garden-house with fifteen hundred pounds in notes. The twenty pounds reserve was left with Joe Glee, in the Turf Commission deposit.

"You see, it's all right, uncle, when I'm *sure!* Then we go strong, for all we're worth. Don't we, Bassett?"

"We do that, Master Paul."

"And when are you sure?" said the uncle, laughing.

"Oh, well, sometimes I'm *absolutely* sure, like about Daffodil," said the boy; "and sometimes I have an idea; and sometimes I haven't even an idea, have I, Bassett? Then we're careful, because we mostly go down."

"You do, do you! And when you're sure, like about Daffodil, what makes you sure, sonny?"

"Oh, well, I don't know," said the boy uneasily. "I'm sure, you know, uncle; that's all."

"It's as if he had it from heaven, sir," Bassett reiterated.

"I should say so!" said the uncle.

But he became a partner. And when the Leger was coming on, Paul was "sure" about Lively Spark, which was a quite inconsiderable horse. The boy insisted on putting a thousand on the horse, Bassett went for five hundred, and Oscar Cresswell two hundred. Lively Spark came in first, and the betting had been ten to one against him. Paul had made ten thousand.

"You see," he said, "I was absolutely sure of him."

Even Oscar Cresswell had cleared two thousand.

"Look here, son," he said, "this sort of thing makes me nervous."

"It needn't, uncle! Perhaps I shan't be sure again for a long time."

"But what are you going to do with your money?" asked the uncle.

"Of course," said the boy, "I started it for mother. She said she had no luck, because father is unlucky, so I thought if *I* was lucky, it might stop whispering."

"What might stop whispering?"

"Our house. I *hate* our house for whispering."

"What does it whisper?"

"Why—why"—the boy fidgeted—"why, I don't know. But it's always short of money, you know, uncle."

"I know it, son, I know it."

"You know people send mother writs, don't you, uncle?"

"I'm afraid I do," said the uncle.

"And then the house whispers, like people laughing at you behind your back. It's awful, that is! I thought if I was lucky . . ."

"You might stop it," added the uncle.

The boy watched him with big blue eyes, that had an uncanny cold fire in them, and he said never a word.

"Well, then!" said the uncle. "What are we doing?"

"I shouldn't like mother to know I was lucky," said the boy.

"Why not, son?"

"She'd stop me."

"I don't think she would."

"Oh!"—and the boy writhed in an odd way—"I *don't* want her to know, uncle."

"All right, son! We'll manage it without her knowing."

They managed it very easily. Paul, at the other's suggestion, handed over five thousand pounds to his uncle, who deposited it with the family lawyer, who was then to inform Paul's mother that a relative had put five thousand pounds into his hands, which sum was to be paid out a thousand pounds at a time, on the mother's birthday, for the next five years.

"So she'll have a birthday present of a thousand pounds for five successive years," said Uncle Oscar. "I hope it won't make it all the harder for her later."

Paul's mother had her birthday in November. The house had been "whispering" worse than ever lately, and, even in spite of his luck, Paul could not bear up against it. He was very anxious to see the effect of the birthday letter, telling his mother about the thousand pounds.

When there were no visitors, Paul now took his meals with his parents, as he was beyond the nursery control. His mother went into town nearly every day. She had discovered that she had an odd knack of sketching furs and dress materials, so she worked secretly in the studio of a friend who was the chief "artist" for the leading drapers. She drew the figures of ladies in furs and ladies in silk and sequins for the newspaper advertisements. This young woman artist earned several thousand pounds a year, but Paul's mother only made several hundreds, and she was again dissatisfied. She so wanted to be first in something, and she did not succeed, even in making sketches for drapery advertisements.

She was down to breakfast on the morning of her birthday. Paul watched her face as she read her letters. He knew the lawyer's letter. As his mother read it, her face hardened and became more expressionless. Then a cold, determined look came on her mouth. She hid the letter under the pile of others, and said not a word about it.

"Didn't you have anything nice in the post for your birthday, mother?" said Paul.

"Quite moderately nice," she said, her voice cold and absent.

She went away to town without saying more.

But in the afternoon Uncle Oscar appeared. He said Paul's mother had had a long interview with the lawyer, asking if the whole five thousand could not be advanced at once, as she was in debt.

"What do you think, uncle?" said the boy.

"I leave it to you, son."

"Oh, let her have it, then! We can get some more with the other," said the boy.

"A bird in the hand is worth two in the bush, laddie!" said Uncle Oscar.

"But I'm sure to *know* for the Grand National; or the Lincolnshire; or else the Derby. I'm sure to know for *one* of them," said Paul.

So Uncle Oscar signed the agreement, and Paul's mother touched the whole five thousand. Then something very curious happened. The voices in the house suddenly went mad, like a chorus of frogs on a spring evening. There were certain new furnishings, and Paul had a tutor. He was *really* going to Eton, his father's school, in the following autumn. There were flowers in the winter, and a blossoming of the luxury Paul's mother had been used to. And yet the voices in the house, behind the sprays of mimosa and almond blossom, and from under the piles of iridescent cushions, simply trilled and screamed in a sort of ecstasy: "There *must* be more money! Oh-h-h; there *must* be more money. Oh, now, now-w! Now-w-w—there *must* be more money!—more than ever! More than ever!"

It frightened Paul terribly. He studied away at his Latin and Greek with his tutors. But his intense hours were spent with Bassett. The

Grand National had gone by: he had not "known," and had lost a hundred pounds. Summer was at hand. He was in agony for the Lincoln. But even for the Lincoln he didn't "know," and he lost fifty pounds. He became wild-eyed and strange, as if something were going to explode in him.

"Let it alone, son! Don't you bother about it!" urged Uncle Oscar. But it was as if the boy couldn't really hear what his uncle was saying.

"I've got to know for the Derby! I've got to know for the Derby!" the child reiterated, his big blue eyes blazing with a sort of madness.

His mother noticed how overwrought he was.

"You'd better go to the seaside. Wouldn't you like to go now to the seaside, instead of waiting? I think you'd better," she said, looking down at him anxiously, her heart curiously heavy because of him.

But the child lifted his uncanny blue eyes.

"I couldn't possibly go before the Derby, mother!" he said. "I couldn't possibly!"

"Why not?" she said, her voice becoming heavy when she was opposed. "Why not? You can still go from the seaside to see the Derby with your Uncle Oscar, if that's what you wish. No need for you to wait here. Besides, I think you care too much about these races. It's a bad sign. My family has been a gambling family, and you won't know till you grow up how much damage it has done. But it has done damage. I shall have to send Bassett away, and ask Uncle Oscar not to talk racing to you, unless you promise to be reasonable about it; go away to the seaside and forget it. You're all nerves!"

"I'll do what you like, mother, so long as you don't send me away till after the Derby," the boy said.

"Send you away from where? Just from this house?"

"Yes," he said gazing at her.

"Why, you curious child, what makes you care about this house so much, suddenly? I never knew you loved it."

He gazed at her without speaking. He had a secret within a secret, something he had not divulged, even to Bassett or to his Uncle Oscar.

But his mother, after standing undecided and a little bit sullen for some moments, said:

"Very well, then! Don't go to the seaside till after the Derby, if you don't wish it. But promise me you won't let your nerves go to pieces. Promise you won't think so much about horse-racing and *events*, as you call them!"

"Oh, no," said the boy casually. "I won't think much about them, mother. You needn't worry. I wouldn't worry, mother, if I were you."

"If you were me and I were you," said his mother, "I wonder what we *should* do!"

"But you know you needn't worry, mother, don't you?" the boy repeated.

"I should be awfully glad to know it," she said wearily.

"Oh, well, you *can*, you know. I mean, you *ought* to know you needn't worry," he insisted.

"Ought I? Then I'll see about it," she said.

Paul's secret of secrets was his wooden horse, that which had no name. Since he was emancipated from a nurse and a nursery-governess, he had had his rocking-horse removed to his own bedroom at the top of the house.

"Surely, you're too big for a rocking-horse!" his mother had remonstrated.

"Well, you see, mother, till I can have a *real* horse, I like to have *some* sort of animal about," had been his quaint answer.

"Do you feel he keeps you company?" she laughed.

"Oh, yes! He's very good, he always keeps me company, when I'm there," said Paul.

So the horse, rather shabby, stood in an arrested prance in the boy's bedroom.

The Derby was drawing near, and the boy grew more and more tense. He hardly heard what was spoken to him, he was very frail, and his eyes were really uncanny. His mother had sudden strange seizures of uneasiness about him. Sometimes, for half-an-hour, she would feel a sudden anxiety about him that was almost anguish. She wanted to rush to him at once, and know he was safe.

Two nights before the Derby, she was at a big party in town, when one of her rushes of anxiety about her boy, her first-born, gripped her heart till she could hardly speak. She fought with the feeling, might and main, for she believed in common-sense. But it was too strong. She had to leave the dance and go downstairs to telephone to the country. The children's nursery-governess was terribly surprised and startled at being rung up in the night.

"Are the children all right, Miss Wilmot?"

"Oh, yes, they are quite all right."

"Master Paul? Is he all right?"

"He went to bed as right as a trivet. Shall I run up and look at him?"

"No," said Paul's mother reluctantly. "No! Don't trouble. It's all right. Don't sit up. We shall be home fairly soon." She did not want her son's privacy intruded upon.

"Very good," said the governess.

It was about one o'clock when Paul's mother and father drove up to their house. All was still. Paul's mother went to her room and slipped off her white fur cloak. She had told her maid not to wait up for her. She heard her husband downstairs, mixing a whisky-and-soda.

And then, because of the strange anxiety at her heart, she stole upstairs to her son's room. Noiselessly she went along the upper corridor. Was there a faint noise? What was it?

She stood, with arrested muscles, outside his door, listening. There was a strange, heavy, and yet not loud noise. Her heart stood still. It was a soundless noise, yet rushing and powerful. Something huge, in violent, hushed motion. What was it? What in God's name was it? She ought to know. She felt that she knew the noise. She knew what it was.

Yet she could not place it. She couldn't say what it was. And on and on it went, like a madness.

Softly, frozen with anxiety and fear, she turned the door-handle.

The room was dark. Yet in the space near the window, she heard and saw something plunging to and fro. She gazed in fear and amazement.

Then suddenly she switched on the light, and saw her son, in his green pyjamas, madly surging on the rocking-horse. The blaze of light suddenly lit him up, as he urged the wooden horse, and lit her up, as she stood, blonde, in her dress of pale green and crystal, in the doorway.

"Paul!" she cried. "Whatever are you doing?"

"It's Malabar!" he screamed, in a powerful, strange voice. "It's Malabar!"

His eyes blazed at her for one strange and senseless second, as he ceased urging his wooden horse. Then he fell with a crash to the ground, and she, all her tormented motherhood flooding upon her, rushed to gather him up.

But he was unconscious, and unconscious he remained, with some brain-fever. He talked and tossed, and his mother sat stonily by his side.

"Malabar! It's Malabar! Bassett, Bassett, I *know!* It's Malabar!"

So the child cried, trying to get up and urge the rocking-horse that gave him his inspiration.

"What does he mean by Malabar?" asked the heart-frozen mother.

"I don't know," said the father stonily.

"What does he mean by Malabar?" she asked her brother Oscar.

"It's one of the horses running for the Derby," was the answer.

And, in spite of himself, Oscar Cresswell spoke to Bassett, and himself put a thousand on Malabar: at fourteen to one.

The third day of the illness was critical: they were waiting for a change. The boy, with his rather long, curly hair, was tossing ceaselessly on the pillow. He neither slept nor regained consciousness, and his eyes were like blue stones. His mother sat, feeling her heart had gone, turned actually into a stone.

In the evening, Oscar Cresswell did not come, but Bassett sent a message, saying could he come up for one moment, just one moment? Paul's mother was very angry at the intrusion, but on second thought she agreed. The boy was the same. Perhaps Bassett might bring him to consciousness.

The gardener, a shortish fellow with a little brown moustache, and sharp little brown eyes, tip-toed into the room, touched his imaginary cap to Paul's mother, and stole to the bedside, staring with glittering, smallish eyes, at the tossing, dying child.

"Master Paul!" he whispered. "Master Paul! Malabar came in first all right, a clean win. I did as you told me. You've made over seventy thousand pounds, you have; you've got over eighty thousand. Malabar came in all right, Master Paul."

"Malabar! Malabar! Did I say Malabar, mother? Did I say Malabar? Do you think I'm lucky, mother? I knew Malabar, didn't I? Over eighty thousand pounds! I call that lucky, don't you, mother? Over eighty thousand pounds! I knew, didn't I know I knew? Malabar came in all right. If I ride my horse till I'm sure, then I tell you, Bassett, you can go as high as you like. Did you go for all you were worth, Bassett?"

"I went a thousand on it, Master Paul."

"I never told you, mother, that if I can ride my horse, and *get there,* then I'm absolutely sure—oh, absolutely! Mother, did I ever tell you? I *am* lucky!"

"No, you never did," said the mother.

But the boy died in the night.

And even as he lay dead, his mother heard her brother's voice saying to her: "My God, Hester, you're eighty-odd thousand to the good, and a poor devil of a son to the bad. But, poor devil, poor devil, he's best gone out of a life where he rides his rocking-horse to find a winner."

by Robert Penn Warren

BLACKBERRY WINTER

Robert Penn Warren was born on April 24, 1905, in Guthrie, Kentucky. He attended Vanderbilt (B.A., 1925), the University of California (M.A., 1927), and, after a year of graduate study at Yale, Oxford (B. Litt., 1930) as a Rhodes Scholar. He has published seven novels, several volumes of poetry and essays, and (with Cleanth Brooks) has written influential textbooks in literature and rhetoric. His one volume of short stories, The Circus in the Attic, *appeared in 1948. In addition to several honorary doctorates, Mr. Warren has received many awards and fellowships for both his poetry and his prose, including the Chair of Poetry of the Library of Congress and the Pulitzer Prize (1947) for* All the King's Men.

Much of Mr. Warren's fiction has been concerned with the human sense of history, the awful burden of time. For the nine-year-old boy of "Blackberry Winter," time "is not a movement, a flowing, a wind . . . , but is, rather, a kind of climate in which things are. . . ." In one day the odd weather, the flood, sickness, and the violent stranger propel him into the stream of time and responsibility. "Hit is the change," says Big Jebb, ostensibly in another connection. "Hit is the change of life and time."

IT was getting into June and past eight o'clock in the morning, but there was a fire—even if it wasn't a big fire, just a fire of chunks—on the hearth of the big stone fireplace in the living room. I was standing on the hearth, almost into the chimney, hunched over the fire, working my bare toes slowly on the warm stone. I relished the heat which made the skin of my bare legs warp and creep and tingle, even as I called to my mother, who was somewhere back in the dining room or kitchen, and said: "But it's June, I don't have to put them on!"

"You put them on if you are going out," she called.

I tried to assess the degree of authority and conviction in the tone, but at that distance it was hard to decide. I tried to analyze the tone, and then I thought what a fool I had been to start out the back door and let her see that I was barefoot. If I had gone out the front door or the side door she would never have known, not till dinner time anyway, and by then the day would have been half gone and I would have been all over the farm to see what the storm had done and down to the creek to see the flood. But it had never crossed my mind that they would try to stop you from going barefoot in June, no matter if there had been a gully-washer and a cold spell.

Nobody had ever tried to stop me in June as long as I could remember, and when you are nine years old, what you remember seems forever; for you remember everything and everything is important and stands big and full and fills up Time and is so solid that you can walk around and around it like a tree and look at it. You are aware that time passes, that there is a movement in time, but that is not what Time is. Time is not a movement, a flowing, a wind then, but is, rather, a kind of climate in which things are, and when a thing happens it begins to live and keeps on living and stands solid in Time like the tree that you can walk around. And if there is a movement, the movement is not Time itself, any more than a breeze is climate, and all the breeze does is to shake a little the leaves on the tree which is alive and solid. When you are nine, you know that there are things that you don't know, but you know that when you know something you know it. You know how a thing has been and you know that you can go barefoot in June. You do not under stand that voice from back in the kitchen which says that you can not go barefoot outdoors and run to see what has happened and rub your feet over the wet shivery grass and make the perfect mark of your foot in the smooth, creamy, red mud and then muse upon it as though you had suddenly come upon that single mark on the glistening auroral beach of the world. You have never seen a beach, but you have read the book and how the footprint was there.

The voice had said what it had said, and I looked savagely at the black stockings and the strong, scuffed brown shoes which I had brought from my closet as far as the hearth rug. I called once more, "But it's June," and waited.

"It's June," the voice replied from far away, "but it's blackberry winter."

I had lifted my head to reply to that, to make one more test of what was in that tone, when I happened to see the man.

The fireplace in the living room was at the end; for the stone chimney was built, as in so many of the farmhouses in Tennessee, at the end of a gable, and there was a window on each side of the chimney. Out of the window on the north side of the fireplace I could see the man. When I saw the man I did not call out what I had intended, but, engrossed by the strangeness of the sight, watched him, still far off, come along the path by the edge of the woods.

What was strange was that there should be a man there at all. That path went along the yard fence, between the fence and the woods which came right down to the yard, and then on back past the chicken runs and on by the woods until it was lost to sight where the woods bulged out and cut off the back field. There the path disappeared into the woods. It led on back, I knew, through the woods and to the swamp, skirted the swamp where the big trees gave way to sycamores and water oaks and willows and tangled cane, and then led on to the river. Nobody ever went back there except people who wanted to gig frogs in the swamp or to fish in the river or to hunt in the woods, and those people, if they didn't have a standing permission from my father, always stopped to ask permission to cross the farm. But the man whom I now saw wasn't, I could tell even at that distance, a sportsman. And what would a sportsman have been doing down there after a storm? Besides, he was coming from the river, and nobody had gone down there that morning. I knew that for a fact, because if anybody had passed, certainly if a stranger had passed, the dogs would have made a racket and would have been out on him. But this man was coming up from the river and had come up through the woods. I suddenly had a vision of him moving up the grassy path in the woods, in the green twilight under the big trees, not making any sound on the path, while now and then, like drops off the eaves, a big drop of water would fall from a leaf or bough and strike a stiff oak leaf lower down with a small, hollow sound like a drop of water hitting tin. That sound, in the silence of the woods, would be very significant.

When you are a boy and stand in the stillness of woods, which can be so still that your heart almost stops beating and makes you want to stand there in the green twilight until you feel your very feet sinking into and clutching the earth like roots and your body breathing slow through its pores like the leaves—when you stand there and wait for the next drop to drop with its small, flat sound to a lower leaf, that sound seems to measure out something, to put an end to something, to begin something, and you cannot wait for it to happen and are afraid it will not happen, and then when it has happened, you are waiting again, almost afraid.

But the man whom I saw coming through the woods in my mind's eye did not pause and wait, growing into the ground and breathing with the enormous, soundless breathing of the leaves. Instead, I saw him moving at that very moment along the path by the edge of the woods, coming toward the house. He was moving steadily, but not fast, with his shoulders hunched a little and his head thrust forward, like a man who has come a long way and has a long way to go. I shut my eyes for a couple of seconds, thinking that when I opened them he would not be there at all. There was no place for him to have come from, and there was no reason for him to come where he was coming, toward our house. But I opened my eyes, and there he was, and he was coming steadily along the side of the woods. He was not yet even with the back chicken yard.

"Mama," I called.

"You put them on," the voice said.

"There's a man coming," I called, "out back."

She did not reply to that, and I guessed that she had gone to the kitchen window to look. She would be looking at the man and wondering who he was and what he wanted, the way you always do in the country, and if I went back there now she would not notice right off whether or not I was barefoot. So I went back to the kitchen.

She was standing by the window. "I don't recognize him," she said, not looking around at me.

"Where could he be coming from?" I asked.

"I don't know," she said.

"What would he be doing down at the river? At night? In the storm?"

She studied the figure out the window, then said, "Oh, I reckon maybe he cut across from the Dunbar place."

That was, I realized, a perfectly rational explanation. He had not been down at the river in the storm, at night. He had come over this morning. You could cut across from the Dunbar place if you didn't mind breaking through a lot of elder and sassafras and blackberry bushes which had about taken over the old cross path, which nobody ever used any more. That satisfied me for a moment, but only for a moment. "Mama," I asked, "what would he be doing over at the Dunbar place last night?"

Then she looked at me, and I knew I had made a mistake, for she was looking at my bare feet. "You haven't got your shoes on," she said.

But I was saved by the dogs. That instant there was a bark which I recognized as Sam, the collie, and then a heavier, churning kind of bark which was Bully, and I saw a streak of white as Bully tore round the corner of the back porch and headed out for the man. Bully was a big, bone-white bull dog, the kind of dog that they used to call a farm bull dog but that you don't see any more, heavy chested and heavy headed, but with pretty long legs. He could take a fence as light as a hound. He had just cleared the white paling fence toward the woods when my mother ran out to the back porch and began calling, "Here you, Bully! Here you!"

Bully stopped in the path, waiting for the man, but he gave a few more of those deep, gargling, savage barks that reminded you of something down a stone-lined well. The red clay mud, I saw, was splashed up over his white chest and looked exciting, like blood.

The man, however, had not stopped walking even when Bully took the fence and started at him. He had kept right on coming. All he had done was to switch a little paper parcel which he carried from the right hand to the left, and then reach into his pants pocket to get something. Then I saw the glitter and knew that he had a knife in his hand, probably the kind of mean knife just made for devilment and nothing else, with a blade as long as the blade of a frog-sticker, which will snap out ready when you press a button in the handle. That knife must have had a button in the handle, or else how could he have had the blade out glittering so quick and with just one hand?

Pulling his knife against the dogs was a funny thing to do, for Bully was a big, powerful brute and fast, and Sam was all right. If those dogs had meant business, they might have knocked him down and ripped him before he got a stroke in. He ought to have picked up a big stick, something to take a swipe at them with and something which they could see and respect when they came at him. But he apparently did not know much about dogs. He just held the knife blade close against the right leg, low down, and kept on moving down the path.

Then my mother had called, and Bully had stopped. So the man let the blade of the knife snap back into the handle, and dropped it into his pocket, and kept on coming. Many women would have been afraid with the strange man who they knew had that knife in his pocket. That is, if they were alone in the house with nobody but a nine-year-old boy. And my mother was alone, for my father had gone off, and Dellie, the cook, was down at her cabin because she wasn't feeling well. But my mother wasn't afraid. She wasn't a big woman, but she was clear and brisk about everything she did and looked everybody and everything right in the eye from her own blue eyes in her tanned face. She had been the first woman in the county to ride a horse astride (that was back when she was a girl and long before I was born), and I have seen her snatch up a pump gun and go out and knock a chicken hawk out of the air like a busted skeet when he came over her chicken yard. She was a steady and self-reliant woman, and when I think of her now after all the years she has been dead, I think of her brown hands, not big, but somewhat square for a woman's hands, with square-cut nails. They looked, as a matter of fact, more like a young boy's hands than a grown woman's. But back then it never crossed my mind that she would ever be dead.

She stood on the back porch and watched the man enter the back gate, where the dogs (Bully had leaped back into the yard) were dancing and muttering and giving sidelong glances back to my mother to see if she meant what she had said. The man walked right by the dogs, almost brushing them, and didn't pay them any attention. I could see now that he wore old khaki pants, and a dark wool coat with stripes in it, and a gray felt hat. He had on a gray shirt with blue stripes in it, and no tie. But I could see a tie, blue and reddish, sticking in his side coat-pocket. Everything was wrong about what he wore. He ought to have been wearing blue jeans or overalls, and a straw hat or an old black felt hat, and the coat, granting that he might have been wearing a wool coat and not a jumper, ought not to have had those stripes. Those clothes, despite the fact that they were old enough and dirty enough for any tramp, didn't belong there in our back yard, coming down the path, in Middle Tennessee, miles away from any big town, and even a mile off the pike.

When he got almost to the steps, without having said anything, my mother, very matter-of-factly, said, "Good morning."

"Good morning," he said, and stopped and looked her over. He did not take off his hat, and under the brim you could see the perfectly unmemorable face, which wasn't old and wasn't young, or thick or thin. It was grayish and covered with about three days of stubble. The eyes were a kind of nondescript, muddy hazel, or something like that, rather bloodshot. His teeth, when he opened his mouth, showed yellow and uneven. A couple of them had been knocked out. You knew that they had been knocked out, because there was a scar, not very old, there on the lower lip just beneath the gap.

"Are you hunting work?" my mother asked him.

"Yes," he said—not "yes, mam"—and still did not take off his hat.

"I don't know about my husband, for he isn't here," she said, and didn't mind a bit telling the tramp, or whoever he was, with the mean knife in his pocket, that no man was around, "but I can give you a few things to do. The storm has drowned a lot of my chicks. Three coops of them. You can gather them up and bury them. Bury them deep so the dogs won't get at them. In the woods. And fix the coops the wind blew over. And down yonder beyond that pen by the edge of the woods are some drowned poults. They got out and I couldn't get them in. Even after it started to rain hard. Poults haven't got any sense."

"What are them things—poults?" he demanded, and spat on the brick walk. He rubbed his foot over the spot, and I saw that he wore a black, pointed-toe low shoe, all cracked and broken. It was a crazy kind of shoe to be wearing in the country.

"Oh, they're young turkeys," my mother was saying. "And they haven't got any sense. I oughtn't to try to raise them around here with so many chickens, anyway. They don't thrive near chickens, even in separate pens. And I won't give up my chickens." Then she stopped herself and resumed briskly on the note of business. "When you finish that, you can fix my flower beds. A lot of trash and mud and gravel has washed down. Maybe you can save some of my flowers if you are careful."

"Flowers," the man said, in a low, impersonal voice which seemed to have a wealth of meaning, but a meaning which I could not fathom. As I think back on it, it probably was not pure contempt. Rather, it was a kind of impersonal and distant marveling that he should be on the verge of grubbing in a flower bed. He said the word, and then looked off across the yard.

"Yes, flowers," my mother replied with some asperity, as though she would have nothing said or implied against flowers. "And they were very fine this year." Then she stopped and looked at the man. "Are you hungry?" she demanded.

"Yeah," he said.

"I'll fix you something," she said, "before you get started." She turned to me. "Show him where he can wash up," she commanded, and went into the house.

I took the man to the end of the porch where a pump was and where a couple of wash pans sat on a low shelf for people to use before they went into the house. I stood there while he laid down his little parcel wrapped in newspaper and took off his hat and looked around for a nail to hang it on. He poured the water and plunged his hands into it. They were big hands, and strong looking, but they did not have the creases and the earth-color of the hands of men who work outdoors. But they were dirty, with black dirt ground into the skin and under the nails. After he had washed his hands, he poured another basin of water and washed his face. He dried his face, and with the towel still dangling in his grasp, stepped over to the mirror on the house wall. He rubbed one hand over the stubble on his face. Then he carefully inspected his face, turning first one side and then the other, and stepped back and settled his striped coat down on his shoulders. He had the movements of a man who has just dressed up to go to church or a party—the way he settled his coat and smoothed it and scanned himself in the mirror.

Then he caught my glance on him. He glared at me for an instant out of the bloodshot eyes, then demanded in a low, harsh voice, "What are you looking at?"

"Nothing," I managed to say, and stepped back a step from him.

He flung the towel down, crumpled, on the shelf, and went toward the kitchen door and entered without knocking.

My mother said something to him which I could not catch. I

started to go in again, then thought about my bare feet, and decided to go back of the chicken yard, where the man would have to come to pick up the dead chicks. I hung around behind the chicken house until he came out.

He moved across the chicken yard with a fastidious, not quite finicking motion, looking down at the curdled mud flecked with bits of chicken-droppings. The mud curled up over the soles of his black shoes. I stood back from him some six feet and watched him pick up the first of the drowned chicks. He held it up by one foot and inspected it.

There is nothing deader looking than a drowned chick. The feet curl in that feeble, empty way which back when I was a boy, even if I was a country boy who did not mind hog-killing or frog-gigging, made me feel hollow in the stomach. Instead of looking plump and fluffy, the body is stringy and limp with the fluff plastered to it, and the neck is long and loose like a little string of rag. And the eyes have that bluish membrane over them which makes you think of a very old man who is sick about to die.

The man stood there and inspected the chick. Then he looked around as though he didn't know what to do with it.

"There's a great big old basket in the shed," I said, and pointed to the shed attached to the chicken house.

He inspected me as though he had just discovered my presence, and moved toward the shed.

"There's a spade there, too," I added.

He got the basket and began to pick up the other chicks, picking each one up slowly by a foot and then flinging it into the basket with a nasty, snapping motion. Now and then he would look at me out of the blood shot eyes. Every time he seemed on the verge of saying something, but he did not. Perhaps he was building up to say something to me, but I did not wait that long. His way of looking at me made me so uncomfortable that I left the chicken yard.

Besides, I had just remembered that the creek was in flood, over the bridge, and that people were down there watching it. So I cut across the farm toward the creek. When I got to the big tobacco field I saw that it had not suffered much. The land lay right and not many tobacco plants had washed out of the ground. But I knew that a lot of tobacco round the country had been washed right out. My father had said so at breakfast.

My father was down at the bridge. When I came out of the gap in the osage hedge into the road, I saw him sitting on his mare over the heads of the other men who were standing around, admiring the flood. The creek was big here, even in low water; for only a couple of miles away it ran into the river, and when a real flood came, the red water got over the pike where it dipped down to the bridge, which was an iron bridge, and high over the floor and even the side railings of the bridge. Only the upper iron work would show, with the water boiling and frothing red and white around it. That creek rose so fast and so heavy because a few miles back it came down out of the hills, where the gorges filled up with water in no time when a rain came. The creek ran in a deep bed with limestone bluffs along both sides until it got within three quarters of a mile of the bridge, and when it came out from between those bluffs in flood it was boiling and hissing and steaming like water from a fire hose.

Whenever there was a flood, people from half the county would come down to see the sight. After a gully-washer there would not be any work to do anyway. If it didn't ruin your crop, you couldn't plow and you felt like taking a holiday to celebrate. If it did ruin your crop, there wasn't anything to do except to try to take your mind off the mortgage, if you were rich enough to have a mortgage, and if you couldn't afford a mortgage you needed something to take your mind off how hungry you would be by Christmas. So people would come down to the bridge and look at the flood. It made something different from the run of days.

There would not be much talking after the first few minutes of trying to guess how high the water was this time. The men and kids just stood around, or sat their horses or mules, as the case might be, or stood up in the wagon beds. They looked at the strangeness of the flood for an hour or two, and then somebody would say that he had better be getting on home to dinner and would start walking down the gray, puddled limestone pike, or would touch heel to his mount and start off. Everybody always knew what it would be like when he got down to the bridge, but people always came. It was like church or a funeral. They always came, that is, if it was summer and the flood unexpected. Nobody ever came down in winter to see high water.

When I came out of the gap in the bodock hedge, I saw the crowd, perhaps fifteen or twenty men and a lot of kids, and saw my father sitting his mare, Nellie Grey. He was a tall, limber man and carried himself well. I was always proud to see him sit a horse, he was so quiet and straight, and when I stepped through the gap of the hedge that morning, the first thing that happened was, I remember, the warm feeling I always had when I saw him up on a horse, just sitting. I did not go toward him, but skirted the crowd on the far side, to get a look at the creek. For one thing, I was not sure what he would say about the fact that I was barefoot. But the first thing I knew, I heard his voice calling, "Seth!"

I went toward him, moving apologetically past the men, who bent their large, red or thin, sallow faces above me. I knew some of the men, and knew their names, but because those I knew were there in a crowd, mixed with the strange faces, they seemed foreign to me, and not friendly. I did not look up at my father until I was almost within touching distance of his heel. Then I looked up and tried to read his face, to see if he was angry about my being barefoot. Before I could decide anything from that impassive, high-boned face, he had leaned over and reached a hand to me. "Grab on," he commanded.

I grabbed on and gave a little jump, and he said, "Up-see-daisy!" and whisked me, light as a feather, up to the pommel of his McClellan saddle.

"You can see better up here," he said, slid back on the cantle a little to make me more comfortable, and then, looking over my head at the swollen, tumbling water, seemed to forget all about me. But his right hand was laid on my side, just above my thigh, to steady me.

I was sitting there as quiet as I could, feeling the faint stir of my father's chest against my shoulders as it rose and fell with his breath, when I saw the cow. At first, looking up the creek, I thought it was just another big piece of driftwood steaming down the creek in the ruck of water, but all at once a pretty good-size boy who had climbed part way up a telephone pole by the pike so that he could see better yelled out, "Golly-damn, look at that-air cow!"

Everybody looked. It was a cow all right, but it might just as well have been driftwood; for it was dead as a chunk, rolling and roiling down the creek, appearing and disappearing, feet up or head up, it didn't matter which.

The cow started up the talk again. Somebody wondered whether it would hit one of the clear places under the top girder of the bridge and get through or whether it would get tangled in the drift and trash that had piled against the upright girders and braces. Somebody remembered how about ten years before so much driftwood had piled up on the bridge that it was knocked off its foundations. Then the cow hit. It hit the edge of the drift against one of the girders, and hung there. For a few seconds it seemed as though it might tear loose, but then we saw that it was really caught. It bobbed and heaved on its side there in a slow, grinding, uneasy fashion. It had a yoke around its neck, the kind made out of a forked stick to keep a jumper behind fence.

"She shore jumped one fence," one of the men said.

And another: "Well, she done jumped her last one, fer a fack."

Then they began to wonder about whose cow it might be. They decided it must belong to Milt Alley. They said that he had a cow that was a jumper, and kept her in a fenced-in piece of ground up the creek. I had never seen Milt Alley, but I knew who he was. He was a squatter and lived up the hills a way, on a shirt-tail patch of set-on-edge land, in a cabin. He was pore white trash. He had lots of children. I had seen the children at school, when they came. They were thin-faced, with straight, sticky-looking, dough-colored hair, and they smelled something like old sour buttermilk, not because they drank so much buttermilk but because that is the sort of smell which children out of those cabins tend to have. The big Alley boy drew dirty pictures and showed them to the little boys at school.

That was Milt Alley's cow. It looked like the kind of cow he would have, a scrawny, old, sway-backed cow, with a yoke around her neck. I wondered if Milt Alley had another cow.

"Poppa," I said, "do you think Milt Alley has got another cow?"

"You say 'Mr. Alley,' " my father said quietly.

"Do you think he has?"

"No telling," my father said.

Then a big gangly boy, about fifteen, who was sitting on a scraggly little old mule with a piece of croker sack thrown across the saw-tooth spine, and who had been staring at the cow, suddenly said to nobody in particular, "Reckin anybody ever et drownt cow?"

He was the kind of boy who might just as well as not have been the son of Milt Alley, with his faded and patched overalls ragged at the bottom of the pants and the mud-stiff brogans hanging off his skinny, bare ankles at the level of the mule's belly. He had said what he did, and then looked embarrassed and sullen when all the eyes swung at him. He hadn't meant to say it, I am pretty sure now. He would have been too proud to say it, just as Milt Alley would have been too proud. He had just been thinking out loud, and the words had popped out.

There was an old man standing there on the pike, an old man with a white beard. "Son," he said to the embarrassed and sullen boy on the mule, "you live long enough and you'll find a man will eat anything when the time comes."

"Time gonna come fer some folks this year," another man said.

"Son," the old man said, "in my time I et things a man don't like to think on. I was a sojer and I rode with Gin'l Forrest, and them things we et when the time come. I tell you. I et meat what got up and run when you taken out yore knife to cut a slice to put on the fire. You had to knock it down with a carbeen butt, it was so active. That-air meat would jump like a bullfrog, it was so full of skippers."

But nobody was listening to the old man. The boy on the mule turned his sullen sharp face from him, dug a heel into the side of the mule and went off up the pike with a motion which made you think that any second you would hear mule bones clashing inside that lank and scrofulous hide.

"Cy Dundee's boy," a man said, and nodded toward the figure going up the pike on the mule.

"Reckin Cy Dundee's young-uns seen times they'd settle fer drownt cow," another man said.

The old man with the beard peered at them both from his weak, slow eyes, first at one and then at the other. "Live long enough," he said, "and a man will settle fer what he kin git."

Then there was silence again, with the people looking at the red, foam-flecked water.

My father lifted the bridle rein in his left hand, and the mare turned and walked around the group and up the pike. We rode on up to our big gate, my father dismounted to open it and let me myself ride Nellie Gray through. When he got to the lane that led off from the drive about two hundred yards from our house, my father said, "Grab on." I grabbed on, and he let me down to the ground. "I'm going to ride down and look at my corn," he said. "You go on." He took the lane, and I stood there on the drive and watched him ride off. He was wearing cowhide boots and an old hunting coat, and I thought that that made him look very military, like a picture. That and the way he rode.

I did not go to the house. Instead, I went by the vegetable garden and crossed behind the stables, and headed down for Dellie's cabin. I wanted to go down and play with Jebb, who was Dellie's little boy about two years older than I was. Besides, I was cold. I shivered as

I walked, and I had goose-flesh. The mud which crawled up between my toes with every step I took was like ice. Dellie would have a fire, but she wouldn't make me put on shoes and stockings.

Dellie's cabin was of logs, with one side, because it was on a slope, set on limestone chunks, with a little porch attached to it, and had a little whitewashed fence around it and a gate with plow-points on a wire to clink when somebody came in, and had two big white oaks in the yard and some flowers and a nice privy in the back with some honeysuckle growing over it. Dellie and Old Jebb, who was Jebb's father and who lived with Dellie and had lived with her for twenty-five years even if they never had got married, were careful to keep everything nice around their cabin. They had the name all over the community for being clean and clever Negroes. Dellie and Jebb were what they used to call "white-folks' niggers." There was a big difference between their cabin and the other two cabins farther down where the other tenants lived. My father kept the other cabins weatherproof, but he couldn't undertake to go down and pick up after the litter they strewed. They didn't take the trouble to have a vegetable patch like Dellie and Jebb or to make preserves from wild plum, and jelly from crab apple the way Dellie did. They were shiftless, and my father was always threatening to get shed of them. But he never did. When they finally left, they just up and left on their own, for no reason, to go and be shiftless somewhere else. Then some more came. But meanwhile they lived down there, Matt Rawson and his family, and Sid Turner and his, and I played with their children all over the farm when they weren't working. But when I wasn't around they were mean sometimes to Little Jebb. That was because the other tenants down there were jealous of Dellie and Jebb.

I was so cold that I ran the last fifty yards to Dellie's gate. As soon as I had entered the yard, I saw that the storm had been hard on Dellie's flowers. The yard was, as I have said, on a slight slope, and the water running across had gutted the flower beds and washed out all the good black woods-earth which Dellie had brought in. What little grass there was in the yard was plastered sparsely down on the ground, the way the drainage water had left it. It reminded me of the way the fluff was plastered down on the skin of the drowned chicks that the strange man had been picking up, up in my mother's chicken yard.

I took a few steps up the path to the cabin, and then I saw that the drainage water had washed a lot of trash and filth out from under Dellie's house. Up toward the porch, the ground was not clean any more. Old pieces of rag, two or three rusted cans, pieces of rotten rope, some hunks of old dog dung, broken glass, old paper, and all sorts of things like that had washed out from under Dellie's house to foul her clean yard. It looked just as bad as the yards of the other cabins, or worse. It was worse, as a matter of fact, because it was a surprise. I had never thought of all that filth being under Dellie's house. It was not anything against Dellie that the stuff had been under the cabin. Trash will get under any house. But I did not think of that when I saw the foulness which had washed out on the ground which Dellie sometimes used to sweep with a twig broom to make nice and clean.

I picked my way past the filth, being careful not to get my bare feet on it, and mounted to Dellie's door. When I knocked, I heard her voice telling me to come in.

It was dark inside the cabin, after the daylight, but I could make out Dellie piled up in bed under a quilt, and Little Jebb crouched by the hearth, where a low fire simmered. "Howdy," I said to Dellie, "how you feeling?"

Her big eyes, the whites surprising and glaring in the black face, fixed on me as I stood there, but she did not reply. It did not look like Dellie, or act like Dellie, who would grumble and bustle around our kitchen, talking to herself, scolding me or Little Jebb, clanking pans, making all sorts of unnecessary noises and mutterings like an old-fashioned black steam thrasher engine when it has got up an extra head of steam and keeps popping the governor and rumbling and shaking on its wheels. But now Dellie just lay up there on the bed, under the patch-work quilt, and turned the black face, which I scarcely recognized, and the glaring white eyes to me.

"How you feeling?" I repeated.

"I'se sick," the voice said croakingly out of the strange black face which was not attached to Dellie's big, squat body, but stuck out from under a pile of tangled bedclothes. Then the voice added: "Mighty sick."

"I'm sorry," I managed to say.

The eyes remained fixed on me for a moment, then they left me and the head rolled back on the pillow. "Sorry," the voice said, in a flat way which wasn't question or statement of anything. It was just the empty word put into the air with no meaning or expression, to float off like a feather or a puff of smoke, while the big eyes, with the whites like the peeled white of hard-boiled eggs, stared at the ceiling.

"Dellie," I said after a minute, "there's a tramp up at the house. He's got a knife."

She was not listening. She closed her eyes.

I tiptoed over to the hearth where Jebb was and crouched beside him. We began to talk in low voices. I was asking him to get out his train and play train. Old Jebb had put spool wheels on three cigar boxes and put wire links between the boxes to make a train for Jebb. The box that was the locomotive had the top closed and a length of broom stick for a smoke stack. Jebb didn't want to get the train out, but I told him I would go home if he didn't. So he got out the train, and the colored rocks, and fossils of crinoid stems, and other junk he used for the load, and we began to push it around, talking the way we thought trainmen talked, making a chuck-chucking sound under the breath for the noise of the locomotive and now and then uttering low, cautious toots for the whistle. We got so interested in playing train that the toots got louder. Then, before he thought, Jebb gave a good, loud *toot-toot*, blowing for a crossing.

"Come here," the voice said from the bed.

Jebb got up slow from his hands and knees, giving me a sudden, naked, inimical look.

"Come here!" the voice said.

Jebb went to the bed. Dellie propped herself weakly up on one arm, muttering, "Come closer."

Jebb stood closer.

"Last thing I do, I'm gonna do it," Dellie said. "Done tole you to be quiet."

Then she slapped him. It was an awful slap, more awful for the kind of weakness which it came from and brought to focus. I had seen her slap Jebb before, but the slapping had always been the kind of easy slap you would expect from a good-natured, grumbling Negro woman like Dellie. But this was different. It was awful. It was so awful that Jebb didn't make a sound. The tears just popped out and ran down his face, and his breath came sharp, like gasps.

Dellie fell back. "Cain't even be sick," she said to the ceiling. "Git sick and they won't even let you lay. They tromp all over you. Cain't even be sick." Then she closed her eyes.

I went out of the room. I almost ran getting to the door, and I did run across the porch and down the steps and across the yard, not caring whether or not I stepped on the filth which had washed out from under the cabin. I ran almost all the way home. Then I thought about my mother catching me with the bare feet. So I went down to the stables.

I heard a noise in the crib, and opened the door. There was Big Jebb, sitting on an old nail keg, shelling corn into a bushel basket. I went in, pulling the door shut behind me, and crouched on the floor near him. I crouched there for a couple of minutes before either of us spoke, and watched him shelling the corn.

He had very big hands, knotted and grayish at the joints, with calloused palms which seemed to be streaked with rust with the rust coming up between the fingers to show from the back. His hands were so strong and tough that he could take a big ear of corn and rip the grains right off the cob with the palm of his hand, all in one motion, like a machine. "Work long as me," he would say, "and the good Lawd'll give you a hand lak cass-ion won't nuthin' hurt." And his hands did look like cast iron, old cast iron streaked with rust.

He was an old man, up in his seventies, thirty years or more older than Dellie, but he was strong as a bull. He was a squat sort of man, heavy in the shoulders, with remarkably long arms, the kind of build they say the river natives have on the Congo from paddling so much in their boats. He had a round bullet-head, set on powerful shoulders. His skin was very black, and the thin hair on his head was now grizzled like tufts of old cotton batting. He had small eyes and a flat nose, not big, and the kindest and wisest old face in the world, the blunt, sad, wise face of an old animal peering tolerantly out on the goings-on of the merely human creatures before him. He was a good man, and I loved him next to my mother and father. I crouched there on the floor of the crib and watched him shell corn with the rusty cast-iron hands, while he looked down at me out of the little eyes set in the blunt face.

"Dellie says she's might sick," I said.

"Yeah," he said.

"What's she sick from?"

"Woman-mizry," he said.

"What's woman-mizry?"

"Hit comes on 'em," he said. "Hit just comes on 'em when the time comes."

"What is it?"

"Hit is the change," he said. "Hit is the change of life and time."

"What changes?"

"You too young to know."

"Tell me."

"Time come and you find out everthing."

I knew that there was no use in asking him any more. When I asked him things and he said that, I always knew that he would not tell me. So I continued to crouch there and watch him. Now that I had sat there a little while, I was cold again.

"What you shiver fer?" he asked me.

"I'm cold. I'm cold because it's blackberry winter," I said.

"Maybe 'tis and maybe 'tain't," he said.

"My mother says it is."

"Ain't sayen Miss Sallie doan know and ain't sayen she do. But folks doan know everthing."

"Why isn't it blackberry winter?"

"Too late fer blackberry winter. Blackberries done bloomed."

"She said it was."

"Blackberry winter just a leetle cold spell. Hit come and then hit go away, and hit is growed summer of a sudden lak a gunshot. Ain't no tellen hit will go way this time."

"It's June," I said.

"June," he replied with great contempt. "That what folks say. What June mean? Maybe hit is come cold to stay."

"Why?"

"Cause this-here old yearth is tahrd. Hit is tahrd and ain't gonna perduce. Lawd let hit come rain one time forty days and forty nights, 'cause He was tahrd of sinful folks. Maybe this-here old yearth say to the Lawd, Lawd, I done plum tahrd, Lawd, lemme rest. And Lawd say, Yearth, you done yore best, you give 'em cawn and you give 'em taters, and all they think on is they gut, and, Yearth, you kin take a rest."

"What will happen?"

"Folks will eat up everthing. The yearth won't perduce no more. Folks cut down all the trees and burn 'em cause they cold, and the yearth won't grow no more. I been tellen 'em. I been tellen folks. Sayen, maybe this year, hit is the time. But they doan listen to me, how the yearth is tahrd. Maybe this year they find out."

"Will everything die?"

"Everthing and everbody, hit will be so."

"This year?"

"Ain't no tellen. Maybe this year."

"My mother said it is blackberry winter," I said confidently, and got up.

"Ain't sayen nuthin' agin Miss Sallie," he said.

I went to the door of the crib. I was really cold now. Running, I had got up a sweat and now I was worse.

I hung on the door, looking at Jebb, who was shelling corn again.

"There's a tramp came to the house," I said. I had almost forgotten the tramp.

"Yeah."

"He came by the back way. What was he doing down there in the storm?"

"They comes and they goes," he said, "and ain't no tellen."

"He had a mean knife."

"The good ones and the bad ones, they comes and they goes. Storm or sun, light or dark. They is folks and they comes and they goes lak folks."

I hung on the door, shivering.

He studied me a moment, then said, "You git on to the house. You ketch yore death. Then what yore mammy say?"

I hesitated.

"You git," he said.

When I came to the back yard, I saw that my father was standing by the back porch and the tramp was walking toward him. They began talking before I reached them, but I got there just as my father was saying, "I'm sorry, but I haven't got any work. I got all the hands on the place I need now. I won't need any extra until wheat thrashing."

The stranger made no reply, just looked at my father.

My father took out his leather coin purse, and got out a half-dollar. He held it toward the man. "This is for half a day," he said.

The man looked at the coin, and then at my father, making no motion to take the money. But that was the right amount. A dollar a day was what you paid them back in 1910. And the man hadn't even worked half a day.

Then the man reached out and took the coin. He dropped it into the right side pocket of his coat. Then he said, very slowly and without feeling: "I didn't want to work on your —— farm."

He used the word which they would have frailed me to death for using.

I looked at my father's face and it was streaked white under the sunburn. Then he said, "Get off this place. Get off this place or I won't be responsible."

The man dropped his right hand into his pants pocket. It was the pocket where he kept the knife. I was just about to yell to my father about the knife when the hand came back out with nothing in it. The man gave a kind of twisted grin, showing where the teeth had been knocked out above the new scar. I thought that instant how maybe he had tried before to pull a knife on somebody else and had got his teeth knocked out.

So now he just gave that twisted, sickish grin out of the unmemorable, grayish face, and then spat on the brick path. The glob landed just about six inches from the toe of my father's right boot. My father looked down at it, and so did I. I thought that if the glob had hit my father's boot something would have happened. I looked down and saw the bright glob, and on one side of it my father's strong cowhide boots, with the brass eyelets and the leather thongs, heavy boots splashed with good red mud and set solid on the bricks, and on the other side the pointed-toe, broken, black shoes, on which the mud looked so sad and out of place. Then I saw one of the black shoes move a little, just a twitch first, then a real step backward.

The man moved in a quarter circle to the end of the porch, with my father's steady gaze upon him all the while. At the end of the porch, the man reached up to the shelf where the wash pans were to get his little newspaper-wrapped parcel. Then he disappeared around the corner of the house and my father mounted the porch and went into the kitchen without a word.

I followed around the house to see what the man would do. I wasn't afraid of him now, no matter if he did have the knife. When I got around in front, I saw him going out the yard gate and starting up the drive toward the pike. So I ran to catch up with him. He was sixty yards or so up the drive before I caught up.

I did not walk right up even with him at first, but trailed him, the way a kid will, about seven or eight feet behind, now and then running two or three steps in order to hold my place against his longer stride. When I first came up behind him, he turned to give me a look, just a meaningless look, and then fixed his eyes up the drive and kept on walking.

When we had got around the bend in the drive which cut the house from sight, and were going along by the edge of the woods, I decided to come up even with him. I ran a few steps, and was by his side, or almost, but some feet off to the right. I walked along in this position for a while, and he never noticed me. I walked along until we got within sight of the big gate that let on the pike.

Then I said: "Where did you come from?"

He looked at me then with a look which seemed almost surprised that I was there. Then he said, "It ain't none of yore business."

We went on another fifty feet.

Then I said, "Where are you going?"

He stopped, studied me dispassionately for a moment, then suddenly took a step toward me and leaned his face down at me. The lips jerked back, but not in any grin, to show where the teeth were knocked out and to make the scar on the lower lip come white with the tension.

He said: "Stop following me. You don't stop following me and I cut yore throat, you little son-of-a-bitch."

Then he went on to the gate, and up the pike.

That was thirty-five years ago. Since that time my father and mother have died. I was still a boy, but a big boy, when my father got cut on the blade of a mowing machine and died of lockjaw. My mother sold the place and went to town to live with her sister. But she never took hold after my father's death, and she died within three years, right in middle life. My aunt always said, "Sallie just died of a broken heart, she was so devoted." Dellie is dead, too, but she died, I heard, quite a long time after we sold the farm.

As for Little Jebb, he grew up to be a mean and ficey Negro. He killed another Negro in a fight and got sent to the penitentiary, where he is yet, the last I heard tell. He probably grew up to be mean and ficey from just being picked on so much by the children of the other tenants, who were jealous of Jebb and Dellie for being thrifty and clever and being white-folks' niggers.

Old Jebb lived forever. I saw him ten years ago and he was about a hundred then, and not looking much different. He was living in town then, on relief—that was back in the Depression—when I went to see him. He said to me: "Too strong to die. When I was a young feller just comen on and seen how things wuz, I prayed the Lawd. I said, Oh, Lawd, gimme strength and meke me strong fer to do and to indure. The Lawd hearkened to my prayer. He give me strength. I was in-duren proud fer being strong and me much man. The Lawd give me my prayer and my strength. But now He done gone off and fergot me and left me alone with my strength. A man doan know what to pray fer, and him mortal."

Jebb is probably living yet, as far as I know.

That is what has happened since the morning when the tramp leaned his face down at me and showed his teeth and said: "Stop following me. You don't stop following me and I cut yore throat, you little son-of-a-bitch." That was what he said, for me not to follow him. But I did follow him, all the years.

by John Cheever

THE SORROWS OF GIN

John Cheever was born on May 27, 1912, in Quincy, Massachusetts. His formal education did not extend past high school; he has been writing for publication since he was sixteen. A frequent contributor to the New Yorker, *Mr. Cheever has published four collections of short stories, of which the most recent is* Some People, Places and Things That Will Not Appear in My Next Novel *(1961).* The Wapshot Chronicle, *his only novel to date, received the National Book Award. Mr. Cheever lives not far from New York, with his wife and children.*

The Lawtons in "The Sorrows of Gin" are typical of the families lately analyzed in such books as William Whyte's The Organization Man *and David Riesman's* The Lonely Crowd*—apparently prosperous, apparently comfortable, but really not secure. Even to the eye of a child this life has "the gloss and the monotony" of a club car. Just as Amy Lawton sometimes imitated a drunk and was "not unhappy at having lost for a second her ability to see the world," so her father, in a sober fantasy, is liberated for a second "from the literal symbols of his life." It is in this that Mr. Cheever, unlike the sociologists, finds the Lawtons objects of sympathy—and admiration.*

IT was a Sunday afternoon, and from her bedroom Amy could hear the Beardens coming in, followed a little while later by the Farquarsons and the Parminters. She went on reading *Black Beauty* until she felt in her bones that they might be eating something good. Then she closed her book and went down the stairs. The living-room door was shut, but through it she could hear the noise of loud talk and laughter. They must have been gossiping or worse, because they all stopped talking when she entered the room.

"Hi, Amy," Mr. Farquarson said.

"Mr. Farquarson spoke to you, Amy," her father said.

"Hello, Mr. Farquarson," she said. By standing outside the group for a minute, until they had resumed their conversation, and then by slipping past Mrs. Farquarson, she was able to swoop down on the nut dish and take a handful.

"Amy!" Mr. Lawton said.

"I'm sorry, Daddy," she said, retreating out of the circle, toward the piano.

"Put those nuts back," he said.

"I've handled them, Daddy," she said.

"Well, pass the nuts, dear," her mother said sweetly. "Perhaps someone else would like nuts."

Amy filled her mouth with the nuts she had taken, returned to the coffee table, and passed the nut dish.

"Thank you, Amy," they said, taking a peanut or two.

"How do you like your new school, Amy?" Mrs. Bearden asked.

"I like it," Amy said. "I like private schools better than public schools. It isn't so much like a factory."

"What grade are you in?" Mr. Bearden asked.

"Fourth," she said.

Her father took Mr. Parminter's glass and his own, and got up to go into the dining room and refill them. She fell into the chair he had left vacant.

"Don't sit in your father's chair, Amy," her mother said, not realizing that Amy's legs were worn out from riding a bicycle, while her father had done nothing but sit down all day.

As she walked toward the French doors, she heard her mother beginning to talk about the new cook. It was a good example of the interesting things they found to talk about.

"You'd better put your bicycle in the garage," her father said, returning with the fresh drinks. "It looks like rain."

Amy went out onto the terrace and looked at the sky, but it was not very cloudy, it wouldn't rain, and his advice, like all the advice he gave her, was superfluous. They were always at her. "Put your bicycle away." "Open the door for Grandmother, Amy." "Feed the cat." "Do your homework." "Pass the nuts." "Help Mrs. Bearden with her parcels." "Amy, please try and take more pains with your appearance."

They all stood, and her father came to the door and called her. "We're going over to the Parminters' for supper," he said. "Cook's here, so you won't be alone. Be sure and go to bed at eight like a good girl. And come and kiss me good night."

After their cars had driven off, Amy wandered through the kitchen to the cook's bedroom beyond it and knocked on the door. "Come in," a voice said, and when Amy entered, she found the cook, whose name was Rosemary, in her bathrobe, reading the Bible. Rosemary smiled at Amy. Her smile was sweet and her old eyes were blue. "Your parents have gone out again?" she asked. Amy said that they had, and the old woman invited her to sit down. "They do seem to enjoy themselves, don't they? During the four days I've been here, they've been out every night, or had people in." She put the Bible face down on her lap and smiled, but not at Amy. "Of course, the drinking that goes on here is all sociable, and what your parents do is none of my business, is it? I worry about drink more than most people, because of my poor sister. My poor sister drank too much. For ten years, I went to visit her on Sunday afternoons, and most of the time she was *non compos mentis*. Sometimes I'd find her huddled up on the floor with one or two sherry bottles empty beside her. Sometimes she'd seem sober enough to a stranger, but I could tell in a second by the way she spoke her words that she'd drunk enough not to be herself any more. Now my poor sister is gone, I don't have anyone to visit at all."

"What happened to your sister?" Amy asked.

"She was a lovely person, with a peaches-and-cream complexion and fair hair." Rosemary said. "Gin makes some people gay—it makes them laugh and cry—but with my sister it only made her sullen and withdrawn. When she was drinking, she would retreat into herself. Drink made her contrary. If I'd say the weather was fine, she'd tell me I was wrong. If I'd say it was raining, she'd say it was clearing. She'd correct me about everything I said, however small it was. She died in Bellevue Hospital one summer when I was working in Maine. She was the only family I had."

The directness with which Rosemary spoke had the effect on Amy of making her feel grown, and for once politeness came to her easily. "You must miss your sister a great deal," she said.

"I was just sitting here now thinking about her. She was in service, like me, and it's lonely work. You're always surrounded by a family, and yet you're never a part of it. Your pride is often hurt. The Madams seems condescending and inconsiderate. I'm not blaming the ladies I've worked for. It's just in the nature of the relationship. They order chicken salad, and you get up before dawn to get ahead of yourself, and just as you've finished the chicken salad, they change their minds and want crab-meat soup."

"My mother changes her mind all the time," Amy said.

"Sometimes you're in a country place with nobody else in help. You're tired, but not too tired to feel lonely. You go out onto the servants' porch when the pots and pans are done, planning to enjoy God's creation, and although the front of the house may have a fine view of the lake or the mountains, the view from the back is never much. But there is the sky and the trees and the stars and the birds singing and the pleasure of resting your feet. But then you hear them in the front of the house, laughing and talking with their guests and their sons and daughters. If you're new and they whisper, you can be sure they're talking about you. That takes all the pleasure out of the evening."

"Oh," Amy said.

"I've worked in all kinds of places—places where there were eight or nine in help and places where I was expected to burn the rubbish myself, on winter nights, and shovel the snow. In a house where there's a lot in help, there's usually some devil among them—some old butler or parlormaid—who tries to make your life miserable from the beginning. 'The Madam doesn't like it this way,' and 'The Madam doesn't like it that way,' and 'I've been with the Madam for twenty years,' they tell you. It takes a diplomat to get along. Then there is the rooms they give you, and every one of them I've ever seen is cheerless. If you have a bottle in your suitcase, it's a terrible temptation in the beginning not to take a drink to raise your spirits. But I have a strong character. It was different with my poor sister. She used to complain about nervousness, but, sitting here thinking about her tonight, I wonder if she suffered from nervousness at all. I wonder if she didn't make it all up. I wonder if she just wasn't meant to be in service. Toward the end, the only work she could get was out in the country, where nobody else would go, and she never lasted much more than a week or two. She'd take a little gin for her nervousness, then a little for her tiredness, and when she'd drunk her own bottle and everything she could steal, they'd hear about it in the front part of the house. There was usually a scene, and my poor sister always liked to have the last word. Oh, if I had had my way, they'd be a law against it! It's not my business to advise you to take anything from your father, but I'd be proud of you if you'd empty his gin bottle into the sink now and then—the filthy stuff! But it's made me feel better to talk with you, sweetheart. It's made me not miss my poor sister so much. Now I'll read a little more in my Bible, and then I'll get you some supper."

The Lawtons had had a bad year with cooks—there had been five of them. The arrival of Rosemary had made Marcia Lawton think back to a vague theory of dispensations; she had suffered, and now she was being rewarded. Rosemary was clean, industrious, and cheerful, and her table—as the Lawtons said—was just like the Chambord. On Wednesday night after dinner, she took the train to New York, promising to return on the evening train Thursday. Thursday morning, Marcia went into the cook's room. It was a distasteful but a habitual precaution. The absence of anything personal in the room—a package of cigarettes, a fountain pen, an alarm clock, a radio, or anything else that could tie the old woman to the place—gave her the uneasy feeling that she was being deceived, as she had so often been deceived by cooks in the past. She opened the closet door and saw a single uniform hanging there and, on the closet floor, Rosemary's old suitcase and the white shoes she wore in the kitchen. The suitcase was locked, but when Marcia lifted it, it seemed to be nearly empty.

Mr. Lawton and Amy drove to the station after dinner on Thursday to meet the eight-sixteen train. The top of the car was down, and the brisk air, the starlight, and the company of her father made the little girl feel kindly toward the world. The railroad station in Shady Hill resembled the railroad stations in old movies she had seen on television, where detectives and spies, bluebeards and their trusting victims, were met to be driven off to remote country estates. Amy liked the station, particularly toward dark. She imagined that the people who traveled on the locals were engaged on errands that were more urgent and sinister than commuting. Except when there was a heavy fog or a snowstorm, the club car that her father traveled on seemed to have the gloss and the monotony of the rest of his life. The locals that ran at odd hours belonged to a world of deeper contrasts, where she would like to live.

They were a few minutes early, and Amy got out of the car and stood on the platform. She wondered what the fringe of string that hung above the tracks at either end of the station was for, but she knew enough not to ask her father, because he wouldn't be able to tell her. She could hear the train before it came into view, and the noise excited her and made her happy. When the train drew in to the station and stopped, she looked in the lighted windows for Rosemary and didn't see her. Mr. Lawton got out of the car and joined Amy on the platform. They could see the conductor bending over someone in a seat, and finally the cook rose. She clung to the conductor as he led her out to the platform of the car, and she was crying. "Like peaches and cream," Amy heard her sob. "A lovely, lovely person." The conductor spoke to her kindly, put his arm around her shoulders, and eased her down the steps. Then the train pulled out, and she stood there drying her tears. "Don't say a word, Mr. Lawton," she said, "and I won't say anything." She held out a small paper bag. "Here's a present for you, little girl."

"Thank you, Rosemary," Amy said. She looked into the paper bag and saw that it contained several packets of Japanese water flowers.

Rosemary walked toward the car with the caution of someone who can hardly find the way in the dim light. A sour smell came from her. Her best coat was spotted with mud and ripped in the back. Mr. Lawton told Amy to get in the back seat of the car, and made the cook sit in front, beside him. He slammed the car door shut after her angrily, and then went around to the driver's seat and drove home. Rosemary reached into her handbag and took out a Coca-Cola bottle with a cork stopper and took a drink. Amy could tell by the smell that the Coca-Cola bottle was filled with gin.

"Rosemary!" Mr. Lawton said.

"I'm lonely," the cook said. "I'm lonely, and I'm afraid, and it's all I've got."

He said nothing more until he had turned in to their drive and brought the car around to the back door. "Go and get your suitcase, Rosemary," he said. "I'll wait here in the car."

As soon as the cook had staggered into the house, he told Amy to go in by the front door. "Go upstairs to your room and get ready for bed."

Her mother called down the stairs when Amy came in, to ask if Rosemary had returned. Amy didn't answer. She went to the bar, took an open gin bottle, and emptied it into the pantry sink. She was nearly crying when she encountered her mother in the living room, and told her that her father was taking the cook back to the station.

When Amy came home from school the next day, she found a heavy, black-haired woman cleaning the living room. The car Mr. Lawton usually drove to the station was at the garage for a check-up, and Amy drove to the station with her mother to meet him. As he came across the station platform, she could tell, by the lack of color in his face, that he had had a hard day. He kissed her mother, touched Amy on the head, and got behind the wheel.

"You know," her mother said, "there's something terribly wrong with the guest-room shower."

"Damn it, Marcia," he said, "I wish you wouldn't always greet me with bad news!"

His grating voice oppressed Amy, and she began to fiddle with the button that raised and lowered the window.

"Stop that, Amy!" he said.

"Oh, well, the shower isn't important," her mother said. She laughed weakly.

"When I got back from San Francisco last week," he said, "you couldn't wait to tell me that we need a new oil burner."

"Well, I've got a part-time cook. That's good news."

"Is she a lush?" her father asked.

"Don't be disagreeable, dear. She'll get us some dinner and wash the dishes and take the bus home. We're going to the Farquarsons'."

"I'm really too tired to go anywhere," he said.

"Who's going to take care of me?" Amy asked.

"You always have a good time at the Farquarsons'," her mother said.

"Well, let's leave early," he said.

"Who's going to take care of me?" Amy asked.

"Mrs. Henlein," her mother said.

When they got home, Amy went over to the piano.

Her father washed his hands in the bathroom off the hall and then went to the bar. He came into the living room holding the empty gin bottle. "What's her name?" he asked.

"Ruby," her mother said.

"She's exceptional. She's drunk a quart of gin on her first day."

"Oh, dear!" her mother said. "Well, let's not make any trouble now."

"Everybody is drinking my liquor," her father shouted, "and I am God-damned sick and tired of it!"

"There's plenty of gin in the closet," her mother said. "Open another bottle."

"We paid that gardener three dollars an hour and all he did was sneak in here and drink up my Scotch. The sitter we had before we got Mrs. Henlein used to water my bourbon, and I don't have to remind you about Rosemary. The cook before Rosemary not only drank everything in my liquor cabinet but she drank all the rum, kirsch, sherry, and wine that we had in the kitchen for cooking. Then, there's that Polish woman we had last summer. Even the old laundress. *And* the painters. I think they must have put some kind of a mark on my door. I think the agency must have checked me off as an easy touch."

"Well, let's get through dinner, and then you can speak to her."

"The hell with that!" he said. "I'm not going to encourage people to rob me. *Ruby!*" He shouted her name several times but she didn't answer. Then she appeared in the dining-room doorway, wearing her hat and coat.

"I'm sick," she said. Amy could see that she was frightened.

"I should think you would be," her father said.

"I'm sick," the cook mumbled, "and I can't find anything around here, and I'm going home."

"Good," he said. "Good! I'm through with paying people to come in here and drink my liquor."

The cook started out the front way, and Marcia Lawton followed her into the front hall to pay her something. Amy had watched this scene from the piano bench, a position that was withdrawn but that still gave her a good view. She saw her father get a fresh bottle of gin and make a shaker of Martinis. He looked very unhappy.

"Well," her mother said when she came back into the room. "You know, she didn't look drunk."

"Please don't argue with me, Marcia," her father said. He poured two cocktails, said, "Cheers," and drank a little. "We can get some dinner at Orfeo's," he said.

"I suppose so," her mother said. "I'll rustle up something for Amy." She went into the kitchen, and Amy opened her music to "Reflets d'Automne." "COUNT," her music teacher had written. "COUNT and lightly, lightly . . ." Amy began to play. Whenever she made a mistake, she said "Darn it!" and started at the beginning again. In the middle of "Reflets d'Automne" it struck her that *she* was the one who had emptied the gin bottle. Her perplexity was so intense that she stopped playing, but her feelings did not go beyond perplexity, although she did not have the strength to continue playing the piano. Her mother relieved her. "Your supper's in the kitchen, dear," she said. "And you can take a popsicle out of the deep freeze for dessert. Just one."

Marcia Lawton held her empty glass toward her husband, who filled it from the shaker. Then she went upstairs. Mr. Lawton remained in the room, and, studying her father closely, Amy saw that his tense look had begun to soften. He did not seem so unhappy any more, and as she passed him on her way to the kitchen, he smiled at her tenderly and patted her on the top of the head.

When Amy had finished her supper, eaten her popsicle, and exploded the bag it came in, she returned to the piano and played "Chopsticks" for a while. Her father came downstairs in his evening clothes, put his drink on the mantelpiece, and went to the French doors to look at his terrace and his garden. Amy noticed that the transformation that had begun with a softening of his features was even more advanced. At last, he seemed happy. Amy wondered if he was drunk, although his walk was not unsteady. If anything it was more steady.

Her parents never achieved the kind of rolling, swinging gait that she saw impersonated by a tightrope walker in the circus each year while the band struck up "Show Me the Way to Go Home" and that she liked to imitate herself sometimes. She liked to turn round and round and round on the lawn, until, staggering and a little sick, she would whoop, "I'm drunk! I'm a drunken man!" and reel over the grass, righting herself as she was about to fall and finding herself not unhappy at having lost for a second her ability to see the world. But she had never seen her parents like that. She had never seen them hanging on to a lamppost and singing and reeling, but she had seen them fall down. They were never indecorous—they seemed to get more decorous and formal the more they drank—but sometimes her father would get up to fill everybody's glass and he would walk straight enough but his shoes would seem to stick to the carpet. And sometimes, when he got to the dining-room door, he would miss it by a foot or more. Once, she had seen him walk into the wall with such force that he collapsed onto the floor and broke most of the glasses he was carrying. One or two people laughed, but the laughter was not general or hearty, and most of them pretended that he had not fallen down at all. When her father got to his feet, he went right on to the bar as if nothing had happened. Amy had once seen Mrs. Farquarson miss the chair she was about to sit in, by a foot, and thump down onto the floor, but nobody laughed then, and they pretended that Mrs. Farquarson hadn't fallen down at all. They seemed like actors in a play. In the school play, when you knocked over a paper tree you were supposed to pick it up without showing what you were doing, so that you would not spoil the illusion of being in a deep forest, and that was the way *they* were when somebody fell down.

Now her father had that stiff, funny walk that was so different from the way he tramped up and down the station platform in the morning, and she could see that he was looking for something. He was looking for his drink. It was right on the mantelpiece, but he didn't look there. He looked on all the tables in the living room. Then he went out onto the terrace and looked there, and then he came back into the living room and looked on all the tables again. Then he went back onto the terrace, and then back over the living-room tables, looking three times in the same place, although he was always telling her to look intelligently when she lost her sneakers or her raincoat. "Look for it, Amy," he was always saying. "Try and remember where you left it. I can't buy you a new raincoat every time it rains." Finally he gave up and poured himself a cocktail in another glass. "I'm going to get Mrs. Henlein," he told Amy, as if this were an important piece of information.

Amy's only feeling for Mrs. Henlein was indifference, and when her father returned with the sitter, Amy thought of the nights, stretching into weeks—the years, almost—when she had been cooped up with Mrs. Henlein. Mrs. Henlein was very polite and was always telling Amy what was ladylike and what was not. Mrs. Henlein also always wanted to know where Amy's parents were going and what kind of a party it was, although it was none of her business. She always sat down on the sofa as if she owned the place, and talked about people she had never even been introduced to, and asked Amy to bring her the newspaper, although she had no authority at all.

When Marcia Lawton came down, Mrs. Henlein wished her good evening. "Have a lovely party," she called after the Lawtons as they went out the door. Then she turned to Amy. "Where are your parents going, sweetheart?"

"I don't know," Amy said.

"But you must know, sweetheart. Put on your thinking cap and try and remember. Are they going to the club?"

"No," Amy said.

"I wonder if they could be going to the Trenchers'," Mrs. Henlein said. "The Trenchers' house was lighted up when we came by."

"They're not going to the Trenchers'," Amy said. "They hate the Trenchers."

"Well, where are they going, sweetheart?" Mrs. Henlein asked.

"They're going to the Farquarsons'," Amy said.

"Well, that's all I wanted to know, sweetheart," Mrs. Henlein said. "Now get me the newspaper and hand it to me politely. *Politely,*" she said, as Amy approached her with the paper. "It don't mean anything when you do things for your elders unless you do them politely." She put on her glasses and began to read the paper.

Amy went upstairs to her room. In a glass on her table were the Japanese flowers that Rosemary had brought her, blooming stalely in water that was colored pink from the dyes. Amy went down the back stairs and through the kitchen into the dining room. Her father's cocktail things were spread over the bar. She emptied the gin bottle into the pantry sink and then put it back where she found it. It was too late to ride her bicycle and too early to go to bed, and she knew that if she got anything interesting on the television, like a murder, Mrs. Henlein would make her turn it off. Then she remembered that her father had brought her home from his trip West a book about horses, and she ran cheerfully up the back stairs to read her new book.

It was after two when the Lawtons returned. Mrs. Henlein, asleep on the living-room sofa dreaming about a dusty attic, was awakened by their voices in the hall. Marcia Lawton paid her, and thanked her, and asked if anyone had called, and then went upstairs. Mr. Lawton was in the dining room, rattling the bottles around. Mrs.

Henlein, anxious to get into her own bed and back to sleep, prayed that he wasn't going to pour himself another drink, as they so often did. She was driven home night after night by drunken gentlemen. He stood in the door of the dining room, holding an empty bottle in his hand. "You must be stinking, Mrs. Henlein," he said.

"Hmm," she said. She didn't understand.

"You drank a full quart of gin," he said.

The lackluster old woman—half between wakefulness and sleep—gathered together her bones and groped for her gray hair. It was in her nature to collect stray cats, pile the bathroom up to the ceiling with interesting and valuable newspapers, rouge, talk to herself, sleep in her underwear in case of fire, quarrel over the price of soup bones, and have it circulated around the neighborhood that when she finally died in her dusty junk heap, the mattress would be full of bankbooks and the pillow stuffed with hundred-dollar bills. She had resisted all these rich temptations in order to appear a lady and she was repaid by being called a common thief. She began to scream at him.

"You take that back, Mr. Lawton! You take back every one of those words you just said! I never stole anything in my whole life, and nobody in my family ever stole anything, and I don't have to stand here and be insulted by a drunk man. Why, as for drinking, I haven't drunk enough to fill an eyeglass for twenty-five years. Mr. Henlein took me to a place of refreshment twenty-five years ago, and I drank two Manhattan cocktails that made me so sick and dizzy that I've never liked the stuff ever since. How dare you speak to me like this! Calling me a thief and a drunken woman! Oh, you disgust me—you disgust me in your ignorance of all the trouble I've had. Do you know what I had for Christmas dinner last year? I had a bacon sandwich. Son of a bitch!" She began to weep. "I'm glad I said it!" she screamed. "It's the first time I've used a dirty word in my whole life and I'm glad I said it. Son of a bitch!" A sense of liberation, as if she stood at the bow of a great ship, came over her. "I lived in this neighborhood my whole life. I can remember when it was full of good farming people and there was fish in the rivers. My father had four acres of sweet meadowland and a name that was known far and wide, and on my mother's side I'm descended from patroons, Dutch nobility. My mother was the spit and image of Queen Wilhelmina. You think you can get away with insulting me, but you're very, very, very much mistaken." She went to the telephone and, picking up the receiver, screamed, "Police! Police! Police! This is Mrs. Henlein, and I'm over at the Lawtons'. He's drunk, and he's calling me insulting names, and I want you to come over here and arrest him!"

The voices woke Amy, and, lying in her bed, she perceived vaguely the pitiful corruption of the adult world; how crude and frail it was, like a piece of worn burlap, patched with stupidities and mistakes, useless and ugly, and yet they never saw its worthlessness, and when you pointed it out to them, they were indignant. But as the voices went on and she heard the cry "Police! Police!" she was frightened. She did not see how they could arrest her, although they could find her fingerprints on the empty bottle, but it was not her own danger that frightened her but the collapse, in the middle of the night, of her father's house. It was all her fault, and when she heard her father speaking into the extension telephone in the library, she felt sunk in guilt. Her father tried to be good and kind—oh, she knew he never meant to be anything else—and, remembering the expensive illustrated book about horses that he had brought her from the West, she had to set her teeth to keep from crying. She covered her head with a pillow and realized miserably that she would have to go away. She had plenty of friends from the time when they used to live in New York, or she could spend the night in the Park or hide in a museum. She would have to go away.

"Good morning," her father said at breakfast. "Ready for a good day!" Cheered by the swelling light in the sky, by the recollection of the manner in which he had handled Mrs. Henlein and kept the police from coming, refreshed by his sleep, and pleased at the thought of playing golf, Mr. Lawton spoke with feeling, but the words seemed to Amy offensive and fatuous; they took away her appetite, and she slumped over her cereal bowl, stirring it with a spoon. "Don't slump, Amy," he said. Then she remembered the night, the screaming, the resolve to go. His cheerfulness refreshed her memory. Her decision was settled. She had a ballet lesson at ten, and she was going to have lunch with Lillian Towele. Then she would leave.

Children prepare for a sea voyage with a toothbrush and a Teddy bear; they equip themselves for a trip around the world with a pair of odd socks, a conch shell, and a thermometer; books and stones and peacock feathers, candy bars, tennis balls, soiled handkerchiefs, and skeins of old string appear to them to be the necessities of travel, and Amy packed, that afternoon, with the impulsiveness of her kind. She was late coming home from lunch, and her getaway was delayed, but she didn't mind. She could catch one of the late-afternoon locals; one of the cooks' trains. Her father was playing golf and her mother was off somewhere. A part-time worker was cleaning the living room. When Amy had finished packing, she went into her parents' bathroom and flushed the toilet. While the water murmured, she took a twenty-dollar bill from her mother's desk. Then she went downstairs and left the house and walked around Blenhollow Circle and down Alewives Lane to the station. No regrets or good-bys formed in her mind. She went over the names of the friends she had in the city, in case she decided not to spend the night in a museum. When she opened the door of the waiting room, Mr. Flanagan, the stationmaster, was poking his coal fire.

"I want to buy a ticket to New York," Amy said.

"One-way or round-trip?"

"One-way, please."

Mr. Flanagan went through the door into the ticket office and raised the glass window. "I'm afraid I haven't got a half-fare ticket for you, Amy," he said. "I'll have to write one."

"That's all right," she said. She put the twenty-dollar bill on the counter.

"And in order to change that," he said, "I'll have to go over to the other side. Here's the four-thirty-two coming in now, but you'll be able to get the five-ten." She didn't protest, and went and sat beside her cardboard suitcase, which was printed with European hotel and place names. When the local had come and gone, Mr. Flanagan shut his glass window and walked over the footbridge to the north-bound platform and called the Lawtons'. Mr. Lawton had just come in from his game and was mixing himself a cocktail. "I think your daughter's planning to take some kind of a trip," Mr. Flanagan said.

It was dark by the time Mr. Lawton got down to the station. He saw his daughter through the station window. The girl sitting on the bench, the rich names on her paper suitcase, touched him as it was in her power to touch him only when she seemed helpless or when she was very sick. Someone had walked over his grave! He shivered with longing, he felt his skin coarsen as when, driving home late and alone, a shower of leaves on the wind crossed the beam of his headlights, liberating him for a second at the most from the literal symbols of his life—the buttonless shirts, the vouchers and bank statements, the order blanks, and the empty glasses. He seemed to listen—God knows for what. Commands, drums, the crackle of signal fires, the music of the glockenspiel—how sweet it sounds on the Alpine air—singing from a tavern in the pass, the honking of wild swans; he seemed to smell the salt air in the churches of Venice. Then, as it was with the leaves, the power of her figure to trouble him was ended; his gooseflesh vanished. He was himself. Oh, why should she want to run away? Travel—and who knew better than a man who spent three days of every fortnight on the road—was a world of overheated plane cabins and repetitious magazines, where even the coffee, even the champagne, tasted of plastics. How could he teach her that home sweet home was the best place of all?

by E. M. Forster

THE CELESTIAL OMNIBUS

E. M. Forster was born on January 1, 1879, and educated at King's College, Cambridge (of which he is now an honorary fellow). In 1905 he published his first novel, Where Angels Fear to Tread. *Three others followed before the completion, in 1924, of* A Passage to India, *his most famous novel, on which he had been working intermittently since 1912. He has since published several volumes of essays, criticism, and biography, and a libretto for Benjamin Britten's opera* Billy Budd. *His short stories, originally collected as* The Celestial Omnibus *(1911) and* The Eternal Moment *(1928), were reissued in one volume in 1946. In 1953 he was made a Companion of Honour by Queen Elizabeth II.*

"The Celestial Omnibus" is a bookish story. It places in opposition two views of how literature should be "used." For Mr. Bons (whose name, spelled backwards, gives him away) a knowledge of poetry is a badge of culture. For the boy, poetry is not something one has knowledge of: it is knowledge itself. And though unskilled in Latin inflections (and much else besides), he understands better than might the pedantic Bons the first words of Sir Thomas Browne, the heavenly coachman, "Omnibus est." It is everything.

THE boy who resided at Agathox Lodge, 28, Buckingham Park Road, Surbiton, had often been puzzled by the old sign-post that stood almost opposite. He asked his mother about it, and she replied that it was a joke, and not a very nice one, which had been made many years back by some naughty young men, and that the police ought to remove it. For there were two strange things about this sign-post: firstly, it pointed up a blank alley, and, secondly, it had painted on it, in faded characters, the words, "To Heaven."

"What kind of young men were they?" he asked.

"I think your father told me that one of them wrote verses, and was expelled from the University and came to grief in other ways. Still, it was a long time ago. You must ask your father about it. He will say the same as I do, that it was put up as a joke."

"So it doesn't mean anything at all?"

She sent him up-stairs to put on his best things, for the Bonses were coming to tea, and he was to hand the cake-stand.

It struck him, as he wrenched on his tightening trousers, that he might do worse than ask Mr. Bons about the sign-post. His father, though very kind, always laughed at him—shrieked with laughter whenever he or any other child asked a question or spoke. But Mr. Bons was serious as well as kind. He had a beautiful house and lent one books, he was a churchwarden, and a candidate for the County Council; he had donated to the Free Library enormously, he presided over the Literary Society, and had Members of Parliament to stop with him—in short, he was probably the wisest person alive.

Yet even Mr. Bons could only say that the sign-post was a joke—the joke of a person named Shelley.

"Of course!" cried the mother; "I told you so, dear. That was the name."

"Had you never heard of Shelley?" asked Mr. Bons.

"No," said the boy, and hung his head.

"But is there no Shelley in the house?"

"Why, yes!" exclaimed the lady, in much agitation. "Dear Mr. Bons, we aren't such Philistines as that. Two at the least. One a wedding present, and the other, smaller print, in one of the spare rooms."

"I believe we have seven Shelleys," said Mr. Bons, with a slow smile. Then he brushed the cake crumbs off his stomach, and, together with his daughter, rose to go.

The boy, obeying a wink from his mother, saw them all the way to the garden gate, and when they had gone he did not at once return to the house, but gazed for a little up and down Buckingham Park Road.

His parents lived at the right end of it. After No. 39 the quality of the houses dropped very suddenly, and 64 had not even a separate servants' entrance. But at the present moment the whole road looked rather pretty, for the sun had just set in splendour, and the inequalities of rent were drowned in a saffron afterglow. Small birds twittered, and the breadwinners' train shrieked musically down through the cutting—that wonderful cutting which has drawn to itself the whole beauty out of Surbiton, and clad itself, like any Alpine valley, with the glory of the fir and the silver birch and the primrose. It was this cutting that had first stirred desires within the boy—desires for something just a little different, he knew not what, desires that would return whenever things were sunlit, as they were this evening, running up and down inside him, up and down, up and down, till he would feel quite unusual all over, and as likely as not would want to cry. This evening he was even sillier, for he slipped across the road towards the sign-post and began to run up the blank alley.

The alley runs between high walls—the walls of the gardens of "Ivanhoe" and "Belle Vista" respectively. It smells a little all the way, and is scarcely twenty yards long, including the turn at the end. So not unnaturally the boy soon came to a standstill. "I'd like to kick that Shelley," he exclaimed, and glanced idly at a piece of paper which was pasted on the wall. Rather an odd piece of paper, and he read it carefully before he turned back. This is what he read:

S. AND C. R. C. C.

Alteration in Service.

Owing to lack of patronage the Company are regretfully compelled to suspend the hourly service, and to retain only the

Sunrise and Sunset Omnibuses,

which will run as usual. It is to be hoped that the public will patronize an arrangement which is intended for their convenience. As an extra inducement, the Company will, for the first time, now issue

Return Tickets!

(available one day only), which may be obtained of the driver. Passengers are again reminded that *no tickets are issued at the other end,* and that no complaints in this connection will receive consideration from the Company. Nor will the Company be responsible for any negligence or stupidity on the part of Passengers, nor for Hailstorms, Lightning, Loss of Tickets, nor for any Act of God.

For the Direction.

Now he had never seen this notice before, nor could he imagine where the omnibus went to. S. of course was for Surbiton, and R.C.C. meant Road Car Company. But what was the meaning of the other C.? Coombe and Malden, perhaps, or possibly "City." Yet it could not hope to compete with the South-Western. The whole thing, the boy reflected, was run on hopelessly unbusiness-like lines. Why no tickets from the other end? And what an hour to start! Then he realized that unless the notice was a hoax, an omnibus must have been starting just as he was wishing the Bonses good-bye. He peered at the ground through the gathering dusk, and there he saw what might or might not be the marks of wheels. Yet nothing had come out of the alley. And he had never seen an omnibus at any time in the Buckingham Park Road. No: it must be a hoax, like the sign-posts, like the fairy tales, like the dreams upon which he would wake suddenly in the night. And with a sigh he stepped from the alley—right into the arms of his father.

Oh, how his father laughed! "Poor, poor Popsey!" he cried. "Diddums! Diddums! Diddums think he'd walky-palky up to Evvink!" And his mother, also convulsed with laughter, appeared on the steps of Agathox Lodge. "Don't, Bob!" she gasped. "Don't be so naughty! Oh, you'll kill me! Oh, leave the boy alone!"

But all that evening the joke was kept up. The father implored to be taken too. Was it a very tiring walk? Need one wipe one's shoes on the door-mat? And the boy went to bed feeling faint and sore, and thankful for only one thing—that he had not said a word about the omnibus. It was a hoax, yet through his dreams it grew more and more real, and the streets of Surbiton, through which he saw it driving, seemed instead to become hoaxes and shadows. And very early in the morning he woke with a cry, for he had had a glimpse of its destination.

He struck a match, and its light fell not only on his watch but also on his calendar, so that he knew it to be half-an-hour to sunrise. It was pitch dark, for the fog had come down from London in the night, and all Surbiton was wrapped in its embraces. Yet he sprang out and dressed himself, for he was determined to settle once for all which was real: the omnibus or the streets. "I shall be a fool one way or the other," he thought, "until I know." Soon he was shivering in the road under the gas lamp that guarded the entrance to the alley.

To enter the alley itself required some courage. Not only was it horribly dark, but he now realized that it was an impossible terminus for an omnibus. If it had not been for a policeman, whom he heard approaching through the fog, he would never have made the attempt. The next moment he had made the attempt and failed. Nothing. Nothing but a blank alley and a very silly boy gaping at its dirty floor. It *was* a hoax. "I'll tell papa and mamma," he decided. "I deserve it. I deserve that they should know. I am too silly to be alive." And he went back to the gate of Agathox Lodge.

There he remembered that his watch was fast. The sun was not risen; it would not rise for two minutes. "Give the bus every chance," he thought cynically, and returned into the alley.

But the omnibus was there.

It had two horses, whose sides were still smoking from their journey, and its two great lamps shone through the fog against the alley's walls, changing their cobwebs and moss into tissues of fairyland. The driver was huddled up in a cape. He faced the blank wall, and how he had managed to drive in so neatly and so silently was one of the many things that the boy never discovered. Nor could he imagine how ever he would drive out.

"Please," his voice quavered through the foul brown air, "Please, is that an omnibus?"

"Omnibus est," said the driver, without turning round. There was a moment's silence. The policeman passed, coughing, by the entrance of the alley. The boy crouched in the shadow, for he did not want to be found out. He was pretty sure, too, that it was a Pirate; nothing else, he reasoned, would go from such odd places and at such odd hours.

"About when do you start?" He tried to sound nonchalant.

"At sunrise."

"How far do you go?"

"The whole way."

"And can I have a return ticket which will bring me all the way back?"

"You can."

"Do you know, I half think I'll come." The driver made no answer. The sun must have risen, for he unhitched the brake. And scarcely had the boy jumped in before the omnibus was off.

How? Did it turn? There was no room. Did it go forward? There was a blank wall. Yet it was moving—moving at a stately pace through the fog, which had turned from brown to yellow. The thought of warm bed and warmer breakfast made the boy feel faint. He wished he had not come. His parents would not have approved. He would have gone back to them if the weather had not made it impossible. The solitude was terrible; he was the only passenger. And the omnibus, though well-built, was cold and somewhat musty. He drew his coat round him, and in so doing chanced to feel his pocket. It was empty. He had forgotten his purse.

"Stop!" he shouted. "Stop!" And then, being of a polite disposition, he glanced up at the painted notice-board so that he might call the driver by name. "Mr. Browne! stop; Oh, do please stop!"

Mr. Browne did not stop, but he opened a little window and looked in at the boy. His face was a surprise, so kind it was and modest.

"Mr. Browne, I've left my purse behind. I've not got a penny. I can't pay for the ticket. Will you take my watch, please? I am in the most awful hole."

"Tickets on this line," said the driver "whether single or return, can be purchased by coinage from no terrene mint. And a chronometer, though it had solaced the vigils of Charlemagne, or measured the slumbers of Laura, can acquire by no mutation the double-cake that charms the fangless Cerberus of Heaven!" So saying, he handed in the necessary ticket, and, while the boy said "Thank you," continued: "Titular pretensions, I know it well, are vanity. Yet they merit no censure when uttered on a laughing lip, and in an homonymous world are in some sort useful, since they do serve to distinguish one Jack from his fellow. Remember me, therefore, as Sir Thomas Browne."

"Are you a Sir? Oh, sorry!" He had heard of these gentlemen

drivers. "It *is* good of you about the ticket. But if you go on at this rate, however does your bus pay?"

"It does not pay. It was not intended to pay. Many are the faults of my equipage; it is compounded too curiously of foreign woods; its cushions tickle erudition rather than promote repose; and my horses are nourished not on the evergreen pastures of the moment, but on the dried bents and clovers of Latinity. But that it pays!—that error at all events was never intended and never attained."

"Sorry again," said the boy rather hopelessly. Sir Thomas looked sad, fearing that, even for a moment, he had been the cause of sadness. He invited the boy to come up and sit beside him on the box, and together they journeyed on through the fog, which was now changing from yellow to white. There were no houses by the road; so it must be either Putney Heath or Wimbledon Common.

"Have you been a driver always?"

"I was a physician once."

"But why did you stop? Weren't you good?"

"As a healer of bodies I had scant success, and several score of my patients preceded me. But as a healer of the spirit I have succeeded beyond my hopes and my deserts. For though my draughts were not better nor subtler than those of other men, yet, by reason of the cunning goblets wherein I offered them, the queasy soul was ofttimes tempted to sip and be refreshed."

"The queasy soul," he murmured; "if the sun sets with trees in front of it, and you suddenly come strange all over, is that a queasy soul?"

"Have you felt that?"

"Why yes."

After a pause he told the boy a little, a very little, about the journey's end. But they did not chatter much, for the boy, when he liked a person, would as soon sit silent in his company as speak, and this, he discovered, was also the mind of Sir Thomas Browne and of many other with whom he was to be acquainted. He heard, however, about the young man Shelley, who was now quite a famous person, with a carriage of his own, and about some of the other drivers who are in the service of the Company. Meanwhile the light grew stronger, though the fog did not disperse. It was now more like mist than fog, and at times would travel quickly across them, as if it was part of a cloud. They had been ascending, too, in a most puzzling way; for over two hours the horses had been pulling against the collar, and even if it were Richmond Hill they ought to have been at the top long ago. Perhaps it was Epsom, or even the North Downs; yet the air seemed keener than that which blows on either. And as to the name of their destination, Sir Thomas Browne was silent.

Crash!

"Thunder, by Jove!" said the boy, "and not so far off either. Listen to the echoes! It's more like mountains."

He thought, not very vividly, of his father and mother. He saw them sitting down to sausages and listening to the storm. He saw his own empty place. Then there would be questions, alarms, theories, jokes, consolations. They would expect him back at lunch. To lunch he would not come, nor to tea, but he would be in for dinner, and so his day's truancy would be over. If he had had his purse he would have bought them presents—not that he should have known what to get them.

Crash!

The peal and the lightning came together. The cloud quivered as if it were alive, and torn streamers of mist rushed past. "Are you afraid?" asked Sir Thomas Browne.

"What is there to be afraid of? Is it much farther?"

The horses of the omnibus stopped just as a ball of fire burst up and exploded with a ringing noise that was deafening but clear, like the noise of a blacksmith's forge. All the cloud was shattered.

"Oh, listen, Sir Thomas Browne! No, I mean look; we shall get a view at last. No, I mean listen; that sounds like a rainbow!"

The noise had died into the faintest murmur, beneath which another murmur grew, spreading stealthily, steadily, in a curve that widened but did not vary. And in widening curves a rainbow was spreading from the horses' feet into the dissolving mists.

"But how beautiful! What colours! Where will it stop? It is more like the rainbows you can tread on. More like dreams."

The colour and the sound grew together. The rainbow spanned an enormous gulf. Clouds rushed under it and were pierced by it, and still it grew, reaching forward, conquering the darkness, until it touched something that seemed more solid than a cloud.

The boy stood up. "What is that out there?" he called. "What does it rest on, out at that other end?"

In the morning sunshine a precipice shone forth beyond the gulf. A precipice—or was it a castle? The horses moved. They set their feet upon the rainbow.

"Oh, look!" the boy shouted. "Oh, listen! Those caves—or are they gateways? Oh, look between those cliffs at those ledges. I see people! I see trees!"

"Look also below," whispered Sir Thomas. "Neglect not the diviner Acheron."

The boy looked below, past the flames of the rainbow that licked against their wheels. The gulf also had cleared, and in its depths there flowed an everlasting river. One sunbeam entered and struck a green pool, and as they passed over he saw three maidens rise to the surface of the pool, singing, and playing with something that glistened like a ring.

"You down in the water—" he called.

They answered, "You up on the bridge—" There was a burst of music. "You up on the bridge, good luck to you. Truth in the depth, truth on the height."

"You down in the water, what are you doing?"

Sir Thomas Browne replied: "They sport in the mancipiary possession of their gold"; and the omnibus arrived.

The boy was in disgrace. He sat locked up in the nursery of Agathox Lodge, learning poetry for a punishment. His father had said, "My boy! I can pardon anything but untruthfulness," and had caned him, saying at each stroke, "There is *no* omnibus, *no* driver, *no* bridge, *no* mountain; you are a *truant*, a *gutter snipe*, a *liar*." His father could be very stern at times. His mother had begged him to say he was sorry. But he could not say that. It was the greatest day of his life, in spite of the caning and the poetry at the end of it.

He had returned punctually at sunset—driven not by Sir Thomas Browne, but by a maiden lady who was full of quiet fun. They had talked of omnibuses and also of barouche landaus. How far away her gentle voice seemed now! Yet it was scarely three hours since he had left her up the alley.

His mother called through the door. "Dear, you are to come down and to bring your poetry with you."

He came down and found that Mr. Bons was in the smoking-room with his father. It had been a dinner party.

"Here is the great traveller!" said his father grimly. "Here is the young gentleman who drives in an omnibus over rainbows, while young ladies sing to him." Pleased with his wit, he laughed.

"After all," said Mr. Bons, smiling, "there is something a little like it in Wagner. It is odd how, in quite illiterate minds, you will find glimmers of Artistic Truth. The case interests me. Let me plead for the culprit. We have all romanced in our time, haven't we."

"Hear how kind Mr. Bons is," said his mother, while his father said, "Very well. Let him say his Poem, and that will do. He is going away to my sister on Tuesday, and *she* will cure him of this alley-slopering." (Laughter.) "Say your Poem."

The boy began. " 'Standing aloof in giant ignorance.' "

His father laughed again—roared. "One for you, my son! 'Standing aloof in giant ignorance!' I never knew these poets talked sense. Just describes you. Here, Bons, you go in for poetry. Put him through it, will you, while I fetch up the whisky?"

"Yes, give me the Keats," said Mr. Bons. "Let him say his Keats to me."

So for a few moments the wise man and the ignorant boy were left alone in the smoking-room.

" 'Standing aloof in giant ignorance, of thee I dream and of the Cyclades, as one who sits ashore and longs perchance to visit—' "

"Quite right. To visit what?"

" 'To visit dolphin coral in deep seas,' " said the boy, and burst into tears.

"Come, come! why do you cry?"

"Because—because all these words that only rhymed before, now that I've come back they're me."

Mr. Bons laid the Keats down. The case was more interesting than he had expected. "*You*?" he exclaimed. "This sonnet, *you*?"

"Yes—and look further on: 'Aye, on the shores of darkness there is light, and precipices show untrodden green.' It *is* so, sir. All these thing are true."

"I never doubted it," said Mr. Bons, with closed eyes.

"You—then you believe me? You believe in the omnibus and the driver and the storm and that return ticket I got for nothing and—"

"Tut, tut! No more of your yarns, my boy. I meant that I never doubted the essential truth of Poetry. Some day, when you have read more, you will understand what I mean."

"But Mr. Bons, it *is* so. There *is* light upon the shores of darkness. I have seen it coming. Light and a wind."

"Nonsense," said Mr. Bons.

"If I had stopped! They tempted me. They told me to give up my ticket—for you cannot come back if you lose your ticket. They called from the river for it, and indeed I was tempted, for I have never been so happy as among those precipices. But I thought of my mother and father, and that I must fetch them. Yet they will not come, though the road starts opposite our house. It has all happened as the people up there warned me, and Mr. Bons has disbelieved me like every one else. I have been caned. I shall never see that mountain again."

"What's that about me?" said Mr. Bons, sitting up in his chair very suddenly.

"I told them about you, and how clever you were, and how many books you had, and they said, 'Mr. Bons will certainly disbelieve you.' "

"Stuff and nonsense, my young friend. You grow impertinent. I—well—I will settle the matter. Not a word to your father. I will cure you. To-morrow evening I will myself call here to take you for a walk, and at sunset we will go up this alley opposite and hunt for your omnibus, you silly little boy."

His face grew serious, for the boy was not disconcerted, but leapt about the room singing, "Joy! joy! I told them you would believe me. We will drive together over the rainbow. I told them that you would come." After all, could there be anything in the story? Wagner? Keats? Shelley? Sir Thomas Browne? Certainly the case was interesting.

And on the morrow evening, though it was pouring with rain, Mr. Bons did not omit to call at Agathox Lodge.

The boy was ready, bubbling with excitement, and skipping about in a way that rather vexed the President of the Literary Society. They took a turn down Buckingham Park Road, and then—having seen that no one was watching them—slipped up the alley. Naturally enough (for the sun was setting) they ran straight against the omnibus.

"Good heavens!" exclaimed Mr. Bons. "Good gracious heavens!"

It was not the omnibus in which the boy had driven first, nor yet that in which he had returned. There were three horses—black, gray, and white, the gray being the finest. The driver, who turned round at the mention of goodness and of heaven, was a sallow man with terrifying jaws and sunken eyes. Mr. Bons, on seeing him, gave a cry as if of recognition, and began to tremble violently.

The boy jumped in.

"Is it possible?" cried Mr. Bons. "Is the impossible possible?"

"Sir; come in, sir. It is such a fine omnibus. Oh, here is his name—Dan some one."

Mr. Bons sprang in too. A blast of wind immediately slammed the omnibus door, and the shock jerked down all the omnibus blinds, which were very weak on their springs.

"Dan . . . Show me. Good gracious heavens! we're moving."

"Hooray!" said the boy.

Mr. Bons became flustered. He had not intended to be kidnapped. He could not find the door-handle, nor push up the blinds. The omnibus was quite dark, and by the time he had struck a match, night had come on outside also. They were moving rapidly.

"A strange, a memorable adventure," he said, surveying the interior of the omnibus, which was large, roomy, and constructed with extreme regularity, every part exactly answering to every other part. Over the door (the handle of which was outside) was written, "Lasciate ogni baldanza voi che entrate"—at least, that was what was written, but Mr. Bons said that it was Lashy arty something, and that baldanza was a mistake for speranza. His voice sounded as if he was in church. Meanwhile, the boy called to the cadaverous driver for two return tickets. They were handed in without a word. Mr. Bons covered his face with his hand and again trembled. "Do you know who that is!" he whispered, when the little window had shut upon them. "It is the impossible."

"Well, I don't like him as much as Sir Thomas Browne, though I shouldn't be surprised if he had even more in him."

"More in him?" He stamped irritably. "By accident you have made the greatest discovery of the century, and all you can say is that there is more in this man. Do you remember those vellum books in my library, stamped with red lilies? This—sit still, I bring you stupendous news!—*this is the man who wrote them.*"

The boy sat quite still. "I wonder if we shall see Mrs. Gamp?" he asked, after a civil pause.

"Mrs.—?"

"Mrs. Gamp and Mrs. Harris. I like Mrs. Harris. I came upon them quite suddenly. Mrs. Gamp's bandboxes have moved over the rainbow so badly. All the bottoms have fallen out, and two of the pippins off her bedstead tumbled into the stream."

"Out there sits the man who wrote my vellum books!" thundered Mr. Bons, "and you talk to me of Dickens and of Mrs. Gamp?"

"I know Mrs. Gamp so well," he apologized. "I could not help being glad to see her. I recognized her voice. She was telling Mrs. Harris about Mrs. Prig."

"Did you spend the whole day in her elevating company?"

"Oh, no. I raced. I met a man who took me out beyond to a race-course. You run, and there are dolphins out at sea."

"Indeed. Do you remember the man's name?"

"Achilles. No; he was later. Tom Jones."

Mr. Bons sighed heavily. "Well, my lad, you have made a miserable mess of it. Think of a cultured person with your opportunities! A cultured person would have known all these characters and known what to have said to each. He would not have wasted his time with a Mrs. Gamp or a Tom Jones. The creations of Homer, of Shakespeare, and of Him who drives us now, would alone have contented him. He would not have raced. He would have asked intelligent questions."

"But Mr. Bons," said the boy humbly, "you will be a cultured person. I told them so."

"True, true, and I beg of you not to disgrace me when we arrive. No gossiping. No running. Keep close to my side, and never speak to these Immortals unless they speak to you. Yes, and give me the return tickets. You will be losing them."

The boy surrendered the tickets, but felt a little sore. After all, he had found the way to this place. It was hard first to be disbelieved and then to be lectured. Meanwhile, the rain had stopped, and moonlight crept into the omnibus through the cracks in the blinds.

"But how is there to be a rainbow?" cried the boy.

"You distract me," snapped Mr. Bons. "I wish to meditate on beauty. I wish to goodness I was with a reverent and sympathetic person."

The lad bit his lip. He made a hundred good resolutions. He would imitate Mr. Bons all the visit. He would not laugh, or run, or sing, or do any of the vulgar things that must have disgusted his new friends last time. He would be very careful to pronounce their names properly, and to remember who knew whom. Achilles did not know Tom Jones—at least, so Mr. Bons said. The Duchess of Malfi was older than Mrs. Gamp—at least, so Mr. Bons said. He would be self-conscious, reticent, and prim. He would never say he liked any one. Yet, when the blind flew up at a chance touch of his head, all these good resolutions went to the winds, for the omnibus had reached the summit of a moonlit hill, and there was the chasm, and there, across it, stood the old precipices, dreaming, with their feet in the everlasting river. He exclaimed, "The mountain! Listen to the new tune in the water! Look at the camp fires in the ravines," and Mr. Bons, after a hasty glance, retorted, "Water? Camp fires? Ridiculous rubbish. Hold your tongue. There is nothing at all."

Yet, under his eyes, a rainbow formed, compounded not of sunlight and storm, but of moonlight and the spray of the river. The three horses put their feet upon it. He thought it the finest rainbow he had seen, but he did not dare to say so, since Mr. Bons said that nothing was there. He leant out—the window had opened—and sang the tune that rose from the sleeping waters.

"The prelude to Rhinegold?" said Mr. Bons suddenly. "Who taught you these *leit motifs*?" He, too, looked out of the window. Then he behaved very oddly. He gave a choking cry, and fell back on to the omnibus floor. He writhed and kicked. His face was green.

"Does the bridge make you dizzy?" the boy asked.

"Dizzy!" gasped Mr. Bons. "I want to go back. Tell the driver."

But the driver shook his head.

"We are nearly there," said the boy. "They are asleep. Shall I call? They will be so pleased to see you, for I have prepared them."

Mr. Bons moaned. They moved over the lunar rainbow, which ever and ever broke away behind their wheels. How still the night was! Who would be sentry at the Gate?

"I am coming," he shouted, again forgetting the hundred resolutions. "I am returning—I, the boy."

"The boy is returning," cried a voice to other voices, who repeated, "The boy is returning."

"I am bringing Mr. Bons with me."

Silence.

"I should have said Mr. Bons is bringing me with him."

Profound silence.

"Who stands sentry?"

"Achilles."

And on the rocky causeway, close to the springing of the rainbow bridge, he saw a young man who carried a wonderful shield.

"Mr. Bons, it is Achilles, armed."

"I want to go back," said Mr. Bons.

The last fragment of the rainbow melted, the wheels sang upon the living rock, the door of the omnibus burst open. Out leapt the boy—he could not resist—and sprang to meet the warrior, who, stooping suddenly, caught him on his shield.

"Achilles!" he cried, "let me get down, for I am ignorant and vulgar, and I must wait for that Mr. Bons of whom I told you yesterday."

But Achilles raised him aloft. He crouched on the wonderful shield, on heroes and burning cities, on vineyards graven in gold, on every dear passion, every joy, on the entire image of the Mountain that he had discovered, encircled, like it, with an everlasting stream. "No, no," he protested, "I am not worthy. It is Mr. Bons who must be up here."

But Mr. Bons was whimpering, and Achilles trumpeted and cried, "Stand upright upon my shield!"

"Sir, I did not mean to stand! something made me stand. Sir, why do you delay? Here is only the great Achilles, whom you knew."

Mr. Bons screamed, "I see no one. I see nothing. I want to go back." Then he cried to the driver, "Save me! Let me stop in your chariot. I have honoured you. I have quoted you. I have bound you in vellum. Take me back to my world."

The driver replied, "I am the means and not the end. I am the food and not the life. Stand by yourself, as that boy has stood. I cannot save you. For poetry is a spirit; and they that would worship it must worship in spirit and in truth."

Mr. Bons—he could not resist—crawled out of the beautiful omnibus. His face appeared, gaping horribly. His hands followed, one gripping the step, the other beating the air. Now his shoulders emerged, his chest, his stomach. With a shriek of "I see London," he fell—fell against the hard, moonlit rock, fell into it as if it were water, fell through it, vanished, and was seen by the boy no more.

"Where have you fallen to, Mr. Bons? Here is a procession arriving to honour you with music and torches. Here come the men and women whose names you know. The mountain is awake, the river is awake, over the race-course the sea is awaking those dolphins, and it is all for you. They want you——"

There was the touch of fresh leaves on his forehead. Some one had crowned him.

ΤΕΛΟΣ

From the *Kingston Gazette, Surbiton Times,* and
Raynes Park Observer.

The body of Mr. Septimus Bons has been found in a shockingly mutilated condition in the vicinity of the Bermondsey gas-works. The deceased's pockets contained a sovereign-purse, a silver cigar-case, a bijou pronouncing dictionary, and a couple of omnibus tickets. The unfortunate gentleman had apparently been hurled from a considerable height. Foul play is suspected, and a thorough investigation is pending by the authorities.

by Flannery O'Connor

THE ARTIFICIAL NIGGER

Flannery O'Connor was born in Savannah, Georgia, on March 25, 1925. She graduated from Georgia State College for Women and later spent two years at the State University of Iowa studying creative writing. Her first novel, Wise Blood, *appeared in 1952, and in 1955 she brought out* A Good Man Is Hard to Find, *a collection of stories of which "The Artificial Nigger" is one. In 1960 she published her second novel,* The Violent Bear It Away. *At present she lives in Milledgeville, Georgia, where reportedly she raises peacocks. Miss O'Connor received a Ford Foundation fellowship in 1959.*

Miss O'Connor is, she tells us, a writer "with Christian concerns." Like her novels and a number of her other stories, "The Artificial Nigger" concerns the moral passions. Old Mr. Head conceives of the visit to Atlanta as a lesson in evil that his grandson must learn. The infernal sewers underfoot and the blackness of the Negroes are to both of them emblems of that evil. In an odd way their judgment is correct: for them the city is indeed an occasion of sin—of treachery and hatred. At last, forgiving and forgiven, they return forever to their lost countryside, leaving behind the city's appetite for evil, represented for them by the statue of a Negro, the gratuitous expression of a lust for blackness.

MR. Head awakened to discover that the room was full of moonlight. He sat up and stared at the floor boards —the color of silver—and then at the ticking on his pillow, which might have been brocade, and after a second, he saw half of the moon five feet away in his shaving mirror, paused as if it were waiting for his permission to enter. It rolled forward and cast a dignifying light on everything. The straight chair against the wall looked stiff and attentive as if it were awaiting an order and Mr. Head's trousers, hanging to the back of it, had an almost noble air, like the garment some great man had just flung to his servant; but the face on the moon was a grave one. It gazed across the room and out the window where it floated over the horse stall and appeared to contemplate itself with the look of a young man who sees his old age before him.

Mr. Head could have said to it that age was a choice blessing and that only with years does a man enter into that calm understanding of life that makes him a suitable guide for the young. This, at least, had been his own experience.

He sat up and grasped the iron posts at the foot of his bed and raised himself until he could see the face on the alarm clock which sat on an overturned bucket beside the chair. The hour was two in the morning. The alarm on the clock did not work but he was not dependent on any mechanical means to awaken him. Sixty years had not dulled his responses; his physical reactions, like his moral ones, were guided by his will and strong character, and these could be seen plainly in his features. He had a long tube-like face with a long rounded open jaw and a long depressed nose. His eyes were alert but quiet, and in the miraculous moonlight they had a look of composure and of ancient wisdom as if they belonged to one of the great guides of men. He might have been Vergil summoned in the middle of the night to go to Dante, or better, Raphael, awakened by a blast of God's light to fly to the side of Tobias. The only dark spot in the room was Nelson's pallet, underneath the shadow of the window.

Nelson was hunched over on his side, his knees under his chin and his heels under his bottom. His new suit and hat were in the boxes that they had been sent in and these were on the floor at the foot of the pallet where he could get his hands on them as soon as he woke up. The slop jar, out of the shadow and made snow-white in the moonlight, appeared to stand guard over him like a small personal angel. Mr. Head lay back down, feeling entirely confident that he could carry out the moral mission of the coming day. He meant to be up before Nelson and to have the breakfast cooking by the time he awakened. The boy was always irked when Mr. Head was the first up. They would have to leave the house at four to get to the railroad junction by five-thirty. The train was to stop for them at five forty-five and they had to be there on time for this train was stopping merely to accommodate them.

This would be the boy's first trip to the city though he claimed it would be his second because he had been born there. Mr. Head had tried to point out to him that when he was born he didn't have the intelligence to determine his whereabouts but this had made no impression on the child at all and he continued to insist that this was to be his second trip. It would be Mr. Head's third trip. Nelson had said, "I will've already been there twict and I ain't but ten."

Mr. Head had contradicted him.

"If you ain't been there in fifteen years, how you know you'll be able to find your way about?" Nelson had asked. "How you know it hasn't changed some?"

"Have you ever," Mr. Head had asked, "seen me lost?"

Nelson certainly had not but he was a child who was never satisfied until he had given an impudent answer and he replied, "It's nowhere around here to get lost at."

"The day is going to come," Mr. Head prophesied, "when you'll find you ain't as smart as you think you are." He had been thinking about this trip for several months but it was for the most part in moral terms that he conceived it. It was to be a lesson that the boy would never forget. He was to find out from it that he had no cause for pride merely because he had been born in a city. He was to find out that the city is not a great place. Mr. Head meant him to see everything there is to see in a city so that he would be content to stay at home for the rest of his life. He fell asleep thinking how the boy would at last find out that he was not as smart as he thought he was.

He was awakened at three-thirty by the smell of fatback frying and he leaped off his cot. The pallet was empty and the clothes boxes had been thrown open. He put on his trousers and ran into the other room. The boy had a corn pone on cooking and had fried the meat. He was sitting in the half-dark at the table, drinking cold coffee out of a can. He had on his new suit and his new gray hat pulled low over his eyes. It was too big for him but they had ordered it a size large because they expected his head to grow. He didn't say anything but his entire figure suggested satisfaction at having arisen before Mr. Head.

Mr. Head went to the stove and brought the meat to the table in the skillet. "It's no hurry," he said. "You'll get there soon enough and it's no guarantee you'll like it when you do neither," and he sat down across from the boy whose hat teetered back slowly to reveal a fiercely expressionless face, very much the same shape as the old man's. They were grandfather and grandson but they looked enough alike to be brothers and brothers not too far apart in age, for Mr. Head had a youthful expression by daylight, while the boy's look was ancient, as if he knew everything already and would be pleased to forget it.

Mr. Head had once had a wife and daughter and when the wife died, the daughter ran away and returned after an interval with Nelson. Then one morning, without getting out of bed, she died and left Mr. Head with sole care of the year-old child. He had made the mistake of telling Nelson that he had been born in Atlanta. If he hadn't told him that, Nelson couldn't have insisted that this was going to be his second trip.

"You may not like it a bit," Mr. Head continued. "It'll be full of niggers."

The boy made a face as if he could handle a nigger.

"All right," Mr. Head said. "You ain't ever seen a nigger."

"You wasn't up very early," Nelson said.

"You ain't ever seen a nigger," Mr. Head repeated. "There hasn't been a nigger in this county since we run that one out twelve years ago and that was before you were born." He looked at the boy as if he were daring him to say he had ever seen a Negro.

"How you know I never saw a nigger when I lived there before?" Nelson asked. "I probably saw a lot of niggers."

"If you seen one you didn't know what he was," Mr. Head said, completely exasperated. "A six-month-old child don't know a nigger from anybody else."

"I reckon I'll know a nigger if I see one," the boy said and got up and straightened his slick sharply creased gray hat and went outside to the privy.

They reached the junction some time before the train was due to arrive and stood about two feet from the first set of tracks. Mr. Head carried a paper sack with some biscuits and a can of sardines in it for their lunch. A coarse-looking orange-colored sun coming up behind the east range of mountains was making the sky a dull red behind them, but in front of them it was still gray and they faced a gray transparent moon, hardly stronger than a thumbprint and completely without light. A small tin switch box and a black fuel tank were all there was to mark the place as a junction; the tracks were double and did not converge again until they were hidden behind the bends at either end of the clearing. Trains passing appeared to emerge from a tunnel of trees and, hit for a second by the cold sky, vanish terrified into the woods again. Mr. Head had had to make special arrangements with the ticket agent to have this train stop and he was secretly afraid it would not, in which case, he knew Nelson would say, "I never thought no train was going to stop for you." Under the useless morning moon the tracks looked white and fragile. Both the old man and the child stared ahead as if they were awaiting an apparition.

Then suddenly, before Mr. Head could make up his mind to turn back, there was a deep warning bleat and the train appeared, gliding very slowly, almost silently around the bend of trees about two hundred yards down the track, with one yellow front light shining. Mr. Head was still not certain it would stop and he felt it would make an even bigger idiot of him if it went by slowly. Both he and Nelson, however, were prepared to ignore the train if it passed them.

The engine charged by, filling their noses with the smell of hot metal and then the second coach came to a stop exactly where they were standing. A conductor with the face of an ancient bloated bulldog was on the step as if he expected them, though he did not look as if it mattered one way or the other to him if they got on or not. "To the right," he said.

Their entry took only a fraction of a second and the train was already speeding on as they entered the quiet car. Most of the travelers were still sleeping, some with their heads hanging off the chair arms, some stretched across two seats, and some sprawled out with their feet in the aisle. Mr. Head saw two unoccupied seats and pushed Nelson toward them. "Get in there by the winder," he said in his normal voice which was very loud at this hour of the morning.

"Nobody cares if you sit there because it's nobody in it. Sit right there."

"I heard you," the boy muttered. "It's no use in you yelling," and he sat down and turned his head to the glass. There he saw a pale ghost-like face scowling at him beneath the brim of a pale ghost-like hat. His grandfather, looking quickly too, saw a different ghost, pale but grinning, under a black hat.

Mr. Head sat down and settled himself and took out his ticket and started reading aloud everything that was printed on it. People began to stir. Several woke up and stared at him. "Take off your hat," he said to Nelson and took off his own and put it on his knee. He had a small amount of white hair that had turned tobacco-colored over the years and this lay flat across the back of his head. The front of his head was bald and creased. Nelson took off his hat and put it on his knee and they waited for the conductor to come ask for their tickets.

The man across the aisle from them was spread out over two seats, his feet propped on the window and his head jutting into the aisle. He had on a light blue suit and a yellow shirt unbuttoned at the neck. His eyes had just opened and Mr. Head was ready to introduce himself when the conductor came up from behind and growled, "Tickets."

When the conductor had gone, Mr. Head gave Nelson the return half of his ticket and said, "Now put that in your pocket and don't lose it or you'll have to stay in the city."

"Maybe I will," Nelson said as if this were a reasonable suggestion.

Mr. Head ignored him. "First time this boy has ever been on a train," he explained to the man across the aisle, who was sitting up now on the edge of his seat with both feet on the floor.

Nelson jerked his hat on again and turned angrily to the window.

"He's never seen anything before," Mr. Head continued. "Ignorant as the day he was born, but I mean for him to get his fill once and for all."

The boy leaned forward, across his grandfather and toward the stranger. "I was born in the city," he said. "I was born there. This is my second trip." He said it in a high positive voice but the man across the aisle didn't look as if he understood. There were heavy purple circles under his eyes.

Mr. Head reached across the aisle and tapped him on the arm.

"The thing to do with a boy," he said sagely, "is to show him all it is to show. Don't hold nothing back."

"Yeah," the man said. He gazed down at his swollen feet and lifted the left one about ten inches from the floor. After a minute he put it down and lifted the other. All through the car people began to get up and move about and yawn and stretch. Separate voices could be heard here and there and then a general hum. Suddenly Mr. Head's serene expression changed. His mouth almost closed and a light, fierce and cautious both, came into his eyes. He was looking down the length of the car. Without turning, he caught Nelson by the arm and pulled him forward. "Look," he said.

A huge coffee-colored man was coming slowly forward. He had on a light suit and a yellow satin tie with a ruby pin in it. One of his hands rested on his stomach which rode majestically under his buttoned coat, and in the other he held the head of a black walking stick that he picked up and set down with a deliberate outward motion each time he took a step. He was proceeding very slowly, his large brown eyes gazing over the heads of the passengers. He had a small white mustache and white crinkly hair. Behind him there were two young women, both coffee-colored, one in a yellow dress and one in a green. Their progress was kept at the rate of his and they chatted in low throaty voices as they followed him.

Mr. Head's grip was tightening insistently on Nelson's arm. As the procession passed them, the light from a sapphire ring on the brown hand that picked up the cane reflected in Mr. Head's eye, but he did not look up nor did the tremendous man look at him. The group proceeded up the rest of the aisle and out of the car. Mr. Head's grip on Nelson's arm loosened. "What was that?" he asked.

"A man," the boy said and gave him an indignant look as if he were tired of having his intelligence insulted.

"What kind of a man?" Mr. Head persisted, his voice expressionless.

"A fat man," Nelson said. He was beginning to feel that he had better be cautious.

"You don't know what kind?" Mr. Head said in a final tone.

"An old man," the boy said and had a sudden foreboding that he was not going to enjoy the day.

"That was a nigger," Mr. Head said and sat back.

Nelson jumped up on the seat and stood looking backward to the end of the car but the Negro had gone.

"I'd of thought you'd know a nigger since you seen so many when you was in the city on your first visit," Mr. Head continued. "That's his first nigger," he said to the man across the aisle.

The boy slid down into the seat. "You said they were black," he said in an angry voice. "You never said they were tan. How do you expect me to know anything when you don't tell me right?"

"You're just ignorant is all," Mr. Head said and he got up and moved over in the vacant seat by the man across the aisle.

Nelson turned backward again and looked where the Negro had disappeared. He felt that the Negro had deliberately walked down the aisle in order to make a fool of him and he hated him with a fierce raw fresh hate; and also, he understood now why his grandfather disliked them. He looked toward the window and the face there seemed to suggest that he might be inadequate to the day's exactions. He wondered if he would even recognize the city when they came to it.

After he had told several stories, Mr. Head realized that the man he was talking to was asleep and he got up and suggested to Nelson that they walk over the train and see the parts of it. He particularly wanted the boy to see the toilet so they went first to the men's room and examined the plumbing. Mr. Head demonstrated the ice-water cooler as if he had invented it and showed Nelson the bowl with the single spigot where the travelers brushed their teeth. They went through several cars and came to the diner.

This was the most elegant car in the train. It was painted a rich egg-yellow and had a wine-colored carpet on the floor. There were wide windows over the tables and great spaces of the rolling view were caught in miniature in the sides of the coffee pots and in the glasses. Three very black Negroes in white suits and aprons were running up and down the aisle, swinging trays and bowing and bending over the travelers eating breakfast. One of them rushed up to Mr. Head and Nelson and said, holding up two fingers, "Space for two!" but Mr. Head replied in a loud voice. "We eaten before we left!"

The waiter wore large brown spectacles that increased the size of his eye whites. "Stan' aside then please," he said with an airy wave of the arm as if he were brushing aside flies.

Neither Nelson nor Mr. Head moved a fraction of an inch. "Look," Mr. Head said.

The near corner of the diner, containing two tables, was set off from the rest by a saffron-colored curtain. One table was set but empty but at the other, facing them, his back to the drape, sat the tremendous Negro. He was speaking in a soft voice to the two women while he buttered a muffin. He had a heavy sad face and his neck bulged over his white collar on either side. "They rope them off," Mr. Head explained. Then he said, "Let's go see the kitchen," and they walked the length of the diner but the black waiter was coming fast behind them.

"Passengers are not allowed in the kitchen!" he said in a haughty voice. "Passengers are NOT allowed in the kitchen!"

Mr. Head stopped where he was and turned. "And there's good reason for that," he shouted into the Negro's chest, "because the cockroaches would run the passengers out!"

All the travelers laughed and Mr. Head and Nelson walked out, grinning. Mr. Head was known at home for his quick wit and Nelson felt a sudden keen pride in him. He realized the old man would be his only support in the strange place they were approaching. He would be entirely alone in the world if he were ever lost from his grandfather. A terrible excitement shook him and he wanted to take hold of Mr. Head's coat and hold on like a child.

As they went back to their seats they could see through the passing windows that the countryside was becoming speckled with small houses and shacks and that a highway ran alongside the train. Cars sped by on it, very small and fast. Nelson felt that there was less breath in the air than there had been thirty minutes ago. The man across the aisle had left and there was no one near for Mr. Head to hold a conversation with so he looked out the window, through his own reflection, and read aloud the names of the buildings they were passing. "The Dixie Chemical Corp!" he announced. "Southern Maid Flour! Dixie Doors! Southern Belle Cotton Products! Patty's Peanut Butter! Southern Mammy Cane Syrup!"

"Hush up!" Nelson hissed.

All over the car people were beginning to get up and take their luggage off the overhead racks. Women were putting on their coats and hats. The conductor stuck his head in the car and snarled, "Firstopppppmry," and Nelson lunged out of his sitting position, trembling. Mr. Head pushed him down by the shoulder.

"Keep your seat," he said in dignified tones. "The first stop is on the edge of town. The second stop is at the main railroad station." He had come by this knowledge on his first trip when he had got off at the first stop and had had to pay a man fifteen cents to take him into the heart of town. Nelson sat back down, very pale. For the first time in his life, he understood that his grandfather was indispensable to him.

The train stopped and let off a few passengers and glided on as if it had never ceased moving. Outside, behind rows of brown rickety houses, a line of blue buildings stood up, and beyond them a pale rose-gray sky faded away to nothing. The train moved into the railroad yard. Looking down, Nelson saw lines and lines of silver tracks multiplying and criss-crossing. Then before he could start counting them, the face in the window started out at him, gray but distinct, and he looked the other way. The train was in the station. Both he and Mr. Head jumped up and ran to the door. Neither noticed that they had left the paper sack with the lunch in it on the seat.

They walked stiffly through the small station and came out of a heavy door into the squall of traffic. Crowds were hurrying to work. Nelson didn't know where to look. Mr. Head leaned against the side of the building and glared in front of him.

Finally Nelson said, "Well, how do you see what all it is to see?"

Mr. Head didn't answer. Then as if the sight of people passing had given him the clue, he said, "You walk," and started off down the street. Nelson followed, steadying his hat. So many sights and sounds were flooding in on him that for the first block he hardly knew what he was seeing. At the second corner, Mr. Head turned and looked behind him at the station they had left, a putty-colored terminal with a concrete dome on top. He thought that if he could keep the dome always in sight, he would be able to get back in the afternoon to catch the train again.

As they walked along, Nelson began to distinguish details and take note of the store windows, jammed with every kind of equipment—hardware, drygoods, chicken feed, liquor. They passed one that Mr. Head called his particular attention to where you walked in and sat on a chair with your feet upon two rests and let a Negro polish your shoes. They walked slowly and stopped and stood at the entrances so he could see what went on in each place but they did not go into any of them. Mr. Head was determined not to go into any city store because on his first trip here, he had got lost in a large one and had found his way out only after many people had insulted him.

They came in the middle of the next block to a store that had a weighing machine in front of it and they both in turn stepped up on it and put in a penny and received a ticket. Mr. Head's ticket said, "You weigh 120 pounds. You are upright and brave and all your friends admire you." He put the ticket in his pocket, surprised that the machine should have got his character correct but his weight wrong, for he had weighed on a grain scale not long before and knew he weighed 110. Nelson's ticket said, "You weigh 98 pounds. You have a great destiny ahead of you but beware of dark women." Nelson did not know any women and he weighed only 68 pounds but Mr. Head pointed out that the machine had probably printed the number upsidedown, meaning the 9 for a 6.

They walked on and at the end of five blocks the dome of the terminal sank out of sight and Mr. Head turned to the left. Nelson could have stood in front of every store window for an hour if there had not been another more interesting one next to it. Suddenly he said, "I was born here!" Mr. Head turned and looked at him with horror. There was a sweaty brightness about his face. "This is where I come from!" he said.

Mr. Head was appalled. He saw the moment had come for drastic action. "Lemme show you one thing you ain't seen yet," he said and took him to the corner where there was a sewer entrance. "Squat down," he said, "and stick you head in there," and he held the back of the boy's coat while he got down and put his head in the sewer. He drew it back quickly, hearing a gurgling in the depths under the sidewalk. Then Mr. Head explained the sewer system, how the entire city was underlined with it, how it contained all the drainage and was full of rats and how a man could slide into it and be sucked along down endless pitchblack tunnels. At any minute any man in the city might be sucked into the sewer and never heard from again. He described it so well that Nelson was for some seconds shaken. He connected the sewer passages with the entrance to hell and understood for the first time how the world was put together in its lower parts. He drew away from the curb.

Then he said, "Yes, but you can stay away from the holes," and his face took on that stubborn look that was so exasperating to his grandfather. "This is where I come from!" he said.

Mr. Head was dismayed but he only muttered, "You'll get your fill," and they walked on. At the end of two more blocks he turned to the left, feeling that he was circling the dome; and he was correct for in a half-hour they passed in front of the railroad station again.

At first Nelson did not notice that he was seeing the same stores twice but when they passed the one where you put your feet on the rests while the Negro polished your shoes, he perceived that they were walking in a circle.

"We done been here!" he shouted. "I don't believe you know where you're at!"

"The direction just slipped my mind for a minute," Mr. Head said and they turned down a different street. He still did not intend to let the dome get too far away and after two blocks in their new direction, he turned to the left. This street contained two- and three-story wooden dwellings. Anyone passing on the sidewalk could see into the rooms and Mr. Head, glancing through one window, saw a woman lying on an iron bed, looking out, with a sheet pulled over her. Her knowing expression shook him. A fierce-looking boy on a bicycle came driving down out of nowhere and he had to jump to the side to keep from being hit. "It's nothing to them if they knock you down," he said. "You better keep closer to me."

They walked on for some time on streets like this before he remembered to turn again. The houses they were passing now were all unpainted and the wood in them looked rotten; the street between was narrower. Nelson saw a colored man. Then another. Then another. "Niggers live in these houses," he observed.

"Well come on and we'll go somewheres else," Mr. Head said. "We didn't come to look at niggers," and they turned down another street but they continued to see Negroes everywhere. Nelson's skin began to prickle and they stepped along at a faster pace in order to leave the neighborhood as soon as possible. There were colored men in their undershirts standing in the doors and colored women rocking on the sagging porches. Colored children played in the gutters and stopped what they were doing to look at them. Before long they began to pass rows of stores with colored customers in them but they didn't pause at the entrances of these. Black eyes in black faces were watching them from every direction. "Yes," Mr. Head said, "this is where you were born—right here with all these niggers."

Nelson scowled. "I think you done got us lost," he said.

Mr. Head swung around sharply and looked for the dome. It was nowhere in sight. "I ain't got us lost either," he said. "You're just tired of walking."

"I ain't tired, I'm hungry," Nelson said. "Give me a biscuit."

They discovered then that they had lost the lunch.

"You were the one holding the sack," Nelson said. "I would have kepaholt of it."

"If you want to direct this trip, I'll go on by myself and leave you right here," Mr. Head said and was pleased to see the boy turn white. However, he realized they were lost and drifting farther every minute from the station. He was hungry himself and beginning to be thirsty and since they had been in the colored neighborhood, they had both begun to sweat. Nelson had on his shoes and he was unaccustomed to them. The concrete sidewalks were very hard. They both wanted to find a place to sit down but this was impossible and they kept on walking, the boy muttering under his breath. "First you lost the sack and then you lost the way," and Mr. Head growling from time to time, "Anybody wants to be from this nigger heaven can be from it!"

By now the sun was well forward in the sky. The odor of dinners cooking drifted out to them. The Negroes were all at their doors to see them pass. "Whyn't you ast one of these niggers the way?" Nelson said. "You got us lost."

"This is where you were born," Mr. Head said. "You can ast one yourself if you want to."

Nelson was afraid of the colored men and he didn't want to be laughed at by the colored children. Up ahead he saw a large colored woman leaning in a doorway that opened onto the sidewalk. Her hair stood straight out from her head for about four inches all around and she was resting on bare brown feet that turned pink at the sides. She had on a pink dress that showed her exact shape. As they came abreast of her, she lazily lifted one hand to her head and her fingers disappeared into her hair.

Nelson stopped. He felt his breath drawn up by the woman's dark eyes. "How do you get back to town?" he said in a voice that did not sound like his own.

After a minute she said, "You in town now," in a rich low tone that made Nelson feel as if a cool spray had been turned on him.

"How do you get back to the train?" he said in the same reed-like voice.

"You can catch you a car," she said.

He understood she was making fun of him but he was too paralyzed even to scowl. He stood drinking in every detail of her. His eyes traveled up from her great knees to her forehead and then made a triangular path from the glistening sweat on her neck down and across her tremendous bosom and over her bare arm back to where her fingers lay hidden in her hair. He suddenly wanted her to reach down and pick him up and draw him against her and then he wanted to feel her breath on his face. He wanted to look down and down into her eyes while she held him tighter and tighter. He had never had such a feeling before. He felt as if he were reeling down through a pitchblack tunnel.

"You can go a block down yonder and catch you a car take you to the railroad station, Sugarpie," she said.

Nelson would have collapsed at her feet if Mr. Head had not pulled him roughly away. "You act like you don't have any sense!" the old man growled.

They hurried down the street and Nelson did not look back at the woman. He pushed his hat sharply forward over his face which was already burning with shame. The sneering ghost he had seen in the train window and all the foreboding feelings he had on the way returned to him and he remembered that his ticket from the scale had said to beware of dark women and that his grandfather's had said he was upright and brave. He took hold of the old man's hand, a sign of dependence that he seldom showed.

They headed down the street toward the car tracks where a long yellow rattling trolley was coming. Mr. Head had never boarded a streetcar and he let that one pass. Nelson was silent. From time to time his mouth trembled slightly but his grandfather, occupied with his own problems, paid him no attention. They stood on the corner and neither looked at the Negroes who were passing, going about their business just as if they had been white, except that most of them stopped and eyed Mr. Head and Nelson. It occurred to Mr. Head that since the streetcar ran on tracks, they could simply follow the tracks. He gave Nelson a slight push and explained that they would follow the tracks on into the railroad station, walking, and they set off.

Presently to their great relief they began to see white people again and Nelson sat down on the sidewalk against the wall of a building. "I got to rest myself some," he said. "You lost the sack and the direction. You can just wait on me to rest myself."

"There's the tracks in front of us," Mr. Head said. "All we got to do is keep them in sight and you could have remembered the sack as good as me. This is where you were born. This is your old home town. This is your second trip. You ought to know how to do," and he squatted down and continued in this vein but the boy, easing his burning feet out of his shoes, did not answer.

"And standing there grinning like a chim-pan-zee while a nigger woman gives you directions. Great Gawd!" Mr. Head said.

"I never said I was nothing but born here," the boy said in a shaky voice. "I never said I would or wouldn't like it. I never said I wanted to come. I only said I was born here and I never had nothing to do with that. I want to go home. I never wanted to come in the first place. It was all your big idea. How you know you ain't following the tracks in the wrong direction?"

This last had occurred to Mr. Head too. "All these people are white," he said.

"We ain't passed here before," Nelson said. This was a neighborhood of brick buildings that might have been lived in or might not. A few empty automobiles were parked along the curb and there was an occasional passerby. The heat of the pavement came up through Nelson's thin suit. His eyelids began to droop, and after a few minutes his head tilted forward. His shoulders twitched once or twice and then he fell over on his side and lay sprawled in an exhausted fit of sleep.

Mr. Head watched him silently. He was very tired himself but they could not both sleep at the same time and he could not have slept anyway because he did not know where he was. In a few minutes Nelson would wake up, refreshed by his sleep and very cocky, and would begin complaining that he had lost the sack and the way. You'd have a mighty sorry time if I wasn't here, Mr. Head thought; and then another idea occurred to him. He looked at the sprawled figure for several minutes; presently he stood up. He justified what he was going to do on the grounds that it is sometimes necessary to teach a child a lesson he won't forget, particularly when the child is always reasserting his position with some new impudence. He walked without a sound to the corner about twenty feet away and sat down on a covered garbage can in the alley where he could look out and watch Nelson wake up alone.

The boy was dozing fitfully, half conscious of vague noises and black forms moving up from some dark part of him into the light. His face worked in his sleep and he had pulled his knees up under his chin. The sun shed a dull dry light on the narrow street; everything looked like exactly what it was. After a while Mr. Head, hunched like an old monkey on the garbage can lid, decided that if

Nelson didn't wake up soon, he would make a loud noise by bamming his foot against the can. He looked at his watch and discovered that it was two o'clock. Their train left at six and the possibility of missing it was too awful for him to think of. He kicked his foot backwards on the can and a hollow boom reverberated in the alley.

Nelson shot up onto his feet with a shout. He looked where his grandfather should have been and stared. He seemed to whirl several times and then, picking up his feet and throwing his head back, he dashed down the street like a wild maddened pony. Mr. Head jumped off the can and galloped after but the child was almost out of sight. He saw a streak of gray disappearing diagonally a block ahead. He ran as fast as he could, looking both ways down every intersection, but without sight of him again. Then as he passed the third intersection, completely winded, he saw about half a block down the street a scene that stopped him altogether. He crouched behind a trash box to watch and get his bearings.

Nelson was sitting with both legs spread out and by his side lay an elderly woman, screaming. Groceries were scattered about the sidewalk. A crowd of women had already gathered to see justice done and Mr. Head distinctly heard the old woman on the pavement shout, "You've broken my ankle and your daddy'll pay for it! Every nickel! Police! Police!" Several of the women were plucking at Nelson's shoulder but the boy seemed too dazed to get up.

Something forced Mr. Head from behind the trash box and forward, but only at a creeping pace. He had never in his life been accosted by a policeman. The women were milling around Nelson as if they might suddenly all dive on him at once and tear him to pieces, and the old woman continued to scream that her ankle was broken and to call for an officer. Mr. Head came on so slowly that he could have been taking a backward step after each forward one, but when he was about ten feet away, Nelson saw him and sprang. The child caught him around the hips and clung panting against him.

The women all turned on Mr. Head. The injured one sat up and shouted, "You sir! You'll pay every penny of my doctor's bill that your boy has caused. He's a juve-nile delinquent! Where is an officer? Somebody take this man's name and address!"

Mr. Head was trying to detach Nelson's fingers from the flesh in the back of his legs. The old man's head had lowered itself into his collar like a turtle's; his eyes were glazed with fear and caution.

"Your boy has broken my ankle!" the old woman shouted. "Police!"

Mr. Head sensed the approach of the policeman from behind. He stared straight ahead at the women who were massed in their fury like a solid wall to block his escape. "This is not my boy," he said. "I never seen him before."

He felt Nelson's fingers fall out of his flesh.

The women dropped back, staring at him with horror, as if they were so repulsed by a man who would deny his own image and likeness that they could not bear to lay hands on him. Mr. Head walked on, through a space they silently cleared, and left Nelson behind. Ahead of him he saw nothing but a hollow tunnel that had once been the street.

The boy remained standing where he was, his neck craned forward and his hands hanging by his sides. His hat was jammed on his head so that there were no longer any creases in it. The injured woman got up and shook her fist at him and the others gave him pitying looks, but he didn't notice any of them. There was no policeman in sight.

In a minute he began to move mechanically, making no effort to catch up with his grandfather but merely following at about twenty paces. They walked on for five blocks in this way. Mr. Head's shoulders were sagging and his neck hung forward at such an angle that it was not visible from behind. He was afraid to turn his head. Finally he cut a short hopeful glance over his shoulder. Twenty feet behind him, he saw two small eyes piercing into his back like pitchfork prongs.

The boy was not of a forgiving nature but this was the first time he had ever had anything to forgive. Mr. Head had never disgraced himself before. After two more blocks, he turned and called over his shoulder in a high desperately gay voice, "Let's us go get us a Co' Cola somwheres!"

Nelson, with a dignity he had never shown before, turned and stood with his back to his grandfather.

Mr. Head began to feel the depth of his denial. His face as they walked on became all hollows and bare ridges. He saw nothing they were passing but he perceived that they had lost the car tracks. There was no dome to be seen anywhere and the afternoon was advancing. He knew that if dark overtook them in the city, they would be beaten and robbed. The speed of God's justice was only what he expected for himself, but he could not stand to think that his sins would be visited upon Nelson and that even now, he was leading the boy to his doom.

They continued to walk on block after block through an endless section of small brick houses until Mr. Head almost fell over a water spigot sticking up about six inches off the edge of a grass plot. He had not had a drink of water since early morning but he felt he did not deserve it now. Then he thought that Nelson would be thirsty and they would both drink and be brought together. He squatted down and put his mouth to the nozzle and turned a cold stream of water into his throat. Then he called out in the high desperate voice, "Come on and getcher some water!"

This time the child stared through him for nearly sixty seconds. Mr. Head got up and walked on as if he had drunk poison. Nelson, though he had not had water since some he had drunk out of a paper cup on the train, passed by the spigot, disdaining to drink where his grandfather had. When Mr. Head realized this, he lost all hope. His face in the waning afternoon light looked ravaged and abandoned. He could feel the boy's steady hate, traveling at an even pace behind him and he knew that (if by some miracle they escaped being murdered in the city) it would continue just that way for the rest of his life. He knew that now he was wandering into a black strange place where nothing was like it had ever been before, a long old age without respect and an end that would be welcome because it would be the end.

As for Nelson, his mind had frozen around his grandfather's treachery as if he were trying to preserve it intact to present at the final judgment. He walked without looking to one side or the other, but every now and then his mouth would twitch and this was when he felt, from some remote place inside himself, a black mysterious form reach up as if it would melt his frozen vision in one hot grasp.

The sun dropped down behind a row of houses and hardly noticing, they passed into an elegant suburban section where mansions were set back from the road by lawns with birdbaths on them. Here everything was entirely deserted. For blocks they didn't pass even a dog. The big white houses were like partially submerged icebergs in the distance. There were no sidewalks, only drives, and these wound around and around in endless ridiculous circles. Nelson made no move to come nearer to Mr. Head. The old man felt that if he saw a sewer entrance he would drop down into it and let himself be carried away; and he could imagine the boy standing by, watching with only a slight interest, while he disappeared.

A loud bark jarred him to attention and he looked up to see a fat man approaching with two bulldogs. He waved both arms like someone shipwrecked on a desert island. "I'm lost!" he called. "I'm lost and can't find my way and me and this boy have got to catch this train and I can't find the station. Oh Gawd I'm lost! Oh hep me Gawd I'm lost!"

The man, who was bald-headed and had on golf knickers, asked him what train he was trying to catch and Mr. Head began to get out his tickets, trembling so violently he could hardly hold them. Nelson had come up to within fifteen feet and stood watching.

"Well," the fat man said, giving him back the tickets, "you won't have time to get back to town to make this but you can catch it at the suburb stop. That's three blocks from here," and he began explaining how to get there.

Mr. Head stared as if he were slowly returning from the dead and when the man had finished and gone off with the dogs jumping at his heels, he turned to Nelson and said breathlessly, "We're going to get home!"

The child was standing about ten feet away, his face bloodless under the gray hat. His eyes were triumphantly cold. There was no light in them, no feeling, no interest. He was merely there, a small figure, waiting. Home was nothing to him.

Mr. Head turned slowly. He felt he knew now what time would be like without seasons and what heat would be like without light and what man would be like without salvation. He didn't care if he never made the train and if it had not been for what suddenly caught his attention, like a cry out of the gathering dusk, he might have forgotten there was a station to go to.

He had not walked five hundred yards down the road when he saw, within reach of him, the plaster figure of a Negro sitting bent over on a low yellow brick fence that curved around a wide lawn. The Negro was about Nelson's size and he was pitched forward at an unsteady angle because the putty that held him to the wall had cracked. One of his eyes was entirely white and he held a piece of brown watermelon.

Mr. Head stood looking at him silently until Nelson stopped at a little distance. Then as the two of them stood there, Mr. Head breathed, "An artificial nigger!"

It was not possible to tell if the artificial Negro were meant to be young or old; he looked too miserable to be either. He was meant to look happy because his mouth was stretched up at the corners but the chipped eye and the angle he was cocked at gave him a wild look of misery instead.

"An artificial nigger!" Nelson repeated in Mr. Head's exact tone.

The two of them stood there with their necks forward at almost the same angle and their shoulders curved in almost exactly the same way and their hands trembling identically in their pockets. Mr. Head looked like an ancient child and Nelson like a miniature old man. They stood gazing at the artificial Negro as if they were faced with some great mystery, some monument to another's victory that brought them together in their common defeat. They could both feel it dissolving their differences like an action of mercy. Mr. Head had never known before what mercy felt like because he had been too good to deserve any, but he felt he knew now. He looked at Nelson and understood that he must say something to the child to show that he was still wise and in the look the boy returned he saw a hungry need for that assurance. Nelson's eyes seemed to implore him to explain once and for all the mystery of existence.

Mr Head opened his lips to make a lofty statement and heard himself say, "They ain't got enough real ones here. They got to have an artificial one."

After a second, the boy nodded with a strange shivering about his mouth, and said, "Let's go home before we get ourselves lost again."

Their train glided into the suburb stop just as they reached the station and they boarded it together, and ten minutes before it was due to arrive at the junction, they went to the door and stood ready to jump off if it did not stop; but it did, just as the moon, restored to its full splendor, sprang from a cloud and flooded the clearing with light. As they stepped off, the sage grass was shivering gently in shades of silver and the clinkers under their feet glittered with a fresh black light. The treetops, fencing the junction like the protecting walls of a garden, were darker than the sky which was hung with gigantic white clouds illuminated like lanterns.

Mr. Head stood very still and felt the action of mercy touch him again but this time he knew that there were no words in the world that could name it. He understood that it grew out of agony, which is not denied to any man and which is given in strange ways to children. He understood it was all a man could carry into death to give his Maker and he suddenly burned with shame that he had so little of it to take with him. He stood appalled, judging himself with the thoroughness of God, while the action of mercy covered his pride like a flame and consumed it. He had never thought himself a great sinner before but he saw now that his true depravity had been hidden from him lest it cause him despair. He realized that he was forgiven for sins from the beginning of time, when he had conceived in his own heart the sin of Adam, until the present, when he had denied poor Nelson. He saw that no sin was too monstrous for him to claim as his own, and since God loved in proportion as He forgave, he felt ready at that instant to enter Paradise.

Nelson, composing his expression under the shadow of his hat brim, watched him with a mixture of fatigue and suspicion, but as the train glided past them and disappeared like a frightened serpent into the woods, even his face lightened and he muttered, "I'm glad I've went once, but I'll never go back again!"

by Graham Greene

THE INNOCENT

Graham Greene was born on October 2, 1904, in Hertfordshire, where his father was Headmaster of Berkhamstead School. He was educated there and at Balliol College, Oxford. He was received into the Roman Catholic Church in 1926, not long after the publication of his first book, a volume of verse. Since then he has published twelve novels of which The Heart of the Matter *(1948) and* The End of the Affair *(1951) are perhaps the best known, three collections of short stories, three plays, and six "entertainments," the category in which he segregates his very popular spy and adventure stories. Several films have been adapted from his work, including* The Fallen Idol *(from "The Basement Room"),* The Third Man, *and* Our Man in Havana. *Mr. Greene has been an editor for the London* Times *(1926–1930), a film critic for* The Spectator *(1935–1939), and a war correspondent in Indo-China for* The New Republic *(1954). In 1952 he received the Catholic Literary Award.*

In a very few pages "The Innocent" exemplifies the most important motive of much of Mr. Greene's mature fiction—a vision of sin. Here that vision is double: the obscene drawing was, the narrator remembers, conceived in innocence. Only as he is morally acute does he know that experience has soiled him; only as he is spiritually paralyzed does he understand that he is thoroughly damned.

IT was a mistake to take Lola there, I knew it the moment we alighted from the train at the small country station. On an autumn evening one remembers more of childhood than at any other time of year, and her bright veneered face, the small bag which hardly pretended to contain our "things" for the night, simply didn't go with the old grain warehouse across the small canal, the few lights up the hill, the posters of an ancient film. But she said, "Let's go into the country," and Bishop's Hendron was, of course, the first name which came into my head. Nobody would know me there now, and it hadn't occurred to me that it would be I who remembered.

Even the old porter touched a chord. I said, "There'll be a four-wheeler at the entrance," and there was, though at first I didn't notice it, seeing the two taxis and thinking. "The old place is coming on." It was very dark, and the thin autumn mist, the smell of wet leaves and canal water were deeply familiar.

Lola said, "But why did you choose this place? It's grim." It was no use explaining to her why it wasn't grim to me, that that sand heap by the canal had always been there (when I was three I remember thinking it was what other people meant by the seaside). I took the bag (I've said it was light; it was simply a forged passport of respectability) and said we'd walk. We came up over the little hump-backed bridge and passed the almshouses. When I was five I saw a middle-aged man run into one to commit suicide; he carried a knife, and all the neighbours pursued him up the stairs. She said, "I never thought the country was like *this*." They were ugly almshouses, little grey stone boxes, but I knew them as I knew nothing else. It was like listening to music, all that walk.

But I had to say something to Lola. It wasn't her fault that she didn't belong here. We passed the school, the church, and came round into the old wide High Street and the sense of the first twelve years of life. If I hadn't come, I shouldn't have known that sense would be so strong, because those years hadn't been particularly happy or particularly miserable: they had been ordinary years, but now with the smell of wood fires, of the cold striking up from the dark damp paving stones, I thought I knew what it was that held me. It was the smell of innocence.

I said to Lola, "It's a good inn, and there'll be nothing here, you'll see, to keep us up. We'll have dinner and drinks and go to bed." But the worst of it was that I couldn't help wishing that I were alone. I hadn't been back all these years; I hadn't realized how well I remembered the place. Things I'd quite forgotten, like that sand heap, were coming back with an effect of pathos and nostalgia. I could have been very happy that night in a melancholy, autumnal way wandering about the little town, picking up clues to that time of life when, however miserable we are, we have expectations. It wouldn't be the same if I came back again, for then there would be the memories of Lola, and Lola meant just nothing at all. We had happened to pick each other up at a bar the day before and liked each other. Lola was all right, there was no one I would rather spend the night with, but she didn't fit in with *these* memories. We ought to have gone to Maidenhead. That's country too.

The inn was not quite where I remembered it. There was the Town Hall, but they had built a new cinema with a Moorish dome and a café, and there was a garage which hadn't existed in my time. I had forgotten too the turning to the left up a steep, villaed hill.

"I don't believe that road was there in my day," I said.

"Your day?" Lola asked.

"Didn't I tell you? I was born here."

"You must get a kick out of bringing me here," Lola said. "I suppose you used to think of nights like this when you were a boy."

"Yes," I said, because it wasn't her fault. She was all right. I liked her scent. She used a good shade of lipstick. It was costing me a lot, a fiver for Lola and then all the bills and fares and drinks, but I'd have thought it money well spent anywhere else in the world.

I lingered at the bottom of that road. Something was stirring in the mind, but I don't think I should have remembered what, if a crowd of children hadn't come down the hill at that moment into the frosty lamplight, their voices sharp and shrill, their breath fuming as they passed under the lamps. They all carried linen bags, and some of the bags were embroidered with initials. They were in their best clothes and a little self-conscious. The small girls kept to themselves in a kind of compact, beleaguered group, and one thought of hair ribbons and shining shoes and the sedate tinkle of a piano. It all came back to me: they had been to a dancing lesson, just as I used to go, to a small square house with a drive of rhododendrons halfway up the hill. More than ever I wished that Lola were not with me, less than ever did she fit, as I thought "something's missing from the picture," and a sense of pain glowed dully at the bottom of my brain.

We had several drinks at the bar, but there was half an hour before they would agree to serve dinner. I said to Lola, "You don't want to drag round this town. If you don't mind, I'll just slip out for ten minutes and look at a place I used to know." She didn't mind. There was a local man, perhaps a schoolmaster, at the bar simply longing to stand her a drink: I could see how he envied me, coming down with her like this from town just for a night.

I walked up the hill. The first houses were all new. I resented them. They hid things like fields and gates I might have remembered. It was like a map which had got wet in the pocket and pieces had stuck together; when you opened it there were whole patches hidden. But halfway up, there the house really was, the drive; perhaps the same old lady was giving lessons. Children exaggerate age. She may not in those days have been more than thirty-five. I could hear the piano. She was following the same routine. Children under eight, 6–7 P.M. Children eight to thirteen, 7–8. I opened the gate and went in a little way. I was trying to remember.

I don't know what brought it back. I think it was simply the autumn, the cold, the wet frosting leaves, rather than the piano, which had played different tunes in those days. I remembered the small girl as well as one remembers anyone without a photograph to refer to. She was a year older than I was: she must have been just on the point of eight. I loved her with an intensity I have never felt since, I believe, for anyone. At least I have never made the mistake of laughing at children's love. It has a terrible inevitability of separation because there *can* be no satisfaction. Of course one invents tales of houses on fire, of war and forlorn charges which prove one's courage in her eyes, but never of marriage. One knows without being told that that can't happen, but the knowledge doesn't mean that one suffers less. I remembered all the games of blind-man's-buff at birthday parties when I vainly hoped to catch her, so that I might have the excuse to touch and hold her, but I never caught her; she always kept out of my way.

But once a week for two winters I had my chance: I danced with her. That made it worse (it was cutting off our only contact) when she told me during one of the last lessons of the winter that next year she would join the older class. She liked me too, I knew it, but we had no way of expressing it. I used to go to her birthday parties and she would come to mine, but we never even ran home together after the dancing class. It would have seemed odd; I don't think it occurred to us. I had to join my own boisterous teasing male companions, and she the besieged, the hustled, the shrilly indignant sex on the way down the hill.

I shivered there in the mist and turned my coat collar up. The piano was playing a dance from an old C. B. Cochran revue. It seemed a long journey to have taken to find only Lola at the end of it. There *is* something about innocence one is never quite resigned to lose. Now when I am unhappy about a girl, I can simply go and buy another one. Then the best I could think of was to write some passionate message and slip it into a hole (it was extraordinary how I began to remember everything) in the woodwork of the gate. I had once told her about the hole, and sooner or later I was sure she would put in her fingers and find the message. I wondered what the message could have been. One wasn't able to express much, I thought, in those days; but because the expression was inadequate, it didn't mean that the pain was shallower than what one sometimes suffered now. I remembered how for days I had felt in the hole and always found the message there. Then the dancing lessons stopped. Probably by the next winter I had forgotten.

As I went out of the gate I looked to see if the hole existed. It was there. I put in my finger, and, in its safe shelter from the seasons and the years, the scrap of paper rested yet. I pulled it out and opened it. Then I struck a match, a tiny glow of heat in the mist and dark. It was a shock to see by its diminutive flame a picture of crude obscenity. There could be no mistake; there were my initials below the childish, inaccurate sketch of a man and woman. But it woke fewer memories than the fume of breath, the linen bags, a damp leaf, or the pile of sand. I didn't recognize it; it might have been drawn by a dirty-minded stranger on a lavatory wall. All I could remember was the purity, the intensity, the pain of that passion.

I felt at first as if I had been betrayed. "After all," I told myself, "Lola's not so much out of place here." But later that night, when Lola turned away from me and fell asleep, I began to realize the deep innocence of that drawing. I had believed I was drawing something with a meaning unique and beautiful; it was only now after thirty years of life that the picture seemed obscene.

by William Faulkner

BARN BURNING

William Faulkner was born on September 25, 1897, in New Albany, Mississippi, a few miles from Oxford, where he was reared. His formal schooling was perfunctory: he completed the fifth grade, attended high school informally, and studied at the University of Mississippi occasionally. In 1917, when America entered the war, he joined the Canadian Air Force. After the Armistice he did odd jobs, returned to the University for a while, and then left for New Orleans. There he met Sherwood Anderson, who persuaded a publisher to bring out his first novel, Soldier's Pay *(1926). Three years later he published* Sartoris, *the first of a series of novels concerning Yoknapatawpha County, Mr. Faulkner's special microcosm. Mr. Faulkner not long ago told an interviewer for* The Paris Review *that in writing* Sartoris, *"I discovered that my own little postage stamp of native soil was worth writing about and that I would never live long enough to exhaust it, and that by sublimating the actual into the apocryphal I would have complete liberty to use whatever talent I might have to its absolute top." Sixteen novels and approximately seventy-five short stories have followed that discovery, most of them exploiting it. They have earned him the O. Henry Memorial Award (1939), the National Book Award (1955), and the Pulitzer Prize (1955). In 1950 he traveled to Stockholm to accept the Nobel Prize for literature. On July 6, 1962, William Faulkner died.*

"Barn Burning" exemplifies the close relationship between the Yoknapatawpha stories and novels. Early in The Hamlet *(1940) the story is retold by Ratliff, a sewing-machine salesman. Such a shift in the point of view and the consequent transformation of tragedy into comedy are typically Faulknerian. But just as typical and more abiding is Faulkner's belief in man's ability to prevail "because he has a soul, a spirit capable of compassion and sacrifice and endurance." And these values move the boy of "Barn Burning" to the final confrontation with his father, the final alienation.*

THE store in which the Justice of the Peace's court was sitting smelled of cheese. The boy, crouched on his nail keg at the back of the crowded room, knew he smelled cheese, and more: from where he sat he could see the ranked shelves close-packed with the solid, squat, dynamic shapes of tin cans whose labels his stomach read, not from the lettering which meant nothing to his mind but from the scarlet devils and the silver curve of fish—this, the cheese which he knew he smelled and the hermetic meat which his intestines believed he smelled coming in intermittent gusts momentary and brief between the other constant one, the smell and sense just a little of fear because mostly of despair and grief, the old fierce pull of blood. He could not see the table where the Justice sat and before which his father and his father's enemy (*our enemy* he thought in that despair; *ourn! mine and hisn both! He's my father!*) stood, but he could hear them, the two of them that is, because his father had said no word yet:

"But what proof have you, Mr. Harris?"

"I told you. The hog got into my corn. I caught it up and sent it back to him. He had no fence that would hold it. I told him so, warned him. The next time I put the hog in my pen. When he came to get it I gave him enough wire to patch up his pen. The next time I put the hog up and kept it. I rode down to his house and saw the wire I gave him still rolled on to the spool in his yard. I told him he could have the hog when he paid me a dollar pound fee. That evening a nigger came with the dollar and got the hog. He was a strange nigger. He said, 'He say to tell you wood and hay kin burn.' I said, 'What?' 'That whut he say to tell you,' the nigger said. 'Wood and hay kin burn.' That night my barn burned. I got the stock out but I lost the barn."

"Where is the nigger? Have you got him?"

"He was a strange nigger, I tell you. I don't know what became of him."

"But that's not proof. Don't you see that's not proof?"

"Get that boy up here. He knows." For a moment the boy thought too that the man meant his older brother until Harris said, "Not him. The little one. The boy," and, crouching, small for his age, small and wiry like his father, in patched and faded jeans even too small for him, with straight, uncombed, brown hair and eyes gray and wild as storm scud, he saw the men between himself and the table part and become a lane of grim faces, at the end of which he saw the

Justice, a shabby, collarless, graying man in spectacles, beckoning him. He felt no floor under his bare feet; he seemed to walk beneath the palpable weight of the grim turning faces. His father, stiff in his black Sunday coat donned not for the trial but for the moving, did not even look at him. *He aims for me to lie,* he thought, again with that frantic grief and despair. *And I will have to do hit.*

"What's your name, boy?" the Justice said.

"Colonel Sartoris Snopes," the boy whispered.

"Hey?" the Justice said. "Talk louder. Colonel Sartoris? I reckon anybody named for Colonel Sartoris in this country can't help but tell the truth, can they?" The boy said nothing. *Enemy! Enemy!* he thought; for a moment he could not even see, could not see that the Justice's face was kindly nor discern that his voice was troubled when he spoke to the man named Harris: "Do you want me to question this boy?" But he could hear, and during those subsequent long seconds while there was absolutely no sound in the crowded little room save that of quiet and intent breathing it was as if he had swung outward at the end of a grape vine, over a ravine, and at the top of the swing had been caught in a prolonged instant of mesmerized gravity, weightless in time.

"No!" Harris said violently, explosively. "Damnation! Send him out of here!" Now time, the fluid world, rushed beneath him again, the voices coming to him again through the smell of cheese and sealed meat, the fear and despair and the old grief of blood:

"This case is closed. I can't find against you, Snopes, but I can give you advice. Leave this country and don't come back to it."

His father spoke for the first time, his voice cold and harsh, level, without emphasis: "I aim to. I don't figure to stay in a country among people who . . ." he said something unprintable and vile, addressed to no one.

"That'll do," the Justice said. "Take your wagon and get out of this country before dark. Case dismissed."

His father turned, and he followed the stiff black coat, the wiry figure walking a little stiffly from where a Confederate provost's man's musket ball had taken him in the heel on a stolen horse thirty years ago, followed the two backs now, since his older brother had appeared from somewhere in the crowd, no taller than the father but thicker, chewing tobacco steadily, between the two lines of grim-faced men and out of the store and across the worn gallery and down the sagging steps and among the dogs and half-grown boys in the mild May dust, where as he passed a voice hissed:

"Barn burner!"

Again he could not see, whirling; there was a face in a red haze, moonlike, bigger than the full moon, the owner of it half again his size, he leaping in the red haze toward the face, feeling no blow, feeling no shock when his head struck the earth, scrabbling up and leaping again, feeling no blow this time either and tasting no blood, scrabbling up to see the other boy in full flight and himself already leaping into pursuit as his father's hand jerked him back, the harsh, cold voice speaking above him: "Go get in the wagon."

It stood in a grove of locusts and mulberries across the road. His two hulking sisters in their Sunday dresses and his mother and her sister in calico and sunbonnets were already in it, sitting on and among the sorry residue of the dozen and more movings which even the boy could remember—the battered stove, the broken beds and chairs, the clock inlaid with mother-of-pearl, which would not run, stopped at some fourteen minutes past two o'clock of a dead and forgotten day and time, which had been his mother's dowry. She was crying, though when she saw him she drew her sleeve across her face and began to descend from the wagon. "Get back," the father said.

"He's hurt. I got to get some water and wash his . . ."

"Get back in the wagon," his father said. He got in too, over the tail-gate. His father mounted to the seat where the older brother already sat and struck the gaunt mules two savage blows with the peeled willow, but without heat. It was not even sadistic; it was exactly that same quality which in later years would cause his descendants to over-run the engine before putting a motor car into motion, striking and reining back in the same movement. The wagon went on, the store with its quiet crowd of grimly watching men dropped behind; a curve in the road hid it. *Forever* he thought. *Maybe he's done satisfied now, now that he has* . . . stopping himself, not to say it aloud even to himself. His mother's hand touched his shoulder.

"Does hit hurt?" she said.

"Naw," he said. "Hit don't hurt. Lemme be."

"Can't you wipe some of the blood off before hit dries?"

"I'll wash to-night," he said. "Lemme be, I tell you."

The wagon went on. He did not know where they were going. None of them ever did or ever asked, because it was always some where, always a house of sorts waiting for them a day or two days or even three days away. Likely his father had already arranged to make a crop on another farm before he . . . Again he had to stop himself. He (the father) always did. There was something about his wolflike independence and even courage when the advantage was at least neutral which impressed strangers, as if they got from his latent ravening ferocity not so much a sense of dependability as a feeling that his ferocious conviction in the rightness of his own actions would be of advantage to all whose interest lay with his.

That night they camped, in a grove of oaks and beeches where a spring ran. The nights were still cool and they had a fire against it, of a rail lifted from a nearby fence and cut into lengths—a small fire, neat, niggard almost, a shrewd fire; such fires were his father's habit and custom always, even in freezing weather. Older, the boy might have remarked this and wondered why not a big one; why should not a man who had not only seen the waste and extravagance of war, but who had in his blood an inherent voracious prodigality with material not his own, have burned everything in sight? Then he might have gone a step farther and thought that that was the reason: that niggard blaze was the living fruit of nights passed during those four years in the woods hiding from all men, blue or gray, with his strings of horses (captured horses, he called them). And older still, he might have divined the true reason: that the element of fire spoke to some deep mainspring of his father's being, as the element of steel or of powder spoke to other men, as the one weapon for the preservation of integrity, else breath were not worth the breathing, and hence to be regarded with respect and used with discretion.

But he did not think this now and he had seen those same niggard blazes all his life. He merely ate his supper beside it and was already half asleep over his iron plate when his father called him, and once more he followed the stiff back, the stiff and ruthless limp, up the slope and on to the starlit road where, turning, he could see his father against the stars but without face or depth—a shape black, flat, and bloodless as though cut from tin in the iron folds of the frockcoat which had not been made for him, the voice harsh like tin and without heat like tin:

"You were fixing to tell them. You would have told him." He didn't answer. His father struck him with the flat of his hand on the side of the head, hard but without heat, exactly as he had struck the two mules at the store, exactly as he would strike either of them with any stick in order to kill a horse fly, his voice still without heat or anger: "You're getting to be a man. You got to learn. You got to learn to stick to your own blood or you ain't going to have any blood to stick to you. Do you think either of them, any man there this morning, would? Don't you know all they wanted was a chance to get at me because they knew I had them beat? Eh?" Later, twenty years later, he was to tell himself, "If I had said they wanted only truth, justice, he would have hit me again." But now he said nothing. He was not crying. He just stood there. "Answer me," his father said.

"Yes," he whispered. His father turned.

"Get on to bed. We'll be there to-morrow."

To-morrow they were there. In the early afternoon the wagon stopped before a paintless two-room house identical almost with the dozen others it had stopped before even in the boy's ten years, and again, as on the other dozen occasions, his mother and aunt got down and began to unload the wagon, although his two sisters and his father and brother had not moved.

"Likely hit ain't fitten for hawgs," one of the sisters said.

"Nevertheless, fit it will and you'll hog it and like it," his father said. "Get out of them chairs and help your Ma unload."

The two sisters got down, big, bovine, in a flutter of cheap ribbons; one of them drew from the jumbled wagon bed a battered lantern, the other a worn broom. His father handed the reins to the older son and began to climb stiffly over the wheel. "When they get unloaded, take the team to the barn and feed them." Then he said, and at first the boy thought he was still speaking to his brother: "Come with me."

"Me?" he said.

"Yes," his father said. "You."

"Abner," his mother said. His father paused and looked back—the harsh level stare beneath the shaggy, graying, irascible brows.

"I reckon I'll have a word with the man that aims to begin to-morrow owning me body and soul for the next eight months."

They went back up the road. A week ago—or before last night, that is—he would have asked where they were going, but not now. His father had struck him before last night but never before had he paused afterward to explain why; it was as if the blow and the following calm, outrageous voice still rang, repercussed, divulging nothing to him save the terrible handicap of being young, the light weight of his few years, just heavy enough to prevent his soaring free of the world as it seemed to be ordered but not heavy enough to keep him footed solid in it, to resist it and try to change the course of its events.

Presently he could see the grove of oaks and cedars and the other flowering trees and shrubs where the house would be, though not the house yet. They walked beside a fence massed with honeysuckle and Cherokee roses and came to a gate swinging open between two brick pillars, and now, beyond a sweep of drive, he saw the house for the first time and at that instant he forgot his father and the terror and despair both, and even when he remembered his father again (who had not stopped) the terror and despair did not return. Because, for all the twelve movings, they had sojourned until now in a poor country, a land of small farms and fields and houses, and he had never seen a house like this before. *Hit's big as a courthouse,* he thought quietly, with a surge of peace and joy whose reason he could not have thought into words, being too young for that: *They are safe from him. People whose lives are a part of this peace and dignity are beyond his touch, he no more to them than a buzzing wasp: capable of stinging for a little moment but that's all; the spell of this peace and dignity rendering even the barns and stable and cribs which belong to it impervious to the puny flames he might contrive . . .* this, the peace and joy, ebbing for an instant as he looked again at the stiff black back, the stiff and implacable limp of the figure which was not dwarfed by the house, for the reason that it had never looked big anywhere and which now, against the serene columned backdrop, had more than ever that impervious quality of something cut ruthlessly from tin, depthless, as though, sidewise to the sun, it would cast no shadow. Watching him, the boy remarked the absolutely undeviating course which his father held and saw the stiff foot come squarely down in a pile of fresh droppings where a horse had stood in the drive and which his father could have avoided by a simple change of stride. But it ebbed only for a moment, though he could not have thought this into words either, walking on in the spell of the house, which he could even want but without envy, without sorrow, certainly never with that ravening and jealous rage which unknown to him walked in the ironlike black coat before him: *Maybe he will feel it too. Maybe it will even change him now from what maybe he couldn't help but be.*

They crossed the portico. Now he could hear his father's stiff foot as it came down on the boards with clocklike finality, a sound out of all proportion to the displacement of the body it bore and which was not dwarfed either by the white door before it, as though it had attained to a sort of vicious and ravening minimum not to be dwarfed by anything—the flat, wide, black hat, the formal coat of broadcloth which had once been black but which had now that friction-glazed greenish cast of the bodies of old house flies, the lifted sleeve which was too large, the lifted hand like a curled claw. The door opened so promptly that the boy knew the Negro must have been watching them all the time, an old man with neat grizzled hair, in a linen jacket, who stood barring the door with his body, saying, "Wipe yo foots, white man, fo you come in here. Major ain't home nohow."

"Get out of my way, nigger," his father said, without heat too, flinging the door back and the negro also and entering, his hat still on his head. And now the boy saw the prints of the stiff foot on the doorjamb and saw them appear on the pale rug behind the machine-like deliberation of the foot which seemed to bear (or transmit) twice the weight which the body compassed. The Negro was shouting "Miss Lula! Miss Lula!" somewhere behind them, then the boy, deluged as though by a warm wave by a suave turn of carpeted stair and a pendant glitter of chandeliers and a mute gleam of gold frames, heard the swift feet and saw her too, a lady—perhaps he had never seen her like before either—in a gray, smooth gown with lace at the throat and an apron tied at the waist and the sleeves turned back, wiping cake or biscuit dough from her hands with a towel as she came up the hall, looking not at his father at all but at the tracks on the blond rug with an expression of incredulous amazement.

"I tried," the Negro cried. "I tole him to . . ."

"Will you please go away?" she said in a shaking voice. "Major de Spain is not at home. Will you please go away?"

His father had not spoken again. He did not speak again. He did not even look at her. He just stood stiff in the center of the rug, in his hat, the shaggy iron-gray brows twitching slightly above the pebble-colored eyes as he appeared to examine the house with brief deliberation. Then with the same deliberation he turned; the boy watched him pivot on the good leg and saw the stiff foot drag round the arc of the turning, leaving a final long and fading smear. His father never looked at it, he never once looked down at the rug. The Negro held the door. It closed behind them, upon the hysteric and indistinguishable woman-wail. His father stopped at the top of the steps and scraped his boot clean on the edge of it. At the gate he stopped again. He stood for a moment, planted stiffly on the stiff foot, looking back at the house. "Pretty and white, ain't it?" he said. "That's sweat. Nigger sweat. Maybe it ain't white enough yet to suit him. Maybe he wants to mix some white sweat with it."

Two hours later the boy was chopping wood behind the house within which his mother and aunt and the two sisters (the mother and aunt, not the two girls, he knew that; even at this distance and muffled by walls the flat loud voices of the two girls emanated an incorrigible idle inertia) were setting up the stove to prepare a meal, when he heard the hooves and saw the linen-clad man on a fine sorrel mare, whom he recognized even before he saw the rolled rug in front of the Negro youth following on a fat bay carriage horse—a suffused, angry face vanishing, still at full gallop, beyond the corner of the house where his father and brother were sitting in the two tilted chairs; and a moment later, almost before he could have put the axe down, he heard the hooves again and watched the sorrel mare go back out of the yard, already galloping again. Then his father began to shout one of the sisters' names who presently emerged backward from the kitchen door dragging the rolled rug along the ground by one end while the other sister walked behind it.

"If you ain't going to tote, go on and set up the wash pot," the first said.

"You, Sarty!" the second shouted. "Set up the wash pot!" His father appeared at the door, framed against that shabbiness, as he had been against that other bland perfection, impervious to either, the mother's anxious face at his shoulder.

"Go on," the father said. "Pick it up." The two sisters stooped, broad, lethargic; stooping, they presented an incredible expanse of pale cloth and a flutter of tawdry ribbons.

"If I thought enough of a rug to have to git hit all the way from France I wouldn't keep hit where folks coming in would have to tromp on hit," the first said. They raised the rug.

"Abner," the mother said. "Let me do it."

"You go back and git dinner," his father said. "I'll tend to this."

From the woodpile through the rest of the afternoon the boy watched them, the rug spread flat in the dust beside the bubbling wash-pot, the two sisters stooping over it with that profound and lethargic reluctance, while the father stood over them in turn, implacable and grim, driving them though never raising his voice again. He could smell the harsh homemade lye they were using; he saw his mother come to the door once and look toward them with an expression not anxious now but very like despair; he saw his father turn, and he fell to with the axe and saw from the corner of his eye his father raise from the ground a flattish fragment of field stone and examine it and return to the pot, and this time his mother actually spoke: "Abner. Abner. Please don't. Please, Abner."

Then he was done too. It was dusk; the whippoorwills had already begun. He could smell coffee from the room where they would presently eat the cold food remaining from the mid-afternoon meal, though when he entered the house he realized they were having coffee again probably because there was a fire on the hearth, before which the rug now lay spread over the backs of the two chairs. The tracks of his father's foot were gone. Where they had been were now long, water-cloudy scoriations resembling the sporadic course of a lilliputian mowing machine.

It still hung there while they ate the cold food and then went to bed, scattered without order or claim up and down the two rooms, his mother in one bed, where his father would later lie, the older brother in the other, himself, the aunt, and the two sisters on pallets on the floor. But his father was not in bed yet. The last thing the boy remembered was the depthless, harsh silhouette of the hat and coat bending over the rug and it seemed to him that he had not even closed his eyes when the silhouette was standing over him, the fire almost dead behind it, the stiff foot prodding him awake. "Catch up the mule," his father said.

When he returned with the mule his father was standing in the black door, the rolled rug over his shoulder. "Ain't you going to ride?" he said.

"No. Give me your foot."

He bent his knee into his father's hand, the wiry, surprising power flowed smoothly, rising, he rising with it, on to the mule's bare back (they had owned a saddle once; the boy could remember it though not when or where) and with the same effortlessness his father swung the rug up in front of him. Now in the starlight they retraced the afternoon's path, up the dusty road rife with honeysuckle, through the gate and up the black tunnel of the drive to the lightless house, where he sat on the mule and felt the rough warp of the rug drag across his thighs and vanish.

"Don't you want me to help?" he whispered. His father did not answer and now he heard again that stiff foot striking the hollow portico with that wooden and clocklike deliberation, that outrageous overstatement of the weight it carried. The rug, hunched, not flung (the boy could tell that even in the darkness) from his father's shoulder struck the angle of wall and floor with a sound unbelievably loud, thunderous, then the foot again, unhurried and enormous; a light came on in the house and the boy sat, tense, breathing steadily and quietly and just a little fast, though the foot itself did not increase its beat at all, descending the steps now; now the boy could see him.

"Don't you want to ride now?" he whispered. "We kin both ride now," the light within the house altering now, flaring up and sinking. *He's coming down the stairs now,* he thought. He had already ridden the mule up beside the horse block; presently his father was up behind him and he doubled the reins over and slashed the mule across the neck, but before the animal could begin to trot the hard, thin arm came round him, the hard, knotted hand jerking the mule back to a walk.

In the first red rays of the sun they were in the lot, putting plow gear on the mules. This time the sorrel mare was in the lot before he heard it at all, the rider collarless and even bareheaded, trembling, speaking in a shaking voice as the woman in the house had done, his father merely looking up once before stooping again to the hame he was buckling, so that the man on the mare spoke to his stooping back:

"You must realize you have ruined that rug. Wasn't there anybody here, any of your women . . ." he ceased, shaking, the boy watching him, the older brother leaning now in the stable door, chewing, blinking slowly and steadily at nothing apparently. "It cost a hundred dollars. But you never had a hundred dollars. You never will. So I'm going to charge you twenty bushels of corn against your crop. I'll add it in your contract and when you come to the commissary you can sign it. That won't keep Mrs. de Spain quiet but maybe it will teach you to wipe your feet off before you enter her house again."

Then he was gone. The boy looked at his father, who still had not spoken or even looked up again, who was now adjusting the loggerhead in the hame.

"Pap," he said. His father looked at him—the inscrutable face, the shaggy brows beneath which the gray eyes glinted coldly. Suddenly the boy went toward him, fast, stopping as suddenly. "You done the best you could!" he cried. "If he wanted hit done different why didn't he wait and tell you how? He won't git no twenty bushels! He won't git none! We'll gether hit and hide hit! I kin watch . . ."

"Did you put the cutter back in that straight stock like I told you?"

"No, sir," he said.

"Then go do it."

That was Wednesday. During the rest of that week he worked steadily, at what was within his scope and some which was beyond it, with an industry that did not need to be driven nor even commanded twice; he had this from his mother, with the difference that some at least of what he did he liked to do, such as splitting wood with the half-size axe which his mother and aunt had earned, or saved money somehow, to present him with at Christmas. In company with the two older women (and on one afternoon, even one of the sisters), he built pens for the shoat and the cow which were a part of his father's contract with the landlord, and one afternoon, his father being absent, gone somewhere on one of the mules, he went to the field.

They were running a middle buster now, his brother holding the plow straight while he handled the reins, and walking beside the straining mule, the rich black soil shearing cool and damp against his bare ankles, he thought *Maybe this is the end of it. Maybe even that twenty bushels that seems hard to have to pay for just a rug will be a cheap price for him to stop forever and always from being what he used to be;* thinking, dreaming now, so that his brother had to speak sharply to him to mind the mule: *Maybe he even won't collect the twenty bushels. Maybe it will all add up and balance and vanish—corn, rug, fire; the terror and grief, the being pulled two ways like between two teams of horses—gone, done with for ever and ever.*

Then it was Saturday; he looked up from beneath the mule he was harnessing and saw his father in the black coat and hat. "Not that," his father said. "The wagon gear." And then, two hours later, sitting in the wagon bed behind his father and brother on the seat, the wagon accomplished a final curve, and he saw the weathered paintless store with its tattered tobacco- and patent-medicine posters and the tethered wagons and saddle animals below the gallery. He mounted the gnawed steps behind his father and brother, and there again was the lane of quiet, watching faces for the three of them to walk through. He saw the man in spectacles sitting at the plank table and he did not need to be told this was a Justice of the Peace; he sent one glare of fierce, exultant, partisan defiance at the man in collar and cravat now, whom he had seen but twice before in his life, and that on a galloping horse, who now wore on his face an expression not of rage but of amazed unbelief which the boy could not have known was at the incredible circumstance of being sued by one of his own tenants, and came and stood against his father and cried at the Justice: "He ain't done it! He ain't burnt . . ."

"Go back to the wagon," his father said.

"Burnt?" the Justice said. "Do I understand this rug was burned too?"

"Does anybody here claim it was?" his father said. "Go back to the wagon." But he did not, he merely retreated to the rear of the room, crowded as that other had been, but not to sit down this time, instead, to stand pressing among the motionless bodies, listening to the voices:

"And you claim twenty bushels of corn is too high for the damage you did to the rug?"

"He brought the rug to me and said he wanted the tracks washed out of it. I washed the tracks out and took the rug back to him."

"But you didn't carry the rug back to him in the same condition it was in before you made the tracks on it."

His father did not answer, and now for perhaps half a minute there was no sound at all save that of breathing, the faint, steady suspiration of complete and intent listening.

"You decline to answer that, Mr. Snopes?" Again his father did not answer. "I'm going to find against you, Mr. Snopes. I'm going to find that you were responsible for the injury to Major de Spain's rug and hold you liable for it. But twenty bushels of corn seems a little high for a man in your circumstances to have to pay. Major de Spain claims it cost a hundred dollars. October corn will be worth about fifty cents. I figure that if Major de Spain can stand a ninety-five dollar loss on something he paid cash for, you can stand a five-dollar loss you haven't earned yet. I hold you in damages to Major de Spain to the amount of ten bushels of corn over and above your contract with him, to be paid to him out of your crop at gathering time. Court adjourned."

It had taken no time hardly, the morning was but half begun. He thought they would return home and perhaps back to the field, since they were late, far behind all other farmers. But instead his father passed on behind the wagon, merely indicating with his hand for the older brother to follow with it, and crossed the road toward the blacksmith shop opposite, pressing on after his father, overtaking him, speaking, whispering up at the harsh, calm face beneath the weathered hat: "He won't git no ten bushels neither. He won't git one. We'll . . ." until his father glanced for an instant down at him, the face absolutely calm, the grizzled eyebrows tangled above the cold eyes, the voice almost pleasant, almost gentle:

"You think so? Well, we'll wait till October anyway."

The matter of the wagon—the setting of a spoke or two and the tightening of the tires—did not take long either, the business of the tires accomplished by driving the wagon into the spring branch behind the shop and letting it stand there, the mules nuzzling into the water from time to time, and the boy on the seat with the idle reins, looking up the slope and through the sooty tunnel of the shed where the slow hammer rang and where his father sat on an upended cypress bolt, easily, either talking or listening, still sitting there when the boy brought the dripping wagon up out of the branch and halted it before the door.

"Take them on to the shade and hitch," his father said. He did so and returned. His father and the smith and a third man squatting on his heels inside the door were talking, about crops and animals; the boy, squatting too in the ammoniac dust and hoof-parings and scales of rust, heard his father tell a long and unhurried story of the time before the birth of the older brother even when he had been a professional horsetrader. And then his father came up beside him where he stood before a tattered last year's circus poster on the other side of the store, gazing rapt and quiet at the scarlet horses, the incredible poisings and convolutions of tulle and tights and the painted leers of comedians, and said, "It's time to eat."

But not at home. Squatting beside his brother against the front wall, he watched his father emerge from the store and produce from a paper sack a segment of cheese and divide it carefully and deliberately into three with his pocket knife and produce crackers from the same sack. They all three squatted on the gallery and ate, slowly, without talking; then in the store again, they drank from a tin dipper tepid water smelling of the cedar bucket and of living beech trees. And still they did not go home. It was a horse lot this time, a tall rail fence upon and along which men stood and sat and out of which one by one horses were led, to be walked and trotted and then cantered back and forth along the road while the slow swapping and buying went on and the sun began to slant westward, they—the three of them—watching and listening, the older brother with his muddy eyes and his steady, inevitable tobacco, the father commenting now and then on certain of the animals, to no one in particular.

It was after sundown when they reached home. They ate supper by lamplight, then, sitting on the doorstep, the boy watched the night fully accomplish, listening to the whippoorwills and the frogs, when he heard his mother's voice: "Abner! No! No! Oh, God. Oh, God. Abner!" and he rose, whirled, and saw the altered light through the door where a candle stub now burned in a bottle neck on the table and his father, still in the hat and coat, at once formal and burlesque as though dressed carefully for some shabby and ceremonial violence, emptying the reservoir of the lamp back into the five-gallon kerosene can from which it had been filled, while the mother tugged at his arm until he shifted the lamp to the other hand and flung her back, not savagely or viciously, just hard, into the wall, her hands flung out against the wall for balance, her mouth open and in her face the same quality of hopeless despair as had been in her voice. Then his father saw him standing in the door.

"Go to the barn and get that can of oil we were oiling the wagon with," he said. The boy did not move. Then he could speak.

"What . . ." he cried. "What are you . . ."

"Go get that oil," his father said. "Go."

Then he was moving, running, outside the house, toward the stable: this the old habit, the old blood which he had not been permitted to choose for himself, which had been bequeathed him willy nilly and which had run for so long (and who knew where, battening on what outrage and savagery and lust) before it came to him. *I could keep on,* he thought. *I could run on and on and never look back, never need to see his face again. Only I can't. I can't,* the rusted can in his hand now, the liquid sploshing in it as he ran back to the house and into it, into the sound of his mother's weeping in the next room, and handed the can to his father.

"Ain't you going to even send a nigger?" he cried. "At least you sent a nigger before!"

This time his father didn't strike him. The hand came even faster than the blow had, the same hand which had set the can on the table with almost excruciating care flashing from the can toward him too quick for him to follow it, gripping him by the back of his shirt and on to tiptoe before he had seen it quit the can, the face stooping at him in breathless and frozen ferocity, the cold, dead voice speaking over him to the older brother who leaned against the table, chewing with that steady, curious, sidewise motion of cows:

"Empty the can into the big one and go on. I'll catch up with you."

"Better tie him up to the bedpost," the brother said.

"Do like I told you," the father said. Then the boy was moving, his bunched shirt and the hard, bony hand between his shoulder-blades, his toes just touching the floor, across the room and into the other one, past the sisters sitting with spread heavy thighs in the two chairs over the cold hearth, and to where his mother and aunt sat side by side on the bed, the aunt's arms about her mother's shoulders.

"Hold him," the father said. The aunt made a startled movement. "Not you," the father said. "Lennie. Take hold of him. I want to see you do it." His mother took him by the wrist. "You'll hold him better than that. If he gets loose don't you know what he is going to do? He will go up yonder." He jerked his head toward the road. "Maybe I'd better tie him."

"I'll hold him," his mother whispered.

"See you do then." Then his father was gone, the stiff foot heavy and measured upon the boards, ceasing at last.

Then he began to struggle. His mother caught him in both arms, he jerking and wrenching at them. He would be stronger in the end, he knew that. But he had no time to wait for it. "Lemme go!" he cried. "I don't want to have to hit you!"

"Let him go!" the aunt said. "If he don't go, before God, I am going up there myself!"

"Don't you see I can't?" his mother cried. "Sarty! Sarty! No! No! Help me, Lizzie!"

Then he was free. His aunt grasped at him but it was too late. He whirled, running, his mother stumbled forward on to her knees behind him, crying to the nearer sister: "Catch him, Net! Catch him!" But that was too late too, the sister (the sisters were twins, born at the same time, yet either of them now gave the impression of being, encompassing as much living meat and volume and weight as any other two of the family) not yet having begun to rise from the chair, her head, face, alone merely turned, presenting to him in the flying instant an astonishing expanse of young female features untroubled by any surprise even, wearing only an expression of bovine interest. Then he was out of the room, out of the house, in the mild dust of the starlit road and the heavy rifeness of honeysuckle, the pale ribbon unspooling with terrific slowness under his running feet, reaching the gate at last and turning in, running, his heart and lungs drumming, on up the drive toward the lighted house, the lighted door. He did not knock, he burst in, sobbing for breath, incapable for the moment of speech; he saw the astonished face of the Negro in the linen jacket without knowing when the Negro had appeared.

"De Spain!" he cried, panting. "Where's . . ." then he saw the white man too emerging from a white door down the hall. "Barn!" he cried. "Barn!"

"What?" the white man said. "Barn?"

"Yes!" the boy cried. "Barn!"

"Catch him!" the white man shouted.

But it was too late this time too. The Negro grasped his shirt, but the entire sleeve, rotten with washing, carried away, and he was out that door too and in the drive again, and had actually never ceased to run even while he was screaming into the white man's face.

Behind him the white man was shouting, "My horse! Fetch my horse!" and he thought for an instant of cutting across the park and climbing the fence into the road, but he did not know the park nor how high the vine-massed fence might be and he dared not risk it. So he ran on down the drive, blood and breath roaring; presently he was in the road again though he could not see it. He could not hear either: the galloping mare was almost upon him before he heard her, and even then he held his course, as if the very urgency of his wild grief and need must in a moment more find him wings, waiting until the ultimate instant to hurl himself aside and into the weed-choked roadside ditch as the horse thundered past and on, for an instant in furious silhouette against the stars, the tranquil early summer night sky which, even before the shape of the horse and rider vanished, stained abruptly and violently upward: a long, swirling roar incredible and soundless, blotting the stars, and he springing up and into the road again, running again, knowing it was too late yet still running even after he heard the shot and, an instant later, two shots, pausing now without knowing he had ceased to run, crying "Pap! Pap!", running again before he knew he had begun to run, stumbling, tripping over something and scrabbling up again without ceasing to run, looking backward over his shoulder at the glare as he got up, running on among the invisible trees, panting, sobbing, "Father! Father!"

At midnight he was sitting on the crest of a hill. He did not know it was midnight and he did not know how far he had come. But there was no glare behind him now and he sat now, his back toward what he had called home for four days anyhow, his face toward the dark woods which he would enter when breath was strong again, small, shaking steadily in the chill darkness, hugging himself into the remainder of his thin, rotten shirt, the grief and despair now no longer terror and fear but just grief and despair. *Father. My father,* he thought. "He was brave!" he cried suddenly, aloud but not loud, no more than a whisper: "He was! He was in the war! He was in Colonel Sartoris' cav'ry!" not knowing that his father had gone to that war a private in the fine old European sense, wearing no uniform, admitting the authority of and giving fidelity to no man or army or flag, going to war as Malbrouck himself did: for booty—it meant nothing and less than nothing to him if it were enemy booty or his own.

The slow constellations wheeled on. It would be dawn and then sun-up after a while and he would be hungry. But that would be tomorrow and now he was only cold, and walking would cure that. His breathing was easier now and he decided to get up and go on, and then he found that he had been asleep because he knew it was almost dawn, the night almost over. He could tell that from the whippoorwills. They were everywhere now among the dark trees below him, constant and inflectioned and ceaseless, so that, as the instant for giving over to the day birds drew nearer and nearer, there was no interval at all between them. He got up. He was a little stiff, but walking would cure that too as it would the cold, and soon there would be the sun. He went on down the hill, toward the dark woods within which the liquid silver voices of the birds called unceasing—the rapid and urgent beating of the urgent and quiring heart of the late spring night. He did not look back.

by Conrad Aiken

SILENT SNOW, SECRET SNOW

Conrad Aiken was born on August 5, 1889, in Savannah, Georgia. After the violent death of his parents when he was eleven, he was taken to Massachusetts to live. At Harvard he was a member of the class of 1911 (which included T. S. Eliot and Walter Lippmann) and was president of the Advocate *and class poet. He refused to serve in World War I on the grounds that as poet he was engaged in an essential industry.*

Mr. Aiken's first book of poems, Earth Triumphant, *appeared in 1914. More than twenty-five others have followed. He was awarded the Pulitzer Prize for poetry in 1929, the year in which* Prelude *and* Selected Poems *appeared. In 1953 he received the National Book Award for his* Collected Poems *and in 1956 the Bollingen Prize for* A Letter from Li Po. *Though principally a poet, Mr. Aiken has published six novels, three collections of essays, and five volumes of short stories.*

"Silent Snow, Secret Snow," like a considerable number of Mr. Aiken's other stories, is a fantasy—a fantasy rooted in fact and thick with detail. As every day the "snow" (whatever it may be) says its white word to him, Paul eagerly retreats further from a real world of school, eczema ointment ads, parents, and unpolished shoes. Like Wordsworth he experiences "obstinate questionings/Of sense and outward things," but unlike the poet, Paul does not grasp at a wall or a tree to recall himself to reality. Paul does not quite know (and would not care if he did) that he is dying—of his own sensibility, as it were.

JUST why it should have happened, or why it should have happened just when it did, he could not, of course, possibly have said; nor perhaps would it even have occurred to him to ask. The thing was above all a secret, something to be preciously concealed from Mother and Father; and to that very fact it owed an enormous part of its deliciousness. It was like a peculiarly beautiful trinket to be carried unmentioned in one's trouser pocket—a rare stamp, an old coin, a few tiny gold links found trodden out of shape on the path in the park, a pebble of carnelian, a seashell distinguishable from all others by an unusual spot or stripe—and, as if it were any one of these, he carried around with him everywhere a warm and persistent and increasingly beautiful sense of possession. Nor was it only a sense of possession—it was also a sense of protection. It was as if, in some delightful way, his secret gave him a fortress, a wall behind which he could retreat into heavenly seclusion. This was almost the first thing he had noticed about it—apart from the oddness of the thing itself—and it was this that now again, for the fiftieth time, occurred to him, as he sat in the little schoolroom. It was the half-hour for geography. Miss Buell was revolving with one finger, slowly, a huge terrestrial globe which had been placed on her desk. The green and yellow continents passed and repassed, questions were asked and answered, and now the little girl in front of him, Deirdre, who had a funny little constellation of freckles on the back of her neck, exactly like the Big Dipper, was standing up and telling Miss Buell that the equator was the line that ran round the middle.

Miss Buell's face, which was old and grayish and kindly, with gray stiff curls beside the cheeks, and eyes that swam very brightly, like little minnows, behind thick glasses, wrinkled itself into a complication of amusements.

"Ah! I see. The earth is wearing a belt, or a sash. Or someone drew a line round it!"

"Oh no—not that—I mean——"

In the general laughter, he did not share, or only a very little. He was thinking about the Arctic and Antarctic regions, which of course, on the globe, were white. Miss Buell was now telling them about the tropics, the jungles, the steamy heat of equatorial swamps, where the birds and butterflies, and even the snakes, were like living jewels. As he listened to these things, he was already, with a pleasant sense of half-effort, putting his secret between himself and the words. Was it really an effort at all? For effort implied something voluntary, and perhaps even something one did not especially want; whereas this was distinctly pleasant, and came almost of its own accord. All he needed to do was to think of that morning, the first one, and then of all the others——

But it was all so absurdly simple! It had amounted to so little. It was nothing, just an idea—and just why it should have become so wonderful, so permanent, was a mystery—a very pleasant one, to be sure, but also, in an amusing way, foolish. However, without ceasing to listen to Miss Buell, who had now moved up to the north temperate zones, he deliberately invited his memory of the first morning. It was only a moment or two after he had waked up—or perhaps the moment itself. But was there, to be exact, an exact moment? Was one awake all at once? or was it gradual? Anyway, it was after he had stretched a lazy hand up toward the headrail, and yawned, and then relaxed again among his warm covers, all the more grateful on a December morning, that the thing had happened. Suddenly, for no reason, he had thought of the postman, he remembered the postman. Perhaps there was nothing so odd in that. After all, he heard the postman almost every morning in his life—his heavy boots could be heard clumping round the corner at the top of the little cobbled hill-street, and then, progressively nearer, progressively louder, the double knock at each door, the crossings and re-crossings of the street, till finally the clumsy steps came stumbling across to the very door, and the tremendous knock came which shook the house itself.

(Miss Buell was saying, "Vast wheat-growing areas in North America and Siberia."

Deirdre had for the moment placed her left hand across the back of her neck.)

But on this particular morning, the first morning, as he lay there with his eyes closed, he had for some reason *waited* for the postman. He wanted to hear him come round the corner. And that was precisely the joke—he never did. He never came. He never had come—*round the corner*—again. For when at last the steps *were* heard, they had already, he was quite sure, come a little down the hill, to the first house; and even so, the steps were curiously different—they were softer, they had a new secrecy about them, they were muffled and indistinct; and while the rhythm of them was the same, it now said a new thing—it said peace, it said remoteness, it said cold, it said sleep. And he had understood the situation at once—nothing could have seemed simpler—there had been snow in the night, such as all winter he had been longing for; and it was this which had rendered the postman's first footsteps inaudible, and the later ones faint. Of course! How lovely! And even now it must be snowing—it was going to be a snowy day—the long white ragged lines were drifting and sifting across the street, across the faces of the old houses, whispering and hushing, making little triangles of white in the corners between cobblestones, seething a little when the wind blew them over the ground to a drifted corner; and so it would be all day, getting deeper and deeper and silenter and silenter.

(Miss Buell was saying, "Land of perpetual snow.")

All this time, of course (while he lay in bed), he had kept his eyes closed, listening to the nearer progress of the postman, the muffled footsteps thumping and slipping on the snow-sheathed cobbles; and all the other sounds—the double knocks, a frosty far-off voice or two, a bell ringing thinly and softly as if under a sheet of ice—had the same slightly abstracted quality, as if removed by one degree from actuality—as if everything in the world had been insulated by snow. But then at last, pleased, he opened his eyes, and turned them toward the window, to see for himself this long-desired and now so clearly imagined miracle—what he saw instead was brilliant sunlight on a roof; and when, astonished, he jumped out of bed and stared down into the street, expecting to see the cobbles obliterated by the snow, he saw nothing but the bare bright cobbles themselves.

Queer, the effect this extraordinary surprise had had upon him—all the following morning he had kept with him a sense as of snow falling about him, a secret storm of new snow between himself and the world. If he had not dreamed such a thing—and how could he have dreamed it while awake?—how else could one explain it? In any case, the delusion had been so vivid as to affect his entire behavior. He could not now remember whether it was on the first or the second morning—or was it even the third?—that his mother had drawn attention to some oddness in his manner.

"But my darling"—she had said at the breakfast table—"what has come over you? You don't seem to be listening. . . ."

And how often that very thing had happened since!

(Miss Buell was now asking if anyone knew the difference between the North Pole and the Magnetic Pole. Deirdre was holding up her flickering brown hand, and he could see the four white dimples that marked the knuckles.)

Perhaps it hadn't been either the second or third morning—or even the fourth or fifth. How could he be sure? How could he be sure just when the delicious *progress* had become clear? Just when it had really *begun?* The intervals weren't very precise. . . . All he now knew was, that at some point or other—perhaps the second day, perhaps the sixth—he had noticed that the presence of the snow was a little more insistent, the sound of it clearer; and, conversely, the sound of the postman's footsteps more indistinct. Not only could he not hear the steps come round the corner, he could not even hear them at the first house. It was below the first house that he heard them; and then, a few days later, it was below the second house that he heard them; and a few days later again, below the third. Gradually, gradually, the snow was becoming heavier, the sound of its seething louder, the cobblestones more and more muffled. When he found, each morning, on going to the window, after the ritual of listening, that the roofs and cobbles were as bare as ever, it made no difference. This was, after all, only what he had expected. It was even what pleased him, what rewarded him: the thing was his own, belonged to no one else. No one else knew about it, not even his mother and father. There, outside, were the bare cobbles; and here, inside, was the snow. Snow growing heavier each day, muffling the world, hiding the ugly, and deadening increasingly—above all—the steps of the postman.

"But my darling"—she had said at the luncheon table—"what has come over you? You don't seem to listen when people speak to you. That's the third time I've asked you to pass your plate. . . ."

How was one to explain this to Mother? or to Father? There was, of course, nothing to be done about it: nothing. All one could do was to laugh embarrassedly, pretend to be a little ashamed, apologize, and take a sudden and somewhat disingenuous interest in what was being done or said. The cat had stayed out all night. He had a curious swelling on his left cheek—perhaps somebody had kicked him, or a stone had struck him. Mrs. Kempton was or was not coming to tea. The house was going to be housecleaned, or "turned out," on Wednesday instead of Friday. A new lamp was provided for his evening work—perhaps it was eyestrain which accounted for this new and so peculiar vagueness of his—Mother was looking at him with amusement as she said this, but with something else as well. A new lamp? A new lamp. Yes, Mother, No, Mother, Yes, Mother. School is going very well. The geometry is very easy. The history is very dull. The geography is very interesting—particularly when it takes one to the North Pole. Why the North Pole? Oh, well, it would be fun to be an explorer. Another Peary or Scott or Shackleton. And then abruptly he found his interest in the talk at an end, stared at the pudding on his plate, listened, waited, and began once more—ah, how heavenly, too, the first beginnings—to hear or feel—for could he actually hear it?—the silent snow, the secret snow.

(Miss Buell was telling them about the search for the Northwest Passage, about Hendrik Hudson, the *Half Moon.*)

This had been, indeed, the only interesting feature of the new experience; the fact that it so increasingly had brought him into a kind of mute misunderstanding, or even conflict, with his father and mother. It was as if he were trying to lead a double life. On the one hand, he had to be Paul Hasleman, and keep up the appearance of being that person—dress, wash, and answer intelligently when spoken to—; on the other, he had to explore this new world which had been opened to him. Nor could there be the slightest doubt—not the slightest—that the new world was the profounder and more wonderful of the two. It was irresistible. It was miraculous. Its beauty was simply beyond anything—beyond speech as beyond thought—utterly incommunicable. But how then, between the two worlds, of which he was thus constantly aware, was he to keep a balance? One must get up, one must go to breakfast, one must talk with Mother, go to school, do one's lessons—and, in all this, try not to appear too much of a fool. But if all the while one was trying to extract the full deliciousness of another and quite separate existence, one which could not easily (if at all) be spoken of—how was one to manage? How was one to explain? Would it be safe to explain? Would it be absurd? Would it merely mean that he would get into some obscure kind of trouble?

These thoughts came and went, came and went, as softly and secretly as the snow; they were not precisely a disturbance, perhaps they were even a pleasure; he liked to have them; their presence was something almost palpable, something he could stroke with his hand, without closing his eyes, and without ceasing to see Miss Buell and the schoolroom and the globe and the freckles on Deirdre's neck; nevertheless he did in a sense cease to see, or to see the obvious external world, and substituted for this vision the vision of snow, the sound of snow, and the slow, almost soundless, approach of the postman. Yesterday, it had been only at the sixth house that the postman had become audible; the snow was much deeper now, it was falling more swiftly and heavily, the sound of its seething was more distinct, more soothing, more persistent. And this morning, it had been—as nearly as he could figure—just above the seventh house—perhaps only a step or two above; at most, he had heard two or three footsteps before the knock had sounded. . . . And with each such narrowing of the sphere, each nearer approach of the limit at which the postman was first audible, it was odd how sharply was increased the amount of illusion which had to be carried into the ordinary business of daily life. Each day, it was harder to get out of bed, to go to the window, to look out at the—as always—perfectly empty and snowless street. Each day it was more difficult to go through the perfunctory motions of greeting Mother and Father at breakfast, to reply to their questions, to put his books together and go to school. And at school, how extraordinarily hard to conduct with success simultaneously the public life and the life that was secret! There were times when he longed —positively ached—to tell everyone about it—to burst out with it—only to be checked almost at once by a far-off feeling as of some faint absurdity which was inherent in it—but *was* it absurd?—and more importantly by a sense of mysterious power in his very secrecy. Yes; it must be kept secret. That, more and more, became clear. At whatever cost to himself, whatever pain to others——

(Miss Buell looked straight at him, smiling, and said, "Perhaps we'll ask Paul. I'm sure Paul will come out of his daydream long enough to be able to tell us. Won't you, Paul?" He rose slowly from his chair, resting one hand on the brightly varnished desk, and deliberately stared through the snow toward the blackboard. It was an effort, but it was amusing to make it. "Yes," he said slowly, "it was what we now call the Hudson River. This he thought to be the Northwest Passage. He was disappointed." He sat down again, and as he did so Deirdre half turned in her chair and gave him a shy smile, of approval and admiration.)

At whatever pain to others.

This part of it was very puzzling, very puzzling. Mother was very nice, and so was Father. Yes, that was all true enough. He wanted to be nice to them, to tell them everything—and yet, was it really wrong of him to want to have a secret place of his own?

At bed-time, the night before, Mother had said, "If this goes on, my lad, we'll have to see a doctor, we will! We can't have our boy—" But what was it she had said? "Live in another world"? "Live so far away"? The word "far" had been in it, he was sure, and then Mother had taken up a magazine again and laughed a little, but with an expression which wasn't mirthful. He had felt sorry for her. . . .

The bell rang for dismissal. The sound came to him through long curved parallels of falling snow. He saw Deirdre rise, and had himself risen almost as soon—but not quite as soon—as she.

On the walk homeward, which was timeless, it pleased him to see through the accompaniment, or counterpoint, of snow, the items of mere externality on his way. There were many kinds of brick in the sidewalks, and laid in many kinds of pattern. The garden walls, too, were various, some of wooden palings, some of plaster, some of stone. Twigs of bushes leaned over the walls: the little hard green winter-buds of lilac, on gray stems, sheathed and fat; other branches very thin and fine and black and desiccated. Dirty sparrows huddled in the bushes, as dull in color as dead fruit left in leafless trees. A single starling creaked on a weather vane. In the gutter, beside a drain, was a scrap of torn and dirty newspaper, caught in a little delta of filth; the word ECZEMA appeared in large capitals, and below it was a letter from Mrs. Amelia D. Cravath, 2100 Pine Street, Fort Worth, Texas, to the effect that after being a sufferer for years she had been cured by Caley's Ointment. In the little delta, beside the fan-shaped and deeply runneled continent of brown mud, were lost twigs, descended from their parent trees, dead matches, a rusty horse-chestnut burr, a small concentration of eggshell, a streak of yellow sawdust which had been wet and now was dry and congealed, a brown pebble, and a broken feather. Farther on was a cement sidewalk, ruled into geometrical parallelograms, with a brass inlay at one end commemorating the contractors who had laid it, and, halfway across, an irregular and random series of dog-tracks, immortalized in synthetic stone. He knew these well, and always stepped on them; to cover the little hollows with his own foot had always been a queer pleasure; today he did it once more, but perfunctorily and detachedly, all the while thinking of something else. That was a dog, a long time ago, who had made a mistake and walked on the cement while it was still wet. He had probably wagged his tail, but that hadn't been recorded. Now, Paul Hasleman, aged twelve, on his way home from school, crossed the same river, which in the meantime had frozen into rock. Homeward through the snow, the snow falling in bright sunshine. Homeward?

Then came the gateway with the two posts surmounted by egg-shaped stones which had been cunningly balanced on their ends, as if by Columbus, and mortared in the very act of balance; a source of perpetual wonder. On the brick wall just beyond the letter H had been stenciled, presumably for some purpose. H? H.

The green hydrant, with a little green-painted chain attached to the brass screw-cap.

The elm tree, with the great gray wound in the bark, kidney-shaped, into which he always put his hand—to feel the cold but living wood. The injury, he had been sure, was due to the gnawings of a tethered horse. But now it deserved only a passing palm, a merely tolerant eye. There were more important things. Miracles. Beyond the thoughts of trees, mere elms. Beyond the thoughts of sidewalks, mere stone, mere brick, mere cement. Beyond the thoughts even of his own shoes, which trod these sidewalks obediently, bearing a burden—far above—of elaborate mystery. He watched them. They were not very well polished; he had neglected them, for a very good reason: they were one of the many parts of the increasing difficulty of the daily return to daily life, the morning struggle. To get up, having at last opened one's eyes, to go to the window, and discover no snow, to wash, to dress, to descend the curving stairs to breakfast——

At whatever pain to others, nevertheless, one must persevere in severance, since the incommunicability of the experience demanded it. It was desirable, of course, to be kind to Mother and Father, especially as they seemed to be worried, but it was also desirable to be resolute. If they should decide—as appeared likely—to consult the doctor, Doctor Howells, and have Paul inspected, his heart listened to through a kind of dictaphone, his lungs, his stomach—well, that was all right. He would go through with it. He would give them answer for question, too—perhaps such answers as they hadn't expected? No. That would never do. For the secret world must, at all costs, be preserved.

The bird-house in the apple tree was empty—it was the wrong time of year for wrens. The little round black door had lost its pleasure. The wrens were enjoying other houses, other nests, remoter trees. But this too was a notion which he only vaguely and grazingly entertained—as if, for the moment, he merely touched an edge of it; there was something further on, which was already assuming a sharper importance; something which already teased at the corners of his eyes, teasing also at the corner of his mind. It was funny to think that he so wanted this, so awaited it—and yet found himself enjoying this momentary dalliance with the bird-house, as if for a quite deliberate postponement and enhancement of the approaching pleasure. He was aware of his delay, of his smiling and detached and now almost uncomprehending gaze at the little bird-house; he knew what he was going to look at next: it was his own little cobbled hill-street, his own house, the little river at the bottom of the hill, the grocer's shop with the cardboard man in the window—and now, thinking of all this, he turned his head, still smiling, and looking quickly right and left through the snow-laden sunlight.

And the mist of snow, as he had foreseen, was still on it—a ghost of snow falling in the bright sunlight, softly and steadily floating and turning and pausing, soundlessly meeting the snow that covered, as with a transparent mirage, the bare bright cobbles. He loved it—he stood still and loved it. Its beauty was paralyzing—beyond all words, all experience, all dream. No fairy story he had ever read could be compared with it—none had ever given him this extraordinary combination of ethereal loveliness with a something else, unnameable, which was just faintly and deliciously terrifying. What was this thing? As he thought of it, he looked upward toward his own bedroom window, which was open—and it was as if he looked straight into the room and saw himself lying half awake in his bed. There he was—at this very instant he was still perhaps actually there—more truly there than standing here at the edge of the cobbled hill-street, with one hand lifted to shade his eyes against the snow-sun. Had he indeed ever left his room, in all this time? since that very first morning? Was the whole progress still being enacted there, was it still the same morning, and himself not yet wholly awake? And even now, had the postman not yet come round the corner? . . .

This idea amused him, and automatically, as he thought of it, he turned his head and looked toward the top of the hill. There was, of course, nothing there—nothing and no one. The street was empty and quiet. And all the more because of its emptiness it occurred to him to count the houses—a thing which, oddly enough, he hadn't before thought of doing. Of course, he had known there weren't many—many, that is, on his own side of the street, which were the ones that figured in the postman's progress—but nevertheless it came as something of a shock to find that there were precisely *six*, above his own house—his own house was the seventh.

Six!

Astonished, he looked at his own house—looked at the door, on which was the number thirteen—and then realized that the whole thing was exactly and logically and absurdly what he ought to have known. Just the same, the realization gave him abruptly, and even a little frighteningly, a sense of hurry. He was being hurried—he was being rushed. For—he knit his brow—he couldn't be mistaken—it was just above the *seventh* house, his *own* house, that the postman had first been audible this very morning. But in that case—in that case—did it mean that tomorrow he would hear nothing? The knock he had heard must have been the knock of their own door. Did it mean—and this was an idea which gave him a really extraordinary feeling of surprise—that he would never hear the postman again?—that tomorrow morning the postman would already have passed the house, in a snow so deep as to render his footsteps completely inaudible? That he would have made his approach down the snow-filled street so soundlessly, so secretly, that he, Paul Hasleman, there lying in bed, would not have waked in time, or waking, would have heard nothing?

But how could that be? Unless even the knocker should be muffled in the snow—frozen tight, perhaps? . . . But in that case——

A vague feeling of disappointment came over him; a vague sadness as if he felt himself deprived of something which he had long looked forward to, something much prized. After all this, all this beautiful progress, the slow delicious advance of the postman through the silent and secret snow, the knock creeping closer each day, and the footsteps nearer, the audible compass of the world thus daily narrowed, narrowed, narrowed, as the snow soothingly and beautifully encroached and deepened, after all this, was he to be defrauded of the one thing he had so wanted—to be able to count, as it were, the last two or three solemn footsteps, as they finally approached his own door? Was it all going to happen, at the end, so suddenly? or indeed, had it already happened? with no slow and subtle gradations of menace, in which he could luxuriate?

He gazed upward again, toward his own window which flashed in the sun; and this time almost with a feeling that it would be better if he *were* still in bed, in that room; for in that case this must still be the first morning, and there would be six more mornings to come—or, for that matter, seven or eight or nine—how could he be sure?—or even more.

After supper, the inquisition began. He stood before the doctor, under the lamp, and submitted silently to the usual thumpings and tappings.

"Now will you please say 'Ah!'?"

"Ah!"

"Now again, please, if you don't mind."

"Ah."

"Say it slowly, and hold it if you can——"

"Ah-h-h-h-h-h——"

"Good."

How silly all this was. As if it had anything to do with his throat! Or his heart, or lungs!

Relaxing his mouth, of which the corners, after all this absurd stretching, felt uncomfortable, he avoided the doctor's eyes, and stared toward the fireplace, past his mother's feet (in gray slippers) which projected from the green chair, and his father's feet (in brown slippers) which stood neatly side by side on the hearth rug.

"Hm. There is certainly nothing wrong there. . . ."

He felt the doctor's eyes fixed upon him, and, as if merely to be polite, returned the look, but with a feeling of justifiable evasiveness.

"Now, young man, tell me—do you feel all right?"

"Yes, sir, quite all right."

"No headaches? no dizziness?"

"No, I don't think so."

"Let me see. Let's get a book, if you don't mind—yes, thank you, that will do splendidly—and now, Paul, if you'll just read it, holding it as you would normally hold it——"

He took the book and read:

" 'And another praise have I to tell for this city our mother, the gift of a great god, a glory of the land most high; the might of horses, the might of young horses, the might of the sea. . . . For thou, son of Cronus, our lord Poseidon, hath throned herein this pride, since in these roads first thou didst show forth the curb that cures the rage of steeds. And the shapely oar, apt to man's hands, hath a wondrous speed on the brine, following the hundred-footed Nereids. . . . O land that art praised above all lands, now is it for thee to make those bright praises seen in deeds.' "

He stopped, tentatively, and lowered the heavy book.

"No—as I thought—there is certainly no superficial sign of eye-strain."

Silence thronged the room, and he was aware of the focused scrutiny of the three people who confronted him. . . .

"We could have his eyes examined—but I believe it is something else."

"What could it be?" That was his father's voice.

"It's only this curious absent-mindedness—" This was his mother's voice.

In the presence of the doctor, they both seemed irritatingly apologetic.

"I believe it is something else. Now Paul—I would like very much to ask you a question or two. You will answer them, won't you—you know I'm an old, old friend of yours, eh? That's right! . . ."

His back was thumped twice by the doctor's fat fist—then the doctor was grinning at him with false amiability, while with one fingernail he was scratching the top button of his waistcoat. Beyond the doctor's shoulder was the fire, the fingers of flame making light prestidigitation against the sooty fireback, the soft sound of their random flutter the only sound.

"I would like to know—is there anything that worries you?"

The doctor was again smiling, his eyelids low against the little black pupils, in each of which was a tiny white bead of light. Why answer him? why answer him at all? "At whatever pain to others"—but it was all a nuisance, this necessity for resistance, this necessity for attention; it was as if one had been stood up on a brilliantly lighted stage, under a great round blaze of spotlight; as if one were merely a trained seal, or a performing dog, or a fish, dipped out of an aquarium and held up by the tail. It would serve them right if he were merely to bark or growl. And meanwhile, to miss these last few precious hours, these hours of which each minute was more beautiful than the last, more menacing—! He still looked, as if from a great distance, at the beads of light in the doctor's eyes, at the fixed false smile, and then, beyond, once more at his mother's slippers, his father's slippers, the soft flutter of the fire. Even here, even amongst these hostile presences, and in this arranged light, he could see the snow, he could hear it—it was in the corners of the room, where the shadow was deepest, under the sofa, behind the half-opened door which led to the dining room. It was gentler here, softer, its seethe the quietest of whispers, as if, in deference to a drawing room, it had quite deliberately put on its "manners"; it kept itself out of sight, obliterated itself, but distinctly with an air of saying, "Ah, but just wait! Wait till we are alone together! Then I will begin to tell you something new! Something white! something cold! something sleepy! something of cease, and peace, and the long bright curve of space! Tell them to go away. Banish them. Refuse to speak. Leave them, go upstairs to your room, turn out the light and get into bed—I will go with you, I will be waiting for you, I will tell you a better story than Little Kay of the Skates, or The Snow Ghost—I will surround your bed, I will close the windows, pile a deep drift against the door, so that none will ever again be able to enter. Speak to them! . . ." It seemed as if the little hissing voice came from a slow white spiral of falling flakes in the corner by the front window—but he could not be sure. He felt himself smiling, then, and said to the doctor, but without looking at him, looking beyond him still——

"Oh no, I think not——"

"But are you sure, my boy?"

His father's voice came softly and coldly then—the familiar voice of silken warning.

"You needn't answer at once, Paul—remember we're trying to help you—think it over and be quite sure, won't you?"

He felt himself smiling again, at the notion of being quite sure. What a joke! As if he weren't so sure that reassurance was no longer necessary, and all this cross-examination a ridiculous farce, a grotesque parody! What could they know about it? these gross intelligences, these humdrum minds so bound to the usual, the ordinary? Impossible to tell them about it! Why, even now, even now, with the proof so abundant, so formidable, so imminent, so appallingly present here in this very room, could they believe it?—could even his mother believe it? No—it was only too plain that if anything were said about it, the merest hint given, they would be incredulous—they would laugh—they would say "Absurd!"—think things about him which weren't true. . . .

"Why no, I'm not worried—why should I be?"

He looked then straight at the doctor's low-lidded eyes, looked from one of them to the other, from one bead of light to the other, and gave a little laugh.

The doctor seemed to be disconcerted by this. He drew back in his chair, resting a fat white hand on either knee. The smile faded slowly from his face.

"Well, Paul!" he said, and paused gravely, "I'm afraid you don't take this quite seriously enough. I think you perhaps don't quite realize —" He took a deep quick breath, and turned, as if helplessly, at a loss for words, to the others. But Mother and Father were both silent—no help was forthcoming.

"You must surely know, be aware, that you have not been quite yourself, of late? Don't you know that? . . ."

It was amusing to watch the doctor's renewed attempt at a smile, a queer disorganized look, as of confidential embarrassment.

"I feel all right, sir," he said, and again gave the little laugh.

"And we're trying to help you." The doctor's tone sharpened.

"Yes, sir, I know. But why? I'm all right. I'm just *thinking*, that's all."

His mother made a quick movement forward, resting a hand on the back of the doctor's chair.

"Thinking?" she said. "But my dear, about what?"

This was a direct challenge—and would have to be directly met. But before he met it, he looked again into the corner by the door, as if for reassurance. He smiled again at what he saw, at what he heard. The little spiral was still there, still softly whirling, like the ghost of a white kitten chasing the ghost of a white tail, and making as it did so the faintest of whispers. It was all right! If only he could remain firm, everything was going to be all right.

"Oh, about anything, about nothing—*you* know the way you do!"

"You mean—daydreaming?"

"Oh, no—thinking!"

"But thinking about *what?*"

"Anything."

He laughed a third time—but this time, happening to glance upward toward his mother's face, he was appalled at the effect his laughter seemed to have upon her. Her mouth had opened in an expression of horror. . . . This was too bad! Unfortunate! He had known it would cause pain, of course—but he hadn't expected it to be quite so bad as this. Perhaps—perhaps if he just gave them a tiny gleaming hint——?

"About the snow," he said.

"What on earth?" This was his father's voice. The brown slippers came a step nearer on the hearth-rug.

"But my dear, what do you mean?" This was his mother's voice.

The doctor merely stared.

"Just *snow*, that's all. I like to think about it."

"Tell us about it, my boy."

"But that's all it is. There's nothing to tell. *You* know what snow is?"

This he said almost angrily, for he felt that they were trying to corner him. He turned sideways so as no longer to face the doctor, and the better to see the inch of blackness between the window-sill and the lowered curtain—the cold inch of beckoning and delicious night. At once he felt better, more assured.

"Mother—can I go to bed, now, please? I've got a headache."

"But I thought you said——"

"It's just come. It's all these questions—! Can I, mother?"

"You can go as soon as the doctor has finished."

"Don't you think this thing ought to be gone into thoroughly, and *now*?" This was Father's voice. The brown slippers again came a step nearer, the voice was the well-known "punishment" voice, resonant and cruel.

"Oh, what's the use, Norman——"

Quite suddenly, everyone was silent. And without precisely facing them, nevertheless he was aware that all three of them were watching him with an extraordinary intensity—staring hard at him—as if he had done something monstrous, or was himself some kind of monster. He could hear the soft irregular flutter of the flames; the cluck-click-cluck-click of the clock; far and faint, two sudden spurts of laughter from the kitchen, as quickly cut off as begun; a murmur of water in the pipes; and then, the silence seemed to deepen, to spread out, to become world-long and world-wide, to become timeless and shapeless, and to center inevitably and rightly, with a slow and sleepy but enormous concentration of all power, on the beginning of a new sound. What this new sound was going to be, he knew perfectly well. It might begin with a hiss, but it would end with a roar—there was no time to lose—he must escape. It mustn't happen here——

Without another word, he turned and ran up the stairs.

Not a moment too soon. The darkness was coming in long white waves. A prolonged sibilance filled the night—a great seamless seethe of wild influence went abruptly across it—a cold low humming shook the windows. He shut the door and flung off his clothes in the dark. The bare black floor was like a little raft tossed in waves of snow, almost overwhelmed, washed under whitely, up again, smothered in curled billows of feather. The snow was laughing; it spoke from all sides at once; it pressed closer to him as he ran and jumped exulting into his bed.

"Listen to us!" it said. "Listen! We have come to tell you the story we told you about. You remember? Lie down. Shut your eyes, now—you will no longer see much—in this white darkness who could see, or want to see? We will take the place of everything. . . . Listen——"

A beautiful varying dance of snow began at the front of the room, came forward and then retreated, flattened out toward the floor, then rose fountain-like to the ceiling, swayed, recruited itself from a new stream of flakes which poured laughing in through the humming window, advanced again, lifted long white arms. It said peace, it said remoteness, it said cold—it said——

But then a gash of horrible light fell brutally across the room from the opening door—the snow drew back hissing—something alien had come into the room—something hostile. This thing rushed at him, clutched at him, shook him—and he was not merely horrified, he was filled with such a loathing as he had never known. What was this? this cruel disturbance? this act of anger and hate? It was as if he had to reach up a hand toward another world for any understanding of it—an effort of which he was only barely capable. But of that other world he still remembered just enough to know the exorcising words. They tore themselves from his other life suddenly——

"Mother! Mother! Go away! I hate you!"

And with that effort, everything was solved, everything became all right: the seamless hiss advanced once more, the long white wavering lines rose and fell like enormous whispering sea-waves, the whisper becoming louder, the laughter more numerous.

"Listen!" it said. "We'll tell you the last, the most beautiful and secret story—shut your eyes—it is a very small story—a story that gets smaller and smaller—it comes inward instead of opening like a flower—it is a flower becoming a seed—a little cold seed—do you hear? we are leaning closer to you——"

The hiss was now becoming a roar—the whole world was a vast moving screen of snow—but even now it said peace, it said remoteness, it said cold, it said sleep.

by Philip Roth

THE CONVERSION OF THE JEWS

Philip Roth, the youngest writer represented here, was born in 1933 in Newark, New Jersey. He graduated from Bucknell University as a member of Phi Beta Kappa and later received his M.A. from the University of Chicago, where he also taught. Mr. Roth's stories have appeared in such diverse magazines as Esquire *and* Commentary; *he has also written movie reviews for* The New Republic. *In 1958 he was awarded the Aga Khan Prize for Fiction by the editors of the* Paris Review. *Mr. Roth's first novel,* Letting Go, *appeared in 1962; three years earlier he received the National Book Award for his collection of short stories,* Goodbye, Columbus.

"The Conversion of the Jews," collected in that volume, is typical of Mr. Roth's generally successful attempts to make Jewish life in America available to the imagination. For Mr. Roth's characters, being a Jew is not the fulltime job it was as recently as a generation ago; and this cultural advance, like most others, is both a blessing and a disaster. Ozzie, in "The Conversion of the Jews," is one of those increasingly rare people—Jewish or Christian—who take ideas and faith seriously. That is Ozzie's real heresy—"what he wanted to know was different."

"YOU'RE a real one for opening your mouth in the first place," Itzie said. "What do you open your mouth all the time for?"

"I didn't bring it up, Itz, I didn't," Ozzie said.

"What do you care about Jesus Christ for anyway?"

"I didn't bring up Jesus Christ. He did. I didn't even know what he was talking about. Jesus is historical, he kept saying. Jesus is historical." Ozzie mimicked the monumental voice of Rabbi Binder.

"Jesus was a person that lived like you and me," Ozzie continued. "That's what Binder said—"

"Yeah? . . . So what! What do I give two cents whether he lived or not. And what do you gotta open your mouth!" Itzie Lieberman favored closed-mouthedness, especially when it came to Ozzie Freedman's questions. Mrs. Freedman had to see Rabbi Binder twice before about Ozzie's questions and this Wednesday at four-thirty would be the third time. Itzie preferred to keep *his* mother in the kitchen; he settled for behind-the-back subtleties such as gestures, faces, snarls and other less delicate barnyard noises.

"He was a real person, Jesus, but he wasn't like God, and we don't believe he is God." Slowly, Ozzie was explaining Rabbi Binder's position to Itzie, who had been absent from Hebrew School the previous afternoon.

"The Catholics," Itzie said helpfully, "they believe in Jesus Christ, that he's God." Itzie Lieberman used "the Catholics" in its broadest sense—to include the Protestants.

Ozzie received Itzie's remark with a tiny head bob, as though it were a footnote, and went on. "His mother was Mary, and his father probably was Joseph," Ozzie said. "But the New Testament says his real father was God."

"His *real* father?"

"Yeah," Ozzie said, "that's the big thing, his father's supposed to be God."

"Bull."

"That's what Rabbi Binder says, that it's impossible—"

"Sure it's impossible. That stuff's all bull. To have a baby you gotta get laid," Itzie theologized. "Mary hadda get laid."

"That's what Binder says: 'The only way a woman can have a baby is to have intercourse with a man.' "

"He said *that*, Ozz?" For a moment it appeared that Itzie had put the theological question aside. "He said that, intercourse?" A little curled smile shaped itself in the lower half of Itzie's face like a pink mustache. "What you guys do, Ozz, you laugh or something?"

"I raised my hand."

"Yeah? Whatja say?"

"That's when I asked the question."

Itzie's face lit up. "Whatja ask about—intercourse?"

"No, I asked the question about God, how if He could create the heaven and earth in six days, and make all the animals and the fish and the light in six days—the light especially, that's what always gets me, that He could make the light. Making fish and animals, that's pretty good—"

"That's damn good." Itzie's appreciation was honest but unimaginative: it was as though God had just pitched a one-hitter.

"But making light . . . I mean when you think about it, it's really something," Ozzie said. "Anyway, I asked Binder if He could make all that in six days, and He could *pick* the six days he wanted right out of nowhere, why couldn't He let a woman have a baby without having intercourse."

"You said intercourse, Ozz, to Binder?"

"Yeah."

"Right in class?"

"Yeah."

Itzie smacked the side of his head.

"I mean, no kidding around," Ozzie said, "that'd really be nothing. After all that other stuff, that'd practically be nothing."

Itzie considered a moment. "What'd Binder say?"

"He started all over again explaining how Jesus was historical and how he lived like you and me but he wasn't God. So I said I under*stood* that. What I wanted to know was different."

What Ozzie wanted to know was always different. The first time he had wanted to know how Rabbi Binder could call the Jews "The Chosen People" if the Declaration of Independence claimed all men to be created equal. Rabbi Binder tried to distinguish for him between political equality and spiritual legitimacy, but what Ozzie wanted to know, he insisted vehemently, was different. That was the first time his mother had to come.

Then there was the plane crash. Fifty-eight people had been killed in a plane crash at La Guardia. In studying a casualty list in the newspaper his mother had discovered among the list of those dead eight Jewish names (his grandmother had nine but she counted

Miller as a Jewish name); because of the eight she said the plane crash was "a tragedy." During free-discussion time on Wednesday Ozzie had brought to Rabbi Binder's attention this matter of "some of his relations" always picking out the Jewish names. Rabbi Binder had begun to explain cultural unity and some other things when Ozzie stood up at his seat and said that what he wanted to know was different. Rabbi Binder insisted that he sit down and it was then that Ozzie shouted that he wished all fifty-eight were Jews. That was the second time his mother came.

"And he kept explaining about Jesus being historical, and so I kept asking him. No kidding, Itz, he was trying to make me look stupid."

"So what he finally do?"

"Finally he starts screaming that I was deliberately simple-minded and a wise guy, and that my mother had to come, and this was the last time. And that I'd never get bar-mitzvahed if he could help it. Then, Itz, then he starts talking in that voice like a statue, real slow and deep, and he says that I better think over what I said about the Lord. He told me to go to his office and think it over." Ozzie leaned his body towards Itzie. "Itz, I thought it over for a solid hour, and now I'm convinced God could do it."

Ozzie had planned to confess his latest transgression to his mother as soon as she came home from work. But it was a Friday night in November and already dark, and when Mrs. Freedman came through the door she tossed off her coat, kissed Ozzie quickly on the face, and went to the kitchen table to light the three yellow candles, two for the Sabbath and one for Ozzie's father.

When his mother lit the candles she would move her two arms slowly towards her, dragging them through the air, as though persuading people whose minds were half made up. And her eyes would get glassy with tears. Even when his father was alive Ozzie remembered that her eyes had gotten glassy, so it didn't have anything to do with his dying. It had something to do with lighting the candles.

As she touched the flaming match to the unlit wick of a Sabbath candle, the phone rang, and Ozzie, standing only a foot from it, plucked off the receiver and held it muffled to his chest. When his mother lit candles Ozzie felt there should be no noise; even breathing, if you could manage it, should be softened. Ozzie pressed the phone to his breast and watched his mother dragging whatever she was dragging, and he felt his own eyes get glassy. His mother was a round, tired, gray-haired penguin of a woman whose gray skin had begun to feel the tug of gravity and the weight of her own history. Even when she was dressed up she didn't look like a chosen person. But when she lit candles she looked like something better; like a woman who knew momentarily that God could do anything.

After a few mysterious minutes she was finished. Ozzie hung up the phone and walked to the kitchen table where she was beginning to lay the two places for the four-course Sabbath meal. He told her that she would have to see Rabbi Binder next Wednesday at four-thirty, and then he told her why. For the first time in their life together she hit Ozzie across the face with her hand.

All through the chopped liver and chicken soup part of the dinner Ozzie cried; he didn't have any appetite for the rest.

On Wednesday, in the largest of the three basement classrooms of the synagogue, Rabbi Marvin Binder, a tall, handsome, broad-shouldered man of thirty with thick strong-fibered black hair, removed his watch from his pocket and saw that it was four o'clock. At the rear of the room Yakov Blotnik, the seventy-one-year-old custodian, slowly polished the large window, mumbling to himself, unaware that it was four o'clock or six o'clock, Monday or Wednesday. To most of the students Yakov Blotnik's mumbling, along with his brown curly beard, scythe nose, and two heel-trailing black cats, made of him an object of wonder, a foreigner, a relic, towards whom they were alternately fearful and disrespectful. To Ozzie the mumbling had always seemed a monotonous, curious prayer; what made it curious was that old Blotnik had been mumbling so steadily for so many years, Ozzie suspected he had memorized the prayers and forgotten all about God.

"It is now free-discussion time," Rabbi Binder said. "Feel free to talk about any Jewish matter at all—religion, family, politics, sports—"

There was silence. It was a gusty, clouded November afternoon and it did not seem as though there ever was or could be a thing called baseball. So nobody this week said a word about that hero from the past, Hank Greenberg—which limited free discussion considerably.

And the soul-battering Ozzie Freedman had just received from Rabbi Binder had imposed its limitation. When it was Ozzie's turn to read aloud from the Hebrew book the rabbi had asked him petulantly why he didn't read more rapidly. He was showing no progress. Ozzie said he could read faster but that if he did he was sure not to understand what he was reading. Nevertheless, at the rabbi's repeated suggestion Ozzie tried, and showed a great talent, but in the midst of a long passage he stopped short and said he didn't understand a word he was reading, and started in again at a drag-footed pace. Then came the soul-battering.

Consequently when free-discussion time rolled around none of the students felt too free. The rabbi's invitation was answered only by the mumbling of feeble old Blotnik.

"Isn't there anything at all you would like to discuss?" Rabbi Binder asked again, looking at his watch. "No questions or comments?"

There was a small grumble from the third row. The rabbi requested that Ozzie rise and give the rest of the class the advantage of his thought.

Ozzie rose. "I forget it now," he said, and sat down in his place.

Rabbi Binder advanced a seat towards Ozzie and poised himself on the edge of the desk. It was Itzie's desk and the rabbi's frame only a dagger's-length away from his face snapped him to sitting attention.

"Stand up again, Oscar," Rabbi Binder said calmly, "and try to assemble your thoughts."

Ozzie stood up. All his classmates turned in their seats and watched as he gave an unconvincing scratch to his forehead.

"I can't assemble any," he announced, and plunked himself down.

"Stand up!" Rabbi Binder advanced from Itzie's desk to the one directly in front of Ozzie; when the rabbinical back was turned Itzie gave it five-fingers off the tip of his nose, causing a small titter in the room. Rabbi Binder was too absorbed in squelching Ozzie's nonsense once and for all to bother with titters. "Stand up, Oscar. What's your question about?"

Ozzie pulled a word out of the air. It was the handiest word. "Religion."

"Oh, now you remember?"

"Yes."

"What is it?"

Trapped, Ozzie blurted the first thing that came to him. "Why can't He make anything He wants to make!"

As Rabbi Binder prepared an answer, a final answer, Itzie, ten feet behind him, raised one finger on his left hand, gestured it meaningfully towards the rabbi's back, and brought the house down.

Binder twisted quickly to see what had happened and in the midst of the commotion Ozzie shouted into the rabbi's back what he couldn't have shouted to his face. It was a loud, toneless sound that had the timbre of something stored inside for about six days.

"You don't know! You don't know anything about God!"

The rabbi spun back towards Ozzie. "What?"

"You don't know—you don't—"

"Apologize, Oscar, apologize!" It was a threat.

"You don't—"

Rabbi Binder's hand flicked out at Ozzie's cheek. Perhaps it had only been meant to clamp the boy's mouth shut, but Ozzie ducked and the palm caught him squarely on the nose.

The blood came in a short, red spurt on to Ozzie's shirt front.

The next moment was all confusion. Ozzie screamed, "You bastard, you bastard!" and broke for the classroom door. Rabbi Binder lurched a step backwards, as though his own blood had started flowing violently in the opposite direction, then gave a clumsy lurch forward and bolted out the door after Ozzie. The class followed after the rabbi's huge blue-suited back, and before old Blotnik could turn from his window, the room was empty and everyone was headed full speed up the three flights leading to the roof.

If one should compare the light of day to the life of man: sunrise to birth; sunset—the dropping down over the edge—to death; then as Ozzie Freedman wiggled through the trapdoor of the synagogue roof, his feet kicking backwards bronco-style at Rabbi Binder's outstretched arms—at that moment the day was fifty years old. As a rule, fifty or fifty-five reflects accurately the age of late afternoons in November, for it is in that month, during those hours, that one's awareness of light seems no longer a matter of seeing, but of hearing: light begins clicking away. In fact, as Ozzie locked shut the trapdoor in the rabbi's face, the sharp click of the bolt into the lock might momentarily have been mistaken for the sound of the heavier gray that had just throbbed through the sky.

With all his weight Ozzie kneeled on the locked door; any instant he was certain that Rabbi Binder's shoulder would fling it open, splintering the wood into shrapnel and catapulting his body into the sky. But the door did not move and below him he heard only the rumble of feet, first loud then dim, like thunder rolling away.

A question shot through his brain. "Can this be *me?*" For a thirteen-year-old who had just labeled his religious leader a bastard, twice, it was not an improper question. Louder and louder the question came to him—"Is it me? Is it me?"—until he discovered himself no longer kneeling, but racing crazily toward the edge of the roof, his eyes crying, his throat screaming, and his arms flying everywhichway as though not his own.

"Is it me? Is it me Me ME ME ME! It has to be me—but is it!"

It is the question a thief must ask himself the night he jimmies open his first window, and it is said to be the question with which bridegrooms quiz themselves before the altar.

In the few wild seconds it took Ozzie's body to propel him to the edge of the roof, his self-examination began to grow fuzzy. Gazing down at the street he became confused as to the problem beneath the question: was it, is-it-me-who-called-Binder-a-Bastard? or, is-it-me-prancing-around-on-the-roof? However, the scene below settled all, for there is an instant in any action when whether it is you or somebody else is academic. The thief crams the money in his pockets and scoots out the window. The bridegroom signs the hotel register for two. And the boy on the roof finds a streetful of people gaping at him, necks stretched backwards, faces up, as though he were the ceiling of the Hayden Planetarium. Suddenly you know it's you.

"Oscar! Oscar Freedman!" A voice rose from the center of the crowd, a voice that, could it have been seen, would have looked like the writing on a scroll. "Oscar Freedman, get down from there. Immediately!" Rabbi Binder was pointing one arm stiffly up at him; and at the end of that arm, one finger aimed menacingly. It was the attitude of a dictator, but one—the eyes confessed all—whose personal valet had spit neatly in his face.

Ozzie didn't answer. Only for a blink's length did he look towards Rabbi Binder. Instead his eyes began to fit together the world beneath him, to sort out people from places, friends from enemies, participants from spectators. In little jagged starlike clusters his friends stood around Rabbi Binder, who was still pointing. The topmost point on a star compounded not of angels but of five adolescent boys was Itzie. What a world it was, with those stars below, Rabbi Binder below . . . Ozzie, who a moment earlier hadn't been able to control his own body, started to feel the meaning of the word control: he felt Peace and he felt Power.

"Oscar Freedman, I'll give you three to come down."

Few dictators give their subjects three to do anything; but, as always, Rabbi Binder only looked dictatorial.

"Are you ready, Oscar?"

Ozzie nodded his head yes, although he had no intention in the world—the lower one of the celestial one he'd just entered—of coming down even if Rabbi Binder should give him a million.

"All right then," said Rabbi Binder. He ran a hand through his black Samson hair as though it were the gesture prescribed for uttering the first digit. Then, with his other hand cutting a circle out of the small piece of sky around him, he spoke. "One!"

There was no thunder. On the contrary, at that moment, as though "one" was the cue for which he had been waiting, the world's least thunderous person appeared on the synagogue steps. He did not so much come out the synagogue door as lean out, onto the darkening air. He clutched at the doorknob with one hand and looked up at the roof.

"Oy!"

Yakov Blotnik's old mind hobbled slowly, as if on crutches, and though he couldn't decide precisely what the boy was doing on the roof, he knew it wasn't good—that is, it wasn't-good-for-the-Jews. For Yakov Blotnik life had fractionated itself simply: things were either good-for-the-Jews or no-good-for-the-Jews.

He smacked his free hand to his in-sucked cheek, gently. "Oy, Gut!" And then quickly as he was able, he jacked down his head and surveyed the street. There was Rabbi Binder (like a man at an auction with only three dollars in his pocket, he had just delivered a shaky "Two!"); there were the students, and that was all. So far it-wasn't-so-bad-for-the-Jews. But the boy had to come down immediately, before anybody saw. The problem: how to get the boy off the roof?

Anybody who has ever had a cat on the roof knows how to get him down. You call the fire department. Or first you call the operator and you ask her for the fire department. And the next thing there is great jamming of brakes and clanging of bells and shouting of instructions. And then the cat is off the roof. You do the same thing to get a boy off the roof.

That is, you do the same thing if you are Yakov Blotnik and you once had a cat on the roof.

When the engines, all four of them, arrived, Rabbi Binder had four times given Ozzie the count of three. The big hook-and-ladder swung around the corner and one of the firemen leaped from it, plunging headlong towards the yellow fire hydrant in front of the synagogue. With a huge wrench he began to unscrew the top nozzle. Rabbi Binder raced over to him and pulled at his shoulder.

"There's no fire . . ."

The fireman mumbled back over his shoulder and, heatedly, continued working at the nozzle.

"But there's no fire, there's no fire . . ." Binder shouted. When the fireman mumbled again, the rabbi grasped his face with both hands and pointed it up at the roof.

To Ozzie it looked as though Rabbi Binder was trying to tug the fireman's head out of his body, like a cork from a bottle. He had to giggle at the picture they made: it was a family portrait—rabbi in black skullcap, fireman in red fire hat, and the little yellow hydrant squatting beside like a kid brother, bareheaded. From the edge of the roof Ozzie waved at the portrait, a one-handed, flapping, mocking wave; in doing it his right foot slipped from under him. Rabbi Binder covered his eyes with his hands.

Firemen work fast. Before Ozzie had even regained his balance, a big, round, yellowed net was being held on the synagogue lawn. The firemen who held it looked up at Ozzie with stern, feelingless faces.

One of the firemen turned his head towards Rabbi Binder. "What, is the kid nuts or something?"

Rabbi Binder unpeeled his hands from his eyes, slowly, painfully, as if they were tape. Then he checked: nothing on the sidewalk, no dents in the net.

"Is he gonna jump, or what?" the fireman shouted.

In a voice not at all like a statue, Rabbi Binder finally answered. "Yes, Yes, I think so . . . He's been threatening to . . ."

Threatening to? Why, the reason he was on the roof, Ozzie remembered, was to get away; he hadn't even thought about jumping. He had just run to get away, and the truth was that he hadn't really headed for the roof as much as he'd been chased there.

"What's his name, the kid?"

"Freedman," Rabbi Binder answered. "Oscar Freedman."

The fireman looked up at Ozzie. "What is it with you, Oscar? You gonna jump, or what?"

Ozzie did not answer. Frankly, the question had just arisen.

"Look, Oscar, if you're gonna jump, jump—and if you're not gonna jump, don't jump. But don't waste our time, willya?"

Ozzie looked at the fireman and then at Rabbi Binder. He wanted to see Rabbi Binder cover his eyes one more time.

"I'm going to jump."

And then he scampered around the edge of the roof to the corner, where there was no net below, and he flapped his arms at his sides, swishing the air and smacking his palms to his trousers on the downbeat. He began screaming like some kind of engine, "Wheeeee . . . wheeeee," and leaning way out over the edge with the upper half of his body. The firemen whipped around to cover the ground with the net. Rabbi Binder mumbled a few words to Somebody and covered his eyes. Everything happened quickly, jerkily, as in a silent movie. The crowd, which had arrived with the fire engines, gave out a long, Fourth-of-July fireworks oooh-aahhh. In the excitement no one had paid the crowd much heed, except, of course, Yakov Blotnik, who swung from the doorknob counting heads. "Fier und tsvansik . . . finf und tsvantsik . . . Oy, Gut!" It wasn't like this with the cat.

Rabbi Binder peeked through his fingers, checked the sidewalk and net. Empty. But there was Ozzie racing to the other corner. The firemen raced with him but were unable to keep up. Whenever Oscar wanted to he might jump and splatter himself upon the sidewalk, and by the time the firemen scooted to the spot all they could do with their net would be to cover the mess.

"Wheeeee . . . wheeeee . . ."

"Hey, Oscar," the winded fireman yelled, "What the hell is this, a game or something?"

"Wheeeee . . . wheeeee . . ."

"Hey, Oscar—"

But he was off now to the other corner, flapping his wings fiercely. Rabbi Binder couldn't take it any longer—the fire engines from nowhere, the screaming suicidal boy, the net. He fell to his knees, exhausted, and with his hands curled together in front of his chest like a little dome, he pleaded, "Oscar, stop it, Oscar. Don't jump, Oscar. Please come down . . . Please don't jump."

And further back in the crowd a single voice, a single young voice, shouted a lone word to the boy on the roof.

"Jump!"

It was Itzie. Ozzie momentarily stopped flapping.

"Go ahead, Ozz—jump!" Itzie broke off his point of the star and courageously, with the inspiration not of a wise-guy but of a disciple, stood alone. "Jump, Ozz, jump!"

Still on his knees, his hands still curled, Rabbi Binder twisted his body back. He looked at Itzie, then, agonizingly, back to Ozzie.

"OSCAR, DON'T JUMP! PLEASE, DON'T JUMP . . . please please . . ."

"Jump!" This time it wasn't Itzie but another point of the star. By the time Mrs. Freedman arrived to keep her four-thirty appointment with Rabbi Binder, the whole little upside down heaven was shouting and pleading for Ozzie to jump, and Rabbi Binder no longer was pleading with him not to jump, but was crying into the dome of his hands.

Understandably Mrs. Freedman couldn't figure out what her son was doing on the roof. So she asked.

"Ozzie, my Ozzie, what are you doing? My Ozzie, what is it?"

Ozzie stopped wheeeeeing and slowed his arms down to a cruising flap, the kind birds use in soft winds, but he did not answer. He stood against the low, clouded, darkening sky—light clicked down swiftly now, as on a small gear—flapping softly and gazing down at the small bundle of a woman who was his mother.

"What are you doing, Ozzie?" She turned towards the kneeling Rabbi Binder and rushed so close that only a paper-thickness of dusk lay between her stomach and his shoulders.

"What is my baby doing?"

Rabbi Binder gaped up at her but he too was mute. All that moved was the dome of his hands; it shook back and forth like a weak pulse.

"Rabbi, get him down! He'll kill himself. Get him down, my only baby . . ."

"I can't," Rabbi Binder said, "I can't . . ." and he turned his handsome head towards the crowd of boys behind him. "It's them. Listen to them."

And for the first time Mrs. Freedman saw the crowd of boys, and she heard what they were yelling.

"He's doing it for them. He won't listen to me. It's them." Rabbi Binder spoke like one in a trance.

"For them?"

"Yes."

"Why for them?"

"They want him to . . ."

Mrs. Freedman raised her two arms upward as though she were conducting the sky. "For them he's doing it!" And then in a gesture older than pyramids, older than prophets and floods, her arms came slapping down to her sides. "A martyr I have. Look!" She tilted her head to the roof. Ozzie was still flapping softly. "My martyr."

"Oscar, come down, *please*," Rabbi Binder groaned.

In a startlingly even voice Mrs. Freedman called to the boy on the roof. "Ozzie, come down, Ozzie. Don't be a martyr, my baby."

As though it were a litany, Rabbi Binder repeated her words. "Don't be a martyr, my baby. Don't be a martyr."

"Gawhead, Ozz—*be* a Martin!" It was Itzie. "Be a Martin, be a Martin," and all the voices joined in singing for Martindom, whatever *it* was. "Be a Martin, be a Martin . . ."

Somehow when you're on a roof the darker it gets the less you can hear. All Ozzie knew was that two groups wanted two new things: his friends were spirited and musical about what they wanted; his mother and the rabbi were even-toned, chanting, about what they didn't want. The rabbi's voice was without tears now and so was his mother's.

The big net stared up at Ozzie like a sightless eye. The big, clouded sky pushed down. From beneath it looked like a gray corrugated board. Suddenly, looking up into that unsympathetic sky, Ozzie realized all the strangeness of what these people, his friends, were asking: they wanted him to jump, to kill himself; they were singing about it now—it made them that happy. And there was an even greater strangeness: Rabbi Binder was on his knees, trembling. If there was a question to be asked now it was not "Is it me?" but rather "Is it us? . . . Is it us?"

Being on the roof, it turned out, was a serious thing. If he jumped would the singing become dancing? Would it? What would jumping stop? Yearningly, Ozzie wished he could rip open the sky, plunge his hands through, and pull out the sun; and on the sun, like a coin, would be stamped JUMP or DON'T JUMP.

Ozzie's knees rocked and sagged a little under him as though they were setting him for a dive. His arms tightened, stiffened, froze, from shoulders to fingernails. He felt as if each part of his body were going to vote as to whether he should kill himself or not—and each part as though it were independent of *him*.

The light took an unexpected click down and the new darkness, like a gag, hushed the friends singing for this and the mother and rabbi chanting for that.

Ozzie stopped counting votes, and in a curiously high voice, like one who wasn't prepared for speech, he spoke.

"Mamma?"

"Yes, Oscar."

"Mamma, get down on your knees, like Rabbi Binder."

"Oscar—"

"Get down on your knees," he said, "or I'll jump."

Ozzie heard a whimper, then a quick rustling, and when he looked down where his mother had stood he saw the top of a head and beneath that a circle of dress. She was kneeling beside Rabbi Binder.

He spoke again. "Everybody kneel." There was the sound of everybody kneeling.

Ozzie looked around. With one hand he pointed towards the synagogue entrance. "Make *him* kneel."

There was a noise, not of kneeling, but of body-and-cloth stretching. Ozzie could hear Rabbi Binder saying in a gruff whisper, ". . . or he'll *kill* himself," and when next he looked there was Yakov Blotnik off the doornob and for the first time in his life upon his knees in the Gentile posture of prayer.

As for the firemen—it is not as difficult as one might imagine to hold a net taut while you are kneeling.

Ozzie looked around again; and then he called to Rabbi Binder.

"Rabbi?"

"Yes, Oscar."

"Rabbi Binder, do you believe in God."

"Yes."

"Do you believe God can do Anything?" Ozzie leaned his head out into the darkness. "Anything?"

"Oscar, I think—"

"Tell me you believe God can do Anything."

There was a second's hesitation. Then: "God can do Anything."

"Tell me you believe God can make a child without intercourse."

"He can."

"Tell me!"

"God," Rabbi Binder admitted, "can make a child without intercourse."

"Mamma, you tell me."

"God can make a child without intercourse," his mother said.

"Make *him* tell me." There was no doubt who *him* was.

In a few moments Ozzie heard an old comical voice say something to the increasing darkness about God.

Next, Ozzie made everybody say it. And then he made them all say they believed in Jesus Christ—first one at a time, then all together.

When the catechizing was through it was the beginning of evening. From the street it sounded as if the boy on the roof might have sighed.

"Ozzie?" A woman's voice dared to speak. "You'll come down now?"

There was no answer, but the woman waited, and when a voice finally did speak it was thin and crying, and exhausted as that of an old man who has just finished pulling the bells.

"Mamma, don't you see—you shouldn't hit me. He shouldn't hit me. You shouldn't hit me about God, Mamma. You should never hit anybody about God—"

"Ozzie, please come down now."

"Promise me, promise me you'll never hit anybody about God."

He had asked only his mother, but for some reason everyone kneeling in the street promised he would never hit anybody about God.

Once again there was silence.

"I can come down now Mamma," the boy on the roof finally said. He turned his head both ways as though checking the traffic lights. "Now I can come down . . ."

And he did, right into the center of the yellow net that glowed in the evening's edge like an overgrown halo.

by James Joyce

ARABY

James Joyce was born on February 2, 1882, in Rathgar, a suburb of Dublin. He was educated at Jesuit schools, including University College (B.A., 1902), where he studied Latin, French, Italian, and (in order to read Ibsen) Norwegian. After his marriage to Nora Barnacle in 1904, Joyce left Ireland to teach languages in Trieste. During his first year there he wrote most of the stories ("Araby" was one) eventually published as Dubliners. *His impending blindness and the difficulty he had in finding a publisher—his work was allegedly obscene—kept him and his family in almost continual need. With the outbreak of World War I, in which he took neither sides nor interest, he moved to Zurich. In 1920 he settled in Paris.* Ulysses *appeared in 1922, and in 1939 his puzzling masterpiece,* Finnegan's Wake. *When the Germans invaded France in 1940, he again sought refuge in Zurich, but only for a few months: he died on January 13, 1941.*

Almost nothing happens in "Araby." A boy visits a bazaar to buy a present for a girl, finds nothing suitable, and leaves. That is all. But the vapid vulgarity of the shopgirl's conversation, the tawdriness of the hall and its emptiness at that late hour contrast effectively with the exotic promise of the bazaar's name, submitting illusion and vanity and adolescent dreams to the test of experience.

NORTH Richmond Street, being blind, was a quiet street except at the hour when the Christian Brothers' School set the boys free. An uninhabited house of two storeys stood at the blind end, detached from its neighbours in a square ground. The other houses of the street, conscious of decent lives within them, gazed at one another with brown imperturbable faces.

The former tenant of our house, a priest, had died in the back drawing-room. Air, musty from having been long enclosed, hung in all the rooms, and the waste room behind the kitchen was littered with old useless papers. Among these I found a few paper-covered books, the pages of which were curled and damp: *The Abbot,* by Walter Scott, *The Devout Communicant* and *The Memoirs of Vidocq.* I liked the last best because its leaves were yellow. The wild garden behind the house contained a central apple-tree and a few straggling bushes under one of which I found the late tenant's rusty bicycle-pump. He had been a very charitable priest; in his will he had left all his money to institutions and the furniture of his house to his sister.

When the short days of winter came dusk fell before we had well eaten our dinners. When we met in the street the houses had grown sombre. The space of sky above us was the colour of everchanging violet and towards it the lamps of the street lifted their feeble lanterns. The cold air stung us and we played till our bodies glowed. Our shouts echoed in the silent street. The career of our play brought us through the dark muddy lanes behind the houses where we ran the gauntlet of the rough tribes from the cottages, to the back doors of the dark dripping gardens where odours arose from the ashpits, to the dark odorous stables where a coachman smoothed and combed the horse or shook music from the buckled harness. When we returned to the street light from the kitchen windows had filled the areas. If my uncle was seen turning the corner we hid in the shadow until we had seen him safely housed. Or if Mangan's sister came out on the doorstep to call her brother in to his tea we watched her from our shadow peer up and down the street. We waited to see whether she would remain or go in and, if she remained, we left our shadow and walked up to Mangan's steps resignedly. She was waiting for us, her figure defined by the light from the half-opened door. Her brother always teased her before he obeyed and I stood by the railings looking at her. Her dress swung as she moved her body and the soft rope of her hair tossed from side to side.

Every morning I lay on the floor in the front parlour watching her door. The blind was pulled down to within an inch of the sash so that I could not be seen. When she came out on the doorstep my heart leaped. I ran to the hall, seized my books and followed her. I kept her brown figure always in my eye and, when we came near the point at which our ways diverged, I quickened my pace and passed her. This happened morning after morning. I had never spoken to her, except for a few casual words, and yet her name was like a summons to all my foolish blood.

Her image accompanied me even in places the most hostile to romance. On Saturday evenings when my aunt went marketing I had to go to carry some of the parcels. We walked through the flaring streets, jostled by drunken men and bargaining women, amid the curses of labourers, the shrill litanies of shop-boys who stood on guard by the barrels of pigs' cheeks, the nasal chanting of street-singers, who sang a *come-all-you* about O'Donovan Rossa, or a ballad about the troubles in our native land. These noises converged in a single sensation of life for me: I imagined that I bore my chalice safely through a throng of foes. Her name sprang to my lips at moments in strange prayers and praises which I myself did not understand. My eyes were often full of tears (I could not tell why) and at times a flood from my heart seemed to pour itself out into my bosom. I thought little of the future. I did not know whether I would ever speak to her or not or, if I spoke to her, how I could tell her of my confused adoration. But my body was like a harp and her words and gestures were like fingers running upon the wires.

One evening I went into the back drawing-room in which the priest had died. It was a dark rainy evening and there was no sound in the house. Through one of the broken panes I heard the rain impinge upon the earth, the fine incessant needles of water playing in the sodden beds. Some distant lamp or lighted window gleamed below me. I was thankful that I could see so little. All my senses seemed to desire to veil themselves and, feeling that I was about to slip from them, I pressed the palms of my hands together until they trembled, murmuring: "*O love! O love!*" many times.

At last she spoke to me. When she addressed the first words to me I was so confused that I did not know what to answer. She asked me was I going to *Araby*. I forgot whether I answered yes or no. It would be a splendid bazaar, she said she would love to go.

"And why can't you?" I asked.

While she spoke she turned a silver bracelet round and round her wrist. She could not go, she said, because there would be a retreat that week in her convent. Her brother and two other boys were fighting for their caps and I was alone at the railings. She held one of the spikes, bowing her head towards me. The light from the lamp opposite our door caught the white curve of her neck, lit up her hair that rested there and, falling, lit up the hand upon the railing. It fell over one side of her dress and caught the white border of a petticoat, just visible as she stood at ease.

"It's well for you," she said.

"If I go," I said, "I will bring you something."

What innumerable follies laid waste my waking and sleeping thoughts after that evening! I wished to annihilate the tedious intervening days. I chafed against the work of school. At night in my bedroom and by day in the classroom her image came between me and the page I strove to read. The syllables of the word *Araby* were called to me through the silence in which my soul luxuriated and cast an Eastern enchantment over me. I asked for leave to go to the bazaar on Saturday night. My aunt was surprised and hoped it was not some Freemason affair. I answered few questions in class. I watched my master's face pass from amiability to sternness; he hoped I was not beginning to idle. I could not call my wandering thoughts together. I had hardly any patience with the serious work of life which, now that it stood between me and my desire, seemed to me child's play, ugly monotonous child's play.

On Saturday morning I reminded my uncle that I wished to go to the bazaar in the evening. He was fussing at the hallstand, looking for the hat-brush, and answered me curtly:

"Yes, boy, I know."

As he was in the hall I could not go into the front parlour and lie at the window. I felt the house in bad humour and walked slowly towards the school. The air was pitilessly raw and already my heart misgave me.

When I came home to dinner my uncle had not yet been home. Still it was early. I sat staring at the clock for some time and, when its ticking began to irritate me, I left the room. I mounted the staircase and gained the upper part of the house. The high cold empty gloomy rooms liberated me and I went from room to room singing.

From the front window I saw my companions playing below in the street. Their cries reached me weakened and indistinct and, leaning my forehead against the cool glass, I looked over at the dark house where she lived. I may have stood there for an hour, seeing nothing but the brown-clad figure cast by my imagination, touched discreetly by the lamplight at the curved neck, at the hand upon the railings and at the border below the dress.

When I came downstairs again I found Mrs. Mercer sitting at the fire. She was an old garrulous woman, a pawnbroker's widow, who collected used stamps for some pious purpose. I had to endure the gossip of the tea-table. The meal was prolonged beyond an hour and still my uncle did not come. Mrs. Mercer stood up to go: she was sorry she couldn't wait any longer, but it was after eight o'clock and she did not like to be out late, as the night air was bad for her. When she had gone I began to walk up and down the room, clenching my fists. My aunt said:

"I'm afraid you may put off your bazaar for this night of Our Lord."

At nine o'clock I heard my uncle's latchkey in the halldoor. I heard him talking to himself and heard the hallstand rocking when it had received the weight of his overcoat. I could interpret these signs. When he was midway through his dinner I asked him to give me the money to go to the bazaar. He had forgotten.

"The people are in bed and after their first sleep now," he said.

I did not smile. My aunt said to him energetically:

"Can't you give him the money and let him go? You've kept him late enough as it is."

My uncle said he was very sorry he had forgotten. He said he believed in the old saying: "All work and no play makes Jack a dull boy." He asked me where I was going and, when I had told him a second time he asked me did I know *The Arab's Farewell to his Steed.* When I left the kitchen he was about to recite the opening lines of the piece to my aunt.

I held a florin tightly in my hand as I strode down Buckingham Street towards the station. The sight of the streets thronged with buyers and glaring with gas recalled to me the purpose of my journey. I took my seat in a third-class carriage of a deserted train. After an intolerable delay the train moved out of the station slowly. It crept onward among ruinous houses and over the twinkling river.

At Westland Row Station a crowd of people pressed to the carriage doors; but the porters moved them back, saying that it was a special train for the bazaar. I remained alone in the bare carriage. In a few minutes the train drew up beside an improvised wooden platform. I passed out on to the road and saw by the lighted dial of a clock that it was ten minutes to ten. In front of me was a large building which displayed the magical name.

I could not find any sixpenny entrance and, fearing that the bazaar would be closed, I passed in quickly through a turnstile, handing a shilling to a weary-looking man. I found myself in a big hall girdled at half its height by a gallery. Nearly all the stalls were closed and the greater part of the hall was in darkness. I recognized a silence like that which pervades a church after a service. I walked into the centre of the bazaar timidly. A few people were gathered about the stalls which were still open. Before a curtain, over which the words *Café Chantant* were written in coloured lamps, two men were counting money on a salver. I listened to the fall of the coins.

Remembering with difficulty why I had come I went over to one of the stalls and examined porcelain vases and flowered tea-sets. At the door of the stall a young lady was talking and laughing with two young gentlemen. I remarked their English accents and listened vaguely to their conversation.

"O, I never said such a thing!"

"O, but you did!"

"O, but I didn't!"

"Didn't she say that?"

"Yes. I heard her."

"O, there's a . . . fib!"

Observing me the young lady came over and asked me did I wish to buy anything. The tone of her voice was not encouraging; she seemed to have spoken to me out of a sense of duty. I looked humbly at the great jars that stood like eastern guards at either side of the dark entrance to the stall and murmured:

"No, thank you."

The young lady changed the position of one of the vases and went back to the two young men. They began to talk of the same subject. Once or twice the young lady glanced at me over her shoulder.

I lingered before her stall, though I knew my stay was useless, to make my interest in her wares seem the more real. Then I turned away slowly and walked down the middle of the bazaar. I allowed the two pennies to fall against the sixpence in my pocket. I heard a voice call from one end of the gallery that the light was out. The upper part of the hall was now completely dark.

Gazing up into the darkness I saw myself as a creature driven and derided by vanity; and my eyes burned with anguish and anger.

by Eudora Welty

A VISIT OF CHARITY

Eudora Welty was born on April 13, 1909, in Jackson, Mississippi. She attended Mississippi State College for Women for two years, the University of Wisconsin (B.A., 1929), and Columbia University. She returned from New York and an uncongenial job in advertising to Jackson to continue writing short stories. Her first book, A Curtain of Green, *in which* "A Visit of Charity" *was first collected, appeared in 1941. Since then she has published four more volumes of stories* (The Wide Net, 1943; Music from Spain, 1948; The Golden Apples, 1949; *and* The Bride of Innisfallen, 1955) *and three novels* (The Robber Bridegroom, 1942; Delta Wedding, 1946; *and* Ponder Heart, 1954). *She has won the Pulitzer Prize and has twice received the O. Henry Memorial award.*

"A Visit of Charity" displays the rigorously just detachment characteristic of many of Miss Welty's best stories. No one comes off well. The old ladies are pathetic, to be sure—but they are horribly less than human as well. The Campfire Girl—who has to pay a visit to "some old lady . . . any of them will do"—is perhaps not really cruel. But her youth, though it explains her callousness, does not excuse it. After all, she gets what she has come for: "a minimum of three points on her score."

IT was mid-morning—a very cold, bright day. Holding a potted plant before her, a girl of fourteen jumped off the bus in front of the Old Ladies' Home, on the outskirts of town. She wore a red coat, and her straight yellow hair was hanging down loose from the pointed white cap all the little girls were wearing that year. She stopped for a moment beside one of the prickly dark shrubs with which the city had beautified the Home, and then proceeded slowly toward the building, which was of whitewashed brick and reflected the winter sunlight like a block of ice. As she walked vaguely up the steps she shifted the small pot from hand to hand; then she had to set it down and remove her mittens before she could open the heavy door.

"I'm a Campfire Girl. . . . I have to pay a visit to some old lady," she told the nurse at the desk. This was a woman in a white uniform who looked as if she were cold; she had close-cut hair which stood up on the very top of her head exactly like a sea wave. Marian, the little girl, did not tell her that this visit would give her a minimum of only three points in her score.

"Acquainted with any of our residents?" asked the nurse. She lifted one eyebrow and spoke like a man.

"With any old ladies? No—but—that is, any of them will do," Marian stammered. With her free hand she pushed her hair behind her ears, as she did when it was time to study Science.

The nurse shrugged and rose. "You have a nice *multiflora cineraria* there," she remarked as she walked ahead down the hall of closed doors to pick out an old lady.

There was loose, bulging linoleum on the floor. Marian felt as if she were walking on the waves, but the nurse paid no attention to it. There was a smell in the hall like the interior of a clock. Everything was silent until, behind one of the doors, an old lady of some kind cleared her throat like a sheep bleating. This decided the nurse. Stopping in her tracks, she first extended her arm, bent her elbow, and leaned forward from the hips—all to examine the watch strapped to her wrist; then she gave a loud double-rap on the door.

"There are two in each room," the nurse remarked over her shoulder.

"Two what?" asked Marian without thinking. The sound like a sheep's bleating almost made her turn around and run back.

One old woman was pulling the door open in short, gradual jerks, and when she saw the nurse a strange smile forced her old face dangerously awry. Marian, suddenly propelled by the strong, impatient arm of the nurse, saw next the side-face of another old woman, even older, who was lying flat in bed with a cap on and a counterpane drawn up to her chin.

"Visitor," said the nurse, and after one more shove she was off up the hall.

Marian stood tongue-tied; both hands held the potted plant. The old woman, still with that terrible, square smile (which was a smile of welcome) stamped on her bony face, was waiting. . . . Perhaps she said something. The old woman in bed said nothing at all, and she did not look around.

Suddenly Marian saw a hand, quick as a bird claw, reach up in the air and pluck the white cap off her head. At the same time, another claw to match drew her all the way into the room, and the next moment the door closed behind her.

"My, my, my," said the old lady at her side.

Marian stood enclosed by a bed, a washstand and a chair; the tiny room had altogether too much furniture. Everything smelled wet —even the bare floor. She held onto the back of the chair, which was wicker and felt soft and damp. Her heart beat more and more slowly, her hands got colder and colder, and she could not hear whether the old women were saying anything or not. She could not see them very clearly. How dark it was! The window shade was down, and the only door was shut. Marian looked at the ceiling. . . . It was like being caught in a robbers' cave, just before one was murdered.

"Did you come to be our little girl for a while?" the first robber asked.

Then something was snatched from Marian's hand—the little potted plant.

"Flowers!" screamed the old woman. She stood holding the pot in an undecided way. "Pretty flowers," she added.

Then the old woman in bed cleared her throat and spoke. "They are not pretty," she said, still without looking around, but very distinctly.

Marian suddenly pitched against the chair and sat down in it.

"Pretty flowers," the first old woman insisted. "Pretty—pretty . . ."

Marian wished she had the little pot back for just a moment—she had forgotten to look at the plant herself before giving it away. What did it look like?

"Stinkweeds," said the other old woman sharply. She had a bunchy white forehead and red eyes like a sheep. Now she turned them toward Marian. The fogginess seemed to rise in her throat again, and she bleated, "Who—are—you?"

To her surprise, Marian could not remember her name. "I'm a Campfire Girl," she said finally.

"Watch out for the germs," said the old woman like a sheep, not addressing anyone.

"One came out last month to see us," said the first old woman.

A sheep or a germ? wondered Marian dreamily, holding onto the chair.

"Did not!" cried the other old woman.

"Did so! Read to us out of the Bible, and we enjoyed it!" screamed the first.

"Who enjoyed it!" said the woman in bed. Her mouth was unexpectedly small and sorrowful, like a pet's.

"We enjoyed it," insisted the other. "You enjoyed it—I enjoyed it."

"We all enjoyed it," said Marian, without realizing that she had said a word.

The first old woman had just finished putting the potted plant high, high on the top of the wardrobe, where it could hardly be seen from below. Marian wondered how she had ever succeeded in placing it there, how she could ever have reached so high.

"You mustn't pay any attention to old Addie," she now said to the little girl. "She's ailing today."

"Will you shut your mouth?" said the woman in bed. "I am not."

"You're a story."

"I can't stay but a minute—really, I can't," said Marian suddenly. She looked down at the wet floor and thought that if she were sick in here they would have to let her go.

With much to-do the first old woman sat down in a rocking chair —still another piece of furniture!—and began to rock. With the fingers of one hand she touched a very dirty cameo pin on her chest. "What do you do at school?" she asked.

"I don't know . . ." said Marian. She tried to think but she could not.

"Oh, but the flowers are beautiful," the old woman whispered. She seemed to rock faster and faster; Marian did not see how anyone could rock so fast.

"Ugly," said the woman in bed.

"If we bring flowers——" Marian began, and then fell silent. She had almost said that if Campfire Girls brought flowers to the Old Ladies' Home, the visit would count one extra point, and if they took a Bible with them on the bus and read it to the old ladies, it counted double. But the old woman had not listened, anyway; she was rocking and watching the other one, who watched back from the bed.

"Poor Addie is ailing. She has to take medicine—see?" she said, pointing a horny finger at a row of bottles on the table, and rocking so high that her black comfort shoes lifted off the floor like a little child's.

"I am no more sick than you are," said the woman in bed.

"Oh yes you are!"

"I just got more sense than you have, that's all," said the other old woman, nodding her head.

"That's only the contrary way she talks when *you all* come," said the first old lady with sudden intimacy. She stopped the rocker with a neat pat of her feet and leaned toward Marian. Her hand reached over—it felt like a petunia leaf, clinging and just a little sticky.

"Will you hush! Will you hush!" cried the other one.

Marian leaned back rigidly in her chair.

"When I was a little girl like you, I went to school and all," said the old woman in the same intimate, menacing voice. "Not here—another town. . . ."

"Hush!" said the sick woman. "You never went to school. You never came and you never went. You never were anywhere—only here. You never were born! You don't know anything. Your head is empty, your heart and hands and your old black purse are all empty, even that little old box that you brought with you you brought empty—you showed it to me. And yet you talk, talk, talk, talk, talk all the time until I think I'm losing my mind! Who are you? You're a stranger—a perfect stranger! Don't you know you're a stranger? Is it possible that they have actually done a thing like this to anyone—sent them in a stranger to talk, and rock, and tell away her whole long rigmarole? Do they seriously suppose that I'll be able to keep it up, day in, day out, night in, night out, living in the same room with a terrible old woman—forever?"

Marian saw the old woman's eyes grow bright and turn toward her. This old woman was looking at her with despair and calculation in her face. Her small lips suddenly dropped apart, and exposed a half circle of false teeth with tan gums.

"Come here, I want to tell you something," she whispered. "Come here!"

Marian was trembling, and her heart nearly stopped beating altogether for a moment.

"Now, now, Addie," said the first old woman. "That's not polite. Do you know what's really the matter with old Addie today?" She, too, looked at Marian; one of her eyelids drooped low.

"The matter?" the child repeated stupidly. "What's the matter with her?"

"Why, she's mad because it's her birthday!" said the first old woman, beginning to rock again and giving a little crow as though she had answered her own riddle.

"It is not, it is not!" screamed the old woman in bed. "It is not my birthday, no one knows when that is but myself, and will you please be quiet and say nothing more, or I'll go straight out of my mind!" She turned her eyes toward Marian again, and presently she said in the soft, foggy voice, "When the worst comes to the worst, I ring this bell, and the nurse comes." One of her hands was drawn out from under the patched counterpane—a thin little hand with enormous black freckles. With a finger which would not hold still she pointed to a little bell on the table among the bottles.

"How old are you?" Marian breathed. Now she could see the old woman in bed very closely and plainly, and very abruptly, from all sides, as in dreams. She wondered about her—she wondered for a moment as though there was nothing else in the world to wonder about. It was the first time such a thing had happened to Marian.

"I won't tell!"

The old face on the pillow, where Marian was bending over it, slowly gathered and collapsed. Soft whimpers came out of the small open mouth. It was a sheep that she sounded like—a little lamb. Marian's face drew very close, the yellow hair hung forward.

"She's crying!" She turned a bright, burning face up to the first old woman.

"That's Addie for you," the old woman said spitefully.

Marian jumped up and moved toward the door. For the second time, the claw almost touched her hair, but it was not quick enough. The little girl put her cap on.

"Well, it was a real visit," said the old woman, following Marian through the doorway and all the way out into the hall. Then from behind she suddenly clutched the child with her sharp little fingers. In an affected, highpitched whine she cried, "Oh, little girl, have you a penny to spare for a poor old woman that's not got anything of her own? We don't have a thing in the world—not a penny for candy—not a thing! Little girl, just a nickel—a penny——"

Marian pulled violently against the old hands for a moment before she was free. Then she ran down the hall, without looking behind her and without looking at the nurse, who was reading *Field & Stream* at her desk. The nurse, after another triple motion to consult her wrist watch, asked automatically the question put to visitors in all institutions: "Won't you stay and have dinner with *us*?"

Marian never replied. She pushed the heavy door open into the cold air and ran down the steps.

Under the prickly shrub she stooped and quickly, without being seen, retrieved a red apple she had hidden there.

Her yellow hair under the white cap, her scarlet coat, her bare knees all flashed in the sunlight as she ran to meet the big bus rocketing through the street.

"Wait for me!" she shouted. As though at an imperial command, the bus ground to a stop.

She jumped on and took a big bite out of the apple.

by Ernest Hemingway

THE CAPITAL OF THE WORLD

Ernest Hemingway was born on July 21, 1899, in Oak Park, Illinois. For a few months after his graduation from high school in 1917 he worked as a reporter on the Kansas City Star; *then he volunteered for ambulance duty in France. He later joined the Italian infantry, was severely wounded by shrapnel, and was twice decorated for bravery. After the war he worked on the Toronto* Star, *covering disturbances in the Near East, a revolution in Greece, and the Lausanne conference. He settled in Paris for a while and published his early work there. With the publication in 1929 of* A Farewell to Arms *Hemingway established his reputation as a writer. But he was restless: he left the comparative quiet and isolation of the United States to cover Spain and the civil war in 1936 and northern China and the Japanese invasion in 1940. With the outbreak of World War II he volunteered his services: first for anti-submarine patrol duty in Cuban waters and then as a correspondent in France and Germany, where he won the Bronze Star. In 1954 Hemingway was awarded both the Pulitzer Prize and the Nobel Prize for his short novel* The Old Man and the Sea. *He died of a self-inflicted gunshot wound on July 2, 1961.*

Paco, the young hero of "The Capital of the World," lives a life "full of illusions." In this he is like the other characters in the story: the three matadors (a "novelty," a consumptive, a coward), the revolutionary waiter, even his sisters and the priests. All submit to a fraudulent world; each perpetuates a private deception. And Paco's bullfight—at one with the design—is the final mockery. Only the metaphor of his death intrudes.

MADRID is full of boys named Paco, which is the diminutive of the name Francisco, and there is a Madrid joke about a father who came to Madrid and inserted an advertisement in the personal columns of *El Liberal* which said: PACO MEET ME AT HOTEL MONTANA NOON TUESDAY ALL IS FORGIVEN PAPA and how a squadron of Guardia Civil had to be called out to disperse the eight hundred young men who answered the advertisement. But this Paco, who waited on table at the Pension Luarca, had no father to forgive him, nor anything for the father to forgive. He had two older sisters who were chambermaids at the Luarca, who had gotten their place through coming from the same small village as a former Luarca chambermaid who had proven hardworking and honest and hence given her village and its products a good name; and these sisters had paid his way on the auto-bus to Madrid and gotten him his job as an apprentice waiter. He came from a village in a part of Extramadura where conditions were incredibly primitive, food scarce, and comforts unknown and he had worked hard ever since he could remember.

He was a well built boy with very black, rather curly hair, good teeth and a skin that his sisters envied, and he had a ready and unpuzzled smile. He was fast on his feet and did his work well and he loved his sisters, who seemed beautiful and sophisticated; he loved Madrid, which was still an unbelievable place, and he loved his work which, done under bright lights, with clean linen, the wearing of evening clothes, and abundant food in the kitchen, seemed romantically beautiful.

There were from eight to a dozen other people who lived at the Luarca and ate in the dining room but for Paco, the youngest of the three waiters who served at table, the only ones who really existed were the bull fighters.

Second-rate matadors lived at that pension because the address in the Calle San Jeronimo was good, the food was excellent and the room and board was cheap. It is necessary for a bull fighter to give the appearance, if not of prosperity, at least of respectability, since decorum and dignity rank above courage as the virtues most highly prized in Spain, and bull fighters stayed at the Luarca until their last pesetas were gone. There is no record of any bull fighter having left the Luarca for a better or more expensive hotel; second-rate bull fighters never became first rate; but the descent from the Luarca was swift since any one could stay there who was making anything at all and a bill was never presented to a guest unasked until the woman who ran the place knew that the case was hopeless.

At this time there were three full matadors living at the Luarca as well as two very good picadors, and one excellent banderillero. The Luarca was luxury for the picadors and the banderilleros who, with their families in Seville, required lodging in Madrid during the Spring season; but they were well paid and in the fixed employ of fighters who were heavily contracted during the coming season and the three of these subalterns would probably make much more apiece than any of the three matadors. Of the three matadors one was ill and trying to conceal it; one had passed his short vogue as a novelty; and the third was a coward.

The coward had at one time, until he had received a peculiarly atrocious horn wound in the lower abdomen at the start of his first season as a full matador, been exceptionally brave and remarkably skillful and he still had many of the hearty mannerisms of his days of success. He was jovial to excess and laughed constantly with and without provocation. He had, when successful, been very addicted to practical jokes but he had given them up now. They took an assurance that he did not feel. This matador had an intelligent, very open face and he carried himself with much style.

The matador who was ill was careful never to show it and was meticulous about eating a little of all the dishes that were presented at the table. He had a great many handkerchiefs which he laundered himself in his room and, lately, he had been selling his fighting suits. He had sold one, cheaply, before Christmas and another in the first week of April. They had been very expensive suits, had always been well kept and he had one more. Before he had become ill he had been a very promising, even a sensational, fighter and, while he himself could not read, he had clippings which said that in his debut in Madrid he had been better than Belmonte. He ate alone at a small table and looked up very little.

The matador who had once been a novelty was very short and brown and very dignified. He also ate alone at a separate table and he smiled very rarely and never laughed. He came from Valladolid, where the people are extremely serious, and he was a capable matador; but his style had become old-fashioned before he had ever succeeded in endearing himself to the public through his virtues, which were courage and a calm capability, and his name on a poster would draw no one to a bull ring. His novelty had been that he was so short that he could barely see over the bull's withers, but there were other short fighters, and he had never succeeded in imposing himself on the public's fancy.

Of the picadors one was a thin, hawk-faced, gray-haired man, lightly built but with legs and arms like iron, who always wore cattle-men's boots under his trousers, drank too much every evening and gazed amorously at any woman in the pension. The other was huge, dark, brown-faced, good-looking, with black hair like an Indian and enormous hands. Both were great picadors although the first was reputed to have lost much of his ability through drink and dissipation, and the second was said to be too headstrong and quarrelsome to stay with any matador more than a single season.

The banderillero was middle-aged, gray, cat-quick in spite of his years and, sitting at the table, he looked a moderately prosperous business man. His legs were still good for this season, and when they should go he was intelligent and experienced enough to keep regularly employed for a long time. The difference would be that when his speed of foot would be gone he would always be frightened where now he was assured and calm in the ring and out of it.

On this evening every one had left the dining room except the hawk-faced picador who drank too much, the birthmarked-faced auctioneer of watches at the fairs and festivals of Spain, who also drank too much, and two priests from Galicia who were sitting at a corner table and drinking if not too much certainly enough. At that time wine was included in the price of the room and board at the Luarca and the waiters had just brought fresh bottles of Valdepeñas to the tables of the auctioneer, then to the picador and, finally, to the two priests.

The three waiters stood at the end of the room. It was the rule of the house that they should all remain on duty until the diners whose tables they were responsible for should all have left but the one who served the table of the two priests had an appointment to go to an Anarcho-Syndicalist meeting and Paco had agreed to take over his table for him.

Upstairs the matador who was ill was lying face down on his bed alone. The matador who was no longer a novelty was sitting looking out of his window preparatory to walking out to the café. The matador who was a coward had the older sister of Paco in his room with him and was trying to get her to do something which she was laughingly refusing to do. This matador was saying "Come on, little savage."

"No," said the sister. "Why should I?"

"For a favor."

"You've eaten and now you want me for dessert."

"Just once. What harm can it do?"

"Leave me alone. Leave me alone, I tell you."

"It is a very little thing to do."

"Leave me alone, I tell you."

Down in the dining room the tallest of the waiters, who was overdue at the meeting, said "Look at those black pigs drink."

"That's no way to speak," said the second waiter. "They are decent clients. They do not drink too much."

"For me it is a good way to speak," said the tall one. "There are the two curses of Spain, the bulls and the priests."

"Certainly not the individual bull and the individual priest," said the second waiter.

"Yes," said the tall waiter. "Only through the individual can you attack the class. It is necessary to kill the individual bull and the individual priest. All of them. Then there are no more."

"Save it for the meeting," said the other waiter.

"Look at the barbarity of Madrid," said the tall waiter. "It is now half-past eleven o'clock and these are still guzzling."

"They only started to eat at ten," said the other waiter. "As you know there are many dishes. That wine is cheap and these have paid for it. It is not a strong wine."

"How can there be solidarity of workers with fools like you?" asked the tall waiter.

"Look," said the second waiter who was a man of fifty. "I have worked all my life. In all that remains of my life I must work. I have no complaints against work. To work is normal."

"Yes, but the lack of work kills."

"I have always worked," said the older waiter. "Go on to the meeting. There is no necessity to stay."

"You are a good comrade," said the tall waiter. "But you lack all ideology."

"*Mejor si me falta eso que el otro,*" said the older waiter (meaning it is better to lack that than work). "Go on to the *mitin.*"

Paco had said nothing. He did not yet understand politics but it always gave him a thrill to hear the tall waiter speak of the necessity for killing the priests and the Guardia Civil. The tall waiter represented to him revolution and revolution also was romantic. He himself would like to be a good catholic, a revolutionary, and have a steady job like this, while, at the same time, being a bullfighter.

"Go on to the meeting, Ignacio," he said. "I will respond for your work."

"The two of us," said the older waiter.

"There isn't enough for one," said Paco. "Go on to the meeting."

"*Pues, me voy,*" said the tall waiter. "And thanks."

In the meantime, upstairs, the sister of Paco had gotten out of the embrace of the matador as skilfully as a wrestler breaking a hold and said, now angry, "These are the hungry people. A failed bullfighter. With your ton-load of fear. If you have so much of that, use it in the ring."

"That is the way a whore talks."

"A whore is also a woman, but I am not a whore."

"You'll be one."

"Not through you."

"Leave me," said the matador who, now, repulsed and refused, felt the nakedness of his cowardice returning.

"Leave you? What hasn't left you?" said the sister. "Don't you want me to make up the bed? I'm paid to do that."

"Leave me," said the matador, his broad good-looking face wrinkled into a contortion that was like crying. "You whore. You dirty little whore."

"Matador," she said, shutting the door. "My matador."

Inside the room the matador sat on the bed. His face still had the contortion which, in the ring, he made into a constant smile which frightened those people in the first rows of seats who knew what they were watching. "And this," he was saying aloud. "And this. And this."

He could remember when he had been good and it had only been three years before. He could remember the weight of the heavy gold-brocaded fighting jacket on his shoulders on that hot afternoon in May when his voice had still been the same in the ring as in the café, and how he sighted along the point-dipping blade at the place in the top of the shoulders where it was dusty in the short-haired black hump of muscle above the wide, wood-knocking, splintered-tipped horns that lowered as he went in to kill, and how the sword pushed in as easy as into a mound of stiff butter with the palm of his hand pushing the pommel, his left arm crossed low, his left shoulder forward, his weight on his left leg, and then his weight wasn't on his leg. His weight was on his lower belly and as the bull raised his head the horn was out of sight in him and he swung over on it twice before they pulled him off it. So now when he went in to kill, and it was seldom, he could not look at the horns and what did any whore know about what he went through before he fought? And what had they been through that laughed at him? They were all whores and they knew what they could do with it.

Down in the dining room the picador sat looking at the priests. If there were women in the room he stared at them. If there were no women he would stare with enjoyment at a foreigner, *un inglés*, but lacking women or strangers, he now stared with enjoyment and insolence at the two priests. While he stared the birth-marked auctioneer rose and folding his napkin went out, leaving over half the wine in the last bottle he had ordered. If his accounts had been paid up at the Luarca he would have finished the bottle.

The two priests did not stare back at the picador. One of them was saying, "It is ten days since I have been here waiting to see him and all day I sit in the ante-chamber and he well not receive me."

"What is there to do?"

"Nothing. What can one do? One cannot go against authority."

"I have been here for two weeks and nothing. I wait and they will not see me."

"We are from the abandoned country. When the money runs out we can return."

"To the abandoned country. What does Madrid care about Galicia? We are a poor province."

"One understands the action of our brother Basilio."

"Still I have no real confidence in the integrity of Basilio Alvarez."

"Madrid is where one learns to understand. Madrid kills Spain."

"If they would simply see one and refuse."

"No. You must be broken and worn out by waiting."

"Well, we shall see. I can wait as well as another."

At this moment the picador got to his feet, walked over to the priests' table and stood, gray-headed and hawk-faced, staring at them and smiling.

"A torero," said one priest to the other.

"And a good one," said the picador and walked out of the dining room, gray-jacketed, trim-waisted, bow-legged, in tight breeches over his high-heeled cattleman's boots that clicked on the floor as he swaggered quite steadily, smiling to himself. He lived in a small, tight, professional world of personal efficiency, nightly alcoholic triumph, and insolence. Now he lit a cigar and tilting his hat at an angle in the hallway went out to the café.

The priests left immediately after the picador, hurriedly conscious of being the last people in the dining room, and there was no one in the room now but Paco and the middle-aged waiter. They cleared the tables and carried the bottles into the kitchen.

In the kitchen was the boy who washed the dishes. He was three years older than Paco and was very cynical and bitter.

"Take this," the middle-aged waiter said, and poured out a glass of the Valdepeñas and handed it to him.

"Why not?" the boy took the glass.

"Tu, Paco?" the older waiter asked.

"Thank you," said Paco. The three of them drank.

"I will be going," said the middle-aged waiter.

"Good night," they told him.

He went out and they were alone. Paco took a napkin one of the priests had used and standing straight, his heels planted, lowered the napkin and with head following the movement, swung his arms in the motion of a slow sweeping veronica. He turned and advancing his right foot slightly, made the second pass, gained a little terrain on the imaginary bull and made a third pass, slow, perfectly timed and suave, then gathered the napkin to his waist and swung his hips away from the bull in a media-veronica.

The dishwasher, whose name was Enrique, watched him critically and sneeringly.

"How is the bull?" he said.

"Very brave," said Paco. "Look."

Standing slim and straight he made four more passes, smooth, elegant and graceful.

"And the bull?" asked Enrique standing against the sink, holding his wine glass and wearing his apron.

"Still has lots of gas," said Paco.

"You make me sick," said Enrique.

"Why?"

"Look."

Enrique removed his apron and citing the imaginary bull he sculptured four perfect, languid gypsy veronicas and ended up with a rebolera that made the apron swing in a stiff arc past the bull's nose as he walked away from him.

"Look at that," he said. "And I wash dishes."

"Why?"

"Fear," said Enrique. "*Miedo*. The same fear you would have in a ring with a bull."

"No," said Paco. "I wouldn't be afraid."

"*Leche!*" said Enrique. "Every one is afraid. But a torero can control his fear so that he can work the bull. I went in an amateur fight and I was so afraid I couldn't keep from running. Every one thought it was very funny. So would you be afraid. If it wasn't for fear every bootblack in Spain would be a bullfighter. You, a country boy, would be frightened worse than I was."

"No," said Paco.

He had done it too many times in his imagination. Too many times he had seen the horns, seen the bull's wet muzzle, the ear twitching, then the head go down and the charge, the hoofs thudding and the hot bull pass him as he swung the cape, to re-charge as he swung the cape again, then again, and again, and again, to end winding the bull around him in his great media-veronica, and walk swingingly away, with bull hairs caught in the gold ornaments of his jacket from the close passes; the bull standing hypnotized and the crowd applauding. No, he would not be afraid. Others, yes. Not he. He knew he would not be afraid. Even if he ever was afraid he knew that he could do it anyway. He had confidence. "I wouldn't be afraid," he said.

Enrique said, "*Leche*," again.

Then he said, "If we should try it?"

"How?"

"Look," said Enrique. "You think of the bull but you do not think of the horns. The bull has such force that the horns rip like a knife, they stab like a bayonet, and they kill like a club. Look," he opened a table drawer and took out two meat knives. "I will bind these to the legs of a chair. Then I will play bull for you with the chair held before my head. The knives are the horns. If you make those passes then they mean something."

"Lend me your apron," said Paco. "We'll do it in the dining room."

"No," said Enrique, suddenly not bitter. "Don't do it, Paco."

"Yes," said Paco. "I'm not afraid."

"You will be when you see the knives come."

"We'll see," said Paco. "Give me the apron."

At this time, while Enrique was binding the two heavy-bladed razor-sharp meat knives fast to the legs of the chair with two soiled napkins holding the half of each knife, wrapping them tight and then knotting them, the two chambermaids, Paco's sisters, were on their way to the cinema to see Greta Garbo in "Anna Christie." Of the two priests, one was sitting in his underwear reading his breviary and the other was wearing a nightshirt and saying the rosary. All the bullfighters except the one who was ill had made their evening appearance at the Café Fornos, where the big, dark-haired picador was playing billiards, the short, serious matador was sitting at a crowded table before a coffee and milk, along with the middle-aged banderillero and other serious workmen.

The drinking, gray-headed picador was sitting with a glass of cazalas brandy before him staring with pleasure at a table where the matador whose courage was gone sat with another matador who had renounced the sword to become a banderillero again, and two very houseworn-looking prostitutes.

The auctioneer stood on the street corner talking with friends. The tall waiter was at the Anarcho-Syndicalist meeting waiting for an opportunity to speak. The middle-aged waiter was seated on the terrace of the Café Alvarez drinking a small beer. The woman who owned the Luarca was already asleep in her bed, where she lay on her back with the bolster between her legs; big, fat, honest, clean, easy-going, very religious and never having ceased to miss or pray daily for her husband, dead, now, twenty years. In his room, alone, the matador who was ill lay face down on his bed with his mouth against a handkerchief.

Now, in the deserted dining room, Enrique tied the last knot in the napkins that bound the knives to the chair legs and lifted the chair. He pointed the legs with the knives on them forward and held the chair over his head with the two knives pointing straight ahead, one on each side of his head.

"It's heavy," he said. "Look, Paco. It is very dangerous. Don't do it." He was sweating.

Paco stood facing him, holding the apron spread, holding a fold of it bunched in each hand, thumbs up, first finger down, spread to catch the eye of the bull.

"Charge straight," he said. "Turn like a bull. Charge as many times as you want."

"How will you know when to cut the pass?" asked Enrique. "It's better to do three and then a media."

"All right," said Paco. "But come straight. Huh, torito! Come on, little bull!"

Running with head down Enrique came toward him and Paco swung the apron just ahead of the knife blade as it passed close in front of his belly and as it went by it was, to him, the real horn, white-tipped, black, smooth, and as Enrique passed him and turned to rush again it was the hot, blood-flanked mass of the bull that thudded by, then turned like a cat and came again as he swung the cape slowly. Then the bull turned and came again and, as he watched the onrushing point, he stepped his left foot two inches too far forward and the knife did not pass, but had slipped in as easily as into a wineskin and there was a hot scalding rush above and around the sudden inner rigidity of steel and Enrique shouting. "Ay! Ay! Let me get it out! Let me get it out!" and Paco slipped forward on the chair, the apron cape still held, Enrique pulling on the chair as the knife turned in him, in him, Paco.

The knife was out now and he sat on the floor in the widening warm pool.

"Put the napkin over it. Hold it!" said Enrique. "Hold it tight. I will run for the doctor. You must hold in the hemorrhage."

"There should be a rubber cup," said Paco. He had seen that used in the ring.

"I came straight," said Enrique, crying. "All I wanted was to show the danger."

"Don't worry," said Paco, his voice sounding far away. "But bring the doctor."

In the ring they lifted you and carried you, running with you, to the operating room. If the femoral artery emptied itself before you reached there they called the priest.

"Advise one of the priests," said Paco, holding the napkin tight against his lower abdomen. He could not believe that this had happened to him.

But Enrique was running down the Carrera San Jeronimo to the all-night first-aid station and Paco was alone, first sitting up, then huddled over, then slumped on the floor, until it was over, feeling his life go out of him as dirty water empties from a bathtub when the plug is drawn. He was frightened and he felt faint and he tried to say an act of contrition and he remembered how it started but before he had said, as fast as he could, "Oh, my God, I am heartily sorry for having offended Thee who art worthy of all my love and I firmly resolve . . . ," he felt too faint and he was lying face down on the floor and it was over very quickly. A severed femoral artery empties itself faster than you can believe.

As the doctor from the first-aid station came up the stairs accompanied by a policeman who held on to Enrique by the arm, the two sisters of Paco were still in the moving-picture palace of the Gran Via, where they were intensely disappointed in the Garbo film, which showed the great star in miserable low surroundings when they had been accustomed to see her surrounded by great luxury and brilliance. The audience disliked the film thoroughly and were protesting by whistling and stamping their feet. All the other people from the hotel were doing almost what they had been doing when the accident happened, except that the two priests had finished their devotions and were preparing for sleep, and the gray-haired picador had moved his drink over to the table with the two houseworn prostitutes. A little later he went out of the café with one of them. It was the one for whom the matador who had lost his nerve had been buying drinks.

The boy Paco had never known about any of this nor about what all these people would be doing on the next day and on other days to come. He had no idea how they really lived nor how they ended. He did not even realize they ended. He died, as the Spanish phrase has it, full of illusions. He had not had time in his life to lose any of them, nor even, at the end, to complete an act of contrition.

He had not even had time to be disappointed in the Garbo picture which disappointed all Madrid for a week.

by Carson McCullers

WUNDERKIND

Carson McCullers was born on February 19, 1917, in Columbus, Georgia. When she was seventeen she left for New York to study literature and music at Columbia University and the Julliard School of Music, but shortly after registration she lost her money on the subway. She then worked part-time, attended night school, and began to publish short stories. Her first novel, The Heart Is a Lonely Hunter, *appeared when she was twenty-two. Three others have followed:* Reflections in a Golden Eye *(1941),* Member of the Wedding *(1946), and* Clock without Hands *(1961). For the stage version of* Member of the Wedding *Miss McCullers received in 1950 the New York Drama Critics Award.* The Ballad of the Sad Café, *her only collection of short stories, was published in 1951.*

At times the writer of fiction turns inward upon the basic problem of his role as artist. He feels impaled upon the horns of a dilemma: the exacting necessity of his art and the expanding necessity of his humanness. Without the first he has no life; without the second his art is lifeless. This conflict, Miss McCullers implies, becomes taut and dimly pathetic when the scale is reduced, when the artist is a child—child and prodigy, bienchen *and* wunderkind.

SHE came into the living room, her music satchel plopping against her winter-stockinged legs and her other arm weighted down with school books, and stood for a moment listening to the sounds from the studio. A soft procession of piano chords and the tuning of a violin. Then Mister Bilderbach called out to her in his chunky, guttural tones:

"That you, Bienchen?"

As she jerked off her mittens she saw that her fingers were twitching to the motions of the fugue she had practiced that morning. "Yes," she answered. "It's me."

"I," the voice corrected. "Just a moment."

She could hear Mister Lafkowitz talking—his words spun out in a silky, unintelligible hum. A voice almost like a woman's, she thought, compared to Mister Bilderbach's. Restlessness scattered her attention. She fumbled with her geometry book and *Le Voyage de Monsieur Perrichon* before putting them on the table. She sat down on the sofa and began to take her music from the satchel. Again she saw her hands—the quivering tendons that stretched down from her knuckles, the sore finger tip capped with curled, dingy tape. The sight sharpened the fear that had begun to torment her for the past few months.

Noiselessly she mumbled a few phrases of encouragement to herself. A good lesson—a good lesson—like it used to be—Her lips closed as she heard the stolid sound of Mister Bilderbach's footsteps across the floor of the studio and the creaking of the door as it slid open.

For a moment she had the peculiar feeling that during most of the fifteen years of her life she had been looking at the face and shoulders that jutted from behind the door, in a silence disturbed only by the muted, blank plucking of a violin string. Mister Bilderbach. Her teacher, Mister Bilderbach. The quick eyes behind the horn-rimmed glasses; the light, thin hair and the narrow face beneath; the lips full and loose shut and the lower one pink and shining from the bites of his teeth; the forked veins in his temples throbbing plainly enough to be observed across the room.

"Aren't you a little early?" he asked, glancing at the clock on the mantelpiece that had pointed to five minutes of twelve for a month. "Josef's in here. We're running over a little sonatina by someone he knows."

"Good," she said, trying to smile. "I'll listen." She could see her fingers sinking powerless into a blur of piano keys. She felt tired—felt that if he looked at her much longer her hands might tremble.

He stood uncertain, halfway in the room. Sharply his teeth pushed down on his bright, swollen lip. "Hungry, Bienchen?" he asked. "There's some apple cake Anna made, and milk."

"I'll wait till afterward," she said. "Thanks."

"After you finish with a very fine lesson—eh?" His smile seemed to crumble at the corners.

There was a sound from behind him in the studio and Mister Lafkowitz pushed at the other panel of the door and stood beside him.

"Frances?" he said, smiling. "And how is the work coming now?"

Without meaning to, Mister Lafkowitz always made her feel clumsy and overgrown. He was such a small man himself, with a weary look when he was not holding his violin. His eyebrows curved high above his sallow, Jewish face as though asking a question, but the lids of his eyes drowsed languorous and indifferent. Today he seemed distracted. She watched him come into the room for no apparent purpose, holding his pearl-tipped bow in his still fingers, slowly gliding the white horsehair through a chalky piece of rosin. His eyes were sharp bright slits today and the linen handkerchief that flowed down from his collar darkened the shadows beneath them.

"I gather you're doing a lot now," smiled Mister Lafkowitz, although she had not yet answered the question.

She looked at Mister Bilderbach. He turned away. His heavy shoulders pushed the door open wide so that the late afternoon sun came through the window of the studio and shafted yellow over the dusty living room. Behind her teacher she could see the squat long piano, the window, and the bust of Brahms.

"No," she said to Mister Lafkowitz, "I'm doing terribly." Her thin fingers flipped at the pages of her music. "I don't know what's the matter," she said, looking at Mister Bilderbach's stooped muscular back that stood tense and listening.

Mister Lafkowitz smiled. "There are times, I suppose, when one——"

A harsh chord sounded from the piano. "Don't you think we'd better get on with this?" asked Mister Bilderbach.

"Immediately," said Mister Lafkowitz, giving the bow one more scrape before starting toward the door. She could see him pick up his violin from the top of the piano. He caught her eye and lowered the instrument. "You've seen the picture of Heime?"

Her fingers curled tight over the sharp corner of the satchel. "What picture?"

"One of Heime in the *Musical Courier* there on the table. Inside the top cover."

The sonatina began. Discordant yet somehow simple. Empty but with a sharp-cut style of its own. She reached for the magazine and opened it.

There Heime was—in the left-hand corner. Holding his violin with his fingers hooked down over the strings for a pizzicato. With his dark serge knickers strapped neatly beneath his knees, a sweater and rolled collar. It was a bad picture. Although it was snapped in profile his eyes were cut around toward the photographer and his finger looked as though it would pluck the wrong string. He seemed suffering to turn around toward the picture-taking apparatus. He was thinner—his stomach did not poke out now—but he hadn't changed much in six months.

Heime Israelsky, talented young violinist, snapped while at work in his teacher's studio on Riverside Drive. Young Master Israelsky, who will soon celebrate his fifteenth birthday, has been invited to play the Beethoven Concerta with—

That morning, after she had practiced from six until eight, her dad had made her sit down at the table with the family for breakfast. She hated breakfast; it gave her a sick feeling afterward. She would rather wait and get four chocolate bars with her twenty cents lunch money and munch them during school—bringing up little morsels from her pocket under cover of her handkerchief, stopping dead when the silver paper rattled. But this morning her dad had put a fried egg on her plate and she had known that if it burst—so that the slimy yellow oozed over the white—she would cry. And that had happened. The same feeling was upon her now. Gingerly she laid the magazine back on the table and closed her eyes.

The music in the studio seemed to be urging violently and clumsily for something that was not to be had. After a moment her thoughts drew back from Heime and the concerta and the picture—and hovered around the lesson once more. She slid over on the sofa until she could see plainly into the studio—the two of them playing, peering at the notations on the piano, lustfully drawing out all that was there.

She could not forget the memory of Mister Bilderbach's face as he had stared at her a moment ago. Her hands, still twitching unconsciously to the motions of the fugue, closed over her bony knees. Tired, she was. And with a circling, sinking away feeling like the one that often came to her just before she dropped off to sleep on the nights when she had over-practiced. Like those weary half-dreams that buzzed and carried her out into their own whirling space.

A *Wunderkind*—a *Wunderkind*—a *Wunderkind*. The syllables would come out rolling in the deep German way, roar against her ears and then fall to a murmur. Along with the faces circling, swelling out in distortion, diminishing to pale blobs—Mister Bilderbach, Mrs. Bilderbach, Heime, Mister Lafkowitz. Around and around in a circle revolving to the guttural *Wunderkind*. Mister Bilderbach looming large in the middle of the circle, his face urging—with the others around him.

Phrases of music seesawing crazily. Notes she had been practicing falling over each other like a handful of marbles dropped downstairs. Bach, Debussy, Prokofieff, Brahms—timed grotesquely to the far off throb of her tired body and the buzzing circle.

Sometimes—when she had not worked more than three hours or had stayed out from high school—the dreams were not so confused. The music soared clearly in her mind and quick, precise little memories would come back—clear as the sissy "Age of Innocence" picture Heime had given her after their joint concert was over.

A *Wunderkind*—a *Wunderkind*. That was what Mister Bilderbach had called her when, at twelve, she first came to him. Older pupils had repeated the word.

Not that he had ever said the word to her. "Bienchen—" (She had a plain American name but he never used it except when her mistakes were enormous.) "Bienchen," he would say, "I know it must be terrible. Carrying around all the time a head that thick. Poor Bienchen——"

Mister Bilderbach's father had been a Dutch violinist. His mother was from Prague. He had been born in this country and had spent his youth in Germany. So many times she wished she had not been born and brought up in just Cincinnati. How do you say *cheese* in German? Mister Bilderbach, what is Dutch for *I don't understand you?*

The first day she came to the studio. After she played the whole Second Hungarian Rhapsody from memory. The room graying with twilight. His face as he leaned over the piano.

"Now we begin all over," he said that first day. "It—playing music

—is more than cleverness. If a twelve-year-old girl's fingers cover so many keys to a second—that means nothing."

He tapped his broad chest and his forehead with his stubby hand. "Here and here. You are old enough to understand that." He lighted a cigarette and gently blew the first exhalation above her head. "And work—work—work—. We will start now with these Bach Inventions and these little Schumann pieces." His hands moved again—this time to jerk the cord of the lamp behind her and point to the music. "I will show you how I wish this practiced. Listen carefully now."

She had been at the piano for almost three hours and was very tired. His deep voice sounded as though it had been straying inside her for a long time. She wanted to reach out and touch his muscle-flexed finger that pointed out the phrases, wanted to feel the gleaming gold band ring and the strong hairy back of his hand.

She had lessons Tuesday after school and on Saturday afternoons. Often she stayed, when the Saturday lesson was finished, for dinner, and then spent the night and took the streetcar home the next morning. Mrs. Bilderbach liked her in her calm, almost dumb way. She was much different from her husband. She was quiet and fat and slow. When she wasn't in the kitchen, cooking the rich dishes that both of them loved, she seemed to spend all her time in their bed upstairs, reading magazines or just looking with a half-smile at nothing. When they had married in Germany she had been a *lieder* singer. She didn't sing anymore (she said it was her throat). When he would call her in from the kitchen to listen to a pupil she would always smile and say that it was *gut*, very *gut*.

When Frances was thirteen it came to her one day that the Bilderbachs had no children. It seemed strange. Once she had been back in the kitchen with Mrs. Bilderbach when he had come striding in from the studio, tense with anger at some pupil who had annoyed him. His wife stood stirring the thick soup until his hand groped out and rested on her shoulder. Then she turned—stood placid—while he folded his arms about her and buried his sharp face in the white, nerveless flesh of her neck. They stood that way without moving. And then his face jerked back suddenly, the anger diminished to a quiet inexpressiveness, and he had returned to the studio.

After she had started with Mister Bilderbach and didn't have time to see anything of the people at high school, Heime had been the only friend of her own age. He was Mr. Lafkowitz's pupil and would come with him to Mister Bilderbach's on evenings when she would be there. They would listen to their teachers' playing. And often they themselves went over chamber music together—Mozart sonatas or Bloch.

A *Wunderkind*—a *Wunderkind.*

Heime was a *Wunderkind.* He and she, then.

Heime had been playing the violin since he was four. He didn't have to go to school; Mister Lafkowitz's brother, who was crippled, used to teach him geometry and European history and French verbs in the afternoon. When he was thirteen he had as fine a technique as any violinist in Cincinnati—everyone said so. But playing the violin must be easier than the piano. She knew it must be.

Heime always seemed to smell of corduroy pants and the food he had eaten and rosin. Half the time, too, his hands were dirty around the knuckles and the cuffs of his shirts peeped out dingily from the sleeves of his sweater. She always watched his hands when he played —thin only at the joints with the hard little blobs of flesh bulging over the short-cut nails and the babyish-looking crease that showed so plainly in his bowing wrist.

In the dreams, as when she was awake, she could remember the concert only in a blur. She had not known it was unsuccessful for her until months after. True, the papers had praised Heime more than her. But he was much shorter than she. When they stood together on the stage he came only to her shoulders. And that made a difference with people, she knew. Also, there was the matter of the sonata they played together. The Bloch.

"No, no—I don't think that would be appropriate," Mister Bilderbach had said when the Bloch was suggested to end the programme. "Now that John Powell thing—the Sonate Virginianesque."

She hadn't understood then; she wanted it to be the Bloch as much as Mister Lafkowitz and Heime.

Mister Bilderbach had given in. Later, after the reviews had said she lacked the temperament for that type of music, after they called her playing thin and lacking in feeling, she felt cheated.

"That oie oie stuff," said Mister Bilderbach, crackling the newspapers at her. "Not for you, Bienchen. Leave all that to the Heimes and vitses and skys."

A *Wunderkind.* No matter what the papers said, that was what he had called her.

Why was it Heime had done so much better at the concert than she? At school sometimes, when she was supposed to be watching someone do a geometry problem on the blackboard, the question would twist knife-like inside her. She would worry about it in bed, and even sometimes when she was supposed to be concentrating at the piano. It wasn't just the Bloch and her not being Jewish—not entirely. It wasn't that Heime didn't have to go to school and had begun his training so early, either. It was—?

Once she thought she knew.

"Play the Fantasia and Fugue," Mister Bilderbach had demanded one evening a year ago—after he and Mister Lafkowitz had finished reading some music together.

The Bach, as she played, seemed to her well done. From the tail of her eye she could see the calm, pleased expression on Mister Bilderbach's face, see his hands rise climactically from the chair arms and then sink down loose and satisfied when the high points of the phrases had been passed successfully. She stood up from the piano when it was over, swallowing to loosen the bands that the music seemed to have drawn around her throat and chest. But—

"Frances—" Mister Lafkowitz had said then, suddenly, looking at her with his thin mouth curved and his eyes almost covered by their delicate lids. "Do you know how many children Bach had?"

She turned to him, puzzled. "A good many. Twenty some odd."

"Well then—" The corners of his smile etched themselves gently on his pale face. "He could not have been so cold—then."

Mister Bilderbach was not pleased; his guttural effulgence of German words had *Kind* in it somewhere. Mister Lafkowitz raised his eyebrows. She had caught the point easily enough, but she felt no deception in keeping her face blank and immature because that was the way Mister Bilderbach wanted her to look.

Yet such things had nothing to do with it. Nothing very much, at least, for she would grow older. Mister Bilderbach understood that, and even Mister Lafkowitz had not meant just what he said.

In the dreams Mister Bilderbach's face loomed out and contracted in the center of the whirling circle. The lips surging softly, the veins in his temples insisting.

But sometimes, before she slept, there were such clear memories; as when she pulled a hole in the heel of her stocking down, so that her shoe would hide it. "Bienchen, Bienchen!" And bringing Mrs. Bilderbach's work basket in and showing her how it should be darned and not gathered together in a lumpy heap.

And the time she graduated from Junior High.

"What you wear?" asked Mrs. Bilderbach the Sunday morning at breakfast when she told them about how they had practiced to march into the auditorium.

"An evening dress my cousin had last year."

"Ah—Bienchen!" he said, circling his warm coffee cup with his heavy hands, looking up at her with wrinkles around his laughing eyes. "I bet I know what Bienchen wants—"

He insisted. He would not believe her when she explained that she honestly didn't care at all.

"Like this, Anna," he said, pushing his napkin across the table and mincing to the other side of the room, swishing his hips, rolling up his eyes behind his horn-rimmed glasses.

The next Saturday afternoon, after her lessons, he took her to the department stores downtown. His thick fingers smoothed over the filmy nets and crackling taffetas that the saleswomen unwound from their bolts. He held colors to her face, cocking his head to one side, and selected pink. Shoes, he remembered too. He liked best some white kid pumps. They seemed a little like old ladies' shoes to her and the Red Cross label in the instep had a charity look. But it really didn't matter at all. When Mrs. Bilderbach began to cut out the dress and fit it to her with pins, he interrupted his lessons to stand by and suggest ruffles around the hips and neck and a fancy rosette on the shoulder. The music was coming along nicely then. Dresses and commencement and such made no difference.

Nothing mattered much except playing the music as it must be played, bringing out the thing that must be in her, practicing, practicing, playing so that Mister Bilderbach's face lost some of its urging look. Putting the thing into her music that Myra Hess had, and Yehudi Menuhin—even Heime!

What had begun to happen to her four months ago? The notes began springing out with a glib, dead intonation. Adolescence, she thought. Some kids played with promise—and worked and worked until, like her, the least little thing would start them crying, and worn out with trying to get the thing across—the longing thing they felt—something queer began to happen—But not she! She was like Heime. She had to be. She——

Once it was there for sure. And you didn't lose things like that. A *Wunderkind*. . . . A *Wunderkind*. . . . Of her he said it, rolling the words in the sure, deep German way. And in the dreams even deeper, more certain than ever. With his face looming out at her, and the longing phrases of music mixed in with the zooming, circling round, round, round—A *Wunderkind.* A *Wunderkind.* . . .

This afternoon Mister Bilderbach did not show Mister Lafkowitz to the front door, as he usually did. He stayed at the piano, softly pressing a solitary note. Listening, Frances watched the violinist wind his scarf about his pale throat.

"A good picture of Heime," she said, picking up her music. "I got a letter from him a couple of months ago—telling about hearing Schnabel and Huberman and about Carnegie Hall and things to eat at the Russian Tea Room."

To put off going into the studio a moment longer she waited until Mister Lafkowitz was ready to leave and then stood behind him as he opened the door. The frosty cold outside cut into the room. It was growing late and the air was seeped with the pale yellow of winter twilight. When the door swung to on its hinges, the house seemed darker and more silent than ever before she had known it to be.

As she went into the studio Mister Bilderbach got up from the piano and silently watched her settle herself at the keyboard.

"Well, Bienchen," he said, "this afternoon we are going to begin all over. Start from scratch. Forget the last few months."

He looked as though he were trying to act a part in a movie. His solid body swayed from toe to heel, he rubbed his hands together, and even smiled in a satisfied, movie way. Then suddenly he thrust this manner brusquely aside. His heavy shoulders slouched and he began to run through the stack of music she had brought in. "The Bach—no, not yet," he murmured. "The Beethoven? Yes. The Variation Sonata. Opus 26."

The keys of the piano hemmed her in—stiff and white and dead-seeming.

"Wait a minute," he said. He stood in the curve of the piano, elbows propped, and looked at her. "Today I expect something from you. Now this sonata—it's the first Beethoven sonata you ever worked on. Every note is under control—technically—you have nothing to cope with but the music. Only music now. That's all you think about."

He rustled through the pages of her volume until he found the place. Then he pulled his teaching chair halfway across the room, turned it around and seated himself, straddling the back with his legs.

For some reason, she knew, this position of his usually had a good effect on her performance. But today she felt that she would notice him from the corner of her eye and be disturbed. His back was stiffly tilted, his legs looked tense. The heavy volume before him seemed to balance dangerously on the chair back. "Now we begin," he said with a peremptory dart of his eyes in her direction.

Her hands rounded over the keys and then sank down. The first notes were too loud, the other phrases followed dryly.

Arrestingly his hand rose up from the score. "Wait! Think a minute what you're playing. How is this beginning marked?"

"*An-andante.*"

"All right. Don't drag it into an *adagio* then. And play deeply into the keys. Don't snatch it off shallowly that way. A graceful, deep-toned *andante*—"

She tried again. Her hands seemed separate from the music that was in her.

"Listen," he interrupted. "Which of these variations dominates the whole?"

"The dirge," she answered.

"Then prepare for that. This is an *andante*—but it's not salon stuff as you just played it. Start out softly, *piano*, and make it swell out just before the arpeggio. Make it warm and dramatic. And down here —where it's marked *dolce* make the counter melody sing out. You know all that. We've gone over all that side of it before. Now play it. Feel it as Beethoven wrote it down. Feel that tragedy and restraint."

She could not stop looking at his hands. They seemed to rest tentatively on the music, ready to fly up as a stop signal as soon as she would begin, the gleaming flash of his ring calling her to halt. "Mister Bilderbach—maybe if I—if you let me play on through the first variation without stopping I could do better."

"I won't interrupt," he said.

Her pale face leaned over too close to the keys. She played through the first part, and, obeying a nod from him, began the second. There were no flaws that jarred on her, but the phrases shaped from her fingers before she had put into them the meaning that she felt.

When she had finished he looked up from the music and began to speak with dull bluntness: "I hardly heard those harmonic fillings in the right hand. And incidentally, this part was supposed to take on intensity, develop the foreshadowings that were supposed to be inherent in the first part. Go on with the next one, though."

She wanted to start it with subdued viciousness and progress to a feeling of deep, swollen sorrow. Her mind told her that. But her hands seemed to gum in the keys like limp macaroni and she could not imagine the music as it should be.

When the last note had stopped vibrating, he closed the book and deliberately got up from the chair. He was moving his lower jaw from side to side—and between his open lips she could glimpse the pink healthy lane to his throat and his strong, smoke-yellowed teeth. He laid the Beethoven gingerly on top of the rest of her music and propped his elbows on the smooth, black piano top once more. "No," he said simply, looking at her.

Her mouth began to quiver. "I can't help it. I—"

Suddenly he strained his lips into a smile. "Listen, Bienchen," he began in a new, forced voice. "You still play the Harmonious Blacksmith, don't you? I told you not to drop it from your repertoire."

"Yes," she said. "I practice it now and then."

His voice was the one he used for children. "It was among the first things we worked on together—remember. So strongly you used to play it—like a real blacksmith's daughter. You see, Bienchen, I know you so well—as if you were my own girl. I know what you have—I've heard you play so many things beautifully. You used to——"

He stopped in confusion and inhaled from his pulpy stub of cigarette. The smoke drowsed out from his pink lips and clung in a gray mist around her lank hair and childish forehead.

"Make it happy and simple," he said, switching on the lamp behind her and stepping back from the piano.

For a moment he stood just inside the bright circle the light made. Then impulsively he squatted down to the floor. "Vigorous," he said.

She could not stop looking at him, sitting on one heel with the other foot resting squarely before him for balance, the muscles of his strong thighs straining under the cloth of his trousers, his back straight, his elbows staunchly propped on his knees. "Simply now," he repeated with a gesture of his fleshy hands. "Think of the blacksmith—working out in the sunshine all day. Working easily and undisturbed."

She could not look down at the piano. The light brightened the hairs on the backs of his outspread hands, made the lenses of his glasses glitter.

"All of it," he urged. "Now!"

She felt that the marrows of her bones were hollow and there was no blood left in her. Her heart that had been springing against her chest all afternoon felt suddenly dead. She saw it gray and limp and shriveled at the edges like an oyster.

His face seemed to throb out in space before her, come closer with the lurching motion in the veins of his temples. In retreat, she looked down at the piano. Her lips shook like jelly and a surge of noiseless tears made the white keys blur in a watery line. "I can't," she whispered. "I don't know why, but I just can't—can't any more."

His tense body slackened and, holding his hand to his side, he pulled himself up. She clutched her music and hurried past him.

Her coat. The mittens and galoshes. The schoolbooks and the satchel he had given her on her birthday. All from the silent room that was hers. Quickly—before he would have to speak.

As she passed through the vestibule she could not help but see his hands—held out from his body that leaned against the studio door, relaxed and purposeless. The door shut to firmly. Dragging her books and satchel she stumbled down the stone steps, turned in the wrong direction, and hurried down the street that had become confused with noise and bicycles and the games of other children.

by Herbert Gold

SUSANNA AT THE BEACH

Herbert Gold was born in Cleveland, Ohio, on March 9, 1924. He holds an M.A. from Columbia University and has studied as a Fulbright scholar at the Sorbonne. His first novel, Birth of a Hero, *appeared in 1951; he has published another almost every second year since then.* Love and Like, *the collection of his stories in which "Susanna at the Beach" appears, came out in 1960. Mr. Gold has received a Guggenheim fellowship and an award from the National Institute of Arts and Letters. In 1962 he published a collection of essays,* The Age of Happy Problems.

Mr. Gold tells us that "Susanna at the Beach" was the result of "that spasmodic impulse which grips the short story writer—find the truth by finding the meaning of childhood." The truth he finds is characterized by the girl's repeated and singular effort to perfect a graceful dive without regard for "the oily, brackish, waste-ridden" water or the sly obscenities of those around her—the men "with waddling rumps in dank wool," "the veiny old men." As the exercise involves her totally, this rite of penance—for the "sin" of innocence—becomes a hymn to her own sufficiency.

FIRST came the girl. Then one fat man idly floated beside a friend in the water, lolling on his back, spitting, his great trunk rolling in the pleasure of himself. He liked to watch the girl while taking his pleasure.

Finally there were the people on shore. These September loiterers, with thin hocks and thick, with waddling rumps in dank wool or tendoned ones in Hawaiian shorts, with itching faces in devotion to sun or a suave glistening under the equivocation of lotion, all of them squinted and winked and finally moved toward her. They strolled, they turned on their heels, or they merely leaned. They came limping over the hot sand like the good wizards in a story.

The girl over whom the old men watched was diving from the end of a breakwater into the oily, brackish, waste-ridden substance of Lake Erie at Cleveland, Ohio. Her arms, deeply tanned, worked firmly; and heated from within, she scrambled up the rocks in haste after her discipline. She had fled all the billboard schemes of the life of a pretty girl. Lips soft and half-parted for a grand design rather than a Lucky Strike, hands taking the measure of ambition rather than the bottle of Coca-Cola, she had come to perfect her diving in a worn black cotton bathing suit which was already too small after her summer's growth. They were simple exercises, but she wanted them to be perfect. She had an idea of how they should be.

The old men, shaking off the sand flies which had multiplied among the refuse so late in the season, looked jealously to the thin cloth which held this girl and to the water which sheathed her. The girl measured the angle of her imagination against the remembered sting of an imperfect arc. Clean! she had prayed, but her worried brow was reporting, *No, another flop*. The black cloth gleamed in the wet. The droplets of water peeled down her body like broken beads as she climbed to try it again. The smile at the corners of her mouth was a promise to herself: Well! This time, then. Even in the brief instant of her stretching, a crescent-shaped slope at one shoulder flashed dry in the sunlight.

This time she went in straight and slender with the will of perfection.

It was a Tuesday afternoon, and a day of rare Indian summer heat. Still, only the most faithful had returned to the beach: the athletic grandfathers, white-haired and withered, with an eye for the weather; a student with his American history textbook and the glaze of sun in his face meeting the doze of exposure to knowledge; the kids pretending to fish and the dead shad belly-up at the washline of water on the sand; the occasional amorous ones, asking riddles, fondling each other slyly, their pockets a-jingle with desire and streetcar fare; women from the industrial flats nearby, sitting in housedress to recall, complain, worry, and take a sleepy hour's leisure together. Mostly, however, beneath the roar and thump of road construction on the slope above them, almost in the shadow of the Terminal Tower to the east, there were the old men: the salesman sunning himself with neck reaching out and pants rolled above the knee so that by evening he can look "just like Miami Beach, better even"; the flat-thighed wanderer in a straw hat and red woolen trunks with a white canvas belt, his sinewy breasts hanging—he sat in a patch of seaweed to observe the diver and stroke the sand from between his toes; another, the big-bellied swimmer, now paddling and spewing water, shaggily emerged onto the pier in order to get nearer to the girl. His friend accompanied him. Hairy-chested loungers, old-time beaux, their bodies both wasted and swollen, they joined the rest of the men along the breakwater. They watched the girl still diving, still climbing; her deep breathing pressed the erect buds of her adolescence against sleek black cloth, she rocked once on her toes, and then off she sprang.

This girl used herself hard, used her lightness hard; and each man there, turning to her from the beach or the pier, thought it a pity. A waste—her sufficiency unto herself silenced and saddened them and made their arms hang tensely forward. Challenged, they turned up the cards of their own sorts of sufficiencies.

The fat swimmer, swirls of hair on his belly and back, was now switching himself with a green branch as he talked business with his friend. They both studied the girl, and their discussion grew lyrical. They talked business and public affairs. He was saying: "You're John-cue Smith, let's put it, you want to get married—"

"I know! Got the taxes to pay, the down payments, the terms—"

"Yes, that's what I mean, to get ahead in life. The installments."

"I got the cost of living these days, Freddy."

"You got the government."

"Yes, Freddy, I got the taxes, yes—"

"The essentials of life."

"Yes, yes, all of that, yes"—and they both shook their heads mournfully and let their mouths fall open while the tips of the girl's feet, propelled by her dive, wriggled above water as she swam.

"Like to bite off a piece of that one, eh Freddy?"

"I saw it first, me, you want to say I didn't?"

A policeman on horseback looked for purse-snatching, nuisance-making, or drunkenness. Overhead, a pontooned airplane swooped low and up. The traffic rushed past the stillness of sun and beach and water, while, out on the lake, a single leaning sailboat, a visitor from the Clifton Club, kept its distance.

Two women, equipped for conversation with quart bottles of cherry pop, their dresses pulled over their knees and their stockings rolled down to their ankles, agreed on questions of mortality, bereavement, and the pleasures of a city beach. They sat on a log stripped by water and shaded their eyes first toward the industrial flats from which they had emerged, then over the lake and into the horizon and beyond. "My mama she die when she eighty-four," said the tanned younger one. "Just like baby, like new kid, she need milk to drink."

"Yah," sighed her friend, a fat and weary woman with concentric rings of flesh about her eyes. "Look that American girlie on the board, what she think? She hurt herself like that."

"She not able my mother care for herself or nothing."

"I know, dear."

"She die like so—sssst—after long life. She work hard."

"I *know*, dear."

"It ain't right, is it?" She nodded once, decisively, and said, "My father he still strong and smoke big cigar I buy for him. He sleep with woman and give her money and everything. Ain't nice old man like that. He make eye at every young girl—"

"Bad young girlie," said the plump woman to the sand, the water, and the figure now climbing back onto the rocks.

The tanned one pulled at her dress and said, "That's why, here in this country, many people go off on roof for fall down. My children all go away to Detroit and *I* give money to my papa."

"No justice on earth, darling," said the sad plump one.

The girl, the fine diver, went off the rocks again, measuring only with a frown the interior demands of her lonely stunt, absent from the beach on the parapets of ambition. She had scraped the cotton suit on a rock. The small split showed an edge of white breast, the first hard growth of the departure from girlhood. Some of the idlers had gathered in silence on the breakwater to watch her. "You want to tell me no, Freddy? I'm telling *you* no," the fat swimmer insisted.

She did not see them; she had nothing to say to them; her regard was absorbed by the patch of black water and the rules of her skill.

Back on the beach, another immature and pretty girl sat with her feet drawn under her on the sands. No one, not even Freddy, the fat swimmer's friend, gave more than a glance to this one, whose tanned plumpness in stylish knee-length shorts promised an eventual stylish willingness while her profile remained strict, suburban, and pure. Her mother, shriveled to creamed skin rather than casual flesh, squatted like the image of her age by her side, but this was not the reason that the free-ranging eyes of the beach passed over the daughter so lightly. The men sensed that she feared to lie on grass because of disease, dirt, and small animals, that she shuddered at the thought of diving into the tricky, steaming, polluted waters, that despite her prettiness she had put herself apart from the play of caprice, open-mouthed laughter, and the risks of pleasure. "Look at the girl on the pier, the one that's diving again," this cute creature said.

"She's headed for earache, that's for sure," her mother commented with satisfaction. "Maybe she doesn't read the paper and how the water's unsafe. Dangerous for bathing. Full of organisms."

"I'm getting hungry, Mother"—wrinkling her junior-miss nose and hugging herself as her favorite starlet did.

"I *said* we'd stop at the Howard Johnson's."

Meanwhile, the diver scrambled over the rocks, up onto the pier, took three or four mincing, dancing steps, and bent her knees for her renewed essay at a controlled style. Her wide temples glowed pinker and pinker with the blood under her skin and the impact of water. Her innocence—an innocence of lessons—was informed by the heat and by the pressure of her blood which brought her climbing, diving, repeating this gesture again and again past the heaped-up rock. Had she seen them and gone on, it would have spoken for an angry and stubborn pride; but her way was the way of habit, of grace, and of a passionate ignorance, a deep communion with belly-smash on the shore of Lake Erie at Cleveland.

The plump lady from the flats was disturbed. "My doctor say: Playsuit! no stockings! Like that you have no more colds for wintertime. You have upper repertory affection, Doctor Sczymanski say. Neighbor she look at playsuit, close mouth, she say: shame! What can I do, darling?"

"That American girl, *she* have no shame," remarked the tanned woman whose father smoked big cigars. "Everybody is look at her legs"—and they both fell into a musing silence, and looked.

The beach was silent while a skin of complicity tightened like the dry sun about them all. Gradually these visitors to the September sands moved toward the breakwater, each one marvelously hushed because, if they said nothing, it could be presumed to be their habit and their devotion, an abandon to mutism in the heat, a pious thing superior to their daily selves: and thus, if the rip in the girl's suit grew longer, it was not their place to warn her of it. Let each creature hunger for itself alone—Freddy poked his pal to mean this—and thus send only appetite in the pursuit of others. The veiny old men moved fastest.

Within a few moments the beach was almost deserted except for the couple busily twisting and tickling in their well-worn place. The girl sat up with a jerk, spreading sand in an abrupt movement of her thighs, while her friend grinned, saying, "I'm not connerdicting you." He pulled her down again.

The tear in the diver's suit widened; the gash in this black second skin showed, to the fat man, the whiteness of belly, and then, to Freddy's bemusement, the flexing folds of flesh. Just once Freddy saw her fingers feel for the rip, but her body's intelligence calculated on nothing but the demands of perfection, and the thought of care for that clothing which was outside desire did not move further than the impatient, rummaging hand. She did not glance at herself. Turned to her idea, fixed on some inner certainty, she closed the split with her fingers, then forgot it, then let go.

She dived and climbed without liability to the give of cloth or the alteration of her world which Freddy and the big-bellied swimmer brought. She scrambled up dripping, let her eyes roam absently over the tense strollers gathering on the rocks, and dived once more. The pale wetness of her flesh opened to them like a wound under the suit while the girl, if she thought of her body at all, thought only of her skill and of her rehearsals for its sake. She was secure (small splash and ripple) in the exercise of method. She was an expert.

"You trying to tell me no, Freddy?" Behind the fat swimmer and his friend, past the city beach on this September afternoon, the machinery of road construction throbbed and the insect hiss of an afternoon breeze occupied the trees on the slope leading up to the highway past the tables, the shelters, and the park restroom. Because his mouth was dry, the fat man pointed to the girl and whispered, "Lookit." He squeezed the muscles of his friend's arm, thumb and forefinger twanging, and then they both moved forward again. The heat and the effort brought shiny tears to his eyes and a dampness to his forehead. The thickness of his body in swimming trunks, sagging at the middle and the rear, bulging beneath, looked enormous in the sunlight and the intimacy of one leg's motion against the other.

Repetitious, formal, and oblivious, the girl's ambition seemed madness or a mad joke to the watchers. It pleased the fat man; it was a delight to him. He opened his mouth, like a swimmer, and put his tongue sideways to breathe more easily. Freddy—as to him—he could hardly believe it. He wanted to float up an inner tube and go out someplace to think about it.

When she climbed over the rocks once again, the rip widened almost audibly, and still she did not see that her suit was ready to hang in tatters. No one warned her—as we do not warn a madman that he is talking nonsense—but they sighed when she extended her arms for the dive. The fat man sighed. All of them leaned together now, men and women, sharing the girl and sharing each other, waiting for their world's confirmation against the challenge she brought it, an assurance of which they were in need before the return to autumn and the years rapid upon them. A whiteness of breast flashed out, its pink sprouting from the girl's body like a delicate thing nurtured in the dark. But the day was bright and the shadows short. Looking at this tender and abstracted girl, the old Polish woman shivered at her own memories of paleness, of resiliency, of pink colors. The fat man, too, partook of their communion, frowning darkly, the green branch switching at his flanks, his knees slightly bent. He pinched his friend instead of himself. Now, her hair flat on her head and the flush of pleasure high on her cheeks after the repeated slap of her forehead against water, the girl was diving in a diminished rhythm, worn out but blind to risk, finished but unable to stop. The moment when her breast and belly slipped by the surface was the fat man's favorite.

The diver, that object for the vindictive imaginations of old men and old women, seemed to pause to acknowledge their study of her, but saw nothing, saw nothing again, and went on. The fat man's eyelids had dropped. He was moved. As she climbed, dripping and critical, bewitched by mastery of her body, feeling, if the presence of the others had come through to her at all, only a reward of praise earned through the long summer, the fat man released his friend's arm to break the silence at last with a shrill whoop. Then the old Polish woman screamed, "You're nekked, girlie! *Nekked!*"

The fat man, his friend, the salesman, the student, many of them were now yelling their cheers at her. Poised for her dive, she must suddenly have seen them and seen herself in their sight. Her look was one of incredulity. Her eyes turned from herself to their shouting, gaping, heavy-tongued mouths and back to the loose cloth dangling from straps. She did not speak. She turned her face from them. Its stern and peaceful determination hardly altered. Then suddenly the extended arms flashed down: she ran, she did not dive, she jumped and rolled into the oily water. Despite this folding upon herself, their eyes searched out a glimpse of sunlit flesh, white and pink and tender. While the crowd applauded, the student shouted, "She wants to drown herself," and leaped into the water.

"I'll get her! Me too! *Me!*"

The young man reached for her hair and only touched it before she wrenched free. She doubled under, holding herself, and then she was swimming. The crowd was roaring. Four, five, six of the men had pushed to the edge of the breakwater. The girl kicked forward and swam with short, quick, sure strokes, straight out into the lake, while a cluster of young men and old, their smiles strict in pursuit, tumbled down the rocks to be first to catch her. The fat man, paddling furiously, was ahead of Freddy. The righteousness of a mob's laughter urged them to be swift, but the girl was very strong, very skillful, gifted, and encumbered by nothing but her single thought.

by F. Scott Fitzgerald

THE FRESHEST BOY

F. Scott Fitzgerald was born on September 24, 1896, in St. Paul, Minnesota, and was educated at private schools in the East. After four years at Princeton he left without a degree to join the army as an infantry officer. For a short time after the war he worked in an advertising agency. In 1920, the year in which his first and very successful novel, This Side of Paradise, *was published, Fitzgerald married Zelda Sayre. During the twenties they lived on Long Island and the Riviera while Fitzgerald wrote* The Beautiful and the Damned *(1921),* The Great Gatsby *(1925), justly regarded as an American classic, and the short stories collected in* Flappers and Philosophers *(1921),* Tales of the Jazz Age *(1922), and* All the Sad Young Men *(1926). At the end of the decade his wife suffered a severe mental breakdown from which she never fully recovered. In 1934 he published* Tender Is the Night, *in some ways his most ambitious work. Fitzgerald worked unhappily as a script writer in Hollywood from 1937 until his death on December 12, 1940, at the age of forty-four.* The Last Tycoon, *on which he was working at the time of his death, appeared in 1941.*

In "The Freshest Boy" Basil Lee escapes the facts of his failure by daydreaming. When his dreams turn real, when, quite literally, his stars descend to a tea room, he realizes that life for everybody is "a struggle, sometimes magnificent from a distance, but always difficult and surprisingly simple and a little sad." Not unlike the rest of us, he comes to "the point of brightest light."

IT was a hidden Broadway restaurant in the dead of the night, and a brilliant and mysterious group of society people, diplomats and members of the underworld were there. A few minutes ago the sparkling wine had been flowing and a girl had been dancing gaily upon a table, but now the whole crowd were hushed and breathless. All eyes were fixed upon the masked but well-groomed man in the dress suit and opera hat who stood nonchalantly in the door.

"Don't move, please," he said, in a well-bred, cultivated voice that had, nevertheless, a ring of steel in it. "This thing in my hand might—go off."

His glance roved from table to table—fell upon the malignant man higher up with his pale saturnine face, upon Heatherly, the suave secret agent from a foreign power, then rested a little longer, a little more softly perhaps, upon the table where the girl with dark hair and dark tragic eyes sat alone.

"Now that my purpose is accomplished, it might interest you to know who I am." There was a gleam of expectation in every eye. The breast of the dark-eyed girl heaved faintly and a tiny burst of subtle French perfume rose into the air. "I am none other than that elusive gentleman, Basil Lee, better known as the Shadow."

Taking off his well-fitting opera hat, he bowed ironically from the waist. Then, like a flash, he turned and was gone into the night.

"You get up to New York only once a month," Lewis Crum was saying, "and then you have to take a master along."

Slowly, Basil Lee's glazed eyes returned from the barns and billboards of the Indiana countryside to the interior of the Broadway Limited. The hypnosis of the swift telegraph poles faded and Lewis Crum's stolid face took shape against the white slip-cover of the opposite bench.

"I'd just duck the master when I got to New York," said Basil.

"Yes, you would!"

"I bet I would."

"You try it and you'll see."

"What do you mean saying I'll see, all the time, Lewis? What'll I see?"

His very bright dark-blue eyes were at this moment fixed upon his companion with boredom and impatience. The two had nothing in common except their age, which was fifteen, and the lifelong friendship of their fathers—which is less than nothing. Also they were bound from the same Middle-Western city for Basil's first and Lewis' second year at the same Eastern school.

But, contrary to all the best tradition, Lewis the veteran was miserable and Basil the neophyte was happy. Lewis hated school. He had grown entirely dependent on the stimulus of a hearty vital mother, and as he felt her slipping farther and farther away from him, he plunged deeper into misery and homesickness. Basil, on the other hand, had lived with such intensity on so many stories of boarding-school life that, far from being homesick, he had a glad feeling of recognition and familiarity. Indeed, it was with some sense of doing the appropriate thing, having the traditional rough-house, that he had thrown Lewis' comb off the train at Milwaukee last night for no reason at all.

To Lewis, Basil's ignorant enthusiasm was distasteful—his instinctive attempt to dampen it had contributed to the mutual irritation.

"I'll tell you what you'll see," he said ominously. "They'll catch you smoking and put you on bounds."

"No, they won't, because I won't be smoking. I'll be training for football."

"Football! Yeah! Football!"

"Honestly, Lewis, you don't like anything, do you?"

"I don't like football. I don't like to go out and get a crack in the eye." Lewis spoke aggressively, for his mother had canonized all his timidities as common sense. Basil's answer, made with what he considered kindly intent, was the sort of remark that creates lifelong enmities.

"You'd probably be a lot more popular in school if you played football," he suggested patronizingly.

Lewis did not consider himself unpopular. He did not think of it in that way at all. He was astounded.

"You wait!" he cried furiously. "They'll take all that freshness out of you."

"Clam yourself." said Basil, coolly plucking at the creases of his first long trousers. "Just clam yourself."

"I guess everybody knows you were the freshest boy at Country Day!"

"Clam yourself," repeated Basil, but with less assurance. "Kindly clam yourself."

"I guess I know what they had in the school paper about you——"

Basil's own coolness was no longer perceptible.

"If you don't clam yourself," he said darkly, "I'm going to throw your brushes off the train too."

The enormity of this threat was effective. Lewis sank back in his seat, snorting and muttering, but undoubtedly calmer. His reference had been to one of the most shameful passages in his companion's life. In a periodical issued by the boys of Basil's late school there had appeared, under the heading Personals:

If someone will please poison young Basil, or find some other means to stop his mouth, the school at large and myself will be much obliged.

The two boys sat there fuming wordlessly at each other. Then, resolutely, Basil tried to reinter this unfortunate souvenir of the past. All that was behind him now. Perhaps he had been a little fresh, but he was making a new start. After a moment, the memory passed and with it the train and Lewis' dismal presence—the breath of the East came sweeping over him again with a vast nostalgia. A voice called him out of the fabled world; a man stood beside him with a hand on his sweater-clad shoulder.

"Lee!"

"Yes, sir."

"It all depends on you now. Understand?"

"Yes, sir."

"All right," the coach said, "go in and win."

Basil tore the sweater from his stripling form and dashed out on the field. There were two minutes to play and the score was 3 to 0 for the enemy, but at the sight of young Lee, kept out of the game all year by a malicious plan of Dan Haskins, the school bully, and Weasel Weems, his toady, a thrill of hope went over the St. Regis stand.

"33-12-16-22!" barked Midget Brown, the diminutive little quarter-back.

"Oh, gosh!" Basil spoke aloud, forgetting the late unpleasantness. "I wish we'd get there before tomorrow."

St. Regis School, Eastchester,
November 18, 19——

Dear Mother: There is not much to say today, but I thought I would write you about my allowance. All the boys have a bigger allowance than me, because there are a lot of little things I have to get, such as shoe laces etc. School is still very nice and am having a fine time, but football is over and there is not much to do. I am going to New York this week to see a show. I do not know yet what it will be, but probably the Quacker Girl or little boy Blue as they are both very good. Dr. Bacon is very nice and there is a good phycission in the village. No more now as I have to study Algebra.

Your Affectionate Son,

BASIL D. LEE.

As he put the letter in its envelope, a wizened little boy came into the deserted study hall where he sat and stood staring at him.

"Hello," said Basil, frowning.

"I been looking for you," said the little boy, slowly and judicially. "I looked all over—up in your room and out in the gym, and they said you probably might of sneaked off in here."

"What do you want?" Basil demanded.

"Hold your horses, Bossy."

Basil jumped to his feet. The little boy retreated a step.

"Go on, hit me!" he chirped nervously. "Go on, hit me, cause I'm just half your size—Bossy."

Basil winced. "You call me that again and I'll spank you."

"No, you won't spank me. Brick Wales said if you ever touched any of us——"

"But I never did touch any of you."

"Didn't you chase a lot of us one day and didn't Brick Wales——"

"Oh, what do you want?" Basil cried in desperation.

"Doctor Bacon wants you. They sent me after you and somebody said maybe you sneaked in here."

Basil dropped his letter in his pocket and walked out—the little boy and his invective following him through the door. He traversed a long corridor, muggy with that odor best described as the smell of stale caramels that is so peculiar to boys' schools, ascended a stairs and knocked at an unexceptional but formidable door.

Doctor Bacon was at his desk. He was a handsome, red-headed Episcopal clergyman of fifty whose original real interest in boys was now tempered by the flustered cynicism which is the fate of all headmasters and settles on them like green mould. There were certain preliminaries before Basil was asked to sit down—gold-rimmed glasses had to be hoisted up from nowhere by a black cord and fixed on Basil to be sure that he was not an impostor; great masses of paper on the desk had to be shuffled through, not in search of anything but as a man nervously shuffles a pack of cards.

"I had a letter from your mother this morning—ah—Basil." The use of his first name had come to startle Basil. No one else in school had yet called him anything but Bossy or Lee. "She feels that your marks have been poor. I believe you have been sent here at a certain amount of—ah—sacrifice and she expects——"

Basil's spirit writhed with shame, not at his poor marks but that his financial inadequacy should be so bluntly stated. He knew that he was one of the poorest boys in a rich boys' school.

Perhaps some dormant sensibility in Doctor Bacon became aware of his discomfort; he shuffled through the papers once more and began on a new note.

"However, that was not what I sent for you about this afternoon. You applied last week for permission to go to New York on Saturday, to a matinée. Mr. Davis tells me that for almost the first time since school opened you will be off bounds tomorrow."

"Yes, sir."

"That is not a good record. However, I would allow you to go to New York if it could be arranged. Unfortunately, no masters are available this Saturday."

Basil's mouth dropped ajar. "Why, I—why, Doctor Bacon, I know two parties that are going. Couldn't I go with one of them?"

Doctor Bacon ran through all his papers very quickly. "Unfortunately, one is composed of slightly older boys and the other group made arrangements some weeks ago."

"How about the party that's going to the Quaker Girl with Mr. Dunn?"

"It's that party I speak of. They feel that their arrangements are complete and they have purchased seats together."

Suddenly Basil understood. At the look in his eye Doctor Bacon went on hurriedly:

"There's perhaps one thing I can do. Of course there must be several boys in the party so that the expenses of the master can be divided up among all. If you can find two other boys who would like to make up a party, and let me have their names by five o'clock, I'll send Mr. Rooney with you."

"Thank you," Basil said.

Doctor Bacon hesitated. Beneath the cynical incrustations of many years an instinct stirred to look into the unusual case of this boy and find out what made him the most detested boy in school. Among boys and masters there seemed to exist an extraordinary hostility toward him, and though Doctor Bacon had dealt with many sorts of schoolboy crimes, he had neither by himself nor with the aid of trusted sixth-formers been able to lay his hands on its underlying cause. It was probably no single thing, but a combination of things; it was most probably one of those intangible questions of personality. Yet he remembered that when he first saw Basil he had considered him unusually prepossessing.

He sighed. Sometimes these things worked themselves out. He wasn't one to rush in clumsily. "Let us have a better report to send home next month, Basil."

"Yes, sir."

Basil ran quickly downstairs to the recreation room. It was Wednesday and most of the boys had already gone into the village of Eastchester, whither Basil, who was still on bounds, was forbidden to follow. When he looked at those still scattered about the pool tables and piano, he saw that it was going to be difficult to get anyone to go with him at all. For Basil was quite conscious that he was the most unpopular boy at school.

It had begun almost immediately. One day, less than a fortnight after he came, a crowd of the smaller boys, perhaps urged on to it, gathered suddenly around him and began calling him Bossy. Within the next week he had two fights, and both times the crowd was vehemently and eloquently with the other boy. Soon after, when he was merely shoving indiscriminatively, like every one else, to get into the dining room, Carver, the captain of the football team, turned about and, seizing him by the back of the neck, held him and dressed him down savagely. He joined a group innocently at the piano and was told, "Go on away. We don't want you around."

After a month he began to realize the full extent of his unpopularity. It shocked him. One day after a particularly bitter humiliation he went up to his room and cried. He tried to keep out of the way for a while, but it didn't help. He was accused of sneaking off here and there, as if bent on a series of nefarious errands. Puzzled and wretched, he looked at his face in the glass, trying to discover there the secret of their dislike—in the expression of his eyes, his smile.

He saw now that in certain ways he had erred at the outset—he had boasted, he had been considered yellow at football, he had pointed out people's mistakes to them, he had shown off his rather extraordinary fund of general information in class. But he had tried to do better and couldn't understand his failure to atone. It must be too late. He was queered forever.

He had, indeed, become the scapegoat, the immediate villain, the sponge which absorbed all malice and irritability abroad—just as the most frightened person in a party seems to absorb all the others' fear, seems to be afraid for them all. His situation was not helped by the fact, obvious to all, that the supreme self-confidence with which he had come to St. Regis in September was thoroughly broken. Boys taunted him with impunity who would not have dared raise their voices to him several months before.

This trip to New York had come to mean everything to him—surcease from the misery of his daily life as well as a glimpse into the long-awaited heaven of romance. Its postponement for week after week due to his sins—he was constantly caught reading after lights, for example, driven by his wretchedness into such vicarious escapes from reality—had deepened his longing until it was a burning hunger. It was unbearable that he should not go, and he told over the short list of those whom he might get to accompany him. The possibilities were Fat Gaspar, Treadway and Bugs Brown. A quick journey to their rooms showed that they had all availed themselves of the Wednesday permission to go into Eastchester for the afternoon.

Basil did not hesitate. He had until five o'clock and his only chance was to go after them. It was not the first time he had broken bounds, though the last attempt had ended in disaster and an extension of his confinement. In his room, he put on a heavy sweater—an overcoat was a betrayal of intent—replaced his jacket over it and hid a cap in his back pocket. Then he went downstairs and with an elaborately careless whistle struck out across the lawn for the gymnasium. Once there, he stood for a while as if looking in the windows, first the one close to the walk, then one near the corner of the building. From here he moved quickly, but not too quickly, into a grove of lilacs. Then he dashed around the corner, down a long stretch of lawn that was blind from all windows and, parting the strands of a wire fence, crawled through and stood upon the grounds of a neighboring estate. For the moment he was free. He put on his cap against the chilly November wind, and set out along the half-mile road to town.

Eastchester was a suburban farming community, with a small

shoe factory. The institutions which pandered to the factory workers were the ones patronized by the boys—a movie house, a quick-lunch wagon on wheels known as the Dog and the Bostonian Candy Kitchen. Basil tried the Dog first and happened immediately upon a prospect.

This was Bugs Brown, a hysterical boy, subject to fits and strenuously avoided. Years later he became a brilliant lawyer, but at that time he was considered by the boys of St. Regis to be a typical lunatic because of his peculiar series of sounds with which he assuaged his nervousness all day long.

He consorted with boys younger than himself, who were without the prejudices of their elders, and was in the company of several when Basil came in.

"Who-ee!" he cried. "Ee-ee-ee!" He put his hand over his mouth and bounced it quickly, making a wah-wah-wah sound. "It's Bossy Lee! It's Bossy Lee! It's Boss-Boss-Boss-Bossy Lee!"

"Wait a minute, Bugs," said Basil anxiously, half afraid that Bugs would go finally crazy before he could persuade him to come to town. "Say, Bugs, listen. Don't, Bugs—wait a minute. Can you come up to New York Saturday afternoon?"

"Whe-ee-ee!" cried Bugs to Basil's distress. "Whee-ee-ee!"

"Honestly, Bugs, tell me, can you? We could go up together if you could go."

"I've got to see a doctor," said Bugs, suddenly calm. "He wants to see how crazy I am."

"Can't you have him see about it some other day?" said Basil without humor.

"Whee-ee-ee!" cried Bugs.

"All right then," said Basil hastily. "Have you seen Fat Gasper in town?"

Bugs was lost in a shrill noise, but someone had seen Fat; Basil was directed to the Bostonian Candy Kitchen.

This was a gaudy paradise of cheap sugar. Its odor, heavy and sickly and calculated to bring out a sticky sweat upon an adult's palms, hung suffocating over the whole vicinity and met one like a strong moral dissuasion at the door. Inside, beneath a pattern of flies, material as black point lace, a line of boys sat eating heavy dinners of banana splits, maple nut and chocolate marshmallow nut sundaes. Basil found Fat Gaspar at a table on the side.

Fat Gaspar was at once Basil's most unlikely and most ambitious quest. He was considered a nice fellow—in fact he was so pleasant that he had been courteous to Basil and had spoken to him politely all fall. Basil realized that he was like that to everyone, yet it was just possible that Fat liked him, as people used to in the past, and he was driven desperately to take a chance. But it was undoubtedly a presumption, and as he approached the table and saw the stiffened faces which the other two boys turned toward him, Basil's hope diminished.

"Say, Fat——" he said, and hesitated. Then he burst forth suddenly. "I'm on bounds, but I ran off because I had to see you. Doctor Bacon told me I could go to New York Saturday if I could get two other boys to go. I asked Bugs Brown and he couldn't go, and I thought I'd ask you."

He broke off, furiously embarrassed, and waited. Suddenly the two boys with Fat burst into a shout of laughter.

"Bugs wasn't crazy enough!"

Fat Gaspar hesitated. He couldn't go to New York Saturday and ordinarily he would have refused without offending. He had nothing against Basil; nor, indeed, against anybody; but boys have only a certain resistance to public opinion and he was influenced by the contemptuous laughter of the others.

"I don't want to go," he said indifferently. "Why do you want to ask *me*?"

Then, half in shame, he gave a deprecatory little laugh and bent over his ice cream.

"I just thought I'd ask you," said Basil.

Turning quickly away, he went to the counter and in a hollow and unfamiliar voice ordered a strawberry sundae. He ate it mechanically, hearing occasional whispers and snickers from the table behind. Still in a daze, he started to walk out without paying his check, but the clerk called him back and he was conscious of more derisive laughter.

For a moment he hesitated whether to go back to the table and hit one of those boys in the face, but he saw nothing to be gained. They would say the truth—that he had done it because he couldn't get anybody to go to New York. Clenching his fists with impotent rage, he walked from the store.

He came immediately upon his third prospect, Treadway. Treadway had entered St. Regis late in the year and had been put in to room with Basil the week before. The fact that Treadway hadn't witnessed his humiliations of the autumn encouraged Basil to behave naturally toward him, and their relations had been, if not intimate, at least tranquil.

"Hey, Treadway," he cried, still excited from the affair in the Bostonian, "can you come up to New York to a show Saturday afternoon?"

He stopped, realizing that Treadway was in the company of Brick Wales, a boy he had had a fight with and one of his bitterest enemies. Looking from one to the other, Basil saw a look of impatience in Treadway's face and a far-away expression in Brick Wales', and he realized what must have been happening. Treadway, making his way into the life of the school, had just been enlightened as to the status of his roommate. Like Fat Gaspar, rather than acknowledge himself eligible to such an intimate request, he preferred to cut their friendly relations short.

"Not on your life," he said briefly. "So long." The two walked past him into the candy kitchen.

Had these slights, so much the bitterer for their lack of passion, been visited upon Basil in September, they would have been unbearable. But since then he had developed a shell of hardness which, while it did not add to his attractiveness, spared him certain delicacies of torture. In misery enough, and despair and self-pity, he went the other way along the street for a little distance until he could control the violent contortions of his face. Then, taking a roundabout route, he started back to school.

He reached the adjoining estate, intending to go back the way he had come. Half-way through a hedge, he heard foot-steps approaching along the sidewalk and stood motionless, fearing the proximity of masters. Their voices grew nearer and louder; before he knew it he was listening with horrified fascination:

"—so, after he tried Bugs Brown, the poor nut asked Fat Gaspar to go with him and Fat said, 'What do you ask me for?' It serves him right if he couldn't get anybody at all."

It was the dismal but triumphant voice of Lewis Crum.

Up in his room, Basil found a package lying on his bed. He knew its contents and for a long time he had been eagerly expecting it, but such was his depression that he opened it listlessly. It was a series of eight color reproductions of Harrison Fisher girls "on glossy paper, without printing or advertising matter and suitable for framing."

The pictures were named Dora, Marguerite, Babette, Lucille,

Gretchen, Rose, Katherine and Mina. Two of them—Marguerite and Rose—Basil looked at, slowly tore up and dropped in the wastebasket, as one who disposes of the inferior pups from a litter. The other six he pinned at intervals around the room. Then he lay down on his bed and regarded them.

Dora, Lucille and Katherine were blond; Gretchen was medium; Babette and Mina were dark. After a few minutes, he found that he was looking oftenest at Dora and Babette and, to a lesser extent, at Gretchen, though the latter's Dutch cap seemed unromantic and precluded the element of mystery. Babette, a dark little violet-eyed beauty in a tight-fitting hat, attracted him most; his eyes came to rest on her at last.

"Babette," he whispered to himself—"beautiful Babette."

The sound of the word, so melancholy and suggestive, like "Velia" or "I'm going to Maxim's" on the phonograph, softened him and, turning over on his face, he sobbed into the pillow. He took hold of the bed rails over his head and, sobbing and straining, began to talk to himself brokenly—how he hated them and whom he hated—he listed a dozen—and what he would do to them when he was great and powerful. In previous moments like these he had always rewarded Fat Gaspar for his kindness, but now he was like the rest. Basil set upon him, pummelling him unmercifully, or laughed sneeringly when he passed him blind and begging on the street.

He controlled himself as he heard Treadway come in, but did not move or speak. He listened as the other moved about the room, and after a while became conscious that there was an unusual opening of closets and bureau drawers. Basil turned over, his arm concealing his tear-stained face. Treadway had an armful of shirts in his hand.

"What are you doing?" Basil demanded.

His roommate looked at him stonily. "I'm moving in with Wales," he said.

"Oh!"

Treadway went on with his packing. He carried out a suitcase full, then another, took down some pennants and dragged his trunk into the hall. Basil watched him bundle his toilet things into a towel and take one last survey about the room's new barrenness to see if there was anything forgotten.

"Good-by," he said to Basil, without a ripple of expression on his face.

"Good-by."

Treadway went out. Basil turned over once more and choked into the pillow.

"Oh, poor Babette!" he cried huskily. "Poor little Babette! Poor little Babette!"

Babette, svelte and piquant, looked down at him coquettishly from the wall.

Doctor Bacon, sensing Basil's predicament and perhaps the extremity of his misery, arranged it that he should go into New York, after all. He went in the company of Mr. Rooney, the football coach and history teacher. At twenty Mr. Rooney had hesitated for some time between joining the police force and having his way paid through a small New England college; in fact he was a hard specimen and Doctor Bacon was planning to get rid of him at Christmas. Mr. Rooney's contempt for Basil was founded on the latter's ambiguous and unreliable conduct on the football field during the past season—he had consented to take him to New York for reasons of his own.

Basil sat meekly beside him on the train, glancing past Mr. Rooney's bulky body at the Sound and the fallow fields of Westchester County. Mr. Rooney finished his newspaper, folded it up and sank into a moody silence. He had eaten a large breakfast and the exigencies of time had not allowed him to work it off with exercise. He remembered that Basil was a fresh boy, and it was time he did something fresh and could be called to account. This reproachless silence annoyed him.

"Lee," he said suddenly, with a thinly assumed air of friendly interest, "why don't you get wise to yourself?"

"What, sir?" Basil was startled from his excited trance of this morning.

"I said why don't you get wise to yourself?" said Mr. Rooney in a somewhat violent tone. "Do you want to be the butt of the school all your time here?"

"No, I don't," Basil was chilled. Couldn't all this be left behind for just one day?

"You oughtn't to get so fresh all the time. A couple of times in history class I could just about have broken your neck." Basil could think of no appropriate answer. "Then out playing football," continued Mr. Rooney "—you didn't have any nerve. You could play better than a lot of 'em when you wanted, like that day against the Pomfret seconds, but you lost your nerve."

"I shouldn't have tried for the second team," said Basil. "I was too light. I should have stayed on the third."

"You were yellow, that was all the trouble. You ought to get wise to yourself. In class, you're always thinking of something else. If you don't study, you'll never get to college."

"I'm the youngest boy in the fifth form," Basil said rashly.

"You think you're pretty bright, don't you?" He eyed Basil ferociously. Then something seemed to occur to him that changed his attitude and they rode for a while in silence. When the train began to run through the thickly clustered communities near New York, he spoke again in a milder voice and with an air of having considered the matter for a long time:

"Lee, I'm going to trust you."

"Yes, sir."

"You go and get some lunch and then go on to your show. I've got some business of my own I got to attend to, and when I've finished I'll try to get to the show. If I can't, I'll anyhow meet you outside."

Basil's heart leaped up. "Yes, sir."

"I don't want you to open your mouth about this at school—I mean, about me doing some business of my own."

"No, sir."

"We'll see if you can keep your mouth shut for once," he said, making it fun. Then he added, on a note of moral sternness. "And no drinks, you understand that?"

"Oh, no, sir!" The idea shocked Basil. He had never tasted a drink, nor even contemplated the possibility, save the intangible and nonalcoholic champagne of his café dreams.

On the advice of Mr. Rooney he went for luncheon to the Manhattan Hotel, near the station, where he ordered a club sandwich, French fried potatoes and a chocolate parfait. Out of the corner of his eye he watched the nonchalant, debonair, blasé New Yorkers at neighboring tables, investing them with a romance by which these possible fellow citizens of his from the Middle West lost nothing. School had fallen from him like a burden; it was no more than an unheeded clamor, faint and far away. He even delayed opening the letter from the morning's mail which he found in his pocket because it was addressed to him at school.

He wanted another chocolate parfait, but being reluctant to bother the busy waiter any more, he opened the letter and spread it before him instead. It was from his mother:

> Dear Basil: This is written in great haste, as I didn't want to frighten you by telegraphing. Grandfather is going abroad to take the waters and he wants you and me to come too. The idea is that you'll go to school at Grenoble or Montreux for the rest of the year and learn the languages and we'll be close by. That is, if you want to. I know how you like St. Regis and playing football and baseball, and of course there would be none of that; but on the other hand, it would be a nice change, even if it postponed your entering Yale by an extra year. So, as usual, I want you to do just as you like. We will be leaving home almost as soon as you get this and will come to the Waldorf in New York, where you can come in and see us for a few days, even if you decide to stay. Think it over, dear.
>
> With love to my dearest boy,
>
> Mother.

Basil got up from his chair with a dim idea of walking over to the Waldorf and having himself locked up safely until his mother came. Then, impelled to some gesture, he raised his voice and in one of his first basso notes called boomingly and without reticence for the waiter. No more St. Regis! No more St. Regis! He was almost strangling with happiness.

"Oh, gosh!" he cried to himself. "Oh, golly! Oh, gosh! Oh, gosh!" No more Doctor Bacon and Mr. Rooney and Brick Wales and Fat Gaspar. No more Bugs Brown and on bounds and being called Bossy. He need no longer hate them, for they were impotent shadows in the stationary world that he was sliding away from, sliding past, waving his hand. "Good-by!" He pitied them. "Good-by!"

It required the din of Forty-second Street to sober his maudlin joy. With his hand on his purse to guard against the omnipresent pickpocket, he moved cautiously toward Broadway. What a day! He would tell Mr. Rooney—Why, he needn't ever go back! Or perhaps it would be better to go back and let them know what he was going to do, while they went on and on in the dismal, dreary round of school.

He found the theatre and entered the lobby with its powdery feminine atmosphere of a matinée. As he took out his ticket, his gaze was caught and held by a sculptured profile a few feet away. It was that of a well-built blond young man of about twenty with a strong chin and direct gray eyes. Basil's brain spun wildly for a moment and then came to rest upon a name—more than a name—upon a legend, a sign in the sky. What a day! He had never seen the young man before, but from a thousand pictures he knew beyond the possibility of a doubt that it was Ted Fay, the Yale football captain, who had almost single-handed beaten Harvard and Princeton last fall. Basil felt a sort of exquisite pain. The profile turned away; the crowd revolved; the hero disappeared. But Basil would know all through the next hours that Ted Fay was here too.

In the rustling, whispering, sweet-smelling darkness of the theatre he read the program. It was the show of all shows that he wanted to see, and until the curtain actually rose the program itself had a curious sacredness—a prototype of the thing itself. But when the curtain rose it became waste paper to be dropped carelessly to the floor.

ACT I. *The Village Green of a Small Town near New York.*

It was too bright and binding to comprehend all at once, and it went so fast that from the very first Basil felt he had missed things; he would make his mother take him again when she came—next week—tomorrow.

An hour passed. It was very sad at this point—a sort of gay sadness, but sad. The girl—the man. What kept them apart even now? Oh, those tragic errors and misconceptions. So sad. Couldn't they look into each other's eyes and *see?*

In a blaze of light and sound, of resolution, anticipation and imminent trouble, the act was over.

He went out. He looked for Ted Fay and thought he saw him leaning rather moodily on the plush wall at the rear of the theatre, but he could not be sure. He bought cigarettes and lit one, but fancying at the first puff that he heard a blare of music he rushed back inside.

ACT II. *The Foyer of the Hotel Astor.*

Yes, she was, indeed, like that song—a Beautiful Rose of the Night. The waltz buoyed her up, brought her with it to a point of aching beauty and then let her slide back to life across its last bars as a leaf slants to earth across the air. The high life of New York! Who could blame her if she was carried away by the glitter of it all, vanishing into the bright morning of the amber window borders, or into distant and entrancing music as the door opened and closed that led to the ballroom? The toast of the shining town.

Half an hour passed. Her true love brought her roses like herself and she threw them scornfully at his feet. She laughed and turned to the other, and danced—danced madly, wildly. Wait! That delicate treble among the thin horns, the low curving note from the great strings. There it was again, poignant and aching, sweeping like a great gust of emotion across the stage, catching her again like a leaf helpless in the wind:

> Rose—Rose—Rose of the night,
> When the spring moon is bright you'll be fair——

A few minutes later, feeling oddly shaken and exalted, Basil drifted outside with the crowd. The first thing upon which his eyes fell was the almost forgotten and now curiously metamorphosed spectre of Mr. Rooney.

Mr. Rooney had, in fact, gone a little to pieces. He was, to begin with, wearing a different and much smaller hat than when he left Basil at noon. Secondly, his face had lost its somewhat gross aspect and turned a pure and even delicate white, and he was wearing his necktie and even portions of his shirt on the outside of his unaccountably wringing-wet overcoat. How, in the short space of four hours, Mr. Rooney had got himself in such shape is explicable only by the pressure of confinement in a boys' school upon a fiery outdoor spirit. Mr. Rooney was born to toil under the clear light of heaven and, perhaps half consciously, he was headed toward his inevitable destiny.

"Lee," he said dimly, "you ought get wise to y'self. I'm going to put you wise y'self."

To avoid the ominous possibility of being put wise to himself in the lobby, Basil uneasily changed the subject.

"Aren't you coming to the show?" he asked, flattering Mr. Rooney by implying that he was in any condition to come to the show. "It's a wonderful show."

Mr. Rooney took off his hat, displaying wringing-wet matted hair. A picture of reality momentarily struggled for development in the back of his brain.

"We got to get back to school," he said in a sombre and unconvinced voice.

"But there's another act," protested Basil in horror. "I've got to stay for the last act."

Swaying, Mr. Rooney looked at Basil, dimly realizing that he had put himself in the hollow of this boy's hand.

"All righ'," he admitted. "I'm going to get somethin' to eat. I'll wait for you next door."

He turned abruptly, reeled a dozen steps and curved dizzily into a bar adjoining the theatre. Considerably shaken, Basil went back inside.

ACT. III. *The Roof Garden of Mr. Van Astor's House. Night.*

Half an hour passed. Everything was going to be all right, after all. The comedian was at his best now, with the glad appropriateness of laughter after tears, and there was a promise of felicity in the bright tropical sky. One lovely plaintive duet, and then abruptly the long moment of incomparable beauty was over.

Basil went into the lobby and stood in thought while the crowd passed out. His mother's letter and the show had cleared his mind of bitterness and vindictiveness—he was his old self and he wanted to do the right thing. He wondered if it was the right thing to get Mr. Rooney back to school. He walked toward the saloon, slowed up as he came to it and, gingerly opening the swinging door, took a quick peek inside. He saw only that Mr. Rooney was not one of those drinking at the bar. He walked down the street a little way, came back and tried again. It was as if he thought the doors were teeth to bite him, for he had the old-fashioned Middle-Western boy's horror of the saloon. The third time he was successful. Mr. Rooney was sound asleep at a table in the back of the room.

Outside again Basil walked up and down, considering. He would give Mr. Rooney half an hour. If, at the end of that time, he had not come out, he would go back to school. After all, Mr. Rooney had laid for him ever since football season—Basil was simply washing his hands of the whole affair, as in a day or so he would wash his hands of school.

He had made several turns up and down, when, glancing up an alley that ran beside the theatre his eye was caught by the sign, Stage Entrance. He could watch the actors come forth.

He waited. Women streamed by him, but those were the days before Glorification and he took these drab people for wardrobe women or something. Then suddenly a girl came out and with her a man, and Basil turned and ran a few steps up the street as if afraid they would recognize him—and ran back, breathing as if with a heart attack—for the girl, a radiant little beauty of nineteen, was Her and the young man by her side was Ted Fay.

Arm in arm, they walked past him, and irresistibly Basil followed. As they walked, she leaned toward Ted Fay in a way that gave them a fascinating air of intimacy. They crossed Broadway and turned into the Knickerbocker Hotel, and twenty feet behind them Basil followed, in time to see them go into a long room set for afternoon tea. They sat at a table for two, spoke vaguely to a waiter, and then, alone at last, bent eagerly toward each other. Basil saw that Ted Fay was holding her gloved hand.

The tea room was separated only by a hedge of potted firs from the main corridor. Basil went along this to a lounge which was almost up against their table and sat down.

Her voice was low and faltering, less certain than it had been in the play, and very sad: "Of course I do, Ted." For a long time, as their conversation continued, she repeated "Of course I do" or "But I do, Ted." Ted Fay's remarks were too low for Basil to hear.

"—says next month, and he won't be put off any more. . . . I do in a way, Ted. It's hard to explain, but he's done everything for mother and me. . . . There's no use kidding myself. It was a foolproof part and any girl he gave it to was made right then and there. . . . He's been awfully thoughtful. He's done everything for me."

Basil's ears were sharpened by the intensity of his emotion; now he could hear Ted Fay's voice too:

"And you say you love me."

"But don't you see I promised to marry him more than a year ago."

"Tell him the truth—that you love me. Ask him to let you off."

"This isn't musical comedy, Ted."

"That was a mean one," he said bitterly.

"I'm sorry, dear, Ted darling, but you're driving me crazy going on this way. You're making it so hard for me."

"I'm going to leave New Haven, anyhow."

"No, you're not. You're going to stay and play baseball this spring. Why, you're an ideal to all those boys! Why, if you——"

He laughed shortly. "You're a fine one to talk about ideals."

"Why not? I'm living up to my responsibility to Beltzman; you've got to make up your mind just like I have—that we can't have each other."

"Jerry! Think what you're doing! All my life, whenever I hear that waltz—"

Basil got to his feet and hurried down the corridor, through the lobby and out of the hotel. He was in a state of wild emotional confusion. He did not understand all he had heard, but from his clandestine glimpse into the privacy of these two, with all the world that his short experience could conceive of at their feet, he had gathered that life for everybody was a struggle, sometimes magnificent from a distance, but always difficult and surprisingly simple and a little sad.

They would go on. Ted Fay would go back to Yale, put her picture in his bureau drawer and knock out home runs with the bases full this spring—at 8:30 the curtain would go up and she would miss something warm and young out of her life, something she had had this afternoon.

It was dark outside and Broadway was a blazing forest fire as Basil walked slowly along toward the point of brightest light. He looked up at the great intersecting planes of radiance with a vague sense of approval and possession. He would see it a lot now, lay his restless heart upon this greater restlessness of a nation—he would come whenever he could get off from school.

But that was all changed—he was going to Europe. Suddenly Basil realized that he wasn't going to Europe. He could not forego the molding of his own destiny just to alleviate a few months of pain. The conquest of the successive worlds of school, college and New York—why, that was his true dream that he had carried from boyhood into adolescence, and because of the jeers of a few boys he had been about to abandon it and run ignominiously up a back alley! He shivered violently, like a dog coming out of the water, and simultaneously he was reminded of Mr. Rooney.

A few minutes later he walked into the bar, past the quizzical eyes of the bartender and up to the table where Mr. Rooney still sat asleep. Basil shook him gently, then firmly. Mr. Rooney stirred and perceived Basil.

"G'wise to yourself," he muttered drowsily. "G'wise to yourself an' let me alone."

"I am wise to myself," said Basil. "Honest, I am wise to myself, Mr. Rooney. You got to come with me into the washroom and get cleaned up, and then you can sleep on the train again, Mr. Rooney. Come on, Mr. Rooney, please—"

It was a long, hard time. Basil got on bounds again in December and wasn't free again until March. An indulgent mother had given him no habits of work and this was almost beyond the power of anything but life itself to remedy, but he made numberless new starts and failed and tried again.

He made friends with a new boy named Maplewood after Christmas, but they had a silly quarrel; and through the winter term, when a boy's school is shut in with itself and only partly assuaged from its natural savagery by indoor sports, Basil was snubbed and slighted a good deal for his real and imaginary sins, and he was much alone. But on the other hand, there was Ted Fay, and Rose of the Night on the phonograph—"All my life whenever I hear that waltz"—and the remembered lights of New York, and the thought of what he was going to do in football next autumn and the glamorous mirage of Yale and the hope of spring in the air.

Fat Gaspar and a few others were nice to him now. Once when he and Fat walked home together by accident from downtown they had a long talk about actresses—a talk that Basil was wise enough not to presume upon afterward. The smaller boys suddenly decided that they approved of him, and a master who had hitherto disliked him put his hand on his shoulder walking to a class one day. They would all forget eventually—maybe during the summer. There would be new fresh boys in September; he would have a clean start next year.

One afternoon in February, playing basketball, a great thing happened. He and Brick Wales were at forward on the second team and in the fury of the scrimmage the gymnasium echoed with sharp slapping contacts and shrill cries.

"Here yar!"

"Bill! Bill!"

Basil had dribbled the ball down the court and Brick Wales, free, was crying for it.

"Here yar! Lee! Hey! Lee-y!"

Lee-y!

Basil flushed and made a poor pass. He had been called by a nickname. It was a poor makeshift, but it was something more than the stark bareness of his surname or a term of derision. Brick Wales went on playing, unconscious that he had done anything in particular or that he had contributed to the events by which another boy was saved from the army of the bitter, the selfish, the neurasthenic and the unhappy. It isn't given to us to know those rare moments when people are wide open and the lightest touch can wither or heal. A moment too late and we can never reach them any more in this world. They will not be cured by our most efficacious drugs or slain with our sharpest swords.

Lee-y! It could scarcely be pronounced. But Basil took it to bed with him that night, and thinking of it, holding it to him happily to the last, fell easily to sleep.

by Katherine Mansfield

THE GARDEN-PARTY

Katherine Mansfield was born on October 14, 1889, at Wellington, New Zealand. When she was fifteen she was sent to London to complete her education at Queen's College, where she edited the college magazine. She showed an early and varied talent: she published her first short story when she was nine, and she was an accomplished cellist at seventeen. In 1918 she married John Middleton Murry and for a time wrote weekly reviews for the Athenaeum, *which he edited. The appearance of* The Garden-Party *(1922), the last of her books to be published during her lifetime, established her reputation as an author. On January 9, 1923, she died of a pulmonary hemorrhage. Since then three more volumes of short stories, a collection of her verse, a volume of her essays, her scrapbook, and her extraordinarily interesting letters and journal have appeared.*

Juxtaposing social gaiety and personal disaster, "The Garden-Party" concerns (as Miss Mansfield once explained) "the diversity of life, and how we fit in everything, Death included." At the time when the story was composed she had been suffering for several years from the disease that was to kill her; she completed the story late at night on October 14, 1921, her birthday—an occasion that is likely to cause anyone to reflect upon his mortality. She believed, too, that the war had brought her generation "a tragic knowledge" of what, quoting Marvell, she called "deserts of vast eternity." She could not, however, "tell anybody bang out *about these deserts: they are my secret." Perhaps this accounts for Laura's hesitant, half-realized attempt at knowledge: " 'Isn't life,' she stammered, 'isn't life——' "*

AND after all the weather was ideal. They could not have had a more perfect day for a garden-party if they had ordered it. Windless, warm, the sky without a cloud. Only the blue was veiled with a haze of light gold, as it is sometimes in early summer. The gardener had been up since dawn, mowing the lawns and sweeping them, until the grass and the dark flat rosettes where the daisy plants had been seemed to shine. As for the roses, you could not help feeling they understood that roses are the only flowers that impress people at garden-parties; the only flowers that everybody is certain of knowing. Hundreds, yes, literally hundreds, had come out in a single night; the green bushes bowed down as though they had been visited by archangels.

Breakfast was not yet over before the men came to put up the marquee.

"Where do you want the marquee put, mother?"

"My dear child, it's no use asking me. I'm determined to leave everything to you children this year. Forget I am your mother. Treat me as an honoured guest."

But Meg could not possibly go and supervise the men. She had washed her hair before breakfast, and she sat drinking her coffee in a green turban, with a dark wet curl stamped on each cheek. Jose, the butterfly, always came down in a silk petticoat and a kimono jacket.

"You'll have to go, Laura; you're the artistic one."

Away Laura flew, still holding her piece of bread-and-butter. It's so delicious to have an excuse for eating out of doors, and besides, she loved having to arrange things; she always felt she could do it so much better than anybody else.

Four men in their shirt-sleeves stood grouped together on the garden path. They carried staves covered with rolls of canvas, and they had big tool-bags slung on their backs. They looked impressive. Laura wished now that she had not got the bread-and-butter, but there was nowhere to put it, and she couldn't possibly throw it away. She blushed and tried to look severe and even a little bit short-sighted as she came up to them.

"Good morning," she said, copying her mother's voice. But that sounded so fearfully affected that she was ashamed, and stammered like a little girl, "Oh—er—have you come—is it about the marquee?"

"That's right, miss," said the tallest of the men, a lanky, freckled fellow, and he shifted his tool-bag, knocked back his straw hat and smiled down at her. "That's about it."

His smile was so easy, so friendly that Laura recovered. What nice eyes he had, small, but such a dark blue! And now she looked at the others, they were smiling too. "Cheer up, we won't bite," their smile seemed to say. How very nice workmen were! And what a beautiful morning! She mustn't mention the morning; she must be business-like. The marquee.

"Well, what about the lily-lawn? Would that do?"

And she pointed to the lily-lawn with the hand that didn't hold the bread-and-butter. They turned, they stared in the direction. A little fat chap thrust out his under-lip, and the tall fellow frowned.

"I don't fancy it," said he. "Not conspicuous enough. You see, with a thing like a marquee," and he turned to Laura in his easy way, "you want to put it somewhere where it'll give you a bang slap in the eye, if you follow me."

Laura's upbringing made her wonder for a moment whether it was quite respectful of a workman to talk to her of bangs slap in the eye. But she did quite follow him.

"A corner of the tennis-court," she suggested. "But the band's going to be in one corner."

"H'm, going to have a band, are you?" said another of the workmen. He was pale. He had a haggard look as his dark eyes scanned the tennis-court. What was he thinking?

"Only a very small band," said Laura gently. Perhaps he wouldn't mind so much if the band was quite small. But the tall fellow interrupted.

"Look here, miss, that's the place. Against those trees. Over there. That'll do fine."

Against the karakas. Then the karaka-trees would be hidden. And they were so lovely, with their broad, gleaming leaves, and their clusters of yellow fruit. They were like trees you imagined growing on a desert island, proud, solitary, lifting their leaves and fruits to the sun in a kind of silent splendour. Must they be hidden by a marquee?

They must. Already the men had shouldered their staves and were making for the place. Only the tall fellow was left. He bent down, pinched a sprig of lavender, put his thumb and forefinger to his nose and snuffed of the smell. When Laura saw that gesture she forgot all about the karakas in her wonder at him caring for things like that—caring for the smell of lavender. How many men that she knew would have done such a thing? Oh, how extraordinarily nice workmen were, she thought. Why couldn't she have workmen for friends rather than the silly boys she danced with and who came to Sunday night supper? She would get on much better with men like these.

It's all the fault, she decided, as the tall fellow drew something on the back of an envelope, something that was to be looped up or left to hang, of these absurd class distinctions. Well, for her part, she didn't feel them. Not a bit, not an atom. . . . And now there came the chock-chock of wooden hammers. Some one whistled, some one sang out, "Are you right there, matey?" "Matey!" The friendliness of it, the— the—— Just to prove how happy she was, just to show the tall fellow how at home she felt, and how she despised stupid conventions, Laura took a big bite of her bread-and-butter as she stared at the little drawing. She felt just like a work-girl.

"Laura, Laura, where are you? Telephone, Laura!" a voice cried from the house.

"Coming!" Away she skimmed, over the lawn, up the path, up the steps, across the veranda, and into the porch. In the hall her father and Laurie were brushing their hats ready to go to the office.

"I say, Laura," said Laurie very fast, "you might just give a squiz at my coat before this afternoon. See if it wants pressing."

"I will," said she. Suddenly she couldn't stop herself. She ran at Laurie and gave him a small, quick squeeze. "Oh, I do love parties, don't you?" gasped Laura.

"Ra-ther," said Laurie's warm, boyish voice, and he squeezed his sister too, and gave her a gentle push. "Dash off to the telephone, old girl."

The telephone. "Yes, yes; oh yes. Kitty? Good morning, dear. Come to lunch? Do, dear. Delighted of course. It will only be a very scratch meal—just the sandwich crusts and broken meringue-shells and what's left over. Yes, isn't it a perfect morning? Your white? Oh, I certainly should. One moment—hold the line. Mother's calling." And Laura sat back. "What, mother? Can't hear."

Mrs. Sheridan's voice floated down the stairs. "Tell her to wear that sweet hat she had on last Sunday."

"Mother says you're to wear that *sweet* hat you had on last Sunday. Good. One o'clock. Bye-bye."

Laura put back the receiver, flung her arms over her head, took a deep breath, stretched and let them fall. "Huh," she sighed, and the moment after the sigh she sat up quickly. She was still, listening. All the doors in the house seemed to be open. The house was alive with soft, quick steps and running voices. The green baize door that led to the kitchen regions swung open and shut with a muffled thud. And now there same a long, chuckling absurd sound. It was the heavy piano being moved on its stiff castors. But the air! If you stopped to notice, was the air always like this? Little faint winds were playing chase, in at the tops of the windows, out at the doors. And there were two tiny spots of sun, one on the inkpot, one on a silver photograph frame, playing too. Darling little spots. Especially the one on the inkpot lid. It was quite warm. A warm little silver star. She could have kissed it.

The front door bell pealed, and there sounded the rustle of Sadie's print skirt on the stairs. A man's voice murmured; Sadie answered, careless, "I'm sure I don't know. Wait. I'll ask Mrs. Sheridan."

"What is it, Sadie?" Laura came into the hall.

"It's the florist, Miss Laura."

It was indeed. There, just inside the door, stood a wide, shallow tray full of pots of pink lilies. No other kind. Nothing but lilies—canna lilies, big pink flowers, wide open, radiant, almost frighteningly alive on bright crimson stems.

"O-oh, Sadie!" said Laura, and the sound was like a little moan. She crouched down as if to warm herself at that blaze of lilies; she felt they were in her fingers, on her lips, growing in her breast.

"It's some mistake," she said faintly. "Nobody ever ordered so many. Sadie, go and find mother."

But at that moment Mrs. Sheridan joined them.

"It's quite right," she said calmly. "Yes, I ordered them. Aren't they lovely?" She pressed Laura's arm. "I was passing the shop yesterday, and I saw them in the window. And I suddenly thought for once in my life I shall have enough canna lilies. The garden-party will be a good excuse."

"But I thought you said you didn't mean to interfere," said Laura. Sadie had gone. The florist's man was still outside at his van. She put her arm round her mother's neck and gently, very gently, she bit her mother's ear.

"My darling child, you wouldn't like a logical mother, would you? Don't do that. Here's the man."

He carried more lilies still, another whole tray.

"Bank them up, just inside the door, on both sides of the porch, please," said Mrs. Sheridan. "Don't you agree, Laura?"

"Oh, I *do*, mother."

In the drawing-room Meg, Jose and good little Hans had at last succeeded in moving the piano.

"Now, if we put this chesterfield against the wall and move everything out of the room except the chairs, don't you think?"

"Quite."

"Hans, move these tables into the smoking-room, and bring a sweeper to take these marks off the carpet and—one moment, Hans——" Jose loved giving orders to the servants, and they loved obeying her. She always made them feel they were taking part in some drama. "Tell mother and Miss Laura to come here at once."

"Very good, Miss Jose."

She turned to Meg. "I want to hear what the piano sounds like, just in case I'm asked to sing this afternoon. Let's try over 'This Life is Weary.' "

Pom! Ta-ta-ta *Tee*-ta! The piano burst out so passionately that Jose's face changed. She clasped her hands. She looked mournfully and enigmatically at her mother and Laura as they came in.

This Life is *Wee*-ary,
A Tear—a Sigh.
A Love that *Chan*-ges,
This Life is *Wee*-ary,
A Tear—a Sigh.
A Love that *Chan*-ges,
And then . . . Good-bye!

But at the word "Good-bye," and although the piano sounded more desperate than ever, her face broke into a brilliant, dreadfully unsympathetic smile.

"Aren't I in good voice, mummy?" she beamed.

This Life is *Wee*-ary,
Hope comes to Die.
A Dream—a *Wa*-kening.

But now Sadie interrupted them. "What is it, Sadie?"

"If you please, m'm, cook says have you got the flags for the sandwiches?"

"The flags for the sandwiches, Sadie?" echoed Mrs. Sheridan dreamily. And the children knew by her face that she hadn't got them. "Let me see." And she said to Sadie firmly, "Tell cook I'll let her have them in ten minutes."

Sadie went.

"Now, Laura," said her mother quickly. "Come with me into the smoking-room. I've got the names somewhere on the back of an envelope. You'll have to write them out for me. Meg, go upstairs this minute and take that wet thing off your head. Jose, run and finish dressing this instant. Do you hear me, children, or shall I have to tell your father when he comes home to-night? And—and, Jose, pacify cook if you do go into the kitchen, will you? I'm terrified of her this morning."

The envelope was found at last behind the dining-room clock, though how it had got there Mrs. Sheridan could not imagine.

"One of you children must have stolen it out of my bag, because I remember vividly—cream cheese and lemon-curd. Have you done that?"

"Yes."

"Egg and——" Mrs. Sheridan held the envelope away from her. "It looks like mice. It can't be mice, can it?"

"Olive, pet," said Laura, looking over her shoulder.

"Yes, of course, olive. What a horrible combination it sounds. Egg and olive."

They were finished at last, and Laura took them off to the kitchen. She found Jose there pacifying the cook, who did not look at all terrifying.

"I have never seen such exquisite sandwiches," said Jose's rapturous voice. "How many kinds did you say there were, cook? Fifteen?"

"Fifteen, Miss Jose."

"Well, cook, I congratulate you."

Cook swept up crusts with the long sandwich knife, and smiled broadly.

"Godber's has come," announced Sadie, issuing out of the pantry. She had seen the man pass the window.

That meant the cream puffs had come. Godber's were famous for their cream puffs. Nobody ever thought of making them at home.

"Bring them in and put them on the table, my girl," ordered cook.

Sadie brought them in and went back to the door. Of course Laura and Jose were far too grown-up to really care about such things. All the same, they couldn't help agreeing that the puffs looked very attractive. Very. Cook began arranging them, shaking off the extra icing sugar.

"Don't they carry one back to all one's parties?" said Laura.

"I supopse they do," said practical Jose, who never liked to be carried back. "They look beautifully light and feathery, I must say."

"Have one each, my dears," said cook in her comfortable voice. "Yer ma won't know."

Oh, impossible. Fancy cream puffs so soon after breakfast. The very idea made one shudder. All the same, two minutes later Jose and Laura were licking their fingers with that absorbed inward look that only comes from whipped cream.

"Let's go into the garden, out by the back way," suggested Laura. "I want to see how the men are getting on with the marquee. They're such awfully nice men."

But the back door was blocked by cook, Sadie, Godber's man and Hans.

Something had happened.

"Tuk-tuk-tuk," clucked cook like an agitated hen. Sadie had her hand clapped to her cheek as though she had toothache. Hans's face was screwed up in the effort to understand. Only Godber's man seemed to be enjoying himself; it was his story.

"What's the matter? What's happened?"

"There's been a horrible accident," said cook. "A man killed."

"A man killed! Where? How? When?"

But Godber's man wasn't going to have his story snatched from under his very nose.

"Know those little cottages just below here, miss?" Know them? Of course, she knew them. "Well, there's a young chap living there, name of Scott, a carter. His horse shied at a traction-engine, corner of Hawke Street this morning, and he was thrown out on the back of his head. Killed."

"Dead!" Laura stared at Godber's man.

"Dead when they picked him up," said Godber's man with relish. "They were taking the body home as I come up here." And he said to the cook, "He's left a wife and five little ones."

"Jose, come here." Laura caught hold of her sister's sleeve and dragged her through the kitchen to the other side of the green baize door. There she paused and leaned against it. "Jose!" she said, horrified, "however are we going to stop everything?"

"Stop everything, Laura!" cried Jose in astonishment. "What do you mean?"

"Stop the garden-party, of course." Why did Jose pretend?

But Jose was still more amazed. "Stop the garden-party? My dear Laura, don't be so absurd. Of course we can't do anything of the kind. Nobody expects us to. Don't be so extravagant."

"But we can't possibly have a garden-party with a man dead just outside the front gate."

That really was extravagant, for the little cottages were in a lane to themselves at the very bottom of a steep rise that led up to the house. A broad road ran between. True, they were far too near. They were the greatest possible eyesore, and they had no right to be in that neighbourhood at all. They were little mean dwellings painted a chocolate brown. In the garden patches there was nothing but cabbage stalks, sick hens and tomato cans. The very smoke coming out of their chimneys was poverty-stricken. Little rags and shreds of smoke, so unlike the great silvery plumes that uncurled from the Sheridans' chimneys. Washerwomen lived in the lane and sweeps and a cobbler, and a man whose house-front was studded all over with minute bird-cages. Children swarmed. When the Sheridans were little they were forbidden to set foot there because of the revolting language and of what they might catch. But since they were grown up, Laura and Laurie on their prowls sometimes walked through. It was disgusting and sordid. They came out with a shudder. But still one must go everywhere; one must see everything. So through they went.

"And just think of what the band would sound like to that poor woman," said Laura.

"Oh, Laura!" Jose began to be seriously annoyed. "If you're going to stop a band playing every time some one has an accident, you'll lead a very strenuous life. I'm every bit as sorry about it as you. I feel just as sympathetic." Her eyes hardened. She looked at her sister just as she used to when they were little and fighting together. "You won't bring a drunken workman back to life by being sentimental," she said softly.

"Drunk! Who said he was drunk?" Laura turned furiously on Jose. She said, just as they had used to say on those occasions, "I'm going straight up to tell mother."

"Do, dear," cooed Jose.

"Mother, can I come into your room?" Laura turned the big glass door-knob.

"Of course, child. Why, what's the matter? What's given you such a colour?" And Mrs. Sheridan turned round from her dressing-table. She was trying on a new hat.

"Mother, a man's been killed," began Laura.

"*Not* in the garden?" interrupted her mother.

"No, no!"

"Oh, what a fright you gave me!" Mrs. Sheridan sighed with relief, and took off the big hat and held it on her knees.

"But listen, mother," said Laura. Breathless, half-choking, she told the dreadful story. "Of course, we can't have our party, can we?" she pleaded. "The band and everybody arriving. They'd hear us, mother; they're nearly neighbours!"

To Laura's astonishment her mother behaved just like Jose; it was harder to bear because she seemed amused. She refused to take Laura seriously.

"But, my dear child, use your common sense. It's only by accident we've heard of it. If some one had died there normally—and I can't understand how they keep alive in those poky little holes—we should still be having our party, shouldn't we?"

Laura had to say "yes" to that, but she felt it was all wrong. She sat down on her mother's sofa and pinched the cushion frill.

"Mother, isn't it really terribly heartless of us?" she asked.

"Darling!" Mrs. Sheridan got up and came over to her, carrying the hat. Before Laura could stop her she had popped it on. "My child!" said her mother, "the hat is yours. It's made for you. It's much too young for me. I have never seen you look such a picture. Look at yourself!" And she held up her hand-mirror.

"But, mother," Laura began again. She couldn't look at herself; she turned aside.

This time Mrs. Sheridan lost patience just as Jose had done.

"You are being very absurd, Laura," she said coldly. "People like that don't expect sacrifices from us. And it's not very sympathetic to spoil everybody's enjoyment as you're doing now."

"I don't understand," said Laura, and she walked quickly out of the room into her own bedroom. There, quite by chance, the first thing she saw was this charming girl in the mirror, in her black hat trimmed with gold daisies, and a long black velvet ribbon. Never had she imagined she could look like that. Is mother right? she thought.

And now she hoped her mother was right. Am I being extravagant? Perhaps it was extravagant. Just for a moment she had another glimpse of that poor woman and those children, and the body being carried into the house. But it all seemed blurred, unreal, like a picture in the newspaper. I'll remember it again after the party's over, she decided. And somehow that seemed quite the best plan. . . .

Lunch was over by half-past one. By half-past two they were all ready for the fray. The green-coated band had arrived and was established in a corner of the tennis-court.

"My dear!" trilled Kitty Maitland, "aren't they too like frogs for words? You ought to have arranged them round the pond with the conductor in the middle on a leaf."

Laurie arrived and hailed them on his way to dress. At the sight of him Laura remembered the accident again. She wanted to tell him. If Laurie agreed with the others, then it was bound to be all right. And she followed him into the hall.

"Laurie!"

"Hallo!" He was half-way upstairs, but when he turned round and saw Laura he suddenly puffed out his cheeks and goggled his eyes at her. "My word, Laura! You do look stunning," said Laurie. "What an absolutely topping hat!"

Laura said faintly "Is it?" and smiled up at Laurie, and didn't tell him after all.

Soon after that people began coming in streams. The band struck up; the hired waiters ran from the house to the marquee. Wherever you looked there were couples strolling, bending to the flowers, greeting, moving on over the lawn. They were like bright birds that had alighted in the Sheridans' garden for this one afternoon, on their way to—where? Ah, what happiness it is to be with people who all are happy, to press hands, press cheeks, smile into eyes.

"Darling Laura, how well you look!"

"What a becoming hat, child!"

"Laura, you look quite Spanish. I've never seen you look so striking."

And Laura, glowing, answered softly, "Have you had tea? Won't you have an ice? The passion-fruit ices really are rather special." She ran to her father and begged him. "Daddy darling, can't the band have something to drink?"

And the perfect afternoon slowly ripened, slowly faded, slowly its petals closed.

"Never a more delightful garden-party . . ." "The greatest success . . ." "Quite the most . . ."

Laura helped her mother with the good-byes. They stood side by side in the porch till it was all over.

"All over, all over, thank heaven," said Mrs. Sheridan. "Round up the others, Laura. Let's go and have some fresh coffee. I'm exhausted. Yes, it's been very successful. But oh, these parties, these parties! Why will you children insist on giving parties!" And they all of them sat down in the deserted marquee.

"Have a sandwich, daddy dear. I wrote the flag."

"Thanks." Mr. Sheridan took a bite and the sandwich was gone. He took another. "I suppose you didn't hear of a beastly accident that happened to-day?" he said.

"My dear," said Mrs. Sheridan, holding up her hand, "we did. It nearly ruined the party. Laura insisted we should put it off."

"Oh, mother!" Laura didn't want to be teased about it.

"It was a horrible affair all the same," said Mr. Sheridan. "The chap was married too. Lived just below in the lane, and leaves a wife and half a dozen kiddies, so they say."

An awkward little silence fell. Mrs. Sheridan fidgeted with her cup. Really, it was very tactless of father . . .

Suddenly she looked up. There on the table were all those sandwiches, cakes, puffs, all uneaten, all going to be wasted. She had one of her brilliant ideas.

"I know," she said. "Let's make up a basket. Let's send that poor creature some of this perfectly good food. At any rate, it will be the greatest treat for the children. Don't you agree? And she's sure to have neighbours calling in and so on. What a point to have it all ready prepared. Laura!" She jumped up. "Get me the big basket out of the stairs cupboard."

"But, mother, do you really think it's a good idea?" said Laura.

Again, how curious, she seemed to be different from them all. To take scraps from their party. Would the poor woman really like that?

"Of course! What's the matter with you today? An hour or two ago you were insisting on us being sympathetic, and now——"

Oh, well! Laura ran for the basket. It was filled, it was heaped by her mother.

"Take it yourself, darling," said she. "Run down just as you are. No, wait, take the arum lilies too. People of that class are so impressed by arum lilies."

"The stems will ruin her lace frock," said practical Jose.

So they would. Just in time. "Only the basket then. And, Laura!" —her mother followed her out of the marquee—"don't on any account——"

"What, mother?"

No, better not put such ideas into the child's head! "Nothing! Run along."

It was just growing dusky as Laura shut their garden gates. A big dog ran by like a shadow. The road gleamed white, and down below in the hollow the little cottages were in deep shade. How quiet it seemed after the afternoon. Here she was going down the hill to somewhere where a man lay dead, and she couldn't realize it. Why couldn't she? She stopped a minute. And it seemed to her that kisses, voices, tinkling spoons, laughter, the smell of crushed grass were somehow inside her. She had no room for anything else. How strange! She looked up at the pale sky, and all she thought was, "Yes, it was the most successful party."

Now the broad road was crossed. The lane began, smoky and dark. Women in shawls and men's tweed caps hurried by. Men hung over the palings; the children played in the doorways. A low hum came from the mean little cottages. In some of them there was a flicker of light, and a shadow, crab-like, moved across the window. Laura bent her head and hurried on. She wished now she had put on a coat. How her frock shone! And the big hat with the velvet streamer—if only it was another hat! Were the people looking at her? They must be. It was a mistake to have come; she knew all along it was a mistake. Should she go back even now?

No, too late. This was the house. It must be. A dark knot of people stood outside. Beside the gate an old, old woman with a crutch sat in a chair, watching. She had her feet on a newspaper. The voices stopped as Laura drew near. The group parted. It was as though she was expected, as though they had known she was coming here.

Laura was terribly nervous. Tossing the velvet ribbon over her shoulder, she said to a woman standing by, "Is this Mrs. Scott's house?" and the woman, smiling queerly, said, "It is, my lass."

Oh, to be away from this! She actually said, "Help me, God," as she walked up the tiny path and knocked. To be away from those staring eyes, or to be covered up in anything, one of those women's shawls even. I'll just leave the basket and go, she decided. I shan't even wait for it to be emptied.

Then the door opened. A little woman in black showed in the gloom.

Laura said, "Are you Mrs. Scott?" But to her horror the woman answered, "Walk in please, miss," and she was shut in the passage.

"No," said Laura, "I don't want to come in. I only want to leave this basket. Mother sent——"

The little woman in the gloomy passage seemed not to have heard her. "Step this way, please, miss," she said in an oily voice, and Laura followed her.

She found herself in a wretched little low kitchen, lighted by a smoky lamp. There was a woman sitting before the fire.

"Em," said the little creature who had let her in. "Em! It's a young lady." She turned to Laura. She said meaningly, "I'm 'er sister, miss. You'll excuse 'er, won't you?"

"Oh, but of course!" said Laura. "Please, please don't disturb her. I—I only want to leave——"

But at that moment the woman at the fire turned round. Her face, puffed up, red, with swollen eyes and swollen lips, looked terrible. She seemed as though she couldn't understand why Laura was there. What did it mean? Why was this stranger standing in the kitchen with a basket? What was it all about? And the poor face puckered up again.

"All right, my dear," said the other. "I'll thenk the young lady."

And again she began, "You'll excuse her, miss, I'm sure," and her face, swollen too, tried an oily smile.

Laura only wanted to get out, to get away. She was back in the passage. The door opened. She walked straight through into the bedroom, where the dead man was lying.

"You'd like a look at 'im, wouldn't you?" said Em's sister, and she brushed past Laura over to the bed. "Don't be afraid, my lass,—" and now her voice sounded fond and sly, and fondly she drew down the sheet—" 'e looks a picture. There's nothing to show. Come along, my dear."

Laura came.

There lay a young man, fast asleep—sleeping so soundly, so deeply, that he was far, far away from them both. Oh, so remote, so peaceful. He was dreaming. Never wake him up again. His head was sunk in the pillow, his eyes were closed; they were blind under the closed eyelids. He was given up to his dream. What did garden-parties and baskets and lace frocks matter to him? He was far from all those things. He was wonderful, beautiful. While they were laughing and while the band was playing, this marvel had come to the lane. Happy . . . happy. . . . All is well, said that sleeping face. This is just as it should be. I am content.

But all the same you had to cry, and she couldn't go out of the room without saying something to him. Laura gave a loud childish sob.

"Forgive my hat," she said.

And this time she didn't wait for Em's sister. She found her way out of the door, down the path, past all those dark people. At the corner of the lane she met Laurie.

He stepped out of the shadow. "Is that you, Laura?"

"Yes."

"Mother was getting anxious. Was it all right?"

"Yes, quite. Oh, Laurie!" She took his arm, she pressed up against him.

"I say, you're not crying, are you?" asked her brother.

Laura shook her head. She was.

Laurie put his arm round her shoulder. "Don't cry," he said in his warm, loving voice. "Was it awful?"

"No," sobbed Laura. "It was simply marvelous. But, Laurie——" She stopped, she looked at her brother. "Isn't life," she stammered, "isn't life——" But what life was she could not explain. No matter. He quite understood.

"*Isn't it*, darling?" said Laurie.

by John Updike

TOMORROW AND TOMORROW AND SO FORTH

John Updike was born on March 18, 1932, in West Reading, Pennsylvania. He received his early education in the Shillington, Pennsylvania, public schools and attended Harvard and the Ruskin School of Art and Drawing in Oxford. For two years he was on the staff of The New Yorker, *to which he is still a frequent contributor. Mr. Updike's first book,* The Carpentered Hen, *a volume of verse, appeared in 1958. Since then he has published three novels—the most recent is* The Centaur *(1963)—and two collections of short stories,* The Same Door *(1959) and* Pigeon Feathers *(1962). Mr. Updike lives in Ipswich, Massachusetts, with his wife and four children.*

Whatever incisive comments "Tomorrow and Tomorrow and So Forth" makes about high school students and their milieu, *the substance of the story is not local. Both the passage from* Macbeth *and the note Mr. Prosser intercepts seek to define (each in its peculiar rhetoric) a thoroughly human attitude. The passage suggests that time is meaningless; the note suggests, according to Mr. Prosser, that love is meaningless—"It is time we coined a new word." The difference, of course, is that Macbeth has come from his wife's death, Mr. Prosser to the uncertainty of a girl's tears.*

WHIRLING, talking, 11D began to enter Room 109. From the quality of their excitement Mark Prosser guessed it would rain. He had been teaching high school for three years, yet his students still impressed him; they were such sensitive animals. They reacted so infallibly to merely barometric pressure.

In the doorway, Brute Young paused while little Barry Snyder giggled at his elbow. Barry's stagy laugh rose and fell, dipping down toward some vile secret that had to be tasted and retasted, then soaring artificially to proclaim that he, little Barry, shared such a secret with the school's fullback. Being Brute's stooge was precious to Barry. The fullback paid no attention to him; he twisted his neck to stare at something not yet coming through the door. He yielded heavily to the procession pressing him forward.

Right under Prosser's eyes, like a murder suddenly appearing in an annalistic frieze of kings and queens, someone stabbed a girl in the back with a pencil. She ignored the assault saucily. Another hand yanked out Geoffrey Langer's shirt-tail. Geoffrey, a bright student, was uncertain whether to laugh it off or defend himself with anger, and made a weak, half-turning gesture of compromise, wearing an expression of distant arrogance that Prosser instantly coördinated with feelings of fear he used to have. All along the line, in the glitter of key chains and the acute angles of turned-back shirt cuffs, an electricity was expressed which simple weather couldn't generate.

Mark wondered if today Gloria Angstrom wore that sweater, an ember-pink angora, with very brief sleeves. The virtual sleevelessness was the disturbing factor: the exposure of those two serene arms to the air, white as thighs against the delicate wool.

His guess was correct. A vivid pink patch flashed through the jiggle of arms and shoulders as the final knot of youngsters entered the room.

"Take your seats," Mr. Prosser said. "Come on. Let's go."

Most obeyed, but Peter Forrester, who had been at the center of the group around Gloria, still lingered in the doorway with her, finishing some story, apparently determined to make her laugh or gasp. When she did gasp, he tossed his head with satisfaction. His orange hair bobbed. Redheads are all alike, Mark thought, with their white eyelashes and pale puffy faces and thyroid eyes, their mouths always twisted with preposterous self-confidence. Bluffers, the whole bunch.

When Gloria, moving in a considered, stately way, had taken her seat, and Peter had swerved into his, Mr. Prosser said, "Peter Forrester."

"Yes?" Peter rose, scrabbling through his book for the right place.

"Kindly tell the class the exact meaning of the words 'Tomorrow, and tomorrow, and tomorrow/Creeps in this petty pace from day to day.' "

Peter glanced down at the high-school edition of *Macbeth* lying open on his desk. One of the duller girls tittered expectantly from the back of the room. Peter was popular with the girls; girls that age had minds like moths.

"Peter. With your book shut. We have all memorized this passage for today. Remember?" The girl in the back of the room squealed in delight. Gloria laid her own book face-open on her desk, where Peter could see it.

Peter shut his book with a bang and stared into Gloria's. "Why," he said at last, "I think it means pretty much what it says."

"Which is?"

"Why, that tomorrow is something we often think about. It creeps into our conversation all the time. We couldn't make any plans without thinking about tomorrow."

"I see. Then you would say that Macbeth is here referring to the, the date-book aspect of life?"

Geoffrey Langer laughed, no doubt to please Mr. Prosser. For a moment, he *was* pleased. Then he realized he had been playing for laughs at a student's expense.

His paraphrase had made Peter's reading of the lines seem more ridiculous than it was. He began to retract. "I admit—"

But Peter was going on; redheads never know when to quit. "Macbeth means that if we quit worrying about tomorrow, and just lived for today, we could appreciate all the wonderful things that are going on under our noses."

Mark considered this a moment before he spoke. He would not be sarcastic. "Uh, without denying that there is truth in what you say, Peter, do you think it likely that Macbeth, in his situation, would be expressing such"—he couldn't help himself—"such sunny sentiments?"

Geoffrey laughed again. Peter's neck reddened; he studied the floor. Gloria glared at Mr. Prosser, the anger in her face clearly meant for him to see.

Mark hurried to undo his mistake. "Don't misunderstand me,

please," he told Peter. "I don't have all the answers myself. But it seems to me the whole speech, down to 'Signifying nothing,' is saying that life is—well, a *fraud*. Nothing wonderful about it."

"Did Shakespeare really think that?" Geoffrey Langer asked, a nervous quickness pitching his voice high.

Mark read into Geoffrey's question his own adolescent premonitions of the terrible truth. The attempt he must make was plain. He told Peter he could sit down and looked through the window toward the steadying sky. The clouds were gaining intensity. "There is," Mr. Prosser slowly began, "much darkness in Shakespeare's work, and no play is darker than 'Macbeth.' The atmosphere is poisonous, oppressive. One critic has said that in this play, humanity suffocates." This was too fancy.

"In the middle of his career, Shakespeare wrote plays about men like Hamlet and Othello and Macbeth—men who aren't allowed by their society, or bad luck, or some minor flaw in themselves, to become the great men they might have been. Even Shakespeare's comedies of this period deal with a world gone sour. It is as if he had seen through the bright, bold surface of his earlier comedies and histories and had looked upon something terrible. It frightened him, just as some day it may frighten some of you." In his determination to find the right words, he had been staring at Gloria, without meaning to. Embarrassed, she nodded, and, realizing what had happened, he smiled at her.

He tried to make his remarks gentler, even diffident. "But then I think Shakespeare sensed a redeeming truth. His last plays are serene and symbolical, as if he had pierced through the ugly facts and reached a realm where the facts are again beautiful. In this way, Shakespeare's total work is a more complete image of life than that of any other writer, except perhaps for Dante, an Italian poet who wrote several centuries earlier." He had been taken far from the Macbeth soliloquy. Other teachers had been happy to tell him how the kids made a game of getting him talking. He looked toward Geoffrey. The boy was doodling on his tablet, indifferent. Mr. Prosser concluded, "The last play Shakespeare wrote is an extraordinary poem called 'The Tempest.' Some of you may want to read it for your next book reports—the ones due May 10th. It's a short play."

The class had been taking a holiday. Barry Snyder was snicking BBs off the blackboard and glancing over at Brute Young to see if he noticed. "Once more, Barry," Mr. Prosser said, "and out you go."

Barry blushed, and grinned to cover the blush, his eyeballs sliding toward Brute. The dull girl in the rear of the room was putting on lipstick. "Put that away, Alice," Mr. Prosser commanded. She giggled and obeyed. Sejak, the Polish boy who worked nights, was asleep at his desk, his cheek white with pressure against the varnished wood, his mouth sagging sidewise. Mr. Prosser had an impulse to let him sleep. But the impulse might not be true kindness, but just the self-congratulatory, kindly pose in which he sometimes discovered himself. Besides, one breach of discipline encouraged others. He strode down the aisle and shook Sejak awake. Then he turned his attention to the mumble growing at the front of the room.

Peter Forrester was whispering to Gloria, trying to make her laugh. The girl's face, though, was cool and solemn, as if a thought had been provoked in her head. Perhaps at least *she* had been listening to what Mr. Prosser had been saying. With a bracing sense of chivalrous intercession, Mark said, "Peter. I gather from this noise that you have something to add to your theories."

Peter responded courteously. "No, sir. I honestly don't understand the speech. Please, sir, what *does* it mean?"

This candid admission and odd request stunned the class. Every white, round face, eager, for once, to learn, turned toward Mark. He said, "I don't know. I was hoping *you* would tell *me*."

In college, when a professor made such a remark, it was with grand effect. The professor's humility, the necessity for creative interplay between teacher and student were dramatically impressed upon the group. But to 11D, ignorance in an instructor was as wrong as a hole in a roof. It was as if he had held forty strings pulling forty faces taut toward him and then had slashed the strings. Heads waggled, eyes dropped, voices buzzed. Some of the discipline problems, like Peter Forrester, smirked signals to one another.

"Quiet!" Mr. Prosser shouted. "All of you. Poetry isn't arithmetic. There's no single right answer. I don't want to force my impression on you, even if I *have* had much more experience with literature." He made this last clause very loud and distinct, and some of the weaker students seemed reassured. "I know none of *you* want that," he told them.

Whether or not they believed him, they subsided, somewhat. Mark judged he could safely reassume his human-among-humans attitude again. He perched on the edge of the desk and leaned forward beseechingly. "Now, honestly. Don't any of you have some personal feeling about the lines that you would like to share with the class and me?"

One hand, with a flowered handkerchief balled in it, unsteadily rose. "Go ahead, Teresa," Mr. Prosser said encouragingly. She was a timid, clumsy girl whose mother was a Jehovah's Witness.

"It makes me think of cloud shadows," Teresa said.

Geoffrey Langer laughed. "Don't be rude, Geoff," Mr. Prosser said sideways, softly, before throwing his voice forward: "Thank you, Teresa. I think that's an interesting and valid impression. Cloud movement has something in it of the slow, monotonous rhythm one feels in the line 'Tomorrow, and tomorrow, and tomorrow.' It's a very gray line, isn't it, class?" No one agreed or disagreed.

Beyond the windows actual clouds were bunching rapidly, and erratic sections of sunlight slid around the room. Gloria's arm, crooked gracefully above her head, turned gold. "Gloria?" Mr. Prosser asked.

She looked up from something on her desk with a face of sullen radiance. "I think what Teresa said was very good," she said, glaring in the direction of Geoffrey Langer. Geoffrey chuckled defiantly. "And I have a question. What does 'petty pace' mean?"

"It means the trivial day-to-day sort of life that, say, a bookkeeper or a bank clerk leads. Or a schoolteacher," he added, smiling.

She did not smile back. Thought wrinkles irritated her perfect brow. "But Macbeth has been fighting wars, and killing kings, and being a king himself, and all," she pointed out.

"Yes, but it's just these acts Macbeth is condemning as 'nothing.' Can you see that?"

Gloria shook her head. "Another thing I worry about—isn't it silly for Macbeth to be talking to himself right in the middle of this war, with his wife just dead, and all?"

"I don't think so, Gloria. No matter how fast events happen, thought is faster."

His answer was weak; everyone knew it, even if Gloria hadn't mused, supposedly to herself, but in a voice the entire class could hear, "It seems so *stupid*."

Mark winced, pierced by the awful clarity with which his students saw him. Through their eyes, how queer he looked, with his long hands, and his horn-rimmed glasses, and his hair never slicked down, all wrapped up in "literature," where, when things get rough, the king mumbles a poem nobody understands. The delight Mr. Prosser took in such crazy junk made not only his good sense but his masculinity a matter of doubt. It was gentle of them not to laugh him out of the room. He looked down and rubbed his fingertips together, trying to erase the chalk dust. The class noise sifted into unnatural quiet. "It's getting late," he said finally. "Let's start the recitations of the memorized passage. Bernard Amilson, you begin."

Bernard had trouble enunciating, and his rendition began " 'T'mau 'n' t'mau 'n' t'mau.' " It was reassuring, the extent to which the class tried to repress its laughter. Mr. Prosser wrote "A" in his marking book opposite Bernard's name. He always gave Bernard A on recitations, despite the school nurse, who claimed there was nothing organically wrong with the boy's mouth.

It was the custom, cruel but traditional, to deliver recitations from the front of the room. Alice, when her turn came, was reduced to a helpless state by the first funny face Peter Forrester made at her. Mark let her hang up there a good minute while her face ripened to cherry redness, and at last forgave her. She may try it later. Many of the youngsters knew the passage gratifyingly well, though there was a tendency to leave out the line "To the last syllable of recorded time" and to turn "struts and frets" into "frets and struts" or simply "struts and struts." Even Sejak, who couldn't have looked at the passage before he came to class, got through it as far as "And then is heard no more."

Geoffrey Langer showed off, as he always did, by interrupting his own recitation with bright questions. " 'Tomorrow, and tomorrow, and tomorrow,' " he said, " 'creeps in'—shouldn't that be '*creep* in,' Mr. Prosser?"

"It is 'creeps.' The trio is in effect singular. Go on." Mr. Prosser was tired of coddling Langer. If you let them, these smart students will run away with the class. "Without the footnotes."

" 'Creep*sss* in this petty pace from day to day, to the last syllable of recorded time, and all our yesterdays have lighted fools the way to dusty death. Out, out—' "

"No, no!" Mr. Prosser jumped out of his chair. "This is poetry. Don't mushmouth it! Pause a little after 'fools.' " Geoffrey looked genuinely startled this time, and Mark himself did not quite understand his annoyance and, mentally turning to see what was behind him, seemed to glimpse in the humid undergrowth the two stern eyes of the indignant look Gloria had thrown Geoffrey. He glimpsed himself in the absurd position of acting as Gloria's champion in her private war with this intelligent boy. He sighed apologetically. "Poetry is made up of lines," he began, turning to the class. Gloria was passing a note to Peter Forrester.

The rudeness of it! To pass notes during a scolding that she herself had caused! Mark caged in his hand the girl's frail wrist and ripped the note from her fingers. He read it to himself, letting the class see he was reading it, though he despised such methods of discipline. The note went:

Pete— I think you're *wrong* about Mr. Prosser. I think he's wonderful and I get a lot out of his class. He's heavenly with poetry. I think I love him. I really do *love* him. So there.

Mr. Prosser folded the note once and slipped it into his side coat pocket. "See me after class, Gloria," he said. Then, to Geoffrey, "Let's try it again. Begin at the beginning."

While the boy was reciting the passage, the buzzer sounded the end of the period. It was the last class of the day. The room quickly emptied, except for Gloria. The noise of lockers slamming open and books being thrown against metal and shouts drifted in.

"Who has a car?"

"Lend me a cig, pig."

"We can't have practice in this slop."

Mark hadn't noticed exactly when the rain started, but it was coming down fast now. He moved around the room with the window pole, closing windows and pulling down shades. Spray bounced in on his hands. He began to talk to Gloria in a crisp voice that, like his device of shutting the windows, was intended to protect them both from embarrassment.

"About note passing." She sat motionless at her desk in the front of the room, her short, brushed-up hair like a cool torch. From the way she sat, her naked arms folded at her breasts and her shoulders hunched, he felt she was chilly. "It is not only rude to scribble when a teacher is talking, it is stupid to put one's words down on paper, where they look much more foolish than they might have sounded if spoken." He leaned the window pole in its corner and walked toward his desk.

"And about love. 'Love' is one of those words that illustrate what happens to an old, overworked language. These days, with movie stars and crooners and preachers and psychiatrists all pronouncing the word, it's come to mean nothing but a vague fondness for something. In this sense, I love the rain, this blackboard, these desks, you. It means nothing, you see, whereas once the word signified a quite explicit thing—a desire to share all you own and are with someone else. It is time we coined a new word to mean that, and when you think up the word *you* want to use, I suggest that you be economical with it. Treat it as something you can spend only once—if not for your own sake, for the good of the language." He walked over to his own desk and dropped two pencils on it, as if to say, "That's all."

"I'm sorry," Gloria said.

Rather surprised, Mr. Prosser said, "Don't be."

"But you don't understand."

"Of course I don't. I probably never did. At your age, I was like Geoffrey Langer."

"I bet you weren't." The girl was almost crying; he was sure of that.

"Come on, Gloria. Run along. Forget it." She slowly cradled her books between her bare arm and her sweater, and left the room with that melancholy shuffling teen-age gait, so that her body above her thighs seemed to float over the desks.

What was it, Mark asked himself, these kids were after? What did they want? Glide, he decided, the quality of glide. To slip along, always in rhythm, always cool, the little wheels humming under you, going nowhere special. If Heaven existed, that's the way it would be there. "He's heavenly with poetry." They loved the word. Heaven was in half their songs.

"Christ, he's humming." Strunk, the physical ed teacher, had come into the room without Mark's noticing. Gloria had left the door ajar.

"Ah," Mark said, "a fallen angel, full of grit."

"What the hell makes you so happy?"

"I'm not happy, I'm just serene. I don't know why you don't appreciate me."

"Say." Strunk came up an aisle with a disagreeably effeminate waddle, pregnant with gossip. "Did you hear about Murchison?"

"No." Mark mimicked Strunk's whisper.

"He got the pants kidded off him today."

"Oh dear."

Strunk started to laugh, as he always did before beginning a story. "You know what a goddam lady's man he thinks he is?"

"You bet," Mark said, although Strunk said that about every male member of the faculty.

"You have Gloria Angstrom, don't you?"

"You bet."

"Well, this morning Murky intercepts a note she was writing, and the note says what a damn neat guy she thinks Murchison is and how she *loves* him!" Strunk waited for Mark to say something, and then, when he didn't, continued, "You could see he was tickled pink. But —get this—it turns out at lunch that the same damn thing happened to Fryeburg in history yesterday!" Strunk laughed and cracked his knuckles viciously. "The girl's too dumb to have thought it up herself. We all think it was Peter Forrester's idea."

"Probably was," Mark agreed. Strunk followed him out to his locker, describing Murchison's expression when Fryeburg (in all innocence, mind you) told what had happened to him.

Mark turned the combination of his locker, 18-24-3. "Would you excuse me, Dave?" he said. "My wife's in town waiting."

Strunk was too thick to catch Mark's anger. "I got to get over to the gym. Can't take the little darlings outside in the rain; their mommies'll write notes to teacher." He clattered down the hall and wheeled at the far end, shouting, "Now don't tell You-know-who!"

Mr. Prosser took his coat from the locker and shrugged it on. He placed his hat upon his head. He fitted his rubbers over his shoes, pinching his fingers painfully, and lifted his umbrella off the hook. He thought of opening it right there in the vacant hall, as a kind of joke, and decided not to. The girl had been almost crying; he was sure of that.

by Willa Cather

PAUL'S CASE

Willa Cather was born near Winchester, Virginia, probably in 1874. In 1882 she and her family moved to Nebraska to farm. She worked her way through the University as a newspaper correspondent. Soon after her graduation she went East to become drama critic of the Pittsburgh* Daily Leader, *a high school English teacher, and until 1911, managing editor of* McClure's. *From 1911 until her death on April 24, 1947, she devoted herself to independent writing.*

Miss Cather's first book, April Twilights *(1903), a volume of undistinguished, conventional verse, was followed in 1905 by* The Troll Garden, *a collection of stories in which "Paul's Case" appeared. In 1912 her first novel,* Alexander's Bridge, *was published. Over the years she brought out eleven more novels, three more collections of stories, and two volumes of essays.*

The West of her Nebraska childhood and the West of earlier history are the stuff of Miss Cather's best novels. O Pioneers! *(1913) and* My Ántonia *(1918) express her interest in the conflict between the life of her region and the European background of many of its settlers. Similarly, in the immensely popular* Death Comes for the Archbishop *(1927) her imagination seems to have been excited by the interplay between two cultures, the Indian and the Spanish.*

Paul of "Paul's Case," of course, is neither an Indian, a Spaniard, nor a Nebraskan. Nevertheless, like the European settlers of the early novels, he is a stranger in the land. Pittsburgh, the high school, and the office confine him, as the open prison of the plains confines the Russians, Bohemians, and Scandinavians of My Ántonia.

** The date of Miss Cather's birth was nowhere recorded. It has been given as 1875 and 1876; but, perhaps most authoritatively, it has been assigned by Mr. W. W. Glass, the Archivist of Winchester, Virginia, to 1874.*

IT was Paul's afternoon to appear before the faculty of the Pittsburgh High School to account for his various misdemeanours. He had been suspended a week ago, and his father had called at the Principal's office and confessed his perplexity about his son. Paul entered the faculty room suave and smiling. His clothes were a trifle outgrown, and the tan velvet on the collar of his open overcoat was frayed and worn; but for all that there was something of the dandy about him, and he wore an opal pin in his neatly knotted black four-in-hand, and a red carnation in his buttonhole. This latter adornment the faculty somehow felt was not properly significant of the contrite spirit befitting a boy under the ban of suspension.

Paul was tall for his age and very thin, with high, cramped shoulders and a narrow chest. His eyes were remarkable for a certain hysterical brilliancy, and he continually used them in a conscious, theatrical sort of way, peculiarly offensive in a boy. The pupils were abnormally large, as though he were addicted to belladonna, but there was a glassy glitter about them which that drug does not produce.

When questioned by the Principal as to why he was there, Paul stated, politely enough, that he wanted to come back to school. This was a lie, but Paul was quite accustomed to lying; found it, indeed, indispensable for overcoming friction. His teachers were asked to state their respective charges against him, which they did with such a rancour and aggrievedness as evinced that this was not a usual case. Disorder and impertinence were among the offences named, yet each of his instructors felt that it was scarcely possible to put into words the real cause of the trouble, which lay in a sort of hysterically defiant manner of the boy's; in the contempt which they all knew he felt for them, and which he seemingly made not the least effort to conceal. Once, when he had been making a synopsis of a paragraph at the blackboard, his English teacher had stepped to his side and attempted to guide his hand. Paul had started back with a shudder and thrust his hands violently behind him. The astonished woman could scarcely have been more hurt and embarrassed had he struck at her. The insult was so involuntary and definitely personal as to be unforgettable. In one way and another, he had made all his teachers, men and women alike, conscious of the same feeling of physical aversion. In one class he habitually sat with his hand shading his eyes; in another he always looked out of the window during the recitation; in another he made a running commentary on the lecture, with humorous intent.

His teachers felt this afternoon that his whole attitude was symbolized by his shrug and his flippantly red carnation flower, and they fell upon him without mercy, his English teacher leading the pack. He stood through it smiling, his pale lips parted over his white teeth. (His lips were continually twitching, and he had a habit of raising his eyebrows that was contemptuous and irritating to the last degree.) Older boys than Paul had broken down and shed tears under that ordeal, but his set smile did not once desert him, and his only sign of discomfort was the nervous trembling of the fingers that toyed with the buttons of his overcoat, and an occasional jerking of the other hand which held his hat. Paul was always smiling, always glancing about him, seeming to feel that people might be watching him and trying to detect something. This conscious expression, since it was as far as possible from boyish mirthfulness, was usually attributed to insolence or "smartness."

As the inquisition proceeded, one of his instructors repeated an impertinent remark of the boy's, and the Principal asked him whether he thought that a courteous speech to make to a woman. Paul shrugged his shoulders slightly and his eyebrows twitched.

"I don't know," he replied. "I didn't mean to be polite or impolite, either. I guess it's a sort of way I have, of saying things regardless."

The Principal asked him whether he didn't think that a way it would be well to get rid of. Paul grinned and said he guessed so. When he was told that he could go, he bowed gracefully and went out. His bow was like a repetition of the scandalous red carnation.

His teachers were in despair, and his drawing-master voiced the feeling of them all when he declared there was something about the boy which none of them understood. He added: "I don't really believe that smile of his comes altogether from insolence; there's something sort of haunted about it. The boy is not strong, for one thing. There is something wrong about the fellow."

The drawing-master had come to realize that, in looking at Paul, one saw only his white teeth and the forced animation of his eyes. One warm afternoon the boy had gone to sleep at his drawing-board, and his master had noted with amazement what a white, blue-veined face it was; drawn and wrinkled like an old man's about the eyes, the lips twitching even in his sleep.

His teachers left the building dissatisfied and unhappy; humiliated to have felt so vindictive toward a mere boy, to have uttered this feeling in cutting terms, and to have set each other on, as it were, in the gruesome game of intemperate reproach. One of them remembered having seen a miserable street cat set at bay by a ring of tormentors.

As for Paul, he ran down the hill whistling the Soldiers' Chorus from "Faust," looking behind him now and then to see whether some of his teachers were not there to witness his light-heartedness. As it was now late in the afternoon and Paul was on duty that evening as usher at Carnegie Hall, he decided that he would not go home to supper.

When he reached the concert hall, the doors were not yet open. It was chilly outside, and he decided to go up into the picture gallery—always deserted at this hour—where there were some of Raffelli's gay studies of Paris streets and an airy blue Venetian scene or two that always exhilarated him. He was delighted to find no one in the gallery but the old guard, who sat in the corner, a newspaper on his knee, a black patch over one eye and the other closed. Paul possessed himself of the place and walked confidently up and down, whistling under his breath. After a while he sat down before a blue Rico and lost himself. When he bethought him to look at his watch, it was after seven o'clock, and he rose with a start and ran downstairs, making a face at Augustus Caesar, peering out from the cast-room, and an evil gesture at the Venus of Milo as he passed her on the stairway.

When Paul reached the ushers' dressing-room, half a dozen boys were there already, and he began excitedly to tumble into his uniform. It was one of the few that at all approached fitting, and Paul thought it very becoming—though he knew the tight, straight coat accentuated his narrow chest, about which he was exceedingly sensitive. He was always excited while he dressed, twanging all over to the tuning of the strings and the preliminary flourishes of the horns in the music-room; but to-night he seemed quite beside himself, and he teased and plagued the boys until, telling him that he was crazy, they put him down on the floor and sat on him.

Somewhat calmed by his suppression, Paul dashed out to the front of the house to seat the early comers. He was a model usher. Gracious and smiling he ran up and down the aisles. Nothing was too much trouble for him; he carried messages and brought programmes as though it were his greatest pleasure in life, and all the people in his section thought him a charming boy, feeling that he remembered and admired them. As the house filled, he grew more and more vivacious and animated, and the colour came to his cheeks and lips. It was very much as though this were a great reception and Paul were the host. Just as the musicians came out to take their places, his English teacher arrived with cheques for the seats which a prominent manufacturer had taken for the season. She betrayed some embarrassment when she handed Paul the tickets, and a hauteur which subsequently made her feel very foolish. Paul was startled for a moment, and had the feeling of wanting to put her out; what business had she here among all these fine people and gay colours? He looked her over and decided that she was not appropriately dressed and must be a fool to sit downstairs in such togs. The tickets had probably been sent her out of kindness, he reflected, as he put down a seat for her, and she had about as much right to sit there as he had.

When the symphony began, Paul sank into one of the rear seats with a long sigh of relief, and lost himself as he had done before the Rico. It was not that symphonies, as such, meant anything in particular to Paul, but the first sigh of the instruments seemed to free some hilarious spirit within him; something that struggled there like the Genius in the bottle found by the Arab fisherman. He felt a sudden zest of life; the lights danced before his eyes and the concert hall blazed into unimaginable splendour. When the soprano soloist came on, Paul forgot even the nastiness of his teacher's being there, and gave himself up to the peculiar intoxication such personages always had for him. The soloist chanced to be a German woman, by no means in her first youth, and the mother of many children; but she wore a satin gown and a tiara, and she had that indefinable air of achievement, that world-shine upon her, which always blinded Paul to any possible defects.

After a concert was over, Paul was often irritable and wretched until he got to sleep—and to-night he was even more than usually restless. He had the feeling of not being able to let down; of its being impossible to give up this delicious excitement which was the only thing that could be called living at all. During the last number he withdrew and, after hastily changing his clothes in the dressing-room, slipped out to the side door where the singer's carriage stood. Here he began pacing rapidly up and down the walk, waiting to see her come out.

Over yonder the Schenley, in its vacant stretch, loomed big and square through the fine rain, the windows of its twelve stories glowing like those of a lighted cardboard house under a Christmas tree. All the actors and singers of any importance stayed there when they were in Pittsburgh, and a number of the big manufacturers of the place lived there in the winter. Paul had often hung about the hotel, watching the people go in and out, longing to enter and leave schoolmasters and dull care behind him forever.

At last the singer came out, accompanied by the conductor, who helped her into her carriage and closed the door with a cordial *auf wiedersehen*—which set Paul to wondering whether she were not an old sweetheart of his. Paul followed the carriage over to the hotel, walking so rapidly as not to be far from the entrance when the singer alighted and disappeared behind the swinging glass doors which were opened by a Negro in a tall hat and a long coat. In the moment that the door was ajar, it seemed to Paul that he, too, entered. He seemed to feel himself go after her up the steps, into the warm, lighted building, into an exotic, a tropical world of shiny, glistening surfaces and basking ease. He reflected upon the mysterious dishes that were brought into the dining-room, the green bottles in buckets of ice, as he had seen them in the supper-party pictures of the Sunday supplement. A quick gust of wind brought the rain down with sudden vehemence, and Paul was startled to find that he was still outside in the slush of the gravel driveway; that his boots were letting in the water and his scanty overcoat was clinging wet about him; that the lights in front of the concert hall were out, and that the rain was driving in sheets between him and the orange glow of the windows above him. There it was, what he wanted—tangibly before him, like the fairy world of a Christmas pantomime; as the rain beat in his face, Paul wondered whether he were destined always to shiver in the black night outside, looking up at it.

He turned and walked reluctantly toward the car tracks. The end had to come sometime; his father in his night-clothes at the top of the stairs, explanations that did not explain, hastily improvised fictions that were forever tripping him up, his upstairs room and its horrible yellow wallpaper, the creaking bureau with the greasy plush collar-box, and over his painted wooden bed the pictures of George Washington and John Calvin, and the framed motto, "Feed my Lambs," which had been worked in red worsted by his mother, whom Paul could not remember.

Half an hour later, Paul alighted from the Negley Avenue car and went slowly down one of the side streets off the main thoroughfare. It was a highly respectable street, where all the houses were exactly alike, and where business men of moderate means begot and reared large families of children, all of whom went to Sabbath School and learned the shorter catechism, and were interested in arithmetic; all of whom were as exactly alike as their homes, and of a piece with the monotony in which they lived. Paul never went up Cordelia Street without a shudder of loathing. His home was next the house of the Cumberland minister. He approached it to-night with the nerveless sense of defeat, the hopeless feeling of sinking back forever into ugliness and commonness that he had always had when he came home. The moment he turned into Cordelia Street he felt the waters close above his head. After each of these orgies of living, he experienced all the physical depression which follows a debauch; the loathing of respectable beds, of common food, of a house permeated by kitchen odours; a shuddering repulsion for the flavourless, colourless mass of every-day existence; a morbid desire for cool things and soft lights and fresh flowers.

The nearer he approached the house, the more absolutely unequal Paul felt to the sight of it all: his ugly sleeping chamber; the cold bathroom with the grimy zinc tub, the cracked mirror, the dripping spigots; his father, at the top of the stairs, his hairy legs sticking out from his nightshirt, his feet thrust into carpet slippers. He was so much later than usual that there would certainly be enquiries and reproaches. Paul stopped short before the door. He felt that he could not be accosted by his father to-night; that he could not toss again on that miserable bed. He would not go in. He would tell his father that he had no car-fare, and it was raining so hard he had gone home with one of the boys and stayed all night.

Meanwhile, he was wet and cold. He went around to the back of the house and tried one of the basement windows, found it open, raised it cautiously, and scrambled down the cellar wall to the floor. There he stood, holding his breath, terrified by the noise he had made; but the floor above him was silent, and there was no creak on the stairs. He found a soap-box, and carried it over to the soft ring of light that streamed from the furnace door, and sat down. He was horribly afraid of rats, so he did not try to sleep, but sat looking distrustfully at the dark, still terrified lest he might have awakened his father.

In such reactions, after one of the experiences which made days and nights out of the dreary blanks of the calendar, when his senses were deadened, Paul's head was always singularly clear. Suppose his father had heard him getting in at the window and had come down and shot him for a burglar? Then, again, suppose his father had come down, pistol in hand, and he had cried out in time to save himself, and his father had been horrified to think how nearly he had killed him? Then, again, suppose a day should come when his father would remember that night, and wish there had been no warning cry to stay his hand? With this last supposition Paul entertained himself until daybreak.

The following Sunday was fine; the sodden November chill was broken by the last flash of autumnal summer. In the morning Paul had to go to church and Sabbath School, as always. On seasonable Sunday afternoons the burghers of Cordelia Street usually sat out on their front "stoops," and talked to their neighbours on the next stoop, or called to those across the street in neighbourly fashion. The men sat placidly on gay cushions placed upon the steps that led down to the sidewalk, while the women, in their Sunday "waists," sat in rockers on the cramped porches, pretending to be greatly at their ease. The children played in the streets; there were so many of them that the place resembled the recreation grounds of a kindergarten. The men on the steps, all in their shirt-sleeves, their vests unbuttoned, sat with their legs well apart, their stomachs comfortably protruding, and talked of the prices of things, or told anecdotes of the sagacity of their various chiefs and overlords. They occasionally looked over the multitude of squabbling children, listened affectionately to their high-pitched, nasal voices, smiling to see their own proclivities reproduced in their offspring, and interspersed their legends of the iron kings with remarks about their sons' progress at school, their grades in arithmetic, and the amounts they had saved in their toy banks.

On this last Sunday of November, Paul sat all the afternoon on the lowest step of his "stoop," staring into the street, while his sisters, in their rockers, were talking to the minister's daughters next door about how many shirtwaists they had made in the last week, and how many waffles someone had eaten at the last church supper. When the weather was warm, and his father was in a particularly jovial frame of mind, the girls made lemonade, which was always brought out in a red-glass pitcher, ornamented with forget-me-nots in blue enamel. This the girls thought very fine, and the neighbours joked about the suspicious colour of the pitcher.

To-day Paul's father, on the top step, was talking to a young man who shifted a restless baby from knee to knee. He happened to be the young man who was daily held up to Paul as a model, and after whom it was his father's dearest hope that he would pattern. This young man was of a ruddy complexion, with a compressed, red mouth, and faded, near-sighted eyes, over which he wore thick spectacles, with gold bows that curved about his ears. He was clerk to one of the magnates of a great steel corporation, and was looked upon in Cordelia Street as a young man with a future. There was a story that, some five years ago—he was now barely twenty-six—he had been a trifle "dissipated," but in order to curb his appetites and save the loss of time and strength that a sowing of wild oats might have entailed, he had taken his chief's advice, oft reiterated to his employés, and at twenty-one had married the first woman whom he could persuade to share his fortunes. She happened to be an angular schoolmistress, much older than he, who also wore thick glasses, and who had now borne him four children, all near-sighted like herself.

The young man was relating how his chief, now cruising in the Mediterranean, kept in touch with all the details of the business, arranging his office hours on his yacht just as though he were at home, and "knocking off work enough to keep two stenographers busy." His father told, in turn, the plan his corporation was considering, of putting in an electric railway plant at Cairo. Paul snapped his teeth; he had an awful apprehension that they might spoil it all before he got there. Yet he rather liked to hear these legends of the iron kings, that were told and retold on Sundays and holidays; these stories of palaces in Venice, yachts on the Mediterranean, and high play at Monte Carlo appealed to his fancy, and he was interested in the triumphs of cash-boys who had become famous, though he had no mind for the cash-boy stage.

After supper was over, and he had helped to dry the dishes, Paul nervously asked his father whether he could go to George's to get some help in his geometry, and still more nervously asked for car-fare. This latter request he had to repeat, as his father, on principle, did not like to hear requests for money, whether much or little. He asked Paul whether he could not go to some boy who lived nearer, and told him that he ought not to leave his school work until Sunday; but he gave him the dime. He was not a poor man, but he had a worthy ambition to come up in the world. His only reason for allowing Paul to usher was that he thought a boy ought to be earning a little.

Paul bounded upstairs, scrubbed the greasy odour of the dishwater from his hands with the ill-smelling soap he hated, and then shook over his fingers a few drops of violet water from the bottle he kept hidden in his drawer. He left the house with his geometry conspicuously under his arm, and the moment he got out of Cordelia Street and boarded a downtown car, he shook off the lethargy of two deadening days, and began to live again.

The leading juvenile of the permanent stock company which played at one of the downtown theatres was an acquaintance of Paul's, and the boy had been invited to drop in at the Sunday-night rehearsals whenever he could. For more than a year Paul had spent every available moment loitering about Charley Edwards's dressing-room. He had won a place among Edwards's following not only because the young actor, who could not afford to employ a dresser, often found him useful, but because he recognized in Paul something akin to what churchmen term "vocation."

It was at the theatre and at Carnegie Hall that Paul really lived; the rest was but a sleep and a forgetting. This was Paul's fairy tale, and it had for him all the allurement of a secret love. The moment he inhaled the gassy, painty, dusty odour behind the scenes, he breathed like a prisoner set free, and felt within him the possibility of doing or saying splendid, brilliant things. The moment the cracked orchestra beat out the overture from "Martha," or jerked at the serenade from "Rigoletto," all stupid and ugly things slid from him, and his senses were deliciously, yet delicately fired.

Perhaps it was because, in Paul's world, the natural nearly always wore the guise of ugliness, that a certain element of artificiality seemed to him necessary in beauty. Perhaps it was because his experience of life elsewhere was so full of Sabbath-School picnics, petty economies, wholesome advice as to how to succeed in life, and the unescapable odours of cooking, that he found this existence so alluring, these smartly clad men and women so attractive, that he was so moved by these starry apple orchards that bloomed perennially under the limelight. It would be difficult to put it strongly enough how convincingly the stage entrance of that theatre was for Paul the actual portal of Romance. Certainly none of the company ever suspected it, least of all Charley Edwards. It was very like the old stories that used to float about London of fabulously rich Jews, who had subterranean halls, with palms, and fountains, and soft lamps and richly apparelled women who never saw the disenchanting light of London day. So, in the midst of that smoke-palled city, enamoured of figures and grimy toil, Paul had his secret temple, his wishing-carpet, his bit of blue-and-white Mediterranean shore bathed in perpetual sunshine.

Several of Paul's teachers had a theory that his imagination had been perverted by garish fiction; but the truth was, he scarcely ever read at all. The books at home were not such as would either tempt or corrupt a youthful mind, and as for reading the novels that some of his friends urged upon him—well, he got what he wanted much more quickly from music; any sort of music, from an orchestra to a barrel-organ. He needed only the spark, the indescribable thrill that made his imagination master of his senses, and he could make plots and pictures enough of his own. It was equally true that he was not stage-struck—not, at any rate, in the usual acceptation of that expression. He had no desire to become an actor, any more than he had to become a musician. He felt no necessity to do any of these things; what he wanted was to see, to be in the atmosphere, float on the wave of it, to be carried out, blue league after league, away from everything.

After a night behind the scenes, Paul found the schoolroom more than ever repulsive; the bare floors and naked walls; the prosy men who never wore frock coats, or violets in their buttonholes; the women with their dull gowns, shrill voices, and pitiful seriousness about prepositions that govern the dative. He could not bear to have the other pupils think, for a moment, that he took these people seriously; he must convey to them that he considered it all trivial, and was there only by way of a joke, anyway. He had autographed pictures of all the members of the stock company which he showed his classmates, telling them the most incredible stories of his familiarity with these people, of his acquaintance with the soloists who came to Carnegie Hall, his suppers with them and the flowers he sent them. When these stories lost their effect, and his audience grew listless, he would bid all the boys good-bye, announcing that he was going to travel for a while; going to Naples, to California, to Egypt. Then, next Monday, he would slip back, conscious and nervously smiling; his sister was ill, and he would have to defer his voyage until spring.

Matters went steadily worse with Paul at school. In the itch to let his instructors know how heartily he despised them, and how thoroughly he was appreciated elsewhere, he mentioned once or twice that he had no time to fool with theorems; adding—with a twitch of the eyebrows and a touch of that nervous bravado which so perplexed them—that he was helping the people down at the stock company; they were old friends of his.

The upshot of the matter was that the Principal went to Paul's father, and Paul was taken out of school and put to work. The manager at Carnegie Hall was told to get another usher in his stead; the doorkeeper at the theatre was warned not to admit him to the house; and Charley Edwards remorsefully promised the boy's father not to see him again.

The members of the stock company were vastly amused when some of Paul's stories reached them—especially the women. They were hard-working women, most of them supporting indolent husbands or brothers, and they laughed rather bitterly at having stirred the boy to such fervid and florid inventions. They agreed with the faculty and with his father, that Paul's was a bad case.

The east-bound train was ploughing through a January snowstorm; the dull dawn was beginning to show grey when the engine whistled a mile out of Newark. Paul started up from the seat where he had lain curled in uneasy slumber, rubbed the breath-misted window-glass with his hand, and peered out. The snow was whirling in curling eddies above the white bottom lands, and the drifts lay already deep in the fields and along the fences, while here and there the tall dead grass and dried weed stalks protruded black above it. Lights shone from the scattered houses, and a gang of labourers who stood beside the track waved their lanterns.

Paul had slept very little, and he felt grimy and uncomfortable. He had made the all-night journey in a day coach because he was afraid if he took a Pullman he might be seen by some Pittsburgh business man who had noticed him in Denny and Carson's office. When the whistle woke him, he clutched quickly at his breast pocket, glancing about him with an uncertain smile. But the little, clay-bespattered Italians were still sleeping, the slatternly women across the aisle were in open-mouthed oblivion, and even the crumby, crying babies were for the time stilled. Paul settled back to struggle with his impatience as best he could.

When he arrived at the Jersey City station, he hurried through his breakfast, manifestly ill at ease and keeping a sharp eye about him. After he reached the Twenty-Third Street station, he consulted a cabman, and had himself driven to a men's furnishing establishment which was just opening for the day. He spent upward of two hours there, buying with endless reconsidering and great care. His new street suit he put on in the fitting-room; the frock coat and dress clothes he had bundled into the cab with his new shirts. Then he drove to a hatter's and a shoe house. His next errand was at Tiffany's, where he selected silver-mounted brushes and a scarf-pin. He would not wait to have his silver marked, he said. Lastly, he stopped at a trunk shop on Broadway, and had his purchases packed into various travelling-bags.

It was a little after one o'clock when he drove up to the Waldorf, and, after settling with the cabman, went into the office. He registered from Washington; said his mother and father had been abroad, and that he had come down to await the arrival of their steamer. He told his story plausibly and had no trouble, since he offered to pay for them in advance, in engaging his rooms; a sleeping-room, sitting-room, and bath.

Not once, but a hundred times Paul had planned this entry into New York. He had gone over every detail of it with Charley Edwards, and in his scrapbook at home there were pages of description about New York hotels, cut from the Sunday papers.

When he was shown to his sitting-room on the eighth floor, he saw at a glance that everything was as it should be; there was but one detail in his mental picture that the place did not realize, so he rang for the bell-boy and sent him down for flowers. He moved about nervously until the boy returned, putting away his new linen and fingering it delightedly as he did so. When the flowers came, he put them hastily into water, and then tumbled into a hot bath. Presently he came out of his white bathroom, resplendent in his new silk underwear, and playing with the tassels of his red robe. The snow was whirling so fiercely outside his windows that he could scarcely see across the street; but within, the air was deliciously soft and fragrant. He put the violets and jonquils on the tabouret beside the couch, and threw himself down with a long sigh, covering himself with a Roman blanket. He was thoroughly tired; he had been in such haste, he had stood up to such a strain, covered so much ground in the last twenty-four hours, that he wanted to think how it had all come about. Lulled by the sound of the wind, the warm air, and the cool fragrance of the flowers, he sank into deep, drowsy retrospection.

It had been wonderfully simple; when they had shut him out of the theatre and concert hall, when they had taken away his bone, the whole thing was virtually determined. The rest was a mere matter of opportunity. The only thing that at all surprised him was his own courage—for he realized well enough that he had always been tormented by fear, a sort of apprehensive dread which, of late years, as the meshes of the lies he had told closed about him, had been pulling the muscles of his body tighter and tighter. Until now, he could not remember a time when he had not been dreading something. Even when he was a little boy, it was always there—behind him, or before, or on either side. There had always been the shadowed corner, the dark place into which he dared not look, but from which something seemed always to be watching him—and Paul had done things that were not pretty to watch, he knew.

But now he had a curious sense of relief, as though he had at last thrown down the gauntlet to the thing in the corner.

Yet it was but a day since he had been sulking in the traces; but yesterday afternoon that he had been sent to the bank with Denny and Carson's deposit, as usual—but this time he was instructed to leave the book to be balanced. There was above two thousand dollars in cheques, and nearly a thousand in the banknotes which he had taken from the book and quietly transferred to his pocket. At the bank he had made out a new deposit slip. His nerves had been steady enough to permit of his returning to the office, where he had finished his work and asked for a full day's holiday to-morrow, Saturday, giving a perfectly reasonable pretext. The bank book, he knew, would not be returned before Monday or Tuesday, and his father would be out of town for the next week. From the time he slipped the banknotes into his pocket until he boarded the night train for New York, he had not known a moment's hesitation.

How astonishingly easy it had all been; here he was, the thing done; and this time there would be no awakening, no figure at the top of the stairs. He watched the snowflakes whirling by his window until he fell asleep.

When he awoke, it was four o'clock in the afternoon. He bounded up with a start; one of his precious days gone already! He spent nearly an hour in dressing, watching every stage of his toilet carefully in the mirror. Everything was quite perfect; he was exactly the kind of boy he had always wanted to be.

When he went downstairs, Paul took a carriage and drove up Fifth Avenue toward the Park. The snow had somewhat abated; carriages and tradesmen's wagons were hurrying soundlessly to and fro in the winter twilight; boys in woollen mufflers were shovelling off the doorsteps; the Avenue stages made fine spots of colour against the white street. Here and there on the corners whole flower gardens blooming behind glass windows, against which the snowflakes stuck and melted; violets, roses, carnations, lilies-of-the-valley—somehow vastly more lovely and alluring that they blossomed thus unnaturally in the snow. The Park itself was a wonderful stage winter-piece.

When he returned, the pause of the twilight had ceased, and the tune of the streets had changed. The snow was falling faster, lights streamed from the hotels that reared their many stories fearlessly up into the storm, defying the raging Atlantic winds. A long, black stream of carriages poured down the Avenue, intersected here and there by other streams, tending horizontally. There were a score of cabs about the entrance of his hotel, and his driver had to wait. Boys in livery were running in and out of the awning stretched across the sidewalk, up and down the red velvet carpet laid from the door to the street. Above, about, within it all, was the rumble and roar, the hurry and toss of thousands of human beings as hot for pleasure as himself, and on every side of him toward the glaring affirmation of the omnipotence of wealth.

The boy set his teeth and drew his shoulders together in a spasm of realization; the plot of all dramas, the text of all romances, the nerve-stuff of all sensations was whirling about him like the snowflakes. He burnt like a fagot in a tempest.

When Paul came down to dinner, the music of the orchestra floated up the elevator shaft to greet him. As he stepped into the thronged corridor, he sank back into one of the chairs against the wall to get his breath. The lights, the chatter, the perfumes, the bewildering medley of colour—he had, for a moment, the feeling of not being able to stand it. But only for a moment; these were his own people, he told himself. He went slowly about the corridors, through the writing-rooms, smoking-rooms, reception-rooms, as though he were exploring the chambers of an enchanted palace, built and peopled for him alone.

When he reached the dining-room he sat down at a table near a window. The flowers, the white linen, the many-coloured wineglasses, the gay toilettes of the women, the low popping of corks, the undulating repetitions of the "Blue Danube" from the orchestra, all flooded Paul's dream with bewildering radiance. When the roseate tinge of his champagne was added—that cold, precious, bubbling stuff that creamed and foamed in his glass—Paul wondered that there were honest men in the world at all. This was what all the world was fighting for, he reflected; this was what all the struggle was about. He doubted the reality of his past. Had he ever known a place called Cordelia Street, a place where fagged-looking business men boarded the early car? Mere rivets in a machine they seemed to Paul —sickening men, with combings of children's hair always hanging to their coats, and the smell of cooking in their clothes. Cordelia Street ——Ah, that belonged to another time and country! Had he not always been thus, had he not sat here night after night, from as far back as he could remember, looking pensively over just such shimmering textures, and slowly twirling the stem of a glass like this one between his thumb and middle finger? He rather thought he had.

He was not in the least abashed or lonely. He had no especial desire to meet or to know any of these people; all he demanded was the right to look on and conjecture, to watch the pageant. The mere stage properties were all he contended for. Nor was he lonely later in the evening, in his loge at the Opera. He was entirely rid of his nervous misgivings, of his forced aggressiveness, of the imperative desire to show himself different from his surroundings. He felt now that his surroundings explained him. Nobody questioned the purple; he had only to wear it passively. He had only to glance down at his dress coat to reassure himself that here it would be impossible for anyone to humiliate him.

He found it hard to leave his beautiful sitting-room to go to bed that night, and sat long watching the raging storm from his turret window. When he went to sleep, it was with the lights turned on in his bedroom; partly because of his old timidity, and partly so that, if he should wake in the night, there would be no wretched moment of doubt, no horrible suspicion of yellow wallpaper, or of Washington and Calvin above his bed.

On Sunday morning the city was practically snow-bound. Paul breakfasted late, and in the afternoon he fell in with a wild San Francisco boy, a freshman at Yale, who said he had run down for a 'little flyer' over Sunday. The young man offered to show Paul the night side of the town, and the two boys went off together after dinner, not returning to the hotel until seven o'clock the next morning. They had started out in the confiding warmth of a champagne friendship, but their parting in the elevator was singularly cool. The freshman pulled himself together to make his train, and Paul went to bed. He awoke at two o'clock in the afternoon, very thirsty and dizzy, and rang for ice-water, coffee, and the Pittsburgh papers.

On the part of the hotel management, Paul excited no suspicion. There was this to be said for him, that he wore his spoils with dignity and in no way made himself conspicuous. His chief greediness lay in his ears and eyes, and his excesses were not offensive ones. His dearest pleasures were the grey winter twilights in his sitting-room; his quiet enjoyment of his flowers, his clothes, his wide divan, his cigarette, and his sense of power. He could not remember a time when he had felt so at peace with himself. The mere release from the necessity of petty lying, lying every day and every day, restored his self-respect. He had never lied for pleasure, even at school; but to make himself noticed and admired, to assert his difference from other Cordelia Street boys; and he felt a good deal more manly, more honest, even, now that he had no need for boastful pretensions, now that he could, as his actor friends used to say, "dress the part." It was characteristic that remorse did not occur to him. His golden days went by without a shadow, and he made each as perfect as he could.

On the eighth day after his arrival in New York, he found the whole affair exploited in the Pittsburgh papers, exploited with a wealth of detail which indicated that local news of a sensational nature was at a low ebb. The firm of Denny and Carson announced that the boy's father had refunded the full amount of his theft, and that they had no intention of prosecuting. The Cumberland minister had been interviewed, and expressed his hope of yet reclaiming the motherless lad, and Paul's Sabbath-School teacher declared that she would spare no effort to that end. The rumour had reached Pittsburgh that the boy had been seen in a New York hotel, and his father had gone East to find him and bring him home.

Paul had just come in to dress for dinner; he sank into a chair, weak in the knees, and clasped his head in his hands. It was to be worse than jail, even; the tepid waters of Cordelia Street were to close over him finally and forever. The grey monotony stretched before him in hopeless, unrelieved years;—Sabbath-School, Young People's Meeting, the yellow-papered room, the damp dish-towels; it all rushed back upon him with sickening vividness. He had the old feeling that the orchestra had suddenly stopped, the sinking sensation that the play was over. The sweat broke out on his face, and he sprang to his feet, looked about him with his white, conscious smile, and winked at himself in the mirror. With something of the childish belief in miracles with which he had so often gone to class, all his lessons unlearned, Paul dressed and dashed whistling down the corridor to the elevator.

He had no sooner entered the dining-room and caught the measure of the music than his remembrance was lightened by his old elastic power of claiming the moment, mounting with it, and finding it all-sufficient. The glare and glitter about him, the mere scenic accessories had again, and for the last time, their old potency. He would show himself that he was game, he would finish the thing splendidly. He doubted, more than ever, the existence of Cordelia Street, and for the first time he drank his wine recklessly. Was he not, after all, one of these fortunate beings? Was he not still himself, and in his own place? He drummed a nervous accompaniment to the music and looked about him, telling himself over and over that it had paid.

He reflected drowsily, to the swell of the violin and the chill sweetness of his wine, that he might have done it more wisely. He might have caught an outbound steamer and been well out of their clutches before now. But the other side of the world had seemed too far away and too uncertain then; he could not have waited for it; his need had been too sharp. If he had to choose over again, he would do the same thing to-morrow. He looked affectionately about the dining-room, now gilded with a soft mist. Ah, it had paid indeed!

Paul was awakened next morning by a painful throbbing in his head and feet. He had thrown himself across the bed without undressing, and had slept with his shoes on. His limbs and hands were lead-heavy, and his tongue and throat were parched. There came upon him one of those fateful attacks of clear-headedness that never occurred except when he was physically exhausted and his nerves hung loose. He lay still and closed his eyes and let the tide of realities wash over him.

His father was in New York; 'stopping at some joint or other,' he told himself. The memory of successive summers on the front stoop fell upon him like a weight of black water. He had not a hundred dollars left; and he knew now, more than ever, that money was everything, the wall that stood between all he loathed and all he wanted. The thing was winding itself up; he had thought of that on his first glorious day in New York, and had even provided a way to snap the thread. It lay on his dressing-table now; he had got it out last night when he came blindly up from dinner—but the shiny metal hurt his eyes, and he disliked the look of it, anyway.

He rose and moved about with a painful effort, succumbing now and again to attacks of nausea. It was the old depression exaggerated; all the world had become Cordelia Street. Yet somehow he was not afraid of anything, was absolutely calm; perhaps because he had looked into the dark corner at last, and knew. It was bad enough, what he saw there; but somehow not so bad as his long fear of it had been. He saw everything clearly now. He had a feeling that he had made the best of it, that he had lived the sort of life he was meant to live, and for half an hour he sat staring at the revolver. But he told himself that was not the way, so he went downstairs and took a cab to the ferry.

When Paul arrived at Newark, he got off the train and took another cab, directing the driver to follow the Pennsylvania tracks out of the town. The snow lay heavy on the roadways and had drifted deep in the open fields. Only here and there the dead grass or dried weed stalks projected, singularly black, above it.

Once well into the country, Paul dismissed the carriage and walked, floundering along the tracks, his mind a medley of irrelevant things. He seemed to hold in his brain an actual picture of everything he had seen that morning. He remembered every feature of both his drivers, the toothless old woman from whom he had bought the red flowers in his coat, the agent from whom he had got his ticket, and all of his fellow-passengers on the ferry. His mind, unable to cope with vital matters near at hand, worked feverishly and deftly at sorting and grouping these images. They made for him a part of the ugliness of the world, of the ache in his head, and the bitter burning on his tongue. He stooped and put a handful of snow into his mouth as he walked, but that, too, seemed hot. When he reached a little hillside, where the tracks ran through a cut some twenty feet below him, he stopped and sat down.

The carnations in his coat were drooping with the cold, he noticed; their red glory over. It occurred to him that all the flowers he had seen in the show windows that first night must have gone the same way, long before this. It was only one splendid breath they had, in spite of their brave mockery at the winter outside the glass. It was a losing game in the end, it seemed, this revolt against the homilies by which the world is run. Paul took one of the blossoms carefully from his coat and scooped a little hole in the snow, where he covered it up.

Then he dozed awhile, from his weak condition, seeming insensible to the cold.

The sound of an approaching train woke him, and he started to his feet, remembering only his resolution, and afraid lest he should be too late. He stood watching the approaching locomotive, his teeth chattering, his lips drawn away from them in a frightened smile; once or twice he glanced nervously sidewise, as though he were being watched. When the right moment came, he jumped. As he fell, the folly of his haste occurred to him with merciless clearness, the vastness of what he had left undone. There flashed through his brain, clearer than ever before, the blue of Adriatic water, the yellow of Algerian sands.

He felt something strike his chest—his body was being thrown swiftly through the air, on and on, immeasurably far and fast, while his limbs gently relaxed. Then, because the picture-making mechanism was crushed, the disturbing visions flashed into black, and Paul dropped back into the immense design of things.

by Kay Boyle

YOUR BODY IS A JEWEL BOX

Kay Boyle was born on February 19, 1903, in St. Paul, Minnesota, and educated in the East, but she has spent more of her life in England, France, Austria, and Germany than in the United States. Her earliest poems and short stories were published in the little magazines of the twenties, Broom, This Quarter, *and* transition, *and in* Poetry, *where her verse still occasionally appears. In 1934 Miss Boyle received a Guggenheim fellowship, and twice, in 1936 and 1941, she has won the O. Henry Memorial Award for the best short story of the year. Since 1929 she has published six volumes of short stories (among them, in 1936,* The White Horses of Vienna, *in which "Your Body Is a Jewel Box" was first collected), a book of verse, and thirteen novels, of which the most recent is* Generation Without Farewell *(1960). After the war Miss Boyle returned to Europe as a correspondent for* The New Yorker *and lived in Germany, where her husband was with the State Department until 1953.*

Characteristically, Miss Boyle sets "Your Body Is a Jewel Box" in Europe, not America. But the cruel respectability of middle-class life, the baffled inadequacy of the mother, the cheapness of the "good" daughter, the crashing vulgarity of the newspaper poem from which the story takes its title are not un-American. Neither, of course, is the final, disastrous, drunken ride through the winter dark.

THE rain was falling just as it did every day at this time of the year, great handfuls of it flung hard on the windows, and when Olive got out of bed she saw that Mildred was sitting on the roof again, holding her knees in her bare arms and crying in the rain.

"For heaven's sake," said Olive, opening the window, "come in, Mildred. Don't sit there like that. Come in, now, do," she said, reaching her hand out to her sister. The two of them were in their nightgowns still, the dark girl on the roof and the yellow-haired girl standing inside the bedroom. "Come in now, Mildred, and we'll go down to the fire and get dry."

But Mildred only raised her head from her arms and looked in what might have been grief at her sister. But in spite of the tears that ran out of her eyes, it was not grief, for there was no look of sorrow in her face; only the black inhuman look of a wounded beast, even in pain, the small, suspicious, weary eye. Her nightdress was so thin and it clung to her so with the wet that the shape of her breasts and her thighs could be clearly seen. Her short hair was in wringing curls all over her head and down the lower side of her cheek and jaw sprang a little growth of darkness, as on a youth's still virgin face.

"Come in, now do," said Olive at the window, and it was as if an evil, black-eyed man were sitting there on the roof, looking distrustingly at the blond young girl in her nightdress as she leaned out into the rain. "You have no right to do like that!" Olive cried out. "If you catch your death, who is it has to nurse you through? You don't think of anyone. I'm cold here, I'm catching cold."

"I'm not cold," said Mildred, and the animal-dark, animal-wounded eyes looked at Olive, and she drew her knees up closer The shaking of her flesh could be seen, her quivering, dark-haired arms, and the shaking shape of her rain-wet thighs.

"I'm going to call everyone, then," Olive said, hugging herself in her arms for warmth. "I'm going to fetch Dr. Peabody over."

Mildred put her head down on her arms again and she did not answer, and Olive went running downstairs in the little old house. The kitchen was warm, with the fire already red in the kitchener, and Olive ran in and stood shaking in her nightgown with her bare feet on the linoleum floor. The father was eating his breakfast in the kitchen, and the mother was filling the teapot with water from the kettle on the stove.

"Mildred's out on the roof again," she said, rubbing her bare arms in the palms of her hands. Her face was wet from the rain and there were drops of it clinging still in her light, uncombed hair.

"For heaven's sake," said the mother, putting the kettle down, and the two of them ran upstairs after Olive: the mother shaking her short, little hands from her wrists, and the father with egg on his mustaches.

"Come in now, Mildred, do," said the father, standing at the window and looking at his daughter sitting there in the rain. "Come in to us, now, there's a good girl," he said. His hair was gray, but in his mustaches there was still a shade of russet left, like the flash of a fox's tail. He had not put on his collar yet, and there was a brassy collar button holding his striped shirt together at the neck. His eyes, pale and innocently blue, were wide open on his daughter.

"Come in now to your dad," said the mother with her full neck shaking. "Mildred lovey, this is no way to do."

"I'm going to fetch Dr. Peabody over," Olive shouted out impatiently at the window, but Mildred did not lift her head. Olive put on her stockings, pulling them up over her plump, hairless legs and twisting them savagely above her knees. Downstairs, she put on her Wellingtons and her raincoat and ran down the path to the gate. Every house in the block was the same, and the same little pieces of garden ran from the front doors to identical gates on the narrow, quiet street. Dr. Peabody's house was on the other side, set apart in the grounds, with trees around it. He did not lose a moment, and in spite of his sixty years he hurried as fast as Olive across the street and into the house where Mildred was sitting on the roof overlooking the back yards.

"Now, Mildred," he said, standing among the members of the family at the window, "I know you want to please us, Mildred. I know you want to be a good girl, don't you? So you're going to make us all happy, and you're going to come in out of the rain."

Mildred looked up at the sound of his voice, her head quickly lifted and a little cocked to one side, as a dog might at the sound of a whistle he knew. But still she had no intention of coming to them.

"I like it here, Dr. Peabody," she said with the rain falling over her face. Her neck was strong and short, like a man's, and broad, with the Adam's apple riding thick and slow in it as she spoke. "I'm not cold, whatever you say. Like this I don't get time to think about other things. I feel hot when I'm lying in bed. I don't feel sick out here in the air like I do closed up in a room, Dr. Peabody."

Dr. Peabody, Dr. Peabody, save me, said the eyes in the thwarted, manlike face. *Let there be some words for the fire in me, that it be suffocated, that it expire. Dr. Peabody, Dr. Peabody,* asked the black, mistrusting eyes, and Dr. Peabody answered:

"Look at your mother and father here, Mildred, look how you're worrying them. Why don't you make up your mind you're not going to act like this any more? Think how happy they'd be if you didn't act like this, Mildred. They've got everything they need to make for happiness in this life, and so have you. Health, and work, and a nice home to live in." Dr. Peabody stood at the window, leaning his old hands on the sill and talking in his equable voice of these things to her: of health and happiness, of tranquillity and love, as if the sound of these words of the sane would draw her back from the brink of where she was. "Come back, Mildred," he said. "You're freezing to death out there, my dear. You mustn't try to make us think you're not. You mustn't try to deceive us, you know. Now, be a good girl and come along in."

"I'm not trying to deceive you, Dr. Peabody," said Mildred, with her black, hard, animal eye on his in distrust. "I'm not trying to deceive anybody. Only I don't think I'm a girl. I think something's happening to me. I don't think I'm a girl any more."

"Of course, you're a girl," said Dr. Peabody. He looked at the mother's and father's faces and smiled in gentle sympathy as he quietly shook his head. "Enough of this now, Mildred," he said in a brisker tone. "You come right in now and we'll get you warm and dry, and I'll give you a warm drink that'll send you off to sleep for a little while."

"No," said Mildred, putting her head down again on her bare shaking arms. "I want to stay here."

It was as well the time of year for the birds to be flying, and there was a great movement of them now through the rain. There were small black birds of one kind or another passing over the roofs with quick, unswooping strokes of the wing, and these came, as if in curiosity, to settle on the wires that stretched through the back gardens, and now at the windows of the houses behind there were other onlookers gathering. The family could see the shirt sleeves and the aprons of their neighbors moving with guilt behind the curtains of their kitchen or back bedroom windows, watching the sight of Mildred, wearing nothing but a nightgown, sitting on the roof in the rain.

In a little while, the father had to go off to work, and Dr. Peabody left the house to telephone the police station and tell the constables to come. The last time it had been the fire department that came when Mildred set fire to the rug in the dining room. The mother stayed at the window, talking in a low, loving, tremulous voice to her daughter, but Mildred never answered.

"Leave her be, why don't you?" said Olive in anger as she dressed quickly in the bedroom before the constables would come. She put her corsets on over her soft, white, apple flesh, and snapped her stockings fast. "She's just doing it on purpose," she said over her bare shoulder to her mother. She could not bear to think of the neighbors watching the scene on the roof from their houses. "She ought to be ashamed," she said. She was wondering which of the constables would be sent. She combed her hair out quickly and rolled it into a bun at the back of her neck, and then she put on her brown wool dress. Her face was round and sweet-looking in the glass before her, and she put on her brooch with care. "She ought to be ashamed," she said to her mother bitterly, "sitting there showing her legs and everything like that." She looked a good, pure, healthy girl standing there fixing her hair before the mirror, with her backside shaped out broad and soft in her dress.

The mother turned back from the window and looked at Olive with her little eyes.

"I read a thing in the paper last night," she said, and she clasped her swollen little hands together. "Maybe it would bring her to her senses, Olive. You run and get me the paper. I don't know what to do."

She had a blue apron tied around her, and her spectacles were on her nose, and when Olive brought her the paper from the kitchen, she stood pressing herself against the sill of the open window, reading the poem out loud to Mildred on the roof.

"Listen to this, Mildred," she said. "You listen, lovey, to what it says. It goes: 'Your body is a jewel box, Given to you to hold, A gift that is more precious Than rubies, pearl, or gold.' That's pretty, isn't it, now, Mildred?" Olive stood with her back to the window, angrily fastening on her low, brown shoes. " 'Guard it from marauders,' " the mother's voice went on, reading out loud, " 'Let nothing sordid soil it. No smirch of soot or coal. Your body is a jewel box,' " said the mother's shaking voice, and she could see the neighbors watching slyly from their windows. " 'The jewel is your soul.' "

The mother put down the paper, and there were tears standing underneath her spectacles. She said:

"That means you oughtn't to let all those strange people look at you, Mildred, lovey. You ought to be too proud to let them see you haven't got anything on."

The breath was coming short in her breast, and suddenly the constable's head moved up beyond the rain gutter. There were his helmet and his face just above the rain gutter, and then the tops of his shoulders in his waterproof could be seen. He was standing on a ladder, waiting to be told what to do. Dr. Peabody and another constable came up the stairs without ringing the doorbell and came into the bedroom. Olive saw it was the young constable, and she looked swiftly at her reflection in the glass.

"Mildred," said Dr. Peabody from the window, but Mildred gave no sign. "I've called some friends of mine here to persuade you to come in and put some clothes on. But I know you're going to come along without making any more fuss about it."

But in a little while there was nothing for the young constable to do but to squeeze himself through the window and start making his way across the roof in the rain to where Mildred was sitting.

"If she makes a jump for the edge, you get her," he called out to the other constable, who was waiting on the ladder. He was holding on to the rain pipe now and he nodded his head. The young constable slid cautiously along toward the seated girl, and as he came close to this dark, strange, inhuman creature, a rush of excitement filled his heart. He could see everything clearly through her thin white nightdress, and even the color of her flesh where the cloth clung fast.

All the neighbors were watching from their back windows quite openly now, and some of them were laughing as the constable moved along the sloping roof until he had come between Mildred and the edge. There was just place for him to squat down, with his hands holding on to the rain-wet shingles.

"Come on, now, Miss," he said, squatting before her in his raincoat. "You must be cold sitting there like that. You don't want to do a thing like that, you know."

Mildred sat with her face hidden in her arms and the rain falling thick and fast upon her, and in every line of her body, in the naked, dark-haired arms, and the shape of the legs revealed, there was a terrible power that roused and impelled him. And yet he felt that he would be sick if he had to touch her with his hands.

"Just help her up here to the window, Constable, please," said Dr. Peabody, leaning out in the rain. The young constable stood up and moved forward toward Mildred, and put his fingers, a little hesitant, underneath her arm. The skin was cold and wet, and he felt his soul recoil within him, and yet she seemed to him a marvelously strange, marvelously evil thing.

"Come along, now, Miss," he urged with a husky voice, and without a word Mildred rose and went with him back up the roof and in through the open window. She stood in the middle of the bedroom, and *Dr. Peabody,* was her anguish saying, *Dr. Peabody, save me from the down springing up on my face and the heaviness in my groins that I cannot give away.* There was no sign of it in her wary eyes as she stood with the rain dripping from her, looking in distrust from one face to the other, looking at her own mother and at her sister and at the doctor and the constable, as if she could never comprehend them as long as she lived.

The rain had drawn off for a little in the afternoon, but Olive and Mildred were wearing their raincoats when they left the house. The doctor's double-seated car was stopped by the curb, with the light-tan top up over it and the isinglass curtains fastened all around, and because the doctor could not get off that afternoon, his nephew was sitting in the driver's seat. Beside him sat his friend, the chemist's son, a responsible young man, whom the doctor had asked to go. As the girls came down the front walk to the little gate, the young constable, wearing plain clothes now, got out from the back seat and opened the door of the car for them.

"Mildred's very glad to be going for a ride this afternoon," said Olive, looking the young constable full in the face. The color ran up from under his collar and into his ears as he helped Olive in. The two young men in the front seat of the car lifted their hats and said good afternoon to her. "We've been telling Mildred how nice it was of you to ask us driving," she said, and she gave a sly, quick glance out the open door to the sight of Mildred standing there with her head averted.

"I don't want to go," said Mildred, scarcely aloud.

"Of course, you want to come," said Olive, and she leaned forward and smiled wisely at the young men. "We're just going for a little ride, Mildred. You know that's all we're going to do."

"You help Mildred in, now, Fogarty," said the doctor's nephew, nodding to the constable. The mother was standing in the sitting-room bay, watching them, with her handkerchief up to the side of her face. She saw the young constable help Mildred in, and then follow her into the car, and close the door behind them. When the car started down the street, she waved her handkerchief and the tears fell down her face, but no one in the doctor's car looked out through the yellowing, misted glass.

"I don't want to go," said Mildred. She had a white felt hat on, and her hair stood out dark and bushy from underneath the brim. Her nose was small and pinched in her face and her cheeks were as white as candles. She was holding her bare hands clenched between her legs.

"You're fine and dandy here now, Mildred," said Olive, looking across her to the young constable in his plain brown suit sitting on the other side. "You know it was nice of these young men to ask us out, now, wasn't it, Mildred?" she said, and her mild, blue wide-set eyes were on the constable.

"I know where you're taking me," said Mildred. The car took the corner of the street and set out fast on the highway.

"We're taking you for a little drive, Mildred," said the doctor's nephew, looking around from the wheel. "You ought to be tickled to death," he said.

He winked at Olive, and she gave him a broad, quick smile.

"All you have to do is to lean back and stop worrying," said the chemist's son.

"I don't want to go there," said Mildred. She was riding with her hands pressed down between her legs and her eyes fixed on the soiled, worn bit of carpet on the floor. The constable had folded his arms across his chest and he rode with his face turned away from Mildred, his eyes staring straight at the dark isinglass through which nothing could be seen. The air was beginning to fill with the smell of the girls' rubber coats as the five of them rode in the curtained-in, swaying car.

"Everything's going to be all right, you'll just see," said Olive. She looked, half smiling with pleasure, at the two heads and the shoulders of the young men riding before them, and then she glanced at the constable sitting on the other side. "Mildred's being a very good girl, isn't she, Mr. Fogarty?" she said.

"Yes," said the young constable with a start, and then his voice stopped in his throat.

"I don't want to go there," said Mildred, and he could feel her flesh beside him. Their thighs were pressed close in the unwieldy, shaking car, their knees withdrawn, their feet apart, and he sat looking into the strange afternoon of yellow isinglass, his heart stirred by the wild power of her hidden flesh. It might have been the most beautiful woman of all riding there beside him, for the terrible, the unbearable love he had for her as he looked into the isinglass. But when his gaze slid sideways to her face, he saw there was nothing of beauty about her, but only her youth, and something like perversion in her body or mind, and this appetite that was starving in her, and crying for food whenever he turned away.

"We're not taking you anywhere, Mildred," said the doctor's nephew, looking around from the wheel again and smiling at Olive. "You just trust us and there won't be any trouble."

"I think Mildred ought to be very grateful to you for taking the afternoon off like this, Mr. Fogarty," said Olive, looking across her sister to the young constable. Suddenly Mildred turned her head and looked straight at her sister with her small, black, wary eyes.

"Don't take me there, don't take me there," she said quickly. Her two hands were held down tight between her knees. "Don't do it. Don't do it to me," she said. "Don't do it, Olive."

"Come on now, Mildred," said the chemist's son. He turned halfway around in his seat and looked at Mildred. "Look here, we're all good friends of yours," he said. "You know me, and Kingdom and Jim Fogarty riding there beside you. We wouldn't do anything to do you any harm."

"Don't take me there," said Mildred in a low, quick voice. She looked with her small, inhuman eyes at the chemist's son, at the back of the other man at the wheel, and then she turned to the constable, who sat with his arms folded over beside her. "Please don't take me there," she said.

The road was running now along the edge of the lake, and through the glass of the windshield they could see the quiet waters, wide and black and still, as the deep waters of the sea might be. The constable could not bring himself to look into her face, and he sat watching the toes of his shoes on the carpet near the long, black-strapped shoes of the girl who rode beside him in the car. She was so near to him that he thought his heart would burst with his desire, but then when his gaze slid to the side of her face, he saw there was nothing in it to draw a man: there was nothing in the pinched, white nostril, and in the piece of the hard, thick, manlike neck that showed.

They had been an hour driving, and the doctor's nephew turned around from the wheel and nodded wisely at Olive.

"It won't be much longer now," he said.

At the sound of his voice, Mildred started up as if from sleep and her thigh in the raincoat pressed hard against the constable's leg.

"I don't want to go there," she said, and Olive, with her hands folded over in her lap, smiled at the chemist's son.

"Let's have a song," she said. She looked toward the constable. "I'm sure you have a good singing voice, Mr. Fogarty," she said.

"I never sing, I can't sing," said the constable, and the color ran into his neck.

"Oh, I'm sure you're a fine singer, Mr. Fogarty," said Olive, smiling. "I always think a good song makes the time pass quicker, don't you?"

"Well, anyone can sing *Tipperary* or anything like that," said the chemist's son. They had finished the stretch of country now and were coming into a town.

"Here's Sloughcombe," said the doctor's nephew, and Mildred said:

"Don't do it. Don't do it to me, Olive."

The darkness was beginning to come, and here and there along the city street a few of the windows were lighted.

"Getting ready for Christmas," said the doctor's nephew above the sound of the car rattling over the cobbles. There were festoons of green and red paper, and strings of tinsel, strung across a stationer's and a toyshop's glass. In a moment they were out of the town and mounting a hill on the other side, and Mildred said:

"Please don't do this to me."

Her voice came out of the dark to them, small and cold, without entreaty or despair. The doctor's nephew leaned forward and turned on the headlights of the car, and on one side of the road the hedges stood up, as green as if flooded with sunlight.

"We're coming to it now," said the chemist's son under his breath, and the doctor's nephew slowed down the car to take the curve at the gateway. As they drove up the private road of the grounds, they could see the lighted windows of a building hidden in the darkness and trees before them, and Olive took a pair of gloves out of her raincoat pocket and drew them over her hands.

"Put your hat on straight," she said quickly to Mildred.

The car came to a stop at the steps of the building. There were bars at the windows, and an attendant in a white coat opened the door to let them in.

It was seven o'clock at night by the time they had settled everything for Mildred. They left her sitting on a chair in the big hall, and they went out and got in the car again and drove away.

"Well, it all went off without any trouble, after all," said the doctor's nephew at the wheel.

"She was meek as lamb, wasn't she?" said Olive. She was sitting in the back seat alone with the constable now. He sat far from her, in the other corner, and she could just make out the shape of him, sitting erect, with his arms folded over, swaying with the motion of the car.

"We ought to be thankful it passed off the way it did," said the chemist's son. "The time I went there with Weston's brother, it took four of us to hold him down. You never knew what he was going to do next. But that was shell shock. That wasn't the same thing."

"You ought to be glad she's where she's off your hands," said the doctor's nephew, driving. "She'll be better off there than anywhere else. When they're like that, it's all the same to them. They don't know if they're home or where they are. They're living on another plane, you know." He said this easily and with authority, for he was studying to be a doctor himself. "You only have to look at her eyes to know she's not like everybody else," he said, watching the road before him. "There's no use trying to reason with them when they're that way."

The lights of the town were coming up before them, and just within the paved street the chemist's son said:

"Why don't we stop and have a drink?"

"That's just what I need," said the doctor's nephew.

Olive glanced at the constable as the car drew up at the curb before the public house. She could see his profile outlined clearly against the dim, glowing curtain of isinglass. His nose was short, like an Irishman's nose, and his lip was long, and his under-jaw was square and firm. Under his brows there was a fringe, and this was the curving brush of his lashes thrusting thick and ferny against the yellow light.

"Come in and have a drink, Olive," said the chemist's son, opening the door of the car. But Olive shook her head.

"I'll wait here," she said, smiling at them. The young constable made no move to get out of the car.

"You drink, Fogarty?" asked the doctor's nephew.

"No," said the constable, shifting a little. "I don't care about having a drink."

"Don't you think you ought to have one after a ride like this?" said Olive, looking toward his corner.

"No, thank you," said the constable, uneasily. Olive watched the other two go through the door to the public bar.

"I thought the weather was going to clear," said Olive, turning her head again toward Fogarty. "The radio said last night it was going to clear."

"It looks as if it might rain now," said the constable, looking into the isinglass. He cleared his throat, and recrossed his legs. Olive smoothed the front of her raincoat out.

"Well, it passed off very well, didn't it?" she said in a moment.

"Yes," said the constable, starting as he spoke.

"It was the first time I was ever inside an asylum," said Olive, looking toward him brightly. "I suppose it was the first time you were ever inside an asylum, Mr. Fogarty? I think it was a very interesting experience to have."

The two young men came out of the public house and climbed into the car again.

"It certainly sets you up to have a drink like that," said the doctor's nephew. "Fogarty, you and Olive would feel better if you had. We've a long way to go and we won't get home till late."

"You see, I don't like going in," said Fogarty.

"Oh, you're all right without your uniform, aren't you?" said the chemist's son. "Look," he said as the motor started, "I'll run in and get you each a drink. What'll it be, Fogarty?" He opened the front door of the car again and jumped down into the street. "I don't mind having another myself," he said. "What'll it be, Olive?"

"Oh, I'll just have a little whisky," said Olive, "with a splash of soda in it."

"I'll have the same thing," said the constable from the corner of the car.

"Nobody's going to get ahead of me," said the doctor's nephew. He turned the motor off and followed the other man into the bar. Olive and Fogarty sat waiting for their drinks to come.

"They're a pair, the two of them!" said Olive, laughing. But the constable was thinking that if he were a man with a wife there would not be this fear and trembling in him. He was scared of his life that

Olive would sit nearer to him, or that she would reach out and touch him with her hand. "I feel as if a weight had been lifted off me," Olive was saying. "We've been talking for months now about taking Mildred to the asylum, and Dr. Peabody has been urging us to do it. Of course, Mom and the rest of us were against it all the time. But I know it's all for the best, and she'll be in good hands there."

The constable sat erect in the corner of the car, with his arms folded over, not daring to turn his head to her, to speak, not daring to see her, for fear that she stir him as Mildred had done. But even as he took down his drink, and the car started off, even then he could feel her turned toward him in the dark. He could see her face, wide and peach-colored under her felt hat, the yellow hair rolled up from her neck in back, and her lips half open.

"I'm sure we've done the right thing for Mildred," she was saying, and the doctor's nephew looked back from the wheel and said:

"Oh, you don't have to worry about that." He talked with authority to her over his shoulder. "They've got good men there," he said. "The kind of methods they put into operation ought to bring anyone around if there's any hope for them. I wouldn't be surprised to see Mildred walk out of there as sane as you and me at the end of a couple of years."

"I know," said Olive, looking toward the constable in the dark.

"Look, there's a pub along here in a minute," said the chemist's son. "What do you say we all pop in and have a drink?"

"That's a good idea," said the doctor's nephew.

This time the four of them went in, and the constable stood a little apart from the others, tall and clean-looking in his plain brown suit, drinking his whisky quickly down. They had two drinks each, and Olive stood at the bar, laughing, with the two young men. The constable saw her pure-white throat, laughing and bare in the collar of her coat, and the color that was shining on her face. He watched the chemist's son put his arm around her as they went out the door. When they got to the car, he said:

"Say, I'm going to join you two in back, Olive. I think you need a chaperon."

"Ha, ha, ha," laughed Olive, getting into the car, as she sat down, gasping with laughter, between Fogarty and the chemist's son. As the doctor's nephew took his place at the wheel and started the motor she began singing: *I'm in the Mood for Love.*

"It's a shame I've got to drive this car," said the doctor's nephew, looking around at her. The chemist's son put his arm around her again.

"You watch the road, Kingdom!" he called out. "You've got enough to keep you busy driving in this rain."

Fogarty could feel Olive's body close to him on the seat. He could feel the pressing of her heavy thigh in the raincoat beside him, and the seeking of her legs for his while she lay in the other man's arms. She was trying to sing, with her head pulled away from the other man in the corner, and he could feel her eyes, and her legs, and her body turning toward him and seeking him out.

But, as if riding in the car with them, there was Mildred as well: the figure bowed double in the raincoat, the hat that was not white any longer, and the voice saying, the voice repeating. He could see the side of the nostril, the down dark on the jawbone, and the man-like neck descending, bone by bone, to where the small breasts sprang. In a moment, he saw that they had stopped again, and the light from another public house was blurring the yellow isinglass.

"Get us a drink, you, Fogarty," said the chemist's son. "I'm not moving from where I am."

"Come along in with me, Fogarty," said the doctor's nephew. "We'll bring those two their drinks outside."

The constable walked into the bar behind Kingdom and began drinking very fast. He drank three whiskies, and then he carried the two glasses out to Olive and the man in the car. He stood on the side-walk, waiting while they drank, not looking in at them, but lifting his face like a blind man to the fine, fast-falling rain. Kingdom was still drinking when he went back into the bar with the empty glasses, and Fogarty had another glass with him. When he climbed into the back seat of the car again he was thinking of Mildred and how they had left her sitting in the insane-asylum hall.

"Don't, don't, please, don't," came Olive's voice out of the darkness.

"Some chaps have all the luck," said Kingdom from the front seat, jerking his head toward the chemist's son. "You better come up for air, Geoffrey," he said as he started the motor.

"Mind your own business, Kingdom," said the chemist's son in a muffled, tight voice from the depths of the seat of the car.

"I'll call a policeman if you try anything like that," said Olive, laughing. She drew away from him and closer to Fogarty.

"Come on, now, come on," wooed the chemist's son. He was trying to draw her down again into the darkness of the seat. "Come on, come on, now," came his soft whispering, wooing voice as the car went rattling, racing on through the dark and the falling rain.

Fogarty sat upright in the corner, holding his hands fast under his folded arms. Olive's legs were feeling for his, softly, yearningly closing on his as she pulled away from Geoffrey. And if he had a wife, Fogarty was thinking, if he had a wife of his own the fire would not be burning like this in his body. Deeper and deeper, and wilder and wilder burned his blood until he felt that his bones themselves were utterly burned away.

"Say, you chaps back there," said the doctor's nephew with a whine, "you've got all the luck. Who wants to drive this car and let me have a chance?"

"Come on back," Olive called out. "There's always room for one more!"

Suddenly she turned around on the seat and faced the constable in the corner. His leg was running to wax against her, and he could hear the breath in her mouth. The whisky, or madness, or love was swinging in his head as he put his arms in agony around her, and her mouth came wet and moaning to his mouth.

"Hey, Fogarty——" shouted the chemist's son, and Kingdom looked back, whining, from the wheel.

"Say, I've been among the onlookers just about long——" he began, but he did not finish. What they took for a sudden downpouring of the rain hit the glass of the windshield like a wave, and the lights went out with it, without terror, and without sound. The movement of the car had ceased as if a hand had closed upon it in the dark.

It was not until the next afternoon that anyone thought of looking into the lake for the doctor's car, and there it was, sure enough, with the marks showing clearly where it had left the road. The four corpses were sitting in it, the four young people, just as death had found them, inside the curtains of isinglass.

by John Collier

AH, THE UNIVERSITY

John Collier was born in London on May 3, 1901. He was educated privately and never attended a university. He published his first poems, Gemini, *when he was twenty and his first novel,* His Monkey Wife, *almost ten years later. Since then he has collected his short stories under such titles as* The Devil and All *(1934),* A Touch of Nutmeg *(1943), and* Fancies and Goodnights *(1951). Mr. Collier has visited the United States frequently, spending much of his time in Hollywood.*

In an essay on laughter Henri Bergson remarked that "comic absurdity gives us from the outset the impression of playing with ideas. Our first impulse is to join the game. That relieves us from the strain of thinking." Perhaps with this in mind we might quickly dispose of "Ah, the University." It is comic absurdity—in the father's profound egotism and appetite, in his son's dedicated and slipshod scholarship. But these delightful exaggerations compel us to the "strain of thinking." For by mocking father and son and the flagrantly serious business of learning, Mr. Collier deftly puts his foot in "the closing college door."

JUST outside London there lived an old father who dearly loved his only son. Accordingly, when the boy was a youngster of some eighteen years, the old man sent for him and, with a benevolent glimmer of his horn-rimmed spectacles, said, "Well, Jack, you are now done with school. No doubt you are looking forward to going to the university."

"Yes, Dad, I am," said the son.

"You show good judgment," said the father. "The best years of one's whole life are unquestionably those which are spent at the university. Apart from the vast honeycomb of learning, the mellow voices of the professors, the venerable gray buildings, and the atmosphere of culture and refinement, there is the delight of being in possession of a comfortable allowance."

"Yes, Dad," said the son.

"Rooms of one's own," continued the father, "little dinners to one's friends, endless credit with the tradespeople, pipes, cigars, claret, Burgundy, clothes."

"Yes, Dad," said the son.

"There are exclusive little clubs," said the old man, "all sorts of sports, May Weeks, theatricals, balls, parties, rags, binges, scaling of walls, dodging of proctors, fun of every conceivable description."

"Yes! Yes, Dad!" cried the son.

"Certainly nothing in the world is more delightful than being at the university," said the father. "The springtime of life! Pleasure after pleasure! The world seems a whole dozen oysters, each with a pearl in it. Ah, the university! However, I'm not going to send you there."

"Then why the hell do you go on so about it?" said poor Jack.

"I did so in order that you might not think I was carelessly underestimating the pleasures I must call upon you to renounce," said his father. "You see, Jack, my health is not of the best; nothing but champagne agrees with me, and if I smoke a second-rate cigar, I get a vile taste in my mouth. My expenses have mounted abominably and I shall have very little to leave to you, yet my dearest wish is to see you in a comfortable way of life."

"If that is your wish, you might gratify it by sending me to the university," said Jack.

"We must think of the future," said his father. "You will have your living to earn, and in a world where culture is the least marketable of assets. Unless you are to be a schoolmaster or a curate, you will gain no great advantage from the university."

"Then what am I to be?" the young man asked.

"I read only a little while ago," said his father, "the following words, which flashed like sudden lightning upon the gloom in which I was considering your future: 'Most players are weak.' These words came from a little brochure upon the delightful and universally popular game of poker. It is a game which is played for counters, commonly called chips, and each of these chips represents an agreeable sum of money."

"Do you mean that I am to be a card-sharper?" cried the son.

"Nothing of the sort," replied the old man promptly. "I am asking you to be strong, Jack. I am asking you to show initiative, individuality. Why learn what everyone else is learning? You, my dear boy, shall be the first to study poker as systematically as others study languages, science, mathematics, and so forth—the first to tackle it as a student. I have set aside a cosy little room with chair, table, and some completely new packs of cards. A bookshelf contains several standard works on the game, and a portrait of Machiavelli hangs above the mantelpiece."

The young man's protests were vain, so he set himself reluctantly to study. He worked hard, mastered the books, wore the spots off a hundred packs of cards, and at the end of the second year he set out into the world with his father's blessing and enough cash to sit in on a few games of penny ante.

After Jack left, the old man consoled himself with his glass of champagne and his first-rate cigar and those other little pleasures which are the solace of the old and the lonely. He was getting on very well with these when one day the telephone rang. It was an overseas call from Jack, whose existence the old man had all but forgotten.

"Hullo, Dad!" cried the son in tones of great excitement. "I'm in Paris, sitting in on a game of poker with some Americans."

"Good luck to you!" said the old man, preparing to hang up the receiver.

"Listen, Dad!" cried the son. "It's like this. Well—just for once I'm playing without any limit."

"Lord have mercy on you!" said the old man.

"There's two of them still in," said the son. "They've raised me fifty thousand dollars and I've already put up every cent I've got."

"I would rather," groaned the old man, "see a son of mine at the university than in such a situation."

"But I've got four kings!" cried the young man.

"You can be sure the others have aces or straight flushes," said the old man. "Back down, my poor boy. Go out and play for cigarette ends with the habitués of your doss house."

"But listen, Dad!" cried the son. "This is a stud round, and nothing wild. I've seen an ace chucked in. I've seen all the tens and fives chucked in. There isn't a straight flush possible."

"Is that so?" cried the old man. "Never let it be said I didn't stand behind my boy. Hold everything. I'm coming to your assistance."

The son went back to the card table and begged his opponents to postpone matters until his father could arrive, and they, smiling at their cards, were only too willing to oblige him.

A couple of hours later the old man arrived by plane at Le Bourget, and shortly thereafter, he was standing beside the card table, rubbing his hands, smiling, affable, the light glinting merrily upon his horn-rimmed spectacles. He shook hands with the Americans and noted their prosperous appearances. "Now what have we here?" said he, sliding into his son's seat and fishing out his money.

"The bet," said one of the opponents, "stands at fifty thousand dollars. Seen by me. It's for you to see or raise."

"Or run," said the other.

"I trust my son's judgment," said the old man. "I shall raise fifty thousand dollars before I even glance at these cards in my hand." With that he pushed forward a hundred thousand dollars of his own money.

"I'll raise that hundred thousand dollars," said the first of his opponents.

"I'll stay and see," said the other.

The old man looked at his cards. His face turned several colours in rapid succession. A low and quavering groan burst from his lips and he was seen to hesitate for a long time, showing all the signs of an appalling inward struggle. At last he summoned up his courage and, pushing out his last hundred thousand (which represented all the cigars, champagne, and other little pleasures he had to look forward to), he licked his lips several times and said, "I'll see you."

"Four kings," said the first opponent, laying down his hand.

"Hell!" said the second. "Four queens."

"And I," moaned the old man, "have four knaves." With that he turned about and seized his son by the lapels of his jacket, shaking him as a terrier does a rat. "Curse the day," said he, "that I ever became the father of a damned fool!"

"I swear I thought they were kings," cried the young man.

"Don't you know that the 'v' is for valets?" said his father.

"Good God!" the son said. "I thought the 'v' was something to do with French kings. You know, Charles, Louis, V one, V two, V three. Oh, what a pity I was never at the university!"

"Go," said the old man. "Go there, or go to Hell or wherever you wish. Never let me see or hear from you again." And he stamped out of the room before his son or anyone else could say a word, even to tell him it was high-low stud they were playing and that the four knaves had won half the pot.

The young man, pocketing his share, mused that ignorance of every sort is deplorable, and, bidding his companions farewell, left Paris without further delay, and very soon he was entered at the university.

by Lionel Trilling

OF THIS TIME, OF THAT PLACE

Lionel Trilling was born on July 4, 1905, in New York City, and attended local public schools. He received his bachelor's, master's, and doctor's degrees from Columbia University and has taught English and American literature there since 1931. Best known for his Matthew Arnold *(1939) and for critical essays published in such magazines as* The Nation, The New Republic, Partisan Review *and* The Kenyon Review, *Mr. Trilling has written one novel,* The Middle of the Journey *(1947), and another short story, "The Other Margaret."*

"Of This Time, Of That Place" opens and closes with a photograph, much as a shutter snaps—and as deliberately. As Joseph Howe leaves the Aiken house to begin the academic year, Hilda Aiken frames a peach tree in her box camera, the sun over her shoulder, her long shadow in the foreground. Just before commencement, in the closing moments of the story, Hilda poses Howe under a little tree "for a character study with light and shade"; she adjusts a tripod, light meter, tape measure, "a fairly good domestic camera." Mr. Trilling's intention is clear: these scenes suggest the central argument of the story. The relationship of Howe to his students is at once simple and complex, vague and precise, natural and mechanical.

IT was a fine September day. By noon it would be summer again but now it was true autumn with a touch of chill in the air. As Joseph Howe stood on the porch of the house in which he lodged, ready to leave for his first class of the year, he thought with pleasure of the long indoor days that were coming. It was a moment when he could feel glad of his profession.

On the lawn the peach tree was still in fruit and young Hilda Aiken was taking a picture of it. She held the camera tight against her chest. She wanted the sun behind her but she did not want her own long morning shadow in the foreground. She raised the camera but that did not help, and she lowered it but that made things worse. She twisted her body to the left, then to the right. In the end she had to step out of the direct line of the sun. At last she snapped the shutter and wound the film with intense care.

Howe, watching her from the porch, waited for her to finish and called good morning. She turned, startled, and almost sullenly lowered her glance. In the year Howe had lived at the Aikens', Hilda had accepted him as one of her family, but since his absence of the summer she had grown shy. Then suddenly she lifted her head and smiled at him, and the humorous smile confirmed his pleasure in the day. She picked up her bookbag and set off for school.

The handsome houses on the streets to the college were not yet fully awake but they looked very friendly. Howe went by the Bradby house where he would be a guest this evening at the first dinner-party of the year. When he had gone the length of the picket fence, the whitest in town, he turned back. Along the path there was a fine row of asters and he went through the gate and picked one for his buttonhole. The Bradbys would be pleased if they happened to see him invading their lawn and the knowledge of this made him even more comfortable.

He reached the campus as the hour was striking. The students were hurrying to their classes. He himself was in no hurry. He stopped at his dim cubicle of an office and lit a cigarette. The prospect of facing his class had suddenly presented itself to him and his hands were cold, the lawful seizure of power he was about to make seemed momentous. Waiting did not help. He put out his cigarette, picked up a pad of theme paper and went to his classroom.

As he entered, the rattle of voices ceased and the twenty-odd freshmen settled themselves and looked at him appraisingly. Their faces seemed gross, his heart sank at their massed impassivity, but he spoke briskly.

"My name is Howe," he said and turned and wrote it on the blackboard. The carelessness of the scrawl confirmed his authority. He went on, "My office is 412 Slemp Hall and my office-hours are Monday, Wednesday and Friday from eleven-thirty to twelve-thirty."

He wrote, "M., W., F., 11:30-12:30." He said, "I'll be very glad to see any of you at that time. Or if you can't come then, you can arrange with me for some other time."

He turned again to the blackboard and spoke over his shoulder. "The text for the course is Jarman's *Modern Plays*, revised edition. The Co-op has it in stock." He wrote the name, underlined "revised edition" and waited for it to be taken down in the new notebooks.

When the bent heads were raised again he began his speech of prospectus. "It is hard to explain—" he said, and paused as they composed themselves. "It is hard to explain what a course like this is intended to do. We are going to try to learn something about modern literature and something about prose composition."

As he spoke, his hands warmed and he was able to look directly at the class. Last year on the first day the faces had seemed just as cloddish, but as the term wore on they became gradually alive and quite likable. It did not seem possible that the same thing could happen again.

"I shall not lecture in this course," he continued. "Our work will be carried on by discussion and we will try to learn by an exchange of opinion. But you will soon recognize that my opinion is worth more than anyone else's here."

He remained grave as he said it, but two boys understood and laughed. The rest took permission from them and laughed too. All Howe's private ironies protested the vulgarity of the joke but the laughter made him feel benign and powerful.

When the little speech was finished, Howe picked up the pad of paper he had brought. He announced that they would write an extemporaneous theme. Its subject was traditional, "Who I am and why I came to Dwight College." By now the class was more at ease and it gave a ritualistic groan of protest. Then there was a stir as fountain-pens were brought out and the writing arms of the chairs were cleared and the paper was passed about. At last all the heads bent to work and the room became still.

Howe sat idly at his desk. The sun shone through the tall clumsy windows. The cool of the morning was already passing. There was a scent of autumn and of varnish, and the stillness of the room was deep and oddly touching. Now and then a student's head was raised and scratched in the old elaborate students' pantomime that calls the teacher to witness honest intellectual effort.

Suddenly a tall boy stood within the frame of the open door. "Is this," he said, and thrust a large nose into a college catalogue, "is this the meeting place of English 1A? The section instructed by Dr. Joseph Howe?"

He stood on the very sill of the door, as if refusing to enter until he was perfectly sure of all his rights. The class looked up from work, found him absurd and gave a low mocking cheer.

The teacher and the new student, with equal pointedness, ignored the disturbance. Howe nodded to the boy, who pushed his head forward and then jerked it back in a wide elaborate arc to clear his brow of a heavy lock of hair. He advanced into the room and halted before Howe, almost at attention. In a loud clear voice he announced, "I am Tertan, Ferdinand R., reporting at the direction of Head of Department Vincent."

The heraldic formality of this statement brought forth another cheer. Howe looked at the class with a sternness he could not really feel, for there was indeed something ridiculous about this boy. Under his displeased regard the rows of heads dropped to work again. Then he touched Tertan's elbow, led him up to the desk and stood so as to shield their conversation from the class.

"We are writing an extemporaneous theme," he said. "The subject is, 'Who am I and why I came to Dwight College'."

He stripped a few sheets from the pad and offered them to the boy. Tertan hesitated and then took the paper but he held it only tentatively. As if with the effort of making something clear, he gulped, and a slow smile fixed itself on his face. It was at once knowing and shy.

"Professor," he said, "to be perfectly fair to my classmates"—he made a large gesture over the room—"and to you"—he inclined his head to Howe—"this would not be for me an extemporaneous subject."

Howe tried to understand. "You mean you've already thought about it—you've heard we always give the same subject? That doesn't matter."

Again the boy ducked his head and gulped. It was the gesture of one who wishes to make a difficult explanation with perfect candor. "Sir," he said, and made the distinction with great care, "the topic I did not expect but I have given much ratiocination to the subject."

Howe smiled and said, "I don't think that's an unfair advantage. Just go ahead and write."

Tertan narrowed his eyes and glanced sidewise at Howe. His strange mouth smiled. Then in quizzical acceptance, he ducked his head, threw back the heavy dank lock, dropped into a seat with a great loose noise and began to write rapidly.

The room fell silent again and Howe resumed his idleness. When the bell rang, the students who had groaned when the task had been set now groaned again because they had not finished. Howe took up the papers and held the class while he made the first assignment. When he dismissed it, Tertan bore down on him, his slack mouth held ready for speech.

"Some professors," he said, "are pedants. They are Dryasdusts. However, some professors are free souls and creative spirits. Kant, Hegel and Nietzsche were all professors." With this pronouncement he paused. "It is my opinion," he continued, "that you occupy the second category."

Howe looked at the boy in surprise and said with good-natured irony, "With Kant, Hegel and Nietzsche?"

Not only Tertan's hand and head but his whole awkward body waved away the stupidity. "It is the kind and not the quantity of the kind," he said sternly.

Rebuked, Howe said as simply and seriously as he could, "It would be nice to think so." He added, "Of course I am not a professor."

This was clearly a disappointment but Tertan met it. "In the French sense," he said with composure. "Generically, a teacher."

Suddenly he bowed. It was such a bow, Howe fancied, as a stage-director might teach an actor playing a medieval student who takes leave of Abelard—stiff, solemn, with elbows close to the body and feet together. Then, quite as suddenly, he turned and left.

A queer fish, and as soon as Howe reached his office he sifted through the batch of themes and drew out Tertan's. The boy had filled many sheets with his unformed headlong scrawl. "Who am I?" he had begun. "Here, in a mundane, not to say commercialized academe, is asked the question which from time long immemorably out of mind has accreted doubts and thoughts in the psyche of man to pester him as a nuisance. Whether in St. Augustine (or Austin as sometimes called) or Miss Bashkirtsieff or Frederic Amiel or Empedocles, or in less lights of the intellect than these, this posed question has been ineluctable."

Howe took out his pencil. He circled "academe" and wrote "vocab." in the margin. He underlined "time long immemorably out of mind" and wrote "Diction!" But this seemed inadequate for what was wrong. He put down his pencil and read ahead to discover the principle of error in the theme. "Today as ever, in spite of gloomy prophets of the dismal science (economics) the question is uninvalidated. Out of the starry depths of heaven hurtles this spear of query demanding to be caught on the shield of the mind ere it pierces the skull and the limbs be unstrung."

Baffled but quite caught, Howe read on. "Materialism, by which is meant the philosophic concept and not the moral idea, provides no aegis against the question which lies beyond the tangible (metaphysics). Existence without alloy is the question presented. Environment and heredity relegated aside, the rags and old clothes of practical life discarded, the name and the instrumentality of livelihood do not, as the prophets of the dismal science insist on in this connection, give solution to the interrogation which not from the professor merely but veritably from the cosmos is given. I think, therefore I am (cogito etc.) but who am I? Tertan I am, but what is Tertan? Of this time, of that place, of some parentage, what does it matter?"

Existence without alloy: the phrase established itself. Howe put aside Tertan's paper and at random picked up another. "I am Arthur J. Casebeer, Jr.," he read. "My father is Arthur J. Casebeer and my grandfather was Arthur J. Casebeer before him. My mother is Nina Wimble Casebeer. Both of them are college graduates and my father is in insurance. I was born in St. Louis eighteen years ago and we still make our residence there."

Arthur J. Casebeer, who knew who he was, was less interesting than Tertan, but more coherent. Howe picked up Tertan's paper again. It was clear that none of the routine marginal comments, no "sent. str." or "punct." or "vocab." could cope with this torrential rhetoric. He read ahead, contenting himself with underscoring the errors against the time when he should have the necessary "conference" with Tertan.

It was a busy and official day of cards and sheets, arrangements and small decisions and it gave Howe pleasure. Even when it was time to attend the first of the weekly Convocations he felt the charm of the beginning of things when intention is still innocent and uncorrupted by effort. He sat among the young instructors on the platform and joined in their humorous complaints at having to assist at the ceremony but actually he got a clear satisfaction from the ritual of prayer and prosy speech and even from wearing his academic gown. And when Convocation was over the pleasure continued as he crossed the campus, exchanging greetings with men he had not seen since the spring. They were people who did not yet, and perhaps never would, mean much to him, but in a year they had grown amiably to be part of his life. They were his fellow-townsmen.

The day had cooled again at sunset and there was a bright chill in the September twilight. Howe carried his voluminous gown over his arm, he swung his doctoral hood by its purple neckpiece and on his head he wore his mortarboard with its heavy gold tassel bobbing just over his eye. These were the weighty and absurd symbols of his new profession and they pleased him. At twenty-six Joseph Howe had discovered that he was neither so well off nor so bohemian as he had once thought. A small income, adequate when supplemented by a sizable cash legacy, was genteel poverty when the cash was all spent. And the literary life—the room at the Lafayette or the small apartment without a lease, the long summers on the Cape, the long afternoons and the social evenings—began to weary him. His writing filled his mornings and should perhaps have filled his life, yet it did not. To the amusement of his friends and with a certain sense that he was betraying his own freedom, he had used the last of his legacy for a year at Harvard. The small but respectable reputation of his two volumes of verse had proved useful—he continued at Harvard on a fellowship and when he emerged as Dr. Howe he received an excellent appointment, with prospects, at Dwight.

He had his moments of fear when all that had ever been said of the dangers of the academic life had occurred to him. But after a year in which he had tested every possibility of corruption and seduction he was ready to rest easy. His third volume of verse, most of it written in his first year of teaching, was not only ampler but, he thought, better than its predecessors.

There was a clear hour before the Bradby dinner-party and Howe looked forward to it. But he was not to enjoy it, for lying with his mail on the hall table was a copy of this quarter's issue of *Life and Letters*, to which his landlord subscribed. Its severe cover announced that its editor, Frederic Woolley, had this month contributed an essay called "Two Poets," and Howe, picking it up, curious to see who the two poets might be, felt his own name start out at him with cabalistic power—Joseph Howe. As he continued to turn the pages his hand trembled.

Standing in the dark hall, holding the neat little magazine, Howe knew that his literary contempt for Frederic Woolley meant nothing, for he suddenly understood how he respected Woolley in the way of the world. He knew this by the trembling of his hand. And of the little world as well as the great, for although the literary groups of New York might dismiss Woolley, his name carried high authority in the academic world. At Dwight it was even a revered name, for it had been here at the college that Frederic Woolley had made the distinguished scholarly career from which he had gone on to literary journalism. In middle life he had been induced to take the editorship of *Life and Letters,* a literary monthly not widely read but heavily endowed and in its pages he had carried on the defense of what he sometimes called the older values. He was not without wit, he had great knowledge and considerable taste and even in the full movement of the "new" literature he had won a certain respect for his refusal to accept it. In France, even in England, he would have been connected with a more robust tradition of conservatism, but America gave him an audience not much better than genteel. It was known in the college that to the subsidy of *Life and Letters* the Bradbys contributed a great part.

As Howe read, he saw that he was involved in nothing less than an event. When the Fifth Series of *Studies in Order and Value* came to be collected, this latest of Frederic Woolley's essays would not be merely another step in the old direction. Clearly and unmistakably, it was a turning point. All his literary life Woolley had been concerned with the relation of literature to mortality, religion and the private and delicate pieties and he had been unalterably opposed to all that he had called "inhuman humanitarianism." But here, suddenly, dramatically late, he had made an about-face, turning to the public life and to the humanitarian politics he had so long despised. This was the kind of incident the histories of literature make much of. Frederic Woolley was opening for himself a new career and winning a kind of new youth. He contrasted the two poets, Thomas Wormser who was admirable, Joseph Howe who was almost dangerous. He spoke of the "precious subjectivism" of Howe's verse. "In times like ours," he wrote, "with millions facing penury and want, one feels that the qualities of the *tour d'ivoire* are well-nigh inhuman, nearly insulting. The *tour d'ivoire* becomes the *tour d'ivresse* and it is not self-intoxicated poets that our people need." The essay said more: "The problem is one of meaning. I am not ignorant that the creed of the esoteric poets declares that a poem does not and should not *mean* anything, that it *is* something. But poetry is what the poet makes it, and if he is a true poet he makes what his society needs. And what is needed now is the tradition in which Mr. Wormser writes, the true tradition of poetry. The Howes do no harm, but they do no good when positive good is demanded of all responsible men. Or do the Howes indeed do no harm? Perhaps Plato would have said they do, that in some ways theirs is the Phrygian music that turns men's minds from the struggle. Certainly it is true that Thomas Wormser writes in the lucid Dorian mode which sends men into battle with evil."

It was easy to understand why Woolley had chosen to praise Thomas Wormser. The long, lilting lines of *Corn Under Willows* hymned, as Woolley put it, the struggle for wheat in the Iowa fields and expressed the real lives of real people. But why out of the dozen more notable examples he had chosen Howe's little volume as the example of "precious subjectivism" was hard to guess. In a way it was funny, this multiplication of himself into "the Howes." And yet this becoming the multiform political symbol by whose creation Frederic Woolley gave the sign of a sudden new life, this use of him as a sacrifice whose blood was necessary for the rites of rejuvenation, made him feel oddly unclean.

Nor could Howe get rid of a certain practical resentment. As a poet he had a special and respectable place in the college life. But it might be another thing to be marked as the poet of a wilful and selfish obscurity.

As he walked to the Bradbys' Howe was a little tense and defensive. It seemed to him that all the world knew of the "attack" and agreed with it. And indeed the Bradbys had read the essay but Professor Bradby, a kind and pretentious man, said, "I see my old friend knocked you about a bit, my boy," and his wife Eugenia looked at Howe with her childlike blue eyes and said, "I shall *scold* Frederic for the untrue things he wrote about you. You aren't the least obscure." They beamed at him. In their genial snobbery they seemed to feel that he had distinguished himself. He was the leader of Howeism. He enjoyed the dinner-party as much as he had thought he would.

And in the following days, as he was more preoccupied with his duties, the incident was forgotten. His classes had ceased to be mere groups. Student after student detached himself from the mass and required or claimed a place in Howe's awareness. Of them all it was Tertan who first and most violently signalled his separate existence. A week after classes had begun Howe saw his silhouette on the frosted glass of his office door. It was motionless for a long time, perhaps stopped by the problem of whether or not to knock before entering. Howe called, "Come in!" and Tertan entered with his shambling stride.

He stood beside the desk, silent and at attention. When Howe asked him to sit down, he responded with a gesture of head and hand as if to say that such amenities were beside the point. Nevertheless he did take the chair. He put his ragged crammed briefcase between his legs. His face, which Howe now observed fully for the first time, was confusing, for it was made up of florid curves, the nose arched in the bone and voluted in the nostril, the mouth loose and soft and rather moist. Yet the face was so thin and narrow as to seem the very type of asceticism. Lashes of unusual length veiled the eyes and, indeed, it seemed as if there were a veil over the whole countenance. Before the words actually came, the face screwed itself into an attitude of preparation for them.

"You can confer with me now?" Tertan said.

"Yes, I'd be glad to. There are several things in your two themes I want to talk to you about." Howe reached for the packet of themes on his desk and sought for Tertan's. But the boy was waving them away.

"These are done perforce," he said. "Under the pressure of your requirement. They are not significant, mere duties." Again his great hand flapped vaguely to dismiss his themes. He leaned forward and gazed at his teacher.

"You are," he said, "a man of letters? You are a poet?" It was more declaration than question.

"I should like to think so," Howe said.

At first Tertan accepted the answer with a show of appreciation, as though the understatement made a secret between himself and Howe. Then he chose to misunderstand. With his shrewd and disconcerting control of expression, he presented to Howe a puzzled grimace. "What does that mean?" he said.

Howe retracted the irony. "Yes. I am a poet." It sounded strange to say.

"That," Tertan said, "is a wonder." He corrected himself with his ducking head. "I mean that is wonderful."

Suddenly he dived at the miserable briefcase between his legs, put it on his knees and began to fumble with the catch, all intent on the difficulty it presented. Howe noted that his suit was worn thin, his shirt almost unclean. He became aware, even, of a vague and musty odor of garments worn too long in unaired rooms. Tertan conquered the lock and began to concentrate upon a search into the interior. At last he held in his hand what he was after, a torn and crumpled copy of *Life and Letters.*

"I learned it from here," he said, holding it out.

Howe looked at him sharply, his hackles a little up. But the boy's face was not only perfectly innocent, it even shone with a conscious admiration. Apparently nothing of the import of the essay had touched him except the wonderful fact that his teacher was a "man of letters." Yet this seemed too stupid and Howe, to test it, said, "The man who wrote that doesn't think it's wonderful."

Tertan made a moist hissing sound as he cleared his mouth of saliva. His head, oddly loose on his neck, wove a pattern of contempt in the air. "A critic," he said, "who admits *prima facie* that he does not understand." Then he said grandly, "It is the inevitable fate."

It was absurd, yet Howe was not only aware of the absurdity but of a tension suddenly and wonderfully relaxed. Now that the "attack" was on the table between himself and this strange boy and subject to the boy's funny and absolutely certain contempt, the hidden force of his feeling was revealed to him in the very moment that it vanished. All unsuspected, there had been a film over the world, a transparent but discoloring haze of danger. But he had no time to stop over the brightened aspect of things. Tertan was going on. "I also am a man of letters. Putative."

"You have written a good deal?" Howe meant to be no more than polite and he was surprised at the tenderness he heard in his words.

Solemnly the boy nodded, threw back the dank lock and sucked in a deep anticipatory breath. "First, a work of homiletics, which is a defense of the principles of religious optimism against the pessimism of Schopenhauer and the humanism of Nietzsche."

"Humanism? Why do you call it humanism?"

"It is my nomenclature for making a deity of man," Tertan replied negligently. "Then three fictional works, novels. And numerous essays in science, combating materialism. Is it your duty to read these if I bring them to you?"

Howe answered simply, "No, it isn't exactly my duty but I shall be happy to read them."

Tertan stood up and remained silent. He rested his bag on the chair. With a certain compunction—for it did not seem entirely proper that, of two men of letters, one should have the right to blue-pencil the other, to grade him or to question the quality of his "sentence structure"— Howe reached for Tertan's papers. But before he could take them up, the boy suddenly made his bow-to-Abelard, the stiff inclination of the body with the hands seeming to emerge from the scholar's gown. Then he was gone.

But after his departure something was still left of him. The timbre of his curious sentences, the downright finality of so quaint a phrase as "It is the inevitable fate" still rang in the air. Howe gave the warmth of his feeling to the new visitor who stood at the door announcing himself with a genteel clearing of the throat.

"Dr. Howe, I believe?" the student said. A large hand advanced into the room and grasped Howe's hand. "Blackburn, sir, Theodore Blackburn, vice-president of the Student Council. A great pleasure, sir."

Out of a pair of ruddy cheeks a pair of small eyes twinkled good-naturedly. The large face, the large body were not so much fat as beefy and suggested something "typical," monk, politician, or inn-keeper.

Blackburn took the seat beside Howe's desk. "I may have seemed to introduce myself in my public capacity, sir," he said. "But it is really as an individual that I came to see you. That is to say, as one of your students to be."

He spoke with an "English" intonation and he went on, "I was once an English major, sir."

For a moment Howe was startled, for the roast-beef look of the boy and the manner of his speech gave a second's credibility to one sense of his statement. Then the collegiate meaning of the phrase asserted itself, but some perversity made Howe say what was not really in good taste even with so forward a student, "Indeed? What regiment?"

Blackburn stared and then gave a little pouf-pouf of laughter. He waved the misapprehension away. "*Very* good, sir. It certainly is an ambiguous term." He chuckled in appreciation of Howe's joke, then cleared his throat to put it aside. "I look forward to taking your course in the romantic poets, sir," he said earnestly. "To me the romantic poets are the very crown of English literature."

Howe made a dry sound, and the boy, catching some meaning in it, said, "Little as I know them, of course. But even Shakespeare who is so dear to us of the Anglo-Saxon tradition is in a sense but the preparation of Shelley, Keats and Byron. And Wadsworth."

Almost sorry for him, Howe dropped his eyes. With some embarrassment, for the boy was not actually his student, he said softly, "Wordsworth."

"Sir?"

"Wordsworth, not Wadsworth. You said Wadsworth."

"Did I, sir?" Gravely he shook his head to rebuke himself for the error. "Wordsworth, of course—slip of the tongue." Then, quite in command again, he went on. "I have a favor to ask of you, Dr. Howe. You see, I began my college course as an English major,"—he smiled —"as I said."

"Yes?"

"But after my first year I shifted. I shifted to the social sciences. Sociology and government—I find them stimulating and very *real*." He paused, out of respect for reality. "But now I find that perhaps I have neglected the other side."

"The other side?" Howe said.

"Imagination, fancy, culture. A well rounded man." He trailed off as if there were perfect understanding between them. "And so, sir, I have decided to end my senior year with your course in the romantic poets."

His voice was filled with an indulgence which Howe ignored as he said flatly and gravely, "But that course isn't given until the spring term."

"Yes, sir, and that is where the favor comes in. Would you let me take your romantic prose course? I can't take it for credit, sir, my program is full, but just for background it seems to me that I ought to take it. I do hope," he concluded in a manly way, "that you will consent."

"Well, it's no great favor, Mr. Blackburn. You can come if you wish, though there's not much point in it if you don't do the reading."

The bell rang for the hour and Howe got up.

"May I begin with this class, sir?" Blackburn's smile was candid and boyish.

Howe nodded carelessly and together, silently, they walked to the classroom down the hall. When they reached the door Howe stood back to let his student enter, but Blackburn moved adroitly behind him and grasped him by the arm to urge him over the threshold. They entered together with Blackburn's hand firmly on Howe's biceps, the student inducting the teacher into his own room. Howe felt a surge of temper rise in him and almost violently he disengaged his arm and walked to the desk, while Blackburn found a seat in the front row and smiled at him.

The question was, At whose door must the tragedy be laid?

All night the snow had fallen heavily and only now was abating in sparse little flurries. The windows were valanced high with white. It was very quiet, something of the quiet of the world had reached the class and Howe found that everyone was glad to talk or listen. In the room there was a comfortable sense of pleasure in being human.

Casebeer believed that the blame for the tragedy rested with heredity. Picking up the book he read, "The sins of the fathers are visited on their children." This opinion was received with general favor. Nevertheless Johnson ventured to say that the fault was all Pastor Manders' because the Pastor had made Mrs. Alving go back to her husband and was always hiding the truth. To this Hibbard objected with logic enough, "Well then, it was really all her husband's fault. He *did* all the bad things." De Witt, his face bright with an impatient idea, said that the fault was all society's. "By society I don't mean upper-crust society," he said. He looked around a little defiantly, taking in any members of the class who might be members of upper-crust society. "Not in that sense. I mean the social unit."

Howe nodded and said, "Yes, of course."

"If the society of the time had progressed far enough in science," De Witt went on, "then there would be no problem for Mr. Ibsen to write about. Captain Alving plays around a little, gives way to perfectly natural biological urges, and he gets a social disease, a venereal disease. If the disease is cured, no problem. Invent salvarsan and the disease is cured. The problem of heredity disappears and li'l Oswald just doesn't get paresis. No paresis, no problem—no problem, no play."

This was carrying the ark into battle and the class looked at De Witt with respectful curiosity. It was his usual way and on the whole they were sympathetic with his struggle to prove to Howe that science was better than literature. Still, there was something in his reckless manner that alienated them a little.

"Or take birth-control, for instance," De Witt went on. "If Mrs. Alving had some knowledge of contraception, she wouldn't have had to have li'l Oswald at all. No li'l Oswald, no play."

The class was suddenly quieter. In the back row Stettenhover swung his great football shoulders in a righteous sulking gesture, first to the right, then to the left. He puckered his mouth ostentatiously. Intellect was alway ending up by talking dirty.

Tertan's hand went up and Howe said, "Mr. Tertan." The boy shambled to his feet and began his long characteristic gulp. Howe made a motion with his fingers, as small as possible, and Tertan ducked his head and smiled in apology. He sat down. The class laughed. With more than half the term gone, Tertan had not been able to remember that one did not rise to speak. He seemed unable to carry on the life of the intellect without this mark of respect for it. To Howe the boy's habit of rising seemed to accord with the formal shabbiness of his dress. He never wore the casual sweaters and jackets of his classmates. Into the free and comfortable air of the college classroom he brought the stuffy sordid strictness of some crowded metropolitan high school.

"Speaking from one sense," Tertan began slowly, "there is no blame ascribable. From the sense of determinism, who can say where the blame lies? The preordained is the preordained and it cannot be said without rebellion against the universe, a palpable absurdity."

In the back row Stettenhover slumped suddenly in his seat, his heels held out before him, making a loud dry disgusted sound. His body sank until his neck rested on the back of his chair. He folded his hands across his belly and looked significantly out of the window, exasperated not only with Tertan but with Howe, with the class, with the whole system designed to encourage this kind of thing. There was a certain insolence in the movement and Howe flushed. As Tertan continued to speak, Howe stalked casually toward the window and placed himself in the line of Stettenhover's vision. He stared at the great fellow, who pretended not to see him. There was so much power in the big body, so much contempt in the Greek-athlete face under the crisp Greek-athlete curls, that Howe felt almost physical fear. But at last Stettenhover admitted him to focus and under his disapproving gaze sat up with slow indifference. His eyebrows raised high in resignation, he began to examine his hands. Howe relaxed and turned his attention back to Tertan.

"Flux of existence," Tertan was saying, "produces all things, so that judgment wavers. Beyond the phenomena, what? But phenomena are adumbrated and to them we are limited."

Howe saw it for a moment as perhaps it existed in the boy's mind—the world of shadows which are cast by a great light upon a hidden reality as in the old myth of the Cave. But the little brush with Stettenhover had tired him and he said irritably, "But come to the point, Mr. Tertan."

He said it so sharply that some of the class looked at him curiously. For three months he had gently carried Tertan through his verbosities, to the vaguely respectful surprise of the other students, who seemed to conceive that there existed between this strange classmate and their teacher some special understanding from which they were content to be excluded. Tertan looked at him mildly and at once came brilliantly to the point. "This is the summation of the play," he said and took up his book and read, " 'Your poor father never found any outlet for the overmastering joy of life that was in him. And I brought no holiday into his home, either. Everything seemed to turn upon duty and I am afraid I made your poor father's home unbearable to him, Oswald.' Spoken by Mrs. Alving."

Yes, that was surely the "summation" of the play and Tertan had hit it, as he hit, deviously and eventually, the literary point of almost everything. But now, as always, he was wrapping it away from sight. "For most mortals," he said, "there are only joys of biological urgings, gross and crass, such as the sensuous Captain Alving. For certain few there are the transmutations beyond these to a contemplation of the utter whole."

Oh, the boy was mad. And suddenly the word, used in hyperbole, intended almost for the expression of exasperated admiration, became literal. Now that the word was used, it became simply apparent to Howe that Tertan was mad.

It was a monstrous word and stood like a bestial thing in the room.

Yet it so completely comprehended everything that had puzzled Howe, it so arranged and explained what for three months had been perplexing him that almost at once its horror became domesticated. With this word Howe was able to understand why he had never been able to communicate to Tertan the value of a single criticism or correction of his wild, verbose themes. Their conferences had been frequent and long but had done nothing to reduce to order the splendid confusion of the boy's ideas. Yet, impossible though its expression was, Tertan's incandescent mind could always strike for a moment into some dark corner of thought.

And now it was suddenly apparent that it was not a faulty rhetoric that Howe had to contend with. With his new knowledge he looked at Tertan's face and wondered how he could have so long deceived himself. Tertan was still talking and the class had lapsed into a kind of patient unconsciousness, a coma of respect for words which, for all that most of them knew, might be profound. Almost with a suffusion of shame, Howe believed that in some dim way the class had long ago had some intimation of Tertan's madness. He reached out as decisively as he could to seize the thread of Tertan's discourse before it should be entangled further.

"Mr. Tertan says that the blame must be put upon whoever kills the joy of living in another. We have been assuming that Captain Alving was a wholly bad man, but what if we assume that he became bad only because Mrs. Alving, when they were first married, acted toward him in the prudish way she says she did?"

It was a ticklish idea to advance to freshmen and perhaps not profitable. Not all of them were following.

"That would put the blame on Mrs. Alving herself, whom most of you admire. And she herself seems to think so." He glanced at his watch. The hour was nearly over. "What do you think, Mr. De Witt?"

De Witt rose to the idea, he wanted to know if society couldn't be blamed for educating Mrs. Alving's temperament in the wrong way. Casebeer was puzzled, Stettenhover continued to look at his hands until the bell rang.

Tertan, his brows louring in thought, was making as always for a private word. Howe gathered his books and papers to leave quickly. At this moment of his discovery and with the knowledge still raw, he could not engage himself with Tertan. Tertan sucked in his breath to prepare for speech and Howe made ready for the pain and confusion. But at that moment Casebeer detached himself from the group with which he had been conferring and which he seemed to represent. His constituency remained at a tactful distance. The mission involved the time of an assigned essay. Casebeer's presentation of the plea—it was based on the freshmen's heavy duties at the fraternities during Carnival Week—cut across Tertan's preparations for speech. "And so some of us fellows thought," Casebeer concluded with heavy solemnity, "that we could do a better job, give our minds to it more, if we had more time."

Tertan regarded Casebeer with mingled curiosity and revulsion. Howe not only said that he would postpone the assignment but went on to talk about the Carnival and even drew the waiting constituency into the conversation. He was conscious of Tertan's stern and astonished stare, then of his sudden departure.

Now that the fact was clear, Howe knew that he must act on it. His course was simple enough. He must lay the case before the Dean. Yet he hesitated. His feeling for Tertan must now, certainly, be in some way invalidated. Yet could he, because of a word, hurry to assign to official and reasonable solicitude what had been, until this moment, so various and warm? He could at least delay and, by moving slowly, lend a poor grace to the necessary, ugly act of making his report.

It was with some notion of keeping the matter in his own hands that he went to the Dean's office to look up Tertan's records. In the outer office the Dean's secretary greeted him brightly and at his request brought him the manila folder with the small identifying photograph pasted in the corner. She laughed. "He was looking for the birdie in the wrong place," she said.

Howe leaned over her shoulder to look at the picture. It was as bad as all the Dean's-office photographs were, but it differed from all that Howe had ever seen. Tertan, instead of looking into the camera, as no doubt he had been bidden, had, at the moment of exposure, turned his eyes upward. His mouth, as though conscious of the trick played on the photographer, had the sly superior look that Howe knew.

The secretary was fascinated by the picture. "What a funny boy," she said. "He looks like Tartuffe!"

And so he did, with the absurd piety of the eyes and the conscious slyness of the mouth and the whole face bloated by the bad lens.

"Is he *like* that?" the secretary said.

"Like Tartuffe? No."

From the photograph there was little enough comfort to be had. The records themselves gave no clue to madness, though they suggested sadness enough. Howe read of a father, Stanislaus Tertan, born in Budapest and trained in engineering in Berlin, once employed by the Hercules Chemical Corporation—this was one of the factories that dominated the sound end of the town—but now without employment. He read of a mother Erminie (Youngfellow) Tertan, born in Manchester, educated at a Normal School at Leeds, now housewife by profession. The family lived on Greenbriar Street which Howe knew as a row of once elegant homes near what was now the factory district. The old mansions had long ago been divided into small and primitive apartments. Of Ferdinand himself there was little to learn. He lived with his parents, had attended a Detroit high school and had transferred to the local school in his last year. His rating for intelligence, as expressed in numbers, was high, his scholastic record was remarkable, he held a college scholarship for his tuition.

Howe laid the folder on the secretary's desk. "Did you find what you wanted to know?" she asked.

The phrases from Tertan's momentous first theme came back to him. "Tertan I am, but what is Tertan? Of this time, of that place, of some parentage, what does it matter?"

"No, I didn't find it," he said.

Now that he had consulted the sad half-meaningless record he knew all the more firmly that he must not give the matter out of his own hands. He must not release Tertan to authority. Not that he anticipated from the Dean anything but the greatest kindness for Tertan. The Dean would have the experience and skill which he himself could not have. One way or another the Dean could answer the question, "What is Tertan?" Yet this was precisely what he feared. He alone could keep alive—not forever but for a somehow important time—the question, "What is Tertan?" He alone could keep it still a question. Some sure instinct told him that he must not surrender the question to a clean official desk in a clear official light to be dealt with, settled and closed.

He heard himself saying, "Is the Dean busy at the moment? I'd like to see him."

His request came thus unbidden, even forbidden, and it was one of the surprising and startling incidents of his life. Later, when he reviewed the events, so disconnected in themselves or so merely odd, of the story that unfolded for him that year, it was over this moment, on its face the least notable, that he paused longest. It was frequently to be with fear and never without a certainty of its meaning in his own knowledge of himself that he would recall this simple, routine request and the feeling of shame and freedom it gave him as he sent everything down the official chute. In the end, of course, no matter what he did to "protect" Tertan, he would have had to make the same request and lay the matter on the Dean's clean desk. But it would always be a landmark of his life that, at the very moment when he was rejecting the official way, he had been, without will or intention, so gladly drawn to it.

After the storm's last delicate flurry, the sun had come out. Reflected by the new snow, it filled the office with a golden light which was almost musical in the way it made all the commonplace objects of efficiency shine with a sudden sad and noble significance. And the light, now that he noticed it, made the utterance of his perverse and unwanted request even more momentous.

The secretary consulted the engagement pad. "He'll be free any minute. Don't you want to wait in the parlor?"

She threw open the door of the large and pleasant room in which the Dean held his Committee meetings and in which his visitors waited. It was designed with a homely elegance on the masculine side of the eighteenth century manner. There was a small coal-fire in the grate and the handsome mahogany table was strewn with books and magazines. The large windows gave on the snowy lawn and there was such a fine width of window that the white casements and walls seemed at this moment but a continuation of the snow, the snow but an extension of casement and walls. The outdoors seemed taken in and made safe, the indoors seemed luxuriously freshened and expanded.

Howe sat down by the fire and lighted a cigarette. The room had its intended effect upon him. He felt comfortable and relaxed, yet nicely organized, some young diplomatic agent of the eighteenth century, the newly fledged Swift carrying out Sir William Temple's business. The rawness of Tertan's case quite vanished. He crossed his legs and reached for a magazine.

It was that famous issue of *Life and Letters* that his idle hand had found and his blood raced as he sifted through it and the shape of his own name, Joseph Howe, sprang out at him, still cabalistic in its power. He tossed the magazine back on the table as the door of the

Dean's office opened and the Dean ushered out Theodore Blackburn.

"Ah, Joseph!" the Dean said.

Blackburn said, "Good morning, Doctor." Howe winced at the title and caught the flicker of amusement over the Dean's face. The Dean stood with his hand high on the door-jamb and Blackburn, still in the doorway, remained standing almost under his long arm.

Howe nodded briefly to Blackburn, snubbing his eager deference. "Can you give me a few minutes?" he said to the Dean.

"All the time you want. Come in." Before the two men could enter the office, Blackburn claimed their attention with a long full "Er." As they turned to him, Blackburn said, "Can *you* give *me* a few minutes, Dr. Howe?" His eyes sparkled at the little audacity he had committed, the slightly impudent play with hierarchy. Of the three of them Blackburn kept himself the lowest, but he reminded Howe of his subaltern relation to the Dean.

"I mean, of course," Blackburn went on easily, "when you've finished with the Dean."

"I'll be in my office shortly," Howe said, turned his back on the ready "Thank you, sir," and followed the Dean into the inner room.

"Energetic boy," said the Dean. "A bit beyond himself but very energetic. Sit down."

The Dean lighted a cigarette, leaned back in his chair, sat easy and silent for a moment, giving Howe no signal to go ahead with business. He was a young Dean, not much beyond forty, a tall handsome man with sad, ambitious eyes. He had been a Rhodes scholar. His friends looked for great things from him and it was generally said that he had notions of education which he was not yet ready to try to put into practice.

His relaxed silence was meant as a compliment to Howe. He smiled and said, "What's the business, Joseph?"

"Do you know Tertan—Ferdinand Tertan, a freshman?"

The Dean's cigarette was in his mouth and his hands were clasped behind his head. He did not seem to search his memory for the name. He said, "What about him?"

Clearly the Dean knew something and he was waiting for Howe to tell him more. Howe moved only tentatively. Now that he was doing what he had resolved not to do, he felt more guilty at having been so long deceived by Tertan and more need to be loyal to his error.

"He's a strange fellow," he ventured. He said stubbornly, "In a strange way he's very brilliant." He concluded, "But very strange."

The springs of the Dean's swivel chair creaked as he came out of his sprawl and leaned forward to Howe. "Do you mean he's so strange that it's something you could give a name to?"

Howe looked at him stupidly. "What do you mean?" he said.

"What's his trouble?" the Dean said more neutrally.

"He's very brilliant, in a way. I looked him up and he has a top intelligence rating. But somehow, and it's hard to explain just how, what he says is always on the edge of sense and doesn't quite make it."

The Dean looked at him and Howe flushed up. The Dean had surely read Woolley on the subject of "the Howes" and the *tour d'ivresse*. Was that quick glance ironical?

The Dean picked up some papers from his desk and Howe could see that they were in Tertan's impatient scrawl. Perhaps the little gleam in the Dean's glance had come only from putting facts together.

"He sent me this yesterday," the Dean said. "After an interview I had with him. I haven't been able to do more than glance at it. When you said what you did, I realized there was something wrong."

Twisting his mouth, the Dean looked over the letter. "You seem to be involved," he said without looking up. "By the way, what did you give him at mid-term?"

Flushing, setting his shoulders, Howe said firmly, "I gave him A-minus."

The Dean chuckled. "Might be a good idea if some of our nicer boys went crazy—just a little." He said, "Well," to conclude the matter and handed the papers to Howe. "See if this is the same thing you've been finding. Then we can go into the matter again."

Before the fire in the parlor, in the chair that Howe had been occupying, sat Blackburn. He sprang to his feet as Howe entered.

"I said my office, Mr. Blackburn." Howe's voice was sharp. Then he was almost sorry for the rebuke, so clearly and naively did Blackburn seem to relish his stay in the parlor, close to authority.

"I'm in a bit of a hurry, sir," he said, "and I did want to be sure to speak to you, sir."

He was really absurd, yet fifteen years from now he would have grown up to himself, to the assurance and mature beefiness. In banks, in consular offices, in brokerage firms, on the bench, more seriously affable, a little sterner, he would make use of his ability to be administered by his job. It was almost reassuring. Now he was exercising his too-great skill on Howe. "I owe you an apology, sir," he said.

Howe knew that he did but he showed surprise.

"I mean, Doctor, after your having been so kind about letting me attend your class, I stopped coming." He smiled in deprecation. "Extracurricular activities take up so much of my time. I'm afraid I undertook more than I could perform."

Howe had noticed the absence and had been a little irritated by it after Blackburn's elaborate plea. It was an absence that might be interpreted as a comment on the teacher. But there was only one way for him to answer. "You've no need to apologize," he said. "It's wholly your affair."

Blackburn beamed. "I'm so glad you feel that way about it, sir. I was worried you might think I had stayed away because I was influenced by——" He stopped and lowered his eyes.

Astonished, Howe said, "Influenced by what?"

"Well, by ——" Blackburn hesitated and for answer pointed to the table on which lay the copy of *Life and Letters*. Without looking at it, he knew where to direct his hand. "By the unfavorable publicity, sir." He hurried on. "And that brings me to another point, sir. I am vice-president of Quill and Scroll, sir, the student literary society, and I wonder if you would address us. You could read your own poetry, sir, and defend your own point of view. It would be very interesting."

It was truly amazing. Howe looked long and cruelly into Blackburn's face, trying to catch the secret of the mind that could have conceived this way of manipulating him, this way so daring and inept—but not entirely inept—with its malice so without malignity. The face did not yield its secret. Howe smiled broadly and said, "Of course I don't think you were influenced by the unfavorable publicity."

"I'm still going to take—regularly, for credit—your romantic poets course next term," Blackburn said.

"Don't worry, my dear fellow, don't worry about it."

Howe started to leave and Blackburn stopped him with, "But about Quill, sir?"

"Suppose we wait until next term? I'll be less busy then."

And Blackburn said, "Very good, sir, and thank you."

In his office the little encounter seemed less funny to Howe, was even in some indeterminate way disturbing. He made an effort to put it from his mind by turning to what was sure to disturb him more, the Tertan letter read in the new interpretation. He found what he had always found, the same florid leaps beyond fact and meaning, the same headlong certainty. But as his eye passed over the familiar scrawl it caught his own name and for the second time that hour he felt the race of his blood.

"The Paraclete," Tertan had written to the Dean, "from a Greek word meaning to stand in place of, but going beyond the primitive idea to mean traditionally the helper, the one who comforts and assists, cannot without fundamental loss be jettisoned. Even if taken no longer in the supernatural sense, the concept remains deeply in the human consciousness inevitably. Humanitarianism is no reply, for not every man stands in the place of every other man for this other's comrade comfort. But certain are chosen out of the human race to be the consoler of some other. Of these, for example, is Joseph Barker Howe, Ph.D. Of intellects not the first yet of true intellect and lambent instructions, given to that which is intuitive and irrational, not to what is logical in the strict word, what is judged by him is of the heart and not the head. Here is one chosen, in that he chooses himself to stand in the place of another for comfort and consolation. To him more than another I give my gratitude, with all respect to our Dean who reads this, a noble man, but merely dedicated, not consecrated. But not in the aspect of the Paraclete only is Dr. Joseph Barker Howe established, for he must be the Paraclete to another aspect of himself, that which is driven and persecuted by the lack of understanding in the world at large, so that he in himself embodies the full history of man's tribulations and, overflowing upon others, notably the present writer, is the ultimate end."

This was love. There was no escape from it. Try as Howe might to remember that Tertan was mad and all his emotions invalidated, he could not destroy the effect upon him of his student's stern, affectionate regard. He had betrayed not only a power of mind but a power of love. And however firmly he held before his attention the fact of Tertan's madness, he could do nothing to banish the physical sensation of gratitude he felt. He had never thought of himself as "driven and persecuted" and he did not now. But still he could not make meaningless his sensation of gratitude. The pitiable Tertan sternly pitied him, and comfort came from Tertan's never-to-be-comforted mind.

In an academic community, even an efficient one, official matters move slowly. The term drew to a close with no action in the case of

Tertan, and Joseph Howe had to confront a curious problem. How should he grade his strange student, Tertan?

Tertan's final examination had been no different from all his other writing, and what did one "give" such a student? De Witt must have his A, that was clear. Johnson would get a B. With Casebeer it was a question of a B-minus or a C-plus, and Stettenhover, who had been crammed by the team tutor to fill half a blue-book with his thin feminine scrawl, would have his C-minus which he would accept with mingled indifference and resentment. But with Tertan it was not so easy.

The boy was still in the college process and his name could not be omitted from the grade sheet. Yet what should a mind under suspicion of madness be graded? Until the medical verdict was given, it was for Howe to continue as Tertan's teacher and to keep his judgment pedagogical. Impossible to give him an F: he had not failed. B was for Johnson's stolid mediocrity. He could not be put on the edge of passing with Stettenhover, for he exactly did not pass. In energy and richness of intellect he was perhaps even De Witt's superior, and Howe toyed grimly with the notion of giving him an A, but that would lower the value of the A De Witt had won with his beautiful and clear, if still arrogant, mind. There was a notation which the Registrar recognized—Inc. for Incomplete, and in the horrible comedy of the situation, Howe considered that. But really only a mark of M for Mad would serve.

In his perplexity, Howe sought the Dean, but the Dean was out of town. In the end, he decided to maintain the A-minus he had given Tertan at midterm. After all, there had been no falling away from that quality. He entered it on the grade sheet with something like bravado.

Academic time moves quickly. A college year is not really a year, lacking as it does three months. And it is endlessly divided into units which, at their beginning, appear larger than they are—terms, half-terms, months, weeks. And the ultimate unit, the hour, is not really an hour, lacking as it does ten minutes. And so the new term advanced rapidly and one day the fields about the town were all brown, cleared of even the few thin patches of snow which had lingered so long.

Howe, as he lectured on the romantic poets, became conscious of Blackburn emanating wrath. Blackburn did it well, did it with enormous dignity. He did not stir in his seat, he kept his eyes fixed on

Howe in perfect attention, but he abstained from using his notebook, there was no mistaking what he proposed to himself as an attitude. His elbow on the writing-wing of the chair, his chin on the curled fingers of his hand, he was the embodiment of intellectual indignation. He was thinking his own thoughts, would give no public offence, yet would claim his due, was not to be intimidated. Howe knew that he would present himself at the end of the hour.

Blackburn entered the office without invitation. He did not smile, there was no cajolery about him. Without invitation he sat down beside Howe's desk. He did not speak until he had taken the blue-book from his pocket. He said, "What does this mean, sir?"

It was a sound and conservative student tactic. Said in the usual way it meant, "How could you have so misunderstood me?" or "What does this mean for my future in the course?" But there were none of the humbler tones in Blackburn's way of saying it.

Howe made the established reply, "I think that's for you to tell me."

Blackburn continued icy. "I'm sure I can't, sir."

There was a silence between them. Both dropped their eyes to the blue-book on the desk. On its cover Howe had pencilled: "F. This is very poor work."

Howe picked up the blue-book. There was always the possibility of injustice. The teacher may be bored by the mass of papers and not wholly attentive. A phrase, even the student's handwriting, may irritate him unreasonably. "Well," said Howe, "let's go through it."

He opened the first page. "Now here: you write, 'In "The Ancient Mariner," Coleridge lives in and transports us to a honey-sweet world where all is rich and strange, a world of charm to which we can escape from the humdrum existence of our daily lives, the world of romance. Here, in this warm and honey-sweet land of charming dreams we can relax and enjoy ourselves.' "

Howe lowered the paper and waited with a neutral look for Blackburn to speak. Blackburn returned the look boldly, did not speak, sat stolid and lofty. At last Howe said, speaking gently, "Did you mean that, or were you just at a loss for something to say?"

"You imply that I was just 'bluffing'?" The quotation marks hung palpable in the air about the word.

"I'd like to know. I'd prefer believing that you were bluffing to believing that you really thought this."

Blackburn's eyebrows went up. From the height of a great and firm-based idea he looked at his teacher. He clasped the crags for a moment and then pounced, craftily, suavely. "Do you mean, Dr. Howe, that there aren't two opinions possible?"

It was superbly done in its air of putting all of Howe's intellectual life into the balance. Howe remained patient and simple. "Yes, many opinions are possible, but not this one. Whatever anyone believes of 'The Ancient Mariner,' no one can in reason believe that it represents a—a honey-sweet world in which we can relax."

"But that is what I *feel*, sir."

This was well done too. Howe said, "Look, Mr. Blackburn. Do you really relax with hunger and thirst, the heat and the sea-serpents, the dead men with staring eyes, Life in Death and the skeletons? Come now, Mr. Blackburn."

Blackburn made no answer and Howe pressed forward. "Now you say of Wordsworth, 'Of peasant stock himself, he turned from the effete life of the salons and found in the peasant the hope of a flaming revolution which would sweep away all the old ideas. This is the subject of his best poems.' "

Beaming at his teacher with youthful eagerness, Blackburn said, "Yes, sir, a rebel, a bringer of light to suffering mankind. I see him as a kind of Prothemeus."

"A kind of what?"

"Prothemeus, sir."

"Think, Mr. Blackburn. We were talking about him only today and I mentioned his name a dozen times. You don't mean Prothemeus. You mean—" Howe waited but there was no response.

"You mean Prometheus."

Blackburn gave no assent and Howe took the reins. "You've done a bad job here, Mr. Blackburn, about as bad as could be done." He saw Blackburn stiffen and his genial face harden again. "It shows either a lack of preparation or a complete lack of understanding." He saw Blackburn's face begin to go to pieces and he stopped.

"Oh, sir," Blackburn burst out, "I've never had a mark like this before, never anything below a B, never. A thing like this has never happened to me before."

It must be true, it was a statement too easily verified. Could it be that other instructors accepted such flaunting nonsense? Howe wanted to end the interview. "I'll set it down to lack of preparation," he said "I know you're busy. That's not an excuse but it's an explanation. Now suppose you really prepare and then take another quiz in two weeks. We'll forget this one and count the other."

Blackburn squirmed with pleasure and gratitude. "Thank you, sir. You're really very kind, very kind."

Howe rose to conclude the visit. "All right then—in two weeks."

It was that day that the Dean imparted to Howe the conclusion of the case of Tertan. It was simple and a little anticlimactic. A physician had been called in, and had said the word, given the name.

"A classic case, he called it," the Dean said. "Not a doubt in the world," he said. His eyes were full of miserable pity and he clutched at a word. "A classic case, a classic case." To his aid and to Howe's there came the Parthenon and the form of the Greek drama, the Aristotelian logic, Racine and the Well-Tempered Clavichord, the blueness of the Aegean and its clear sky. Classic—that is to say, without a doubt, perfect in its way, a veritable model, and, as the Dean had been told, sure to take a perfectly predictable and inevitable course to a foreknown conclusion.

It was not only pity that stood in the Dean's eyes. For a moment there was fear too. "Terrible," he said, "it is simply terrible."

Then he went on briskly. "Naturally we've told the boy nothing. And naturally we won't. His tuition's paid by his scholarship and we'll continue him on the rolls until the end of the year. That will be kindest. After that the matter will be out of our control. We'll see, of course, that he gets into the proper hands. I'm told there will be no change, he'll go on like this, be as good as this, for four to six months. And so we'll just go along as usual."

So Tertan continued to sit in Section 5 of English 1A, to his classmates still a figure of curiously dignified fun, symbol to most of them of the respectable but absurd intellectual life. But to his teacher he was now very different. He had not changed—he was still the greyhound casting for the scent of ideas and Howe could see that he was still the same Tertan, but he could not feel it. What he felt as he looked at the boy sitting in his accustomed place was the hard blank of a fact. The fact itself was formidable and depressing. But what Howe was chiefly aware of was that he had permitted the metamorphosis of Tertan from person to fact.

As much as possible he avoided seeing Tertan's upraised hand and eager eye. But the fact did not know of its mere factuality, it continued its existence as if it were Tertan, hand up and eye questioning, and one day it appeared in Howe's office with a document.

"Even the spirit who lives egregiously, above the herd, must have its relations with the fellowman," Tertan declared. He laid the document on Howe's desk. It was headed "Quill and Scroll Society of Dwight College. Application for Membership."

"In most ways these are crass minds," Tertan said, touching the paper. "Yet as a whole, bound together in their common love of letters, they transcend their intellectual lacks since it is not a paradox that the whole is greater than the sum of its parts."

"When are the elections?" Howe asked.

"They take place tomorrow."

"I certainly hope you will be successful."

"Thank you. Would you wish to implement that hope?" A rather dirty finger pointed to the bottom of the sheet. "A faculty recommender is necessary," Tertan said stiffly, and waited.

"And you wish me to recommend you?"

"It would be an honor."

"You may use my name."

Tertan's finger pointed again. "It must be a written sponsorship, signed by the sponsor." There was a large blank space on the form under the heading, "Opinion of Faculty Sponsor."

This was almost another thing and Howe hesitated. Yet there was nothing else to do and he took out his fountain pen. He wrote, "Mr. Ferdinand Tertan is marked by his intense devotion to letters and by his exceptional love of all things of the mind." To this he signed his name which looked bold and assertive on the white paper. It disturbed him, the strange affirming power of a name. With a business-like air, Tertan whipped up the paper, folded it with decision and put it into his pocket. He bowed and took his departure, leaving Howe with the sense of having done something oddly momentous.

And so much now seemed odd and momentous to Howe that should not have seemed so. It was odd and momentous, he felt, when he sat with Blackburn's second quiz before him and wrote in an excessively firm hand the grade of C-minus. The paper was a clear, an indisputable failure. He was carefully and consciously committing a cowardice. Blackburn had told the truth when he had pleaded his past record. Howe had consulted it in the Dean's office. It showed no grade lower than a B-minus. A canvass of some of Blackburn's previous instructors had brought vague attestations to the adequate powers of a student imperfectly remembered and sometimes surprise that his abilities could be questioned at all.

As he wrote the grade, Howe told himself that his cowardice sprang from an unwillingness to have more dealings with a student he disliked. He knew it was simpler than that. He knew he feared Blackburn: that was the absurd truth. And cowardice did not solve the matter after all. Blackburn, flushed with a first success, attacked at once. The minimal passing grade had not assuaged his feelings and he sat at Howe's desk and again the blue-book lay between them. Blackburn said nothing. With an enormous impudence, he was waiting for Howe to speak and explain himself.

At last Howe said sharply and rudely, "Well?" His throat was tense and the blood was hammering in his head. His mouth was tight with anger at himself for his disturbance.

Blackburn's glance was almost baleful. "This is impossible, sir."

"But there it is," Howe answered.

"Sir?" Blackburn had not caught the meaning but his tone was still haughty.

Impatiently Howe said, "There it is, plain as day. Are you here to complain again?"

"Indeed I am, sir." There was surprise in Blackburn's voice that Howe should ask the question.

"I shouldn't complain if I were you. You did a thoroughly bad job on your first quiz. This one is a little, only a very little, better." This was not true. If anything, it was worse.

"That might be a matter of opinion, sir."

"It is a matter of opinion. Of my opinion."

"Another opinion might be different, sir."

"You really believe that?" Howe said.

"Yes." The omission of the "sir" was monumental.

"Whose, for example?"

"The Dean's, for example." Then the fleshy jaw came forward a little. "Or a certain literary critic's, for example."

It was colossal and almost too much for Blackburn himself to handle. The solidity of his face almost crumpled under it. But he withstood his own audacity and went on. "And the Dean's opinion might be guided by the knowledge that the person who gave me this mark is the man whom a famous critic, the most eminent judge of literature in this country, called a drunken man. The Dean might think twice about whether such a man is fit to teach Dwight students."

Howe said in quiet admonition, "Blackburn, you're mad," meaning no more than to check the boy's extravagance.

But Blackburn paid no heed. He had another shot in the locker. "And the Dean might be guided by the information, of which I have evidence, documentary evidence,"—he slapped his breastpocket twice —"that this same person personally recommended to the college literary society, the oldest in the country, that he personally recommended a student who is crazy, who threw the meeting into an uproar, a psychiatric case. The Dean might take that into account."

Howe was never to learn the details of that "uproar." He had always to content himself with the dim but passionate picture which at that moment sprang into his mind, of Tertan standing on some abstract height and madly denouncing the multitude of Quill and Scroll who howled him down.

He sat quiet a moment and looked at Blackburn. The ferocity had entirely gone from the student's face. He sat regarding his teacher almost benevolently. He had played a good card and now, scarcely at all unfriendly, he was waiting to see the effect. Howe took up the blue-book and negligently sifted through it. He read a page, closed the book, struck out the C-minus and wrote an F.

"Now you may take the paper to the Dean," he said. "You may tell him that after reconsidering it, I lowered the grade."

The gasp was audible. "Oh sir!" Blackburn cried. "Please!" His face was agonized. "It means my graduation, my livelihood, my future. Don't do this to me."

"It's done already."

Blackburn stood up. "I spoke rashly, sir, hastily. I had no intention, no real intention, of seeing the Dean. It rests with you—entirely, entirely. I *hope* you will restore the first mark."

"Take the matter to the Dean or not, just as you choose. The grade is what you deserve and it stands."

Blackburn's head dropped. "And will I be failed at midterm, sir?"

"Of course."

From deep out of Blackburn's great chest rose a cry of anguish. "Oh sir, if you want me to go down on my knees to you, I will, I will."

Howe looked at him in amazement.

"I will. I will. On my knees, sir. This mustn't, mustn't happen."

He spoke so literally, meaning so very truly that his knees and exactly his knees were involved and seeming to think that he was offering something of tangible value to his teacher, that Howe, whose head had become icy clear in the nonsensical drama, thought, "The boy is mad," and began to speculate fantastically whether something in himself attracted or developed aberration. He could see himself standing absurdly before the Dean and saying, "I've found another. This time it's the Vice-president of the Council, the manager of the debating team and secretary of Quill and Scroll."

One more such discovery, he thought, and he himself would be discovered! And there, suddenly, Blackburn was on his knees with a thump, his huge thighs straining his trousers, his hand outstretched in a great gesture of supplication.

With a cry, Howe shoved back his swivel chair and it rolled away on its casters half across the little room. Blackburn knelt for a moment to nothing at all, then got to his feet.

Howe rose abruptly. He said, "Blackburn, you will stop acting like an idiot. Dust your knees off, take your paper and get out. You've behaved like a fool and a malicious person. You have half a term to do a decent job. Keep your silly mouth shut and try to do it. Now get out."

Blackburn's head was low. He raised it and there was a pious light in his eyes. "Will you shake hands, sir?" he said. He thrust out his hand.

"I will not," Howe said.

Head and hand sank together. Blackburn picked up his blue-book and walked to the door. He turned and said, "Thank you, sir." His back, as he departed, was heavy with tragedy and stateliness.

After years of bad luck with the weather, the College had a perfect day for Commencement. It was wonderfully bright, the air so transparent, the wind so brisk that no one could resist talking about it.

As Howe set out for the campus he heard Hilda calling from the back yard. She called, "Professor, professor," and came running to him.

Howe said, "What's this 'professor' business?"

"Mother told me," Hilda said. "You've been promoted. And I want to take your picture."

"Next year," said Howe. "I won't be a professor until next year. And you know better than to call anybody 'professor.' "

"It was just in fun," Hilda said. She seemed disappointed.

"But you can take my picture if you want. I won't look much different next year." Still, it was frightening. It might mean that he was to stay in this town all his life.

Hilda brightened. "Can I take it in this?" she said, and touched the gown he carried over his arm.

Howe laughed. "Yes, you can take it in this."

"I'll get my things and meet you in front of Otis," Hilda said. "I have the background all picked out."

On the campus the Commencement crowd was already large. It stood about in eager, nervous little family groups. As he crossed, Howe was greeted by a student, capped and gowned, glad of the chance to make an event for his parents by introducing one of his teachers. It was while Howe stood there chatting that he saw Tertan.

He had never seen anyone quite so alone, as though a circle had been woven about him to separate him from the gay crowd on the campus. Not that Tertan was not gay, he was the gayest of all. Three weeks had passed since Howe had last seen him, the weeks of examination, the lazy week before Commencement, and this was now a different Tertan. On his head he wore a panama hat, broadbrimmed and fine, of the shape associated with South American planters. He wore a suit of raw silk, luxurious but yellowed with age and much too tight, and he sported a whangee cane. He walked sedately, the hat tilted at a devastating angle, the stick coming up and down in time to his measured tread. He had, Howe guessed, outfitted himself to greet the day in the clothes of that ruined father whose existence was on record in the Dean's office. Gravely and arrogantly he surveyed the scene—in it, his whole bearing seemed to say, but not of it. With his haughty step, with his flashing eye, Tertan was coming nearer. Howe did not wish to be seen. He shifted his position slightly. When he looked again, Tertan was not in sight.

The chapel clock struck the quarter hour. Howe detached himself from his chat and hurried to Otis Hall at the far end of the campus. Hilda had not yet come. He went up into the high portico and, using the glass of the door for a mirror, put on his gown, adjusted the hood on his shoulders and set the mortarboard on his head. When he came down the steps Hilda had arrived.

Nothing could have told him more forcibly that a year had passed than the development of Hilda's photographic possessions from the box camera of the previous fall. By a strap about her neck was hung a leather case, so thick and strong, so carefully stitched and so molded to its contents that it could only hold a costly camera. The appearance was deceptive, Howe knew, for he had been present at the Aikens' pre-Christmas conference about its purchase. It was only a fairly good domestic camera. Still, it looked very impressive. Hilda carried another leather case from which she drew a collapsible tripod. Decisively she extended each of its gleaming legs and set it up on the path. She removed the camera from its case and fixed it to the tripod. In its compact efficiency the camera almost had a life of its own, but Hilda treated it with easy familiarity, looked into its eye, glanced casually at its gauges. Then from a pocket she took still another leather case and drew from it a small instrument through which she looked first at Howe, who began to feel inanimate and lost, and then at the sky. She made some adjustment on the instrument, then some adjustment on the camera. She swept the scene with her eye, found a spot and pointed the camera in its direction. She walked to the spot, stood on it and beckoned to Howe. With each new leather case, with each new instrument and with each new adjustment she had grown in ease and now she said, "Joe, will you stand here?"

Obediently Howe stood where he was bidden. She had yet another instrument. She took out a tape-measure on a mechanical spool. Kneeling down before Howe, she put the little metal ring of the tape under the tip of his shoe. At her request, Howe pressed it with his toe. When she had measured her distance, she nodded to Howe who released the tape. At a touch, it sprang back into the spool. "You have to be careful if you're going to get what you want," Hilda said. "I don't believe in all this snap-snap-snapping," she remarked loftily. Howe nodded in agreement, although he was beginning to think Hilda's care excessive.

Now at last the moment had come. Hilda squinted into the camera, moved the tripod slightly. She stood to the side, holding the plunger of the shutter-cable. "Ready," she said. "Will you relax, Joseph, please?" Howe realized that he was standing frozen. Hilda stood poised and precise as a setter, one hand holding the little cable, the other extended with curled dainty fingers like a dancer's, as if expressing to her subject the precarious delicacy of the moment. She pressed the plunger and there was the click. At once she stirred to action, got behind the camera, turned a new exposure. "Thank you," she said. "Would you stand under that tree and let me do a character study with light and shade?"

The childish absurdity of the remark restored Howe's ease. He went to the little tree. The pattern the leaves made on his gown was what Hilda was after. He had just taken a satisfactory position when he heard in the unmistakable voice, "Ah, Doctor! Having your picture taken?"

Howe gave up the pose and turned to Blackburn who stood on the walk, his hands behind his back, a little too large for his bachelor's gown. Annoyed that Blackburn should see him posing for a character study in light and shade, Howe said irritably, "Yes, having my picture taken."

Blackburn beamed at Hilda. "And the little photographer," he said. Hilda fixed her eyes on the ground and stood closer to her brilliant and aggressive camera. Blackburn, teetering on his heels, his hands behind his back, wholly prelatical and benignly patient, was not abashed at the silence. At last Howe said, "If you'll excuse us, Mr. Blackburn, we'll go on with the picture."

"Go right ahead, sir. I'm running along." But he only came closer. "Dr. Howe," he said fervently, "I want to tell you how glad I am that I was able to satisfy your standards at last."

Howe was surprised at the hard insulting brightness of his own voice and even Hilda looked up curiously as he said, "Nothing you have ever done has satisfied me and nothing you could ever do would satisfy me, Blackburn."

With a glance at Hilda, Blackburn made a gesture as if to hush Howe—as though all his former bold malice had taken for granted a kind of understanding between himself and his teacher, a secret which must not be betrayed to a third person. "I only meant, sir," he said, "that I was able to pass your course after all."

Howe said, "You didn't pass my course. I passed you out of my course. I passed you without even reading your paper. I wanted to be sure the college would be rid of you. And when all the grades were in and I did read your paper, I saw I was right not to have read it first."

Blackburn presented a stricken face. "It was very bad, sir?"

But Howe had turned away. The paper had been fantastic. The paper had been, if he wished to see it so, mad. It was at this moment that the Dean came up behind Howe and caught his arm. "Hello, Joseph," he said. "We'd better be getting along, it's almost late."

He was not a familiar man, but when he saw Blackburn, who approached to greet him, he took Blackburn's arm too. "Hello, Theodore," he said. Leaning forward on Howe's arm and on Blackburn's, he said, "Hello, Hilda, dear." Hilda replied quietly, "Hello, Uncle George."

Still clinging to their arms, still linking Howe and Blackburn, the Dean said, "Another year gone, Joe, and we've turned out another crop. After you've been here a few years, you'll find it reasonably upsetting—you wonder how there can be so many graduating classes while you stay the same. But of course you don't stay the same." Then he said, "Well," sharply, to dismiss the thought. He pulled Blackburn's arm and swung him around to Howe. "Have you heard about Teddy Blackburn?" he asked. "He has a job already, before graduation, the first man of his class to be placed." Expectant of congratulations, Blackburn beamed at Howe. Howe remained silent.

"Isn't that good?" the Dean said. Still Howe did not answer and the Dean, puzzled and put out, turned to Hilda. "That's a very fine-looking camera, Hilda." She touched it with affectionate pride.

"Instruments of precision," said a voice. "Instruments of precision." Of the three with joined arms, Howe was the nearest to Tertan, whose gaze took in all the scene except the smile and the nod which Howe gave him. The boy leaned on his cane. The broadbrimmed hat, canting jauntily over his eye, confused the image of his face that Howe had established, suppressed the rigid lines of the ascetic and brought out the baroque curves. It made an effect of perverse majesty.

"Instruments of precision," said Tertan for the last time, addressing no one, making a casual comment to the universe. And it occurred to Howe that Tertan might not be referring to Hilda's equipment. The sense of the thrice-woven circle of the boy's loneliness smote him fiercely. Tertan stood in majestic jauntiness, superior to all the scene, but his isolation made Howe ache with a pity of which Tertan was more the cause than the object, so general and indiscriminate was it.

Whether in his sorrow he made some unintended movement toward Tertan which the Dean checked or whether the suddenly tightened grip on his arm was the Dean's own sorrow and fear, he did not know. Tertan watched them in the incurious way people watch a photograph being taken and suddenly the thought that, to the boy, it must seem that the three were posing for a picure together made Howe detach himself almost rudely from the Dean's grasp.

"I promised Hilda another picture," he announced—needlessly, for Tertan was no longer there, he had vanished in the last sudden flux of visitors who, now that the band had struck up, were rushing nervously to find seats.

"You'd better hurry," the Dean said. "I'll go along, it's getting late for me." He departed and Blackburn walked stately by his side.

Howe again took his position under the little tree which cast its shadow over his face and gown. "Just hurry, Hilda, won't you?" he said. Hilda held the cable at arm's length, her other arm crooked and her fingers crisped. She rose on her toes and said "Ready," and pressed the release. "Thank you," she said gravely and began to dismantle her camera as he hurried off to join the procession.

by Sherwood Anderson

I'M A FOOL

Sherwood Anderson was born on September 13, 1876, in Camden, Ohio. His formal education was often interrupted by the odd jobs he took to help out his large and impoverished family and was ended before he was fourteen. After serving in Cuba during the Spanish-American War, he became manager of a paint factory in Ohio and an advertising copywriter in Chicago. Two novels and a book of poems preceded the publication, in 1919, of Winesburg, Ohio, *a collection of short stories. In 1923 he brought out* Horses and Men, *in which "I'm a Fool" appeared. After a few years in Europe, New Orleans, and New York, he finally settled in Marion, Virginia, where he edited the town's two newspapers, one Republican and one Democratic, and continued to write. In all, he produced twelve novels, one book of verse, three collections of short stories, and five volumes of autobiographical writings. He died on March 8, 1941, in Panama, at the beginning of a goodwill trip to South America.*

"I'm a Fool" reveals Sherwood Anderson's characteristically American fascination with manners and style. Clothes, habits of speech, and "deportment" are not mere externals; they are the necessary and dependable signs by which we "place" people. The distinctions, though subtle, are finally clear. "I like a man to be a man and dress up"; but a "fellow with a cane and a Windsor tie on" is a dude and contemptible. The girl "could talk proper grammar"—a suspicious circumstance; however, she does so "without being like a schoolteacher." The catastrophe of the story occurs when the boy himself displays false signs—his huge bet, his glib, disastrous lie.

IT was a hard jolt for me, one of the most bitterest I ever had to face. And it all came about through my own foolishness, too. Even yet sometimes, when I think of it, I want to cry or swear or kick myself. Perhaps, even now, after all this time, there will be a kind of satisfaction in making myself look cheap by telling of it.

It began at three o'clock one October afternoon as I sat in the grand stand at the fall trotting and pacing meet at Sandusky, Ohio.

To tell the truth, I felt a little foolish that I should be sitting in the grand stand at all. During the summer before I had left my home town with Harry Whitehead and, with a nigger named Burt, had taken a job as swipe with one of the two horses Harry was campaigning through the fall race meets that year. Mother cried and my sister Mildred, who wanted to get a job as a school teacher in our town that fall, stormed and scolded about the house all during the week before I left. They both thought it something disgraceful that one of our family should take a place as a swipe with race horses. I've an idea Mildred thought my taking the place would stand in the way of her getting the job she'd been working so long for.

But after all I had to work, and there was no other work to be got. A big lumbering fellow of nineteen couldn't just hang around the house and I had got too big to mow people's lawns and sell newspapers. Little chaps who could get next to people's sympathies by their sizes were always getting jobs away from me. There was one fellow who kept saying to everyone who wanted a lawn mowed or a cistern cleaned, that he was saving money to work his way through college, and I used to lay awake nights thinking up ways to injure him without being found out. I kept thinking of wagons running over him and bricks falling on his head as he walked along the street. But never mind him.

I got the place with Harry and I liked Burt fine. We got along splendid together. He was a big nigger with a lazy sprawling body and soft, kind eyes, and when it came to a fight he could hit like Jack Johnson. He had Bucephalus, a big black pacing stallion that could do 2.09 or 2.10 if he had to, and I had a little gelding named Doctor Fritz that never lost a race all fall when Harry wanted him to win.

We set out from home late in July in a box car with the two horses and after that, until late November, we kept moving along to the race meets and the fairs. It was a peachy time for me, I'll say that. Sometimes now I think that boys who are raised regular in houses, and never have a fine nigger like Burt for best friend, and go to high schools and college, and never steal anything, or get drunk a little, or learn to swear from fellows who know how, or come walking up in front of a grand stand in their shirt sleeves and with dirty horsey pants on when the races are going on and the grand stand is full of people all dressed up—What's the use of talking about it? Such fellows don't know nothing at all. They've never had no opportunity.

But I did. Burt taught me how to rub down a horse and put the bandages on after a race and steam a horse out and a lot of valuable things for any man to know. He could wrap a bandage on a horse's leg so smooth that if it had been the same color you would think it was his skin, and I guess he'd have been a big driver, too, and got to the top like Murphy and Walter Cox and the others if he hadn't been black.

Gee whizz, it was fun. You got to a county seat town, maybe say on a Saturday or Sunday, and the fair began the next Tuesday and lasted until Friday afternoon. Doctor Fritz would be, say in the 2.25 trot on Tuesday afternoon and on Thursday afternoon Bucephalus would knock 'em cold in the "free-for-all" pace. It left you a lot of time to hang around and listen to horse talk, and see Burt knock some yap cold that got too gay, and you'd find out about horses and men and pick up a lot of stuff you could use all the rest of your life, if you had some sense and salted down what you heard and felt and saw.

And then at the end of the week when the race meet was over, and Harry had run home to tend up to his livery stable business, you and Burt hitched the two horses to carts and drove slow and steady across country, to the place for the next meeting, so as to not over-heat the horses, etc., etc., you know.

Gee whizz, Gosh amighty, the nice hickorynut and beechnut and oaks and other kinds of trees along the roads, all brown and red, and the good smells, and Burt singing a song that was called Deep River, and the country girls at the windows of houses and everything. You can stick your colleges up your nose for all me. I guess I know where I got my education.

Why, one of those little burgs of towns you come to on the way, say now on a Saturday afternoon, and Burt says, "let's lay up here." And you did.

And you took the horses to a livery stable and fed them, and you got your good clothes out of a box and put them on.

And the town was full of farmers gaping, because they could see you were race horse people, and the kids maybe never see a nigger before and was afraid and run away when the two of us walked down their main street.

And that was before prohibition and all that foolishness, and so you went into a saloon, the two of you, and all the yaps come and stood around, and there was always someone pretended he was horsey and knew things and spoke up and began asking questions, and all you did was to lie and lie all you could about what horses you had, and I said I owned them, and then some fellow said "will you have a drink of whiskey" and Burt knocked his eye out the way he could say, offhand like. "Oh well, all right, I'm agreeable to a little nip. I'll split a quart with you." Gee whizz.

But that isn't what I want to tell my story about. We got home late in November and I promised mother I'd quit the race horses for good. There's a lot of things you've got to promise a mother because she don't know any better.

And so, there not being any work in our town any more than when I left there to go to the races, I went off to Sandusky and got a pretty good place taking care of horses for a man who owned a teaming and delivery and storage and coal and real estate business there. It was a pretty good place with good eats, and a day off each week, and sleeping on a cot in a big barn, and mostly just shovelling in hay and oats to a lot of big good-enough skates of horses, that couldn't have trotted a race with a toad. I wasn't dissatisfied and I could send money home.

And then, as I started to tell you, the fall races come to Sandusky and I got the day off and I went. I left the job at noon and had on my good clothes and my new brown derby hat, I'd just bought the Saturday before, and a stand-up collar.

First of all I went down-town and walked about with the dudes. I've always thought to myself, "put up a good front" and so I did it. I had forty dollars in my pocket and so I went into the West House, a big hotel, and walked up to the cigar stand. "Give me three twenty-five cent cigars," I said. There was a lot of horsemen and strangers and dressed-up people from other towns standing around in the lobby and in the bar, and I mingled amongst them. In the bar there was a fellow with a cane and a Windsor tie on, that it made me sick to look at him. I like a man to be a man and dress up, but not to go put on that kind of airs. So I pushed him aside, kind of rough, and had me a drink of whiskey. And then he looked at me, as though he thought maybe he'd get gay, but he changed his mind and didn't say anything. And then I had another drink of whiskey, just to show him something, and went out and had a hack out to the races, all to myself, and when I got there I bought myself the best seat I could get up in the grand stand, but didn't go in for any of these boxes. That's putting on too many airs.

And so there I was, sitting up in the grand stand as gay as you please and looking down on the swipes coming out with their horses, and with their dirty horsey pants on and the horse blankets swung over their shoulders, same as I had been doing all the year before. I liked one thing about the same as the other, sitting up there and feeling grand and being down there and looking up at the yaps and feeling grander and more important, too. One thing's about as good as another, if you take it just right. I've often said that.

Well, right in front of me, in the grand stand that day, there was a fellow with a couple of girls and they was about my age. The young fellow was a nice guy all right. He was the kind maybe that goes to college and then comes to be a lawyer or maybe a newspaper editor or something like that, but he wasn't stuck on himself. There are some of that kind are all right and he was one of the ones.

He had his sister with him and another girl and the sister looked around over his shoulder, accidental at first, not intending to start anything—she wasn't that kind—and her eyes and mine happened to meet.

You know how it is. Gee, she was a peach! She had on a soft dress, kind of a blue stuff and it looked carelessly made, but was well sewed and made and everything. I knew that much. I blushed when she looked right at me and so did she. She was the nicest girl I've ever seen in my life. She wasn't stuck on herself and she could talk proper grammar without being like a school teacher or something like that. What I mean is, she was O. K. I think maybe her father was well-to-do, but not rich to make her chesty because she was his daughter, as some are. Maybe he owned a drug store or a drygoods store in their home town, or something like that. She never told me and I never asked.

My own people are all O. K. too, when you come to that. My grandfather was Welsh and over in the old country, in Wales he was—— But never mind that.

The first heat of the first race come off and the young fellow setting there with the two girls left them and went down to make a bet. I knew what he was up to, but he didn't talk big and noisy and let everyone around know he was a sport, as some do. He wasn't that kind. Well, he come back and I heard him tell the two girls what horse he'd bet on, and when the heat was trotted they all half got to their feet and acted in the excited, sweaty way people do when they've got money down on a race, and the horse they bet on is up there pretty close at the end, and they think maybe he'll come on with a rush, but he never does because he hasn't got the old juice in him, come right down to it.

And then, pretty soon, the horses came out for the 2.18 pace and there was a horse in it I knew. He was a horse Bob French had in his string but Bob didn't own him. He was a horse owned by a Mr. Mathers down at Marietta, Ohio.

This Mr. Mathers had a lot of money and owned some coal mines or something, and he had a swell place out in the country, and he was stuck on race horses, but was a Presbyterian or something, and I think more than likely his wife was one, too, maybe a stiffer one than himself. So he never raced his horses hisself, and the story round the Ohio race tracks was that when one of his horses got ready to go to the races he turned him over to Bob French and pretended to his wife he was sold.

So Bob had the horses and he did pretty much as he pleased and you can't blame Bob, at least, I never did. Sometimes he was out to win and sometimes he wasn't. I never cared much about that when I was swiping a horse. What I did want to know was that my horse had the speed and could go out in front, if you wanted him to.

And, as I'm telling you, there was Bob in this race with one of Mr. Mathers' horses, was named "About Ben Ahem" or something like that, and was fast as a streak. He was a gelding and had a mark of 2.21, but could step in .08 or .09.

Because when Burt and I were out, as I've told you, the year before, there was a nigger, Burt knew, worked for Mr. Mathers and we went out there one day when we didn't have no race on at the Marietta Fair and our boss Harry was gone home.

And so everyone was gone to the fair but just this one nigger and he took us all through Mr. Mathers' swell house and he and Burt tapped a bottle of wine Mr. Mathers had hid in his bedroom, back in a closet, without his wife knowing, and he showed us this Ahem horse. Burt was always stuck on being a driver but didn't have much chance to get to the top, being a nigger, and he and the other nigger gulped that whole bottle of wine and Burt got a little lit up.

So the nigger let Burt take this About Ben Ahem and step him a mile in a track Mr. Mathers had all to himself, right there on the farm. And Mr. Mathers had one child, a daughter, kinda sick and not very good looking, and she came home and we had to hustle and get Ben Ahem stuck back in the barn.

I'm only telling you to get everything straight. At Sandusky, that afternoon I was at the fair, this young fellow with the two girls was fussed, being with the girls and losing his bet. You know how a fellow is that way. One of them was his girl and the other his sister. I had figured that out.

"Gee whizz," I says to myself, "I'm going to give him the dope."

He was mighty nice when I touched him on the shoulder. He and the girls were nice to me right from the start and clear to the end. I'm not blaming them.

And so he leaned back and I give him the dope on About Ben Ahem. "Don't bet a cent on this first heat because he'll go like an oxen hitched to a plow, but when the first heat is over go right down and lay on your pile." That's what I told him.

Well, I never saw a fellow treat any one sweller. There was a fat man sitting beside the little girl, that had looked at me twice by this time, and I at her, and both blushing, and what did he do but have the nerve to turn and ask the fat man to get up and change places with me so I could set with his crowd.

Gee whizz, craps amighty. There I was. What a chump I was to go and get gay up there in the West House bar, and just because that dude was standing there with a cane and that kind of a necktie on, to go and get all balled up and drink that whiskey, just to show off.

Of course she would know, me setting right beside her and letting her smell of my breath. I could have kicked myself right down out of that grand stand and all around that race track and made a faster record than most of the skates of horses they had there that year.

Because that girl wasn't any mutt of a girl. What wouldn't I have give right then for a stick of chewing gum to chew, or a lozenger, or some liquorice, or most anything. I was glad I had those twenty-five cent cigars in my pocket and right away I give that fellow one and lit one myself. Then that fat man got up and we changed places and there I was, plunked right down beside her.

They introduced themselves and the fellow's best girl, he had with him, was named Miss Elinor Woodbury, and her father was a manufacturer of barrels from a place called Tiffin, Ohio. And the fellow himself was named Wilbur Wessen and his sister was Miss Lucy Wessen.

I suppose it was their having such swell names got me off my trolley. A fellow, just because he has been a swipe with a race horse, and works taking care of horses for a man in the teaming, delivery, and storage business, isn't any better or worse than any one else. I've often thought that, and said it too.

But you know how a fellow is. There's something in that kind of nice clothes, and the kind of nice eyes she had, and the way she had looked at me, awhile before, over her brother's shoulder, and me looking back at her, and both of us blushing.

I couldn't show her up for a boob, could I?

I made a fool of myself, that's what I did. I said my name was Walter Mathers from Marietta, Ohio, and then I told all three of them the smashingest lie you ever heard. What I said was that my father owned the horse About Ben Ahem and that he had let him out to this Bob French for racing purposes, because our family was proud and had never gone into racing that way, in our own name, I mean. Then I had got started and they were all leaning over and listening, and Miss Lucy Wessen's eyes were shining, and I went the whole hog.

I told about our place down at Marietta, and about the big stables and the grand brick house we had on a hill, up above the Ohio River, but I knew enough not to do it in no bragging way. What I did was to start things and then let them drag the rest out of me. I acted just as reluctant to tell as I could. Our family hasn't got any barrel factory, and, since I've known us, we've always been pretty poor, but not asking anything of any one at that, and my grandfather, over in Wales—but never mind that.

We set there talking like we had known each other for years and years, and I went and told them that my father had been expecting maybe this Bob French wasn't on the square, and had sent me up to Sandusky on the sly to find out what I could.

And I bluffed it through I had found out all about the 2.18 pace, in which About Ben Ahem was to start.

I said he would lose the first heat by pacing like a lame cow and then he would come back and skin 'em alive after that. And to back up what I said I took thirty dollars out of my pocket and handed it to Mr. Wilbur Wessen and asked him, would he mind, after the first heat, to go down and place it on About Ben Ahem for whatever odds he could get. What I said was that I didn't want Bob French to see me and none of the swipes.

Sure enough the first heat come off and About Ben Ahem went off his stride, up the back stretch, and looked like a wooden horse or a sick one, and come in to be last. Then this Wilbur Wessen went down to the betting place under the grand stand and there I was with the two girls, and when that Miss Woodbury was looking the other way once, Lucy Wessen kinda, with her shoulder you know, kinda touched me. Not just tucking down, I don't mean. You know how a woman can do. They get close, but not getting gay either. You know what they do. Gee whizz.

And then they give me a jolt. What they had done, when I didn't know, was to get together, and they had decided Wilbur Wessen would bet fifty dollars, and the two girls had gone and put in ten dollars each, of their own money, too. I was sick then, but I was sicker later.

About the gelding, About Ben Ahem, and their winning their money, I wasn't worried a lot about that. It come out O. K. Ahem stepped the next three heats like a bushel of spoiled eggs going to market before they could be found out, and Wilbur Wessen had got nine to two for the money. There was something else eating at me.

Because Wilbur come back, after he had bet the money, and after that he spent most of his time talking to that Miss Woodbury, and Lucy Wessen and I was left alone together like on a desert island. Gee, if I'd only been on the square or if there had been any way of getting myself on the square. There ain't any Walter Mathers, like I said to her and them, and there hasn't ever been one, but if there was, I bet I'd go to Marietta, Ohio, and shoot him to-morrow.

There I was, big boob that I am. Pretty soon the race was over, and Wilbur had gone down and collected our money, and we had a hack down-town, and he stood us a swell supper at the West House, and a bottle of champagne beside.

And I was with that girl and she wasn't saying much, and I wasn't saying much either. One thing I know. She wasn't stuck on me because of the lie about my father being rich and all that. There's a way you know. . . . Craps amighty. There's a kind of girl, you see just once in your life, and if you don't get busy and make hay, then you're gone for good and all, and might as well go jump off a bridge. They give you a look from inside of them somewhere, and it ain't no vamping, and what it means is—you want that girl to be your wife, and you want nice things around her like flowers and swell clothes, and you want her to have the kids you're going to have, and you want good music played and no rag time. Gee whizz.

There's a place over near Sandusky, across a kind of bay, and it's called Cedar Point. And after we had supper we went over to it in a launch, all by ourselves. Wilbur and Miss Lucy and that Miss Woodbury had to catch a ten o'clock train back to Tiffin, Ohio, because, when you're out with girls like that you can't get careless and miss any trains and stay out all night, like you can with some kinds of Janes.

And Wilbur blowed himself to the launch and it cost him fifteen cold plunks, but I wouldn't never have knew if I hadn't listened. He wasn't no tin horn kind of a sport.

Over at the Cedar Point place, we didn't stay around where there was a gang of common kind of cattle at all.

There was big dance halls and dining places for yaps, and there was a beach you could walk along and get where it was dark, and we went there.

She didn't talk hardly at all and neither did I, and I was thinking how glad I was my mother was all right, and always made us kids learn to eat with a fork at table, and not swill soup, and not be noisy and rough like a gang you see around a race track that way.

Then Wilbur and his girl went away up the beach and Lucy and I sat down in a dark place, where there was some roots of old trees, the water had washed up, and after that the time, till we had to go back in the launch and they had to catch their trains, wasn't nothing at all. It went like winking your eye.

Here's how it was. The place we were setting in was dark, like I said, and there was the roots from that old stump sticking up like arms, and there was a watery smell, and the night was like—as if you could put your hand out and feel it—so warm and soft and dark and sweet like an orange.

I most cried and I most swore and I most jumped up and danced, I was so mad and happy and sad.

When Wilbur come back from being alone with his girl, and she saw him coming, Lucy she says, "we got to go to the train now," and she was most crying too, but she never knew nothing I knew, and she couldn't be so all busted up. And then, before Wilbur and Miss Woodbury got up to where we was, she put her face up and kissed me quick and put her head up against me and she was all quivering and —Gee whizz.

Sometimes I hope I have cancer and die. I guess you know what I mean. We went in the launch across the bay to the train like that, and it was dark, too. She whispered and said it was like she and I could get out of the boat and walk on the water, and it sounded foolish, but I knew what she meant.

And then quick we were right at the depot, and there was a big gang of yaps, the kind that goes to the fairs, and crowded and milling around like cattle, and how could I tell her? "It won't be long because you'll write and I'll write to you." That's all she said.

I got a chance like a hay barn afire. A swell chance I got.

And maybe she would write me, down at Marietta that way, and the letter would come back, and stamped on the front of it by the U.S.A. "there ain't any such guy," or something like that, whatever they stamp on a letter that way.

And me trying to pass myself off for a bigbug and a swell—to her, as decent a little body as God ever made. Craps amighty—a swell chance I got!

And then the train come in, and she got on it, and Wilbur Wessen he come and shook hands with me, and that Miss Woodbury was nice too and bowed to me, and I at her, and the train went and I busted out and cried like a kid.

Gee, I could have run after the train and made Dan Patch look like a freight train after a wreck but, socks amighty, what was the use? Did you ever see such a fool?

I'll bet you what—if I had an arm broke right now or a train had run over my foot—I wouldn't go to no doctor at all. I'd go set down and let her hurt and hurt—that's what I'd do.

I'll bet you what—if I hadn't a drunk that booze I'd a never been such a boob as to go tell such a lie—that couldn't never be made straight to a lady like her.

I wish I had that fellow right here that had on a Windsor tie and carried a cane. I'd smash him for fair. Gosh darn his eyes. He's a big fool—that's what he is.

And if I'm not another you just go find me one and I'll quit working and be a bum and give him my job. I don't care nothing for working, and earning money, and saving it for no such boob as myself.

by John Steinbeck

FLIGHT

John Steinbeck was born on February 27, 1902, in Salinas, California. He attended local schools and studied intermittently at Stanford University, leaving in 1925 without a degree. Prior to his success as a novelist, he was a reporter, hod carrier, painter, chemist, surveyor, and fruit picker. Mr. Steinbeck's first novel, Cup of Gold, *appeared in 1929, but not until he published* Tortilla Flat *(1935) did his work receive any acclaim. In 1939* Grapes of Wrath *appeared, winning him the 1940 Pulitzer Prize. During World War II, Mr. Steinbeck was a foreign correspondent and wrote recruiting materials for the Army Air Force. Since then he has written seven novels—*The Winter of Our Discontent *is the latest—two plays, and a diary of observations on America,* Travels with Charley *(1962). Mr. Steinbeck was awarded the Nobel Prize for literature in 1962.*

Monterey County, the author's birthplace, is the scene of "Flight," as it is of much of his other fiction. But Mr. Steinbeck is no mere local colorist. Though Pepé's flight is a journey through vividly actual mountains and underbrush, the mountains bare their "jagged rotten teeth," the underbrush grabs at his legs with "sharp brittle fingers." And it is a like transmutation of the actual into the symbolic that makes his a flight not only from a murder he must own, but from a childhood he must leave. His final act recognizes these commitments: in a gesture of heroic acceptance, he "stands erect."

About fifteen miles below Monterey, on the wild coast, the Torres family had their farm, a few sloping acres above a cliff that dropped to the brown reefs and to the hissing white waters of the ocean. Behind the farm the stone mountains stood up against the sky. The farm buildings huddled like little clinging aphids on the mountain skirts, crouched low to the ground as though the wind might blow them into the sea. The little shack, the rattling, rotting barn were grey-bitten with sea salt, beaten by the damp wind until they had taken on the color of the granite hills. Two horses, a red cow and a red calf, half a dozen pigs and a flock of lean, multicolored chickens stocked the place. A little corn was raised on the sterile slope, and it grew short and thick under the wind, and all the cobs formed on the landward sides of the stalks.

Mama Torres, a lean, dry woman with ancient eyes, had ruled the farm for ten years, ever since her husband tripped over a stone in the field one day and fell full length on a rattlesnake. When one is bitten on the chest there is not much that can be done.

Mama Torres had three children, two undersized black ones of twelve and fourteen, Emilio and Rosy, whom Mama kept fishing on the rocks below the farm when the sea was kind and when the truant officer was in some distant part of Monterey County. And there was Pepé, the tall smiling son of nineteen, a gentle, affectionate boy, but very lazy. Pepé had a tall head, pointed at the top, and from its peak, coarse black hair grew down like a thatch all around. Over his smiling little eyes Mama cut a straight bang so he could see. Pepé had sharp Indian cheek bones and an eagle nose, but his mouth was as sweet and shapely as a girl's mouth, and his chin was fragile and chiseled. He was loose and gangling, all legs and feet and wrists, and he was very lazy. Mama thought him fine and brave, but she never told him so. She said, "Some lazy cow must have got into thy father's family, else how could I have a son like thee." And she said, "When I carried thee, a sneaking lazy coyote came out of the brush and looked at me one day. That must have made thee so."

Pepé smiled sheepishly and stabbed at the ground with his knife to keep the blade sharp and free from rust. It was his inheritance, that knife, his father's knife. The long heavy blade folded back into the black handle. There was a button on the handle. When Pepé pressed the button, the blade leaped out ready for use. The knife was with Pepé always, for it had been his father's knife.

One sunny morning when the sea below the cliff was glinting and blue and the white surf creamed on the reef, when even the stone mountains looked kindly, Mama Torres called out the door of the shack, "Pepé, I have a labor for thee."

There was no answer. Mama listened. From behind the barn she heard a burst of laughter. She lifted her full long skirt and walked in the direction of the noise.

Pepé was sitting on the ground with his back against a box. His white teeth glistened. On either side of him stood the two black ones, tense and expectant. Fifteen feet away a redwood post was set in the ground. Pepé's right hand lay limply in his lap, and in the palm the big black knife rested. The blade was closed back into the handle. Pepé looked smiling at the sky.

Suddenly Emilio cried, "Ya!"

Pepé's wrist flicked like the head of a snake. The blade seemed to fly open in mid-air, and with a thump the point dug into the redwood post, and the black handle quivered. The three burst into excited laughter. Rosy ran to the post and pulled out the knife and brought it back to Pepé. He closed the blade and settled the knife carefully in his listless palm again. He grinned self-consciously at the sky.

"Ya!"

The heavy knife lanced out and sunk into the post again. Mama moved forward like a ship and scattered the play.

"All day you do foolish things with the knife, like a toy-baby," she stormed. "Get up on thy huge feet that eat up shoes. Get up!" She took him by one loose shoulder and hoisted at him. Pepé grinned sheepishly and came half-heartedly to his feet. "Look!" Mama cried. "Big lazy, you must catch the horse and put on him thy father's saddle. You must ride to Monterey. The medicine bottle is empty. There is no salt. Go thou now, Peanut! Catch the horse."

A revolution took place in the relaxed figure of Pepé. "To Monterey, me? Alone? Sí, Mama."

She scowled at him. "Do you think, big sheep, that you will buy candy. No, I will give you only enough for the medicine and the salt."

Pepé smiled. "Mama, you will put the hatband on the hat?"

She relented then. "Yes, Pepé. You may wear the hatband."

His voice grew insinuating, "And the green handkerchief, Mama?"

"Yes, if you go quickly and return with no trouble, the silk green handkerchief will go. If you make sure to take off the handkerchief when you eat so no spot may fall on it. . . ."

"Sí, Mama. I will be careful. I am a man."

"Thou? A man? Thou art a peanut."

He went into the rickety barn and brought out a rope, and he walked agilely enough up the hill to catch the horse.

When he was ready and mounted before the door, mounted on his father's saddle that was so old that the oaken frame showed through torn leather in many places, then Mama brought out the round black hat with the tooled leather band, and she reached up and knotted the green silk handkerchief about his neck. Pepé's blue denim coat was much darker than his jeans, for it had been washed much less often.

Mama handed up the big medicine bottle and the silver coins. "That for the medicine," she said, "and that for the salt. That for a candle to burn for the papa. That for *dulces* for the little ones. Our friend Mrs. Rodriguez will give you dinner and maybe a bed for the night. When you go to the church say only ten Paternosters and only twenty-five Ave Marias. Oh! I know, big coyote. You would sit there flapping your mouth over Aves all day while you looked at the candles and the holy pictures. That is not good devotion to stare at the pretty things."

The black hat, covering the high pointed head and black thatched hair of Pepé, gave him dignity and age. He sat the rangy horse well. Mama thought how handsome he was, dark and lean and tall. "I would not send thee now alone, thou little one, except for the medicine," she said softly. "It is not good to have no medicine, for who knows when the toothache will come, or the sadness of the stomach. These things are."

"Adios, Mama," Pepé cried. "I will come back soon. You may send me often alone. I am a man."

"Thou art a foolish chicken."

He straightened his shoulders, flipped the reins against the horse's shoulder and rode away. He turned once and saw that they still watched him, Emilio and Rosy and Mama. Pepé grinned with pride and gladness and lifted the tough buckskin horse to a trot.

When he had dropped out of sight over a little dip in the road, Mama turned to the black ones, but she spoke to herself. "He is nearly a man now," she said. "It will be a nice thing to have a man in the house again." Her eyes sharpened on the children. "Go to the rocks now. The tide is going out. There will be abalones to be found." She put the iron hooks into their hands and saw them down the steep trail to the reefs. She brought the smooth stone *metate* to the doorway and sat grinding her corn to flour and looking occasionally at the road over which Pepé had gone. The noonday came and then the afternoon, when the little ones beat the abalones on a rock to make them tender and Mama patted the tortillas to make them thin. They ate their dinner as the red sun was plunging down toward the ocean. They sat on the doorsteps and watched the big white moon come over the mountain tops.

Mama said, "He is now at the house of our friend Mrs. Rodriguez. She will give him nice things to eat and maybe a present."

Emilio said, "Some day I too will ride to Monterey for medicine. Did Pepé come to be a man today?"

Mama said wisely, "A boy gets to be a man when a man is needed. Remember this thing. I have known boys forty years old because there was no need for a man."

Soon afterwards they retired, Mama in her big oak bed on one side of the room, Emilio and Rosy in their boxes full of straw and sheepskins on the other side of the room.

The moon went over the sky and the surf roared on the rocks. The roosters crowed the first call. The surf subsided to a whispering surge against the reef. The moon dropped toward the sea. The roosters crowed again.

The moon was near down to the water when Pepé rode on a winded horse to his home flat. His dog bounced out and circled the horse yelping with pleasure. Pepé slid off the saddle to the ground. The weathered little shack was silver in the moonlight and the square shadow of it was black to the north and east. Against the east the piling mountains were misty with light; their tops melted into the sky.

Pepé walked wearily up the three steps and into the house. It was dark inside. There was a rustle in the corner.

Mama cried out from her bed, "Who comes? Pepé, is it thou?"

"Sí, Mama."

"Did you get the medicine?"

"Sí, Mama."

"Well, go to sleep, then. I thought you would be sleeping at the house of Mrs. Rodriguez." Pepé stood silently in the dark room. "Why do you stand there, Pepé? Did you drink wine?"

"Sí, Mama."

"Well, go to bed then and sleep out the wine."

His voice was tired and patient, but very firm. "Light the candle, Mama. I must go away into the mountains."

"What is this, Pepé? You are crazy." Mama struck a sulphur match and held the little blue burr until the flame spread up the stick. She set light to the candle on the floor beside her bed. "Now, Pepé, what is this you say?" She looked anxiously into his face.

He was changed. The fragile quality seemed to have gone from his chin. His mouth was less full than it had been, the lines of the lips were straighter, but in his eyes the greatest change had taken place. There was no laughter in them any more, nor any bashfulness. They were sharp and bright and purposeful.

He told her in a tired monotone, told her everything just as it happened. A few people came into the kitchen of Mrs. Rodriguez. There was wine to drink. Pepé drank wine. The little quarrel—the man started toward Pepé and then the knife—it went almost by itself. It flew, it darted before Pepé knew it. As he talked, Mama's face grew stern, and it seemed to grow more lean. Pepé finished. "I am a man now, Mama. The man said names to me I could not allow."

Mama nodded. "Yes, thou art a man, my poor little Pepé. Thou art a man. I have seen it coming on thee. I have watched you throwing the knife into the post, and I have been afraid." For a moment her face had softened, but now it grew stern again. "Come! We must get you ready. Go. Awaken Emilio and Rosy. Go quickly."

Pepé stepped over to the corner where his brother and sister slept among the sheepskins. He leaned down and shook them gently. "Come, Rosy! Come, Emilio! The mama says you must arise."

The little black ones sat up and rubbed their eyes in the candlelight. Mama was out of bed now, her long black skirt over her nightgown. "Emilio," she cried. "Go up and catch the other horse for Pepé. Quickly, now! Quickly." Emilio put his legs in his overalls and stumbled sleepily out the door.

"You heard no one behind you on the road?" Mama demanded.

"No, Mama. I listened carefully. No one was on the road."

Mama darted like a bird about the room. From a nail on the wall she took a canvas water bag and threw it on the floor. She stripped a blanket from her bed and rolled it into a tight tube and tied the ends with string. From a box beside the stove she lifted a flour sack half full of black stringy jerky. "Your father's black coat, Pepé. Here, put it on."

Pepé stood in the middle of the floor watching her activity. She reached behind the door and brought out the rifle, a long 38-56, worn shiny the whole length of the barrel. Pepé took it from her and held it in the crook of his elbow. Mama brought a little leather bag and counted the cartridges into his hand. "Only ten left," she warned. "You must not waste them."

Emilio put his head in the door. " '*Qui 'st 'l caballo,* Mama."

"Put on the saddle from the other horse. Tie on the blanket. Here, tie the jerky to the saddle horn."

Still Pepé stood silently watching his mother's frantic activity. His chin looked hard, and his sweet mouth was drawn and thin. His little eyes followed Mama about the room almost suspiciously.

Rosy asked softly, "Where goes Pepé?"

Mama's eyes were fierce. "Pepé goes on a journey. Pepé is a man now. He has a man's thing to do."

Pepé straightened his shoulders. His mouth changed until he looked very much like Mama.

At last the preparation was finished. The loaded horse stood outside the door. The water bag dripped a line of moisture down the bay shoulder.

The moonlight was being thinned by the dawn and the big white moon was near down to the sea. The family stood by the shack. Mama confronted Pepé. "Look, my son! Do not stop until it is dark again. Do not sleep even though you are tired. Take care of the horse in order that he may not stop of weariness. Remember to be careful with the bullets—there are only ten. Do not fill thy stomach with jerky or it will make thee sick. Eat a little jerky and fill thy stomach with grass. When thou comest to the high mountains, if thou seest any of the dark watching men, go not near to them nor try to speak to them. And forget not thy prayers." She put her lean hands on Pepé's shoulders, stood on her toes and kissed him formally on both cheeks, and Pepé kissed her on both cheeks. Then he went to Emilio and Rosy and kissed both of their cheeks.

Pepé turned back to Mama. He seemed to look for a little softness, a little weakness in her. His eyes were searching, but Mama's face remained fierce. "Go now," she said. "Do not wait to be caught like a chicken."

Pepé pulled himself into the saddle. "I am a man," he said.

It was the first dawn when he rode up the hill toward the little canyon which let a trail into the mountains. Moonlight and daylight fought with each other, and the two warring qualities made it difficult to see. Before Pepé had gone a hundred yards, the outlines of his figure were misty; and long before he entered the canyon, he had become a grey, indefinite shadow.

Mama stood stiffly in front of her doorstep, and on either side of her stood Emilio and Rosy. They cast furtive glances at Mama now and then.

When the grey shape of Pepé melted into the hillside and disappeared, Mama relaxed. She began the high, whining keen of the death wail. "Our beautiful—our brave," she cried. "Our protector, our son is gone." Emilio and Rosy moaned beside her. "Our beautiful—our brave, he is gone." It was the formal wail. It rose to a high piercing whine and subsided to a moan. Mama raised it three times and then she turned and went into the house and shut the door.

Emilio and Rosy stood wondering in the dawn. They heard Mama whimpering in the house. They went out to sit on the cliff above the ocean. They touched shoulders. "When did Pepé come to be a man?" Emilio asked.

"Last night," said Rosy. "Last night in Monterey." The ocean clouds turned red with the sun that was behind the mountains.

"We will have no breakfast," said Emilio. "Mama will not want to cook." Rosy did not answer him. "Where is Pepé gone?" he asked.

Rosy looked around at him. She drew her knowledge from the quiet air. "He has gone on a journey. He will never come back."

"Is he dead? Do you think he is dead?"

Rosy looked back at the ocean again. A little steamer, drawing a line of smoke sat on the edge of the horizon. "He is not dead," Rosy explained. "Not yet."

Pepé rested the big rifle across the saddle in front of him. He let the horse walk up the hill and he didn't look back. The stony slope took on a coat of short brush so that Pepé found the entrance to a trail and entered it.

When he came to the canyon opening, he swung once in his saddle and looked back, but the houses were swallowed in the misty light. Pepé jerked forward again. The high shoulder of the canyon closed in on him. His horse stretched out its neck and sighed and settled to the trail.

It was a well-worn path, dark soft leaf-mould earth strewn with broken pieces of sandstone. The trail rounded the shoulder of the canyon and dropped steeply into the bed of the stream. In the shallows the water ran smoothly, glinting in the first morning sun. Small round stones on the bottom were as brown as rust with sun moss. In the sand along the edges of the stream the tall, rich wild mint grew, while in the water itself the cress, old and tough, had gone to heavy seed.

The path went into the stream and emerged on the other side. The horse sloshed into the water and stopped. Pepé dropped his bridle and let the beast drink of the running water.

Soon the canyon sides became steep and the first giant sentinel redwoods guarded the trail, great round red trunks bearing foliage as green and lacy as ferns. Once Pepé was among the trees, the sun was lost. A perfumed and purple light lay in the pale green of the underbrush. Gooseberry bushes and blackberries and tall ferns lined the stream, and overhead the branches of the redwoods met and cut off the sky.

Pepé drank from the water bag, and he reached into the flour sack and brought out a black string of jerky. His white teeth gnawed at the string until the tough meat parted. He chewed slowly and drank occasionally from the water bag. His little eyes were slumberous and tired, but the muscles of his face were hard set. The earth of the trail was black now. It gave up a hollow sound under the walking hoofbeats.

The stream fell more sharply. Little waterfalls splashed on the stones. Five-fingered ferns hung over the water and dripped spray from their fingertips. Pepé rode half over in his saddle, dangling one leg loosely. He picked a bay leaf from a tree beside the way and put it into his mouth for a moment to flavor the dry jerky. He held the gun loosely across the pommel.

Suddenly he squared in his saddle, swung the horse from the trail and kicked it hurriedly up behind a big redwood tree. He pulled up the reins tight against the bit to keep the horse from whinnying. His face was intent and his nostrils quivered a little.

A hollow pounding came down the trail, and a horseman rode by, a fat man with red cheeks and a white stubble beard. His horse put down its head and blubbered at the trail when it came to the place where Pepé had turned off. "Hold up!" said the man and he pulled up his horse's head.

When the last sound of the hoofs died away, Pepé came back into the trail again. He did not relax in the saddle any more. He lifted the big rifle and swung the lever to throw a shell into the chamber, and then he let down the hammer to half cock.

The trail grew very steep. Now the redwood trees were smaller and their tops were dead, bitten dead where the wind reached them. The horse plodded on; the sun went slowly overhead and started down toward the afternoon.

Where the stream came out of a side canyon, the trail left it. Pepé dismounted and watered his horse and filled up his water bag. As soon as the trail had parted from the stream, the trees were gone and only the thick brittle sage and manzanita and chaparral edged the trail. And the soft black earth was gone, too, leaving only the light tan broken rock for the trail bed. Lizards scampered away into the brush as the horse rattled over the little stones.

Pepé turned in his saddle and looked back. He was in the open now: he could be seen from a distance. As he ascended the trail the country grew more rough and terrible and dry. The way wound about the bases of great square rocks. Little grey rabbits skittered in the brush. A bird made a monotonous high creaking. Eastward the bare rock mountaintops were pale and powder-dry under the dropping sun. The horse plodded up and up the trail toward a little V in the ridge which was the pass.

Pepé looked suspiciously back every minute or so, and his eyes sought the tops of the ridges ahead. Once, on a white barren spur, he saw a black figure for a moment, but he looked quickly away, for it was one of the dark watchers. No one knew who the watchers were, nor where they lived, but it was better to ignore them and never to show interest in them. They did not bother one who stayed on the trail and minded his own business.

The air was parched and full of light dust blown by the breeze from the eroding mountains. Pepé drank sparingly from his bag and corked it tightly and hung it on the horn again. The trail moved up the dry shale hillside, avoiding rocks, dropping under clefts, climbing in and out of old water scars. When he arrived at the little pass he stopped and looked back for a long time. No dark watchers were to be seen now. The trail behind was empty. Only the high tops of the redwoods indicated where the stream flowed.

Pepé rode on through the pass. His little eyes were nearly closed with weariness, but his face was stern, relentless and manly. The high mountain wind coasted sighing through the pass and whistled on the edges of the big blocks of broken granite. In the air, a red-tailed hawk sailed over close to the ridge and screamed angrily. Pepé went slowly through the broken jagged pass and looked down on the other side.

The trail dropped quickly, staggering among broken rock. At the bottom of the slope there was a dark crease, thick with brush, and on the other side of the crease a little flat, in which a grove of oak trees grew. A scar of green grass cut across the flat. And behind the flat another mountain rose, desolate with dead rocks and starving little black bushes. Pepé drank from the bag again for the air was so dry that it encrusted his nostrils and burned his lips. He put the horse down the trail. The hooves slipped and struggled on the steep way, starting little stones that rolled off into the brush. The sun was gone behind the westward mountain now, but still it glowed brilliantly on the oaks and on the grassy flat. The rocks and the hillsides still sent up waves of the heat they had gathered from the day's sun.

Pepé looked up to the top of the next dry withered ridge. He saw a dark form against the sky, a man's figure standing on top of a rock, and he glanced away quickly not to appear curious. When a moment later he looked up again, the figure was gone.

Downward the trail was quickly covered. Sometimes the horse floundered for footing, sometimes set his feet and slid a little way. They came at last to the bottom where the dark chaparral was higher than Pepé's head. He held up his rifle on one side and his arm on the other to shield his face from the sharp brittle fingers of the brush.

Up and out of the crease he rode, and up a little cliff. The grassy flat was before him, and the round comfortable oaks. For a moment he studied the trail down which he had come, but there was no movement and no sound from it. Finally he rode out over the flat, to the green streak, and at the upper end of the damp he found a little spring welling out of the earth and dropping into a dug basin before it seeped out over the flat.

Pepé filled his bag first, and then he let the thirsty horse drink out of the pool. He led the horse to the clump of oaks, and in the middle of the grove, fairly protected from sight on all sides, he took off the saddle and the bridle and laid them on the ground. The horse stretched his jaws sideways and yawned. Pepé knotted the lead rope about the horse's neck and tied him to a sapling among the oaks, where he could graze in a fairly large circle.

When the horse was gnawing hungrily at the dry grass, Pepé went to the saddle and took a black string of jerky from the sack and strolled to an oak tree on the edge of the grove, from under which he could watch the trail. He sat down in the crisp dry oak leaves and automatically felt for his big black knife to cut the jerky, but he had no knife. He leaned back on his elbow and gnawed at the tough strong meat. His face was blank, but it was a man's face.

The bright evening light washed the eastern ridge, but the valley was darkening. Doves flew down from the hills to the spring, and the quail came running out of the brush and joined them, calling clearly to one another.

Out of the corner of his eye Pepé saw a shadow grow out of the bushy crease. He turned his head slowly. A big spotted wildcat was creeping toward the spring, belly to the ground, moving like thought.

Pepé cocked his rifle and edged the muzzle slowly around. Then he looked apprehensively up the trail and dropped the hammer again. From the ground beside him he picked an oak twig and threw it toward the spring. The quail flew up with a roar and the doves whistled away. The big cat stood up: for a long moment he looked at Pepé with cold yellow eyes, and then fearlessly walked back into the gulch.

The dusk gathered quickly in the deep valley. Pepé muttered his prayers, put his head down on his arm and went instantly to sleep.

The moon came up and filled the valley with cold blue light, and the wind swept rustling down from the peaks. The owls worked up and down the slopes looking for rabbits. Down in the brush of the gulch a coyote gabbled. The oak trees whispered softly in the night breeze.

Pepé started up, listening. His horse had whinnied. The moon was just slipping behind the western ridge, leaving the valley in darkness behind it. Pepé sat tensely gripping his rifle. From far up the trail he heard an answering whinny and the crash of shod hooves on the broken rock. He jumped to his feet, ran to his horse and let it under the trees. He threw on the saddle and cinched it tight for the steep trail, caught the unwilling head and forced the bit into the mouth. He felt the saddle to make sure the water bag and the sack of jerky were there. Then he mounted and turned up the hill.

It was velvet dark. The horse found the entrance to the trail where it left the flat, and started up, stumbling and slipping on the rocks. Pepé's hand rose up to his head. His hat was gone. He had left it under the oak tree.

The horse had struggled far up the trail when the first change of dawn came into the air, a steel greyness as light mixed thoroughly with dark. Gradually the sharp snaggled edge of the ridge stood out above them, rotten granite tortured and eaten by the winds of time. Pepé had dropped his reins on the horn, leaving direction to the horse. The brush grabbed at his legs in the dark until one knee of his jeans was ripped.

Gradually the light flowed down over the ridge. The starved brush and rocks stood out in the half light, strange and lonely in high perspective. Then there came warmth into the light. Pepé drew up and looked back, but he could see nothing in the darker valley below. The sky turned blue over the coming sun. In the waste of the mountainside, the poor dry brush grew only three feet high. Here and there, big outcroppings of unrotted granite stood up like mouldering houses. Pepé relaxed a little. He drank from his water bag and bit off a piece of jerky. A single eagle flew over, high in the light.

Without warning Pepé's horse screamed and fell on its side. He was almost down before the rifle crash echoed up from the valley. From a hole behind the struggling shoulder, a stream of bright crimson blood pumped and stopped and pumped and stopped. The hooves threshed on the ground. Pepé lay half stunned beside the horse. He looked slowly down the hill. A piece of sage clipped off beside his head and another crash echoed up from side to side of the canyon. Pepé flung himself frantically behind a bush.

He crawled up the hill on his knees and one hand. His right hand held the rifle up off the ground and pushed it ahead of him. He moved with the instinctive care of an animal. Rapidly he wormed his way toward one of the big outcroppings of granite on the hill above him. Where the brush was high he doubled up and ran, but where the cover was slight he wriggled forward on his stomach, pushing the rifle ahead of him. In the last little distance there was no cover at all. Pepé poised and then he darted across the space and flashed around the corner of the rock.

He leaned panting against the stone. When his breath came easier he moved along behind the big rock until he came to a narrow split that offered a thin section of vision down the hill. Pepé lay on his stomach and pushed the rifle barrel through the slit and waited.

The sun reddened the western ridges now. Already the buzzards were settling down toward the place where the horse lay. A small brown bird scratched in the dead sage leaves directly in front of the rifle muzzle. The coasting eagle flew back toward the rising sun.

Pepé saw a little movement in the brush far below. His grip tightened on the gun. A little brown doe stepped daintily out on the trail and crossed it and disappeared into the brush again. For a long time Pepé waited. Far below he could see the little flat and the oak trees and the slash of green. Suddenly his eyes flashed back at the trail again. A quarter of a mile down there had been a quick movement in the chaparral. The rifle swung over. The front sight nestled in the v of the rear sight. Pepé studied for a moment and then raised the rear sight a notch. The little movement in the brush came again. The sight settled on it. Pepé squeezed the trigger. The explosion crashed down the mountain and up the other side, and came rattling back. The whole side of the slope grew still. No more movement. And then a white streak cut into the granite of the slit and a bullet whined away and a crash sounded up from below. Pepé felt a sharp pain in his right hand. A sliver of granite was sticking out from between his first and second knuckles and the point protruded from his palm. Carefully he pulled out the sliver of stone. The wound bled evenly and gently. No vein nor artery was cut.

Pepé looked into a little dusty cave in the rock and gathered a handful of spider web, and he pressed the mass into the cut, plastering the soft web into the blood. The flow stopped almost at once.

The rifle was on the ground. Pepé picked it up, levered a new shell into the chamber. And then he slid into the brush on his stomach. Far to the right he crawled, and then up the hill, moving slowly and carefully, crawling to cover and resting and then crawling again.

In the mountains the sun is high in its arc before it penetrates the gorges. The hot face looked over the hill and brought instant heat with it. The white light beat on the rocks and reflected from them and rose up quivering from the earth again, and the rocks and bushes seemed to quiver behind the air.

Pepé crawled in the general direction of the ridge peak, zig-zagging for cover. The deep cut between his knuckles began to throb. He crawled close to a rattlesnake before he saw it, and when it raised its dry head and made a soft beginning whirr, he backed up and took another way. The quick grey lizards flashed in front of him, raising a tiny line of dust. He found another mass of spider web and pressed it against his throbbing hand.

Pepé was pushing the rifle with his left hand now. Little drops of sweat ran to the ends of his coarse black hair and rolled down his cheeks. His lips and tongue were growing thick and heavy. His lips writhed to draw saliva into his mouth. His little dark eyes were uneasy and suspicious. Once when a grey lizard paused in front of him on the parched ground and turned its head sideways he crushed it flat with a stone.

When the sun slid past noon he had not gone a mile. He crawled exhaustedly a last hundred yards to a patch of high sharp manzanita, crawled desperately, and when the patch was reached he wriggled in among the tough gnarly trunks and dropped his head on his left arm. There was little shade in the meager brush, but there was cover and safety. Pepé went to sleep as he lay and the sun beat on his back. A few little birds hopped close to him and peered and hopped away. Pepé squirmed in his sleep and he raised and dropped his wounded hand again and again.

The sun went down behind the peaks and the cool evening came, and then the dark. A coyote yelled from the hillside, Pepé started awake and looked about with misty eyes. His hand was swollen and heavy; a little thread of pain ran up the inside of his arm and settled in a pocket in his armpit. He peered about and then stood up, for the mountains were black and the moon had not yet risen. Pepé stood up in the dark. The coat of his father pressed on his arm. His tongue was swollen until it nearly filled his mouth. He wriggled out of the coat and dropped it in the brush, and then he struggled up the hill, falling over rocks and tearing his way through the brush. The rifle knocked against stones as he went. Little dry avalanches of gravel and shattered stone went whispering down the hill behind him.

After a while the old moon came up and showed the jagged ridge top ahead of him. By moonlight Pepé traveled more easily. He bent forward so that his throbbing arm hung away from his body. The journey uphill was made in dashes and rests, a frantic rush up a few yards and then a rest. The wind coasted down the slope rattling the dry stems of the bushes.

The moon was at meridian when Pepé came at last to the sharp backbone of the ridge top. On the last hundred yards of the rise no soil had clung under the wearing winds. The way was on solid rock. He clambered to the top and looked down on the other side. There was a draw like the last below him, misty with moonlight, brushed with dry struggling sage and chaparral. On the other side the hill rose up sharply and at the top the jagged rotten teeth of the mountain showed against the sky. At the bottom of the cut the brush was thick and dark.

Pepé stumbled down the hill. His throat was almost closed with thirst. At first he tried to run, but immediately he fell and rolled. After that he went more carefully. The moon was just disappearing behind the mountains when he came to the bottom. He crawled into the heavy brush feeling with his fingers for water. There was no water in the bed of the stream, only damp earth. Pepé laid his gun down and scooped up a handful of mud and put it in his mouth, and then he spluttered and scraped the earth from his tongue with his finger, for the mud drew at his mouth like a poultice. He dug a hole in the stream bed with his fingers, dug a little basin to catch water; but before it was very deep his head fell forward on the damp ground and he slept.

The dawn came and the heat of the day fell on the earth, and still Pepé slept. Late in the afternoon his head jerked up. He looked slowly around. His eyes were slits of wariness. Twenty feet away in the heavy brush a big tawny mountain lion stood looking at him. Its long thick tail waved gracefully, its ears were erect with interest, not laid back dangerously. The lion squatted down on its stomach and watched him.

Pepé looked at the hole he had dug in the earth. A half inch of muddy water had collected in the bottom. He tore the sleeve from his hurt arm, with his teeth ripped out a little square, soaked it in the water and put it in his mouth. Over and over he filled the cloth and sucked it.

Still the lion sat and watched him. The evening came down but there was no movement on the hills. No birds visited the dry bottom of the cut. Pepé looked occasionally at the lion. The eyes of the yellow beast drooped as though he were about to sleep. He yawned and his long thin red tongue curled out. Suddenly his head jerked around and his nostrils quivered. His big tail lashed. He stood up and slunk like a tawny shadow into the thick brush.

A moment later Pepé heard the sound, the faint far crash of horses' hooves on gravel. And he heard something else, a high whining yelp of a dog.

Pepé took his rifle in his left hand and he glided into the brush almost as quietly as the lion had. In the darkening evening he crouched up the hill toward the next ridge. Only when the dark came did he stand up. His energy was short. Once it was dark he fell over the rocks and slipped to his knees on the steep slope, but he moved on and on up the hill, climbing and scrabbling over the broken hillside.

When he was far up toward the top, he lay down and slept for a little while. The withered moon, shining on his face, awakened him. He stood up and moved up the hill. Fifty yards away he stopped and turned back, for he had forgotten his rifle. He walked heavily down and poked about in the brush, but he could not find his gun. At last he lay down to rest. The pocket of pain in his armpit had grown more sharp. His arm seemed to swell out and fall with every heartbeat. There was no position lying down where the heavy arm did not press against his armpit.

With the effort of a hurt beast, Pepé got up and moved again toward the top of the ridge. He held his swollen arm away from his body with his left hand. Up the steep hill he dragged himself, a few steps and a rest, and a few more steps. At last he was nearing the top. The moon showed the uneven sharp back of it against the sky.

Pepé's brain spun in a big spiral up and away from him. He slumped to the ground and lay still. The rock ridge top was only a hundred feet above him.

The moon moved over the sky. Pepé half turned on his back. His tongue tried to make words, but only a thick hissing came from between his lips.

When the dawn came, Pepé pulled himself up. His eyes were sane again. He drew his great puffed arm in front of him and looked at the angry wound. The black line ran up from his wrist to his armpit. Automatically he reached in his pocket for the big black knife, but it was not there. His eyes searched the ground. He picked up a sharp blade of stone and scraped at the wound, sawed at the proud flesh and then squeezed the green juice out in big drops. Instantly he threw back his head and whined like a dog. His whole right side shuddered at the pain, but the pain cleared his head.

In the grey light he struggled up the last slope to the ridge and crawled over and lay down behind a line of rocks. Below him lay a deep canyon exactly like the last, waterless and desolate. There was no flat, no oak trees, not even heavy brush in the bottom of it. And on the other side a sharp ridge stood up, thinly brushed with starving sage, littered with broken granite. Strewn over the hill there were giant outcroppings, and on the top the granite teeth stood out against the sky.

The new day was light now. The flame of the sun came over the ridge and fell on Pepé where he lay on the ground. His coarse black hair was littered with twigs and bits of spider web. His eyes had retreated back into his head. Between his lips the tip of his black tongue showed.

He sat up and dragged his great arm into his lap and nursed it, rocking his body and moaning in his throat. He threw back his head and looked up into the pale sky. A big black bird circled nearly out of sight, and far to the left another was sailing near.

He lifted his head to listen, for a familiar sound had come to him from the valley he had climbed out of; it was the crying yelp of hounds, excited and feverish, on a trail.

Pepé bowed his head quickly. He tried to speak rapid words but only a thick hiss came from his lips. He drew a shaky cross on his breast with his left hand. It was a long struggle to get to his feet. He crawled slowly and mechanically to the top of a big rock on the ridge peak. Once there, he arose slowly, swaying to his feet, and stood erect. Far below he could see the dark brush where he had slept. He braced his feet and stood there, black against the morning sky.

There came a ripping sound at his feet. A piece of stone flew up and a bullet droned off into the next gorge. The hollow crash echoed up from below. Pepé looked down for a moment and then pulled himself straight again.

His body jarred back. His left hand fluttered helplessly toward his breast. The second crash sounded from below. Pepé swung forward and toppled from the rock. His body struck and rolled over and over, starting a little avalanche. And when at last he stopped against a bush, the avalanche slid slowly down and covered up his head.

by Bernard Malamud

A SUMMER'S READING

Bernard Malamud was born on April 26, 1914, in Brooklyn. He attended the College of the City of New York and received an M.A. in English from Columbia University. His first novel, The Natural, *was published in 1952. Since then two more of his novels have appeared; the most recent is* A New Life *(1961).* The Magic Barrel, *the collection of stories from which "A Summer's Reading" is taken, received the National Book Award in 1959. Mr. Malamud has taught in New York City high schools and at Oregon State College. At present he lives in Vermont.*

"A Summer's Reading" moves quietly, relentlessly, like the sultry days in August. The boy in the story is, like his neighbors, "wilting and listless, waiting for a breeze." And it comes: he practices an easy deception upon them. He does this to gain their smiles and their respect, the repeated and somewhat incongruous demands of his still and dull life. But his satisfaction is brief; he grows uncomfortable in his lie. When an old neighbor's kindness saves him from exposure, he comes to another realization and a new discomfort.

GEORGE Stoyonovich was a neighborhood boy who had quit high school on an impulse when he was sixteen, run out of patience, and though he was ashamed everytime he went looking for a job, when people asked him if he had finished and he had to say no, he never went back to school. This summer was a hard time for jobs and he had none. Having so much time on his hands, George thought of going to summer school, but the kids in his classes would be too young. He also considered registering in a night high school, only he didn't like the idea of the teachers always telling him what to do. He felt they had not respected him. The result was he stayed off the streets and in his room most of the day. He was close to twenty and had needs with the neighborhood girls, but no money to spend, and he couldn't get more than an occasional few cents because his father was poor, and his sister Sophie, who resembled George, a tall bony girl of twenty-three, earned very little and what she had she kept for herself. Their mother was dead, and Sophie had to take care of the house.

Very early in the morning George's father got up to go to work in a fish market. Sophie left about eight for her long ride in the subway to a cafeteria in the Bronx. George had his coffee by himself, then hung around in the house. When the house, a five-room railroad flat above a butcher store, got on his nerves he cleaned it up—mopped the floors with a wet mop and put things away. But most of the time he sat in his room. In the afternoons he listened to the ball game. Otherwise he had a couple of old copies of the *World Almanac* he had bought long ago, and he liked to read in them and also the magazines and newspapers that Sophie brought home, that had been left on the tables in the cafeteria. They were mostly picture magazines about movie stars and sports figures, also usually the *News* and *Mirror*. Sophie herself read whatever fell into her hands, although she sometimes read good books.

She once asked George what he did in his room all day and he said he read a lot too.

"Of what besides what I bring home? Do you ever read any worthwhile books?"

"Some," George answered, although he really didn't. He had tried to read a book or two that Sophie had in the house but found he was in no mood for them. Lately he couldn't stand made-up stories, they got on his nerves. He wished he had some hobby to work at—as a kid he was good in carpentry, but where could he work at it?

Sometimes during the day he went for walks, but mostly he did his walking after the hot sun had gone down and it was cooler in the streets.

In the evening after supper George left the house and wandered in the neighborhood. During the sultry days some of the storekeepers and their wives sat in chairs on the thick, broken sidewalks in front of their shops, fanning themselves, and George walked past them and the guys hanging out on the candy store corner. A couple of them he had known his whole life, but nobody recognized each other. He had no place special to go, but generally, saving it till the last, he left the neighborhood and walked for blocks till he came to a darkly lit little park with benches and trees and an iron railing, giving it a feeling of privacy. He sat on a bench here, watching the leafy trees and the flowers blooming on the inside of the railing, thinking of a better life for himself. He thought of the jobs he had had since he had quit school—delivery boy, stock clerk, runner, lately working in a factory—and he was dissatisfied with all of them. He felt he would someday like to have a good job and live in a private house with a porch, on a street with trees. He wanted to have some dough in his pocket to buy things with, and a girl to go with, so as not to be so lonely, especially on Saturday nights. He wanted people to like and respect him. He thought about these things often but mostly when he was alone at night. Around midnight he got up and drifted back to his hot and stony neighborhood.

One time while on his walk George met Mr. Cattanzara coming home very late from work. He wondered if he was drunk but then could tell he wasn't. Mr. Cattanzara, a stocky, bald-headed man who worked in a change booth on an IRT station, lived on the next block after George's, above a shoe repair store. Nights, during the hot weather, he sat on his stoop in an undershirt, reading the *New York Times* in the light of the shoemaker's window. He read it from the first page to the last, then went up to sleep. And all the time he was reading the paper, his wife, a fat woman with a white face, leaned out of the window, gazing into the street, her thick white arms folded under her loose breast, on the window ledge.

Once in a while Mr. Cattanzara came home drunk, but it was a quiet drunk. He never made any trouble, only walked stiffly up the street and slowly climbed the stairs into the hall. Though drunk, he looked the same as always, except for his tight walk, the quietness, and that his eyes were wet. George liked Mr. Cattanzara because he remembered him giving him nickels to buy lemon ice with when he was a squirt. Mr. Cattanzara was a different type than those in the neighborhood. He asked different questions than the others when he met you, and he seemed to know what went on in all the newspapers. He read them, as his fat sick wife watched from the window.

"What are you doing with yourself this summer, George?" Mr. Cattanzara asked. "I see you walkin' around at nights."

George felt embarrassed. "I like to walk."

"What are you doin' in the day now?"

"Nothing much just right now, I'm waiting for a job." Since it shamed him to admit he wasn't working, George said, "I'm staying home—but I'm reading a lot to pick up my education."

Mr. Cattanzara looked interested. He mopped his hot face with a red handkerchief.

"What are you readin'?"

George hesitated, then said, "I got a list of books in the library once, and now I'm gonna read them this summer." He felt strange and a little unhappy saying this, but he wanted Mr. Cattanzara to respect him.

"How many books are there on it?"

"I never counted them. Maybe around a hundred."

Mr. Cattanzara whistled through his teeth.

"I figure if I did that," George went on earnestly, "it would help me in my education. I don't mean the kind they give you in high school. I want to know different things than they learn there, if you know what I mean."

The change maker nodded. "Still and all, one hundred books is a pretty big load for one summer."

"It might take longer."

"After you're finished with some, maybe you and I can shoot the breeze about them?" said Mr. Cattanzara.

"When I'm finished," George answered.

Mr. Cattanzara went home and George continued on his walk. After that, though he had the urge to, George did nothing different from usual. He still took his walks at night, ending up in the little park. But one evening the shoemaker on the next block stopped George to say he was a good boy, and George figured that Mr. Cattanzara had told him all about the books he was reading. From the shoemaker it must have gone down the street, because George saw a couple of people smiling kindly at him, though nobody spoke to him personally. He felt a little better around the neighborhood and liked it more, though not so much he would want to live in it forever. He had never exactly disliked the people in it, yet he had never liked them very much either. It was the fault of the neighborhood. To his surprise, George found out that his father and Sophie knew about his reading too. His father was too shy to say anything about it—he was never much of a talker in his whole life—but Sophie was softer to George, and she showed him in other ways she was proud of him.

As the summer went on George felt in a good mood about things. He cleaned the house every day, as a favor to Sophie, and he enjoyed the ball games more. Sophie gave him a buck a week allowance, and though it still wasn't enough and he had to use it carefully, it was a helluva lot better than just having two bits now and then. What he bought with the money—cigarettes mostly, an occasional beer or movie ticket—he got a big kick out of. Life wasn't so bad if you knew how to appreciate it. Occasionally he bought a paperback book from the news-stand, but he never got around to reading it, though he was glad to have a couple of books in his room. But he read thoroughly Sophie's magazines and newspapers. And at night was the most enjoyable time, because when he passed the storekeepers sitting outside their stores, he could tell they regarded him highly. He walked erect, and though he did not say much to them, or they to him, he could feel approval on all sides. A couple of nights he felt so good that he skipped the park at the end of the evening. He just wandered in the neighborhood, where people had known him from the time he was a kid playing punchball whenever there was a game of it going; he wandered there, then came home and got undressed for bed, feeling fine.

For a few weeks he had talked only once with Mr. Cattanzara, and though the change maker had said nothing more about the books, asked no questions, his silence made George a little uneasy. For a while George didn't pass in front of Mr. Cattanzara's house anymore, until one night, forgetting himself, he approached it from a different direction than he usually did when he did. It was already past midnight. The street, except for one or two people, was deserted, and George was surprised when he saw Mr. Cattanzara still reading his newspaper by the light of the street lamp overhead. His impulse was to stop at the stoop and talk to him. He wasn't sure what he wanted to say, though he felt the words would come when he began to talk; but the more he thought about it. the more the idea scared him, and he decided he'd better not. He even considered beating it home by another street, but he was too near Mr. Cattanzara, and the change maker might see him as he ran, and get annoyed. So George unobtrusively crossed the street, trying to make it seem as if he had to look in a store window on the other side, which he did, and then went on, uncomfortable at what he was doing. He feared Mr. Cattanzara would glance up from his paper and call him a dirty rat for walking on the other side of the street, but all he did was sit there, sweating through his undershirt, his bald head shining in the dim light as he read his *Times*, and upstairs his fat wife leaned out of the window, seeming to read the paper along with him. George thought she would spy him and yell out to Mr. Cattanzara, but she never moved her eyes off her husband.

George made up his mind to stay away from the change maker until he had got some of his softback books read, but when he started them and saw they were mostly story books, he lost his interest and didn't bother to finish them. He lost his interest in reading other things too. Sophie's magazines and newspapers went unread. She saw them piling up on a chair in his room and asked why he was no longer looking at them, and George told her it was because of all the other reading he had to do. Sophie said she had guessed that was it. So for most of the day, George had the radio on, turning to music when he was sick of the human voice. He kept the house fairly neat, and Sophie said nothing on the days when he neglected it. She was still kind and gave him his extra buck, though things weren't so good for him as they had been before.

But they were good enough, considering. Also his night walks invariably picked him up, no matter how bad the day was. Then one night George saw Mr. Cattanzara coming down the street toward him. George was about to turn and run but he recognized from Mr. Cattanzara's walk that he was drunk, and if so, probably he would not even bother to notice him. So George kept on walking straight ahead until he came abreast of Mr. Cattanzara and though he felt wound up enough to pop into the sky, he was not surprised when Mr. Cattanzara passed him without a word, walking slowly, his face and body stiff. George drew a breath in relief at his narrow escape, when he heard his name called, and there stood Mr. Cattanzara at his elbow, smelling like the inside of a beer barrel. His eyes were sad as he gazed at George, and George felt so intensely uncomfortable he was tempted to shove the drunk aside and continue on his walk.

But he couldn't act that way to him, and, besides, Mr. Cattanzara took a nickel out of his pants pocket and handed it to him.

"Go buy yourself a lemon ice, Georgie."

"It's not that time anymore, Mr. Cattanzara," George said, "I am a big guy now."

"No, you ain't," said Mr. Cattanzara, to which George made no reply he could think of.

"How are all your books comin' along now?" Mr. Cattanzara asked. Though he tried to stand steady, he swayed a little.

"Fine, I guess," said George, feeling the red crawling up his face.

"You ain't sure?" The change maker smiled slyly, a way George had never seen him smile.

"Sure I'm sure. They're fine."

Though his head swayed in little arcs, Mr. Cattanzara's eyes were steady. He had small blue eyes which could hurt if you looked at them too long.

"George," he said, "name me one book on that list that you read this summer, and I will drink to your health."

"I don't want anybody drinking to me."

"Name me one so I can ask you a question on it. Who can tell, if it's a good book maybe I might wanna read it myself."

George knew he looked passable on the outside, but inside he was crumbling apart.

Unable to reply, he shut his eyes, but when—years later—he opened them, he saw that Mr. Cattanzara had, out of pity, gone away, but in his ears he still heard the words he had said when he left: "George, don't do what I did."

The next night he was afraid to leave his room, and though Sophie argued with him he wouldn't open the door.

"What are you doing in there?" she asked.

"Nothing."

"Aren't you reading?"

"No."

She was silent a minute, then asked, "Where do you keep the books you read? I never see any in your room outside of a few cheap trashy ones."

He wouldn't tell her.

"In that case you're not worth a buck of my hard-earned money. Why should I break my back for you? Go on out, you bum, and get a job."

He stayed in his room for almost a week, except to sneak into the kitchen when nobody was home. Sophie railed at him, then begged him to come out, and his old father wept, but George wouldn't budge, though the weather was terrible and his small room stifling. He found it very hard to breathe, each breath was like drawing a flame into his lungs.

One night, unable to stand the heat anymore, he burst into the street at one A.M., a shadow of himself. He hoped to sneak to the park without being seen, but there were people all over the block, wilted and listless, waiting for a breeze. George lowered his eyes and walked, in disgrace, away from them, but before long he discovered they were still friendly to him. He figured Mr. Cattanzara hadn't told on him. Maybe when he woke up out of his drunk the next morning, he had forgotten all about meeting George. George felt his confidence slowly come back to him.

That same night a man on a street corner asked him if it was true that he had finished reading so many books, and George admitted he had. The man said it was a wonderful thing for a boy his age to read so much.

"Yeah," George said, but he felt relieved. He hoped nobody would mention the books anymore, and when, after a couple of days, he accidentally met Mr. Cattanzara again, *he* didn't, though George had the idea he was the one who had started the rumor that he had finished all the books.

One evening in the fall, George ran out of his house to the library, where he hadn't been in years. There were books all over the place, wherever he looked, and though he was struggling to control an inward trembling, he easily counted off a hundred, then sat down at a table to read.

by Truman Capote

A TREE OF NIGHT

Truman Capote was born on September 30, 1924, in New Orleans, and attended schools in New York and Connecticut. Thoroughly relieved to be graduated from high school, he never sought a college education but decided instead to devote himself to writing. He published his first story at seventeen. In 1948 his first novel, Other Voices, Other Rooms, *appeared, and the next year he brought out his first collection of stories,* A Tree of Night. *Mr. Capote has spent considerable time in Haiti, Paris, Tangiers, Venice, and Sicily, and has written scripts for motion pictures (most notably the highly comic* Beat the Devil*) and the book for a musical comedy. In 1959 he received an award from the National Institute of Arts and Letters.*

The girl in "A Tree of Night" picks her way through a strange and yet familiar world. Though icicles hang along the station-house eaves "like some crystal monster's vicious teeth" and the train lurches in "a ghost of steam," the odor of "discarded sandwiches, apple cores, and orange hulls" infects the dying smoke of the coach, where a man dozes, his legs in the aisle, and a child cries out in his sleep. The two dimensions of that world are best seen in the side-show performer: his name, Lazarus, pulls one way; the Mickey Mouse watch strapped around his wrist, the other. But the disparity is only apparent, for both name and watch share the same quality, the bizarre. On this common center Mr. Capote works his mischief and his meaning.

IT was winter. A string of naked light bulbs, from which it seemed all warmth had been drained, illuminated the little depot's cold, windy platform. Earlier in the evening it had rained, and now icicles hung along the station-house eaves like some crystal monster's vicious teeth. Except for a girl, young and rather tall, the platform was deserted. The girl wore a gray flannel suit, a raincoat, and a plaid scarf. Her hair, parted in the middle and rolled up neatly on the sides, was rich blondish-brown; and, while her face tended to be too thin and narrow, she was, though not extraordinarily so, attractive. In addition to an assortment of magazines and a gray suede purse on which elaborate brass letters spelled Kay, she carried conspicuously a green Western guitar.

When the train, spouting steam and glaring with light, came out of the darkness and rumbled to a halt, Kay assembled her paraphernalia and climbed up into the last coach.

The coach was a relic with a decaying interior of ancient red-plush seats, bald in spots, and peeling iodine-colored woodwork. An old-time copper lamp, attached to the ceiling, looked romantic and out of place. Gloomy dead smoke sailed the air; and the car's heated closeness accentuated the stale odor of discarded sandwiches, apple cores, and orange hulls: this garbage, including Lily cups, soda-pop bottles, and mangled newspapers, littered the long aisle. From a water cooler, embedded in the wall, a steady stream trickled to the floor. The passengers, who glanced up wearily when Kay entered, were not, it seemed, at all conscious of any discomfort.

Kay resisted a temptation to hold her nose and threaded her way carefully down the aisle, tripping once, without disaster, over a dozing fat man's protruding leg. Two nondescript men turned an interested eye as she passed; and a kid stood up in his seat, squalling, "Hey, Mama, look at de banjo! Hey, lady, lemme play ya banjo!" till a slap from Mama quelled him.

There was only one empty place. She found it at the end of the car in an isolated alcove occupied already by a man and woman who were sitting with their feet settled lazily on the vacant seat opposite. Kay hesitated a second then said, "Would you mind if I sat here?"

The woman's head snapped up as if she had not been asked a simple question, but stabbed with a needle, too. Nevertheless, she managed a smile. "Can't say as I see what's to stop you, honey," she said, taking her feet down and also, with a curious impersonality, removing the feet of the man who was staring out the window, paying no attention whatsoever.

Thanking the woman, Kay took off her coat, sat down, and arranged herself with purse and guitar at her side, magazines in her lap: comfortable enough, though she wished she had a pillow for her back.

The train lurched; a ghost of steam hissed against the window; slowly the dingy lights of the lonesome depot faded past.

"Boy, what a jerkwater dump," said the woman. "No town, no nothin'."

Kay said, "The town's a few miles away."

"That so? Live there?"

No. Kay explained she had been at the funeral of an uncle. An uncle who, though she did not of course mention it, had left her nothing in his will but the green guitar. Where was she going? Oh, back to college.

After mulling this over, the woman concluded, "What'll you ever learn in a place like that? Let me tell you, honey, I'm plenty educated and I never saw the inside of no college."

"You didn't?" murmured Kay politely and dismissed the matter by opening one of her magazines. The light was dim for reading and none of the stories looked in the least compelling. However, not wanting to become involved in a conversational marathon, she continued gazing at it stupidly till she felt a furtive tap on her knee.

"Don't read," said the woman. "I need somebody to talk to. Naturally, it's no fun talking to *him*." She jerked a thumb toward the silent man. "He's afflicted: deaf and dumb, know what I mean?"

Kay closed the magazine and looked at her more or less for the first time. She was short; her feet barely scraped the floor. And like many undersized people she had a freak of structure, in her case an enormous, really huge head. Rouge so brightened her sagging, fleshy-featured face it was difficult even to guess at her age: perhaps fifty, fifty-five. Her big sheep eyes squinted, as if distrustful of what they saw. Her hair was an obviously dyed red, and twisted into parched, fat corkscrew curls. A once-elegant lavender hat of impressive size flopped crazily on the side of her head, and she was kept busy brushing back a drooping cluster of celluloid cherries sewed to the brim. She wore a plain, somewhat shabby blue dress. Her breath had a vividly sweetish gin smell.

"You do wanna talk to me, don't you, honey?"

"Sure," said Kay, moderately amused.

"Course you do. You bet you do. That's what I like about a train. Bus people are a close-mouthed buncha dopes. But a train's the place for putting your cards on the table, that's what I always say." Her voice was cheerful and booming, husky as a man's. "But on accounta *him,* I always try to get us this here seat; it's more private, like a swell compartment, see?"

"It's very pleasant," Kay agreed. "Thanks for letting me join you."

"Only too glad to. We don't have much company; it makes some folks nervous to be around him."

As if to deny it, the man made a queer, furry sound deep in his throat and plucked the woman's sleeve. "Leave me alone, dear-heart," she said, as if she were talking to an inattentive child. "I'm O.K. We're just having us a nice little ol' talk. Now behave yourself or this pretty girl will go away. She's very rich; she goes to college." And winking, she added, "He thinks I'm drunk."

The man slumped in the seat, swung his head sideways, and studied Kay intently from the corners of his eyes. These eyes, like a pair of clouded milky-blue marbles, were thickly lashed and oddly beautiful. Now, except for a certain remoteness, his wide, hairless face had no real expression. It was as if he were incapable of experiencing or reflecting the slightest emotion. His gray hair was clipped close and combed forward into uneven bangs. He looked like a child aged abruptly by some uncanny method. He wore a frayed blue serge suit, and he had anointed himself with a cheap, vile perfume. Around his wrist was strapped a Mickey Mouse watch.

"He thinks I'm drunk," the woman repeated. "And the real funny part is, I am. Oh, shoot—you gotta do something, ain't that right?" She bent closer. "Say, ain't it?"

Kay was still gawking at the man; the way he was looking at her made her squeamish, but she could not take her eyes off him. "I guess so," she said.

"Then let's have us a drink," suggested the woman. She plunged her hand into an oilcloth satchel and pulled out a partially filled gin bottle. She began to unscrew the cap but, seeming to think better of this, handed the bottle to Kay. "Gee, I forgot about you being company," she said. "I'll go get us some nice paper cups."

So, before Kay could protest that she did not want a drink, the woman had risen and started none too steadily down the aisle toward the water cooler.

Kay yawned and rested her forehead against the windowpane, her fingers idly strumming the guitar: the strings sang a hollow, lulling tune, as monotonously soothing as the Southern landscape, smudged in darkness, flowing past the window. An icy winter moon rolled above the train across the night sky like a thin white wheel.

And then, without warning, a strange thing happened: the man reached out and gently stroked Kay's cheek. Despite the breathtaking delicacy of this movement, it was such a bold gesture Kay was at first too startled to know what to make of it: her thoughts shot in three or four fantastic directions. He leaned forward till his queer eyes were very near her own; the reek of his perfume was sickening. The guitar was silent while they exchanged a searching gaze. Suddenly, from some spring of compassion, she felt for him a keen sense of pity; but also, and this she could not suppress, an overpowering disgust, an absolute loathing: something about him, an elusive quality she could not quite put a finger on, reminded her of—of what?

After a little, he lowered his hand solemnly and sank back in his seat, an asinine grin transfiguring his face, as if he had performed a clever stunt for which he wished applause.

"Giddyup! Giddyup! my little bucker-ROOS . . ." shouted the woman. And she sat down, loudly proclaiming to be, "Dizzy as a witch! Dog tired! Whew!" From a handful of Lily cups she separated two and casually thrust the rest down her blouse. "Keep 'em safe and dry, ha ha ha. . . ." A coughing spasm seized her, but when it was over she appeared calmer. "Has my boy friend been entertaining?" she asked, patting her bosom reverently. "Ah, he's so sweet." She looked as if she might pass out. Kay rather wished she would.

"I don't want a drink," Kay said, returning the bottle. "I never drink: I hate the taste."

"Mustn't be a kill-joy," said the woman firmly. "Here now, hold your cup like a good girl."

"No, please . . ."

"Formercysake, hold it still. Imagine, nerves at your age! Me, I can shake like a leaf, I've got reasons. Oh, Lordy, have I got 'em."

"But . . ."

A dangerous smile tipped the woman's face hideously awry. "What's the matter? Don't you think I'm good enough to drink with?"

"Please, don't misunderstand," said Kay, a tremor in her voice.

"It's just that I don't like being forced to do something I don't want to. So look, couldn't I give this to the gentleman?"

"Him? No sirree: he needs what little sense he's got. Come on, honey, down the hatch."

Kay, seeing it was useless, decided to succumb and avoid a possible scene. She sipped and shuddered. It was terrible gin. It burned her throat till her eyes watered. Quickly, when the woman was not watching, she emptied the cup out into the sound hole of the guitar. It happened, however, that the man saw; and Kay, realizing it, recklessly signaled to him with her eyes a plea not to give her away. But she could not tell from his clear-blank expression how much he understood.

"Where you from, kid?" resumed the woman presently.

For a bewildered moment, Kay was unable to provide an answer. The names of several cities came to her all at once. Finally, from this confusion, she extracted: "New Orleans. My home is in New Orleans."

The woman beamed. "N.O.'s where I wanna go when I kick off. One time, oh, say 1923, I ran me a sweet little fortune-telling parlor there. Let's see, that was on St. Peter Street." Pausing, she stooped and set the empty gin bottle on the floor. It rolled into the aisle and rocked back and forth with a drowsy sound. "I was raised in Texas—on a big ranch—my papa was rich. Us kids always had the best; even Paris, France, clothes. I'll bet you've got a big swell house, too. Do you have a garden? Do you grow flowers?"

"Just lilacs."

A conductor entered the coach, preceded by a cold gust of wind that rattled the trash in the aisle and briefly livened the dull air. He lumbered along, stopping now and then to punch a ticket or talk with a passenger. It was after midnight. Someone was expertly playing a harmonica. Someone else was arguing the merits of a certain politician. A child cried out in his sleep.

"Maybe you wouldn't be so snotty if you knew who we was," said the woman, bobbing her tremendous head. "We ain't nobodies, not by a long shot."

Embarrassed, Kay nervously opened a pack of cigarettes and lighted one. She wondered if there might not be a seat in a car up ahead. She could not bear the woman, or, for that matter, the man, another minute. But she had never before been in a remotely comparable situation. "If you'll excuse me now," she said, "I have to be leaving. It's been very pleasant, but I promised to meet a friend on the train. . . ."

With almost invisible swiftness the woman grasped the girl's wrist. "Didn't your mama ever tell you it was sinful to lie?" she stage-whispered. The lavender hat tumbled off her head but she made no effort to retrieve it. Her tongue flicked out and wetted her lips. And, as Kay stood up, she increased the pressure of her grip. "Sit down, dear . . . there ain't any friend . . . Why, we're your only friends and we wouldn't have you leave us for the world."

"Honestly, I wouldn't lie."

"Sit down, dear."

Kay dropped her cigarette and the man picked it up. He slouched in the corner and became absorbed in blowing a chain of lush smoke rings that mounted upward like hollow eyes and expanded into nothing.

"Why, you wouldn't want to hurt his feelings by leaving us, now, would you, dear?" crooned the woman softly. "Sit down—down—now, that's a good girl. My, what a pretty guitar. What a pretty, pretty guitar . . ." Her voice faded before the sudden whooshing, static noise of a second train. And for an instant the lights in the coach went off; in the darkness the passing train's golden windows winked black-yellow-black-yellow-black-yellow. The man's cigarette pulsed like the glow of a firefly, and his smoke rings continued rising tranquilly. Outside, a bell pealed wildly.

When the lights came on again, Kay was massaging her wrist where the woman's strong fingers had left a painful bracelet mark. She was more puzzled than angry. She determined to ask the conductor if he would find her a different seat. But when he arrived to take her ticket, the request stuttered on her lips incoherently.

"Yes, miss?"

"Nothing," she said.

And he was gone.

The trio in the alcove regarded one another in mysterious silence till the woman said, "I've got something here I wanna show you, honey." She rummaged once more in the oilcloth satchel. "You won't be so snotty after you get a gander at this."

What she passed to Kay was a handbill, published on such yellowed, antique paper it looked as if it must be centuries old. In fragile, overly fancy lettering, it read:

LAZARUS

The Man Who Is Buried Alive

A MIRACLE

SEE FOR YOURSELF

Adults, 25¢—Children, 10¢

"I always sing a hymn and read a sermon," said the woman. "It's awful sad: some folks cry, especially the old ones. And I've got me a perfectly elegant costume: a black veil and a black dress, oh, very becoming. *He* wears a gorgeous made-to-order bridegroom suit and a turban and lotsa talcum on his face. See, we try to make it as much like a bonafide funeral as we can. But shoot, nowadays you're likely to get just a buncha smart alecks come for laughs—so sometimes I'm real glad he's afflicted like he is accounta otherwise his feelings would be hurt, maybe."

Kay said, "You mean you're with a circus or a sideshow or something like that?"

"Nope, us alone," said the woman as she reclaimed the fallen hat. "We've been doing it for years and years—played every tank town in the South: Singasong, Mississippi—Spunky, Louisiana—Eureka, Alabama . . ."—these and other names rolled off her tongue musically, running together like rain. "After the hymn, after the sermon, we bury him."

"In a coffin?"

"Sort of. It's gorgeous, it's got silver stars painted all over the lid."

"I should think he would suffocate," said Kay, amazed. "How long does he stay buried?"

"All told it takes maybe an hour—course that's not counting the lure."

"The lure?"

"Uh huh. It's what we do the night before a show. See, we hunt up a store, any ol' store with a big glass window'll do, and get the owner to let *him* sit inside this window, and, well, hypnotize himself. Stays there all night stiff as a poker and people come and look: scares the livin' hell out of 'em. . . ." While she talked she jiggled a finger in her ear, withdrawing it occasionally to examine her find. "And one time this ol' bindlestiff Mississippi sheriff tried to . . ."

The tale that followed was baffling and pointless: Kay did not bother to listen. Nevertheless, what she had heard already inspired a reverie, a vague recapitulation of her uncle's funeral; an event which, to tell the truth, had not much affected her since she had scarcely known him. And so, while gazing abstractedly at the man, an image of her uncle's face, white next the pale silk casket pillow, appeared in her mind's eye. Observing their faces simultaneously, both the man's and uncle's, as it were, she thought she recognized an odd parallel: there was about the man's face the same kind of shocking, embalmed, secret stillness, as though, in a sense, he were truly an exhibit in a glass cage, complacent to be seen, uninterested in seeing.

"I'm sorry, what did you say?"

"I said: I sure wish they'd lend us the use of a regular cemetery. Like it is now we have to put on the show wherever we can . . . mostly in empty lots that are nine times outa ten smack up against some smelly fillin' station, which ain't exactly a big help. But like I say, we got us a swell act, the best. You oughta come see it if you get a chance."

"Oh, I should love to," Kay said, absently.

"Oh, I should love to," mimicked the woman. "Well, who ask you? Anybody ask you?" She hoisted up her skirt and enthusiastically blew her nose on the ragged hem of a petticoat. "Bu-leeve me, it's a hard way to turn a dollar. Know what our take was last month? Fifty-three bucks! Honey, you try living on that sometime." She sniffed and re-arranged her skirt with considerable primness. "Well, one of these days my sweet boy's sure enough going to die down there; and even then somebody'll say it was a gyp."

At this point the man took from his pocket what seemed to be a finely shellacked peach seed and balanced it on the palm of his hand. He looked across at Kay and, certain of her attention, opened his eyelids wide and began to squeeze and caress the seed in an undefinably obscene manner.

Kay frowned. "What does he want?"

"He wants you to buy it."

"But what is it?"

"A charm," said the woman. "A love charm."

Whoever was playing the harmonica stopped. Other sounds, less unique, became at once prominent: someone snoring, the gin bottle seesaw rolling, voices in sleepy argument, the train wheels' distant hum.

"Where could you get love cheaper, honey?"

"It's nice. I mean it's cute . . ." Kay said, stalling for time. The man rubbed and polished the seed on his trouser leg. His head was lowered at a supplicating, mournful angle, and presently he stuck the seed between his teeth and bit it, as if it were a suspicious piece of silver. "Charms always bring me bad luck. And besides . . . please, can't you make him stop acting that way?"

"Don't look so scared," said the woman, more flat-voiced than ever. "He ain't gonna hurt you."

"Make him stop, damn it!"

"What can I do?" asked the woman, shrugging her shoulders. "You're the one that's got money. You're rich. All he wants is a dollar, one dollar."

Kay tucked her purse under her arm. "I have just enough to get back to school," she lied, quickly rising and stepping out into the aisle. She stood there a moment, expecting trouble. But nothing happened.

The woman, with rather deliberate indifference, heaved a sigh and closed her eyes; gradually the man subsided and stuck the charm back in his pocket. Then his hand crawled across the seat to join the woman's in a lax embrace.

Kay shut the door and moved to the front of the observation platform. It was bitterly cold in the open air, and she had left her raincoat in the alcove. She loosened her scarf and draped it over her head.

Although she had never made this trip before, the train was traveling through an area strangely familiar: tall trees, misty, painted pale by malicious moonshine, towered steep on either side without a break or clearing. Above, the sky was a stark, unexplorable blue thronged with stars that faded here and there. She could see streamers of smoke trailing from the train's engine like long clouds of ectoplasm. In one corner of the platform a red kerosene lantern cast a colorful shadow.

She found a cigarette and tried to light it: the wind snuffed match after match till only one was left. She walked to the corner where the lantern burned and cupped her hands to protect the last match: the flame caught, sputtered, died. Angrily she tossed away the cigarette and empty folder; all the tension in her tightened to an exasperating pitch and she slammed the wall with her fist and began to whimper softly, like an irritable child.

The intense cold made her head ache, and she longed to go back inside the warm coach and fall asleep. But she couldn't, at least not yet; and there was no sense in wondering why, for she knew the answer very well. Aloud, partly to keep her teeth from chattering and partly because she needed the reassurance of her own voice, she said: "We're in Alabama now, I think, and tomorrow we'll be in Atlanta and I'm nineteen and I'll be twenty in August and I'm a sophomore. . . ." She glanced around at the darkness, hoping to see a sign of dawn, and finding the same endless wall of trees, the same frosty moon. "I hate him, he's horrible and I hate him. . . ." She stopped, ashamed of her foolishness and too tired to evade the truth: she was afraid.

Suddenly she felt an eerie compulsion to kneel down and touch the lantern. Its graceful glass funnel was warm, and the red glow seeped through her hands, making them luminous. The heat thawed her fingers and tingled along her arms.

She was so preoccupied she did not hear the door open. The train wheels roaring clickety-clack-clackety-click hushed the sound of the man's footsteps.

It was a subtle zero sensation that warned her finally; but some seconds passed before she dared look behind.

He was standing there with a mute detachment, his head tilted, his arms dangling at his sides. Staring up into his harmless, vapid face, flushed brilliant by the lantern light, Kay knew of what she was afraid: it was a memory, a childish memory of terrors that once, long ago, had hovered above her like haunted limbs on a tree of night. Aunts, cooks, strangers—each eager to spin a tale or teach a rhyme of spooks and death, omens, spirits, demons. And always there had been the unfailing threat of the wizard man: stay close to the house, child, else a wizard man'll snatch and eat you alive! He lived everywhere, the wizard man, and everywhere was danger. At night, in bed, hear him tapping at the window? Listen!

Holding onto the railing, she inched upward till she was standing erect. The man nodded and waved his hand toward the door. Kay took a deep breath and stepped forward. Together they went inside.

The air in the coach was numb with sleep: a solitary light now illuminated the car, creating a kind of artificial dusk. There was no motion but the train's sluggish sway, and the stealthy rattle of discarded newspapers.

The woman alone was wide awake. You could see she was greatly excited: she fidgeted with her curls and celluloid cherries, and her plump little legs, crossed at the ankles, swung agitatedly back and forth. She paid no attention when Kay sat down. The man settled in the seat with one leg tucked beneath him and his arms folded across his chest.

In an effort to be casual, Kay picked up a magazine. She realized the man was watching her, not removing his gaze an instant: she knew this though she was afraid to confirm it, and she wanted to cry out and waken everyone in the coach. But suppose they did not hear? What if they were not really *asleep?* Tears started in her eyes, magnifying and distorting the print on a page till it became a hazy blur. She shut the magazine with fierce abruptness and looked at the woman.

"I'll buy it," she said. "The charm, I mean. I'll buy it, if that's all—just all you want."

The woman made no response. She smiled apathetically as she turned toward the man.

As Kay watched, the man's face seemed to change form and recede before her like a moon-shaped rock sliding downward under a surface of water. A warm laziness relaxed her. She was dimly conscious of it when the woman took away her purse, and when she gently pulled the raincoat like a shroud above her head.

by Joseph Conrad

YOUTH

Joseph Conrad (Josef Teodor Konrad Nalęcz Korzeniowski) was born on December 3, 1857, in Podolia, one of the Ukrainian provinces of czarist Poland. Both his parents, exiled political revolutionists, died before he was twelve. At sixteen he shipped on a French merchantman at Marseilles; at twenty he taught himself English. Less than ten years later he had earned his certificate as a master mariner and had become a British subject. From 1893, when he left the sea, until his death on August 3, 1924, Conrad devoted his life to writing. During those years he published fourteen novels, most notably The Nigger of the "Narcissus" *(1897),* Lord Jim *(1900),* Nostromo *(1904),* The Secret Agent *(1907), and* Victory *(1915). His essays appeared in four volumes and his stories in seven, of which the second, published in 1902, contains as its title story "Youth."*

"'Youth,'" Conrad tells us in his prefatory note to that volume, "is a feat of memory." In its outlines the story is the narrative of Conrad's first voyage as second mate, aboard the old barque Palestine. *It is more than that, however. As Marlow, Conrad's narrator, remarks, there are "those voyages . . . that might stand for a symbol of existence," and this is one of them. Now, no longer youthfully unreflective, Marlow can supply the similes (however unremarkable in themselves) for the ambiguous, symbolic East, "full of danger and promise," that faced him then: "silent like death, dark like a grave." Here as elsewhere Conrad elegiacally celebrates the sanguine expectations and the glamour of youth because they have, in one critic's words, "the beauty of threatened things."*

THIS could have occurred nowhere but in England, where men and sea interpenetrate, so to speak—the sea entering into the life of most men, and the men knowing something or everything about the sea, in the way of amusement, of travel, or of bread-winning.

We were sitting round a mahogany table that reflected the bottle, the claret-glasses, and our faces as we leaned on our elbows. There was a director of companies, an accountant, a lawyer, Marlow, and myself. The director had been a *Conway* boy, the accountant had served four years at sea, the lawyer—a fine crusted Tory, High Churchman, the best of old fellows, the soul of honour—had been chief officer in the P. & O. service in the good old days when mail-boats were square-rigged at least on two masts, and used to come down the China Sea before a fair monsoon with stun'-sails set alow and aloft. We all began life in the merchant service. Between the five of us there was the strong bond of the sea, and also the fellowship of the craft, which no amount of enthusiasm for yachting, cruising, and so on can give, since one is only the amusement of life and the other is life itself.

Marlow (at least I think that is how he spelt his name) told the story, or rather the chronicle, of a voyage:—

"Yes, I have seen a little of the Eastern seas; but what I remember best is my first voyage there. You fellows know there are those voyages that seem ordered for the illustration of life, that might stand for a symbol of existence. You fight, work, sweat, nearly kill yourself, sometimes do kill yourself, trying to accomplish something—and you can't. Not from any fault of yours. You simply can do nothing, neither great nor little—not a thing in the world—not even marry an old maid, or get a wretched 600-ton cargo of coal to its port of destination.

"It was altogether a memorable affair. It was my first voyage to the East, and my first voyage as second mate; it was also my skipper's first command. You'll admit it was time. He was sixty if a day; a little man, with a broad, not very straight back, with bowed shoulders and one leg more bandy than the other, he had that queer twisted-about appearance you see so often in men who work in the fields. He had a nut-cracker face—chin and nose trying to come together over a sunken mouth—and it was framed in iron-gray fluffy hair, that looked like a chin-strap of cotton-wool sprinkled with coal-dust. And he had blue eyes in that old face of his, which were amazingly like a boy's, with that candid expression some quite common men preserve to the end of their days by a rare internal gift of simplicity of heart and rectitude of soul. What induced him to accept me was a wonder. I had come out of a crack Australian clipper, where I had been third officer, and he seemed to have a prejudice against crack clippers as aristocratic and high-toned. He said to me, 'You know, in this ship you will have to work.' I said I had to work in every ship I had ever been in. 'Ah, but this is different, and you gentlemen out of them big ships; . . . but there! I dare say you will do. Join to-morrow.'

"I joined to-morrow. It was twenty-two years ago; and I was just twenty. How time passes! It was one of the happiest days of my life. Fancy! Second mate for the first time—a really responsible officer! I wouldn't have thrown up my new billet for a fortune. The mate looked me over carefully. He was also an old chap, but of another stamp. He had a Roman nose, a snow-white, long beard, and his name was Mahon, but he insisted that it should be pronounced Mann. He was well connected; yet there was something wrong with his luck, and he had never got on.

"As to the captain he had been for years in coasters, then in the Mediterranean, and last in the West Indian trade. He had never been round the Capes. He could just write a kind of sketchy hand, and didn't care for writing at all. Both were thorough good seamen of course, and between those two old chaps I felt like a small boy between two grandfathers.

"The ship also was old. Her name was the *Judea*. Queer name, isn't it? She belonged to a man Wilmer, Wilcox—some name like that; but he has been bankrupt and dead these twenty years or more, and his name don't matter. She had been laid up in Shadwell basin for ever so long. You may imagine her state. She was all rust, dust, grime—soot aloft, dirt on deck. To me it was like coming out of a palace into a ruined cottage. She was about 400 tons, had a primitive windlass, wooden latches to the doors, not a bit of brass about her, and a big square stern. There was on it, below her name in big letters, a lot of scrollwork, with the gilt off, and some sort of a coat of arms, with the motto 'Do or Die' underneath. I remember it took my fancy immensely. There was a touch of romance in it, something that made me love the old thing—something that appealed to my youth!

"We left London in ballast—sand ballast—to load a cargo of coal in a northern port for Bankok. Bankok! I thrilled. I had been six years at sea, but had only seen Melbourne and Sydney, very good places, charming places in their way—but Bankok!

"We worked out of the Thames under canvas, with a North Sea pilot on board. His name was Jermyn, and he dodged all day long about the galley drying his handkerchief before the stove. Apparently he never slept. He was a dismal man, with a perpetual tear sparkling at the end of his nose, who either had been in trouble, or was in trouble, or expected to be in trouble—couldn't be happy unless something went wrong. He mistrusted my youth, my common-sense, and my seamanship, and made a point of showing it in a hundred little ways. I dare say he was right. It seems to me I knew very little then, and I know not much more now; but I cherish a hate for that Jermyn to this day.

"We were a week working up as far as Yarmouth Roads, and then we got into a gale—the famous October gale of twenty-two years ago. It was wind, lightning, sleet, snow, and a terrific sea. We were flying light, and you may imagine how bad it was when I tell you we had smashed bulwarks and a flooded deck. On the second night she shifted her ballast into the lee bow, and by that time we had been blown off somewhere on the Dogger Bank. There was nothing for it but go below with shovels and try to right her, and there we were in that vast hold, gloomy like a cavern, the tallow dips stuck and flickering on the beams, the gale howling above, the ship tossing about like mad on her side; there we all were, Jermyn, the captain, every one, hardly able to keep our feet, engaged on that gravedigger's work, and trying to toss shovelfuls of wet sand up to windward. At every tumble of the ship you could see vaguely in the dim light men falling down with a great flourish of shovels. One of the ship's boys (we had two), impressed by the weirdness of the scene, wept as if his heart would break. We could hear him blubbering somewhere in the shadows.

"On the third day the gale died out, and by-and-by a north-country tug picked us up. We took sixteen days in all to get from London to the Tyne! When we got into dock we had lost our turn for loading, and they hauled us off to a pier where we remained for a month. Mrs. Beard (the captain's name was Beard) came from Colchester to see the old man. She lived on board. The crew of runners had left, and there remained only the officers, one boy and the steward, a mulatto who answered to the name of Abraham. Mrs. Beard was an old woman, with a face all wrinkled and ruddy like a winter apple, and the figure of a young girl. She caught sight of me once, sewing on a button, and insisted on having my shirts to repair. This was something different from the captains' wives I had known on board crack clippers. When I brought her the shirts, she said: 'And the socks? They want mending, I am sure, and John's—Captain Beard's—things are all in order now. I would be glad of something to do.' Bless the old woman. She overhauled my outfit for me, and meantime I read for the first time *Sartor Resartus* and Burnaby's *Ride to Khiva.* I didn't understand much of the first then; but I remember I preferred the soldier to the philosopher at the time; a preference which life has only confirmed. One was a man, and the other was either more—or less. However, they are both dead and Mrs. Beard is dead, and youth, strength, genius, thoughts, achievements, simple hearts—all dies. . . . No matter.

"They loaded us at last. We shipped a crew. Eight able seamen and two boys. We hauled off one evening to the buoys at the dock-gates, ready to go out, and with a fair prospect of beginning the voyage next day. Mrs. Beard was to start for home by a late train. When the ship was fast we went to tea. We sat rather silent through the meal—Mahon, the old couple, and I. I finished first, and slipped away for a smoke, my cabin being in a deck-house just against the poop. It was high water, blowing fresh with a drizzle; the double dock-gates were opened, and the steam-colliers were going in and out in the darkness with their lights burning bright, a great plashing of propellers, rattling of winches, and a lot of hailing on the pier-heads. I watched the procession of head-lights gliding high and of green lights gliding low in the night, when suddenly a red gleam flashed at me, vanished, came into view again, and remained. The fore-end of a steamer loomed up close. I shouted down the cabin, 'Come up, quick!' and then heard a startled voice saying afar in the dark, 'Stop her, sir.' A bell jingled. Another voice cried warningly, 'We are going right into that barque, sir.' The answer to this was a gruff 'All right,' and the next thing was a heavy crash as the steamer struck a glancing blow with the bluff of her bow about our fore-rigging. There was a moment of confusion, yelling, and running about. Steam roared. Then somebody was heard saying, 'All clear, sir.' . . . 'Are you all right?' asked the gruff voice. I had jumped forward to see the damage, and hailed back, 'I think so.' 'Easy astern,' said the gruff voice. A bell jingled. 'What steamer is that?' screamed Mahon. By that time she was no more to us than a bulky shadow manœuvring a little way off. They shouted at us some name—a woman's name, Miranda or

Melissa—or some such thing. 'This means another month in this beastly hole,' said Mahon to me, as we peered with lamps about the splintered bulwarks and broken braces. 'But where's the captain?'

"We had not heard or seen anything of him all that time. We went aft to look. A doleful voice arose hailing somewhere in the middle of the dock, '*Judea* ahoy!' . . . How the devil did he get there? . . . 'Hallo!' we shouted. 'I am adrift in our boat without oars,' he cried. A belated water-man offered his services, and Mahon struck a bargain with him for half-a-crown to tow our skipper alongside; but it was Mrs. Beard that came up the ladder first. They had been floating about the dock in that mizzly cold rain for nearly an hour. I was never so surprised in my life.

"It appears that when he heard my shout 'Come up' he understood at once what was the matter, caught up his wife, ran on deck, and across, and down into our boat, which was fast to the ladder. Not bad for a sixty-year-old. Just imagine that old fellow saving heroically in his arms that old woman—the woman of his life. He set her down on a thwart, and was ready to climb back on board when the painter came adrift somehow, and away they went together. Of course in the confusion we did not hear him shouting. He looked abashed. She said cheerfully, 'I suppose it does not matter my losing the train now?' 'No, Jenny—you go below and get warm,' he growled. Then to us: 'A sailor has no business with a wife—I say. There I was, out of the ship. Well, no harm done this time. Let's go and look at what that fool of a steamer smashed.'

"It wasn't much, but it delayed us three weeks. At the end of that time, the captain being engaged with his agents, I carried Mrs. Beard's bag to the railway-station and put her all comfy into a third-class carriage. She lowered the window to say, 'You are a good young man. If you see John—Captain Beard—without his muffler at night, just remind him from me to keep his throat well wrapped up.' 'Certainly, Mrs. Beard,' I said. 'You are a good young man; I noticed how attentive you are to John—to Captain——' The train pulled out suddenly; I took my cap off to the old woman: I never saw her again. . . . Pass the bottle.

"We went to sea next day. When we made that start for Bankok we had been already three months out of London. We had expected to be a fortnight or so—at the outside.

"It was January, and the weather was beautiful—the beautiful sunny winter weather that has more charm than in the summer-time, because it is unexpected, and crisp, and you know it won't, it can't, last long. It's like a windfall, like a godsend, like an unexpected piece of luck.

"It lasted all down the North Sea, all down Channel; and it lasted till we were three hundred miles or so to the westward of the Lizards: then the wind went round to the sou'west and began to pipe up. In two days it blew a gale. The *Judea*, hove to, wallowed on the Atlantic like an old candle-box. It blew day after day: it blew with spite, without interval, without mercy, without rest. The world was nothing but an immensity of great foaming waves rushing at us, under a sky low enough to touch with the hand and dirty like a smoked ceiling. In the stormy place surrounding us there was as much flying spray as air. Day after day and night after night there was nothing round the ship but the howl of the wind, the tumult of the sea, the noise of water pouring over her deck. There was no rest for her and no rest for us. She tossed, she pitched, she stood on her head, she sat on her tail, she rolled, she groaned, and we had to hold on while on deck and cling to our bunks when below, in a constant effort of body and worry of mind.

"One night Mahon spoke through the small window of my berth. It opened right into my very bed, and I was lying there sleepless, in my boots, feeling as though I had not slept for years, and could not if I tried. He said excitedly—

" 'You got the sounding-rod in here, Marlow? I can't get the pumps to suck. By God! it's no child's play.'

"I gave him the sounding-rod and lay down again, trying to think of various things—but I thought only of the pumps. When I came on deck they were still at it, and my watch relieved at the pumps. By the light of the lantern brought on deck to examine the sounding-rod I caught a glimpse of their weary, serious faces. We pumped all the four hours. We pumped all night, all day, all the week—watch and watch. She was working herself loose, and leaked badly—not enough to drown us at once, but enough to kill us with the work at the pumps. And while we pumped the ship was going from us piecemeal: the bulwarks went, the stanchions were torn out, the ventilators smashed, the cabin-door burst in. There was not a dry spot in the ship. She was being gutted bit by bit. The long-boat changed, as if by magic, into matchwood where she stood in her gripes. I had lashed her myself, and was rather proud of my handiwork, which had withstood so long the malice of the sea. And we pumped. And there was no break in the weather. The sea was white like a sheet of foam, like a caldron of boiling milk; there was not a break in the clouds, no—not the size of a man's hand—no, not for so much as ten seconds. There was for us no sky, there were for us no stars, no sun, no universe—nothing but angry clouds and an infuriated sea. We pumped watch and watch, for dear life; and it seemed to last for months, for years, for all eternity, as though we had been dead and gone to a hell for sailors. We forgot the day of the week, the name of the month, what year it was, and whether we had ever been ashore. The sails blew away, she lay broadside on under a weather-cloth, the ocean poured over her, and we did not care. We turned those handles, and had the eyes of idiots. As soon as we had crawled on deck I used to take a round turn with a rope about the men, the pumps, and the mainmast, and we turned, we turned incessantly, with the water to our waists, to our necks, over our heads. It was all one. We had forgotten how it felt to be dry.

"And there was somewhere in me the thought: By Jove! this is the deuce of an adventure—something you read about; and it is my first voyage as second mate—and I am only twenty—and here I am lasting it out as well as any of these men, and keeping my chaps up to the mark. I was pleased. I would not have given up the experience for worlds. I had moments of exultation. Whenever the old dismantled craft pitched heavily with her counter high in the air, she seemed to me to throw up, like an appeal, like a defiance, like a cry to the clouds without mercy, the words written on her stern: '*Judea*, London. Do or Die.'

"O youth! The strength of it, the faith of it, the imagination of it! To me she was not an old rattle-trap carting about the world a lot of coal for a freight—to me she was the endeavour, the test, the trial of life. I think of her with pleasure, with affection, with regret—as you would think of someone dead you have loved. I shall never forget her. . . . Pass the bottle.

"One night when tied to the mast, as I explained, we were pumping on, deafened with the wind, and without spirit enough in us to wish ourselves dead, a heavy sea crashed aboard and swept clean over us. As soon as I got my breath I shouted, as in duty bound, 'Keep on, boys!' when suddenly I felt something hard floating on deck strike the calf of my leg. I made a grab at it and missed. It was so dark we could not see each other's faces within a foot—you understand.

"After that thump the ship kept quiet for a while, and the thing, whatever it was, struck my leg again. This time I caught it—and it was a saucepan. At first, being stupid with fatigue and thinking of nothing but the pumps, I did not understand what I had in my hand. Suddenly it dawned upon me, and I shouted, 'Boys, the house on deck is gone. Leave this, and let's look for the cook.'

"There was a deck-house forward, which contained the galley, the cook's berth, and the quarters of the crew. As we had expected for days to see it swept away, the hands had been ordered to sleep in the cabin—the only safe place in the ship. The steward, Abraham, however, persisted in clinging to his berth, stupidly, like a mule—from sheer fright I believe, like an animal that won't leave a stable falling in an earthquake. So we went to look for him. It was chancing death, since once out of our lashings we were as exposed as if on a raft. But we went. The house was shattered as if a shell had exploded inside. Most of it had gone overboard—stove, men's quarters, and their property, all was gone; but two posts, holding a portion of the bulkhead to which Abraham's bunk was attached, remained as if by a miracle. We groped in the ruins and came upon this, and there he was, sitting in his bunk, surrounded by foam and wreckage, jabbering cheerfully to himself. He was out of his mind; completely and for ever mad, with this sudden shock coming upon the fag-end of his endurance. We snatched him up, lugged him aft, and pitched him head-first down the cabin companion. You understand there was no time to carry him down with infinite precautions and wait to see how he got on. Those below would pick him up at the bottom of the stairs all right. We were in a hurry to go back to the pumps. That business could not wait. A bad leak is an inhuman thing.

"One would think that the sole purpose of that fiendish gale had been to make a lunatic of that poor devil of a mulatto. It eased before morning, and next day the sky cleared, and as the sea went down the leak took up. When it came to bending a fresh set of sails the crew demanded to put back—and really there was nothing else to do. Boats gone, decks swept clean, cabin gutted, men without a stitch but what they stood in, stores spoiled, ship strained. We put her head for home, and—would you believe it? The wind came east right in our teeth. It blew fresh, it blew continuously. We had to beat up every inch of the way, but she did not leak so badly, the water keeping comparatively smooth. Two hours' pumping in every four is no joke—but it kept her afloat as far as Falmouth.

"The good people there live on casualties of the sea, and no doubt they were glad to see us. A hungry crowd of shipwrights sharpened their chisels at the sight of that carcass of a ship. And, by Jove! they had pretty pickings off us before they were done. I fancy the owner was already in a tight place. There were delays. Then it was decided to take part of the cargo out and caulk her topsides. This was done, the repairs finished, cargo reshipped; a new crew came on board, and we went out—for Bankok. At the end of a week we were back again. The crew said they weren't going to Bankok—a hundred and fifty days' passage—in a something hooker that wanted pumping eight hours out of the twenty-four; and the nautical papers inserted again the little paragraph: '*Judea*. Barque. Tyne to Bankok; coals; put back to Falmouth leaky and with crew refusing duty.'

"There were more delays—more tinkering. The owner came down for a day, and said she was as right as a little fiddle. Poor old Captain Beard looked like the ghost of a Geordie skipper—through the worry and humiliation of it. Remember he was sixty, and it was his first command. Mahon said it was a foolish business, and would end badly. I loved the ship more than ever, and wanted awfully to get to Bankok. To Bankok! Magic name, blessed name. Mesopotamia wasn't a patch on it. Remember I was twenty, and it was my first second-mate's billet, and the East was waiting for me.

"We went out and achored in the outer roads with a fresh crew—the third. She leaked worse than ever. It was as if those confounded shipwrights had actually made a hole in her. This time we did not even go outside. The crew simply refused to man the windlass.

"They towed us back to the inner harbour, and we became a fixture, a feature, an institution of the place. People pointed us out to visitors as 'That 'ere barque that's going to Bankok—has been here six months—put back three times.' On holidays the small boys pulling about in boats would hail, '*Judea*, ahoy!' and if a head showed above the rail shouted, 'Where you bound to?—Bankok?' and jeered. We were only three on board. The poor old skipper mooned in the cabin. Mahon undertook the cooking, and unexpectedly developed all a Frenchman's genius for preparing nice little messes. I looked languidly after the rigging. We became citizens of Falmouth. Every shopkeeper knew us. At the barber's or tobacconist's they asked familiarly, 'Do you think you will ever get to Bankok?' Meantime the owner, the underwriters, and the charterers squabbled amongst themselves in London, and our pay went on. . . . Pass the bottle.

"It was horrid. Morally it was worse than pumping for life. It seemed as though we had been forgotten by the world, belonged to nobody, would get nowhere; it seemed that, as if bewitched, we would have to live for ever and ever in that inner harbour, a derision and a by-word to generations of long-shore loafers and dishonest boatmen. I obtained three months' pay and a five days' leave, and made a rush for London. It took me a day to get there and pretty well another to come back—but three months' pay went all the same. I don't know what I did with it. I went to a music-hall, I believe, launched, dined, and supped in a swell place in Regent Street, and was back to time, with nothing but a complete set of Byron's works and a new railway rug to show for three months' work. The boat-man who pulled me off to the ship said: 'Hallo! I thought you had left the old thing. *She* will never get to Bankok.' 'That's all *you* know about it,' I said, scornfully—but I didn't like that prophecy at all.

"Suddenly a man, some kind of agent to somebody, appeared with full powers. He had grog-blossoms all over his face, an indomitable energy, and was a jolly soul. We leaped into life again. A hulk came alongside, took our cargo, and then we went into dry dock to get our copper stripped. No wonder she leaked. The poor thing, strained beyond endurance by the gale, had, as if in disgust, spat out all the oakum of her lower seams. She was recaulked, new coppered, and made as tight as a bottle. We went back to the hulk and reshipped our cargo.

"Then, on a fine moonlight night, all the rats left the ship.

"We had been infested with them. They had destroyed our sails, consumed more stores than the crew, affably shared our beds and our dangers, and now, when the ship was made seaworthy, concluded to clear out. I called Mahon to enjoy the spectacle. Rat after rat appeared on our rail, took a last look over his shoulder, and leaped with a hollow thud into the empty hulk. We tried to count them, but soon lost the tale. Mahon said: 'Well, well! don't talk to me about the intelligence of rats. They ought to have left before, when we had that narrow squeak from foundering. There you have the proof how silly is the superstition about them. They leave a good ship for an old rotten hulk, where there is nothing to eat, too, the fools! . . . I don't believe they know what is safe or what is good for them, any more than you or I.'

"And after some more talk we agreed that the wisdom of rats had been grossly overrated, being in fact no greater than that of men.

"The story of the ship was known, by this, all up the Channel from

Land's End to the Forelands, and we could get no crew on the south coast. They sent us one all complete from Liverpool, and we left once more—for Bankok.

"We had fair breezes, smooth water right into the tropics, and the old *Judea* lumbered along in the sunshine. When she went eight knots everything cracked aloft, and we tied our caps to our heads; but mostly she strolled on at the rate of three miles an hour. What could you expect? She was tired—that old ship. Her youth was where mine is—where yours is—you fellows who listen to this yarn; and what friend would throw your years and your weariness in your face? We didn't grumble at her. To us aft, at least, it seemed as though we had been born in her, reared in her, had lived in her for ages, had never known any other ship. I would just as soon have abused the old village church at home for not being a cathedral.

"And for me there was also my youth to make me patient. There was all the East before me, and all life, and the thought that I had been tried in that ship and had come out pretty well. And I thought of men of old who, centuries ago, went that road in ships that sailed no better, to the land of palms, and spices, and yellow sands, and of brown nations ruled by kings more cruel than Nero the Roman, and more splendid than Solomon the Jew. The old bark lumbered on, heavy with her age and the burden of her cargo, while I lived the life of youth in ignorance and hope. She lumbered on through an interminable procession of days; and the fresh gilding flashed back at the setting sun, seemed to cry out over the darkening sea the words painted on her stern, '*Judea*, London. Do or Die.'

"Then we entered the Indian Ocean and steered northerly for Java Head. The winds were light. Weeks slipped by. She crawled on, do or die, and people at home began to think of posting us as overdue.

"One Saturday evening, I being off duty, the men asked me to give them an extra bucket of water or so—for washing clothes. As I did not wish to screw on the fresh-water pump so late, I went forward whistling, and with a key in my hand to unlock the forepeak scuttle, intending to serve the water out of a spare tank we kept there.

"The smell down below was as unexpected as it was frightful. One would have thought hundreds of paraffin-lamps had been flaring and smoking in that hole for days. I was glad to get out. The man with me coughed and said, 'Funny smell, sir.' I answered negligently, 'It's good for the health they say,' and walked aft.

"The first thing I did was to put my head down the square of the midship ventilator. As I lifted the lid a visible breath, something like a thin fog, a puff of faint haze, rose from the opening. The ascending air was hot, and had a heavy, sooty, paraffiny smell. I gave one sniff, and put down the lid gently. It was no use choking myself. The cargo was on fire.

"Next day she began to smoke in earnest. You see it was to be expected, for though the coal was of a safe kind, that cargo had been so handled, so broken up with handling, that it looked more like smithy coal than anything else. Then it had been wetted—more than once. It rained all the time we were taking it back from the hulk, and now with this long passage it got heated, and there was another case of spontaneous combustion.

"The captain called us into the cabin. He had a chart spread on the table, and looked unhappy. He said, 'The coast of West Australia is near, but I mean to proceed to our destination. It is the hurricane month, too; but we will just keep her head for Bankok, and fight the fire. No more putting back anywhere, if we all get roasted. We will try first to stifle this 'ere damned combustion by want of air.'

"We tried. We battened down everything, and still she smoked. The smoke kept coming out through imperceptible crevices; it forced itself through bulkheads and covers; it oozed here and there and everywhere in slender threads, in an invisible film, in an incomprehensible manner. It made its way into the cabin, into the forecastle; it poisoned the sheltered places on the deck, it could be sniffed as high as the mainyard. It was clear that if the smoke came out the air came in. This was disheartening. This combustion refused to be stifled.

"We resolved to try water, and took the hatches off. Enormous volumes of smoke, whitish, yellowish, thick, greasy, misty, choking, ascended as high as the trucks. All hands cleared out aft. Then the poisonous cloud blew away, and we went back to work in a smoke that was no thicker now than that of an ordinary factory chimney.

"We rigged the force-pump, got the hose along, and by-and-by it burst. Well, it was as old as the ship—a prehistoric hose, and past repair. Then we pumped with the feeble head-pump, drew water with buckets, and in this way managed in time to pour lots of Indian Ocean into the main hatch. The bright stream flashed in sunshine, fell into a layer of white crawling smoke, and vanished on the black surface of coal. Steam ascended mingling with the smoke. We poured salt water as into a barrel without a bottom. It was our fate to pump in that ship, to pump out of her, to pump into her; and after keeping water out of her to save ourselves from being drowned, we frantically poured water into her to save ourselves from being burnt.

"And she crawled on, do or die, in the serene weather. The sky was a miracle of purity, a miracle of azure. The sea was polished, was blue, was pellucid, was sparkling like a precious stone, extending on all sides, all round to the horizon—as if the whole terrestrial globe had been one jewel, one colossal sapphire, a single gem fashioned into a planet. And on the lustre of the great calm waters the *Judea* glided imperceptibly, enveloped in languid and unclean vapours, in a lazy cloud that drifted to leeward, light and slow; a pestiferous cloud defiling the splendour of sea and sky.

"All this time of course we saw no fire. The cargo smouldered at the bottom somewhere. Once Mahon, as we were working side by side, said to me with a queer smile: 'Now, if she only would spring a tidy leak—like that time when we first left the Channel—it would put a stopper on this fire. Wouldn't it?' I remarked irrelevantly, 'Do you remember the rats?'

"We fought the fire and sailed the ship too as carefully as though nothing had been the matter. The steward cooked and attended on us. Of the other twelve men, eight worked while four rested. Everyone took his turn, captain included. There was equality, and if not exactly fraternity, then a deal of good feeling. Sometimes a man, as he dashed a bucketful of water down the hatchway, would yell out, 'Hurrah for Bankok!' and the rest laughed. But generally we were taciturn and serious—and thirsty. Oh! how thirsty! And we had to be careful with the water. Strict allowance. The ship smoked, the sun blazed. . . . Pass the bottle.

"We tried everything. We even made an attempt to dig down to the fire. No good, of course. No man could remain more than a minute below. Mahon, who went first, fainted there, and the man who went to fetch him out did likewise. We lugged them out on deck. Then I leaped down to show how easily it could be done. They had learned wisdom by that time, and contented themselves by fishing for me with a chain-hook tied to a broom-handle, I believe. I did not offer to go and fetch up my shovel, which was left down below.

"Things began to look bad. We put the long-boat into the water. The second boat was ready to swing out. We had also another, a 14-foot thing, on davits aft, where it was quite safe.

"Then, behold, the smoke suddenly decreased. We redoubled our efforts to flood the bottom of the ship. In two days there was no smoke at all. Everybody was on the broad grin. This was on a Friday. On Saturday no work, but sailing the ship of course, was done. The men washed their clothes and their faces for the first time in a fortnight, and had a special dinner given them. They spoke of spontaneous combustion with contempt, and implied *they* were the boys to put out combustions. Somehow we all felt as though we each had inherited a large fortune. But a beastly smell of burning hung about the ship. Captain Beard had hollow eyes and sunken cheeks. I had never noticed so much before how twisted and bowed he was. He and Mahon prowled soberly about the hatches and ventilators, sniffing. It struck me suddenly poor Mahon was a very, very old chap. As to me, I was as pleased and proud as though I had helped to win a great naval battle. O! Youth!

"The night was fine. In the morning a homeward-bound ship passed us hull down—the first we had seen for months; but we were nearing land at last, Java Head being about 190 miles off, and nearly due north.

"Next day it was my watch on deck from eight to twelve. At breakfast the captain observed, 'It's wonderful how that smell hangs about the cabin.' About ten, the mate being on the poop, I stepped down on the main-deck for a moment. The carpenter's bench stood abaft the mainmast: I leaned against it sucking at my pipe, and the carpenter, a young chap, came to talk to me. He remarked, 'I think we have done very well, haven't we?' and then I perceived with annoyance the fool was trying to tilt the bench. I said curtly, 'Don't, Chips,' and immediately became aware of a queer sensation, of an absurd delusion,—I seemed somehow to be in the air. I heard all round me like a pent-up breath released—as if a thousand giants simultaneously had said Phoo!—and felt a dull concussion which made my ribs ache suddenly. No doubt about it—I was in the air, and my body was describing a short parabola. But short as it was, I had the time to think several thoughts in, as far as I can remember, the following order: 'This can't be the carpenter—What is it?—Some accident—Submarine volcano?—Coals, gas!—By Jove! we are being blown up—Everybody's dead—I am falling into the after-hatch—I see fire in it.'

"The coal-dust suspended in the air of the hold had glowed dull-red at the moment of the explosion. In the twinkling of an eye, in an infinitesimal fraction of a second since the first tilt of the bench, I was sprawling full length on the cargo. I picked myself up and scrambled out. It was quick like a rebound. The deck was a wilderness of smashed timber, lying crosswise like trees in a wood after a hurricane; an immense curtain of solid rags waved gently before me—it was the mainsail blown to strips. I thought, The masts will be toppling over directly; and to get out of the way bolted on all-fours towards the poop-ladder. The first person I saw was Mahon, with eyes like saucers, his mouth open, and the long white hair standing straight on end round his head like a silver halo. He was just about to go down when the sight of the main-deck stirring, heaving up, and changing into splinters before his eyes, petrified him on the top step. I stared at him in unbelief, and he stared at me with a queer kind of shocked curiosity. I did not know that I had no hair, no eyebrows, no eyelashes, that my young moustache was burnt off, that my face was black, one cheek laid open, my nose cut, and my chin bleeding. I had lost my cap, one of my slippers, and my shirt was torn to rags. Of all this I was not aware. I was amazed to see the ship still afloat, the poop-deck whole—and, most of all, to see anybody alive. Also the peace of the sky and the serenity of the sea were distinctly surprising. I suppose I expected to see them convulsed with horror. . . . Pass the bottle.

"There was a voice hailing the ship from somewhere—in the air, in the sky—I couldn't tell. Presently I saw the captain—and he was mad. He asked me eagerly, 'Where's the cabin-table?' and to hear such a question was a frightful shock. I had just been blown up, you understand, and vibrated with that experience,—I wasn't quite sure whether I was alive. Mahon began to stamp with both feet and yelled at him, 'Good God! don't you see the deck's blown out of her?' I found my voice, and stammered out as if conscious of some gross neglect of duty, 'I don't know where the cabin-table is.' It was like an absurd dream.

"Do you know what he wanted next? Well, he wanted to trim the yards. Very placidly, and as if lost in thought, he insisted on having the foreyard squared. 'I don't know if there's anybody alive,' said Mahon, almost tearfully. 'Surely,' he said, gently, 'there will be enough left to square the foreyard.'

"The old chap, it seems, was in his own berth winding up the chronometers, when the shock sent him spinning. Immediately it occurred to him—as he said afterwards—that the ship had struck something, and ran out into the cabin. There, he saw, the cabin-table had vanished somewhere. The deck being blown up, it had fallen down into the lazarette of course. Where we had our breakfast that morning he saw only a great hole in the floor. This appeared to him so awfully mysterious, and impressed him so immensely, that what he saw and heard after he got on deck were mere trifles in comparison. And, mark, he noticed directly the wheel deserted and his barque off her course—and his only thought was to get that miserable, stripped, undecked, smouldering shell of a ship back again with her head pointing at her port of destination. Bankok! That's what he was after. I tell you this quiet, bowed, bandy-legged, almost deformed little man was immense in the singleness of his idea and in his placid ignorance of our agitation. He motioned us forward with a commanding gesture, and went to take the wheel himself.

"Yes; that was the first thing we did—trim the yards of that wreck! No one was killed, or even disabled, but everyone was more or less hurt. You should have seen them! Some were in rags, with black faces, like coal-heavers, like sweeps, and had bullet heads that seemed closely cropped, but were in fact singed to the skin. Others, of the watch below, awakened by being shot out from their collapsing bunks, shivered incessantly, and kept on groaning even as we went about our work. But they all worked. That crew of Liverpool hard cases had in them the right stuff. It's my experience they always have. It is the sea that gives it—the vastness, the loneliness surrounding their dark stolid souls. Ah! Well! we stumbled, we crept, we fell, we barked our shins on the wreckage, we hauled. The masts stood, but we did not know how much they might be charred down below. It was nearly calm, but a long swell ran from the west and made her roll. They might go at any moment. We looked at them with apprehension. One could not foresee which way they would fall.

"Then we retreated aft and looked about us. The deck was a tangle of planks on edge, of planks on end, of splinters, of ruined woodwork. The masts rose from that chaos like big trees above a matted undergrowth. The interstices of that mass of wreckage were full of something whitish, sluggish, stirring—of something that was like a greasy fog. The smoke of the invisible fire was coming up again, was trailing, like a poisonous thick mist in some valley choked with dead wood. Already lazy wisps were beginning to curl upwards amongst the mass of splinters. Here and there a piece of timber, stuck upright, resembled a post. Half of a fife-rail had been shot through the foresail, and the sky made a patch of glorious blue in the ignobly soiled canvas. A portion of several boards holding together had fallen across the rail, and one end protruded overboard, like a gangway leading upon nothing, like a gangway leading over the deep sea, leading to death—as if inviting us to walk the plank at once and be done with our ridiculous troubles. And still the air, the sky—a ghost, something invisible was hailing the ship.

"Someone had the sense to look over, and there was the helmsman, who had impulsively jumped overboard, anxious to come back. He yelled and swam lustily like a merman, keeping up with the ship. We threw him a rope, and presently he stood amongst us streaming with water and very crestfallen. The captain had surrendered the wheel, and apart, elbow on rail and chin in hand, gazed at the sea wistfully. We asked ourselves, What next? I thought, Now, this is something like. This is great. I wonder what will happen. O youth!

"Suddenly Mahon sighted a steamer far astern. Captain Beard said, 'We may do something with her yet.' We hoisted two flags, which said in the international language of the sea, 'On fire. Want immediate assistance.' The steamer grew bigger rapidly, and by-and-by spoke with two flags on her foremast, 'I am coming to your assistance.'

"In half an hour she was abreast, to windward, within hail, and rolling slightly, with her engines stopped. We lost our composure, and yelled all together with excitement, 'We've been blown up.' A man in a white helmet, on the bridge, cried, 'Yes! All right! all right!' and he nodded his head, and smiled, and made soothing motions with his hand as though at a lot of frightened children. One of the boats dropped in the water, and walked towards us upon the sea with her long oars. Four Calashes pulled a swinging stroke. This was my first sight of Malay seamen. I've known them since, but what struck me then was their unconcern: they came alongside, and even the bowman standing up and holding to our main-chains with the boathook did not deign to lift his head for a glance. I thought people who had been blown up deserved more attention.

"A little man, dry like a chip and agile like a monkey, clambered up. It was the mate of the steamer. He gave one look, and cried, 'O boys—you had better quit.'"

"We were silent. He talked apart with the captain for a time,—seemed to argue with him. Then they went away together to the steamer.

"When our skipper came back we learned that the steamer was the

Somerville, Captain Nash, from West Australia to Singapore *via* Batavia with mails, and that the agreement was she should tow us to Anjer or Batavia, if possible, where we could extinguish the fire by scuttling, and then proceed on our voyage—to Bankok! The old man seemed excited. 'We will do it yet,' he said to Mahon, fiercely. He shook his fist at the sky. Nobody else said a word.

"At noon the steamer began to tow. She went ahead slim and high, and what was left of the *Judea* followed at the end of seventy fathom of tow rope,—followed her swiftly like a cloud of smoke with mastheads protruding above. We went aloft to furl the sails. We coughed on the yards, and were careful about the bunts. Do you see the lot of us there, putting a neat furl on the sails of that ship doomed to arrive nowhere? There was not a man who didn't think that at any moment the masts would topple over. From aloft we could not see the ship for smoke, and they worked carefully, passing the gaskets with even turns. 'Harbour furl—aloft there!' cried Mahon from below.

"You understand this? I don't think one of those chaps expected to get down in the usual way. When we did I heard them saying to each other, 'Well, I thought we would come down overboard, in a lump—sticks and all—blame me if I didn't.' 'That's what I was thinking to myself,' would answer wearily another battered and bandaged scarecrow. And, mind, these were men without the drilled-in habit of obedience. To an onlooker they would be a lot of profane scallywags without a redeeming point. What made them do it—what made them obey me when I, thinking consciously how fine it was, made them drop the bunt of the foresail twice to try and do it better? What? They had no professional reputation—no examples, no praise. It wasn't a sense of duty; they knew well enough how to shirk, and laze, and dodge—when they had a mind to it—and mostly they had. Was it the two pounds ten a-month that sent them there? They didn't think their pay half good enough. No; it was something in them, something inborn and subtle and everlasting. I don't say positively that the crew of a French or German merchantman wouldn't have done it, but I doubt whether it would have been done in the same way. There was a completeness in it, something solid like a principle, and masterful like an instinct—a disclosure of something secret—of that hidden something, that gift of good or evil that makes racial difference, that shapes the fate of nations.

"It was that night at ten that, for the first time since we had been fighing it, we saw the fire. The speed of the towing had fanned the smouldering destruction. A blue gleam appeared forward, shining below the wreck of the deck. It wavered in patches, it seemed to stir and creep like the light of a glowworm. I saw it first, and told Mahon. 'Then the game's up,' he said. 'We had better stop this towing, or she will burst out suddenly fore and aft before we can clear out.' We set up a yell; rang bells to attract their attention; they towed on. At last Mahon and I had to crawl forward and cut the rope with an axe. There was not time to cast off the lashings. Red tongues could be seen licking the wilderness of splinters under our feet as we made our way back to the poop.

"Of course they very soon found out in the steamer that the rope was gone. She gave a loud blast of her whistle, her lights were seen sweeping in a wide circle, she came up ranging close alongside, and stopped. We were all in a tight group on the poop looking at her. Every man had saved a little bundle or a bag. Suddenly a conical flame with a twisted top shot up forward and threw upon the black sea a circle of light, with the two vessels side by side and heaving gently in its centre. Captain Beard had been sitting on the gratings still and mute for hours, but now he rose slowly and advanced in front of us, to the mizzen-shrouds. Captain Nash hailed: 'Come along! Look sharp. I have mail-bags on board. I will take you and your boats to Singapore.'

" 'Thank you! No!' said our skipper. 'We must see the last of the ship.'

" 'I can't stand by any longer,' shouted the other. 'Mails—you know.'

" 'Ay! ay! We are all right.'

" 'Very well! I'll report you in Singapore. . . . Good-bye!'

"He waved his hand. Our men dropped their bundles quietly. The steamer moved ahead, and passing out of the circle of light, vanished at once from our sight, dazzled by the fire which burned fiercely. And then I knew that I would see the East first as commander of a small boat. I thought it fine; and the fidelity to the old ship was fine. We should see the last of her. Oh, the glamour of youth! Oh, the fire of it, more dazzling than the flames of the burning ship, throwing a magic light on the wide earth, leaping audaciously to the sky, presently to be quenched by time, more cruel, more pitiless, more bitter than the sea—and like the flames of the burning ship surrounded by an impenetrable night.

"The old man warned us in his gentle and inflexible way that it was part of our duty to save for the underwriters as much as we could of the ship's gear. Accordingly we went to work aft, while she blazed forward to give us plenty of light. We lugged out a lot of rubbish. What didn't we save? An old barometer fixed with an absurd quantity of screws nearly cost me my life: a sudden rush of smoke came upon me, and I just got away in time. There were various stores, bolts of canvas, coils of rope; the poop looked like a marine bazaar, and the boats were lumbered to the gunwales. One would have thought the old man wanted to take as much as he could of his first command with him. He was very, very quiet, but off his balance evidently. Would you believe it? He wanted to take a length of old stream-cable and a kedge-anchor with him in the long-boat. We said, 'Ay, ay, sir,' deferentially, and on the quiet let the things slip overboard. The heavy medicine-chest went that way, two bags of green coffee, tins of paint—fancy, paint!—a whole lot of things. Then I was ordered with two hands into the boats to make a stowage and get them ready against the time it would be proper for us to leave the ship.

"We put everything straight, stepped the long-boat's mast for our skipper, who was to take charge of her, and I was not sorry to sit down for a moment. My face felt raw, every limb ached as if broken, I was aware of all my ribs and would have sworn to a twist in the backbone. The boats, fast astern, lay in a deep shadow, and all around I could see the circle of the sea lighted by the fire. A gigantic flame arose forward straight and clear. It flared fierce, with noises like the whirr of wings, with rumbles as of thunder. There were cracks, detonations, and from the cone of flame the sparks flew upwards, as man is born to trouble, to leaky ships, and to sails that burn.

"What bothered me was that the ship, lying broadside to the swell and to such wind as there was—a mere breath—the boats would not keep astern where they were safe, but persisted, in a pig-headed way boats have, in getting under the counter and then swinging alongside. They were knocking about dangerously and coming near the flame, while the ship rolled on them, and, of course, there was always the danger of the masts going over the side at any moment. I and my two boat-keepers kept them off as best we could, with oars and boat-hooks; but to be constantly at it became exasperating, since there was no reason why we should not leave at once. We could not see those on board, nor could we imagine what caused the delay. The boat-keepers were swearing feebly, and I had not only my share of th[illegible]d to keep at it two men who showed a constant [illegible]nselves down and let things slide. [illegible]leck there,' and someone looked over. 'We're [illegible]ad disappeared, and very soon popped up [illegible]right, sir, and to keep the boats well [illegible]

[illegible]here was a frightful racket, rattle, cla[illegible] millions of sparks flew up into the s[illegible]od leaning slightly above the ship. T[illegible]nd the two red-hot anchors had gone [illegible]hem two hundred fathoms of red-hot ch[illegible]ss of flame swayed as if ready to collap[illegible]ast fell. It darted down like an arrow of [illegible]antly leaping up within an oar's-length of the b[illegible]quietly, very black on the luminous sea. I hailed the deck [illegible]After some time a man in an unexpectedly cheerful but also mu[illegible]ed tone, as though he had been trying to speak with his mouth shut, informed me, 'Coming directly, sir,' and vanished. For a long time I heard nothing but the whirr and roar of the fire. There were also whistling sounds. The boats jumped, tugged at the painters, ran at each other playfully, knocked their sides together, or, do what we would, swung in a bunch against the ship's side. I couldn't stand it any longer, and swarming up a rope, clambered aboard over the stern.

"It was as bright as day. Coming up like this, the sheet of fire facing me was a terrifying sight, and the heat seemed hardly bearable at first. On a settee cushion dragged out of the cabin Captain Beard, his legs drawn up and one arm under his head, slept with the light playing on him. Do you know what the rest were busy about? They were sitting on deck right aft, round an open case, eating bread and cheese and drinking bottled stout.

"On the background of flames twisting in fierce tongues above their heads they seemed at home like salamanders, and looked like a band of desperate pirates. The fire sparkled in the whites of their eyes, gleamed on patches of white skin seen through the torn shirts. Each had the marks as of a battle about him—bandaged heads, tied-up arms, a strip of dirty rag round a knee—and each man had a bottle between his legs and a chunk of cheese in his hand. Mahon got up. With his handsome and disreputable head, his hooked profile, his long white beard, and with an uncorked bottle in his hand, he resembled one of those reckless sea-robbers of old making merry amidst violence and disaster. 'The last meal on board,' he explained solemnly. 'We had nothing to eat all day, and it was no use leaving all this.' He flourished the bottle and indicated the sleeping skipper. 'He said he couldn't swallow anything, so I got him to lie down,' he went on; and as I stared, 'I don't know whether you are aware, young fellow, the man had no sleep to speak of for days—and there will be dam' little sleep in the boats.' 'There will be no boats by-and-by if you fool about much longer,' I said, indignantly. I walked up to the skipper and shook him by the shoulder. At last he opened his eyes, but did not move. 'Time to leave her, sir,' I said quietly.

"He got up painfully, looked at the flames, at the sea sparkling round the ship, and black, black as ink farther away; he looked at the stars shining dim through a thin veil of smoke in a sky black, black as Erebus.

" 'Youngest first,' he said.

"And the ordinary seaman, wiping his mouth with the back of his hand, got up, clambered over the taffrail, and vanished. Others followed. One, on the point of going over, stopped short to drain his bottle, and with a great swing of his arm flung it at the fire. 'Take this!' he cried.

"The skipper lingered disconsolately, and we left him to commune alone for a while with his first command. Then I went up again and brought him away at last. It was time. The ironwork on the poop was hot to the touch.

"Then the painter of the long-boat was cut, and the three boats, tied together, drifted clear of the ship. It was just sixteen hours after the explosion when we abandoned her. Mahon had charge of the second boat, and I had the smallest—the 14-foot thing. The long-boat would have taken the lot of us; but the skipper said we must save as much property as we could—for the underwriters—and so I got my first command. I had two men with me, a bag of biscuits, a few tins of meat, and a breaker of water. I was ordered to keep close to the long-boat, that in case of bad weather we might be taken into her.

"And do you know what I thought? I thought I would part company as soon as I could. I wanted to have my first command all to myself. I wasn't going to sail in a squadron if there were a chance for independent cruising. I would make land by myself. I would beat the other boats. Youth! All youth! The silly, charming, beautiful youth.

"But we did not make a start at once. We must see the last of the ship. And so the boats drifted about that night, heaving and setting on the swell. The men dozed, waked, sighed, groaned. I looked at the burning ship.

"Between the darkness of earth and heaven she was burning fiercely upon a disc of purple sea shot by the blood-red play of gleams; upon a disc of water glittering and sinister. A high, clear flame, an immense and lonely flame, ascended from the ocean, and from its summit the black smoke poured continuously at the sky. She burned furiously; mournful and imposing like a funeral pile kindled in the night, surrounded by the sea, watched over by the stars. A magnificent death had come like a grace, like a gift, like a reward to that old ship at the end of her laborious days. The surrender of her weary ghost to the keeping of stars and sea was stirring like the sight of a glorious triumph. The masts fell just before daybreak, and for a moment there was a burst and turmoil of sparks that seemed to fill with flying fire the night patient and watchful, the vast night lying silent upon the sea. At daylight she was only a charred shell, floating still under a cloud of smoke and bearing a glowing mass of coal within.

"Then the oars were got out, and the boats forming in a line moved round her remains as if in procession—the long-boat leading. As we pulled across her stern a slim dart of fire shot out viciously at us, and suddenly she went down, head first, in a great hiss of steam. The unconsumed stern was the last to sink; but the paint had gone, had cracked, had peeled off, and there were no letters, there was no word, no stubborn device that was like her soul, to flash at the rising sun her creed and her name.

"We made our way north. A breeze sprang up, and about noon all the boats came together for the last time. I had no mast or sail in mine, but I made a mast out of a spare oar and hoisted a boat-awning for a sail, with a boat-hook for a yard. She was certainly over-masted, but I had the satisfaction of knowing that with the wind aft I could beat the other two. I had to wait for them. Then we all had a look at the captain's chart, and, after a sociable meal of hard bread and water, got our last instructions. These were simple: steer north, and keep together as much as possible. 'Be careful with that jury-rig, Marlow,' said the captain; and Mahon, as I sailed proudly past his boat, wrinkled his curved nose and hailed, 'You will sail that ship of yours under water, if you don't look out, young fellow.' He was a malicious old man—and may the deep sea where he sleeps now rock him gently, rock him tenderly to the end of time!

"Before sunset a thick rain-squall passed over the two boats, which were far astern, and that was the last I saw of them for a time. Next day I sat steering my cockle-shell—my first command—with nothing but water and sky around me. I did sight in the afternoon the upper sails of a ship far away, but said nothing, and my men did not notice her. You see I was afraid she might be homeward bound, and I had no mind to turn back from the portals of the East. I was steering for Java—another blessed name—like Bankok, you know. I steered many days.

"I need not tell you what it is to be knocking about in an open boat. I remember nights and days of calm, when we pulled, we pulled, and the boat seemed to stand still, as if bewitched within the circle of the sea horizon. I remember the heat, the deluge of rain-squalls that kept us baling for dear life (but filled our water-cask), and I remember sixteen hours on end with a mouth dry as a cinder and a steering-oar over the stern to keep my first command head on to a breaking sea. I did not know how good a man I was till then. I remember the drawn faces, the dejected figures of my two men, and I remember my youth and the feeling that will never come back any more—the feeling that I could last for ever, outlast the sea, the earth, and all men; the deceitful feeling that lures us on to joys, to perils, to love, to vain effort—to death; the triumphant conviction of strength, the heat of life in the handful of dust, the glow in the heart that with every year grows dim, grows cold, grows small, and expires—and expires, too soon, too soon—before life itself.

"And this is how I see the East. I have seen its secret places and have looked into its very soul; but now I see it always from a small boat, a high outline of mountains, blue and afar in the morning; like faint mist at noon; a jagged wall of purple at sunset. I have the feel of the oar in my hand, the vision of a scorching blue sea in my eyes. And I see a bay, a wide bay, smooth as glass and polished like ice, shimmering in the dark. A red light burns far off upon the gloom of the land, and the night is soft and warm. We drag at the oars with aching arms, and suddenly a puff of wind, a puff faint and tepid and laden with strange odours of blossoms, of aromatic wood, comes out of the still night—the first sigh of the East on my face. That I can never forget. It was impalpable and enslaving, like a charm, like a whispered promise of mysterious delight.

"We had been pulling this finishing spell for eleven hours. Two pulled, and he whose turn it was to rest sat at the tiller. We had made out the red light in that bay and steered for it, guessing it must mark some small coasting port. We passed two vessels, outlandish and high-sterned, sleeping at anchor, and, approaching the light, now very dim, ran the boat's nose against the end of a jutting wharf. We were blind with fatigue. My men dropped the oars and fell off the thwarts as if dead. I made fast to a pile. A current rippled softly. The scented obscurity of the shore was grouped into vast masses, a density of colossal clumps of vegetation, probably—mute and fantastic shapes. And at their foot the semicircle of a beach gleamed faintly, like an illusion. There was not a light, not a stir, not a sound. The mysterious East faced me, perfumed like a flower, silent like death, dark like a grave.

"And I sat weary beyond expression, exulting like a conqueror, sleepless and entranced as if before a profound, a fateful enigma.

"A splashing of oars, a measured dip reverberating on the level of water, intensified by the silence of the shore into loud claps, made me jump up. A boat, a European boat, was coming in. I invoked the name of the dead; I hailed: *Judea* ahoy! A thin shout answered.

"It was the captain. I had beaten the flagship by three hours, and I was glad to hear the old man's voice again, tremulous and tired. 'Is it you, Marlow?' 'Mind the end of that jetty, sir,' I cried.

"He approached cautiously, and brought up with the deep-sea lead-line which we had saved—for the underwriters. I eased my painter and fell alongside. He sat, a broken figure at the stern, wet with dew, his hands clasped in his lap. His men were asleep already. 'I had a terrible time of it,' he murmured. 'Mahon is behind—not very far.' We conversed in whispers, in low whispers, as if afraid to wake up the land. Guns, thunder, earthquakes would not have awakened the men just then.

"Looking round as we talked, I saw away at sea a bright light travelling in the night. 'There's a steamer passing the bay,' I said. She was not passing, she was entering, and she even came close and anchored. 'I wish,' said the old man, 'you would find out whether she is English. Perhaps they could give us a passage somewhere.' He seemed nervously anxious. So by dint of punching and kicking I started one of my men into a state of somnambulism, and giving him an oar, took another and pulled towards the lights of the steamer.

"There was a murmur of voices in her, metallic hollow clangs of the engine-room, footsteps on the deck. Her ports shone, round like dilated eyes. Shapes moved about, and there was a shadowy man high up on the bridge. He heard my oars.

"And then, before I could open my lips, the East spoke to me, but it was in a Western voice. A torrent of words was poured into the enigmatical, the fateful silence; outlandish, angry words, mixed with words and even whole sentences of good English, less strange but even more surprising. The voice swore and cursed violently; it riddled the solemn peace of the bay by a volley of abuse. It began by calling me Pig, and from that went crescendo into unmentionable adjectives —in English. The man up there raged aloud in two languages, and with a sincerity in his fury that almost convinced me I had, in some way, sinned against the harmony of the universe. I could hardly see him, but began to think he would work himself into a fit.

"Suddenly he ceased, and I could hear him snorting and blowing like a porpoise. I said—

" 'What steamer is this, pray?'

" 'Eh? What's this? And who are you?'

" 'Castaway crew of an English barque burnt at sea. We came here to-night. I am the second mate. The captain is in the long-boat, and wishes to know if you would give us a passage somewhere.'

" 'Oh, my goodness! I say. . . . This is the *Celestial* from Singapore on her return trip. I'll arrange with your captain in the morning, . . . and, . . . I say, . . . did you hear me just now?'

" 'I should think the whole bay heard you.'

" 'I thought you were a shore-boat. Now, look here—this infernal lazy scoundrel of a caretaker has gone to sleep again—curse him. The light is out, and I nearly ran foul of the end of this damned jetty. This is the third time he plays me this trick. Now, I ask you, can anybody stand this kind of thing? It's enough to drive a man out of his mind. I'll report him. . . . I'll get the Assistant Resident to give him the sack, by . . . ! See—there's no light. It's out, isn't it? I take you to witness the light's out. There should be a light, you know. A red light on the——'

" 'There was a light,' I said, mildly.

" 'But it's out, man! What's the use of talking like this? You can see for yourself it's out—don't you? If you had to take a valuable steamer along this God-forsaken coast you would want a light, too. I'll kick him from end to end of his miserable wharf. You'll see if I don't. I will——'

"'So I may tell my captain you'll take us?' I broke in.

"'Yes, I'll take you. Good-night,' he said, brusquely.

"I pulled back, made fast again to the jetty, and then went to sleep at last. I had faced the silence of the East. I had heard some of its language. But when I opened my eyes again the silence was as complete as though it had never been broken. I was lying in a flood of light, and the sky had never looked so far, so high, before. I opened my eyes and lay without moving.

"And then I saw the men of the East—they were looking at me. The whole length of the jetty was full of people. I saw brown, bronze, yellow faces, the black eyes, the glitter, the colour of an Eastern crowd. And all these beings stared without a murmur, without a sigh, without a movement. They stared down at the boats, at the sleeping men who at night had come to them from the sea. Nothing moved. The fronds of palms stood still against the sky. Not a branch stirred along the shore, and the brown roofs of hidden houses peeped through the green foliage, through the big leaves that hung shining and still like leaves forged of heavy metal. This was the East of the ancient navigators, so old, so mysterious, resplendent and sombre, living and unchanged, full of danger and promise. And these were the men. I sat up suddenly. A wave of movement passed through the crowd from end to end, passed along the heads, swayed the bodies, ran along the jetty like a ripple on the water, like a breath of wind on a field—and all was still again. I see it now—the wide sweep of the bay, the glittering sands, the wealth of green infinite and varied, the sea blue like the sea of a dream, the crowd of attentive faces, the blaze of vivid colour—the water reflecting it all, the curve of the shore, the jetty, the high-sterned outlandish craft floating still, and the three boats with the tired men from the West sleeping, unconscious of the land and the people and of the violence of sunshine. They slept thrown across the thwarts, curled on bottom-boards, in the careless attitudes of death. The head of the old skipper, leaning back in the stern of the long-boat, had fallen on his breast, and he looked as though he would never wake. Farther out old Mahon's face was upturned to the sky, with the long white beard spread out on his breast, as though he had been shot where he sat at the tiller; and a man, all in a heap in the bows of the boat, slept with both arms embracing the stem-head and with his cheek laid on the gunwale. The East looked at them without a sound.

"I have known its fascination since; I have seen the mysterious shores, the still water, the lands of brown nations, where a stealthy Nemesis lies in wait, pursues, overtakes so many of the conquering race, who are proud of their wisdom, of their knowledge, of their strength. But for me all the East is contained in that vision of my youth. It is all in that moment when I opened my young eyes on it. I came upon it from a tussle with the sea—and I was young—and I saw it looking at me. And this is all that is left of it! Only a moment; a moment of strength, of romance, of glamour—of youth! . . . A flick of sunshine upon a strange shore, the time to remember, the time for a sigh, and—good-bye!—Night—Good-bye . . . !"

He drank.

"Ah! The good old time—the good old time. Youth and the sea. Glamour and the sea! The good, strong sea, the salt, bitter sea, that could whisper to you and roar at you and knock your breath out of you."

He drank again.

"By all that's wonderful it is the sea, I believe, the sea itself—or is it youth alone? Who can tell? But you here—you all had something out of life: money, love—whatever one gets on shore—and, tell me, wasn't that the best time, that time when we were young at sea; young and had nothing, on the sea that gives nothing, except hard knocks—and sometimes a chance to feel your strength—that only—what you all regret?"

And we all nodded at him: the man of finance, the man of accounts, the man of law, we all nodded at him over the polished table that like a still sheet of brown water reflected our faces, lined, wrinkled; our faces marked by toil, by deceptions, by success, by love; our weary eyes looking still, looking always, looking anxiously for something out of life, that while it is expected is already gone—has passed unseen, in a sigh, in a flash—together with the youth, with the strength, with the romance of illusions.

by Delmore Schwartz

IN DREAMS BEGIN RESPONSIBILITIES

Delmore Schwartz was born on December 8, 1913, in Brooklyn, New York, and educated at Columbia, Wisconsin, and New York University. His first book of poems appeared in 1938 and has been followed by four others. He has published two volumes of short stories, The World Is a Wedding *(1948) and* Successful Love *(1961). Mr. Schwartz was for twelve years an editor of* Partisan Review; *his criticism has appeared in a number of small magazines. He has taught at Harvard, Kenyon, Princeton, and the University of Chicago. Mr. Schwartz has received awards from* Poetry *(1950) and the National Academy of Arts and Letters (1953).*

The poet's aptness of phrase is perhaps what strikes one first on reading "In Dreams Begin Responsibilities." A streetcar, the narrator tells us, "skates and gnaws, slowly progressing"; he hears a horse's hooves "falling like stones." But the story is more than a record of observations. Who are the dreamers for whom responsibility begins? The narrator, of course, is one, dreaming away the last night of childhood and awakening on his twenty-first birthday to the weight of the adult world. So, too, are his father and mother, who in their romantic visions, their temper, and their stubbornness are beginning something that matters, as the usher in their son's dream puts it, "too much."

I THINK it is the year 1909. I feel as if I were in a motion picture theatre, the long arm of light crossing the darkness and spinning, my eyes fixed on the screen. This is a silent picture as if an old Biograph one, in which the actors are dressed in ridiculously old-fashioned clothes, and one flash succeeds another with sudden jumps. The actors too seem to jump about and walk too fast. The shots themselves are full of dots and rays, as if it were raining when the picture was photographed. The light is bad.

It is Sunday afternoon, June 12th, 1909, and my father is walking down the quiet streets of Brooklyn on his way to visit my mother. His clothes are newly pressed and his tie is too tight in his high collar. He jingles the coins in his pockets, thinking of the witty things he will say. I feel as if I had by now relaxed entirely in the soft darkness of the theatre; the organist peals out the obvious and approximate emotions on which the audience rocks unknowingly. I am anonymous, and I have forgotten myself. It is always so when one goes to the movies, it is, as they say, a drug.

My father walks from street to street of trees, lawns and houses, once in a while coming to an avenue on which a street-car skates and gnaws, slowly progressing. The conductor, who has a handle-bar mustache helps a young lady wearing a hat like a bowl with feathers on to the car. She lifts her long skirts slightly as she mounts the steps. He leisurely makes change and rings his bell. It is obviously Sunday, for everyone is wearing Sunday clothes, and the street-car's noises emphasize the quiet of the holiday. Is not Brooklyn the City of Churches? The shops are closed and their shades drawn, but for an occasional stationery store or drug-store with great green balls in the window.

My father has chosen to take this long walk because he likes to walk and think. He thinks about himself in the future and so arrives at the place he is to visit in a state of mild exaltation. He pays no attention to the houses he is passing, in which the Sunday dinner is being eaten, nor to the many trees which patrol each street, now coming to their full leafage and the time when they will room the whole street in cool shadow. An occasional carriage passes, the horse's hooves falling like stones in the quiet afternoon, and once in a while an automobile, looking like an enormous upholstered sofa, puffs and passes.

My father thinks of my mother, of how nice it will be to introduce her to his family. But he is not yet sure that he wants to marry her, and once in a while he becomes panicky about the bond already established. He reassures himself by thinking of the big men he admires who are married: William Randolph Hearst, and William Howard Taft, who has just become President of the United States.

My father arrives at my mother's house. He has come too early and so is suddenly embarrassed. My aunt, my mother's sister, answers the loud bell with her napkin in her hand, for the family is still at dinner. As my father enters, my grandfather rises from the table and shakes hands with him. My mother has run upstairs to tidy herself. My grandmother asks my father if he has had dinner, and tells him that Rose will be downstairs soon. My grandfather opens the conversation by remarking on the mild June weather. My father sits uncomfortably near the table, holding his hat in his hand. My grandmother tells my aunt to take my father's hat. My uncle, twelve years old, runs into the house, his hair touseled. He shouts a greeting to my father, who has often given him a nickel, and then runs upstairs. It is evident that the respect in which my father is held in this household is tempered by a good deal of mirth. He is impressive, yet he is very awkward.

Finally my mother comes downstairs, all dressed up, and my father being engaged in conversation with my grandfather becomes uneasy, not knowing whether to greet my mother or continue the conversation. He gets up from the chair clumsily and says "hello" gruffly. My grandfather watches, examining their congruence, such as it is, with a critical eye, and meanwhile rubbing his bearded cheek roughly, as he always does when he reflects. He is worried; he is afraid that my father will not make a good husband for his oldest daughter. At this point something happens to the film, just as my father is saying something funny to my mother; I am awakened to myself and my unhappiness just as my interest was rising. The audience begins to clap impatiently. Then the trouble is cared for but the film has been returned to a portion just shown, and once more I see my grandfather rubbing his bearded cheek and pondering my father's character. It is difficult to get back into the picture once more and forget myself, but as my mother giggles at my father's words, the darkness drowns me.

My father and mother depart from the house, my father shaking hands with my mother once more, out of some unknown uneasiness. I stir uneasily also, slouched in the hard chair of the theatre. Where is the older uncle, my mother's older brother? He is studying in his bedroom upstairs, studying for his final examination at the College of the City of New York, having been dead of rapid pneumonia for the last twenty-one years. My mother and father walk down the same quiet streets once more. My mother is holding my father's arm and telling him of the novel which she has been reading; and my father utters judgments of the characters as the plot is made clear to him. This is a habit which he very much enjoys, for he feels the utmost superiority and confidence when he approves and condemns the behavior of other people. At times he feels moved to utter a brief "Ugh,"—whenever the story becomes what he would call sugary. This tribute is paid to his manliness. My mother feels satisfied by the interest which she has awakened; she is showing my father how intelligent she is, and how interesting.

They reach the avenue, and the street-car leisurely arrives. They are going to Coney Island this afternoon, although my mother considers that such pleasures are inferior. She has made up her mind to indulge only in a walk on the boardwalk and a pleasant dinner, avoiding the riotous amusements as being beneath the dignity of so dignified a couple.

My father tells my mother how much money he has made in the past week, exaggerating an amount which need not have been exaggerated. But my father has always felt that actualities somehow fall short. Suddenly I begin to weep. The determined old lady who sits next to me in the theatre is annoyed and looks at me with an angry face, and being intimidated, I stop. I drag out my handkerchief and dry my face, licking the drop which has fallen near my lips. Meanwhile I have missed something, for here are my mother and father alighting at the last stop, Coney Island.

They walk toward the boardwalk, and my father commands my mother to inhale the pungent air from the sea. They both breathe in deeply, both of them laughing as they do. They have in common a great interest in health, although my father is strong and husky, my mother frail. Their minds are full of theories of what is good to eat and not good to eat, and sometimes they engage in heated discussions of the subject, the whole matter ending in my father's announcement, made with a scornful bluster, that you have to die sooner or later anyway. On the boardwalk's flagpole, the American flag is pulsing in an intermittent wind from the sea.

My father and mother go to the rail of the boardwalk and look down on the beach where a good many bathers are casually walking about. A few are in the surf. A peanut whistle pierces the air with its pleasant and active whine, and my father goes to buy peanuts. My mother remains at the rail and stares at the ocean. The ocean seems merry to her; it pointedly sparkles and again and again the pony waves are released. She notices the children digging in the wet sand, and the bathing costumes of the girls who are her own age. My father returns with the peanuts. Overhead the sun's lightning strikes and strikes, but neither of them are at all aware of it. The boardwalk is full of people dressed in their Sunday clothes and idly strolling. The tide does not reach as far as the boardwalk, and the strollers would feel no danger if it did. My mother and father lean on the rail of the boardwalk and absently stare at the ocean. The ocean is becoming rough; the waves come in slowly, tugging strength from far back. The moment before they somersault, the moment when they arch their backs so beautifully, showing green and white veins amid the black, that moment is intolerable. They finally crack, dashing fiercely upon the sand, actually driving, full force downward, against the sand, bouncing upward and forward, and at last petering out into a small stream which races up the beach and then is recalled. My parents gaze absentmindedly at the ocean, scarcely interested in its harshness. The sun overhead does not disturb them. But I stare at the terrible sun which breaks up sight, and the fatal, merciless, passionate ocean, I forget my parents. I stare fascinated and finally, shocked by the indifference of my father and mother, I burst out weeping once more. The old lady next to me pats me on the shoulder and says "There, there, all of this is only a movie, young man, only a movie," but I look up once more at the terrifying sun and the terrifying ocean, and being unable to control my tears, I get up and go to the men's room, stumbling over the feet of the other people seated in my row.

When I return, feeling as if I had awakened in the morning sick for lack of sleep, several hours have apparently passed and my parents are riding on the merry-go-round. My father is on a black horse, my mother on a white one, and they seem to be making an eternal circuit for the single purpose of snatching the nickel rings which are attached to the arm of one of the posts. A hand-organ is playing; it is one with the ceaseless circling of the merry-go-round.

For a moment it seems that they will never get off the merry-go-round because it will never stop. I feel like one who looks down on the avenue from the 50th story of a building. But at length they do get off; even the music of the hand-organ has ceased for a moment. My father has acquired ten rings, my mother only two, although it was my mother who really wanted them.

They walk on along the boardwalk as the afternoon descends by imperceptible degrees into the incredible violet of dusk. Everything fades into a relaxed glow, even the ceaseless murmuring from the beach, and the revolutions of the merry-go-round. They look for a place to have dinner. My father suggests the best one on the boardwalk and my mother demurs, in accordance with her principles.

However they do go to the best place, asking for a table near the window, so that they can look out on the boardwalk and the mobile ocean. My father feels omnipotent as he places a quarter in the waiter's hand as he asks for a table. The place is crowded and here too there is music, this time from a kind of string trio. My father orders dinner with a fine confidence.

As the dinner is eaten, my father tells of his plans for the future, and my mother shows with expressive face how interested she is, and how impressed. My father becomes exultant. He is lifted up by the waltz that is being played, and his own future begins to intoxicate him. My father tells my mother that he is going to expand his business, for there is a great deal of money to be made. He wants to settle down. After all, he is twenty-nine, he has lived by himself since he was thirteen, he is making more and more money, and he is envious of his married friends when he visits them in the cozy security of their homes, surrounded, it seems, by the calm domestic pleasures, and by delightful children, and then, as the waltz reaches the moment when all the dancers swing madly, then, then with awful daring, then he asks my mother to marry him, although awkwardly enough and puzzled, even in his excitement, at how he had arrived at the proposal, and she, to make the whole business worse, begins to cry, and my father looks nervously about, not knowing at all what to do now, and my mother says: "It's all I've wanted from the moment I saw you," sobbing, and he finds all of this very difficult, scarcely to his taste, scarcely as he had thought it would be, on his long walks over Brooklyn Bridge in the revery of a fine cigar, and it was then that I stood up in the theatre and shouted: "Don't do it It's not too late to change your minds, both of you. Nothing good will come of it, only remorse, hatred, scandal, and two children whose characters are monstrous." The whole audience turned to look at me, annoyed, the usher came hurrying down the aisle flashing his searchlight, and the old lady next to me tugged me down into my seat, saying: "Be quiet. You'll be put out, and you paid thirty-five cents to come in." And so I shut my eyes because I could not bear to see what was happening. I sat there quietly.

But after awhile I begin to take brief glimpses, and at length I watch again with thirsty interest, like a child who wants to maintain his sulk although offered the bribe of candy. My parents are now having their picture taken in a photographer's booth along the boardwalk. The place is shadowed in the mauve light which is apparently necessary. The camera is set to the side on its tripod and looks like a Martian man. The photographer is instructing my parents in how to pose. My father has his arm over my mother's shoulder, and both of them smile emphatically. The photographer brings my mother a bouquet of flowers to hold in her hand but she holds it at the wrong angle. Then the photographer covers himself with the black cloth which drapes the camera and all that one sees of him is one protruding arm and his hand which clutches the rubber ball which he will squeeze when the picture is finally taken. But he is not satisfied with their appearance. He feels with certainty that somehow there is something wrong in their pose. Again and again he issues from his hidden place with new directions. Each suggestion merely makes matters worse. My father is becoming impatient. They try a seated pose. The photographer explains that he has pride, he is not interested in all of this for the money, he wants to make beautiful pictures. My father says: "Hurry up, will you? We haven't got all night." But the photographer only scurries about apologetically, and issues new directions. The photographer charms me. I approve of him with all my heart, for I know just how he feels, and as he criticizes each revised pose according to some unknown idea of rightness, I become quite hopeful. But then my father says angrily: "Come on, you've had enough time, we're not going to wait any longer." And the photographer, sighing unhappily, goes back under his black covering, holds out his hand, says: "One, two, three, Now!", and the picture is taken, with my father's smile turned to a grimace and my mother's bright and false. It takes a few minutes for the picture to be developed and as my parents sit in the curious light they become quite depressed.

They have passed a fortune-teller's booth, and my mother wishes to go in, but my father does not. They begin to argue about it. My mother becomes stubborn, my father once more impatient, and then they begin to quarrel, and what my father would like to do is walk off and leave my mother there, but he knows that that would never do. My mother refuses to budge. She is near to tears, but she feels an uncontrollable desire to hear what the palm-reader will say. My father consents angrily, and they both go into a booth which is in a way like the photographer's, since it is draped in black cloth and its light is shadowed. The place is too warm, and my father keeps saying this is all nonsense, pointing to the crystal ball on the table. The fortune-teller, a fat, short woman, garbed in what is supposed to be Oriental robes, comes into the room from the back and greets them, speaking with an accent. But suddenly my father feels that the whole thing is intolerable; he tugs at my mother's arm, but my mother refuses to budge. And then, in terrible anger, my father lets go of my mother's arm and strides out, leaving my mother stunned. She moves to go after my father, but the fortune-teller holds her arm tightly and begs her not to do so, and I in my seat am shocked more than can ever be said, for I feel as if I were walking a tight-rope a hundred feet over a circus-audience and suddenly the rope is showing signs of breaking, and I get up from my seat and begin to shout once more the first words I can think of to communicate my terrible fear and once more the usher comes hurrying down the aisle flashing his searchlight, and the old lady pleads with me, and the shocked audience has turned to stare at me, and I keep shouting: "What are they doing? Don't they know what they are doing? Why doesn't my mother go after my father? If she does not do that, what will she do? Doesn't my father know what he is doing?"—But the usher has seized my arm and is dragging me away, and as he does so, he says: "What are *you* doing? Don't you know that you can't do whatever you want to do? Why should a young man like you, with your whole life before you, get hysterical like this? Why don't you *think* of what you're doing? You can't act like this even if other people aren't around! You will be sorry if you do not do what you should do, you can't carry on like this, it is not right, you will find that out soon enough, everything you do matters too much," and he said that dragging me through the lobby of the theatre into the cold light, and I woke up into the bleak winter morning of my 21st birthday, the windowsill shining with its lip of snow, and the morning already begun.